W9-ATB-985

TOGETHER IN ONE VOLUME FOR THE FIRST TIME

THE ECOLITAN OPERATION
AND
THE ECOLOGIC SECESSION

The Galactic Empire is old and corrupt. No human or alien forces have ever been able to stand up against its powers. But now, at the Ecolitan Institute on the planet Accord, the seeds of change are being sown. The Institute may look like an innocent academy of ecology, but it's actually much more. . . .

Back in print at last, these two linked SF adventures are the perfect entry point to L. E. Modesitt's engrossing series, The Ecolitan Matter. If you enjoyed Isaac Asimov's Foundation trilogy, you don't want to miss this story of heroism and historic change.

"L. E. Modesitt, Jr., is a writer deeply concerned for the impact of humanity on the world. This concern shows clearly in fantasies such as *The Order War* and science fiction such as *The Ecologic Envoy*. . . . The space adventure side of the tale will be all that many readers want, and they will be thoroughly satisfied. Modesitt never fails on that level. But he is more than an adventure writer; he is also quite a thoughtful fellow, and I found his musings on the need for responsibility in a high-tech society the more fascinating aspect of this novel."

—*Analog* on *Gravity Dreams*

"*The Ecolitan Enigma* can be enjoyed as a first-rate political-adventure tale, as a continuation of a long-running SF conversation, or as an examination of human nature. . . . It's an outstanding work, and I plan to reread it."

—*SFSite.com*

"Modesitt's talent for writing SF-slanted political-military intrigue has grown over the years. . . . Tyros are advised to seek out the earlier volumes. The effort will be rewarding, since Modesitt's talent also extends to characterization and dialogue."

–*Starlog*

TOR BOOKS BY L. E. MODESITT, JR.

THE SPELLSONG CYCLE

The Soprano Sorceress	*Darksong Rising*
The Spellsong War	*The Shadow Sorceress*

THE SAGA OF RECLUCE

The Magic of Recluce	*The Chaos Balance*
The Towers of the Sunset	*The White Order*
The Magic Engineer	*Colors of Chaos*
The Order War	*Magi'i of Cyador*
The Death of Chaos	*Scion of Cyador*
Fall of Angels	

THE ECOLITAN MATTER

The Ecologic Envoy	*The Ecologic Secession*
The Ecolitan Operation	*The Ecolitan Enigma*

THE FOREVER HERO
contains

Dawn for a Distant Earth	*In Endless Twilight*
The Silent Warrior	

TIMEGODS' WORLD
contains

The Timegod	*Timediver's Dawn*

Of Tangible Ghosts	*The Ghost of the Revelator*
Ghost of the White Nights*	

The Green Progression	*The Parafaith War*
Hammer of Darkness	*Adiamante*
Gravity Dreams	*The Octagonal Raven*

*Forthcoming

KATEY
JANE

1

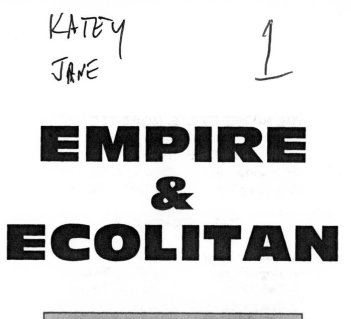

EMPIRE
&
ECOLITAN

THE ECOLITAN OPERATION

THE ECOLOGIC SECESSION

L. E. Modesitt, Jr.

TOR®

A TOM DOHERTY ASSOCIATES BOOK
NEW YORK

This is a work of fiction. All the characters and events portrayed in these novels are either fictitious or are used fictitiously.

EMPIRE & ECOLITAN
Copyright © 2001 by L. E. Modesitt, Jr.

The Ecolitan Operation, copyright © 1989 by L. E. Modesitt, Jr.
The Ecologic Secession, copyright © 1990 by L. E. Modesitt, Jr.

All rights reserved, including the right to reproduce this book, or portions thereof, in any form.

This book is printed on acid-free paper.

A Tor Book
Published by Tom Doherty Associates, LLC
175 Fifth Avenue
New York, NY 10010

www.tor.com

Tor® is a registered trademark of Tom Doherty Associates, LLC.

Library of Congress Cataloging-in-Publication Data

ISBN 978-0-312-87879-5

Printed in the United States of America

P1

CONTENTS

THE ECOLITAN OPERATION

To Elizabeth Leanore,
For her love
of words,
of the books that contain them,
and of her father who writes them.

THE MAN IN the power technician's white jumpsuit scanned the control board with the same bored ease and critical eye that the real technician would have used.

His forearms rested lightly on the angled and flat gray padding at the base of the control board as his eyes continued their scan.

Technically, the failsafe systems were supposed to catch any imbalances long before they showed on the main board, but the destruction of the Newton quarter on Einstein had not been forgotten over the three centuries since it had occurred. There, the failsafes had not functioned, and the duty technician had gone with the plant when the magfield had contracted a magnitude more than the plant had ever been designed to handle.

The man who had replaced the duty technician smiled a bored smile as he waited for the failure he knew would come. His eyes flicked to the time readout in the center of the board.

2146—two standard minutes until the magfield began a series of pulses so minute that they would not be perceived for another twenty minutes outside of central control. More important, it was 2146 on Landing Eve, forty-six minutes after the Grand Commandant had arrived at the Military Pavilion to begin the celebration. Nearly the entire Halstani government would be present.

The Military Pavilion was twenty-five kays from the power station—well beyond the maximum damage capabilities of a malfunctioning fusion bottle—but not beyond range of the EMP factors that had been designed into the fluctuations, nor of the power pulses that the fusion system would begin to feed into the power net.

2147—the man in the technician's suit surveyed the board again, following the pattern he had rehearsed so carefully, leaning forward slightly, his elbow brushing the square plate in the middle of the right side of the board.

He lifted his head perhaps three centimeters as he eased back and began the scan pattern again.

2148—his eyes crossed the feedback constriction loop indicator as the fluid bar flickered minutely. He did not nod, but continued his scan pattern.

At the end of another scan circuit, he turned as if to wipe a speck of dirt, an eyelash, from the inside corner of his right eye with the forefinger of his right hand. He leaned forward as he did so, and his elbow tapped another control plate, this time in the second row.

The replacement technician leaned back, as if satisfied with the readings displayed across the board, all of which continued to appear normal. The duplicate readings in the backup control center, in power control central, and at Military Central also would continue to appear normal.

2150—a second pulse registered on the feedback constriction loop, larger only to an eye looking for the minute difference. The man in the operator's control seat could feel the beginning of dampness on his palms, but his face was as impassive as it had been when he had assumed the duty nearly two standard hours earlier. His heartbeat remained unchanged, as was absolutely necessary. The chair in which he sat monitored the vital signs of the operator, and his departure from that chair, until relieved, would trigger alarms in five separate locales.

The operator repressed a smile, taking a deep breath of the carefully filtered air, as he thought about the special circuitry woven into the suit which he wore and the special modules in the heels of his boots. The air, despite the filtration, carried a tang of ozone and metal.

He stretched, carefully, to ensure his weight remained in the chair, then returned to scanning the board, his professional look glued firmly in place, waiting for the hidden, but routine, 2200 military scan.

2152—a third pulse on the feedback loop, this time larger, almost above the noise level.

Click.

The light pen slipped from the narrow front ledge of the control console and dropped onto the floor. Bending forward and carefully leaving his body weight on the seat, the operator reached for the instrument.

He paused to touch the back of his right boot heel, detaching the bottom section in a single motion and slipping it into the prepared pocket on the inside of the jumpsuit's right trouser hem. The special conducting male and female couplers slipped together soundlessly. The operator sat up, stylus in hand, and scanned the board quickly, to assure himself that he had missed nothing.

2154—a fourth pulse on the feedback loop, this time edging barely above the normal noise range.

The operator rested his left hand on his knee, letting his breath out slowly as he invoked his internal-system function control disciplines.

2156—a fifth pulse, clearly into the high noise range.

The operator looked toward the sealed portal, as if checking to see that no one had entered. His left elbow touched another control plate, this time in the third row on the left side.

2158—a sixth pulse, high, but now masked by a higher energy noise level since the automatic signal dampers had been disengaged.

2200—a seventh pulse, fractionally above the highest of the damped noise levels. The operator continued to breathe normally, now concentrating more upon maintaining normal bodily function signals than upon the board before him, as he waited for the double pulse on the output monitor line that signified a full data pull by the HALDEFNET monitors.

2202—the feedback loop pulse was clearly reaching above the noise level. The operator spent exactly the same amount of time checking the readout as he had for each previous scan.

2203—on the fourth panel from the left in the second row down, twin pulses wavered for an instant and were gone.

The operator took a deep breath, then shook his head as if disoriented, and dropped it between his knees, out of sight of the direct visual monitors. His hands detached the left boot heel, guiding it into the pocket on the left trouser leg of the single-piece coverall. Once again the couplings in the pocket and those on the heel slipped together without a sound.

He had less than half a standard minute to complete the next phase of his mission.

Squinting his eyelids shut tightly, and still keeping his head down, he tossed two small squarish cubes over the top of the control console.

Flrrrt.

A flare of intense light flooded the room, a brilliance that seared the monitors into uselessness. Even as the glare continued, the operator, eyes closed, taped down the seat cushion on four edges. While the pressure would not be as great as if he remained sitting there, it would be adequate to convince outsiders that the operator was slumped halfway out of the seat. Next he jerked open the front closures on the singlesuit and wriggled out, carefully leaving the suit itself in the operator's chair, where the electrical circuits he had connected would now continue to mimic the bodily patterns of an unconscious man. The chair would dutifully report that an injured operator remained within the control room.

Eyes still closed, he walked twenty measured steps through the glare to the portal, slipping the counterfeit of the special military key into place, and easing out into the lock. Once the portal closed on the searing light, he opened his eyes and placed the beret of the Halstani Marines on his head to complete the uniform he had worn under the technician's suit. The only substantial difference between his replicated uniform and the standard Halstani Marine Major's uniform was that all the insignia and accoutrements were comprised of plastics transparent to the metal sensors used by the Halstani security systems.

Outside the lock, as he had calculated, the immediate area was vacant. He turned and slapped a thin line of instant-weld taping across the portal. Breaking it would require a laser cutter. He turned and began to walk down the corridor. His steps were precise, clicking as he marched down the tech access corridor and turned right at the first intersection, then left at the second.

The power station's main security checkpoint, the only one in operation on holidays, was less than fifty meters before him. Less than fifty meters and two guards, neither of whom was likely to let him go unchallenged. One was on the inside of the security portal, waiting for him. The other, unseen for now, was on the outside.

He did not shrug, but he could have, as he maintained his stiff posture all the way to the first security checkpoint.

"Who . . . pardon, Major? What are you doing—?"

The false Major launched himself over the low console.

Thud.

Clank.

The uniform had obtained for him momentary respect, the extra instants he had needed to disable the guard.

He frowned, not liking the next step, as he retrieved the standard-issue stunner, the one the guard had dropped.

Thrummm!

The unconscious soldier twitched before his breathing lightened. Then the man in the Major's uniform began to reprogram the security console, setting it to seal the lock behind him. As he stepped forward to enter the lock to the outer security station, he touched the "execute" key.

Thrumm!

Thrummm!

Clank.

Again the Major had been faster than the guard. He rubbed his sore knee as he lurched to his feet from the dive he had taken out of the lock.

The second guard lay sprawled across his console, stunner scattered a good meter away where it had skidded across the hard plastone flooring. The Major eased the guard off the console and laid him down out of sight. Once more the Major's fingers flew across the console, adding a series of codes. Next he retrieved the stunner and pocketed it before straightening up and marching toward the exit, less than five meters away.

As he approached, the automatic door swung open. Though he carried one stunner ready to use, the ramp and the groundcar lot it led to both appeared virtually empty under the searing blue glare of the arc lights. The summer evening air was warm on his face as he headed down the ramp.

With a wrinkle of his nose at the dank smell of the nearby Feloose Swamp, he glanced back over his shoulder, realizing that he should not have done so. Trying to make the glance casual, he returned his gaze to the lot ahead.

The technician's car was where he had left it, and he eased himself inside, taking off the beret as he closed the door. As the electric whined into operation, he slipped out of the uniform tunic and into the travel tunic that he had left folded on the other front seat.

By now he was well out of the lot and onto the highway away from the city and toward the shuttleport. After stuffing the uniform tunic under the seat, he began to peel the plastic striping off the pseudo-military trousers.

One-handed, he continued to drive as he took a small towel from the dashboard storage box and began to wipe his hair. The mahogany-red hair color broke down under the enzyme, and a muddy brown color, not his own, replaced it. The rest of the changes were complete by the time he parked the electrocar at the tube station that served the shuttleport. He locked the car and walked briskly into the station and onto the downward ramp leading to the tube platform below for the five-minute ride to the port.

Ignoring the flashing full-color hologram that asked whether he was "man enough to give your best for Halston? Can you meet the test of the best Marines this side of the Arm?" he slipped the system pass into the gate.

Hmmmmmm.

The bars turned to allow him onto the platform. At the same time, the identity of the pass holder was automatically flashed into the movement control section of the planetary police monitoring network. Since the pass holder was clearly not on duty or supposed to be at work, the automatic alerts did not flag one of the duty officers.

The man who was not the pass holder smiled faintly as he waited on the empty platform. A faint vibration and an even fainter high-pitched humming notified him of the approaching maglev tube train.

Still alone on the platform when the doors on the two-car train hissed open, he stepped inside and took a seat near the doors, letting his eyes skip over the single other passenger, a rumpled-looking technician in a gray suit, to the train security officer in his shielded booth. The doors hissed closed.

The power fluctuations would not be noticeable for another twenty minutes, nor would the explosion occur until he was well clear of Halston—assuming that things went as planned.

The maglev arrived at the port two stops and four minutes later. He and the other technician both departed, heading for two different concourses.

The man who had been Major, technician, and several other roles along the course of his efforts took the last seat on the 2300 shuttle.

The two explosions occurred nearly simultaneously.

The main power station went at 2257.

Military Central, and eighty-five percent of the Halstani High Command, went at 2258, when the EMP set off three tacheads stored nearby, tacheads whose fusing systems had been modified for electrical pulse detonation.

The beta shuttle for Halston orbit control had lifted at 2259, carrying a man with muddy brown hair.

At 2330, Planetary Police Movement Control, under orders from the acting senior Military Commandant, declared a state of emergency and suspended all off-planet travel.

AFTER PLACING THE plastic square into the public comm console, the man with the muddy brown hair and incipient paunch began to code his message, slowly, almost laboriously, his tongue protruding from his lips as he punched in each word. He seemed to grunt slightly, from time to time, with the effort.

The clerk behind the transmission counter shook her head slowly, wondering how the man had ever gathered enough funds for the message, let alone for the trip he was obviously about to take, or had just taken.

At last he finished and pressed the display button to check his handiwork.

MALENDR FRISTIL
DROP 23A
HIGH CITY
ALPHANE
SECTOR BLUE, EMPIRE

AUNT MALENDR,
FINISHED THE REPLACEMENT OF THE TRIM. THE CABINET WAS COMPLETELY ROTTEN NEAR THE TOP. THE JOB REQUIRED REMOVING THE ENTIRE TOP. I HAD TO USE POWER TOOLS, AND THEY PROBABLY LEFT SCARS ON THE INSIDE.
I AM TAKING MY VACATION NOW, AND I WILL SEE YOU WHEN I GET BACK.

THORIN

He nodded at his work with a pleased smile and punched the eject stud, taking the plastic square in his hand to the dispatch clerk.

"Alphane, Sector Blue," he mumbled apologetically to the woman.

She inserted the card in the reader, scanned the number of characters, weight, and routings.

"Twenty-three credits."

The workman fumbled through his battered pouch, finally coming up with a stained twenty and three chips, all of which he plopped on the counter.

"Thank you." Her voice was simultaneously warm and bored.

The man bobbed his head. "How long, miss?"

"Let's see. The Alphane run goes through Scandia. No more than two days at the outside."

"Much obliged."

The cabinetmaker smiled a toothy grin, almost a leer, before he picked up his traveling satchel and headed back into the orbit control concourse.

The clerk routinely bypassed the privacy safeguards, as she had been taught by Halstani Security, and was reading his message to Aunt Malendr even before he had disappeared into the sparse crowd swirling through the station's curved corridors.

She had forgotten the cabinetmaker within a few minutes, her fading memory of yet another nondescript traveler blotted out by the news of the disaster on Halston below when the carefully scripted presentations of the explosions began to flash across the station's main screens.

■■■

WHILE THE GLAMOUR of the *Empress Katerina* had not entirely departed the ship, most of the old moneyed passengers who had once sworn by the *Empress* on the run between Halston and New Avalon had. Instead, they took the newer *General Tsao*, even while deploring the stark lines and functional decor of the newer ship.

The man who currently bore the name of Thorin Woden, sitting in the dark-paneled, but cramped, lounge of the *Empress*, enjoyed the faded ambience of the about-to-be-retired dowager ship.

In his hand was a well-thumbed manual on woodworking, although both hand and book lay along the arm of the heavy-appearing armchair. The chair was bolted to the deck, the mountings concealed beneath the thin but rich-looking carpet that was beginning to fray. Neither old nor heavy, the chair was a lightweight imitation comprised of well-connected struts, stiffened fabric, and first-class plastwood veneer. Thorin Woden appreciated both the appearance and the illusion, for reasons beyond the ambience.

"For those passengers with a destination of New Avalon, we will be entering orbit in fifteen standard minutes. On behalf of the *Empress*, we wish you a pleasant stay in New Avalon.

"Passengers continuing to Tinhorn should remain on board. Because of delays in returning to Halston, the New Avalon orbit station requests that only those passengers actually bound for New Avalon leave the *Empress*."

Thorin Woden shook his head slowly, surveying the near empty lounge. Through passengers preferred the observation deck, where remote screens relayed the approach to orbit control, while most departing passengers were gathering their belongings, luggage, and spouses or offspring.

The man called Woden had little enough to gather, and while his vacation on New Avalon would be brief, he intended to enjoy it. He was too well aware that each vacation could be his last.

Finally, a faint *clink* ran through the hull, and he stood, holding a satchel and a nondescript carrying bag generally filled with clothes.

"We regret to announce that there will be a short delay before departing passengers can disembark. This delay is caused by the lack of available lock capacity. The *Empress* regrets the delay, but we are informed that it will be minimal."

Woden frowned.

Lack of an available lock or docking capacity normally meant waiting off-station, not locking in and waiting. Lock capacity wasn't the real problem.

New Avalon enjoyed chilly relations with Halston. So the delay could not be at the request of Halstani officials. New Avalon was too proud of its quiet efficiency to deliberately allow anything to halt smooth passenger services.

Woden's hands moved to the heavy workman's belt, his fingertips skimming over the hidden openings. Then he lifted his luggage and stepped toward the lounge exit.

Abruptly, he stepped back into the lounge just in time to avoid two figures moving quickly toward the minimal amenities passenger cabins, more accurately termed closets, he reflected.

The first was a flushed and angry junior officer of the *Empress Katerina*, a third pilot by the stripes on her sleeves, flanked by an Imperial Marine Commander, who also looked out of sorts.

Woden frowned again, then forced his face to relax and headed toward the disembarkation lock.

If there were to be a confrontation, he needed witnesses.

Smiling thinly as he heard the heavy pounding on the cabin he had left hours earlier, he continued in the opposite direction, toward the main lock, where he was certain he would find another Imperial functionary of sorts.

"Wrong," he muttered to himself as he reached the central section of the hull where all the corridors connected.

A crowd of passengers stood lined up before the lock, which was flanked by a pair of Imperial Marine guards in combat suits, their stunners unholstered.

Each passenger faced a credentials check, followed by a full-body scan, designed to compare the passenger against a preselected body profile. That was not the public explanation for the scanner, which was touted universally as a routine method for discovering internal body smuggling and for concealed weapons. Other methods, less conspicuous and just as effective, if unpublicized, already detected smuggling and unauthorized weapons.

The man called Woden let out his breath slowly, shaking his head, and letting his bags droop in his hands.

"You there. Either wait until you're cleared or get in line," snapped the Marine on the right.

The cabinetmaker grinned.

"I said to get in line." The guard raised her stunner, as if to emphasize the command.

"That won't be necessary," suggested the cabinetmaker. "You can either take my word that I'm the one you're looking for, or you can put me through the scanner first."

"You wait your turn."

"Fine, and you'll spend your next turn on Adark, both for ignoring a reasonable suggestion and for unnecessarily delaying debarkation from an innocent commercial—"

"What's this?"

The cabinetmaker turned toward the red-faced Commander, the one who had already been pounding on cabin doors.

"Major Wright, Commander. Jimjoy Wright. Presume you're looking for me?"

The Commander's mouth dropped momentarily, and his nose wrinkled as if the air smelled of rancid fish.

"How . . . yes, Major. The Service does happen to be looking for you."

"Too good to believe I might get leave after all. The mess on Halston?"

The Commander swallowed, as if to say something, then choked it back, finally answering, "If you wouldn't mind the scanner, Major?"

"Not at all. Only have my word I'm me."

With that, the Major picked up his two bags and handed them to the officious Marine. "Take care of these, please. Thank you."

Next he stepped in front of a bewildered young woman, black-haired and thin-faced, wearing a purple shipsuit that made her look even more washed out than her apparently natural pallor.

"Excuse me, miss, but this will speed up everyone's departure." He half bowed, smiled, and stepped through the scanner, then glanced at the technician operating the equipment.

She avoided looking at him and tried to catch the eye of the Commander, who was now engaged in conversation with the ship's third officer. The Commander did not look up, and the technician tried to keep from looking at the strange Major.

The ship's officer's voice was low, but intense.

". . . dangerous, you said . . . need to block the ship . . . quarantine the station . . . and he announces himself . . . Regency Lines . . . protest . . . consider the matter of compensation . . ."

The third officer was leaning toward the Commander, who took one step backward, then another.

The Major let a faint smile cross his face as he watched the Commander endure the civilian pilot's complaints. He had no doubt that he would hear from the Commander in turn.

"Commander?" asked the Major, loud enough to break into the pilot's monologue. "Believe your technician has something to say."

"Yes, Aldora?" asked the Commander, half turning from the pilot, who glared at both the Commander and the Major, switching her glance from one to the other.

"The Major . . . I mean . . . the comparison . . . he's Major Wright," stammered the technician.

"Thank you." The cabinetmaker and Major inclined his head to the technician.

"I can believe it," announced the Marine Commander. Turning back to the pilot, he inclined his head. "Thank you, Officer Shipstaad. A pleasure to work with you."

The third pilot inclined her head stiffly. "My pleasure, Commander." The words came out harshly.

The Major noted that the Marine guards appeared more tense, rather than less, now that he had been positively identified.

"Major?" The Commander gestured toward the ship's lock, where yet another pair of Marine guards waited.

The Major nodded and marched toward the lock and the second set of guards. He had no doubt that he could have escaped, but there was no reason to, not now.

He'd only done his duty, if not exactly in the way in which he had been ordered. But he had completed the job, and about that, High Command couldn't quibble.

On the other side of the *Empress*'s lock, inside orbit control station, waited a third pair of guards.

The Major shook his head. All this to deny him his hard-earned leave. He grinned at the pair, who had leveled their stunners at him and motioned for him to stop.

"If I'd decided to take your toys away, technicians, you'd be long gone." His smile was friendly, and so was his tone, but the man on his right paled slightly. The woman aimed directly at his midsection, in approved Service fashion.

"Major, I would greatly appreciate it if you would refrain from threatening my personnel. They might believe you, and I would have a hard time explaining why I was shipping your body, rather than you."

"Commander, I appreciate your suggestion and solicitude, but I do need some relaxation now that High Command has decided unilaterally to cancel my hard-earned leave."

The Commander coughed.

"Where to?" the Major asked.

"Lock six. To your left. There's a courier waiting."

The Major who had briefly been a technician, a Halstani officer, a cabinetmaker, and assorted other occupations smiled again, briefly, and turned to his left.

A trailing guard raised an eyebrow at the other guard, the one who had arrived carrying the Major's bags. The baggage-carrying guard glared at the other, who looked away.

A third guard whispered, "The Major's supposedly a Special Operative. You wouldn't argue either."

A handful of civilian passengers, cordoned off behind a rope, viewed the military procession with open eyes and closed faces, waiting for the Imperials to leave so they could get on board the *Empress* and on with their trip to Tinhorn.

IV

A MAN WHO believes in nothing will support the status quo, not oppose it.

A man who believes in himself first can be trained to support his society.

The true believer will place his ideals above action, because no action can attain the perfection of his ideals.

These are the people who compose most of society.

The others? The criminals, idiots, writers, politicians, and fanatics?

The politicians pose some danger because they are interesting and employ popular vanity and the illusion of ideals to make small changes in society. Small does not necessarily mean insignificant, and for this reason the politicians must be watched.

Of the remainder, the greatest danger comes from the altruistic fanatic, who believes simultaneously in himself, his ideals, and the need for action. Such individuals should be killed at birth, if they could but be identified that early.

Failing that, they should be made military heroes and given the first possible chance at a glorious death. That is the Empire's current policy.

Unfortunately, someday one of those heroes will survive . . .

Private Observations
Sanches D. P. Kwixot
New Augusta, 2456 A.E.F.F.

V

CLING.

At the sound of the console chime, the officer in dress grays stiffened, though he did not leave the straight-backed chair.

"Yes, Commander. Yes, sir."

The orderly's voice, soft as it was, carried through the outer office, a room empty except for the orderly and a Major in a gray uniform and recently cut black hair.

"Major Wright?"

"Yes." The Major stood, flexing his broad shoulders, shoulders that did not seem as broad as they were in view of his equally broad torso and muscular lower body. He looked through the orderly, who avoided looking in the direction of his eyes.

"You may go in, sir. Commander Hersnik is ready to see you . . . sir."

"Thank you." The Major's voice was expressionless.

The orderly continued avoiding any eye-to-eye contact with the Major until the Special Operative had passed him and was stepping through the security portal to the Commander's office.

The security portal flashed green, signifying that the Major carried neither weapons nor energy concentrations on his body, not that he would have required either to deal with the single senior Commander who awaited him.

Major Wright stepped from the portal ramp onto the deep gray carpet and halted, coming to attention before the Commander. The Commander sat behind a wide wooden console with an inset screen.

To the Major's right was a wide-screen reproduction of New Augusta, as seen from the air, distant as it was from the Intelligence Service station, showing the broad boulevards and clear golden sunlight of the Imperial City on a cloudless summer day.

The Major repressed a cynical smile. The view had been carefully chosen to avoid showing the blighted areas that remained on Old Earth, whose ecology still remained fragile.

"Major Jimjoy Earle Wright, Special Operations, reporting as ordered."

"Commander Hersnik, Major Wright. Have a seat." The Commander, black-haired, black-eyed, olive-skinned, neat, and proper, did not leave his swivel, and presumably the energy-defense screens mounted in the console, but gestured toward a straight-backed armchair across the console from him.

"Thank you, sir." Once again, the Major's tone was politely expressionless as he took the proffered seat.

"You are wondering, no doubt, Major, why you were diverted from your scheduled leave to report to Intelligence Headquarters." Commander Hersnik, elbows on the arms of his swivel, steepled his fingers together, then rested his chin on them as he waited for the Special Operative's answer.

"Figured it had to be important, to risk my cover. Did wonder about it . . . sir . . . Especially when your . . . security forces . . . delayed an entire civilian ship and insisted on my immediate return. Seemed . . . unusual."

"Unusual. Yes, that would be one way of putting it." The Commander paused. "Tell me, Major, your own evaluation of your last mission, the Halston mission."

Jimjoy Wright shrugged. "Instructions were clear-cut. Halstani Military was ready to annex the Gilbi systems. Need to immobilize them to give us time to deal with the situation appropriately." He smiled self-deprecatingly. "My efforts along the immobilization line never got far. Once they had those accidents outside the capital, it didn't seem there was much else I could do."

"Uhhh . . . accidents?"

"They had to be accidents, didn't they, Commander? Who would possibly conceive of deliberately turning a fusion power system into a nuclear mishap on purpose? And coincidental detonation of tactical nuclear weapons followed the power failure, according to the fax reports. Attempting to create that kind of EMP-induced accident would have been awfully chancy, even if it had been deliberate."

"I see . . ." The Commander frowned. "Assuming these accidents . . . they were rather unfortunate accidents from the viewpoint of the Halstani *Military*, wouldn't you say?"

The Major ignored the emphasized word, shifted his weight in the straight-backed chair, and looked straight into the Commander's eyes. His own eyes were flat and expressionless. "Most large-scale accidents with fatalities are unfortunate, sir. Some have minor consequences, except for the casualties themselves. Others have major impacts."

"If such an accident had not occurred, then, Major, I take it that you had a plan that would have been more targeted?"

The Major smiled widely, seemingly enjoying the falsity of his expression. "Can't say that I did, Commander. That's the problem with trying to stop a government's war machine. You remove the top admiral, the marshal, whoever . . . and someone else takes up the gauntlet. And they have a martyr to make it even easier. Even if I could have destroyed a goodly section of their fleets, why . . . they'd rebuild."

"So the accidents were rather fortunate, at least from Intelligence's point of view. And from mine, I'd guess. Looked like an impossible job for any conventional approach."

The Commander's lips pursed, and he drew into himself, as if he were repressing a shiver.

"Are you disclaiming the credit for accomplishing your assignment, Major?"

"Not disclaiming, Commander. Wouldn't be true, either. Just suggesting that it continue to be classified as a regrettable accident, and one for which the Emperor sends his heartfelt condolences."

"Then you take the responsibility for fifty thousand casualties, many of them civilians?"

"You know, Commander, you have a rather unusual approach to a poor Special Operative who managed to carry off an assignment that at least four others had failed to accomplish."

"How did you—never mind. I asked you a question, Major. Do you take the responsibility for fifty thousand casualties?" Hersnik's chin was now off his hands, and he leaned intently toward the Major.

"My orders specifically required that I not consider casualties, Commander. Obviously, every Special Operative will be held accountable and responsible for his actions. War creates casualties. When a system supports a warlike government, the distinction between civilians and military personnel becomes semantic. Under the circumstances, we do what we can, sir."

"Were I the strictest of military traditionalists, Major, I would find your attitude less than perfectly acceptable."

Major Jimjoy Earle Wright said nothing, but retained the open and falsely expansive smile as he waited for the Commander to get to the main point.

Commander Hersnik coughed, steepled his fingers together again before looking at the captured panorama of New Augusta to his left. He kept his glance well above the broad shoulders of the not-quite-stocky Special Operative.

"The Fuardians have begun to annex Gilbi, Major. And there's nothing we can do about it. Not now."

The Major's smile vanished. He shrugged, but did not comment.

"Would you like to say something now, Major, about the fortuitousness of your 'accidents'? Would you?" Commander Hersnik's voice was soft, cultured.

"Not much to say, is there, Commander? Except that Special Operatives aren't theorists. We're operatives, and we solve the problems we're handed. Wasn't told I had to worry about being successful."

"Major Wright," continued the Commander even more softly, "it's worse than that. The Woman's Party has taken control of the Halstani government. Military Central was the only group strong enough to hold them off. Now there's no military presence to speak of, not with political expertise."

Wright shrugged again. What could he say?

"The Woman's Party has made known in the past their extreme displeasure with the Empire. They are far more likely to take a hard line than Military Central did."

"Why?"

"Because the Halstani military relied on hardware and did not have complete heavy-weapons design and manufacturing capability. The Woman's Party is more inclined, shall we say, toward more economic attacks."

"So why didn't someone suggest to the former Halstani military leaders that they leave Gilbi alone?"

"It was suggested, I am told. On more than one occasion. The Halstani military refused to believe that the Empire was cold-blooded enough to act. Now the Woman's Party is claiming that we had a hand in the 'accident' and that any further Imperial interference in the Gilbi area will be proof enough of that."

"But you want me to single-handedly stop the Fuard annexation anyway?"

The Commander smiled a smile even more false than the early smiles of the Special Operative. "That is not a bad idea, and one which I enthusiastically supported, Major, since you and the Fuards seem tailor-made for each other. But High Command would like the real estate in the Gilbi sector to remain undamaged.

"That leaves us with the question of your next mission, Major Wright, and one which, given the circumstances of your . . . diversion . . . should be nonactive and relatively distant from your last episode. High Command has such a mission. Strictly reconnaissance." The Commander paused again. "Does the name Accord mean anything to you?"

"The eco-freaks out on the Arm?"

"The very same. It has come to our attention that they are beginning to develop a rather nasty biotech system that could prove, shall we say, rather difficult. You are to determine whether that is in fact the case. You are to report back with your findings without taking *any* action. Any action at all. Do you understand?"

"I understand, Commander." The Major's flat blue eyes were flatter than ever, as was his voice.

"Fine, Major. Fine. My orderly has your new orders and briefing package. You may go."

The Special Operative slid from the chair to attention, waiting.

"You may go, Major. And let us hope that you are tougher than the eco-freaks, for our sake, if not for yours . . ."

Jimjoy Wright could follow the train of unspoken thoughts beyond the words, but did not comment, even in his expression, as he turned to leave the Intelligence Service officer.

"Thank you, sir."

"My pleasure, Major. My pleasure."

VI

"WHAT ARE YOU going to do about him?"

"Nothing."

"Nothing?" The one Commander shrugged to the other. "At least, not until he's on Accord. Then . . ."

"Perhaps, but will he make it that far?"

"With the new Matriarchy, the Fuards, and a few others all looking for him? I doubt it."

"He's good."

"At destruction, but not necessarily at the undercover business. You told me that yourself."

"You're probably right, but I think we'll prepare. Just in case he turns out to be better than you think."

"I think? That was your assessment."

"That was then. After seeing the report on the New Avalon encounter, I wonder."

"He turned himself in, didn't he?"

"Exactly . . . when he didn't have to. That bothers me, because he used the situation to dominate it."

"You handle it, then."

"I always do. I always do."

VII

"SPACE AVAILABLE PASSENGER. White . . . Space Available Passenger White . . . please report to control lock three. Please report to control lock three."

A muscular man, no longer quite young yet not middle-aged, stood. He wore the too tight clothes affected mainly by graduate students aping the Slavonian muscle elite. Unlike most graduate students, he and his obviously exercised upper-body muscles would have passed on Slavonia as well.

Unfortunately, his cheap clothes would have marked him as nonelite, as did the muddy brown hair and the tightness around his eyes. The

Slavonian elite wore only the finest in natural fabrics and leathers. Their oiled golden, or black, hair glistened above carefully relaxed expressions.

The man, easy on his feet, and the subject of not a few not-so-covert gazes by a handful of female passengers and by at least one interested male passenger, hefted a pair of crew bags and turned toward the counter waiting under a larger number three on the corridor wall.

As he turned, his eyes traversed the rows of seated passengers, all waiting to embark upon the *Morgan*, without stopping to study any single individual until he locked gazes with a woman who had shoulder-length black hair. He smiled faintly but, without waiting for a response, turned his concentration back toward the lock control counter he had almost reached.

The counter held only a screen, a speaker, and a scanner.

"White," he said softly to the screen.

A face appeared on the formerly blank screen, the face of a pleasant young woman.

"May I help you, citizen?"

"You called me. Space Available Passenger White."

"May I help you, citizen?" the screen repeated mindlessly, the carefully constructed female face showing the proper degree of abstracted concern, dark eyebrows rising with the words' inflection.

"Yes. My name is Hale White." The man looked down at the keyboard, finally touching one of the studs.

"Yes, citizen White," the computer persona answered. "There has been a late cancellation. If you will accept a minimal amenities cabin, Republic Interstellar can fulfill your request for transportation to Haversol on the *J. P. Morgan*. If you accept, please depress the lighted panel on the console and insert your credtab."

The man called White tapped the "inquiry" stud instead.

"You have a further question?"

"Price. My funds are limited." At the same time, he touched the "Cr" button, followed by another tap on the "inquiry" stud.

"The total price, including Imperial tax, Haversolian entry fees, pilotage surcharges, and minimal sustenance charges, will be Cr 1,087. If you accept, please insert your credtab."

He reluctantly pulled the thin strip from his belt and inserted it into the slot.

"Your funds are sufficient, and your place on the *J. P. Morgan* is confirmed. Place your hand on the scanner."

A flash followed, creating a combined record of handprint and picture, against which any passenger claiming to be Hale White could be compared at the actual lock entry control port.

"Thank you for choosing Republic Interstellar. The *J. P. Morgan* is currently disembarking passengers through lock three. We anticipate beginning boarding passengers within one standard hour. Your boarding time will be in approximately one and one half standard hours. Please be at lock port three by 1430 Imperial Standard time."

The muscled man, who could have been a Solarian tough, an out-of-work steel-bending spacer, or someone even less reputable, turned away from the now blank screen and picked up the set of heavy bags, almost with contempt. Crossing the corridor back to the waiting area for lock port three, he ignored the scrutiny of women too young and too old, and another admirer of roughly the right age but the wrong sex.

From the handful of empty chairs, he picked one away from the single large wall screen displaying the planet below, and nearer the lock port itself, where shortly the departing passengers would be entering the station for either shuttle service planetside or transfer to another ship.

"Down on luck, spacer?" asked the white-haired and thin man in the flimsy chair next to him. His eyes were shielded behind heavy old-fashioned, black-lensed glasses.

"Not yet," the younger muscular man grunted. "Actinic burns?"

"Laser."

The younger man shifted in his seat carefully, as if he were worried that the thin tubes and stretched fabric would collapse under him. He noted the thin wires running from the mirrored glasses to the bioplugs behind the older man's ears.

"Scanner glasses? How do they work?"

"All right. Can't do color, and they blur clothes. Some places shut me down. Don't like broadcast energy, even low power. Hell on shapes, though. You look like ex-commando pilot type. Sort of like Dubnik."

"Dubnik? Friend of yours?"

"Dubnik? That spineless musclehead? Hardly. When I was chief on the *Alvarado*, he gave me these scanners. Used to paint—old-fashioned watercolors. You know what these are . . . can I paint now? Sculpture, but it's not the same.

"No, that bastard had to use lasers, had to. The Serianese threw high-speed torps. Dubnik put the screens back up. Didn't tell the laser battery chief. That was me."

In spite of himself, the younger man winced. "You still here?"

"You see me, spacer. But you don't. Half flesh, half synth. Better than not being here. Dubnik . . . he didn't make it. Still spineless mus-clehead. Torps never even brushed the screens. Serianese couldn't shoot then. Can't now. That's why they belong to the Fuards."

The spacer did not look away, but had nothing to say.

The lock door had opened, and the first passenger out was a young woman in a Republic Interstellar glide chair guided by a man in the uniform of a steward, light gray, with green stripes down the sleeves and trouser seams.

"She's a grav-field para," announced the ex-technician.

"Anything you don't see, chief?"

"Not much. Don't call me chief. Call me anything; call me Arto. Hell-fired pun, but it's my name."

"What about that woman sitting on the end over there, with the case by her feet? She really that muscular?"

"Legs are. Shoulders, too, but she's got something wrapped around her middle. Not much density. Sort of like rope, I'd guess."

"Cernadine rope. Ship scan will pick that up."

"Won't do anything. Cernadine's legal on Haversol. Empire doesn't care much about it anyway."

"Does seem that way." A hint of bitterness tinged the spacer's words.

"For now, spacer."

"Stow the spacer. Name's White. Flitter driver—till I told a Special Op suicide wasn't my department. His maybe."

"And you're still here?" asked the older man ironically.

"He was easy on me. Lots of bruises, concussion, and a month in rehab. He didn't like suicide either. Went off and did it, though."

"Him or you?"

"I was out cold. He went. Didn't come back. None of them did. Teryla two episode."

"Heard about it. Two men cashiered. Rest dead; one casualty before the drop."

"Me. Casualty. Career and respect."

"Sounds like Haversol is just a transfer point."

"Does, doesn't it?"

The last of the departing passengers left the *Morgan*. The door to the lock closed.

"Embarkation on the *J. P. Morgan* will begin in fifteen standard minutes. In fifteen minutes, those passengers holding gold status accommodations will be embarked."

"Wonder how many of this group rates gold?" asked the younger spacer.

"To Haversol? Not many."

"What about the blonde? Sorry . . . the thinnish woman in the middle of the second row, the one sitting taller than the others?"

"Built like a Special Operative herself, under all that fluff. Muscles like yours, just not quite as obvious. Has a plate in her shoulder, and some sort of metal behind her left eyes."

"Probably is a Special Op with all that."

"Not Imperial," answered Arto. "Empire makes sure their boys got no metal anywhere. All plastics, if anything. Second, never saw a female Special Op. Fuards, Halstanis, Serianese—everyone else uses women. Best we do is commando corps. Should be the other way around. Bulk counts for commandos, doesn't count near as much for undercover sneak and thief."

"Wonder who?"

"With all those muscles and height, probably Halstani. One of their flamed sisters."

"Could be. Won't the lock scanners catch her?"

"Sure. But the Empire's not at war. So the crew just forgets she's there. Just like the Fuardian and the Halstani flag lines forget about our ops, unless there's trouble."

"Makes sense, I guess. But why's she here?"

"Not here, White. Haversol. Haversol's a happy hunting ground for everyone—us, them, the outies, even see some of the Ursans once in a while. Good reason to be careful there."

"Why are you headed there?"

"Not headed there. Headed to Accord. Understand they *might* be able to fix my eyes. Good biologics there."

"Like the genetic wars under the Directorate?"

Arto shook his head. "No. Not quite the same, the way I understand it. The Directorate tried to create superkillers. Accord works with what already exists."

"Not what I heard." The younger man shrugged, and let his eyes check the still-closed lock port. "But I guess you hear what they want you to hear."

"Isn't that the truth," snorted Arto. "Never changes."

In the lull in the conversation that followed, both men looked around the waiting area.

"Attention, please. Your attention, please. In just a few standard minutes, we will be embarking full status passengers on the *J. P. Morgan* through lock port three. Those passengers with gold status should be prepared to embark. Those passengers with gold status should be prepared to embark."

Arto glanced from the far seats back at the man beside him. "Wouldn't mind that kind of status."

"No. Beats the stand-up closet I got."

"Bet you spend most of your time in the common lounges."

"No bet."

"Be careful, White. You look just enough like an Imperial agent to get in trouble, and you haven't got any metal plates in you. Every two-bit operator, like that sister, or like the fellow over on the end with the heavy boots—bet he's a Fuard with the steel tubes built into his forearms—will be angling to find you out. Doesn't matter that you're what you say you are. Because only an Impie agent could have cover that good."

"Hades! That why everyone keeps looking at me? Thought it might be my good looks."

"Just a guess, friend." The scanner glasses, their mirrored surface impenetrable, looked away from the spacer and toward the lock.

"So who do you work for? Knowing all the agents and what makes them tick?"

"Me? I work for me, no one else. Couldn't afford it otherwise. One stun beam my way and I'm blind. Direct hit and I'm out for a week, with a headache for a month afterward."

The spacer nodded, ignoring the evasion. "So what should I do? Act my normal dumb self? Hope someone doesn't decide I'm am Impie agent? Pretend I am? Pray?"

"Prayer won't help. Neither will playing the agent unless you can carry it off. Acting innocent might, particularly if you are. At least until you land on Haversol. Then all bets are off."

"Wonderful." The brown-haired man shook his head, lifted both shoulders as if trying to relax them.

"And that shielded personal kit in your bag would make anyone suspicious, at least anyone with a scanner."

The other shook his head again. "That why I've opened the damned thing every time I've turned around?"

"Your attention, please," interrupted the message system. "Your attention, please. Republic Interstellar is now embarking gold status passengers on the *J. P. Morgan*. Gold status passengers only. Through lock port three. Would those passengers with silver status please prepare to embark? Passengers with silver status prepare to embark."

Arto reached down and pulled a single kit back toward his feet. "Time for us to separate, White."

"Have a good trip. Good luck with the eyes."

"Hope to, and thank you." The older man stood, then leaned toward the younger spacer. "Someone's out for you, but it won't be me. Good luck."

With that, Arto was up and in the waiting line of passengers, his bag in one hand.

The man called White did not shake his head, but studied the remaining passengers waiting to board the *Morgan*.

So someone was already looking for him? That was scarcely the most auspicious beginning he could have hoped for. Not at all.

He shrugged and brushed back his hair with his left hand, not that his hair was long enough or messed enough to require attention.

"Standard amenities passengers, please stand by for boarding. Standard amenities passengers, please stand by for boarding on the *Morgan*. Destination Haversol."

The level of deference in the carefully controlled voice announcing the passenger boarding schedule was definitely declining.

The apparent Halstani Intelligence Operative glanced in his direction before standing. Her eyes passed over him, but he had no doubt that the woman already knew who he was. Her look was confirmation, not search.

He would have liked to sigh, but that wouldn't have been in character.

His supposedly uneventful trip to Haversol was looking less and less uneventful.

VIII

JIMJOY STRETCHED AS he studied the small room.

One double bed, scratched plastic drawers built into the wall next to a narrow closet with dual doors—bent—which looked as if they squeaked every time they were opened. A lopsided and cracked plastic table squatted in front of two armchairs that would have been out of style three centuries earlier in most of the Empire. The drapes, spread, upholstery, and floor padding were all either brown or orange or both, and the two colors, faded as they were, clashed.

The Imperiale was anything but imperial, though in character for the itinerant pilot/electrical worker outlined in Jimjoy's cover papers.

He shook his head. Hale Vale White—whoever had saddled him with such an absurd cover name should be on the mission, rather than the overtired and overworked Major who was.

Lifting the single hanging bag from the floor, he opened the closet doors.

Skkreeett.

Wincing, he hung up the bag, but did not close the door. Instead, he glanced over at the other bag, squat and lumpy. With a sigh, he dragged it over and used his right foot to give it a final shove inside the shallow closet, where it barely fit.

Then he sat on the edge of the bed, which sank alarmingly under his weight, and pulled off his dusty boots, letting them clump to the floor.

He half turned, half eased himself back into the central valley in the bed, the depression created by his own weight. Even sleeping one night at the Imperiale was likely to give him a backache, and there was no guarantee that he would escape with a single night. But he wasn't up to trying the floor, or to fighting with what might appear on it once the lights were out.

With the first Accord ship not available for two days, and with supposedly few credits, the poor pilot named White could be expected to catch a few hours' sleep, especially in the warm midday of Haversol. Besides, if Arto were right, the longer he stayed around Haversol, the more he would have to be on his guard. The sleep he got now might be his best.

At least the Imperiale had climate control, reflected Jimjoy as he adjusted the pillow under his head. He hoped that no one would bother him, not yet. The last thing he needed was his combat reflexes jolting him into full awareness because some cheap hotel's valet wasn't certain who belonged where.

In a more affluent system, he wouldn't have had to even leave the orbit station, but Haversol had no quarters in orbit, except for the extraordinarily wealthy, which raised the costs of travel beyond Haversol considerably. And the Empire certainly wouldn't help Haversol out, not to improve transit toward the Arm. Neither was it in Haversol's interest.

Jimjoy shook his head and let the economics lapse.

The dim light of late afternoon angling into his eyes woke him from the latest in a series of nightmares.

He recalled only the last, in which he had commandeered a slow freighter and was being chased toward some system jump point by a full Imperial flotilla, all because he had failed to give Commander Hersnik the proper salute.

"Must be a moral in that," he muttered as he struggled up into a sitting position to wipe his dripping forehead with the back of his sleeve. He eased his feet over the side of the bed, his back to the narrow single window, cradling his aching head in his hands.

Finally, he stood and made his way into the antique bathroom, where he began to splash the lukewarm water that was ostensibly cold over his face. Slowly, he wiped his face dry.

Then, taking a deep breath, he stepped back into the empty floor space next to the bed and began the muscular relaxation exercises designed to relieve tight muscles and the symptoms of tension.

The sagging bed had left his back stiff, but not actually sore—not yet.

The exercises relieved that stiffness, as well as the remnants of the nightmare-induced headache.

Once he had completed the exercise pattern, he returned to the bathroom and cleaned up. Then he extracted a clean, but slightly faded, tunic from the hanging bag, leaving the squeak-prone closet door still open. He pulled on the tunic.

He bent down and touched the squat kit bag, as if to adjust the clasp, and then straightened, stepping away from the shallow closet again and toward the door that represented the single exit from the room. With a glance around the not-quite-shabbiness, he touched his hand to the door, then listened before actually opening it.

No one seemed to be outside in the hallway.

Feeling more rested and slightly more relaxed than when he had entered the dingy room hours earlier, Jimjoy started down the empty hallway toward the center stairs, avoiding the ancient elevator.

Four flights down and he stood in the dusty lobby, inhabited by one bored clerk hunched behind a faded plastone-facaded counter, and a white-haired man who stared at the main doors.

Jimjoy touched his chin, wondering whether to try the equally aged saloon or to chance finding something nearby which might be even more dismal and expensive.

The Special Operative walked over to the open portals, the first actual portals he had seen so far on Haversol, and peered in. Despite the early hour, nearly half the tables were taken, and the majority of the patrons were actually eating.

He shrugged. The posted prices were reasonable, and he was no more likely to find trouble in his hotel than outside it.

Scarcely inside the portal, he found a tough-faced woman in a gray tunic before him.

"Dinner or drinks? Or both?"

"Dinner . . . maybe drinks later."

"Unhh-hunnnn," mumbled the hostess as she turned.

Jimjoy shrugged again and followed her, letting himself amble along in the style of his current persona. The walk was that of an outwardly careless man who had actually never let down his guard. For all that the style reflected Jimjoy's current feelings, the motion was more obvious than he would have normally used. But he had the strong feeling that he was being tracked closely.

"Here," grunted the green-haired tough who had led the way. The small table was in a corner, jammed under a planter from which a tattered nightfern spilled over the sides and brushed Jimjoy's shoulder as he ducked under it in moving behind the smeared and nonreflecting black table.

The would-be out-of-luck spacer eased himself into the straight-backed wooden chair on the back side, glancing at the two dark-bearded and burly men and their companion at the nearest table. The first looked up from his mug of ale. The second continued to stare at the tabletop. Their companion, a younger male with collar-length blond hair, was clean-shaven and held a heavy wineglass.

The four tables on the other side, to his right, each designed for four, were filled, and all were lined up with minimal space between the tables and the rear wall.

Even as he positioned himself in the battered chair to survey the saloon, he could feel the chair back grate against the already scraped and dented paneling behind him. Although the planter stand projected nearly half a meter from the wall, he still had a good view of the threesome to his left. He edged the chair farther away from the planter to give himself a bit more room, hoping he wouldn't need it.

Another woman, tired-looking, wiry, with white-streaked black hair, dropped a bill slate on the adjoining table and turned, in two swift jerks, to face him.

"Eats? Or drinks?"

"Eats. What do you have?"

"Here." She slapped a cube on the table, which projected the menu right into the air before Jimjoy. "Be back in a minute."

She jerked back toward the three men who hunched around the table to Jimjoy's left. The younger man was still drinking from the wineglass, but the two bearded men had drained their heavy and transparent mugs.

Jimjoy glanced at the blond man and decided that he was a she . . . despite the masculine appearance and garb.

Jimjoy frowned as he watched the hard-looking blond woman proffer a handful of credit discs to the waitress before standing with a sudden movement.

"Let's go . . ." The low and gravelly voice grated on Jimjoy's nerves, and he wished the woman and her two bearded friends would depart quickly. He also hoped that the adjoining table would remain empty, but with the saloon filling up so early in the evening, he doubted that.

"Come on," said the blond woman. Standing, she was taller than Jimjoy.

One man, the one closest to the Special Operative, rose quickly. The other did not.

Jimjoy's mouth opened. He closed it quickly.

"Now!" snapped the blond, as her right hand reached down and lifted the man who had remained seated from his chair and onto his feet.

The waitress scuttled backward, nearly upsetting Jimjoy's small table, at the sight of the tall woman yanking a nearly hundred-kilo man from his chair as if he had been a disobedient infant.

"We're going . . ." said the tall woman, quietly this time.

The laggard male did not look at her, but nodded . . . after mumbling "Sorry" under his breath.

The waitress slid sideways past Jimjoy's table in an effort to avoid the argument and brushed into the shoulder of another woman, violet-haired and hard-eyed, who immediately looked up with a glare. The violet-haired woman's look softened as she realized it was the waitress, even as both watched the blond woman escorting her male friends toward the doorway.

". . . used to be a Hand of the Mother . . ." That whispered scrap of information came drifting down from the line of tables to his right.

The woman was not massively built. Solid, but certainly not heavy, and if that episode had been the casual effort of a retired or resigned Hand, Jimjoy would just as soon avoid one on any terms, but especially on professional terms.

Quite suddenly, Commander Hersnik's concerns about the Matriarchal takeover of Halston seemed much more believable.

"You decided?" asked the waitress. Her tired voice sounded as though nothing in the world had happened minutes before, even though the Halstani trio were not quite out of the saloon.

"Samburg steak, whatever else goes with it."

"Salad or local veggies."

"What do you recommend?"

"Local veggies."

"I'll take them."

"Drink?"

"El Parma, with dinner."

He hoped the local beer was palatable, but the out-of-luck pilot of his cover would not have wasted credits on anything more elaborate. Hale Vale White indeed.

He snorted.

By now almost all the tables were taken. As he watched, the green-haired hostess escorted two couples to the table next to him, barely before the glasses had been removed and the table surface further smeared by the quick hand of a scarred youth wearing a faded brown singlesuit.

As the four sat down and were quickly abandoned by the hostess once she had gestured at the table, Jimjoy glanced from one face to the next. He wrinkled his nose, afraid he might sneeze, so heavy was the scent of rose perfume emanating from the false blonde. She and the spurious redhead were obvious joygirls bent on separating the younger men from their paychecks and whatever else could be separated.

Jimjoy sighed at the lustful innocence in the face of both men, wondering how long before they lost more than innocence, wondering if lust was ever innocent for all its singlemindedness.

Rather than dwell further on the neighboring set of mismatched couples whose companionships were doubtless financially based, he began to study people at other tables.

Across the nonreflecting tabletop toward his right and past the three closer tables was a corner table, pulled out fractionally. At it sat three people: a silver-haired woman, apparently in her late twenties or early thirties, as measured in standard Terran years; a dark-haired and slender man whose age seemed indeterminate in the dim light; and another woman, clearly older and heavier. Although he could not have said why, Jimjoy felt that the younger woman's silver hair color was natural. He knew of no world where such color was widespread, but it looked natural—and not the natural color that came with age or premature aging.

The woman looked in his direction momentarily, although he could not tell whether she had actually looked at him.

Jimjoy dismissed the urge to smile and continued to survey the room. The table closest to him on his right held four men, all bearded, silently chewing on their main course, occasionally swallowing gulps of beer. One, his red beard shot with silver, thumped his heavy mug on the table, empty, wiped his mouth and beard with the back of his faded gray sleeve, and waved wildly toward the tired-looking waitress.

She looked at the bearded man, who held up the empty mug. With a nod toward the bar, she accepted his order.

For all the diversity in the saloon, Jimjoy became aware of one thing. The two couples next to him did not fit. Nowhere else could he see such an obviously commercial relationship.

Slowly he edged his chair back until it rested firmly against the wall behind him. Then he quietly shifted his weight until his legs were coiled under him.

"What you doing, bud?" demanded the nearest of the young men.

Jimjoy recognized the accent and coldly looked at him, bringing his hands up under the edge of the table.

"Nothing."

The other man began to move.

With that, Jimjoy yanked the table up to interpose as a momentary shield between him and the other two, or four, agents.

Crash.

Pssss.

Water splattered from somewhere, as if sprayed.

SSSSSZZZZzzzzztttttt.

"AAAeeeiiii!"

Jimjoy cleared the table area, spraying the remaining chairs aside and landing in the open dance area. He glanced back at the two couples, ignoring the pain in his right bicep, which felt like a low-grade burn.

A smell of smoldering electronics permeated the area.

The agent who had received the table struggled to his feet, half cradling his arms against him. Either wrists or forearms, or some combination of both, were broken or unusable.

The others?

The second man and his female companion were sprawled facedown against the table, while a set of cubes sputtered and sparked on the floor under the table. The second woman edged away from the table, as if the cubes were about to explode.

Jimjoy wanted to touch his injured arm, but just looked down at the narrow slit in his sleeve as he slipped away from his table. He tried to implement the relaxation techniques he had learned years earlier as he moved. His concentration was unequal to the task, and besides, he needed to finish getting out of the way before someone focused on him rather than on the devastation he had inadvertently created.

"Screamers!"

WWHHHEEEEeeeeeee!

Belatedly, the saloon alarm had gone off, and two blocky men carrying riot sticks and tangleweb guns burst through the tables to level their equipment at the table where the four agents had been.

Jimjoy eased himself into a vacant stool at the long bar.

The woman with the fake red hair had disappeared, but the riot police grabbed the man with the injured arms from a corner table after gestures from several patrons and a nod from the bartender.

"See that?" asked the man on the adjoining stool. "Weren't you sitting there?"

"Next table. Place exploded when I got up." Jimjoy shook his head. "Needed to use the facilities. Just lost my samburg steak."

"Didn't miss much. Should have ordered the grilled colpork. What happened anyway? They say anything?"

Jimjoy ignored half the questions.

"Thanks for the tip on the steak. She doesn't find me, and I'll have the colpork instead."

The Imperial Special Operative shook his head again, doing his best to look confused, which wasn't difficult, since he was anyway. He still couldn't understand how the Fuards had found him so quickly. Or been able to arrange the table next to him on such short notice.

"Buster . . . you ordered samburg?"

Jimjoy repressed a rueful smile at the efficiency of the tired-looking waitress, who didn't wait for his reply to start setting his order on the bar.

"That's fine. No way I'm going back there."

"Can't say I blame you . . . Say, you're bleeding . . . What happened?"

"Flame!" Jimjoy looked at his arm. He could see some blood, and the tunic sleeve was darker above the cut on his upper arm. The wound still burned. "Must have been cut by all the flying glass." He eased the fabric away from the skin. From what he could see, the wound looked like a combination between a razor knife cut and a tangler burn, but was little more than skin deep. It would probably leave a bruise covering most of his upper arm within a few days.

"Just a cut. Got some spray?"

"Cost you . . ."

"If it's just a few creds, fine. Otherwise, I'll just bleed until I finish eating."

"Five credits."

"Spray it."

"Cryl, spray here." The waitress's voice was low, but carried to the bartender.

Jimjoy realized that the saloon had quieted as the two men with the riot gear had been joined by three other men in dark black uniforms.

The waitress took the thin can from the bartender and sprayed the heal/seal solution through the slit sleeve and right over the threads of blood running down his arm. Jimjoy bit his tongue to repress a shudder at the pain. Definitely a nerve scrambler of some sort.

"So what happened?" asked the waitress in the same low voice.

Jimjoy did not look back over his shoulder at the methodical cleanup he knew had to be going on, but anticipated a tap on the shoulder at any second. He took a bite of the samburg steak, managing to choke it down. Colpork couldn't have been any worse. He looked for the El Parma and swallowed more than he should have. Between a steak that made sawdust taste good and the bruise and burning in his arm, not to mention his being a target for who knew how many agents, things were definitely headed downhill, if not farther.

He managed to clear his throat and recall the woman's question.

"Oh . . . hadesfire if I know. Got up . . . to use the facilities, and the big guy grabbed at my table. Then there was water everywhere. Somebody screamed, and the guy let go of me . . . ducked away . . ."

"All right . . . cart them off . . ." The voice of one of the men in the dark uniforms stilled the room.

Jimjoy realized that the local authorities had not attempted more than a perfunctory questioning of the people at the few adjoining tables, and were basically just cleaning up the mess.

The two blocky men tossed the two bodies on a stretcher which was quickly covered with a stained gray cloth. One of the dark-uniformed men escorted out the man with the injured arms. And no one even looked for the missing redhead.

"... swear there were four there ..." he muttered, trying to see if the waitress would comment.

"One of the women's gone. Havvies don't care ... so long as types like that don't cause more trouble ..."

"Don't care?"

"How could they? You want to be a target of every system's sneaks?" With that, the waitress was gone, heading for the table where the four agents had been sitting. She picked up a battered pitcher from beside the table and handed it contemptuously to the youth in the singlesuit who was cleaning up the rest of the mess around the table, waiting for the two Havvies to finish.

"... water ... who threw it ..."

Jimjoy had seen the pitcher, had felt the water. But who had thrown it? And why?

His forehead furrowed as he glanced over his shoulder, scanning the area. The table where the silver-haired woman and her two companions had been sitting was vacant, without a water pitcher. More interesting was the service station next to the table, without any water pitchers either.

The remaining two uniformed men were gingerly collecting the two fused cubes of metal. They ignored a second battered water pitcher on the floor.

He returned his glance to the plate in front of him.

"... be even worse if you don't eat it warm," offered the talkative man.

"Thanks," mumbled Jimjoy as he took a mouthful, though he failed to see how the samburg could be any worse cold.

The threesome had been the only ones close enough to have reached the water pitchers, but why had they bothered? Were they somehow tracking the Fuards?

He shook his head again as he methodically chewed the so-called steak. The advice had been correct. The cooler the samburg got, the more it tasted like oily sawdust, as opposed to hot sawdust.

The two Haversol officials completed their cleanup, scooped up their equipment, and left. The waitress and the busboy finished resetting the table, and the green-haired hostess showed a threesome to the smeared tabletop.

The conversations around the room returned to normal chaotic volume, as if the scene had happened before and would again.

Jimjoy was becoming more aware, minute by minute, of his aching right arm. Within another hour, it would be virtually useless for at least a day. And that meant he would have to be even more careful when returning to his room. At the same time he doubted that more than two pairs of agents would be tracking him in such an out-of-the-way place as Haversol.

The silver-haired woman's group had wanted either him alive or the Fuards out of the picture, for which he was grateful, if puzzled. The remaining Fuard was in no shape to want anything, and by the time he could summon much aid, Jimjoy would be on Accord. That left the Havvies themselves, and from what he could tell they didn't take sides.

He pushed aside the inedible remnants of samburg and took a series of swallows from the bottle of El Parma. Then he tried the vegetables, which were far better than the samburg. He finished them all, then swigged the last of the local brew.

He forced himself to use his right hand in signaling the waitress, who never seemed to look his way.

"Here." Still without more than a sidelong glance, she slapped the bill on the counter.

Jimjoy could feel her apprehension, but he ignored it and turned to the bartender.

"You or her."

"Either. Leave her hers."

Jimjoy handed the rail-thin man the Imperial twenty-credit note, waited for the change, and left two small notes on the counter. He did not look back as he headed for the still-open portals.

He found the effort to keep from wincing increasingly difficult as he climbed the stairs to his room. The arm was like a series of knives ripping at his shoulder, although the heal/seal had stopped the blood from the thin parallel cuts.

Slamming the door open, Jimjoy staggered in, ready to use his left hand, and the palm weapon it held, if necessary.

His room was empty, dust showing it as untouched as when he had left. Either that or the lightest footed or fingered of intruders had come and gone. He was scarcely up to analyzing the situation as he bolted the door and swallowed one of the emergency painkillers from his kit . . . before sinking into the valley in the center of the too soft bed.

IX

He was running, arms pumping, chest heaving, sweat streaming from his forehead down his face, blurring his vision, burning the corners of his eyes.

His right arm dangled useless, broken in two places, and each step jarred it, sending a fresh wave of pain into his shoulder.

Thrummmm!

The stunner bolt hummed past him, close enough to spur his already flagging steps.

He could feel the pair of Imperial Special Operatives closing in as he tried to reach the tube train station from the Grand Park.

Thrummmm!

His right leg buckled with the stunner paralysis, and he pitched forward, headfirst down the ramp toward the platform, trying to tuck himself into the approved combat roll, but hampered by the broken arm and unresponsive leg.

Thrummmmmmmmmmmmmmmm!

Another stunner bolt chased him, the sound rolling like thunder after him as he tumbled helplessly toward the stone wall where the ramp made a half circle down and around toward the tube train platform.

Crack!

A projectile ricocheted off the stone.

Crackkkk . . .

The sweat was still running off his face, and the throbbing in his arm continued to send waves of pain into and up through his shoulder, but Jimjoy realized he was lying on his back.

On his back? Where? Had Hersnik caught him?

Crack. Tap.

"Room cleaning."

Room cleaning?

He shook his head to clear his thoughts. The Imperiale . . . was he still there?

Glancing around the darkened room, he noted the still-open metal closet doors, his pack on the floor.

"You want your room cleaned?" repeated the voice through the closed door.

"No," he croaked. "Not now."

"No later. Maybe tomorrow."

"Maybe tomorrow," he responded through his all-too-dry throat.

Thrummmmmmmmmmmmmmmm. The muted roar of the cleaning machine continued down the corridor away from his room.

Slowly, he eased himself into a sitting position, using his good arm. Then he eased off the tunic, blinking back the involuntary tears when the fabric ripped away from the cuts and the heal/seal.

Surprisingly, his upper right arm appeared only slightly swollen. Although the throbbing intensified when he moved his arm or fingers, he could move them, a good sign so soon after the injury.

He shifted his weight and let his legs dangle over the side of the bed, taking one deep breath, then another.

The nightmare memory of the chase was clear, terribly clear, although he had never been on either end of such a pursuit in real life.

He started to shrug, then aborted the motion as he felt the pain from his arm increase. Instead, he gingerly slid from the bed to a standing position, then took a step toward the dingy bathroom. He needed to feel clean.

X

THE NARROW SCREEN beside the lock port flickered, then changed from a blank gray to a fuzzy image of the Accordan ship as it edged in toward the lock.

With its bulbous shape and plasteen plates, the Accordan vessel had certainly not been designed for anything besides full space work, or much beyond service as a transport. Jimjoy doubted that the structure could have taken much more than a full gee under any circumstances.

As his eyes surveyed the screen image beside the inner lock portal, he could not help but note the symmetry and the smooth plate joints that proclaimed a level of workmanship higher than technically or practically necessary.

"Stand by for locking." The metallic voice rasped through the compartment where he stood with two dozen others, including the silver-haired woman with the enigmatic smile. He had noticed that she also had green eyes, eyes which seemed to bore into his back when he wasn't able to check whether she was looking at him or not. Then again, it could have been his imagination.

He turned suddenly as a flutter of white in the corner of his eye caught his attention . . . and wished he hadn't made the motion quite so abruptly as a sharp ache in his right arm reminded him again of his first night on Haversol.

The second night had been far less eventful, if more painful. But he had not seen any of the characters from his first dinner, including the silver lady, since then. Not until he had gotten off the shuttle and caught a glimpse of her hair in the corridor of the small orbit station. But while the pain of whatever stunner or nervetangler that had raked his arm had subsided, it was far from gone, particularly when he used his right arm or moved suddenly.

Whunnnkkk.

The dull thudding sound echoed through the closed space, and the floor vibrated, but not enough to cause any of the travelers even to have to shift their footing.

"Locks linked," the unseen speaker announced unnecessarily. "Have your passcards ready for boarding."

Jimjoy took a deep breath and fumbled with the thin folder he carried, turning to his left just enough to catch sight of the silver-haired woman—the young silver-haired woman, he corrected himself. This time he caught her eyes momentarily before she looked past him without a glint of recognition. She had her passcard ready as well.

"Please enter the portal in single file. Your passcard will be taken once you are in the lock." The voice from the overhead speaker was a new one, a voice with an accent, as if the speaker used Panglais as a second language.

After all the polite jostling, Jimjoy Wright discovered that the silver-haired woman, as well as a number of others, had ended up in front of him. His bemused smile faded as he began to wonder.

He was assuming that she was the woman from the Imperiale. What was the likelihood of her being in both places, en route to Accord, merely by chance? If not by circumstance, then for whom did she work? Hersnik? The Matriarchy? Was she a contract agent for Hersnik?

He nearly shook his head, but repressed the gesture. After all, he was merely an itinerant pilot and technician—that was all he was.

The short line moved quickly. The dozen-odd people before him had disappeared through the inner lock portal so swiftly that he had to take three long steps to close the gap before stepping inside.

He held up his card.

"White?"

"Yes?"

The ship's officer ignored his response, instead waiting for an answer from a second official, who stood behind and to the right of the card checker.

"Have him stand aside."

"Would you please stand here, Ser White?" asked the checker with a polite smile on her lips. "We need to discuss several matters with you before you embark."

"What matters?" responded Jimjoy, equally as formally.

"Nothing wrong. We just would prefer you understand your options on Accord before the fact." With that she gestured for Jimjoy to move to the side, even as she took the next pass.

"Fliereo?"

"Clear."

"Simones?"

"Clear."

When the remaining ten men and women and the sole child, a boy of perhaps ten standard years, had been passed on by the officials, Jimjoy found himself standing with the two Accordan ship personnel and a thin and red-haired woman.

"Ser White. You first. Your credentials sheet indicates background and experience in various piloting duties, including flitters, skitters, and even space scout craft. You also claim experience as a journeyman electronics technician. We'll pass on the obvious Imperial connection and take you at face value." The checker pursed her thin lips and nodded her head at the man who had first suggested that he step aside.

"Afraid I don't understand," interrupted Jimjoy.

"It's not a question of understanding. Accord is a new planet with colonization started less than two centuries ago. The current and potential food supply system, and the entire economy, are geared to that development level. The native hydrocarbons and metals are on the light side. That means that there isn't much industry, except in the satellite community off Four. So there isn't much demand for pilots or electronics types, and that job market is rather tight right now. That makes you category three—useful but not in high demand."

"So how does that affect me?"

"There's a bond requirement . . ."

"Bond?" Jimjoy frowned. This didn't sound like the happy-go-lucky, back-to-the-trees bunch that rumors had portrayed or that all the Havvies had been talking about. They sounded much more like the hardened and practical would-be rebels that Headquarters feared—and that he had discounted. "Still don't understand."

"Because you may not be able to support yourself as an unofficial immigrant, you must post a bond equivalent to the passage cost to the nearest system which will employ you. In your case, that is relatively low, since Haversol needs both pilots and electronics types."

Jimjoy sighed.

"How much? With whom?"

"Five thousand Imperial credits."

"That's incredible." This time he did shake his head.

"Can you post it or not? Do you choose to?"

"You don't take immigrants?"

"Unless or until you take the immigrant aptitude tests, Accord takes no responsibility for your employability. Anyone who does not have verified long-term current employment must either post bond or take the tests."

"You can't win, Major," added the woman checker.

After a moment of shock, barely managing to keep his jaw in place, Jimjoy laughed. She was right.

"I'll post the bond."

"Since you're being reasonable, Ser . . . White . . . by being relatively direct, in turn, we'll spare you any delusions about our lack of vigilance."

The thin red-haired woman's eyes went back and forth in puzzlement as she watched the byplay between Jimjoy and the ship's officers.

"Assuming I am what you think I am, I'd be interested in the basis for your statement."

The checker grinned before answering.

"We test all immigrants for skills and aptitudes. The profile would tell us what your passcard shows, and a great deal more. That would go on the record, of course, which is periodically inspected by the various Imperial services, since Accord is a dutiful colony, fully aware of its indebtedness to the Empire."

Jimjoy refrained from grinning in return and shrugged. "What next?"

The man responded this time, nodding at the woman. "Cerla is the third officer. Doubles as purser, customs, immigration, and tourism.

Technically, once you post bond, you're a tourist, although we don't stop anyone who wants to from working. But you're a tourist even if you stay your whole life, with no local citizenship rights unless you officially change your mind and go through testing." He added, "Cerla will guide you through the formalities in her office."

Cerla, her short brown hair bouncing slightly, turned and headed through the inner ship lock into the Accord vessel, assuming he would follow.

He did, but not before overhearing the beginning of the conversation between the man and the red-haired woman.

"Sher Masdra, you have no skills beyond the commerce . . . shall we say . . . of your own person . . ."

When it came right down to it, reflected Jimjoy absently as he followed the purser, neither did he or anyone else. Especially, it appeared, on Accord. He hurried in pursuit of Cerla.

By the time he had caught up with the quick-moving purser, she had stopped by a portal that was beginning to open.

"My office, quarters, and general place of business." The woman gestured for him to enter.

Jimjoy slipped inside, ready for anything—except for the four-by-four-meter room, tastefully accented in shades of blue and cream, with a console and four small screens on one wall, a recessed double bunk on the opposite wall, a small table and two chairs. His eyes lighted on the built-in beverage dispenser, then flicked to the overhead lighting strips.

"Everything from business to pleasure," he noted dryly.

"Have a seat." Her tone ignored his sarcasm.

The Special Operative looked over the choice. Either the luxurious and padded sink chair or the utilitarian swivel before the console.

He settled into the sink chair, since he knew she would not sit down if he took the swivel. As he eased himself into the chair, he inadvertently put his weight on his right arm, and was rewarded with a renewed throb from the muscle all the way into his shoulder.

"You looked like you were sitting for an execution, Major."

"What's the Major bit? The name's White."

Cerla raised an eyebrow. "I thought we'd gone through that already. No charades, as I recall."

Jimjoy smiled expansively from the depths of the padded sink chair, designed clearly to keep upstart passengers from leaping at the purser/government agent. "Only admitted I wasn't an immigrant. Didn't deny

I had Imperial ties. You said that I was a Major . . . or whatever."

Cerla shook her head, and her bobbed brown hair bounced away from her round face and suddenly flat brown eyes.

"All right. You are Major Jimjoy Earle Wright the Third, Imperial Space Service, Special Operative, Intelligence Service, on special detail for reconnaissance of Accord. Your cover name is Hale Vale White. You have orders limiting you to strict observation, without any specific time limits.

"You graduated from Malestra College with an I.S.S. scholarship, completed pilot training at Saskan during the '43 emergency, served one tour as junior second pilot on the courier *Rimbaud* before being transferred to Headquarters staff for independent assignments. You are qualified to pilot virtually every class of atmospheric and space vehicle. You are persona non grata to the Fuards, the Halstanis, the Orknarlians. You are the tempter incarnate on *IFoundIt!* And your profile has been circulated to every non-Imperial world by the Comsis Co-Op.

"Besides, even if you aren't exactly *who* we think you are, there's absolutely no doubt about *what* you are."

Jimjoy frowned. "Care to explain that?"

Cerla smiled faintly. "I probably shouldn't, but you've obviously been set up. That means that the Empire either wants you dead or to create an incident. It also means that the Empire won't listen to anything beyond an in-depth factual report, if that. Something as ossified as the Empire cannot afford to change, not beyond the cosmetic."

"Hope you're going to explain," Jimjoy pursued. He was annoyed by the woman's patronizing attitude—even as attractive and friendly as she projected herself. Even if what she said made a certain disturbing kind of sense. He took a breath slightly deeper than normal and tried to relax.

"Yes . . . although I am tempted not to."

"Appreciate it if you would. I'm too Imperial not to be put off by your rather patronizing attitude toward the Empire. Even if you turn out to be right."

This time the purser smiled more than faintly, pursed her lips, and cleared her throat. "It's really very simple, so simple that anyone could use the technique, not that we had to in your case. First is the question of identity." She paused. "I'm getting there, Major. Believe me, I am. But there are a lot of pieces of information you need, and it's not exactly easy to blurt out these things, even though it's necessary now." Her smile was broad, but somehow forced.

While he appreciated the effort, and the smile, Jimjoy was leaning forward, wondering what came next, a cold chill settling inside him, reinforced by the hot throbbing of his still-unhealed arm.

"Every Imperial Special Operative falls within certain clearly defined parameters—male, with an optimum muscle, fat, and bone ratio that never varies by more than five percent; never less than one hundred eighty-one centimeters nor more than one hundred ninety-five centimeters; primarily Caucasian genetic background; strong technical education and mechanical skills; generally between twenty-eight and forty-five standard years; and always with a surface carriage index of between seven and eight."

Jimjoy looked at the purser blankly.

She said nothing more.

Finally, he spoke. "I understood everything until you got to the last item."

"I thought everyone knew about surface carriage indices." He could see the steel in her eyes and repressed a shudder, not quite sure how he had thought she might be friendly. Or was she just being mischievous?

"Afraid I'm rather uninformed."

"Surface carriage index is a measure of underlying muscular tension and emotional stability. It was originally developed by Alregord's psychiatrists as an attempt to provide a long-range visual indication of intentions. For that, it was a failure, because the only thing the index is really good for is showing the unconscious attitude of the individual toward humanity in general. The higher the number, the less socially oriented the individual. This gets complicated because the index varies with some individuals depending on their surroundings. For our purposes it doesn't make much difference, because the variations are generally less toward either end of the scale. Above ten, and a person is sociopathic or psychopathic. Below two, and there's almost no individual identity. The seven-to-eight range indicates a loner with little or no interest in permanent attachments to people."

"Sounds like psychosocial mumbo jumbo."

"Think about it, Major. Compare my description to any Special Operatives you may know before you condemn the analysis."

Jimjoy felt cold. If Accord had discovered such a readily apparent pattern, who else knew? His thoughts returned to the meeting with the retired spacer. Arto, had that been his name? Had he been an Accord operative? Or had he seen part of the pattern?

Jimjoy was brought back to the present by Cerla's next question.

"Now . . . do we continue the charade, or do you want to give me some idea of what you happen to be looking for?"

Jimjoy nodded. He'd been set up, at least to some degree, because his actions were a problem to the Empire . . . or the Service. It almost seemed as though no one wanted him to be successful. Every time he'd pulled off the difficult, they'd given him something tougher. The apparent ease of the Accord assignment should have been a signal, especially now, after the incident on Haversol.

The quiet of the cabin was punctuated only by the hissing of the ventilators, and by a dull *thunk* that echoed through the ship, indicating that the ship had unlocked from the Haversol orbit control station.

"While you're still deciding, would you like a drink?"

"I'll pass on the drink for now. How about a piece of information? I know your name. Period. You seem to know everything about me. Seems you'd have to be a part of colonial intelligence or armed forces . . . or that Institute . . . but why does anyone care?"

Cerla poured herself a goblet of a lime-green fluid and set the other glass back in the rack by the dispenser.

"Anything the Empire does affects us. How could anyone concerned not care?"

"Suppose you're right—"

"And you still haven't decided whether you're going to play it straight. What other options do you have? We know who and what you are. And . . ."

"And . . . ?"

". . . you're intelligent enough to see that."

Jimjoy was positive she had been about to say something else, but there was no way to determine what.

"Reluctant to affirm or deny," he said with a half smile. "If I deny I'm this Wright character, I have to spend forever proving I am who I am. And you won't believe me. If I lie outright, that's trouble. If I agree, that's a confession, and people have been known to disappear for less. This Wright character sounds like he's on everyone's hit list. Very popular man."

"You make a good point. Good . . . but irrelevant."

As she spoke, Jimjoy eased himself forward in the depths of the chair, trying to shift his weight in a way not to seem too obvious, yet ready for action if necessary. He doubted that he could escape untouched, but he had to try.

Cerla ignored his tension and sat in the anchored swivel less than a meter away. After speaking, she sipped from the goblet, swallowed, and cleared her throat.

"I will make one further observation which might help you decide. While Accord is not unknown for its ability to obtain intelligence, the background on you was there for the taking, laid out. This leads to certain disturbing conclusions, which is why you were warned on Haversol."

"Warned?"

Cerla said nothing, but waited.

"I see," temporized Jimjoy.

"Not totally, but we can always hope that you will." She stood, swiftly, though so gracefully that Jimjoy did not move. "Are you sure you wouldn't like something?"

"How about some juice?"

The purser/agent filled the second goblet and tendered it to him before reseating herself on the swivel, one leg tucked under her.

Her posture reassured the Special Operative . . . slightly. The sink chair felt somehow sticky under him and he shifted his position again.

"So where does that leave us?" he asked.

"You refuse to admit anything, and we're forced to take you on faith, at least in part. Assuming you are who we think you are, Accord would like to see that your visit is successful and that you return safely from our poor colonial outpost to your headquarters."

"And how much will you hide?" He didn't bother with questioning their assumption of his being an Imperial agent. That was probably all that was keeping him alive, even if he were being stubborn and not wanting to admit it outright.

"Nothing. We obviously will not volunteer anything, but should you find something or wish to observe something, we will certainly not hinder you in any way."

"That bad?"

"Yes."

"And who are 'we'? You talk about some group, but you've never identified who you are."

Jimjoy took a sip from the goblet. The green juice reminded him of a combination of orange and lime with a hint of cinnamon, except the combined taste was somehow whole and clean.

"We?" he prompted.

"Let us just say that most of Accord has a vested interest in your safe return, including the colonial forces, the local government, and the Institute."

Jimjoy wanted to shake his head. The situation sounded far worse than Hersnik or the briefing tapes had portrayed, and he wasn't even on Accord yet. Instead of commenting, he chose the inane.

"Very good drink. What is it?"

"Lerrit. Native."

She waited.

He waited.

"The *Carson* is approaching jump point. Approaching jump point."

The announcement from the hidden speaker was the first indication Jimjoy had of actual operation since the delocking maneuver. The crew was smooth . . . very smooth. And that brought up the question of why a ship's officer was spending so very much time with an apparent down-and-almost-out spacer—even one thought to be an Imperial operative.

Jimjoy had a momentary feeling of being into something over his head, very far over his head. He ignored it.

"So you fear the Empire—and my safe return, with whatever information I pick up, allows the Empire no pretexts, whereas my demise would allow them to blast two orbs with one bolt?"

"That's half of what the—what we had determined."

"And the other half?"

"If you're such a headache to your own Service, we're certainly not out to do them any favors." This time the smile was nearly malicious.

Jimjoy took a deep swallow of the lerrit, and waited again.

"What about all that noise about the bond requirement?"

"Forget it. That was for public consumption. Besides, the Empire might not clear any credit line or voucher you wrote, and that would be just another problem for us."

Jimjoy looked over at Cerla dubiously.

"We will, of course," Cerla continued, as she shifted her weight in the swivel and placed her nearly empty goblet on the console, "claim that you did post bond, and customs records will show that it was posted and returned to you when you left."

Jimjoy could see Hersnik causing problems over that transaction, but since it would be a while before he had to break that particular orbit, he said nothing about it. Instead he took another gulp of the lerrit, nearly finishing it.

"Would you like some more?"

"Not now." He looked for some place to put the goblet down, but finding nowhere within arm's reach, retained it. "Aren't you afraid I'll find something?"

"We're certain you will. We just don't think it will do the Empire much good."

"You obviously know it won't," concluded Jimjoy. "That means you either intend—" He broke off his statement, not sure where his words might carry him.

"We think it won't. We don't know. What were you going to say?"

Her last question had been idly asked, but Jimjoy did not miss the sharpening of attention.

"Not sure. Except that when something is this clear, there's more than meets the eye."

Cling!

"Standing by for jump."

The announcement was delivered in a bored tone from the same unseen speaker.

Cling! Cling!

The ship's interior was flooded with the pitch blackness that accompanied every jump, a blackness that seemed instantaneous and eternal all at once.

Normal lighting returned just as instantaneously.

"The next jump shift will occur in approximately one half standard hour."

Cerla picked up her goblet to drain the last half sip. Then she set it back on the console.

Thud.

The sound echoed through the quietness of the cabin.

Jimjoy avoided looking at the woman and tilted the goblet back to drain the last drops out.

"Are you sure you wouldn't like some more?"

"No, thanks." He extended the empty goblet with his left hand. His right arm was beginning to throb once more.

She took it and set it next to hers.

Thud.

"So where do all of these orbits within orbits leave me?"

"You're cleared into Accord. Your papers are here." She gestured vaguely at her console. "Once we arrive, the shuttle from orbit control will deposit you at the port outside Harmony. You're free to pursue your observations and inquiries. If you need special assistance or transportation to places not served by normal commercial channels, we suggest that you request such transportation through the Institute, rather than flying yourself in equipment of potentially dubious performance. If you prefer to be the pilot, the Institute will provide a flitter and a backup pilot.

"In return for this openness, Accord will know what you see, or at least have a good idea."

"Being unduly generous?"

"Practical. Short of assassinating you, Major, which would be easy enough to do, no one could stop you. We'd rather you didn't expire on our watch." She fixed his eyes with hers.

Jimjoy found their opacity disturbing in their intensity.

"We may also request that you actually observe other activities, from time to time, if we feel you may be missing information for your report."

"Indoctrination now?"

"Hardly. We hope for a limited balance in your findings, and more information shouldn't exactly hurt you. Your report will need to be more than brilliant, in any case."

Jimjoy smiled wryly. In that respect, Cerla was right. Dead right.

"That it?" He stood, ignoring the burning in his right arm.

"Almost." She stood and turned back toward the console, where she picked up the folder from the flat top. She took two steps back toward Jimjoy and extended the documents. "Those are your clearances, as well as a list of fax numbers you may find helpful. At the end are the particulars circulated on you, which you may find of some interest."

Cerla inclined her head toward the portal. "That's it, Major. Turn to the left as you leave. Your cabin is the last on the left. You won't need it that long, though. This is a short hop. Less than twenty-four hours before we swing orbit." She paused again. "And, Major, you might consider that being a loner is not the same as being independent."

"I'll think about it. Sleep on it, in fact, since that's what I need most right now."

Cerla raised her eyebrows, but said nothing. She continued to extend the documents.

Jimjoy took them, meeting her eyes. He nodded and stepped away, turning.

The portal opened before he approached and stepped through, heading to the left. He could feel the purser's eyes on his back as he departed, knew she was watching since he had not heard her close the portal. She was interested in him, but not in any romantic or sensual way.

Her parting comment bothered him, even more than the implications about Accord's use of the so-called surface carriage index. While Accord could have invented the concept just to fluster him, that didn't make sense either.

He found himself shaking his head again. Accord wasn't going to be any picnic, not if they were all as sharp as he'd seen so far. And that was scary for another reason. Accord wasn't even independent. Just a colony with a few scattered colonial forces, a colonial council, and a ragtag Institute pretending to be a university.

XI

ANY POWER WHICH merely opposes its own destruction or the loss of its territory almost never wins the ensuing conflict unless it defines its objectives beyond survival or the perpetuation of the status quo.

In warfare, status never remains quo. All things change, and success for the defender rests on the ability to shift the fight from defense to offense, to place its attacker or attackers on the defensive.

Without such a de facto switch in positions, the most that can be gained is a stalemate, and the result of such a stalemate is inevitably a change in the actual governments of both attacker and defender, even if the outward forms remain apparently unaltered.

Thus, the eventual outcome of any war is a change in the government of at least one of the parties. For this reason, no war should be undertaken by any government interested in its survival without change, not unless the alternative is wide-scale death and destruction.

Patterns of Politics
Exton Land
Halston, 3123 N.E.

XII

JIMJOY STEPPED THROUGH the shuttle portal and onto the open ramp that led down to the white tarmac below.

No impenetrable plastarmac, no lines of shuttles, and no throngs, either of officials or of welcomers. Just a handful of men and women. And, also unlike the central systems of the Empire, there was no baggage handling. Jimjoy carried both his hanging bag and the heavier and bulkier bag which contained equipment, folded clothes, and personal items.

"Excuse me . . ."

He looked back as he realized that his hesitation was blocking the other passengers.

The woman who had spoken was the silver-haired one, the one he suspected of lofting the water pitcher onto the Fuards to help him.

"You did a very nice job," he said, trying not to let the sarcasm creep into his voice. "Thank you."

"Just my job, Major. Now . . . if you will excuse me . . ."

"Sorry." He stepped aside, gestured broadly for her to proceed, following quickly. By now the upper right arm only ached, although it would be days before the bruise disappeared.

". . . about time . . ." Jimjoy ignored the whispered complaint from the heavyset man who had been standing behind the Accord agent. Except, he wondered, how could she be an agent? As an Imperial colony, Accord could not operate an intelligence service, nor any armed forces other than the domestic police forces.

Jimjoy had been operating outside the Empire too long and had totally missed that simple fact. Yet the woman, as well as the ship's purser and the other ship's officers, had acted as though she were representing *something*. Did the Ecologic Institute, or whatever it was called, actually run the colony? Was that what worried Hersnik?

He filed the thought and hurried to keep close to the silver-haired woman.

From the scattered group of people waiting a woman stepped forward, her tanned face and short-cropped blond hair giving her the appearance of an outdoor professional of some sort. "Thelina!"

"Meryl!"

The two women exchanged hugs, and Jimjoy fixed both faces in his mind as he skirted them and headed for the transportation terminal ahead. He could hear them talking as they followed in the same general direction, but he could not make out anything beyond pleasantries.

Thelina—that had been what the blond woman had called the Accord/Institute agent. He mentally noted the name. Then he took a deep breath and lengthened his stride, trying to ignore the tired feeling in his right arm.

The air was crisp, with a tang, not salty like the sea, but like a mountaintop above a fir forest. The shuttleport was west of Harmony, on a plateau of sorts, but certainly not one high enough to qualify as a mountain. Jimjoy looked up in front of him toward the west, where he could see a hint of clouds above the peaks on the horizon.

The gravity was a shade stronger than Terra-norm, but not enough to bother him, certainly not the way it would have on Mara or on the Fuard heavy planets.

He entered the transport terminal, glanced up at the high ceilings supported by arched wooden beams, and realized that the open area was both dimmer and cooler than he would have expected without climate control.

"Ser Wright?"

Jimjoy looked at the young man, scarcely more than a schoolboy, who wore a forest-green tunic and matching trousers.

"Yes." His voice was noncommittal.

"I am apprentice Dorfman, from the Institute. Your flitter is waiting to take you either to your hotel or to quarters at the Institute, if you prefer."

"The Ecologic or Ecolitan Institute?"

"Yes, ser."

"I plan to visit the Institute later, but I think I will take commercial transport to my hotel."

"Very good, ser. I hope we will see you later. The commercial transport sector is to your left."

With that, the apprentice turned and left.

Had there been a certain relief in the young man's expression? Had the Institute hoped he would refuse its offer? He shook his head and continued toward the ground-transport gates before him.

Once through the four-meter-wide polished wood gates that looked as though they were never closed, he put down both bags with relief, shrugging his shoulders, particularly the right one. Although he wanted to rub the still-tender muscles, he did not, instead leaning down as if to check the heavy squat bag.

Although he had been the first passenger from the shuttle through the gates, he waited until several others, in groups of twos and threes, began to appear and line up for transportation. He inserted himself third in line, watching to see whether any prearranged groundcar pulled into line to pick him up. None did.

He got the third car in the lineup. As the driver, a slender, white-haired man, opened the door, Jimjoy swung the bags into the rear seat with him.

"Your destination, ser?"

"Colonial Grande."

"Colonial Grande it is."

The electrocar hummed as it slowly built up speed leaving the shuttleport, turning right on the first boulevard, which contained a center parkway lined on each side with ten-meter-high trees. Each tree was the same, with a thick black trunk that rose five meters before branching out into stubby black branches. Along each branch, particularly at the end, sprouted long and thin fronds of yellow and green, enormous narrow leaves that swayed in the gentle breeze.

"The trees?" asked the Imperial Operative.

"Corran. They almost look T-type until you study them up close. They shimmer in the sun after a good rain, like they had a light of their own."

From the first boulevard the driver made another right turn onto a second, less expansive boulevard with a narrower center parkway that held but a single line of the corran trees.

Gray stone slabs, finely cut, composed the walks on the edge of the boulevard, and the grass was emerald green and neatly trimmed. For all the careful design of the streets, the dwellings abutting them were modest, muted in color, and generally of one story.

Almost as if it were a scene from the past, reflected the Special Operative, without metals, synthetics, and plastarmac, when people built with wood and stone and brick.

He asked no more questions as the car hummed through the morning quiet of Harmony, instead concentrating on gathering impressions of Accord. He could see the people, could even see an occasional small child, too young to be in school. Although he saw one or two individuals in a hurry, the general impression he received was of a peaceful town. Too peaceful?

There was none of the haste and self-importance of Tinhorn, or Madeira, or New Washton, or even of New Avalon. Certainly none of the lurking impression of power conveyed by New Augusta, or even the hidden fantaticism of smaller capitals—such as *IFoundIt!*

"Colonial Grande coming up on the left, ser."

Jimjoy recalled himself from his dreaming mood and took a deep breath.

As the groundcar hummed up to the Colonial Grande, which, with its plank-and-stone facing and heavy walls, resembled a lodge more than a hotel, Jimjoy surveyed the circular entry driveway, more from habit than from any feeling of need.

His eyes swept past the thin man working on the wide flower bed beside the main entry, then halted and looked back. No reason for a gardener not to be working on a nice morning, but something about the man bothered Jimjoy.

Instinctively, he checked the concealed belt knife, whose plastics would trigger no detectors, and the small stunner the Accord officials had pointedly ignored and probably should not have let him keep.

The electrocar purred to a stop.

Jimjoy watched the gardener, who had arranged his weeding chores so that he faced the entry canopy.

"The Colonial Grande, ser."

"Oh . . . yes. Thank you. How much?"

"Nineteen credits, ser."

Jimjoy fumbled a twenty note and a five-credit piece from his belt while still watching the gardener. Finally, he opened the door with his right hand, his left poised to use whatever might be necessary.

As the morning sun struck his face, Jimjoy caught the look of recognition on the gardener's face.

Zing!

Thrummm!

Even while flying toward the turf on the right-hand side of the entry pillar, Jimjoy fired one charge from the stunner.

A quick look around the base of the pillar reassured him that, while the other agent's needler had missed, he had not. Scrambling to his feet, ignoring the scrapes that his knees had taken even through his trousers, he scanned the area, checking the roofline.

"Hades . . . and . . ."

He launched himself back behind the next pillar.

Zing! Zing! Zing!

Chips from several needle darts sprayed around the pillar and into the area where he had first flung himself. They had come at an angle from behind the gardener.

Thrumm! Thrumm! Thrumm!

Several stunners responded to the needler, even before Jimjoy looked around the pillar to catch sight of a figure disappearing over the roofline. He pulled himself up, then lurched forward toward the inert form in the garden.

A small squad of men and women dressed in forest-green tunics and trousers, without insignia, had deployed across the entry area, appearing as if by magic. Their stunners had clearly been those responding to the rooftop sniper.

As Jimjoy finally reached the man, who was not breathing, so did a familiar figure, one with silver hair, but still wearing her traveling clothes.

"No warning from you this time."

"You didn't seem to need it," observed Thelina.

Jimjoy noted with amusement that Thelina had apparently made a dive similar to his and was now brushing the dirt and dust from her tunic.

Jimjoy took in the needle dart in the gardener's back, recognizing the dead man's facial structure through the disguise and changed hair color. He glanced back up at the roofline.

"Did you tell anyone where you were going?"

"Hardly." He looked around. The groundcar was gone, his two bags lying in a heap. "Except the driver."

"That wouldn't have counted," responded the woman flatly. "That leaves exactly one possibility, Major. I suggest you think about it."

Jimjoy didn't like that possibility at all, not at all. He looked away from the woman to see an armored groundcar purr into the circular entrance drive.

"Institute?"

"Yes."

"All right if I change my mind about lodgings?" He wondered if he were making a mistake, but so far, his opposition was treating him much better than the Empire had.

"Took you long enough, Major." His title was delivered almost in a tone of contempt.

"So I'm a slow learner."

Thelina flipped her shoulder-length hair away from her thin face, mumbling under her breath.

". . . damned hair . . . nuisance . . ."

"I rather like it, Thelina."

"Ecolitan Andruz to you, Major Wright."

"I rather like it, Ecolitan Andruz." He stooped to check what he already knew. Commander Allen had disposed of another disposable partner. Some other lieutenant, since anyone with seniority avoided the Commander whenever possible. That meant either that the Service didn't want to reveal to the colonials the need to dispose of one Major Wright or that two Special Operatives were acting independently. The second possibility was laughable.

Jimjoy shivered, feeling lucky that he had never had to work with the Commander. Allen and Hersnik both after him—just what he needed.

"You know him?"

"No," answered Jimjoy, "but I'd seen him before. That was enough."

"Nice partner. That last needle wasn't exactly an accident."

"Doesn't look like it, but you or I will take the blame. Do you think your people will find him?"

"No. Too professional, unless we did a total search, and that would leak out. Besides, that would lead to another embarrassment."

"Embarrassment? Is that all you people think about?"

"Considering that you are relying on that same protection, Major, I wouldn't push too hard. You're here . . ."

Jimjoy shrugged. "Defer to your wisdom, Ecolitan Andruz." He tried to keep his voice level. Clearly, the Institute had little love for any Imperials, or at least Thelina Andruz had little affection for either him or Commander Allen.

Jimjoy glanced back at the roof from which the Commander had disappeared, wondering when Allen would make another attempt. Probably not until Jimjoy left Accord, or until Allen had another expendable partner.

That left Jimjoy—and the Institute—some time.

He just hoped he was reading the situation right. It would be rather embarrassing, to say the least, if the Institute had set all the circumstances to encourage him to visit the Institute right off. On the other hand, maybe the good Commander did not want Jimjoy at the Institute.

He shook his head. No matter what, he was probably wrong.

"Head shaking won't help, Major. Here's your transport." She gestured at a second groundcar purring into the drive.

With a last look at the dead man, Jimjoy straightened up and walked slowly back to where the commercial driver had dumped his bags. He picked up both to carry them to the second groundcar, now waiting behind the armored one.

"Are you coming, Ecolitan Andruz?"

"No. Someone has to clean up the Imperial messes, Major, even coming off leave."

"Appreciate your efforts, Ecolitan Andruz, and I do like your hair, even if it's not fashionable to take compliments."

"I do take compliments, Major. From friends . . . or good enemies." She began to turn to face a younger man in the dark green uniform of the Institute. "Perhaps we can get around to clarifying your status as an enemy of sorts, at least by the next time we meet."

Jimjoy wondered whether he had caught the hint of a smile, or if he were just imagining things.

XIII

JIMJOY OPENED THE rear door of the groundcar and glanced inside, then stood back.

The driver was female, dark-haired, and tanned, wearing the same sort of uniform as the apprentice who had offered him a ride from the shuttleport.

The Imperial Major looked aside, then back at Thelina Andruz. She was already turning away, as if her duty were complete. She still wore the informal green shipsuit in which she had left the *Carson*, and she wore it with the authority of an Imperial Commodore.

Seeing that the Ecolitan had already dismissed him, Jimjoy returned his attention to the groundcar, realizing that his right arm was beginning to stiffen up from holding the heavy kit bag while he stood there.

Thelina continued her conversation with a young trooper, her voice low enough that Jimjoy could not pick up more than fragments of words. The uniform worn by the man was unfamiliar, as was the single insignia on the collar, a dark green triangle within a silver circle. Because planetary police and local Imperial reserves normally adopted Imperial-style uniforms, Jimjoy decided that the man, with the tunic's similarity to that of the driver's, had to be some sort of member of the Institute.

The idea of an Institute with a range of uniforms indicated more than tailoring, as did the lack of insignia.

"Are you coming, Major Wright? Ser?" The driver's voice was low, polite, and mildly insistent.

"In a moment." Jimjoy decided that Thelina was not about to halt her conversation for good-byes or other pleasantries, and swung the heavy kit bag through the open door of the groundcar. He then slung the hanging bag into the car, leaning inside to drape it over the kit bag. After another look at the oblivious Ecolitan Andruz, he swung himself into the groundcar, closing the door behind him.

Thudd!!

He repressed a wince at the force with which he had shut the door and decided against rubbing his still-sore arm.

The Ecolitan behind the wheel did not blink as she let the vehicle hum smoothly away from the circular drive of the Colonial Grande.

Jimjoy refrained from looking back, but settled himself as comfortably as possible on the rather firm and drab green rear seat.

"Standard transport?" he asked.

"Hardly, Major," answered the young driver. Her response seemed to be in Old American.

Jimjoy frowned. Had he addressed the question in Panglais or Old American?

While the Panglais of the Empire was the official language of Accord, since it was part of the Empire, most of the settlers had been refugees from the ecollapse of the western hemisphere of Old Earth, assisted and joined by the remnants of the marginally successful colony on Columbia. Yet until the driver had spoken, all he had heard, he was certain, had been Panglais.

"Old American the normal language at the Institute?" He phrased his question in Old American.

"We still call it Anglish, Major. But . . . yes."

"How did you know I understood it?"

The driver did not take her eyes off the road, but Jimjoy thought he saw a faint flush at the back of her neck, under the dark skin he had thought was tanned but now suspected was a naturally dark complexion.

She swallowed once, then answered. "I didn't. I thought you must if you were coming to visit the Institute."

Jimjoy nodded. A full background on one Major Jimjoy Earle Wright had been circulated. What hadn't been broadcast to the winds?

"How far is it?"

"By groundcar? Another two standard hours."

"Are we going all the way by groundcar?"

"I was told you were adverse to Institute flitters, and that you wanted to see as much of Accord as possible. The car was available."

Jimjoy sighed silently, letting himself enjoy a rueful smile. The transportation arrangements had to have been the idea of one certain Ecolitan Andruz.

Why, he couldn't say. Not yet, at least. But he would have bet that her sense of humor was warped, or warped enough for her to enjoy the thought of his sitting on a hard groundcar bench for two hours rather than spending a few minutes in a flitter. The object lesson was clear, intended or not.

He turned his eyes outside. Already the car was leaving Harmony, with only a few scattered homes along the still-broad boulevard that stretched ahead. Two hours! He owed the striking lady something.

Thelina—yes, the lady was certainly striking. Natural silver hair that reminded him of Accord's sunlight, green eyes, and a complexion that seemed like silvered bronze.

Striking indeed.

His mouth dropped open. Of course she was striking. She had been put there for him to notice. To distract him from noticing others. Once he had been allowed to discover she was an Institute member or agent, he would find it difficult, if not impossible, to recall who else might have been observing him, who else might be tracking him.

He shivered. Such an obvious ploy, and he had swallowed it whole. The undercover business was clearly not his. Clearly. So why was he in it?

He shook his head. A bit late for him to be understanding the difference between espionage and Special Operations.

"You do want to see as much of Accord as possible, Major, don't you?" asked the driver, interrupting his belated understanding of Thelina's role.

He forced a grin. "That's the way it's been presented. Would you like to provide some commentary on the sights we are passing? Their economic, historical, and military significance?"

"I'll do my best, Major," replied the driver without looking back at him.

Jimjoy straightened himself in the seat.

"We are now turning onto the Grand Highway. The highway climbs gradually west from Harmony and is the most direct route between the east and west coasts of Atlantal, at least in the mid-latitudes."

The Imperial Special Operative concentrated, trying to bring back into clear mental focus the screens upon screens of map projections he had studied.

Atlantal, the main and first settled continent, ran from nearly the north polar ocean to past the planetary equator, the only continent with such a great north-south range. Harmony was roughly forty degrees above the equator, with a temperate climate moderated further by its seaside position on Muir Bay and by the prevailing winds.

Jimjoy did not immediately recall the Grand Highway, but then the Imperial maps had been climate- and relief-based, rather than showing highways or local political jurisdictions.

"Grand . . ." he muttered, struggling to recall whether there had been an east-west range of hills or mountains near the latitude of the Accord planetary capital.

"Officially, the highway is called the Ridge Continental Transit Corridor. Basically, it follows the mid-continent ridge from coast to coast," the driver elaborated as she completed a sweeping turn onto an empty highway even wider than the boulevard they had just left.

Jimjoy nodded, visualizing the geography and remembering the odd intersection of continental plates that had left Atlantal with both east-west and north-south lines of mountains.

South of Harmony, the mountains ran generally in east-west bands. North of the capital, the even older hills swept north-south, climbing into the Saradocks, which peaked near the northernmost point of Atlantal.

He pursed his lips briefly as he returned his full attention to the driver and the scenery.

Outside, the well-tended but forest-bordered fields displayed a range of green and dark green plants. The space between the individual plants indicated to Jimjoy that the growing season had a while to go before harvest—certainly consistent with the local calendar of early summer. He saw few dwellings. Given the small total population of Accord, that wasn't surprising, although he personally would have suspected a larger population center than Harmony. Yet the capital was by far the largest urban area.

Most surprising was the highway. Far too wide and smooth and with far too little traffic for such an impressive engineering work.

Ahead, the road arrowed straight into the haze that cloaked the horizon and muted the dark green of the more distant hills and peaks.

"Rather an imposing highway . . . for so little traffic."

"It wasn't our idea, Major. A legacy of the Empire. Look at it closely." The driver was smiling.

He shrugged and flexed his shoulders, trying to unstiffen the sore arm and to get more comfortable on the hard seat.

Item: The pavement itself was smooth, without visible joints.

Item: The highway was straight, even when the geography would have dictated some curves

Item: The cuts through the hills were glassy smooth, so smooth that no vegetation had taken hold.

Item: Tall local trees towered over the edges of the highway shoulder, where the pavement ended, as if cut by a knife.

Jimjoy almost slapped his forehead. He was getting flamed tired of missing everything.

"Imperial Engineers? Another Road to Nowhere?"

The driver nodded.

"Suppose it dates back a good two–three centuries."

"Almost two. The Institute figures it will last another 2,000 years before the underlying stresses reach the total structure break point."

"Wouldn't want to be around then." Jimjoy laughed harshly.

"Not much chance of that, Major."

"Suppose you're right there."

Impervious to virtually all natural forces except the basic stresses of geology, used or unused, the road would outlast them both. And the resources used to build it probably represented close to as much as the total colonization effort. Needless to say, there had only been two Roads to Nowhere built, according to the footnotes in Engineer history. One was on Tinhorn, and the other had not been mentioned. Obviously, it was on Accord.

Just as obviously, there was more to Accord, far more, than he was seeing, or likely to see. And someone in the Imperial forces didn't want him to see it.

XIV

AFTER NEARLY TWO hours in the groundcar, Jimjoy was more than willing to admit that his inadvertent refusal of an Institute flitter had been a terrible choice, not even considering the near assassination. Unhappily, he had not thought that turning down the flitter had meant making a choice between ground and air transport.

For the last sixty minutes the highway had not only continued straight but remained absolutely level, roughly five hundred meters below the highest points on the ridge lines of the mountains to the south. Neither had the vegetation visible from the car changed much, nor the tenor of his desultory conversation with the Ecolitan driver.

He was only relieved that his trip had encompassed less than ten percent of the highway's length, and hoped that it would not encompass much more. The dull silver of the pavement was boring, engineering masterpiece or not.

"Mera, how much farther? What's on the other side of the hills to our right?"

"Major, we're less than ten minutes from the Institute. On the other side of the hills are the grounds belonging to the Institute. Training areas, research farm plots, some specialty forests, all sorts of things like that."

"Airstrips?" he asked innocently.

"A few, but just for transport and medical emergencies. We're still pretty thinly populated up here."

Jimjoy smiled wryly. The cadet, or Ecolitan, or whatever they called senior student types, hadn't liked the idea of driving him all the way on the ground either and had used the incredible smoothness of the highway to best advantage, moving close to the speed of a slow—very slow—flitter, and well above the recommended speed for a groundcar.

During the trip, they had seen only three or four other vehicles, all slow and bulky cargo carriers with wide tires.

"Steamers," according to Mera, running on actual old-fashioned external combustion engines.

"Why not?" she had answered his question. "They're cheap, efficient, nonpolluting, and suited to the road. They represent maximum efficient use of resources."

The last comment had puzzled the Imperial Major. Accord would not have to worry about resource shortages for centuries, if even then, especially with some of the metal-rich moons circling the fourth and fifth planets in the system. So why were the Accordans so preoccupied with resource efficiency, rather than in building up their manufacturing and technical infrastructure as quickly as possible?

That also scarcely sounded like a colony planning revolt, especially when Mera had pointed out that Accord was attempting to develop the fewest number of mines and mineral extraction sites and was investigating "other" extraction processes.

The young Ecolitan could have been lying, but Jimjoy didn't think so. "Other?"

"Biological. You'll have to get that from the research fellows. They can lead you through the details, Major."

Jimjoy paid more attention to the outside surroundings again as the groundcar began to slow. He could see a break in the hillside ahead and to the right, as well as a green triangle perched upon a wooden pole beside the road, and set perhaps two meters above the level of the smooth road surface.

"We here?"

"Another few minutes once we leave the Grand Highway."

"Grand Highway? Thought it was the Ridge Corridor."

"We're not quite so prone to take Imperial terminology literally. Besides, what else would you call it?"

Although he shrugged at the young woman's cavalier references to a great engineering feat, he was a little surprised at her flippant tone with him. Her feelings he could understand. The highway might be a great engineering wonder, but it didn't exactly appear to be necessary. He decided to push further.

"The Grand Fiasco?"

"Not totally. It does make coast-to-coast surface cargo traffic both practical and economic, so long as you don't have to factor in the amortization of the construction costs, which we don't."

Jimjoy kept his jaw in place. The driver, young as she appeared, had been educated in more than mere ecology, that was certain.

"Economics, yet?"

"If you can't make something economical, its ecology or engineering doesn't matter. Except for something like the Grand Highway."

Jimjoy agreed silently—with reservations—and braced himself

when the groundcar slowed as it took the banked curve through the narrow cut in the hill. The steeply sloped sides of the exit road were covered with vegetation, a sure sign that the exit road postdated the highway.

The much narrower road they now traveled did not follow the imperious straight-line example of the Engineers' masterpiece, but arced around the more imposing hills in wide, sweeping curves, gradually descending.

"How far?"

"Another five kays. Just around that last curve and downhill from there."

Although he saw one short and low stone wall, Jimjoy noted the general absence of fences, as well as a mixture of familiar and unfamiliar flora. He saw no animals.

"Animals?"

"The Institute research farm is farther west. Most native animals are nocturnal, those that the Engineers left." While her voice was carefully neutral, that neutrality provided a clear contrast to her previous tone.

"I take it the Institute has questioned the Engineers' policy of limiting local fauna?"

"That was before our time, and there's not too much we can do about it, except to modify things to fill in the gaps."

"Gaps?"

"Ecological gaps. If you need a predator, one will evolve. In the meantime, you discover something else overpopulates its range, usually with negative consequences.

"Here we have the additional problem of fitting in Terran flora and fauna necessary for our own food chain. We don't need as much as the Imperial Engineers calculated. But they always thought bigger was better."

Jimjoy listened, but concentrated more on his surroundings as they presumably neared the Institute.

No power lines, often common on developing planets, marred the landscape. Nor did he detect any overt air pollution, not even any smoke plumes. No glints of metal or rusted hunks of discarded machines.

The bluish-tinged trees with the angular leaves had a well-tended look. Interspersed with the native trees he could see Terran-style evergreens, but nothing which looked like T-type deciduous stock.

The Accord-built road, although narrower than the Grand Highway and curving, appeared equally smooth, without a sign of patching or buckling.

"How active is Accord? Geologically?"

"Slightly less than Terra, but the geologists claim that the current era is the most stable in several eons. And a geologic disaster is waiting in a decaying orbit."

"When does the disaster begin?"

"I understand we have somewhere between twenty thousand and fifty thousand years local."

Jimjoy caught just a glimmer of a smile as she answered his last question.

Mera had slowed the groundcar evenly as they neared the next curve. Jimjoy tensed, wondering if he were about to be ambushed or whether they were merely nearing their destination.

As the car decelerated to slightly faster than a quick walk, it came around a wide curve and through two cylindrical pillars, one on each side of the road. Each rose five meters and was topped with a bronze triangle set inside a dark metal circle. The dark gray stones were set so tightly that the joints were hairline cracks. No mortar was visible.

Below, in a circular valley, stood the Institute. The placement of the low buildings, the muted greens and browns, and the symmetry of the landscaping all stated that the valley housed an institute. Beyond the buildings, the ground rose to a lake, then to a series of small hills that flanked the lake before climbing into a series of foothills, then into low mountains nearly as high as those whose flanks had been scored by the Grand Highway of the Imperial Engineers.

"Impressive."

"You think so?"

"Yes. Very powerful."

"Powerful?"

Jimjoy nodded before speaking. "Tremendous sense of power, of knowledge, of purpose. Especially purpose."

"So that's why you're here."

"I'm not sure I know why I'm here myself, young lady. Would you care to explain?"

"I shouldn't have spoken out."

"No reason to stop now, and besides, your thoughts won't doom either one of us."

The driver laughed lightly, uneasily. "No." Her voice turned more serious. "Not this time. I suppose I do owe you some explanation." She did not look back at him as she let the groundcar roll down the curving drive toward a circular building at the front of the Institute. "Most visitors make some comment about how rustic the Institute is, or how isolated, or how beautiful. All that's true, but it's not why we're here. You're the first I know of who instinctively saw—really saw—it as it is."

Jimjoy wondered if she had shivered or merely shifted position as she completed her admission.

"Are you as dangerous as they say, Major Wright?"

Jimjoy repressed a smile. After more than two hours, Mera had finally used her own admitted weakness as a lever to ask a question to which she had wanted an answer.

"Don't know who *they* are. Or what they say. Done some dangerous things, and a lot of stupid things. Probably more dangerous to me than to anybody else. Don't know how else to answer your question."

Mera nodded. She pursed her lips, then licked them and looked at the building she was guiding the car toward.

Jimjoy followed her glance, realized that he had seen but a handful of vehicles. He was betting that some of the gentle hills were artificial and housed both aircraft and groundcars.

"Major . . ."

Jimjoy waited.

"If you're dangerous to yourself . . . what you learn here can only make that worse . . ."

He frowned and opened his mouth to question her observation.

"Here we are, Major. It looks like the Prime himself is here to greet you. That's quite an honor, you know."

Jimjoy focused on the silver-haired and slender man in an unmarked forest-green tunic and trousers who was walking from the circular building down the walkway lined with a flowering hedge. The tiny flowers were a brilliant yellow.

Both car and Ecolitan would arrive nearly together.

Jimjoy smiled wryly, briefly.

Mera's pause on the hilltop overlooking the Institute had been for more than just letting him get a good look at the facilities. He just wondered what other signals he would discover after the fact while he was at the Institute.

XV

"HE'S ADDRESSED AS 'Prime,' " noted Mera, as Jimjoy reached for the groundcar's door latch.

"Prime what?"

"Just 'Prime.' He's the Prime Ecolitan."

The Imperial Major shrugged, then opened the door.

"Don't worry about your bags. We'll get them to your quarters. Besides, you don't need to drag them out."

Jimjoy released his grip. "All right . . . Thank you."

"No problem, Major. No problem."

He looked at the approaching Ecolitan, then back at the driver. "And thank you for the scenic tour."

"Anytime, Major." She was already looking at the driveway before her.

Jimjoy closed the door and straightened, absently deciding that, even had he been in uniform, a salute would have somehow been improper.

"Honored to meet you," he stated, with what might have passed for a slight bow to the slender man who stood waiting.

The Ecolitan seemed several centimeters taller than Jimjoy, but whether the differential was created by an effortlessly perfect carriage or by actual physical dimensions, Jimjoy wasn't immediately certain.

"The honor is mine, Major Wright. It is not often we receive Imperial officers here at our isolated and rather provincial outpost of erudition."

The statement was delivered by the lightly tanned man without even the hint of a smile, although Jimjoy thought he caught the hint of a twinkle in the dark green eyes as the Prime extended his hand. "Welcome to the Institute."

"Pleased to be here. Not certain I had all that much choice, under the circumstances, but look forward to learning all about the Institute."

"We would be more than pleased to offer what we have, although what you find may not be what you seek."

"Mysteries within mysteries," noted Jimjoy with a shrug.

The Prime smiled. "No mysteries. My name is Samuel. Samuel Lastborne Hall. I am called Ecolitan Hall, Prime, Supreme Obfuscator, and

other terms less endearing. Also Sam, mostly by dear friends and enemies."

"Pleased to meet you, Sam." Jimjoy nodded again. "I've also been
called by a number of names."

"Currently . . . Jimjoy Earle Wright, Major, Imperial Service, or
Hale Vale White, unemployed pilot?"

"Whichever you prefer. I'd prefer not to acknowledge anything."

"I trust you will not object if we use your real name, Major Wright."

Jimjoy felt as though he were fencing on the edge of a cliff, rather
than standing on a gray stone walkway lined with a flowered hedge,
and bathed in a weak sunshine that struggled through the high, thin
clouds.

"Can't control what you acknowledge," he finally admitted with a
smile.

Jimjoy realized that the groundcar had not left, even though he had
shut the door.

"We need to continue our talk, Major, but it's rather impolite to
keep you standing here. My office is not far."

The Prime Ecolitan turned.

Jimjoy followed.

As the two men headed back toward the low two-storied, stone-
walled building, the electrocar began to whine as it rolled away toward
its storage spot or next assignment. Jimjoy wondered when he would
run across Mera again, or if he would.

The main doors to the Institute building, simply carved, were the
old-fashioned manual type. No automatic portals for the Ecolitans.

Holding one open for Jimjoy, the Prime used just his fingertips,
indicating the apparently well-designed counterbalancing of the heavy
wood.

Jimjoy stepped through, then slowed to wait for his escort.

"My spaces are at the head of those stairs."

The air was as fresh as that outdoors, if slightly cooler, and the stone
underfoot was identical to that of the outdoor walkway except for the
wax or plastic film that protected the interior stone and imparted a faint
sheen.

Heavy, open wooden slabs, smoothed to a satin finish and protected
with a transparent coating that neither was slick nor showed any signs
of wear, composed the stairs.

Despite his intentionally heavy tread, Jimjoy could feel absolutely
no give in the three-meter-wide staircase. He did not nod to himself at

the craftsmanship, but added that assessment to those of the doors and the stonework.

Double doors to the Prime's office stood open, and the Prime made no move to close them after he and Jimjoy entered the simply furnished room.

Jimjoy had seen no one else except Samuel Lastborne Hall since leaving the groundcar.

Besides the wide one-drawered table that served as a desk, the all-wooden armchair behind it, and the three wooden straight-backed armchairs for visitors, the only other furniture in the modest room consisted of built-in bookcases, which lined all the wall space, except for three wide windows reaching floor to ceiling. The half-open tinted glass windows were flanked by simple-working inside wooden shutters. Although the woods in the room's furnishings showed differing grains, all were light, nearly blond.

The Prime gestured to the chairs before the table.

"You'll pardon me if I take the most comfortable, but these days I am not quite as limber as I once was."

Jimjoy sat in the chair on the far right, closest to the middle window.

Smiling as he seated himself in his own chair, the Prime slowly let the smile fade.

In turn, saying nothing, Jimjoy deliberately scanned the rows and rows of bookshelves, picking up the eclectic flavor of the titles arrayed there. Most he did not recognize, but the titles showed an impressive range. At last he returned his glance to the head Ecolitan, waiting.

"Did you wonder why I met you myself? Why there were no subordinates? Or have you thought about those implications?"

"Didn't think about it one way or another."

Ecolitan Hall smiled faintly again. "The behavior of those in power is reflected in their actions. So . . . perhaps I have no power.

"In any case, I would like you to consider several points while you remain here at the Institute. First, while we do believe you should stay for at least a few days, we hope you will remain longer. How long you stay is entirely up to you."

"Not entirely," interjected Jimjoy wryly, his attention directed at the Prime even though he could hear a flitter approaching and wanted to turn to check it out.

"True. You do owe some allegiance to a higher authority, such as it is, but you do have some leeway. It is in your interest, and in ours, for you to understand the Institute as fully as possible.

"Second, we would like you to talk to as many people as possible, as often and as deeply as you feel comfortable.

"Third, any and all classes here at the Institute are open to you, and the entire staff has been instructed to answer all your questions. Completely, I might add."

Jimjoy continued looking past the Prime toward the bookshelves behind the man, wishing he had chosen the chair farthest from the window to be able to see the incoming flitter while still looking at the Prime.

"Completely? Doubt that. Should be at least a few secrets around here."

The whine of the incoming flitter sounded military, with the fuller sound and overtones of maximum-performance turbines.

"There are quite a number of secrets here, Major. If you can find them, you are welcome to inform the Imperial Service of them all, should you choose to do so."

"Assuming I were an Imperial officer . . . not seriously suggesting I would be able to hide anything from any superiors I might have?"

"I am not suggesting anything, Major. Your report is your report. We are providing some incentive for you to stay, and I personally feel that any additional information you obtain will be of benefit both to you and to the Institute. We should both end up profiting from the experience."

Jimjoy returned his full attention to the Ecolitan as the flitter landed, and its turbines whispered away into silence.

"Why would such a peaceful organization as the Institute require military-style flitters? Would you care to answer questions like that?"

"Might I first inquire if that is theoretical or based upon your own observations? Or upon rumor?"

"Observation."

"You have actually seen a military-style flitter? Here? I don't see how." The Prime shook his head rather dubiously.

"If we're splitting neutrons, honored Prime Ecolitan, I should state that my observations have not noted an actual military flitter, but only one flitter with full military engine and lift capabilities."

The Prime nodded. "You are well above average in your observations, as well as basically honest. It may be too bad for you that you were not born on Accord. Then again, it may be better for all of us that you were not."

"Do I get an answer? For all the supposed openness?"

The older man shifted in the wooden armchair, smiled easily, and nodded.

"We do not operate any armed flitters at the Institute, but all our flitters are built with full armor-composite fuselages and are powered with the highest-powered turbines possible for each class. We manufacture our own fuel through a modified biological process which, although time-consuming, is based on renewable feedstocks and is relatively less expensive than synthetic fuel engineering. That process is also much cleaner in environmental terms."

"Armor implies defense, and defense implies attacks. There are no reports of attacks."

"Defense . . . true. But defense against what? Against more severe weather, against a wilder ecology in some ways, and against early breakdown. Also, there has been some sabotage, and you yourself were the subject of an armed attack."

Jimjoy pulled at his chin. "That wasn't exactly a complete answer."

"Your follow-up question was not based on either fact or observation."

"So I have to know at least part of the question before anyone will answer?"

"For me, that is true, but I am sure that the students and most of the instructors will answer most of your questions, whether or not you know what you are asking about, to the best of their knowledge."

Jimjoy grinned. "Sounds like you really want me to learn what you're doing. Either that or you don't intend for me to ever leave."

"Major, we cannot afford for you not to return. You, Major Jimjoy Earle Wright, will return able to report and discuss anything and everything about the Institute."

The assurance sounded absolute.

Jimjoy tried not to frown.

The Prime stood, then walked around the desk table.

In return, Jimjoy stood. "Appreciate your hospitality. And the transport."

"Let me know personally should you find any trace of inhospitality. And I do mean that." The Prime's handshake was firm. "Now I will be taking you to meet Ecolitan Thorson, who will take care of your quarters and any other logistical and scheduling requirements you may have while you are here."

Jimjoy followed the Prime back down the wide wooden stairs that should have been slippery and were not, trying to keep from shaking his head.

XVI

"GAVIN THORSON," OFFERED the painfully thin man in greens. His freckled face and smooth complexion gave the impression of a man younger than he had to be.

"Hale White or Jimjoy Wright, depending on whose word you take," answered Jimjoy, extending his hand.

"Major Wright, a pleasure to see you. I must admit that you look less fearsome in person than on paper." He took Jimjoy's hand and gave it a healthy squeeze, then stepped back. His smile, like that of the Prime Ecolitan, Samuel Lastborne Hall, was open and friendly.

"Careful, Gavin," interjected the Prime from near the doorway. "That's part of his effectiveness. All the while he looks at you guilelessly, he listens, and more important, he understands. Then he analyzes what he hears."

"Too much credit," said Jimjoy with a laugh.

"There he goes again. Watch out for your secrets."

"Thought you said there weren't any, or none that I couldn't ask about."

"Gavin will tell you anything you want to know, provided you can ask the question to show you know what you're talking about."

Jimjoy glanced back at Thorson, who had remained next to his comparatively cluttered desk.

"The Major should have one of the standard staff rooms in the short-term quarters."

"That's no problem. Anything else, Sam?"

The familiarity caught Jimjoy off guard.

"We don't stand on ceremony around here. I do put up with the students and junior staff calling me Prime, and I reluctantly have to insist that all the staff be accorded some deference by the students, although that's never been a problem after the first two weeks anyway." The Prime Ecolitan nodded as he returned his gaze to the thinner Ecolitan. "The Major is a visiting lecturer and staff member. He may observe, or he may choose to share some knowledge with us. That is entirely his decision."

The older man glanced back at Jimjoy. "Now, if you will excuse me, there are a few things still pressing on me."

Jimjoy inclined his head and waited until the Prime had left.

"Amazing man, Sam is. Hard to believe he's nearly ninety."

"Ninety! He looks scarcely fifty." Jimjoy paused, then added, "Is that a benefit of Accord biotechnology?"

"Probably, but not in the way you would suppose. Diet, physical condition, genetics, and mental outlook are still the best retardants of age. Sam just comes from good stock, and he's taken care of himself."

The Imperial Major could not restrain a skeptical glance at the gangly Ecolitan.

"Ah, yes, the Empire is concerned about our great biotechnology secrets. I only wish we had them."

"What I've read indicates you've already done plenty."

Thorson brushed the remark aside with a gesture as he suddenly stepped away from the puddle of sunlight where he had been standing.

"We have. We certainly have. But not with humans. We've accomplished a great deal in integrated ecologic studies, experimental plant genetic manipulation, and the development of Accord-specific plant crossbreeds. We've even managed some limited tissue clones and some success in suppressing the genetic reaction syndrome. But conquer the aging process? Hardly. Do you have any idea how complex that is?" The fussy-looking Thorson nodded his head. "Now, I need to get you to your quarters, and we need to get you some greens. Street clothes just won't do, and while we could probably find Imperial uniforms, I doubt that you really want to wear them, not after that nasty incident in Harmony."

"Greens would be fine."

"Come along, then. After that, I need to have you assigned an I.D. number and plugged into the information net for schedules, library access, and all the little details that you need to know about. Then there's an account to use your funds . . ."

"Details . . . ?" But Jimjoy was talking to the Ecolitan's back. He turned to follow the thin man.

Thorson bounded down the wide stairs two at a time, his feet scarcely seeming to touch the wood.

Jimjoy felt like his steps shook the building.

"Where—"

"First, your quarters, where Mera should have put your bags."

Jimjoy had wondered about that, but had let the young woman take his bags, particularly since there was nothing absolutely vital in them. While some material was convenient, it all could be replaced, with a little effort. What would be interesting was whether it was all there, and how deeply the Ecolitans had snooped.

He shook his head. It would all be there, with the seals intact.

Two doorways, two covered walkways, and what seemed a half a kay later, Thorson flapped down a corridor and flung open a doorway.

"Here you are."

The sandy-haired man was not even breathing hard, despite the breakneck pace he had set. If an older administrator were in such good shape, what conditioning would he find in Ecolitans who could take the field? And would he find Ecolitans who were trained to take the field?

Jimjoy looked around the room, which had a single wide window and four-meter-square floor space.

"Not exactly a palace, but it should be sufficient for your stay. I am pleased to see Mera has delivered your two bags."

Jimjoy looked down, convinced that they had not been touched. The two bags had been laid next to the narrow bed. The bed was unmade, but a set of linens and a heavy dark green quilt were folded at one end.

Beneath the window, which was closed off by blond wooden shutters, were a study table and chair. On the desk was a bronze lamp with a parchment shade. The chair was carved and straight-backed. Both table and chair were of matched bronze woods, slightly darker than the shutters.

White plaster walls lightened the room. From what Jimjoy could see, the exterior walls were solid stone, but whether the plaster had been applied directly to the stone or whether there was an extensive internal wooden support structure was another question. He wasn't immediately ready to start thumping or probing the room's walls to make that determination.

A rectangular gold rug, edged with a dark green border, covered most of the gray stone flooring. A second bronze lamp was attached to the wall beyond the foot of the bed. The bed itself was against the right, or north, wall, while a built-in closet and drawers were on the left-hand side.

Crossing the soft rug, Jimjoy walked toward the window, glancing down at the triangular design in the center of the gold central section.

"That's the Institute's emblem," answered Thorson to the unspoken question.

Jimjoy stopped in front of the window and unhooked the shutter latch, folding the hinged shutters back against the casement. The sunlight outside had begun to fade as the clouds from the west crept along the mountains.

The base of the window, more than a meter wide, stood about one and a half meters above the neatly clipped grass. The lawn sloped gently downhill toward a garden. On the far side of the garden, the ground again rose toward another single-story building, one which had the look of classrooms, or laboratories, with close-spaced and near continuous windows.

Turning back to Thorson, Jimjoy nodded. "Very pleasant. These are short-term quarters?"

"Short-term staff quarters. Provided for Ecolitans who are here for a few weeks, or at most a few months. The longer-term quarters range in size from two or three rooms with kitchen and bath facilities to separate houses in the family quarters section."

Jimjoy nodded again.

Thorson smiled his awkward smile. "This is more central to all that's going on here, and Sam was most specific that he wanted you to be able to see everything.

"Now . . . I need to show you the dining area, and we need to get you over to the tailor to pick up your greens, and then to Data Central to provide you with an I.D. to use the datanet system."

Jimjoy grinned as the tall, thin Ecolitan flew down the corridor like a giant stork. Then he shrugged, closed the door—which had no lock, he noted in passing—and followed the older man.

XVII

THE STOCKY MAN who was in fact a muscular thin man puffed up the ramp into the shuttle.

The embarking officer glanced at the checker, who batted her eyelashes and turned to address the boarding passenger.

"Ser Blanko . . . so glad you enjoyed your stay on Accord."

"Who said I enjoyed it? Business is business is business. That's my motto." He swung his case around.

"If you wouldn't mind, Ser Blanko . . ."

"Mind what?" grumbled the stocky man with a touch of a whine to his response.

"Just being careful with the case until you get home. That's all.

After your partner, we wouldn't want you to have any problems . . ."

Barely an instant's stiffness froze the man. "You got the wrong person, officer. Never had a partner, never will. Business is business, like I say. No time to educate someone else. Just enough time to get the sale made."

"So sorry, Ser Blanko. We hope you have a pleasant trip back to Alphane."

The man did not correct the embarking officer.

Although his destination was Alphane, his card indicated Frostbreak.

XVIII

"THELINA . . ." HE ROLLED the sound of her name out into the whispers of the night, his voice scarcely more than a murmur.

As he walked toward the experimental orchard, he wondered why he had spoken the woman's name. After all, she had scarcely said more than a handful of words to him, and he was certainly no more attractive than a score of senior Ecolitans, all intelligent, well muscled, and tanned. Most important, in her brief words to him, Thelina Andruz had made it perfectly clear that she was less than thrilled with his success at wholesale and individual murder and civil disruption.

He frowned in the darkness, not that darkness had concealed anything in the centuries since the development of night vision scanners and snooperscopes. He concentrated on stretching his legs, trying to make each stride perfectly even, perfectly balanced, trying to feel his way across the uneven ground without looking.

Training his body to operate as independently of conscious perceptions as possible, he had practiced the technique for years. While he still had to scan the terrain, he did not have to spend time consciously plotting his route or progress.

Jimjoy paused to listen, catching again the sound of someone trying to match his stops. The unseen watcher continued to miss the irregular pauses on a continuing basis.

The Imperial Major grinned. Obviously, some poor apprentice or student had been assigned the task, probably either as penalty or to improve clearly deficient skills.

Jimjoy suddenly broke into a full sprint toward the orchard, still at least a half kilometer away.

A faint gasp whispered across the high grasses from his left, and he grinned as he concentrated on breaking away—at least momentarily.

Within three steps he was close to full speed. Tempted as he was to come to a full stop and listen to the chaos that might result from his tracker's lack of ability, he did not. Jimjoy was a sprinter by build and should have been doing more distance running, far more distance running, than he had been doing recently.

Training was boring, inanely boring. This time, with someone trailing him, he could make it into a game. If the tracker were a good distance runner with a lighter build, by the time that Jimjoy reached the orchard, the odds would be that his pursuer would be catching up, no matter how hard Jimjoy pressed.

He tried to keep his breathing deep and even, matching breath to strides, once the early exhilaration passed and his legs began to feel heavier.

Listening as he ran, he tried to pick up the sounds of his shadow but could hear nothing beyond the sounds of his own footsteps, his own breath rasping in his throat and chest.

As the low stone wall separating the meadow from the road drew closer, he darted a glance back over his shoulder down the gentle incline up which he had run. No sign of the other person.

Looking across the wall and to the left and right, he hurdled the waist-high barrier, landing relatively lightly, for him, on the pavement. Two more steps, and another hurdle, and he was running between the rows of the orange/trilia trees. With the level ground underfoot, the effort was not quite as great, although he was becoming more aware of the fractionally higher Accord gravity with each step.

The trees were past the blossom stage, and in the daylight only green buds would show where the full fruits would be by autumn. In the starlight, Jimjoy could not see those buds, only know that they were there, only smell in passing the faintest hint of the bittersweet odor of trilia.

The more he thought about it, step after hard step, the more he wondered about the sound of the gasp he had heard as he had sprinted away.

With a shake of his head, he slowed and made a circuit around a tree and headed back toward the walled road and the meadow beyond.

As he passed the trees closest to the road, he checked for traffic on the road, even though he saw no lights, before hurdling the first wall. He landed heavily, his feet thudding down one after the other. The pavement felt hard, much harder than on the way uphill. He forced the second hurdle, which became half jump/half hurdle, and stumbled as he landed on the softer meadow ground.

His breathing was close to gasping. His steps were shortening, and his feet were hitting the ground with almost no spring. The knee-to-waist-high meadow grass seemed more of a drag than on even the uphill sprint, but he forced the pace and adjusted his direction toward the spot where he thought he would find his would-be pursuer.

Short of the area, he slowed his stride into little more than a jog and began to look, listening for any sign.

He stopped, then began to inch forward, drinking in the sounds around him, trying to pinpoint any area of silence where the night insects did not chitter or whisper, where only the sighing of the grass occurred.

A faint crackle from the left caught his attention.

Wondering how much he should play the role, he decided, with a grin, to overplay it to the hilt.

With that, he eased down into the grass and began to edge silently toward his unseen target.

Something promptly bit him on the neck, not once but three times. He tightened his lips and continued his inching along. The silence ahead was perceptible.

Several sharp stones jabbed into his legs, but Jimjoy ignored them, still easing himself forward.

A warbling call echoed across the night.

In spite of himself, Jimjoy nodded. Almost perfect, but not quite.

So the person in the grass before him had a partner.

A froglike sound chirruped perhaps five meters ahead, to his left.

The warbling call repeated.

So did the chirrup.

Neither changed position, and Jimjoy edged forward, listening as he moved.

In time, he could sense a figure stretched out in the grass, could hear the lightly ragged breathing of someone trying to use breath exercises to control pain. Less than two meters from the youngster now, he suspected the youth was male.

"Twisted your ankle . . . or do you think it's broken?" he asked conversationally.

A sharp intake of breath was the only response.

"Look, young man. This isn't war . . . it's training. Besides, if I'd been after you, you'd have been out of the way long before I started running."

Jimjoy stood and, with two quick steps, knocked the truncheon/short staff from the young man's hands with a quick blow.

Even in the darkness, Jimjoy could see that his would-be tracker was in a great deal of pain from trying to sit up.

"Damned fool . . ." mumbled Jimjoy. "Never attack when you're wounded, especially in training. Not unless you're dead anyway. Now lie back and let me look at that leg.

"And signal your partner that you need help," he added. "I assume that bird call was from her."

The student's body posture answered both questions, but he still refused to answer.

"Idiot . . ." Jimjoy cupped his hand to his mouth and rendered a credible imitation of the imitation bird call.

"Major . . . I wish you hadn't done that. That will only get us both in trouble."

"Not in any more trouble than you're in already." He gently edged the youth's leg from its doubled position. "Hades if I can figure out how you did it, but looks like you've got at least one broken bone there. Not to mention some severely torn muscles."

"Can't. Need the credit."

"So I was an extra-credit assignment. Wish I'd known. What course? Field training?"

"Stet."

"Ecolitan Andruz?"

"No. Sabatini."

"I'll have to talk to him."

"Her. I really prefer that you didn't, Major."

Jimjoy ignored the comment.

"Is there anything . . . hovercraft . . . that can track out over this soft ground?"

"Never seen anything here. Maybe nearer Harmony." Even in the dimness, he was ghost-white.

The Major studied the meadow, concentrating on the section from which he had originally come, where it sloped upward toward the trees that separated the meadow proper from the low quarters buildings.

He warbled again, more urgently.

"That about right?"

"Nightcaller is a little higher-pitched. Two short and a trail-off."

Jimjoy tried again.

"Pretty good, Major."

Jimjoy could see a figure at the edge of the trees.

"Come on down. Your partner's broken his leg!"

The figure disappeared into the trees.

"Hades! Now she's convinced that I destroy students. Hang on."

Jimjoy picked up the youngster, who was bigger than he looked, perhaps as much as eighty percent of Jimjoy's own mass.

"Major, you can't carry me."

"Don't sell me short."

Jimjoy took one step, then another, concentrating on maintaining his footing as he made his way up the hillside toward the footpath that wound through the trees.

The young man wore blacks, he observed absently, which were really too dark for night work.

"How's the leg?"

"It hurts."

"Any more than before I lifted you?"

"A little less, except when you sway."

By now they were approaching the trees. Jimjoy heard several sets of footsteps.

Three people emerged from the shadows as he neared the path—one in blacks and two in greens.

All dark-haired. That disappointed him.

"Suspect your student will be laid up for a while, Ecolitan Sabatini."

"Practicing your night combat skills, Major?" The woman's voice was low. The sarcasm was undisguised.

"No. Did try some night running. Didn't think any real Ecolitan would put so much pressure on a student that he'd lie silently in the grass with a broken and twisted leg."

"Excuses, now?"

"Sabatini, you want a fight . . . I'll give it to you. You want an apology . . . we'll talk about it. After you point me to the infirmary. Or the hospital or whatever."

Jimjoy could see the pallor on the older woman's face, even in the dimness of the starlight. The two standing beside her were students, one female and one male. The female wore black coveralls.

"And by the way, black doesn't work that well in a night wilderness setting. Not natural out here."

Sabatini said nothing, but he could see the tenseness in her body posture.

"You two . . . it's been a long night already. Where's the infirmary?"

The woman student nodded to the right, where the path meandered back toward the instructional buildings.

Jimjoy shrugged his shoulders gently. The one arm, where he had taken the hit on Haversol, was beginning to tighten up. He walked around the three without a word and marched forward, using his anger as fuel for his quick strides.

A single set of steps followed his along the smooth stones.

"What's your partner's name?"

"Mariabeth."

"Mariabeth? Come on up here and lead the way."

She said nothing, but darted around him and his burden and briskly set the pace. At the first fork, she followed the left-hand branch.

So did Jimjoy, hoping that the health care facilities were not too much farther, since both arms were beginning to ache. But Hades would freeze over before he would let any of the stiff-necked Ecolitans know that.

Ahead, one of the doors in a long and low building showed a faint glow.

Mariabeth took the stone walk that led there.

Jimjoy followed, breathing deeply, wondering if he'd been a damned fool or merely an idiot for dressing down Sabatini before students.

Mariabeth held the door. In the glow of the shaded lamp, she turned out to be a muscular girl with black hair and black eyes, a mouth that could probably scowl, pout, or smile with equal facility and expressiveness, and shoulders that could bear the weight of the Institute's regime without too much trouble.

Jimjoy squinted hard as he stepped inside. Even though the interior light was still dim, his night vision was scarcely ready for the abrupt change.

The waiting area was empty, but a wheeled stretcher stood vacant on the far side of the room.

After taking the last three steps with his burden, Jimjoy laid the young man on the white cover of the stretcher trying not to express too much relief as he eased the youngster down.

Taking a deep breath instead of sighing, he glanced around.

Mariabeth pushed the "Emergency Call" plate as he watched, and

Jimjoy squinted even more as the light level in the room rose again. He could feel the involuntary tears as his eyes adjusted once more.

"Thank you, Major."

"No problem. Some ways, I caused your injury. Not that I meant to."

"I understand."

Mariabeth stood waiting by the interior door.

"What's the problem?"

Jimjoy's eyes turned toward the newcomer, another Ecolitan, male, and about his own age.

"I'd guess that the young man has at least one broken bone in the right leg, if not a compound fracture. Probably some ripped muscle tissue when he tried to stand on it and hadn't realized how badly he was hurt."

The newcomer took in Jimjoy, then moved to the stretcher.

"How did it happen?"

"Running in the dark," answered Jimjoy.

"How did it happen?" repeated the medical man.

"The Major happens to be right . . . oooohhhh . . ."

"Sorry. Looks like the Major was right about several things . . . First, who are you, just for the record?"

"Oh . . . Elting, Elias Winden, Student Third, Fifth Wing."

"Been here recently . . . any other injuries . . . any drug allergies . . ."

Jimjoy waited to see if the medical type needed anything else from him.

". . . well . . . the Major was apparently right about several things . . . but why did you try to run on this leg?"

"Sabatini—"

"That was my fault, Doctor. He was trying to keep up, and I didn't realize he was hurt that badly when he fell."

"He came back for me as soon as he knew . . ."

"He carried Elias all the way from the meadow." Mariabeth's soft voice cut off both Jimjoy and Elias.

"That's nearly a kilo . . ."

"That's right. And that was after he'd sprinted more than a kilo already," added Elias.

Jimjoy managed to keep from frowning, not certain where the two students were going.

"Well, young man, you certainly aren't going to be doing too much with that leg for a while." The doctor looked back at Jimjoy and Mariabeth. "Either of you coming?"

"I am. Elias is my partner."

"Major?"

"He's in good hands with you two. Not much I can add now. Just wanted to get him here. Stay with him, Mariabeth." Jimjoy didn't know why he had added the last words, but he did not retract them.

"I will, Major. I will."

"Thanks, Major. For . . . just thanks."

Jimjoy did not turn until the three disappeared into the corridor down to the treatment center. Then he took three deep breaths.

He slowly turned, walked to the door, and opened it, listening before stepping outside. The path was quiet, deathly silent, and he took another deep breath, another step, flexing his shoulders, trying to loosen the muscles. His steps kept him in the center of the three-meter-wide pavement as he directed himself back toward his own small room.

Three minutes—that was the minimum he needed for night vision adaptation, even forcing it, and he wondered if he would get that much.

Stopping for a moment, he rubbed his chin, then shrugged his shoulders once again. The slightest hiss behind him indicated a foot set down gently, but not quite silently, in the grass to the side of the walkway.

He continued walking, slowly, breathing evenly.

After a time, he looked up briefly, scanning the midnight skies. The afternoon clouds never lasted into late night. By now the stars of the Arm were low in the western sky. Above the Arm was the Rift, a jagged half-heaven width of starless black running overhead north to south. In the east shimmered a few double handfuls of stars.

He lowered his eyes. Someone was waiting, ready to follow. The muted sounds of the local insects told him that much.

Jimjoy shrugged again, glancing down the empty path ahead to his room. Whether he liked it or not, if the Institute itself wanted him dead, he was dead. Which meant that his big worry was the amateurs, assuming he could tell the difference.

He picked up his pace abruptly, straining for the sound of steps, but he heard no sounds at all.

He stopped nearly in mid-stride, but still heard nothing.

With a wry smile, he resumed his strategic withdrawal toward his room, and perhaps sleep.

Just before he stepped inside the quarters building, he looked back at the night sky overhead, at the wide sleeve of sooty darkness that comprised the Rift, and then at the Arm. Rift and Arm. Arm and Rift.

He shook his head and opened the door. The inside corridor was as empty as the stone walk behind him, as empty as the Rift overhead.

As empty as the future before him.

XIX

FOR A MOMENT Jimjoy did not move. Finally he squinted, yawned, and dragged himself upright, at last swinging his feet from the narrow bed and onto the dark green of the rug.

"Hades . . ."

He did not shake his head, but glanced at the partly open window. The small room held a hint of chill. Flexing his shoulders to relieve some soreness, he sat for a moment longer, then stood swiftly.

A glance at the white square of paper half underneath his door told him that his suggested daily schedule had been silently delivered, as usual. Some poor student or junior faculty member delivered it sometime after midnight, but well before the time he woke, even on the few mornings he had risen before the summer sun.

Jimjoy, bare-chested, hairy, wore only briefs. His unshaven black beard imparted a faintly sinister look. His forced smile as he reached for the heavy shower robe did nothing to dispel the sinister impression. He bent down and retrieved the schedule.

"Microcellular biologics—permanent genetic alterations . . . theory of unified ecological balances . . . practical analysis of the Imperial political structure . . . linguistics as a predicate for cultural analysis . . . field training briefing . . ."

He paused at the last item.

"Field training briefing . . . instructor . . . Regulis . . . too bad it isn't Andruz . . ."

After laying the schedule on the desk, he pulled his shaving kit off the shelf and draped the heavy towel over his shoulder. With a tuneless whistle, he opened the door onto the empty corridor and trudged, barefoot, down toward the washroom and showers.

How much of the biology he would understand was uncertain, but try he would, if only to see what the Ecolitans seemed to be able to do.

He shrugged his shoulders again.

XX

As THE CHIMES rang the second time, Jimjoy put down the orientation manual he had coerced from the librarian and stood, watching the student Ecolitans flow quietly from the library carrels and the frozen data screens toward the open double doors of the main corridor.

The silence amazed him. Although he had not been an Academy graduate, he had visited the Alphane Academy, with its iron discipline, and the Imperial cadets resembled rowdy toughs compared with the student Ecolitans. Yet the Accord students appeared to be in at least as good a physical condition, and they certainly did not hesitate in questioning their instructors. Politely phrased as those questions were, many constituted direct challenges to the instructors' beliefs or conclusions.

He glanced at the orientation manual, one of the few hard documents on the Institute itself, then at the dwindling stream of young men and women in greens.

Shrugging, he tucked the manual under his arm and headed for the doors himself.

"Major," called the librarian, a stocky man with silver hair, "please feel free to keep that as long as you need it." There was no sarcasm in his voice.

"Thank you." Jimjoy nodded and marched out the door after a pair of students, both male, as they silently marched toward the main servarium.

After slightly more than a week at the Institute, the Imperial Major still felt confused. The daily printout offered a choice of classes and activities to observe. Without its guidance, he would merely have been shooting blind. There were no class schedules printed anywhere. Everyone seemed to know where to go. Only notices for special activities appeared on the computer bulletin boards or the scattered public notice boards around the Institute.

Jimjoy had used the library terminals to access the main schedules, and all the abbreviations and schedules there matched those in the master course file. But like all university catalogs, the brief course descriptions told him little enough, particularly since he didn't share the same cultural background.

So he had attended the majority of recommended classes, ranging from hand-to-hand combat, where he had observed but not participated, to an advanced seminar on techniques of cellular manipulation, where he understood only enough to come away fascinated and awed.

The Ecolitans were adequate in the martial arts, better than any other colonies or any of the independent systems, with the exception of the Fuard Commandos and the Halstani Hands of the Mother. While Jimjoy would have hated to deal with the Commandos or the Hands, he would have given the edge to most of the Imperial Marine Commandos and virtually all Special Operatives. Nonetheless, the Institute looked to have a large number of well-trained personnel, especially considering it wasn't even supported, at least officially, by a planetary government.

Even more impressive were the apparent skills of the Ecolitans in ecology, biology, and all the related sciences. Though not a scientist himself, he would have bet that their understanding of the ecologically related fields would shame virtually all the top Imperials in the field.

He shook his head as the two junior students slipped into the servarium and into the quickly moving line of students on the right.

Jimjoy paused, as he always seemed to do, then walked to the left, toward the shorter line reserved for Institute staff.

No menu was ever posted.

"Yes, Major Wright?"

Jimjoy grinned. Every last member of the Institute had to have been briefed on his appearance and presence, down to the lowest cook.

"Whatever's good."

"Both the parfish and the baked scampig are good."

"Scampig."

The cook handed him the heavy earthenware plate, pale green, and Jimjoy placed a salad and a glass of the iced liftea on the tray with the plate.

Surprisingly, every staff table had at least one occupant.

He studied the tables.

"Major Wright?"

The voice seemed familiar, and he turned to the right.

"Here, Major."

Temmilan, one of the younger history instructors, motioned to him, pointed to a vacant seat.

He nearly shrugged, but moved easily through the widely spaced tables toward her. Smiling wryly, he reflected on the spaciousness of everything on Accord, from the city of Harmony to the table spacing at the Institute. Even his room was far more spacious than anything the Academy would have granted a visitor.

The spaciousness—and the grant of personal space without the chill of the Empire—still amazed him. The Accordans granted each other personal space without crowding or ignoring one another.

"You look bemused," observed Temmilan, as Jimjoy pulled out the wooden chair.

"More like amazed."

"Amazed . . . what an interesting choice of words."

Jimjoy did not immediately answer, but set his dishes and glass on the polished wood and placed the tray, also wooden, in the rack in the middle of the table, which immediately sank slightly under the impact.

"Surprised, whatever," he finally answered. "The business of friendly quiet."

"Quiet isn't exactly business."

Jimjoy grinned. He wondered who the others were at the table, particularly the older redheaded man with the analytical appearance. Instead of asking, he took a sip of the liftea.

"And friendship certainly should have elements of quiet . . ." pursued the thin-faced instructor. Her straight black hair was cut short, and her eyes seemed to slant more than their natural inclination when she smiled.

Jimjoy frowned, then readjusted his chair.

Temmilan waited, then added in a low voice, "If you do not mind, I would like to introduce you to some other philosophy staff members."

"Thought you were history . . ." mumbled Jimjoy, caught with a mouthful of bitterroot salad.

"You cannot separate history and philosophy. We try not to make such an artificial distinction. History inevitably reflects the philosophy of the historian." She paused, with a sheepish look on her face. "But that makes us sound so pedantic."

"But we are pedagogues," added the older man.

"Next to you is Sergel Firion. He's the head philosopher, so to speak."

"Or the head historian," chuckled the department head, "if you believe in the impartiality of historians." His blue eyes twinkled under a short-cut thatch of red hair shot with silver.

"Across the table is Marlen Smyther, and you know who I am," concluded Temmilan.

Jimjoy swallowed another mouthful of bitterroot salad. "Temmilan, also teaching history or philosophy or whatever."

"We'll make it complete, then, Major Wright." The smile disappeared. "I am Temmilan Danaan, instructor in history and moral philosophy and practicing Ecolitan."

At the words "practicing Ecolitan," Jimjoy caught a trace of a frown on the face of the woman whom Temmilan had introduced as Marlen.

"I thought all Ecolitans practiced what you preach, or is there organized hypocrisy as well?" Jimjoy regretted the sarcasm as he spoke, but he still wanted to see any reaction.

"Practicing Ecolitans," answered Sergel Firion, still with a hint of laughter in his voice, "take themselves much more seriously than the rest of the Institute. They like to extol the virtues of our little school to outsiders and to anyone else who will listen."

"If you're teaching here, how?"

"Through example," responded Temmilan. "We take sabbaticals on a regular basis and go where we are needed." She smiled. "That's not always where we would like to go, I assure you."

Jimjoy speared another mouthful of salad. He could see that the majority of student Ecolitans were already finishing up, although he had barely started his meal.

"No need to hurry," observed Temmilan. "None of us have a class right after lunch."

The Special Operative managed not to shiver. He disliked espionage because he was so transparent in personal interactions. The history instructor's comment reminded him all too clearly how out of his depth he was. Demolition, piloting, problem-solving—those he could handle. But not people problems, and he was sitting among the individuals comprising perhaps the biggest people problem facing the Empire with an assignment to *do* nothing. Just report. He did have to return first, and that might prove a problem.

KKCHHhhewww!!

Jimjoy started at the sneeze from Sergel.

"Excuse me. That shouldn't have happened. I'll have to check my antiallergen levels."

"Some of us are still not fully adapted to a few of the local histamines," added Temmilan.

Jimjoy nodded, although something about the comment bothered him, and took a bite of the scampig, which remained warm under a coating of tangy cheese. The meat was far tastier than the salad. He had tasted better weeds on some survival-level assignments.

Another odd fact tickled his brain with the third bite of scampig. He had not seen a single dessert in his stay at the Institute. Fruits, yes. Cheeses, yes. But no cakes or sugared pastries or the equivalent.

Perhaps because he avoided desserts, as a result of their all-too-positive impact on his waistline, he had not noted their absence earlier. The observation brought him up short. What else was he missing?

"Why the frown?" asked Temmilan.

"Not sure." He shrugged as if to pass it off, then sipped the iced liftea. The taste was somewhat bitter, but remained as palate clearing and refreshing as usual.

"Are you really a member of the Imperial Intelligence Service?" blurted Temmilan.

Jimjoy debated whether he should even reply, then smiled. "I could deny it, but there's probably not much point in that, since virtually everyone at the Institute seems to be convinced that I am."

"You didn't exactly answer the question."

"The answer is sufficient, but I'll amplify a bit. As the entire galaxy from Haversol to Accord apparently knows, I am a Major in something connected with the Empire. I did not graduate from the Academy on Alphane. I have seen service on a number of worlds, the latest of which is Accord."

Jimjoy coughed to clear his throat, then inclined his head to Temmilan. "And what is the real reason why the Institute combines philosophy and history?"

He hoped she would answer at enough length so that he could finish more of his meal.

He waited, taking another mouthful of the scampig. She did not answer. So he took another bite, then another. The meat remained tasty, for all that it was now cool.

A nod, which Jimjoy ignored, passed from Sergel to Temmilan.

She finally spoke. "It may be as much tradition as it is anything, but Jimbank, the first Ecolitan on Old Earth before his corruption, is reputed to have said that without history, philosophy is meaningless, and without philosophy, history is irrelevant.

"Certainly, history is determined in large part by the philosophy of those who wrote it, and how it is recorded is determined in even larger measure by those who record it."

"Victors write history," mumbled Jimjoy through another and final mouthful of scampig. "Nothing new about that."

"Not all history is written by the victors, Major. And much history is rewritten once the losers later triumphed. And that rewrite may have been rewritten even later."

Jimjoy held up a hand, swallowing quickly, to speak before the conversation moved further.

"All true," he admitted. "But what's the point? Does understanding the philosophy of the historian change what happened? What happened happened. Your historian can write all he wants about two hundred deaths in a battle, but if three thousand soldiers died, three thousand died. All the words and tapes around won't change the real number of deaths. Or what power controls the territory in the end."

"You're absolutely right, Major," interjected Sergel, "so far as your argument goes."

For some reason, Jimjoy felt feverish, yet strangely clear headed. He blinked several times.

Marlen nodded to Temmilan.

"A moment yet," said Sergel to no one in particular. "We may be able to integrate the entire proceeding." He focused on the Special Operative.

"Major, is it not true that all successful governments, directly or indirectly, control the curriculum of public education? In fact, is it not true that one time-honored purpose of education is indoctrination in the system in which one lives?"

Jimjoy frowned, trying to grapple with the words.

"Yes . . . in some cases." He felt he should say more, but he could only respond to questions.

"Don't you feel, deep inside, that the Empire has changed the way it presents history to show itself in a more favorable light?"

Jimjoy nodded. It was easier than talking.

"Is not the Academy designed as much to instill loyalty as to educate? And is that not the reason why few Imperial officers who are not educated at the Academy ever make the most senior ranks?"

"Yes . . . probably . . . makes sense . . ."

"Do you think that your not being an Academy graduate made it easier for your superiors to send you to Accord?"

"Yes . . . maybe . . . not—not sure . . ." he stammered, wondering why he was answering the question at all.

"Then why were you sent here? And why was every outsystem intelligence service allowed to discover your posting?"

"Thought it was because I was too direct. Hersnik implied I was being punished for undermining the Halstani Militarists and allowing the Matriarchy to take control."

Jimjoy noted Marlen's mouth drop open, but it seemed unimportant. It was crystal clear to him, and the Ecolitans ought to be bright enough to figure that one out.

"How did you undermine the Militarists? Did you do that because you believed that the historical picture you received showed them as undesirable?" pressed Sergel.

"How?" fumbled Jimjoy. "Not hard. Redid the controls on the main fusactor system. Set a delay constriction for the mag bottle. Created a critical mass. Then used the EMP to trigger some loose tacheads they weren't supposed to have. They couldn't complain because they were already breaking the Concordat."

"But why did you do it? Just because you were ordered to?"

"Mostly. You either believe in a system or you don't. You believe, and you obey. You don't . . . you run like hades."

Jimjoy could feel the sweat breaking out on his forehead, but the clearheaded feeling seemed to come and go.

"Do you still believe in the Empire?"

"No." Jimjoy wanted to shiver at the matter-of-fact way his damning admission had slipped out.

"Do you really think anyone here believes in the Empire?"

"No. Not unless someone's a spy."

Sergel nodded at Temmilan, who asked the next question.

"But aren't you a spy?"

"Yes. You know that."

"Are you here to destroy something like you did on Halston?"

"No. Forbidden to destroy. Just observe."

"You no longer believe," interjected Sergel, "and now you doubt. Doesn't that show how what you are taught affects your own philosophy?"

"Not sure about that."

"We are," continued Sergel. "That is why we feel that philosophy and history should not be separated. Do you see why?"

Jimjoy could feel the clearheaded feeling leaving him. He wiped his forehead, took a deep breath, then shivered. But he found himself answering. "I think so. You argue . . . philosophy controls . . . both what is taught and how it is taught."

"Exactly," added Temmilan brightly. "If you understand philosophy, you can understand why history is written the way it is or was. More important, you can analyze today's events and see why they become the type of history that they do."

"But people are still people. Deaths still happen, and the dead are just as dead," responded Jimjoy, wondering why he bothered. With all the admissions he had just made, he was probably as dead as the history they were discussing.

"We are not certain all those deaths have to happen, Major. Philosophical analysis of history can be a projective tool as well. One can project the impacts of a culture's interpretation of history into the future. A culture that blames the rest of the world or the rest of the galaxy for its ills is likely to stoop to anything. One which is obsessed with explaining legalities will have to justify itself before acting, which could provide some restraint.

"Those, of course, are gross examples . . ."

"Does that apply to individual behavior?" asked Jimjoy. He was getting a headache and afraid he knew exactly why.

"Not really," answered Marlen, an edge to her voice. "An individual can be a contradiction—honorable and a trained killer. Or dishonest, but compelled to act honorably."

"And individuals change," added Temmilan, "which seldom happens with established cultures—except through force."

"I'm not sure that individuals are any different," reflected the Imperial Major. "They do react more quickly to the threat of force." He wiped his forehead with the napkin. This time his skin stayed dry.

Jimjoy looked around the dining area. No one remained except those at his table and a man and a woman at a corner table. He glanced away from the pair as he recognized their function.

"Do the practitioners of moral philosophy and history have any overriding ethical obligations?" he asked almost casually, not wanting to acknowledge overtly the effectiveness of whatever they had slipped into his liftea, but wanting to twist some of their supposed ethic back at them.

"I would suppose so," responded Sergel. "They should live in accord with their moral code, if at all possible. But in any culture, survival transcends morality, or there is no culture. The danger there, of course, is that if one stoops to anything for survival, one may become one's own greatest danger."

Jimjoy laughed, once, harshly. "As if man is not always his own worst enemy?"

Sergel nodded slowly.

"Some merely have to worry about their place in the Empire . . ." murmured Marlen.

"That's true," offered Jimjoy evenly, fixing her eyes with his. "Especially those of us who have to return."

He stood abruptly. "I appreciate the education, both practical and theoretical. I do not doubt that you all have given me a great deal to consider." He scooped up the orientation manual and tucked it back under his arm. Then, half bowing, he smiled quickly and falsely at the three before turning and walking quickly toward the doors that opened onto the main garden.

As he passed by the pair in the corner, he half waved, half saluted, then continued onward.

"What else can you do?" he asked himself. "What else could you do?"

He hoped that the three were not a problem, but the rule of three probably held.

Where there are three rebels, one is a spy for the government.

The question was which one. He would have picked Marlen, but he knew his judgment of character in women was suspect. Why else would he keep hoping to attract Thelina Andruz?

"Check . . . and mate." He shook his head as he stepped into the garden.

He glanced around and had to smile. The Institute and its gardeners had a way with plants. That he could not deny.

XXI

THROUGH THE PREDAWN mists of the upland valley slipped Jimjoy, his long and even strides silent as he moved through the parklike forests west of the Institute.

His quick steps took him toward the taller hill he had noted earlier, and as he progressed, he glanced overhead. The mist, swirling and green-gray, was already thinning as if anticipating the sun.

Before him, the ground changed from spongy green turf into a sparser grass barely covering the rocky and dark red clay that slanted upward in a progressively steeper incline.

Terwhit . . . terwhitttt . . .

The gentle call whispered from the woods behind him. He halted for a moment to pinpoint the direction, but the call was not repeated.

Sccrrrttt . . .

The scraping sound was distant, but clear in the muted time before sunrise. Jimjoy shook his head and continued the climb. Let whoever it was follow as they wished. He hoped that his followers would be more careful, and this time he would not run.

He stepped up his pace again, to a walk that bordered upon the speed of a trot. His breathing quickened, yet remained regular at an effort that would have prostrated most others.

Crunnch . . .

This time the sound paralleled his course.

He nodded without breaking stride. As he had suspected, there was a trail up to the hilltop. He hoped that the view from the overlook shown on the contours map was as good as the map indicated. Still . . . the hike was good exercise, if nothing more.

He grinned and broke into a trot. That shouldn't push anyone into a careless mistake. Trail or no trail, he intended to be there before his shadow. Either of his shadows, the one that presently trailed him or the one that would arrive with the sunrise.

The faint sounds dropped back, although he knew his own progress was certainly no longer silent. But that was usually the case. Difficult as hades to be both quick and quiet, whether on foot or in a courier or a scout.

Jimjoy could feel the hillside steepen further, then after fifty meters flatten out as he neared the clump of trees that seemed to begin just short of the hill crest.

He was now panting slightly as he entered the copse of trees with the blue-black trunks, irregular and heavy branches, and needle-pointed green leaves. Then, all the trees on Accord had blue-green or yellow-green leaves—never just plain green—except for the obvious Terran imports, which didn't seem to be that widespread.

His shoulder itched, and he absentmindedly rubbed it. The trees.

The hard clay of the lower slope had become a softer humus under the trees, easier on his booted feet. A stickiness seemed to ooze from the branches, like a fine mist parted by his passage.

Ahead, he could see where the trees ended, and between the gaps at the edges of the grove before him, the swirling mist. Through the mist he could see the outlines of the lower hills on the eastern side of the Institute. The gap of the Grand Highway was partly visible to the right.

Terwhit . . .

veranda. On the veranda stood several tables set for breakfast. Set, but without occupants.

After passing the tables, he turned under the colonnade and in through the open portal to a wide carpeted corridor leading through the lobby of the Regency.

"May I help you, ser?"

"No. Just passing through."

The doorman stepped back with a puzzled look on his face, although the man had spoken in Anglish.

Without another word, Jimjoy, taller than the average Accordan, though not noticeably so, proceeded through the lobby and out onto the front walkway leading to the Avenue of Anselad. His steps picked up as he left the hotel. And upon reaching the avenue, he abruptly turned left, heading downhill toward the mastercraft shops.

From the near silence surrounding the hotel he walked into a gradually increasing number of Accordans, apparently on their way either to work or to transact some sort of business.

The first shop he passed bore a simple sign—"Waltar's Implements."

He half smiled as he looked in the wide window at the range of hand tools displayed, and at the limited power tools. But he did not stop, passing in succession an electronics emporium, a small cafe, and a decorator's shop with paint, fabric, and paper wall coverings displayed in coordinated settings.

The next doorway opened into a bookstore, which was still closed, although he could see a man apparently getting ready to open for business.

Rather than wait on the street, he continued forward, studying the surroundings. Most of the buildings were built from a native stone, a grayish granite, and finished and framed with wood or timbers. The roofs uniformly bore pale green slate shingles. All the walks were finished stone, with central panels of the dark stone surrounded by a narrower border of a white-green similar in color to that of the shingles, all carefully fitted together with a minimum of mortar.

Flower boxes, as much greenery as flowers, were everywhere, and even the Avenue of Anselad itself, the central business-and-shopping area, was split by a central mall of trees, hedges, and grass—nearly twenty meters wide. All told, the avenue was nearly seventy meters wide.

Farther north, the central parkway widened into a square flanked by three imposing stone buildings. Jimjoy could see only their tops from where he stood, but it was clear that all three were considerably taller than anything else in Harmony.

The clean smell of baked goods wafted his way, reminding him that he had eaten little before catching the flitter from the Institute.

"Christina's" was all the sign stated, but there were several cases heaped with breads, muffins, turnovers, ellars, and ghoshtis. He stepped inside, noting that although a number of people were waiting at the display cases, several small tables were vacant.

"Try the ellars, especially the greaseberry ones . . ."

". . . have two loaves of the spicebread . . ."

". . . told me that she would quit . . . Ansart will be furious . . . all he wants is for her to support him anyway . . ."

". . . and one more turnover . . ."

"Can I eat it now, daddy? . . ."

"Yes, ser, may I help you?" The woman was light-haired, youngish, but with slight circles under her eyes and a pleasant smile. Like the two men helping her at the counter, she wore khaki trousers, a pale yellow shirt, and a wide black belt.

"Just wanted something warm and filling. Any possibility of getting some liftea with it?"

"The tea's on the end of the counter there. Just help yourself. The nutbread muffins are the best, if you like nuts. If not, the berry ellars are good." She pointed to a tray of lightly browned pastries. Each appeared to be tied in a knot, but the slight differences in each indicated their handmade origin.

"Two ellars and the tea."

"Two creds fifty, ser." She handed him an earthenware plate with the ellars on it. "Hope you like them."

"Sure I will," he answered, again in Anglish, handing her a five-credit piece.

"Don't see many of these," she observed, making change.

"The coins?"

"They only mint small coins here. Here's your change."

He nodded and made his way to one of the small empty tables, where he set down the plate before moving back to the counter to pour some liftea from the heavy crockery teapot into an equally heavy and large earthenware mug. The mug itself was bright yellow with a green sprout as decoration. He did not recognize the type of vegetation depicted.

". . . must be from the Institute . . . but no stripe . . ."

". . . don't recognize him . . ."

"Mommy . . . want a turnie . . . now!"

". . . and a loaf of the rye . . ."

He sat at the table and took a sip of the steaming tea, then another, savoring both the warmth and the taste, even though he had not been cold to begin with.

"Is that order ready . . . for the Colonial Grande . . . ?"

". . . shipped him off to Four for a research assignment of some sort . . . talks, but I never understand—yes, the mixed rye and the spicebread, please—so what can you do . . ."

". . . is that one over there? In the corner . . ."

"The same uniform, I think . . ."

"Here you are, ser. Will there be anything else?"

The ellars were a mixture of two kinds of pastry, a light and flaky crust twisted together with a heavier and richer one, wrapped around the filling. He finished both and almost licked the crumbs off his fingers.

"Pardon me, ser . . . if you're through with the plate, I'll take it."

"Are you Christina?"

"No . . . I'm Laura. Christina's my aunt." She lifted the plate, then turned back to him. "You are from the Institute, aren't you?"

He thought for a moment before answering. "For now, at least. I'm classified as a visiting instructor."

"I didn't know they had any outsider professors . . ."

"May be the first . . . but that's probably up to Sam . . ."

"Sam?"

"The Prime."

The sandy-blonde paused. "How long will you be here?"

"In town? Just for the day. Hadn't seen much of Harmony."

"You from Parundia?"

"A bit farther than that, I'm afraid."

"Off-planet?"

He nodded.

"But you speak Anglish, not Panglais. That why I figured you were from one of the out-continents."

Her last statement seemed forced.

He shrugged. "The Institute invited, and it seemed . . . so I accepted."

"Do you intend to stay at the Institute?"

He laughed, gently. "Now, that is not my choice, one way or the other."

"I suppose not." She paused again. "How did you like the ellars?"

"Good. Quite good."

She nodded and headed back into the kitchen area, through a swinging door, still carrying the earthenware plate.

The crowd at the display cases had diminished, and only a single man stood there.

"Order for Waltar's."

"The usual?"

"Same as always."

"Here you go."

Aware as he was of the Ecolitan-style uniform, Jimjoy forced himself to sip the last of the liftea before slipping a fifty-unit piece next to the mug when he finally finished the liftea and stood. One youngster, also in khaki and yellow, waited behind the counter.

"Quite good."

"Thank you, ser. Come again."

"I hope to."

Outside on the avenue, there were fewer people. The temperature was at least another five degrees warmer, and steamier than at the Institute. He shrugged and headed back to the bookstore.

"Readables." That was the name of the establishment, and despite the modest title, the shop was even bigger than the implement store, with shelf after shelf of bound hard-copy books. The disc-and-cube section comprised less than one-fifth of the floor space.

Jimjoy began at one end of the hard-copy section, scanning the titles one after another, listening as he did to the half dozen people scattered throughout the shop.

"Do you have . . . *Politics and the Age of Power?*"

"Section three on the right, about the fourth shelf down."

". . . can you believe he said that . . . to her, of all people . . . and right after she finished hand-to-hand . . ."

". . . mangle him? . . ."

". . . didn't bother, but when he realized . . . should have seen his face . . ."

". . . all of them out there like that? . . ."

". . . guess so—oh, look over there . . ."

"So how is the weather in Parundia?"

He smiled as he continued with his survey of the bookshelves, noting a wide array of volumes openly displayed which were unavailable even in the restricted section of Alphane Academy library.

He reached for a small volume. *The Integrated Planetary Ecology*, Samuel L. Hall, The Institute Press, Harmony, Accord. He scanned the title page. Eighth Printing.

"Hmm." He slipped the book under his arm as he continued his study.

"Are you looking for something in particular?" The young woman addressed him in Panglais.

He repressed a smile and looked at her blankly.

She repeated the question in Anglish.

"No. Just looking."

"That's fine. Let me know if you need help." She returned to her position behind the counter by the door.

A few moments later, an older man joined her. The two whispered. Jimjoy listened as he browsed.

". . . doesn't acknowledge Panglais . . . Parundian accent in Anglish . . . but official dress tunic . . ."

"One of their specialists? . . . Growing so big you don't know them all anymore . . ."

". . . said that there's even an Impie there now . . ."

"Him?"

". . . speaks Anglish . . ."

Cling!

"Readables, this is Tracel. May I help you? . . .

"No, we don't have that right now. If we get the cubes on the next downship, we can have it bound and on the shelves by next week. If you have disc or cube, we'll have that the day after . . .

"That's no problem. Let me take down your name . . ."

Jimjoy moved across to the compact cube-and-disc section, checking off the titles. While the technical and professional titles seemed about the same, the hard-copy fictional and poetry sections, not to mention crafts and hobbies, were more extensive.

He nodded to himself and stepped up to the counter, laying Sam Hall's book on the counter, along with a twenty-credit note.

Tracel finished entering something on the small terminal and looked up.

"That's an old one . . . seventeen-fifty, please."

"But still popular, I see."

"Is it still required reading at the Institute?"

He shrugged. "Couldn't say. Just a visiting lecturer. But it was recommended."

"My sister said it was pretty interesting. I never read it, though." Tracel made change and handed him three coins. "Do you need a bag?"

"No, thank you." He nodded politely and left.

Outside, the temperature was even warmer, with correspondingly fewer people on the streets. With several hours before he was to meet the Institute flitter, he crossed the avenue between the infrequent groundcars and began to wander northward again, listening and taking in the shops.

Sometimes, sometimes, just walking and listening taught as much as anything, if not more.

XXIII

" . . . TWO, THREE, FOUR . . . two, three, four . . . two, three, four . . ."

Jimjoy whispered the cadences to himself as he wound up the exercise routine. Sweat poured down over his forehead, as much a consequence of the humidity and stillness of the air in the room as of any real heat.

Outside, the rain poured down, more like a tropical storm on most T-type planets. On Accord, the storm qualified as the normal evening shower. The summer pattern was relatively constant—cool, crisp mornings, increasing warmth and humidity as the day unfolded until late afternoon or early evening, when the clouds piled up and poured over the low mountains to the west and saturated the Institute. Once in a while, there were days that remained clear into the night, and when that happened the temperature dropped another ten degrees.

Not that the rains seemed to stop Institute activities. The only concession was the number of covered walkways between the major buildings. That and the solid construction, although Jimjoy wondered why all the buildings consisted solely of natural materials, either woods or stone. No synthetics, no metals, and no buildings of more than two stories.

That had been true in Harmony as well. Only the buildings housing the Council, the Court, and the Governor had exceeded that height.

He pushed away the delaying thoughts and squared himself for the next series of exercises, designed to exercise his combat training reflexes. They did little more than keep his skills from deteriorating too rapidly. Jimjoy needed practice with others, and used the Service facilities on Alphane or elsewhere to the maximum whenever possible. By himself, he found it hard to push hard enough to keep the edge he needed. Solitary exercises were neither fun, interesting, nor competitive. Only necessary.

Outside the window, the even sound of the heavy rain lessened as the evening storm began to lift. Jimjoy noted the decreasing precipitation, but doggedly continued his regime, pausing briefly every so often to wipe the sweat from his eyes with the short sleeves of his exercise shirt.

As the rainfall drizzled to a halt, so did the Special Operative, panting from a routine that should not have left him quite so exhausted, although his endurance had improved slightly since he had first arrived at the Institute. He hoped the better condition would balance somewhat his lack of combat practice.

He swallowed, still finding it hard to accept that the marginally higher gravity of Accord should have made such a difference. It did not seem that much greater than T-norm, not enough to affect short bursts of exercise, but it still took a toll during prolonged exertion.

"Wonder if it would make a difference in combat troops . . ."

Shaking his head at the unconscious verbalization, he pulled off the soaked exercise gear and laid it on the rack in the closet. Then he pulled on the standard heavy cloth robe supplied by the Institute and draped a towel over his shoulder.

He trudged out the door that had no lock and down the hall toward the showers, wondering once again why there were no showers attached to individual rooms.

"No locks, no theft, no showers . . ."

There was no theft at the Institute, or so he had been told. And he had lost nothing. As far as he could determine, no one had even entered his room while he was gone, not even for cleaning. Each resident was responsible for that.

Jimjoy smiled. No Imperial officer ever had to clean his own base quarters. With his limited cleaning experience, Jimjoy doubted that his room matched the sparkling state of the student rooms, but neither was it obviously cluttered or grubby.

The showers were empty, and Jimjoy sighed as he immersed himself in the stream of hot water. At least the ecological purists had not done away with the basic pleasures of a hot shower and soap.

Unfortunately, each shower was vented with liberal quantities of cool fresh air coming from outside through angled louvers. The Special Operative decided he did not want to be showering there in winter.

He shivered anyway as he cut off the water and began to towel himself dry—quickly. He wrapped the heavy robe around himself, grateful for the warmth of the thick cloth.

Thlap, thlap, thlap.

The shower clogs, also Institute supplied, were big and heavy, announcing his presence with every step back toward his room. Half the time, especially in the morning, he just went barefoot.

Back inside his room, he stuffed his exercise clothes into the bag he used for laundry, estimating that he had another day before he had to take care of the mundane business of wash.

Given his lack of previous experience, he was glad he was using the Institute-supplied uniforms rather than his own.

He smiled faintly as he sat down on the narrow but comfortable bed, still wearing nothing but robe and clogs, and reflected on how sharp most of the senior Ecolitans looked in the same tunics he wore. He had watched some of them wash them right alongside Jimjoy, but somehow they didn't look like the end of the day the first thing in the morning.

With a sigh, he stood up and walked back to the closet, where he stripped off the robe and pulled on a pair of briefs. Even though he had been informed that most Ecolitans slept in the nude, with nothing but a sheet and a standard quilt, that was one accommodation Jimjoy found himself unable to make.

By now, with the window completely open, both the temperature and the humidity in the room had dropped, and there was already a hint of night chill. The Imperial Major turned off the lights, wondering again at their concession to modernity, and settled into his bed, drawing the heavy comforter around him.

Aside from a few murmurs, occasional light footsteps, and the calls of night insects, the Institute was still. So still that virtually every night the quiet left him thinking. Was it the architecture, with the solid walls and natural materials? Or were the Ecolitans all ghostlike and silent people?

He turned over as the faint sound of footsteps came down the hallway from the shower rooms.

He sat up as the footsteps stopped outside his door, swung his bare
feet onto the rug as the door opened noiselessly. In the backlight from
the hall he could see a figure in a robe sliding inside the doorway and
the door closing as noiselessly as it had opened.

Just as noiselessly, he hoped, Jimjoy slid to the foot of the bed,
hoping to catch the intruder unaware.

The robed figure moved toward the bed.

Jimjoy jumped—to find himself holding all too closely the warm
figure of a woman who was clearly wearing nothing beneath the robe.

"Do you always attack so directly, Major?" The voice was low, almost
breathless, with the hint of a laugh . . . somehow familiar to the Special
Operative.

Not Thelina. No . . . Jimjoy released his hold and stepped back, to
find the woman close against his chest again, her arms going around
his neck.

"Are you always . . . this . . . direct?"

"My secret . . ." Her voice was low in his left ear.

"Temmilan—" he blurted.

"It took you long enough." Her lips brushed his earlobe.

Jimjoy's hands slid down to her waist and lifted her away and onto
the bed. Sitting, not lying, he told himself. He sat down next to her,
conscious now of her warmth and his chill. He stifled a shiver.

Her arm went around him, her fingers digging into his right shoulder, drawing him closer.

He disengaged himself and stood up, crossing the room to get his
robe, knowing that if he had not immediately separated himself he
never would, knowing how vulnerable he was to her softness and
warmth. This time, as he reached for the robe, he did shiver.

After momentarily debating whether to turn on the lights, he decided against it, but belted his robe firmly and sat down at the foot of
the bed, keeping some distance between them.

"You don't accept gifts, Major? Even willing ones?"

"I enjoy the packaging, Temmilan," he answered, knowing that what
he said was stupid, but trying to say something that would neither
entice nor antagonize the Ecolitan. She could make his mission even
more impossible if she chose.

"Someone else, or someone left at home, then?"

"Something like that." He paused. "Not that I don't appreciate the
thought . . . and the interest."

"Not enough, apparently."

He winced at the bitter edge to her voice, glad she could not see more than his profile, he hoped.

"Too single-minded, I guess . . ."

"*Most* men are."

Jimjoy had to repress a laugh at her attempt to insinuate that his rejection was tied to his lack of masculinity. He wondered what attack would be next.

"I can only share the weaknesses of my sex," he added.

"You do have them, I'm sure."

"You know them already, or you wouldn't be here."

"Perhaps you have more than I guessed."

Jimjoy stood, then walked over to the study table, where he turned on the small lamp.

"Should I shed some light on the subject in question?" He turned back to the Ecolitan historian. "Assuming you would like to have some illumination."

"Puns, and erudition yet, and from a clandestine ki—source."

Jimjoy picked up the straight-backed wooden chair and twisted it. He sat down with his forearms resting on the back, facing Temmilan, who had let her robe fall open. He avoided the view, instead looking her in the eyes.

"Too many assumptions, Temmilan."

"Oh?"

"Assume that because I'm clandestine, I'm inherently a killer. That because I'm alone, I'm vulnerable to the advances of an extraordinarily attractive woman. That because I don't respond unthinkingly, I can't." He paused. "Shall I go on?"

"You do reason well." She pushed a stray lock of her jet-black hair back over her right ear. "You have obviously had to learn to rationalize on a grand scale. Not that it's surprising."

"So . . . what do you really want?"

"Haven't I made that clear?" She lifted her weight and let the robe gape further.

Jimjoy kept his expression bemused, struggling to keep his eyes well above her shoulders, and trying to figure out the strange contradiction between seduction and hostility.

"I suppose so . . . though why is still a bit unclear . . ."

"Perhaps I think you need conversation of a less violent nature, Major."

"That's true. We Imperials eat children for breakfast. Raw, preferably, and then ravage the women."

"Major . . ."

"And we go in for whips and chains as well, even while we remember the last books we read, perhaps a decade earlier . . ."

"Major Wright . . ."

"But I don't understand . . . do I? One look from a lovely lady is supposed to turn me around. One promise of rapture . . . and this Imperial officer will be defenseless."

This time, Jimjoy waited for a response.

"You want me to say you're impossible. You know, that would be the standard feminine line—"

"And if there's something you can't stand, it's being predictably feminine." His voice was soft. "Even if you've just set up a predictably feminine situation."

He was rewarded with a laugh, slightly ragged, but a laugh nonetheless.

"Sometimes, Major, just sometimes, you show flashes of inspiration."

Temmilan's right hand drew the robe close enough to cut off the most provocative angle of the too revealing view, as she straightened up and shifted her weight on the bed.

Jimjoy tensed fractionally, wondering why Temmilan was dragging out the situation, rather than either throwing herself at him or withdrawing gracefully.

Was there a sound in the corridor?

"Only sometimes?" he countered, easing himself off the chair gradually and standing, then shrugging his shoulders, inching backward.

"Fishing for compliments?"

"Hardly. Just fishing." As he spoke, he reached the door, opened it quickly, and grabbed the fully dressed Ecolitan leaning toward it.

Crunch!

Clannk!

The green-clad man stared at the stunner on the tiles and shook his wrist.

"Sorry about that, friend," said Jimjoy conversationally. "Now, Temmilan," he began, as if to finish his talk with her.

Sccr—

"Ooooffff." The Ecolitan collapsed in mid-leap from the force of the Major's kick.

"This is getting all too predictable. Temmilan, why don't you take this poor fellow back to whichever garbage heap he came from . . . and jump in with him."

Jimjoy yanked the white-faced young Ecolitan from the rug and set him on his feet.

"Very clever, Major. Is dragging in poor bystanders and abusing them your idea of impressing me?"

Jimjoy sighed. Loudly.

"Spare me the posturing, and get the hades out of here."

Temmilan slowly got up, again letting the robe gape open, nearly baring her breasts and swaying slightly as she did so.

Jimjoy ignored the brazen motion, stepping back and kicking the stunner into the corridor and shoving the still-gasping Ecolitan after the weapon.

"Keep your hands to yourself, killer." Her voice was so low that only Jimjoy could have heard the words.

"I always intended to."

Jimjoy waited in the doorway, watching, until the pair disappeared around the corridor corner ten meters away. He almost laughed when he saw Temmilan begin to console the younger man.

Then he closed the door, shaking his head.

The setup was brazen, so brazen, so unlike the underlying sophistication and simplicity he associated with the Accord and the Institute.

He shivered as he understood the full implications.

Then he chuckled, realizing that neither he nor Temmilan could say anything, for exactly the same reasons.

Shaking his head again, he propped the straight-backed chair under the door lever, not that he expected more visitors. But he decided he did need a bit of warning the way things were going.

He took off his robe once more, turned off the light, and climbed back into bed. Intrigue within intrigue or not, he needed some sleep.

XXIV

JIMJOY ANGLED ALONG the corridor, following the young man he had seen the night before—and who seemed vaguely familiar. From what he could tell, the man was an apprentice Ecolitan—one who had finished all his course work and was now assisting various instructors for roughly a year before being sent on a field assignment.

Not all apprentices remained at the Institute, but exactly where the others went, Jimjoy had yet to discover. As for field assignments, that could mean just about anything.

The program of studies only noted that "apprenticeships may occur at the Institute or at other Ecolitan facilities." The library held no actual listing of such facilities under the apprenticeship notation, but did list separately two dozen small ecological field stations, two weather satellites, and a half-dozen satellite and on-system but off-planet research centers.

The apprentice strode out through the double doors and under the covered walkway that led to the physical training facilities.

The walkway was virtually without traffic. Jimjoy raised his eyebrows and stepped through the doors, following the brown-haired man.

About fifty meters away from the covered training arena, the Ecolitan apprentice glanced back over his shoulder.

Jimjoy smiled broadly, then watched the other stiffen as he looked away and continued toward the training complex. Jimjoy wiped the smile from his face and increased his steps to narrow the gap. He noted a number of students approaching on the intersecting walkway from the southern classroom complex.

Apparently, the apprentice was assigned to help with a physical training class.

The apprentice disappeared through the staff doorway.

Jimjoy grinned. His own locker lay through the very same doorway.

Before entering, he paused, listening, then flung the door open and marched through, watching two instructors look up in surprise from their conversation at the small table in the center of the room.

"Can we help you, Major?" asked the one on the right, a muscular blond woman with the triangle of senior staff on her short-sleeved and three-quarter-length, padded martial arts clothing.

The apprentice was quietly dressing in the far left corner of the room, sandwiched between two rows of lockers.

"Just like to observe, perhaps work out a little."

The blonde smiled. "I'm Kerin Sommerlee. You're certainly welcome. We're probably not up to your caliber."

Jimjoy and the instructor both ignored the snort from the apprentice.

"Have to see. Not in the shape I should be. You don't mind?"

"Not at all." She pointed toward a rack on her right. "You might want to change, though. Take whatever fits."

"Appreciate it." He nodded. "When do you start?"

"As soon as the students finish straggling in. Take any locker that doesn't have a silver triangle."

"Thanks. I have one at the end." He moved toward the rack and studied the choice of available jackets and trousers, finally selecting one of each. As he carried them toward his own locker in the corner opposite the apprentice, Jimjoy noted a locker with both name and silver triangle—Andruz. He also noted, once again, that while the showers were individual, the locker areas were common, at least for the staff, without separate dressing areas by sex.

He shrugged as he pulled off tunic, trousers, and boots, and slipped on the padded short jacket and trousers. He went barefoot, although his feet were no longer as tough as he would have liked.

He did not miss the once-over by Kerin Sommerlee, or by the other instructor, a blocky man with the muscles of a powerlifter. At one hundred and ninety centimeters, Jimjoy was neither outstandingly tall nor replete with bulging muscles. But technique was another question, and why he worried about losing touch without continual practice. For him, timing was especially important.

"Warm-up mats?" he asked the blocky man, since Kerin had already left.

"I'm Geoff Aspan, Major," answered the Ecolitan. "The warm-up area is through that door. That's where the class is meeting."

"Appreciate it."

"Our honor."

Jimjoy found the nameless apprentice and Kerin talking quietly as the two watched students arrive and begin their warm-ups. Again he felt he had seen the young man before, but could not remember where. He had seen so many faces wearing the forest-green tunics lately, and his thoughts had not been primarily on the student or apprentice Ecolitans.

He pushed away the questions of where he had seen the apprentice and what he might be discussing with the blond instructor and decided to warm up. Taking a vacant mat, he began his own routine, concentrating especially on stretching out his all-too-tight back and leg muscles. The backs of his thighs were always tight, too tight, and even in tip-top condition and limberness, he had trouble touching his toes easily.

Jimjoy repressed a grin as the nameless apprentice watched in disbelief while Jimjoy struggled to put his hands flat on the floor with straight knees and legs. The young man did not quite shake his head at the obviously poor shape of the Imperial Major.

Continuing through his routine, Jimjoy concentrated on stomach-centered exercise as the students completed filtering in. Finally he stood up and shrugged his shoulders, moving toward the wall as Kerin Sommerlee walked toward the center of the mat. The powerlifter stood behind her, and the apprentice next to him.

"Today is basically a review class. We'll break you into groups and evaluate your progress individually . . ."

Jimjoy looked over the students—obviously one of the youngest classes at the Institute. Several of the girls were repressing giggles at something, and the casualness of the boys was too artificial to be real.

He watched as Sommerlee split the class apart, carefully separating the gigglers into different groups. All the groups had varying sex mixes, but none was of a single sex.

"Now . . . responses . . . one at a time."

Sommerlee stood before one group, the muscular man before another, and the apprentice before another, as each student reacted to an attack by the instructor.

The near mechanical student responses almost brought a smile to the Major's lips as he recalled his own sessions years earlier. Perhaps five of the twenty students in the class showed some flair, either from a natural ability or from earlier training. One was a petite redheaded girl, who used the muscular instructor's own weight and momentum to considerable advantage.

Thud.

Even Jimjoy winced, but the muscular Ecolitan smiled.

"Nice, Jerrite, nice. Don't forget to keep your position. You won't usually be facing just one single attacker."

Nodding at that, Jimjoy looked over the progress of the other groups, easing along the back of the mats, studying the moves used and the instructions given.

He frowned. Something about the course nagged at him, but he couldn't immediately say why. Looking at the open-worked beams overhead, their smooth workmanship, did not help his concentration. So he looked at Kerin Sommerlee, who was busy "attacking" one of the larger male students.

Then Jimjoy slowly nodded, understanding what about the course, about most courses, had bothered him.

He frowned, debating whether he should share the insight, or how he could convey the message.

Ambling toward Sommerlee, he waited for a break in the class pattern.

"Major . . . care to play attacker?"

"No . . . thank you." He paused. "Not for a moment, anyway. But if you'd care for a match . . . no one defined as attacker or defender . . ."

"The class isn't ready for free form yet."

"Understand. But . . . like to claim the right to share something. And I can't share it without a demonstration. Also, without a demonstration first, I doubt if my unsupported word would have much credibility. It might be better if . . ." Jimjoy gestured toward the heavily muscled instructor.

"No . . . you don't get off that easily. Geoff has yet to take me, even with a handicap."

"All right. Rules?"

"What do you suggest?"

"No gouging. No broken bones, and no action once someone's on the mat."

Sommerlee frowned in return. "Of course. We wouldn't do that normally."

"Thought so, but I haven't worked out here."

"All right." She raised her voice. "Gather round, everyone."

Jimjoy waited.

The students were silent as they ringed the mat.

"Major Wright has requested a free-form demonstration. Some of what you see will be beyond your current ability. *Do not try it.* Trying something without the fundamentals is a quick way to break your neck, if not worse.

"We are fortunate to have Major Wright here, and since he will not be able to stay until you are ready to try some of what he may show you, try to remember the basis of what you see for *future* reference."

Sommerlee backed away and faced Jimjoy.

He took a deep breath, then moved, aiming at her right, then cutting left.

Keeping a balanced stance, which he had calculated, she countered—and Jimjoy struck.

Thud.

Sommerlee shook her head groggily.

"Whoa . . ."

"You all right?" he asked evenly.

"In a moment."

Jimjoy ignored the whispers.

". . . so fast . . ."

". . . and she's the best . . ."

". . . used his weight . . ."

He offered her his hand, knowing she might attempt to throw him with it.

She did, and he went into a dive carrying her along. At the last instant, he twisted and released her hand.

Thud.

Jimjoy came out of the roll and looked back at Sommerlee. She did not move, but she was breathing evenly. After a moment, she sat up very slowly.

"I think you have made your point, Major, whatever it was."

"I don't, Ecolitan Sommerlee."

Jimjoy did not bother to hold back his smile at the apprentice's comments.

"Would you like a chance at the Major, apprentice Dorfman?"

"Yes, please, Ecolitan Sommerlee."

"Try to take it easy on him, Major." Kerin Sommerlee got up gingerly and walked to the side of the mat.

Jimjoy faced Dorfman, realizing where he had seen the apprentice before last night—on his arrival at the Institute. Maybe it had been better that he had taken the cab.

The younger man did not move for a moment, then tried to flank Jimjoy.

The Major moved, as if to avoid the pass, then lashed out with a foot.

Dorfman twisted, but could not undo his momentum, finally turning it into a twisting roll. Coming out of the roll, he launched himself back at the Major, in an imitation of the attack Jimjoy had used earlier.

Thud.

"Had enough, Dorfman?" he asked in a deliberately annoying tone.

Sommerlee frowned. So did the other instructor.

Dorfman shook his head, looked down at the mat, and slowly stood, as if unsteady.

This time, Jimjoy waited.

Crack.

Thud.

The openhanded slap had caught Dorfman on the cheek, lifted him, and dropped him into a heap.

"He'll be all right in a moment."

"Are you sure?"

Dorfman twitched, then pulled himself into a sitting position.

"Enough is enough, apprentice Dorfman." Jimjoy's voice was cold enough to penetrate. Dorfman slumped, almost as if in relief.

"Now . . . if no one minds, I'd like to share a few observations. About this class. About hand-to-hand combat. Based on my own training, not that different from yours, but mostly from my experience, which is a great deal different."

"Be our guest, Major."

Jimjoy tried to overlook the edge of bitterness in her tone. He could scarcely have expected charity.

"First . . . watched you train. Something bothered me. Took a minute to see." He glanced out over the students, finally fixing his eyes on Sommerlee.

"Most courses like yours, like my original training, assume the strength of a defensive position, only conceding to overwhelming brute force. That's not necessarily so. The stronger position is the stronger position." He could see the puzzled looks.

"Let me show you. A volunteer?"

The petite redhead stepped forward.

"Take a defensive position, as if I were going to attack. I won't," he added as she looked up at him warily. "But I need to illustrate." He moved to her side. "You're balanced against an attack from roughly here to here. From here—" He touched her shoulder, and she wavered. "So what? Any good martial arts student constantly changes position to present what you could call a 'defense for attack.' That's still a defense.

"You can sit down," he added in a lower voice.

"What I did to both Ecolitan Sommerlee and apprentice Dorfman, in the simplest terms, was force them into a defense that was vulnerable to attack at the time I actually attacked." He paused. "That sounds simple. And it is—*if you think in those terms*. But if you begin by assuming that defense is the best position, you won't think that way."

Jimjoy looked at Dorfman, whose expression was still blank.

"Look. Why do you learn combat? Not to toss someone aside. You learn it to kill or disable someone. Period. No other reason, except exercise, and there are a lot better ways to exercise. If you have to really use your skills, they shouldn't be defensive. The point is disability or death. Period. Not defense. If you don't want someone disabled or dead, don't learn the skills . . . because you'll end up dead instead." He lowered his voice. "Doesn't apply to practice, but your practice should always keep that in mind."

Jimjoy paused again, studying the students, whose faces, if not blank, mirrored subdued shock at his bluntness.

"Put it more bluntly. Most times you use hand-to-hand combat when you've screwed up once already. If you have to kill or disable someone, the worst possible way is to do it hand-to-hand.

"Second point. You will screw up. We all will. I'm human, and you're human. We make mistakes. But the universe doesn't give you three chances in a row, and damned few enemies will give you even two. So you can't risk losing *even once* with hand-to-hand. Fighting has no honor. Except in learning or improving your skills, you fight to win."

He scanned the faces, repressing a sigh at the ignorance, the naïveté.

"That doesn't mean you attack all-out like Dorfman did. See where it got him? It does mean any defense should only be temporary . . . just until you can destroy your opponent. End of sermon."

He half bowed to Sommerlee. "Your class, Ecolitan Sommerlee."

"The Major has just delivered a rather convincing lecture. While we may not share all his political views, what he says about hand-to-hand combat has a great deal of . . . validity."

Jimjoy walked toward the locker area, not certain whether he had hurt or helped himself, but hoping that some of them had listened. Behind him, the exercise area was silent, almost dead silent. The whispers would begin, he suspected, only after he had disappeared into the staff dressing area.

He took a few deep breaths as he stepped through the doorway.

"Another great success, killer?"

Sabatini stood next to the table, her black eyes glinting.

"Another great success, Sabatini. If that's the way you look at it. If any of them listen, it might save their lives. Not into propaganda. Just survival."

"How touching."

He walked past her to his locker, where he pulled off the jacket, then the trousers. He draped a towel over his shoulder and headed for the shower.

Sabatini surveyed him from head to toe as he passed.

"Try the meat market, Sabatini. Steers don't fight back."

"You have a way with words, killer."

"I know. The wrong way."

He turned the shower on as hot as he could stand it, letting the steamy spray bathe him from all sides.

By the time he had toweled off and opened the door, Sabatini was gone. Instead, Kerin Sommerlee was standing by the table, clad only in underwear and examining bruises on leg and thigh.

She shook her head as she saw him. "Hate to face you when you really were out to kill."

"Too enthusiastic out there." Jimjoy mumbled, making sure the towel was clinched firmly around his waist, and avoiding looking directly at the woman's body, far less stocky and more shapely than he had realized. She reminded him of Thelina, though the two looked only vaguely alike.

"Major . . . you pulled the last throw . . . or whatever it was?"

He shifted his weight uneasily, conscious of the dampness of his bare feet on the slightly roughened stone underfoot. "Yes . . . could have killed you otherwise."

"I know. I could feel it. Geoff knows, too. He was white when I looked at him."

"Dorfman doesn't. Most of the students didn't."

"Dorfman's a fool."

He shrugged, not quite looking at her, but toward her face. "And the students?"

"Some were beginning to realize, especially after Geoff's comment."

"Geoff's comment?"

"You didn't hear? He said that the Institute had never had any two people who could have taken you, let alone one. You shook him up a lot. I don't think he ever realized just how good the Special Operatives are."

Jimjoy automatically opened his mouth to protest.

"Please save the objections, Major." Her voice was tired. "After about thirty seconds with you on that mat, I know who and what you are. There aren't half a dozen people on this planet or three others where I've been who could do to me what you did. None that quickly and effortlessly." She winced as she examined her leg. "That's what upset Geoff. Suddenly, you're real. All too real. The kids—that's all they are—can't see that . . . except maybe Jerrite."

"Sorry."

"Don't be. You provided a lesson we couldn't have learned so painlessly—relatively, at least." She pulled her padded robe and trousers back on in quick but smooth motions.

"I have one more class this morning. Then I can soak out what I know is going to be even more sore." She looked up. "You're one of the best. Right?"

Jimjoy said nothing.

"Aren't you?"

"Probably. Not the top, but close."

"Attitude?"

He nodded.

"I thought so." She flexed her shoulders, trying to relax her muscles. "Like to do any instruction here? Say . . . for the advanced classes?"

"Not sure it would be a good idea. I'll think about it."

"Do. And don't worry about Sabatini. She's on her way out. She was under review even before you arrived. She'll blame you, of course, but there's not much the Institute can do about that."

"Whatever's convenient." Jimjoy hitched up his towel and headed for his locker.

"And whoever she is, Major, she's lucky."

Jimjoy shook his head at the nonsequitur, but decided against asking for an explanation. He had too many problems already without asking for another.

XXV

FINDING THELINA ANDRUZ'S quarters had been neither difficult nor helpful. While the silver-haired Ecolitan lived in a separate house with another Ecolitan in the senior staff section of the Institute, and while there were no guards or restrictions, every nonstudent Ecolitan seemed to live on his or her own personal clock. The pathways and corridors of the Institute were never quite completely deserted. Just as frustrating, for his projected schemes, was the lack of centralized personal communications. Without going to her quarters, he could not discover if she were actually there.

After his encounter with the historians, and then his night visit from Temmilan, the last thing he wanted was to broadcast any intentions of anything. Yet it was clear that he was close to transparent to at least some, if not all, of the Ecolitans. Part of that was their training in physical character reading—he'd been fascinated by the classes on surface carriage and physical intent. So interested that he'd actually read through most of the student assignments, hoping that they would prove helpful in the future.

The Major stopped his pacing and sat on the edge of his narrow bed. Then he stood back up again. He frowned. Who else could help him? Could she? Or was he just rationalizing because she intrigued him? How could he possibly learn what he needed to know quietly, when everyone seemed to follow him, to pay attention automatically when he appeared?

Someone seemed to be there to watch his every action, from the books he borrowed to the material he accessed from the datanet, from the classes he attended to the limited instruction he had undertaken. Almost as if they were compiling a dossier on him, or on every Imperial agent. Probably both, he concluded gloomily, and from that would follow a profile of the Imperial Intelligence Service, at least a profile of the Special Operative section.

But that left his problem unsolved. He didn't dare chase Thelina.

"So . . . if you can't go to the mountain, get the mountain to come to you . . ."

Easier said than done. He looked out at the darkness before dawn. Thelina was not about to chase down one Jimjoy Wright. Not from any indication he had seen so far. Not when she had refused to say a single word after sharing a clearly breathtaking sunrise.

What about illusions? Or coincidences? Could he arrange a circumstance where she had to talk to him . . . alone? And would she listen?

Could his maneuvering get her beyond the obvious contempt of him and of the Empire he was bound to represent? Most important, would she help, however inadvertently, to get him on the right path? Before the Empire put him back on the clearly marked path to Hades already reserved for him by Commander Hersnik?

Special Operatives did not just resign. Jimjoy had never heard of a resignation. Some graduated from field work to Intelligence. One or two were medically retired, after a year or two of quarantine duty and extensive psychological "readjustment." But he didn't want the Empire's idea of medial retirement, and movement to Intelligence from the Special Operative section meant a promotion to Commander. And there was no way he would get a promotion, not after the Halstani incident, not after being tagged, he was certain, with complicity in the killing of Commander Allen's partner. Even though Allen had clearly killed his partner to keep the facts behind the assignment from coming out.

If he stayed on Accord, he'd be the target of every spare agent around, from the Empire to the Hands of the Mother. Not to mention the fact that his delay on Accord would give the Empire another excuse to move against Accord. Even his "disappearance" on Accord could trigger that, which was probably why he was still alive and being protected by the Institute. And why Temmilan could do nothing fatal to him, since such an action would blow her cover.

Jimjoy snorted. The Ecolitans had to know about her, or he was missing something. And Temmilan was far from stupid, which meant she had to know they knew. He shook his head, trying to refocus on his own problem.

If he did return on schedule . . . At that, he shuddered. His return would never be noted, and the records would show his disappearance in action, with the finger still firmly pointed at Accord.

He continued to pace, knowing that his time was growing shorter. He stopped, stared at the rough white ceiling, still grayed in the foggy predawn light that misted through the casement. Outside, the whispered shrilling of a dawn lizard punctuated the fog with its intermittent calls.

Muted voices from down the corridor indicated that the junior Ecolitans were rising and beginning their morning routine, a routine he thought not nearly as intense as it should be . . . as if he cared.

In the meantime, his time on Accord continued to dwindle, especially with the good Commander Allen running loose, reporting back and pinning everything on Jimjoy. If he could just saddle Allen and Hersnik with all the problems . . . if . . . if . . .

He looked back out the window, not really focusing, then at the triangle in the middle of the rug.

Jimjoy smiled, tentatively at first, then with nearly unconcealed joy. The whole idea was so preposterous, so silly, that it might work. The longest of long shots, but better than anything else, assuming he could get some limited cooperation from the good Ecolitan Andruz. Assuming he could move quickly enough when the time came . . .

He sat back on the edge of the bed, then swung his feet up and stretched out, since there was nothing he could do.

Not yet.

XXVI

ALTHOUGH JIMJOY WORE the unmarked greens of the Institute and could have been taken for an Ecolitan at first glance, even with the black hair and blue eyes, his lightly tanned complexion had not seen the outdoors to the extent required of Institute faculty and students alike. And the raw and unconcealed intensity in his eyes was not that of the Institute.

The Ecolitan greens had represented a compromise for Jimjoy. He had not brought a uniform, nor did he intend to wear one, or admit publicly that he was an Imperial officer. At the same time, civilian clothes would have been even more out of place.

While the greens had scarcely been a major consideration, they were now critical to his plan. If his calculations were right, the one Ecolitan named Andruz would finally be coming along the walkway before long. If she didn't eat at home or skip lunch like she had for two out of the last four days. Or bring her friend Meryl along again. Or lunch with the entire field training staff . . .

He continued his glances down the ramp until he caught sight of the distinctive silver hair.

At that, he turned away from the old-fashioned bulletin board and started toward the dining area. According to the literature, few people ever considered someone in front of them to be following them, although that was exactly what Jimjoy had in mind. He let the gap between them narrow.

As he entered the dining area, he took the left line, the one always used by the Institute staff, and slowly moved through, listening to see if Thelina, who was alone today, unlike the last time, had any comments. She said nothing.

"What will it be, Major?"

He could have cared less today, but he grinned in spite of himself. The staff behind the counters still seemed to delight in announcing him and his rank.

"What do you have?"

"No meat. Just fish—grubber, parfish, or lingholm."

"Parfish." He'd seen it before, and the Ecolitans seemed to enjoy it.

"The lingholm's better."

"Then I'll take the lingholm."

The student serving as cook's helper grinned broadly back at him.

That was another thing he didn't understand. Virtually the entire Institute took his presence with an amused seriousness, yet denied to outsiders that he even existed. He had heard two beginning students tell, with tears of laughter running down their cheeks, how they had played dense colonials to a Fuardian faxer tracking down a rumor that Imperial officers were being trained by the Institute.

Chalk up another angle for the ubiquitous Commander Allen, getting yet another stooge to do the work. But he was glad the Institute ignored the potential danger and could still laugh.

Jimjoy did not look back. If his scheme were to have a chance, Thelina had to be convinced that he had not seen her.

At the end of the food line, he paused by the salads, as if trying to decide upon fruit or greenery. Finally, after the man behind him had slipped by, he picked a small fruit plate and straightened, blocking Thelina without seeing her.

He turned and carried his tray toward the dining area, slowly scanning the tables as if searching for someone, but carefully avoiding anyone's glance while straddling the aisle. He could feel Thelina moving closer. He stopped momentarily, then leaned forward, as if to head for a table, then stopped again, leaning back.

Her tray jabbed him in the back, and something hot sloshed onto him.

He turned, hoping his calculations had been correct.

"Oh . . ." he said, letting his mouth drop open as he looked at the silver-haired Ecolitan. Then he grinned ruefully. "Still throwing things at us poor Imperials? Were you trying to alert me this time?" His voice was gentle and good-humored.

Thelina Andruz sighed. "It would be you, wouldn't it? I should have guessed."

"Guessed?"

"Who else but you or a visiting dignitary would be ambling around?" She glanced over her shoulder. "We're crowding the aisle. Take that table over there. Your company won't hurt, as long as I can eat quickly."

Jimjoy said nothing, but eased over to the two-person table toward which she had inclined her head.

He took an extra napkin from another table as he passed, and, after setting his tray down, awkwardly tried to mop up the liquid that had splattered across his lower back.

"Scampig broth," explained Thelina as she slid into her chair. "It shouldn't stain anything, and . . ."

Jimjoy nodded. "And I probably deserved it for stalling around, right?"

"Probably," observed Thelina, before taking her first bite out of a thin sandwich.

"Since it's taken me more than a week to engineer this," Jimjoy commented softly as he seated himself, "I hope you'll stay long enough to listen."

"Engineer what?"

"Your running into me."

"You . . . unwhoooo . . ." For a moment, Jimjoy wondered if she were choking or laughing or swallowing, or all three.

The Ecolitan coughed again and cleared her throat, before swallowing and taking a sip of her iced liftea. "For what reason? You certainly could have just walked over to see me. I'm hardly inaccessible."

"That's assuming I wanted the entire world to know I was looking for you."

"That, in turn, means you are up to no good whatsoever, Major Wright." Her voice had turned distinctly cooler.

"Half right," answered Jimjoy, before taking a bite of his salad. He said nothing else and bit into a bright green fruit, trying not to let the large piece pucker his mouth too much.

"First time I've ever seen anyone try to eat an entire sourpear at once."

"Could be the last," mumbled Jimjoy as he reached for his own iced liftea.

"Your half-right proposal, Major?"

He refrained from glancing around the crowded dining area, hoping that the overall noise level and the apparently spontaneous meeting were enough to allow him a quick comment. "I would like your help in leaving Accord and getting to somewhere like Sligo or even Alphane without the Empire being alerted to my departure."

"Why?"

"Because I'm not likely to arrive, otherwise."

"You believe that of the glorious and saintly Empire which you serve?"

"Flamed right." His voice was low.

Thelina did not respond, but cocked her head slightly and took a spoonful of the scampig broth, that which remained. Then she pursed her lips, but still said nothing.

Jimjoy watched the green eyes, noted that the silver hair was twisted up short behind her head in some sort of bun.

"That's right, Major. Worn up or short now that I'm back here in a physically active billet." She took another spoonful of the broth.

Jimjoy repressed a sigh and tried another fruit, a reddish one with a pink interior. Unlike the sourpear, the red fruit was sweet, with only a hint of tartness. He wondered if the tartness were part of the Accord character and fostered by its foods. He continued to eat methodically, occasionally studying the silver-haired woman, but refusing to bring up the subject again until she acknowledged interest or rejected the idea.

"Greetings, Major."

Jimjoy kept from jumping, barely. Instead, he glanced up at the thin-faced professor with mild interest. "Greetings, Temmilan. How is the philosophical history business?"

"About as practical as ever . . . or, as you suggested, as impractical as ever." The historian transferred her study to the Ecolitan across from Jimjoy. "You're in the field unit, and we met last year, but I'm not good with names. Temmilan Danaan."

Thelina nodded. "Thelina Andruz. Field Two."

"Pleased to see you again. You know the Major well?"

"Not terribly well, Temmilan," answered Jimjoy. "This is the second time we've met. She was considering making amends for running into me with a full tray of scampig broth."

"Major Wright is always accurate, Temmilan. It is one of his worse faults."

"You may be right, Thelina. Make what amends you can . . . if he will accept them." Temmilan nodded to them with a pleasant, if distant, smile and eased past the table.

"And what did you do to her?" asked Thelina dryly.

Jimjoy found himself flushing, and shrugged.

"That bad?"

"No. You might say it was what I didn't do."

"That's worse." By now the silver-haired Ecolitan was smiling an indecently broad smile.

Jimjoy looked down at the last few bites of the lingholm and speared a small morsel, gulping it down.

"Well, you have some ethics, if no taste."

"Won't claim either."

"Let's take a walk. Whether you intended to or not, you've just told the whole world you're looking for me. After that confrontation, half the Institute will be told that we're lovers."

"Uhhnn . . ." choked Jimjoy.

"Temmilan's the biggest gossip around, except for old Firion."

The Imperial Special Operative managed to choke down the last of the fish. He followed that with a deep swallow of liftea to clear his throat.

"Am I that unattractive, Major?"

"I believe you mentioned a walk." He stood.

"I did. The main garden would be nice, if you don't mind, the one by the biology quad."

"Lead on, Ecolitan Andruz."

Neither said anything until they had entered the garden and taken the second path to the left, which led toward a bench surrounded by a low hedge on three sides and shaded by a large evergreen.

Jimjoy glanced upward.

"Silft . . . native. This bench is proofed for conversation. Have a seat, Major."

Jimjoy raised his eyebrows, but followed her directions. Thelina seated herself next to him, as closely as he could have wished under other circumstances.

"Look toward that building. See the lack of focus?"

Jimjoy nodded. Obviously the raised hillock on which rested the hedge, and bench contained more than mere earth.

"Why don't you trust the Empire? And why should we help you, assuming we could? Specifics, please, Major."

He took a deep breath before starting. "Simple. My cover was broadcast to every outsystem agent possible. Commander . . . the agent at the hotel . . . were clearly after me. If I leave on any recognized transport, there's no way I can count on recognizing my own assassin. You and your people are clearly able to track me anywhere and keep me from getting off-planet without your consent."

Jimjoy shrugged. "And if I tried to stay here, the Empire would put pressure on you. Insist that you send me back on a planned schedule."

during which I would meet some sort of unfortunate accident. If you stood up to them directly . . . that gives them an excuse to come down hard, say with three or four fleets.

"Doesn't leave you many options. Odds are that if anything happens to me, and that's exactly what the Service wants, they'll tag you with it. I'd like to stay in one piece. You'd like that, too—professionally, at least. That means I have to get off-planet and to a location where I can show up so visibly that the Empire has a problem with me, not with you."

Thelina looked straight ahead, not meeting his eyes. "This one time, Major, I agree with your logic and all your conclusions. You did forget one option."

"My death here by doing something wrong? No . . . that would still get me out of the Empire's hair and allow them to use me as a martyr and a cause to move against you."

"That was not what I had in mind. What if you stayed here, at least for a few weeks longer, then suddenly appeared back at your original duty station?"

"Some risk for the 'local' Major Wright, isn't there?"

"Not if he stays at the Institute."

Jimjoy grinned at the thought of confounding Commander Hersnik.

"What do we get from it, Major?" The Ecolitan's voice was soft but cool.

"What do you want? Editing rights to my report? Future information? My gratitude? Mutual survival? Those are the options, but my chances for future information and long-term survival are slim."

"They're probably nonexistent." Her voice was flat.

"Where there's life . . ."

"I suppose so. You don't offer much."

"Editing my report . . ."

"Major, we would only edit your report to point out factual errors. Frankly, we want it to be as complete and accurate as possible. That is one reason why we would prefer to keep you in good standing, officially, until someone in authority actually reads it." She paused, then added, "That's because the rumors about us are far more deadly than the facts."

And more true, probably, thought the Major, not vocalizing the thought.

"That should do it," concluded Thelina. "Now, put your arm around me for a moment, as if we're about to say good-bye. A bit more affectionately, Major. There will be some speculation as to why we're seen together, and we need to give the gossips the right flavor. You were right about that also."

Jimjoy put his arm around her, as requested, and leaned toward her, although he could feel his eyebrows raised in question.

"How else can I see you? Especially after hours. Everyone will think you've made another conquest, Major."

He could feel himself blushing, and resenting it. She leaned into his arm, briefly resting her head against his. Just as he was beginning to enjoy the feeling, she sat up and looked at her wrist.

"I'll be late, again." Her lips brushed his cheek, and she was gone, leaving him standing by the bench.

He did not shake his head, but he wondered if he had actually had his arm around her.

XXVII

"How long do we wait?"

"You just arrived back. His orders give him up to six standard months. The idea was to let him hang himself. Besides, we still don't have a report from our contact at the Institute."

"That could be a problem. You may not."

"Definitely a possibility, since they clearly know at least one of our contacts. But better one we're allowed than none."

"And you stand for that?"

"You have a better idea? Besides our current operation to force them into the open?"

"You should have sent Wright after them the way he did the Halstanis. Either way, we would have gained something."

"You are rather impatient. Remember, the Emperor and the Senate both frown on blowing up our own colonies. Or have you forgotten that small fact? Besides, Wright was never trained in espionage. Subtle as an old-style cruiser, and he's certainly bound to make mistakes. They don't forgive easily."

"Do we really know that?"

"No." He paused. "But do you have any other explanations for the disappearances? And our inability to plant anyone they don't want planted?"

"Perhaps you picked the wrong people?"

"Wrong people . . . perhaps. Speaking of which, how did you lose the other half of your team? Again, I might add?"

"Wright shot him."

"No. Better to claim *they* shot him. Wright was probably looking for you."

"You know me too well."

"All too well, my friend. All too well. And how will you report the incident?"

"As you suggested. Reconnaissance disrupted by unknown agents, presumably attached to the underground rebel force associated with the Institute. You'll have to explain the need for reconnaissance."

"Unfortunately . . . unfortunately. Is there any way our contact could be persuaded to goad Wright into action? His actions are always so drastic we could probably recoup everything."

"I've suggested that, but no response. And what happens if Wright goes over to the rebels?"

"Then we can move. Claim he was either killed or reconditioned, and that he was destroyed uncovering the rebellion. Get rid of him and them."

"Why bother?"

"You're asking that?"

"Outside of the personal thing, I meant. It would be years before the Institute would be a threat, if ever."

"I wish that were true."

"Then the rumors *are* true."

"It's time for you to file your report. And make sure it's filed correctly, especially this time."

"Don't I always?"

XXVIII

JIMJOY STOOD UP from the table where he had eaten alone. The unmarked Ecolitan greens offered no real protective coloration, although he continued to ignore the low comments from the young man with brown hair seated beside a darker-haired history and moral-philosophy instructor and an older professor.

After glancing absently around the room, Jimjoy flexed his shoulders and walked toward the trio, looking beyond them toward the garden. As he neared the table, he glanced down, casually letting his eyes take in the two Ecolitans and the apprentice.

"Oh, good day, Temmilan, apprentice Dorfman. And you, too, Professor Firion." His voice was pleasantly false, as he had meant it to be.

"Good day, Major," responded Temmilan.

Dorfman did not meet Jimjoy's eyes, instead looked away.

"A very pleasant day, indeed," observed the graying Sergel Firion.

"Yes, it is. A day for cheerful quiet." Jimjoy paused briefly, then added, "Once you said something about friendship being able to rest in quiet, and I questioned that. Now I find, rather surprisingly, that I agree with Temmilan's original assessment."

"My, you're such a quick convert." Temmilan's voice was only slightly warmer than glacial ice.

"We Imperials have no moral philosophy and can be converted quickly." He laughed softly and concluded, "And sometimes we even stay converted." He paused again, then added, "Have a pleasant day." But before he could turn to leave, he found his right arm engaged by a silver-haired woman.

"Major Wright." Despite the formality of the salutation, the words sounded warmer. Much warmer.

Thelina squeezed his upper arm gently before releasing her grip.

"Thel—Ecolitan Andruz." He inclined his head to her.

"He's still rather formal, don't you think, Temmilan?" Thelina Andruz smiled brightly at the two historians and the apprentice.

"Rather."

Thelina turned her bright smile on the Imperial Major. "I'm sorry I couldn't make it in time for lunch, but I do have a few moments. Shall we go?"

"Nice to see you all," Jimjoy said warmly as he nodded to the historians and left with the silver-haired Ecolitan, who had reasserted her grip on his arm.

"You have such a way with words, Major."

"Thank you so much."

The two walked out of the staff area arm in arm. Jimjoy could not resist a grin, even though he knew the scene was a charade.

"The main garden, or somewhere else?"

"Have you seen the small formal garden?"

"No. Don't even know which one it is."

"Then you should, Major. You certainly should. How else could you bring back an accurate picture of the Institute and what it stands for?"

"Guess I couldn't."

"You are absolutely correct *this time*. You couldn't."

He winced at the emphasis in her statement.

Thelina disengaged her arm from his and reached for the door before he could.

"Don't you let a poor Imperial do anything by himself?" Even as he walked through the open door and the words tumbled out, he shook his head.

Thelina was silent. Jimjoy glanced back at her as she let go of the doorway.

In turn, she was shaking her head.

"I know. I know. It's a good thing I don't have to operate just on words."

She nodded in agreement with a solemn smile and stepped back beside him. She did not take his arm. "Take the left walkway."

"Left it is." He decided against offering any more statements. With Thelina, every time he opened his mouth, he seemed to swallow either his tongue or his boots.

Less than ten meters from the doorway, they stepped out from under the covered walkway onto a path with rectangular gray stones which curved in a gentle arc beyond the edge of the nearest academic building, the one that housed the library where Jimjoy had spent more than a few hours wrestling with the Institute's datanet and finding out more than he suspected the Ecolitans would have liked, for all their professions of openness.

Thelina's steps were unhurried, forcing Jimjoy to slow his pace.

"We are not on a field march, Major. You should enjoy the scenery, especially the garden. It's close to a replica of the more famous English formal gardens."

"An Anglish garden? Generally a replica?"

"*English* was the way it was most properly pronounced. And generally a replica because there have been no gardens there for some time." She paused before continuing. "There. The bushes—they should properly be boxwoods, at least chest-high. But boxwoods do not grow well here, if at all. So we have used a dwarf delft on the outer hedges and even lower smallwood on the inside."

"Which path?" he asked as they entered the green chest-high maze. Jimjoy could see that the inner part of the maze consisted of bushes less than waist-high.

"Whichever you wish. There are benches on either side, and this is a symmetrical pattern."

In time they reached a bench, partly concealed, resting on four of the gray paving stones, with the delft on three sides, and a narrow single-stone-width path from the main path to the bench.

Jimjoy started to step across the grass.

"You could take the path, just for the sake of form."

He glanced across to see her smiling gently and brushing a stray wisp of silver over her left ear. Her hair was again twisted up on the back of her head.

"Still long?" His eyes took in the wound silver, which seemed to glint, almost haloing her face, despite the afternoon overcast and the absence of direct sunlight.

"So far, Major. I probably will get around to cutting it one of these days, assuming that I remain here for more than home leave."

He raised his eyebrows. A training slot counted as *leave*.

"The Empire seems to feel that short-haired women are automatically from Halston or Accord. Who needs that kind of attention on field duty?"

That made an unfortunate kind of sense, Jimjoy reflected. He followed her suggestion and walked the curving spiral of stones behind her, putting each foot in the middle of a slate-gray stone and taking a good dozen extra steps to get to the smooth wooden bench.

The bench itself was typical of Accord, smoothly and finely finished, with a high back and with each slat grooved into place.

Jimjoy saw neither bolts nor nails, but only the smoothed traces of well-fitted pegs.

Did the Accordans carry everything to the extreme craft he saw at the Institute? Harmony had certainly looked much the same. Was anything done quickly or without precision and care?

"Why the frown?"

"Just . . . thinking," he murmured.

Thelina gestured toward the space beside her as she sat down. "Might as well sit down and tell me, Major."

Jimjoy sat.

"Closer. You'd think we were strangers, and we certainly aren't that, Major. Are we?"

Jimjoy sat down, puzzled because there was no edge to her statement. Neither was her tone inviting. She had merely stated a fact.

"What were you thinking about?"

"About the degree of craft that goes into everything, even wooden benches."

"You find craftsmanship unusual?"

Jimjoy laid his arm across the back of the bench, above her shoulders but not actually touching her, and leaned slightly closer, as if the conversation were more intimate than it was certain to be.

"Not craftsmanship. Seen nothing here without it. Not sure all things are worth doing well."

"There's a difference between actions and objects, Major. You seem to value the reverse, faulting yourself when your actions are not perfect. Yet you say not all actions need to be done well. If you spend the time to create something, shouldn't it be made honestly and well? Not elaborately, but honestly and well?"

"You may be right. Hadn't considered that distinction."

"You're remarkably open-minded when you're not on the defensive."

"Could be. Seems a few people here want me on the defensive."

Thelina turned in toward him, touched his right shoulder with her left hand, and brushed his cheek with her lips. The semi-kiss, without emotion, was followed by an announcement lower than a whisper. "This is not shielded, but we're making arrangements. We'll be eloping some night in the next week when I visit you."

He leaned closer to her. "Then why here?"

"Why not?" her voice was louder, soft but carrying. "Everyone knows about us."

Jimjoy brought his other arm up, holding her loosely. He felt awkward.

"You're blushing, Major."

He was, he knew, and tried to refocus the conversation before he really got in over his head. More over his head, he corrected himself.

"What can I say?"

"Nothing, Major. Your intentions are completely and totally transparent."

Jimjoy wrenched his thoughts back to what had been bothering him earlier.

"Historian . . . has to be working for Allen . . . has to be . . ."

Jimjoy kept his voice as low as he could, and his arms around Thelina, who felt as responsive as a mannikin, though warmer.

She turned as if to nibble his ear, whispering back, "I can hear you.

So can anyone with a directional cone. Who's Allen?"

He tried to keep his voice even softer. "Man who got away . . . first day here . . . Commander . . . Special Op . . ."

"Cold," she said, half aloud.

"I agree," he answered, not agreeing with anything.

"Why don't you like her?" Thelina moved away from Jimjoy and her question was asked in a normal tone of voice.

He let his arm drop away and shifted his weight. "Too forward. Too obvious."

"Remind me to avoid that pitfall, Major."

"Now we're back to being formal?"

"I'm only allowed so much off-duty time, Major."

Jimjoy shifted his weight totally away from her, stretched his shoulders with a shrugging gesture, and stood up beside the bench. He looked around the garden.

"Well, shouldn't keep you for too long." He kept the puzzled look off his face, though he wondered why Thelina had taken his comments about Temmilan with so little reaction.

She turned on the wooden bench to follow his movement without standing up. Her green eyes focused on him and seemed to sharpen. "You're right, Major. It's time for me to get back to work, and time for you to get back to view any of those classes you missed. You have a lot left to cover, I'm sure."

He nodded. "Always learning something new. Hard to tell what you people don't already know, though. Some things don't surprise you at all. Almost as if you already knew it all and hadn't bothered to let anyone know."

She shook her head as she in turn stretched and stood up. "No. You know military skills and tactics far better than we do. Kerin told me about your little exhibition. You weren't just impressive, she said. You awed a woman who's never impressed, especially by men."

Jimjoy flushed, again, and glanced at the low hedge around the bench. He saw no sign of the blurring that would have signified a distortion screen.

"Then, too, Major, we also watch for reactions, or overreactions. The fact that your judgment was so accurate in heated circumstances was interesting, especially given the 'stress' you were under. We had a bit longer to make our conclusions."

Jimjoy forced a smile. He knew now all too well to what incident she was referring.

"As I suspected, Thelina, you have been ahead of me all the time. Cool and calculating." His voice was almost as cool as hers had been at times.

Thelina was standing facing him, grinning widely. "It makes no difference. Your reactions are unique enough to throw all our calculations off."

He shrugged again, still coolly angry, still aware that he could say nothing that surprised her. He wondered why so many of the Ecolitans, Thelina in particular, left him feeling verbally inadequate.

"Anyway," she added lightly, "I do have a field lesson for the newbies."

"Newbies?" He glanced at her, his eyes picking up on the small monogrammed Ecolitan emblem on her tunic.

Her eyes followed his and, surprisingly, she blushed. "New—new—"

"Brats?" he offered.

"Not exactly, but accurate enough, thank you." Her voice was again moderated and cool, and the momentary color in her face was gone as quickly as it had appeared.

"Field session?" he probed.

"Survival indoctrination . . . edible plants and animals. The usual. Basic principles."

"How many planets' worth?"

"That, Major, depends on how receptive the students are. First, they have to learn this planet. Enough . . . in any case."

Jimjoy could not tell from her tone whether she was putting him down or leading him astray, or both. He did not shrug, though he felt like it.

A brief gust of wind ruffled his hair and pulled several strands of hers loose.

"See you later." He stepped around her, brushing into the hedge, feeling several sharp points digging into his hip. She did not move, though an amused smile played across her lips. He ignored it as he put his feet on the narrow stones and headed back toward the main walkway that would eventually lead him to the physical training facility.

Now that everyone was awed, he obviously couldn't hide anything and might as well get a decent workout. A workout he clearly needed to untangle his thoughts. He hadn't planned on that, but he clearly needed it, for more than one reason.

"Have a good workout, Major."

Jimjoy tightened his jaw, but did not look back or acknowledge the pleasantry as he kept his steps even.

XXIX

"NAME?"

"Laslo Boorck."

"Imperial I.D. or passport?"

The hefty man handed across the Imperial I.D., looking down on the purser from near two hundred centimeters. In turn, the purser placed the flat card in the reader.

"Palmprint."

"Yas . . ." The hand went on the scanner.

The scanner remained silent for a moment, then flickered once, then turned green.

Bleep.

"Welcome aboard, citizen Boorck."

Citizen Boorck ambled a few steps, then waited.

"Next. Name?"

"Lestina Nazdru." The woman, with her red-and-silver-streaked hair, was clearly a different type from the sedate and overweight agricultural specialist whom she accompanied. Her nails glittered, and her eyelids drooped under their own weight.

The purser did his best not to stare at the translucent blouse.

"I.D., please."

"Of course, officer."

She placed her hand on the screen with a practiced motion. The long nails glittered alternating red and silver.

Again the scanner hesitated, but finally flickered green.

Bleep.

"Welcome aboard . . ."

"Thank you." Her voice was low, a shade too hard but pleasant, if vaguely professional.

The purser smiled faintly as the woman rejoined her husband, if their reservations could be believed. He'd seen all types, and a lot of the October-May marriages looked like the pair he had just passed on board the *M. Monroe*. Older and heavier man, wealthy, but with minimal taste, and an attractive wife not that much younger, but of even more questionable taste and background.

Remembering the hesitation of the scanner, he glanced at the short list on his screen to compare profiles, but neither the heavy man nor his companion matched the handful of names and profiles. The automatics were supposed to match names against prints. The list contained individuals for whom various law enforcement or military authorities had placed a detention order. He scanned the list again, then looked up.

"Next."

Behind him, the October-May couple walked toward their silver status stateroom, holding hands casually.

"You like the ship?" asked the man.

"A touch beneath you, Laslo, but it will do." She looked along the narrow corridor. "Shouldn't we turn here somewhere, dear?"

"I believe so, honeydrop. I do believe so."

The man stopped and fumbled with the silver-colored card.

"All passengers. All passengers. The *Monroe* will be leaving orbit station in five standard minutes, bound for Certis three. We will be leaving Accord orbit station in five minutes, bound for Certis three, with a final destination of Alphane four. If you are not bound for Certis three or Alphane four, please contact ship personnel immediately."

The stateroom door opened, and the man withdrew the silver card, gesturing to the woman.

"After you, dear."

"You can be so courtly when you have to, Laslo."

He followed her inside. Two built-in and plush chairs flanked a table. Over the table was a screen. The view on the screen showed the mixed blue-green of planetary continents and water covered with swirls of clouds, as seen from orbit.

The woman closed the door and flopped into one of the chairs.

"Take a load off, Las."

"In a minute . . ."

"They got any entertainment on the screen? Who wants to see a dumb planet every time you travel? Seen one, you've seen them all."

"You're so right, dear. But Accord has such marvelous agricultural techniques. I thought it might look different from orbit."

"Laslo, you dragged me here on business, left me in that tiny hotel while you went running through the countryside. You still smell like manure. Once we get to Alphane . . . We're going to Alphane for some civilized times and some real fun. And some comfort. Freshers with perfume, not old-fashioned showers. Real Tarlian caviar. You promised!"

"So I did. So I did. And where are we? We are on an Imperial ship bound for Alphane."

The silver-and-red-haired woman kicked off one shoe, then the other.

"Are our bags here yet?"

"They should have arrived before us. Let me check." He opened the artificially veneered closet door. Two expensive and expansive black leather bags, matching, were set on the racks, side by side.

"They're here."

"Tell me, Laslo, why was that ship's man looking at his screen every time he checked someone in?"

"Looking for some criminal, I suppose." The heavy man eased himself into the other chair.

"Do they ever look for women?"

"I would suppose that they might. Women break the law as much as men . . . although, dear, I suspect that they do not get caught as often."

He took her left hand, the one on the table.

She disengaged it deftly.

"Laslo, I feel rather tired, and it's likely I will continue to feel tired until after I return to civilization."

The man sighed. "I understand, dear. I do understand."

"You're always so understanding, Laslo. It's one of your great strengths, you know."

"Thank you." The man looked up at the screen. A slight shiver passed underfoot.

"The *Monroe* is now leaving orbit. The *Monroe* is now leaving orbit. The dining room will be open in fifteen standard minutes. The dining room will be open in fifteen standard minutes. Please confirm your reservations in advance. Please confirm your reservations in advance."

The woman smoothed her long hair back over her right ear, then over her left ear, tapped her fingernails on the table.

"You might damage the grain of the wood, dear."

"What grain? Can't you recognize cheap veneer?"

"I suppose it's the principle of the thing." He looked straight into her muddy brown eyes. "Will you be ready for dinner soon?"

"I will be ready for dinner when I am ready. That shouldn't be long."

"In that case, I will meet you in the lounge, dear." The man levered himself out of the chair, straightened his short jacket, and moved to the stateroom door.

"That's a dear."

The doorway opened, then closed with a firm *click*.

XXX

"WELCOME TO ALPHANE station, ser Boorck, lady Nazdru. We hope you enjoy your stay. Will you be taking the shuttle planetside or transshipping?"

"The shuttle . . . for now . . . for . . . some culture . . ." answered the man.

"That we have. That we have. The shuttle concourse is to your left."

"Laslo, you are so masterful," commented the woman with the sparkling red-and-silver hair and the matching nails, blissfully unaware of the stares she was receiving from the conservative Alphane residents returning planetside.

"Thank you, dear. You know how I value your judgment."

"You should, dear. You should."

"But you know I do. Why else would I be here?"

"Now, Laslo, don't get sentimental. We have a shuttle to catch."

The big man sighed, loudly, and motioned for a porter to follow with the two heavy black leather bags.

The three stepped onto the moving strip in the center of the corridor and were carried toward the shuttle concourse. Lady Nazdru continued to draw stares. Few noticed Ser Boorck at all, except as an overweight man obviously dominated by a younger, if experienced, woman.

"You'd think that they'd never seen someone with colored hair, dear."

"Not like you, dear."

"You're so kind, Laslo."

The porter coughed. "Ser . . . lady . . ."

"Oh, yes, thank you." The man stepped off the moving strip and toward one of the staffed counters.

"May I help you, citizen?"

"I unfortunately neglected to arrange for shuttle passage . . ."

"That shouldn't be a problem. Do you have an Imperial I.D. or an outsystem passport?"

He handed over the flat I.D. card.

"Your print, citizen?"

The man complied.

"Does she need mine, too, Laslo?"

The woman behind the counter scanned the red-and-silver-haired woman. "I don't think that will be necessary. Your . . . husband's I.D. is clearly adequate." She shifted her glance back to the man. "How do you wish to pay for passage?"

"How much is it?'

"Three hundred each, plus tax."

"This should do." He handed over a credit voucher.

"Just a moment, citizen." She laid the voucher on the screen.

Bleep.

"That will clearly suffice, ser." Her voice showed much greater respect. "It will take another moment to print out a revised voucher."

"When does the shuttle leave?"

"You should not have to wait long, ser. The next one is for Alphane City. That is in thirty-five standard minutes. The next shuttle after that is the one for Bylero. That is in fifty minutes. If you want the southern continent, take the shuttle for Dyland . . ."

Burp.

"Here is your credit voucher, ser. And your passes. They are good on any shuttle. Just check in at the lock, or make arrangements at any service desk."

"Laslo, have you reconfirmed our accommodations at the Grosvenor Hill?"

"I will, dear, I will, just as soon as I arrange for our shuttle."

The shuttle clerk suppressed a smile as the man motioned to the porter and waddled toward the service counter. With her eyes on the woman, she did not notice that the man made no attempt to reconfirm the accommodations.

The heavy man and the woman leaned toward each other, out of apparent earshot of the shuttle clerk.

"But, Laslo, dear, I did so want to see Dyland *first*."

"I understand, honeydrop . . . I understand."

The shuttle clerk smiled amusedly and returned her attention to the screen.

"You didn't tell me you had *business* in Alphane City." The woman shook her red-and-silver hair.

"Put the bags here." The man nodded at the porter, then extended his hand with a five-credit token.

"Thank you, ser. Will that be all?"

"You promised, Laslo. You promised . . ."

"That will be all."

The porter left with his cart.

"You promised . . ." Her voice trailed off.

"I can only do my best." The man shrugged. "What if I meet you in Dyland . . . the day after tomorrow?"

"Laslo . . ."

"Tomorrow?"

"And you'll take me to the Crimson Palaccio?"

"Yes . . . the Crimson Palaccio."

"You're a dear, Laslo." She threw her arms around him and gave him a theatrical hug, whispering in his ear, "Look behind me." As she broke away, she added more loudly, "And be careful. Don't forget your diet, dear."

"I'll see you then, honeydrop. Don't buy too much . . ."

"I won't, Laslo. You know I won't. And we'll talk about *that* at home." She beckoned to a porter.

He watched as she waltzed away, shaking his head slowly.

XXXI

JIMJOY SQUINTED AS he studied the set of carefully crafted orders. Captain Dunstan Freres, it was. He set the orders on the battered dresser.

Then he sighed. According to his rough calculations of the probabilities, there was literally no chance of another name matching Dunstan Guillaume Freres in the entire Service, but the syllabic and semantic contents were unusual enough to convince the skeptical that no one would create such a name as a cover.

The authorization codes were genuine, taken from the Service's reserve list, which meant that he had roughly three standard weeks before they triggered any alarms. Jimjoy intended to surface before that.

Sighing again, he ran his left hand through his short hair, dark brown to match his temporarily swarthy complexion. Then he looked down at the closed and nearly depleted emergency make-over kit, then back at the uniform on the sagging bed. Next to the uniform lay a baggy and ancient raincoat and a shapeless cap.

One complication led to another. He couldn't exactly walk out of his less-than-modest room in a crisp uniform, but neither did he want to attempt donning the uniform in a public fresher, knowing what he knew about the ways of Special Operatives and the Imperial surveillance network.

"Curses of knowing the work," he muttered under his breath.

Although the gray-green walls, with the scuffs that even the heavy plastic wall coating had been unable to resist, seemed to press in on him, Jimjoy let himself slump onto the edge of the palletlike mattress, avoiding the uniform laid out on the other side.

If he left before the rest of the conapt tenants began to stream out, there was always the chance that someone would notice. More important, the base duty officer was bound to take notice of an early morning arrival.

No Service Captain with any understanding would check in before 0800 or after 1200. Before 0800, and there was the chance that you'd be required to report to your assignment immediately. After 1200, and you were docked the extra day of leave.

As Dunstan G. Freres, Captain, I.S.S. (Logistics), Jimjoy intended to be as forgettable as possible.

Forgettable or not, he was bored. While he could wait, and did, the room was boring, just short of being dingy, and all too typical of the short-term quarters that had surrounded military bases since they first moved from tents to fixed emplacements with roofs and floors.

The bed was nearly the worst he had slept on, except for the one on Haversol. Not that he had gotten much sleep that night, not after the incident in the saloon, when Thelina had indirectly saved him from the hordes of assassins snooping around after the fresh meat he had represented.

The Special Operative smiled a long, slow smile. In time . . . in a comparatively short time, Commanders Allen and Hersnik would get a taste of being on the other end—one way or another.

He stretched and stood up, checking the time, walking back and forth at the foot of the bed.

Checking the time again, he looked at the uniform on top of the bed and perched on the edge once more.

Lack of patience, if anything, had been his undoing before, and now he couldn't afford any undoing. So he looked away from the Service-issue timestrap and began counting the scuffs in the wall plastic, since they were the only finite details within the room.

This time, he lost track around number 277.

"Roughly one quarter of one wall . . . makes a thousand plus twenty-seven times four or a hundred eight . . . eleven hundred eight times three walls is thirty-three twenty-four. Say the short wall's half the others . . . half of eleven hundred eight is five fifty-four . . . added to thirty-three twenty-four . . . thirty-eight seventy-eight. Three thousand, eight hundred and seventy-eight blemishes and scuffs on the walls . . ."

What else could he count? Or should he reflect back on Aurore to see what else he had missed?

Either way, it would be a long, slow early morning.

XXXII

JIMJOY EASED INTO the vacant console, tabbing the proper entry and access codes. His bored appearance and gray-flecked hair matched the rating stripes on his tunic sleeve. Another not-too-bright, but technically skilled, file follower, with the intelligence to ensure that the records of all the officers under his care were complete, that they had current physical examinations and training schedules that matched their promotion profiles, and that they met all the other bureaucratic requirements.

He, as the most recently arrived technician, accessed a series of files, profiling physical examinations. The senior duty tech noted the screen coming on line, nodded, and returned his attention to the problem before him, the question of how to schedule the senior Commander performance review-board interviews within the operational and deployment requirements.

The senior technician did not notice the subfile called up by the technician, nor the immediate split screen, since he was supervising from three cubicles away. Not that he really knew any of the horde of

personnel technicians other than by their files and his reviews of their
data-handling capabilities.

The graying rating with the youngish face accessed another file, this
time adding an item on various positions, subtracting others. He
checked the cycle times, the times at which current masters would be
updated with present file information. At that point, the changes would
be relatively permanent.

He returned the second file to storage, then called up five files con-
secutively, nodding minutely as he did, and as the supporting information was added to each.

In time he returned to the tedious business of transferring and editing, satisfied that Commander Allen's records now showed all his
physical examinations as having been performed by the same physician
in the same Intelligence clinic.

That had been the hard part, reflected Jimjoy, finding a good Service
physician at Headquarters who had recently died of sudden causes. But
he had had three options—debriefing officers, dental officers, or medical
officers. Finally he had located a medical officer, and, not surprisingly,
the late Major Kelb had actually examined Commander Allen after one
mission.

Getting to the actual medical records had been the easy part, for
him.

The major difficulty had been finding the people to impersonate.

He shrugged, touched the console again, and forced a frown.

"System four beta inoperative."

He tapped another access code, and was rewarded with another set
of files. He glanced around to see if the senior technician were nearby.
But the senior tech remained locked in his own cubicle, still wrestling
with the promotion board schedules.

Jimjoy stood, eased back the swivel, and headed down the corridor
toward the fresher facilities, leaving his dress beret beside the screen.
Once around the first corner, he took the left-hand corridor back to the
security desk, pulling another beret from beneath his belt.

"Leaving a bit early, aren't you?"

"Not leaving," he mumbled. "Beta four's down. Need to get a de-
bugger from Tech-Ops."

"Personally?"

"Syndar says I have to explain *personally*. The authorization is on the
screen."

The thin-faced Marine at the shielded console nodded sympathetically at the thought of one personnel technician's having to explain how he had scrambled an entire system.

"Wouldn't want to be in your shoes. Let's see your card."

Jimjoy handed over the plastic oblong.

The guard checked the screen codes and inserted the card into the verifier.

"Handprint."

The verifier, after a moment, flashed green. The Imperial Marine did not remark on the slight hesitation, which could not have been avoided, but handed back the card and touched the portal release, opening the barrier that separated the closed personnel section from the rest of the facility.

"See you later. Good luck."

"Thanks."

"You'll need it."

Jimjoy nodded as he stepped through the portal, then continued his even pace until he was around the next corner, where he entered the public men's fresher.

Shortly, a heavyset Major of Supply waddled forth, proceeding toward the main security gate.

The pair of Marines at the main gate, male and female, passed the Major with bored looks, logging the screen pass into the console and dismissing his average muddy looks and brown hair as soon as his waddling gait had carried him out of sight.

XXXIII

THE WHITE-HAIRED Commodore bustled down the corridor, the tightness of the tunic and trousers indicating either vanity or a recent weight gain. The gold sleeve slashes glittered, indicating a recent promotion, in contrast to the row of faded ribbons across a heavy chest.

He passed a junior officer in exercise shorts and shirt, sweat streaming from his forehead, who stared at the sight of a Commodore in full-dress uniform hurrying through the Intelligence sector's physical training and demonstration facilities.

The Commodore felt the look and withered the unfortunate with a single steely glance, continuing his short quick steps until he arrived at the locked portal. His fingers proffered the entry card, danced over the console to enter a code, and presented a full handprint to the screen.

Bleep.

The portal irised open, and the senior officer hurried through, immediately turning left toward the combat simulation sector.

The multiple-target simulator was behind the third portal on the right side.

Taking a small plate from his belt, the Commodore deftly made two adjustments to the entry log console, then stepped through the portal. The small anteroom was empty, two chairs vacant for users who might have to wait their turn. Two additional closed portals confronted the older-looking officer.

Without hesitation, he took the one on the left, and bounded up the two steps into the simulator control room.

"What . . . Commodore? This—"

Thrummm!

Even before the young technician had collapsed over the console, the Commodore had reached her and pulled her and the swivel in which she had slumped away from the board.

His fingers tapped three studs, and light flooded the simulator below and back up through the armaglass window. He tapped another stud and spoke into the directional cone. "Maintenance problem. The system seems to have dropped the lighting parameters. We should be able to bring the backup on line. Do you want to begin the sequence again, or to continue from where it broke?"

"Hades! Can't you techs ever run anything right?"

The Commodore smiled a wintry smile through the one-way glass as he saw the man in the camouflage suit stand up in the far corner. Another man moved on the far side of the now large and empty room that had been filled with holographic projections not moments before.

"We do our best, sir." The Commodore paused, then continued. "While we're getting back on line, there's a Commodore Thrukma here. He says he needs a moment with Commander Allen, if one of you is Commander Allen."

"Thrukma? Never heard of him. What does he want?" The leaner and older man holstered the needler and turned toward the portal that would lead him back to the anteroom.

"He says that you already know."

Commander Allen frowned, but said nothing as he palmed the portal release. "Be back in a minute, Forstmann. Try the sequence yourself."

The Commodore obliged by rekeying the holotrack and tapping the "resume" stud. Then he turned to the portal through which he had entered, his own needler in hand.

Thring.

Thud.

The man who wore the name Thrukma on his tunic shook his head slowly as he looked at the body sprawled halfway through the portal.

Commander Allen wore the same frown with which he had left the simulator. Not even the neat hole through his forehead had erased all the lines on his face.

The Commodore checked the body, to ensure that the good Commander was as deceased as he looked, to slip several items into the Commander's equipment belt, and to make the changes and adjustments to the two needlers.

Then, moving quickly, he ran his fingers over the console. Next he dragged the body all the way into the control room before locking the control room portal behind him.

Finally, he locked the portal into the simulator, making it difficult, if not impossible, for Lieutenant Forstmann to leave the simulator without outside assistance. That would ensure Forstmann raised no alarm until either someone finally broke into the simulator or the technician recovered.

With a last look around, the Commodore palmed the portal to the main corridor, stepping outside. Without seeming to, he scanned the corridor and, seeing no one, made a final entry on the console portal controls, an entry that effectively locked them to all comers. While the tampering would be recorded under Commodore Thrukma's name, the Commodore would long since have vanished by the time it mattered.

The white-haired man turned from the portal and picked up his short steps toward the less secured section of the Intelligence physical training facility.

With the same deft manipulations, he logged himself out of the secure section and into the regular training area.

He began to bustle toward the main exit.

"Commodore?"

The voice came from a senior Commander, wearing, unfortunately, the Intelligence Service insignia on his collar.

"Yes, Commander." The Commodore's voice was neutral, yet condescending at the same time.

"I do not believe we have met, and your name is not posted to Headquarters . . ."

"Thrukma, Commander. If you check the most recent listing, I believe you will find it. It's spelled T-H-R-U-K-M-A. From Tierna, Fifth Fleet. Had the *Alaric*."

"*Alaric*? That the one—"

"Exactly. The same one, for better or worse." The Commodore's dark gray eyes focused on the Commander. "And you, Commander Persnal, if I recall correctly, were the watch officer on the *Challenger* at Landrik."

A slow flush crept over the collar of the dark-haired Commander, and his jaw tightened.

"Your pass, please, Commodore."

"Of course, Persnal. Of course. You always were a stickler for the rules, and I see you haven't changed at all." The Commodore flashed a purple oblong and nodded toward the main exit. "I believe the nearest verification console is there."

Persnal swallowed, but said nothing, standing well aside from the senior officer. The flush had subsided, and his sallow complexion had become even paler as he trailed the quick-stepping Commodore.

Two Imperial Marines and a duty technician waited behind the shielded consoles, bored looks on all three faces.

"Problems, Commander?"

"Problems, Commodore?"

The Marines had addressed the Commodore. The duty technician had addressed the Commander.

"No," answered the Commodore. "Just posted here, and the Commander does not know me personally. He has suggested, as ranking Intelligence officer, that I verify my clearance and identity." The Commodore stepped up to the console and inserted the purple card, tapped in his codes, and presented his hand to the scanner.

Bleep. The console flashed green, after an almost undetectable pause, and displayed an authorization code. All three ratings scanned it and nodded, virtually simultaneously.

The Commander frowned, studied the screen, studied the Commodore, then checked the screen again.

"Now," suggested the Commodore, "how about verifying who you are?"

"But . . . I'm the duty officer . . ."

"I don't know that . . . and I don't think you look like the Major, I mean Commander Persnal who was . . . on the *Challenger*. So be a good officer and oblige me, Persnal."

The Commander looked at the suddenly blank-faced technician and the impassive Marines, then back at the Commodore. The flush returned to his face, but he extracted a purple card seemingly identical to the one that Commodore had proffered and placed it on the console, adding his own keycode and placing his hand on the scanner.

Bleep.

"Good," noted the Commodore. "Good day, Commander. A pleasure to meet you again and to know you still regard the rules as paramount. I'm sure we'll be seeing more of each other." He palmed the portal release and stepped through, out into the afternoon sunshine.

With a glance at the senior officer quarters, he stepped toward the transportation center, where the dispatch records would indicate that Commodore Thrukma had requisitioned a flitter for Central City.

XXXIV

THE NONDESCRIPT BROWNISH groundcar rolled into the parking area behind the visiting officers' quarters, swinging carefully into an un-numbered and unreserved spot.

After a delay of several minutes, Jimjoy stepped out, wearing the rumpled working ship blues of a Service Captain and carrying a ship bag. He locked the car and stepped away, scanning the area, but saw nothing out of the ordinary.

The cubelike building before him, three stories tall, with its greenish-white permacrete finish, looked like a smaller-scale transplant from Alphane City. The few straggly trees between the parking area and the quarters had managed to hang on to a few handfuls of yellow-green leaves, and the yellowish dust collected around the permacrete walk from the groundcar parking area to the side entrance to the quarters.

Nearer the building were the reserved spaces, only one of which was filled, with an official-looking black car with tinted windows.

Jimjoy smiled. That one had to belong to the Security duty officer. He walked across the spaces, stepping aside as a small blue electric runabout darted toward him. He waved, then waited, as the runabout screeched to a halt.

Another officer, female, also in ship blues, popped out of the runabout.

"Off early, Freres?"

"Off late. Been on since 2400."

"Ooooo. That sounds like you've had a few problems." The solid and pale-skinned Lieutenant shook her head. Her lacquered hair scarcely moved.

Jimjoy grimaced. He didn't have to act. The jungle-flower perfume was overpowering. "Who hasn't, these days?"

"I know what you mean. It seems as though everything is happening. All at once. And the Intelligence types . . . something really has them unglued."

"Can't believe that. Nothing upsets that bunch. Deep-space ice in their hearts."

"Not today. Why, Captain . . . well, I shouldn't say, but they are really turning the base upside down . . . and they won't say a word."

"Still don't think it sounds like them." He turned and matched her shorter strides as they headed for the quarters.

"I suppose they're human. Something must upset them, at least sometimes." She tossed her head again, but the lacquered blond hair under her uniform cap still remained immobile. "And what about you? You up for something later?"

He grinned widely.

"That's not what I meant."

"It isn't?"

"You know it's not."

Jimjoy grinned even more widely.

"You're impossible!"

"That's entirely possible." He swung the bag over his shoulder. "Unfortunately, I have been on my feet—"

"For once."

"—since 2400 this morning. And to be up for anything, possible or impossible . . ."

"You need some sleep. I know. All you do is sleep off duty."

"Not all." He grinned again.

"Let's avoid that. If you actually manage to rouse yourself after obtaining whatever rest is necessary, and are interested in something besides the impossible, you might think about calling me later." She entered the quarters before him.

"Kkkkchewwww . . ." He sneezed from the combination of the perfume in the enclosed area and from the drifting yellow dust that swirled around them as the portal swished behind them.

"Maybe you do need some rest."

"Just dust."

"Think about it, Freres." She smiled warmly as she took the right-hand corridor away from him.

"I will . . . after I get some rest."

Jimjoy admired her spunk, though not necessarily the solidity of either her figure or her makeup. Without the over-abundance of artificial fragrance, it would have been even nicer to chat with her.

He took the left-hand corridor, heading around the corner toward his own small, but adequate, room.

Although he had hoped for a bit more time before the Intelligence community began turning over stones, in some ways he was surprised to have gotten as far as he had before the reaction had become obvious. The fact that it was obvious indicated that they had no real leads—yet.

Still, he let his steps slow as he neared the room where he had spent the last several weeks, on and off.

Quiet. Far too quiet.

"Shoooo . . ."

He turned and moved back around the corner, wearing the disappointed expression of a man who has suddenly remembered that he forgot something. He maintained that disappointed look as he marched back up the hall and out to the small groundcar.

Knowing that his current official identity as the good Captain Dunstan Freres could come under scrutiny at any time, he had left only a few uniforms in the officers' quarters, and a few real and a few spurious papers and documents supporting the identity of one Dunstan Freres.

The additional funds supplied by the Institute had come in very useful in procuring the range of uniforms and accessories necessary to his plans. He'd been more than a little surprised at Thelina's insistence on his accepting the funds.

But he certainly trusted her judgment, at times perhaps more than his own.

His steps clicked lightly on the pavement as he headed back toward the groundcar, hoping that Prullen had not seen him, although she probably wouldn't have thought of his mere return to the car as anything more than a personal rejection—he hoped.

It was almost time for him to surface at Intelligence Headquarters, assuming that his information packages had reached their intended destinations—the key media, the Admiral, and Commander Hersnik.

The media would probably attempt to verify the noncritical sections first, and that would blast a few more orbits, and another Intelligence crew would likely end up nosing around trying to discover who had leaked certain classified material.

Hersnik he trusted not at all, but he needed Hersnik to make the decisions, preferably without too much chance to think things over. So his reemergence and entrance would have to be abrupt enough and public enough to avoid the kind of unpleasant details that the late Commander Allen had specialized in.

He shrugged as he climbed into the groundcar. He had done what he could. Now he would see what kind of fool he had been.

XXXV

COMMANDER HERSNIK HAD been in his office roughly five standard minutes, according to Jimjoy's calculations, when the Special Operative stepped through the Security portal and into the Commander's outer office. In a single fluid motion, his fingers traced a series of patterns over the interior controls of the portal.

"What . . . why did . . . ?"

Jimjoy smiled at the orderly. "Security. Very tight security, Lieutenant."

"I suggest that you unseal that portal, Major—quickly, before the Commander has to summon the necessary assistance." The Lieutenant's hands were moving toward the small red keyboard.

Thrumm.

Clunk.

Jimjoy shook his head as the junior officer slumped over the security console, unconscious. The Special Operative slid around the end of the bank of screens and entered several codes and messages into the system, all indicating that the office was temporarily vacant as a result of a strategy conference and that the Commander would be available at 1500 for his normal appointments.

While there was a risk that Hersnik might be scheduled to meet with a superior, conceivably a Commodore or an Admiral, such immediate postluncheon meetings were rare, or nonexistent.

He smiled as he tapped the access panel.

"Yes?" Hersnik had left the screen blank, but his voice was as annoyingly clear as the last time Jimjoy had visited him.

"Major Wright to see you."

"Wright . . . Major Wright . . . here?"

Jimjoy nodded, then realized that he had left the orderly's screen blank—obviously.

"That is correct. He claims he has some unique information for you, Commander."

"You're not Jillson!"

"No, I'm Wright? Do you want the information, or do you want to face a court-martial?"

"Court-martial? Who are you kidding, Major?"

Jimjoy sighed, loudly, since Hersnik wasn't the type to appreciate subtleties. "Since when have I ever overstated my case, Hersnik?"

"Commander to you, Wright!"

"Hardly, and not much longer, unless you're willing to listen. And don't bother to try your out-lines. They've all been shunted into a delay loop."

Jimjoy waited for Hersnik to realize that he was effectively isolated.

"All right, Wright. Come on in."

Jimjoy smiled at the false levity in Hersnik's tone. The voice patterns told him what he needed to know. As he stepped up to the second portal, the one into the even more secure inner office, he picked up the long-barreled stunner again, touched the access plate, and stepped inside.

Thrumm.

Thriiiimmm.

Clank.

Hersnik was grabbing for the fallen stunner with his left hand as Jimjoy pounced from the portal and swept the weapon away from the Commander's grasp.

"Sit down."

Hersnik looked at Jimjoy, then at the weapon, then slowly eased back into his seat.

"Keep your hands visible, and listen."

Hersnik said nothing, but pursed his lips.

"You know, Commander, you really didn't need the stunner," Jimjoy observed, as he moved to the side where he could see both the consoles and Hersnik's hands. "I really am a loyal Imperial officer, difficult as you seem to be making it for me. And I meant what I said. Check the information on your console under 'Allen, double eff, star-cross.' "

Hersnik's usually neat black hair was slightly mussed, and there were circles under his eyes.

"That's nonsense . . . and how did you get here?"

"Not nonsense, and I got here on schedule, as set forth in my orders. Was there some reason why I should not have been able to return on schedule, Commander?"

Hersnik looked blankly at Jimjoy.

"Let's lay those questions aside for a moment, Commander, and get to the reason why I came back so quietly. That happens to be because Commander Harwood Allen is a Fuardian agent, and because he knows I know that." Jimjoy paused, then shrugged, still watching the Commander's hands and eyes. "And because I really didn't want him to have another shot at assassinating me."

This time, the Intelligence officer behind the wooden-framed consoles swallowed hard. "Allen . . . a Fuardian agent? Ridiculous!"

"That's what I thought, even after the first time he tried to kill me, then killed his partner when the Accord locals had him surrounded. That didn't make sense, you know. They would have had to turn the Lieutenant over to the local Imperial representative. So why didn't he want another arm of Imperial authority to know that he was out to kill off an Imperial Special Operative? Unless there was something strange about their mission? Besides, the Accord types already knew that we kill each other off all the time. So it just couldn't have been that he had hush-hush orders to do me in, could it?"

Hersnik said nothing for a long moment, then, rubbing his numb right hand, cleared his throat. "Go on, Major. That is all pure speculation."

Jimjoy shrugged again.

"When he tried the second time, it seemed rather strange, especially since he usually doesn't work solo. That's probably why his report won't show the second attempt."

Hersnik raised his eyebrows.

"By then, I'd managed to find out a few things on my own, like his connection to Major Kelb, and his hidden credit accounts, and the gaps in his time accounts and early personal history."

"Interesting—if true. But what do those things have to do with you? Or with your ridiculous assertion that he is a Fuardian agent?"

"Commander, isn't it obvious? Commander Allen knows that I know about him. He's tried to kill me twice. If I tried a direct return to base, he would have had me either fried in obscurity or locked away in some dark cell forever." Jimjoy smiled humorlessly. "The options aren't exactly wonderful. I can't desert because Allen leaked who and what I was to every agent within sectors of Accord, and I couldn't come home because some of my own team was laying for me. My only chance was to sneak back here and present the evidence."

"What evidence, Major? I have yet to see a shred of anything remotely resembling factual evidence."

"Oh . . . that. Once I realized what was really going on, that was easy enough to dig up. Bank records, holo shots of Allen with Fuardian muckety-mucks, alterations to service records, even his original birth records, not to mention his off-duty training with the Fuards during his official Imperial leave."

"You have documentation?"

"Brought you some copies. You can tell how good they are. The originals are safely tucked away. The Fuards have some. But everything will stay safely buried unless, of course, I don't show up back on duty pretty quickly.

"But let's get back to Commander Allen and that code. 'Allen, double eff, star-cross.' Remember?"

"What nonsense . . ."

"Commander, no nonsense. Doesn't hurt to look, unless you're in with Allen on this, in which case I'd start running. So don't bother protesting. Key it in. 'Allen, double eff, star-cross.' "

Jimjoy watched as the Commander laboriously tapped out the codes with his left hand. He refrained from shaking his head at desk-bound officers who were nearly helpless if their right hands were incapacitated.

The Commander's eyes widened as he read the material appearing on the screen. Finally, Hersnik swallowed. "Am I supposed to believe this?"

"You can or you can't. That's your choice. The Admiral will receive his transmission in less than two standard hours, and he'll read it because it will come in under the Imperial star coding. His staff also has the same information, and they will ensure, I suspect, he receives that information in his afternoon briefing. That's in less than an hour.

"There's a timedrop to Galactafax and Stellarview first thing in the morning. I came to alert you, and to request immediate reassignment to field duty."

"You what?" blurted the Commander. "You think that will change your . . . destiny?"

Jimjoy grinned once more, widely. "Have to be a gambling man, Commander. My bet is that it will be a lot easier for you to give me an impossible assignment that will probably kill me than to murder me on Service territory and risk a stink, particularly if you think about it."

"Why don't you just let us make the decisions?"

"I am. Just want to give you the complete picture before you do." Jimjoy bent toward the Commander. "Look. I'm good at what I do. Hades good. You can use me or not, but there have to be tough problems where you can. I'm not after diamonds and braid. If I disappear now, you risk a stink, and you can see from the information in the packets that it could involve you personally."

"Me?"

"It's on record that I entered your office, and that you are in charge of both assignments for me and for Commander Allen." Jimjoy paused, surveying the room and the telltales on the consoles.

"Assuming that the Service were out to . . . shall we say . . . make your life difficult . . . what future insurance would you have that the same preposterous set of circumstances might not occur again, purely through chance?"

"None, except for my own abilities and wits." Jimjoy smiled tightly, before adding, "And, of course, some insurance that if I disappear, except on assignment, such information as you see there will appear in various media outlets. There would be enough confirming data to make it sticky."

"Are you through threatening the Service, Major?" Hersnik asked coolly.

"Don't think you understand, Commander. I'm not threatening anyone. I've been threatened. Simply want to do my job, and try to ensure that I have some chance to keep doing it—since it doesn't look like I can do anything else."

"If you felt so threatened, why didn't you just disappear? You certainly have some talent for it."

Jimjoy kept his expression impassive. "For how long? How long could I stay hidden with every Imperial agent, and everyone who owes Intelligence something, on my track?"

Hersnik nodded. "So you accept the extent of Imperial Intelligence?"

"Be a fool if I didn't."

"Then why did you come back? With that power, couldn't Commander Allen have you disappear tomorrow and not ever reappear?"

Jimjoy hid his puzzlement over Hersnik's continued reference to Allen as if the late Commander were still alive. While it was certainly in Jimjoy's favor to act as if Allen were hanging on the other side of the portal, was Hersnik trying to test him? Or could it be that Hersnik didn't know?

"I don't question the Service's power, Commander. My only hope is to set up a situation where it is easier and more profitable to use me than to dispose of me."

Hersnik nodded once more, as if some obscure fact had become clearer. His fingers tapped the console, but he left them in clear view. "You seem to find the Service untrustworthy on one hand and extraordinarily trustworthy on the other. That's either naive or exploitive on your part, isn't it?"

Jimjoy shrugged. "The Service is trustworthy, at least as an institution, Commander. I have found some individuals less than trustworthy, and I have brought back some evidence of their failures. They seem to be out to stop me from bringing back that evidence, but I seriously doubt that most of the Intelligence Service has ever even heard of one Major Wright, much less concerned itself with his fate."

The Commander chuckled mirthlessly. "So what do you want? Really want?"

Jimjoy took a deep breath. "Immediate orders to the toughest assignment possible. Preferably as far from Headquarters as practical."

"How immediate is immediate?"

"Next shuttle off-planet."

Hersnik nodded again.

Jimjoy found the gesture annoying, but did not react.

"I take it you are worried about Commander Allen?"

"Put it this way, Commander. Either you believe me or you don't. If you do, you're going to detain Allen, and the Fuards will be after me. Or you won't, but you'll tell Allen, and he'll be after me."

"Commander Allen is an Imperial officer."

"Commander Allen damned near killed me twice," responded Jimjoy evenly. "Was he under Imperial orders to do so?"

"Hardly," answered Hersnik, with a twist to his lips.

Jimjoy could tell that Hersnik was relieved to be able to answer the question truthfully, since Allen had been ordered to kill Jimjoy once, and only once.

"In that case, Commander, you shouldn't find it that difficult to provide me with orders to do my job somewhere."

"That assumes the Service finds, after an appropriate investigation and inquiry, that your assertions are correct."

"My life is somewhat more important than your inquiries. Do you intend to give me orders or place me under detention—and face an inquiry yourself, along with me?"

"You leave me little choice, Major Wright. Not exactly for the reasons you thought, however. I cannot afford to turn down your generous offer. We've already lost three operatives on New Kansaw." He nodded at the keyboard. "May I?"

"In a moment, when I release some of the blocks."

"You might also be interested to know that we have already discovered the late Commander Allen's double game."

"Late. Late? You mean he's dead? You already tried and executed him?"

"Not exactly. It appears as though someone else found out first. He was shot through the head with a needler in the combat simulator. It seems as if it might have been done by another inside agent. We have some idea who might have killed him, but it would be impossible to prove, especially now, since the needler used was the Commander's own. It was fully charged, and not for simulator work, either."

"Then why did you string me along here?"

Hersnik smiled coldly. "Why not? Your entrance was not exactly designed for friendliness, although, in retrospect, I can understand your concerns. At least you appear willing to handle another assignment, and we have a much better lead on the late Commander's demise.

"As for the New Kansaw assignment, Major, you seem to be the perfect choice, because, frankly, I really don't care how many rebels you butcher. I'd rather not ruin another officer doing it."

Jimjoy forced a frown. "I don't have to like it . . ."

"Neither do I . . ."

"But you get the credit for uncovering Commander Allen's espionage, while I get a black mark, another one, for unconventional behavior, if I'm lucky."

"Don't press your luck, Major. Standard procedures . . ."

"Didn't seem to hamper you when you assigned me to the Accord mess. By the way, that report is completed and filed under 'Accord, biotech one,' with my order code."

"What did you find out?"

"It's all in the report. Basically, they have taken the science of genetics further than anyone in the Empire. I suspect they may even be beyond the accomplishments of Old Earth in the pre-Directorate days. How far only a skilled scientist could tell you. I tried to put all the technical jargon in the report. There probably are future military applications, but the Accord types seem to be concentrating mainly on plant genetics and removal of lethal human genes. They've done a great deal with plants.

"Accord really has no way to disseminate the information beyond its own people. No one outside of the top Imperial scientists seems to understand what they're doing. I suspect that's what led to the Fuardian actions and Commander Allen's presence there, perhaps as a way to get the Empire to crack down on the Institute, rather than learn from it."

"I'm not sure that follows."

"Look at it this way. Only Accord and the Empire have the scientific background to benefit from the Institute's research. Halston's still in an uproar, and the fundamentalist leanings of the Fuards have always prohibited genetic research. If Commander Allen could have persuaded the Service to destroy the Institute *before* gaining the knowledge the Institute has developed, then the Empire could not use that information against the Fuards. And since genetic research is against the Fuard creed, they'd want to destroy the Institute anyway. But since Accord is still an Imperial colony, they can't move directly. Of course, I'm sure you've already figured that out."

"True . . . uh . . . ummm," offered Hersnik, glancing at the small security screen wistfully, and rubbing the numbed fingers of his right hand with his left.

Jimjoy took a step toward Hersnik, who looked up nervously. "Seems to me you have two choices—get me out of here and clean up the mess, or be unavailable when the Admiral is looking for you and wants to know why his staff knows and why you haven't let him know."

"That sounds like blackmail . . ."

"No. Letting the Admiral and the media know is merely insurance." Jimjoy sighed. "If I'm alive and this drags out, you'll always have the chance to blame me for forcing the issue—once you've shunted me off to somewhere like Gilbi or New Kansaw."

Hersnik steepled his fingers, awkwardly, since his right hand seemed not totally controlled. His black eyebrows furrowed. "You forget I could still place you under a security lock."

"You could." Jimjoy laughed, harshly. "But then you'd have to explain that in addition to everything else, and it would look like you were trying to cover up something worse. Do you really want that, Hersnik?"

At the use of his name without its accompanying rank, the Intelligence Commander glared at the Major.

"Explain what?"

Jimjoy leaned forward, with an intensity that forced the Commander to lean back in his swivel. "Do you think that the Admiral is going to explain to the media how a Fuard agent infiltrated the Service's most inner circles? Do you think the Admiral will go before all those fax crews? When the news is bad? When that's your job? When my reports show that the Fuards are manipulating the Intelligence Service?"

"What?"

"A portion of my report was leaked to the media . . . the part that shows Commander Allen was trying to kill me to prevent his identity from being revealed."

"And . . ." said Hersnik slowly.

"If anything happens to me right now, it would seem that you were covering up everything to save your own neck. I doubt it matters to the Admiral one way or another whether you explain your way, or face an inquiry and a possible court-martial. Not to mention explaining my disappearance. Of course, you could just say that everything is well in hand, and that I have been reassigned at my own request . . ."

Jimjoy could finally see the trace of sweat on Hersnik's forehead. He waited.

"You really don't think this will protect you for long, do you?"

"No. As soon as the furor dies down, I imagine someone will try again. But I'm a good enough operative to have a chance. And it will probably cost anyone who tries at least a few good men, which would also have to be explained. And I really don't think you want to make those explanations for a little while."

"That's not enough, Wright. Good try, but it won't wash."

Jimjoy smiled. "All right. I'd hoped you'd be reasonable. Unless I cancel the drop personally, and I won't until and unless I have a courier to my assignment and I'm the copilot, 'Halston Fuse One' will hit the fax circuit."

"Halston Fuse One?"

"Call it up on your Security two base. You can call up from your data banks. You just can't get outside."

Hersnik frowned, but the Commander's hands touched the console. His mouth dropped open.

"Not even the Admiral knows about this, Commander, and if I get safely off-planet in my courier, he won't have to."

Hersnik glared.

"No threats, please." Jimjoy sighed. "I've already had to do more than enough just to carry out my mission."

"Your mission . . . your mission . . ."

"The one you sent me on. The one you didn't want me to return from, Commander. You and I both know who Commander Allen really worked for, and you're far better off this way."

Hersnik's face was blank, and Jimjoy wondered if he had pushed too far.

"Orders to New Kansaw it is. Permanently, as far as the Service is concerned."

"I'll wait right here, after I've released the holds on your system, while you do the authorizations, Commander."

"Suit yourself, Major. Suit yourself. Not that you haven't already. This orbit's yours."

Jimjoy nodded. He just hoped one orbit would be enough.

XXXVI

"ARE YOU CERTAIN, Commander?"

"Of course not, sir. If I could prove it, it would have been handled in the ordinary manner."

The Admiral sighed. "I think we'll refrain from going into that right now." He rested his elbows on the wide expanse of polished wood beside the ornate console, leaning forward to pin the dark-haired Commander with piercing green eyes. "Let me summarize your surmises, and they are surmises, for all the circumstantial evidence you have presented.

"First, Major Wright managed to appear at Intelligence Headquarters without known use of Imperial Service transport or without being intercepted by any of your agents or by any friendly agents. Second, he admitted recognizing two attempts on his life by the late Commander Allen. Third, the health and service records of Commander Allen now in the data banks and the hard copies in Headquarters do not match the hard copies of the records found in the Commander's personal effects. Fourth, Commander Allen should not have had access to all of his own personal records—"

At the open-jawed expression of the Commander, the Admiral smiled and interjected, "My summary is not confined to just those facts you have chosen to present, Commander."

The Intelligence Service Commander closed his mouth without uttering another word.

"Fifth, Commander Allen was killed with the weapon found in his own holster inside a secure military installation by a Commodore who does not exist, but who knew background information known only to the senior watch officer, and not available to Major Wright under normal circumstances. Sixth, Major Wright detected and avoided two other assassination attempts you engineered indirectly and did not report to High Command. For whatever reasons, he chose not to even report all these incidents to you. Seventh, Major Wright still chose to return and to make a full, accurate, and detailed report, albeit with certain 'precautions,' and to request further orders, as far from Intelligence Headquarters as possible. Finally, he sent me a copy of the materials he presumably set aside to ensure his own protection."

The Admiral smiled at the Commander, but the smile had all the warmth of a wolf confronting a wounded stag. "Now, Commander, would you care to draw any additional conclusions from my summary?"

"No, sir. I would be interested in your conclusions."

The Admiral nodded. "I can understand that. First, despite your deviousness, your incredible stupidity, and your colossal egotism, your instincts happen to be correct. Major Wright represents a considerable threat to the Service. Second, your choice of an assignment for the man is also probably correct. And third, that is exactly what Wright wanted."

The Commander swallowed.

The Admiral waited.

"I don't think I follow your logic to the end, sir."

"Major Wright is a threat because he will never see the Empire's need for subtle action. Every direct action reflects poorly and stirs up greater resentment against the Empire. He will also destroy incompetence, one way or another, and most incompetents in the Service have strong political connections. They must be kept isolated and placated, but we do not have the political capital to destroy them."

The Commander squirmed slightly in the hard seat, but continued to listen.

"Major Wright also inspires great loyalty in the able people who recognize his talents. They would emulate him, multiplying the destructive impact the man can create.

"Last, he has no hesitations. He is a deeply ethical man, in his own way, with the same lack of restraint as a psychopath. With him, to think is to act, and no structure, authoritarian or democratic, can react fast enough to counter him."

The Commander cleared his throat softly, as if requesting permission to speak.

"Yes, Commander?"

"You make him sound almost like a hero. But you insist he is a danger, and you say that my actions were correct."

"Correct on all three counts. He is a hero type. He is a danger, and if he cannot be eliminated, he must be kept on isolated and dangerous duty at all costs."

"What if he deserts—" The Commander broke off the question as he saw the Admiral grin. "I see . . . I think. If he deserts, he destroys his credibility within the Service. And if he takes straight butchery assignments, he'll either have to reject them, for which he can be court-martialed or cashiered, or lose his ethics in accepting them. Is that it?"

"More or less, Commander. Although we will attempt, with more subtlety, to render the longer-term issues moot." The Admiral frowned. "That leaves the question of how to deal with Commander Allen. My thought is to leave the murder as unsolved, but to imply that he was indeed a double agent, and that a certain Major solved the Empire's problem. Since that Major will not be around to counter the rumors, that approach will bear double duty."

"Why are you telling me?"

"Because you will make the necessary arrangements, Commander. Need I say more?"

The Commander repressed a groan. "No, sir."

The Admiral stood, with a brief shake of his head, the backlighting glinting through his silvered blond hair. "That will be all, Commander."

XXXVII

STILL FROWNING AFTER his quick look through the station screens at the scout ship in the docking port, Jimjoy sealed his suit and stepped forward.

The *Captain Carpenter* had seen better days. Much better days, but he couldn't say that he was surprised. Obviously, Hersnik wanted to get word to New Kansaw before his favorite Special Operative arrived.

From the looks of the *Carpenter*, the good Commander might not have to worry about Jimjoy's arrival at all.

Jimjoy shrugged within his suit and tapped the access panel.

"*Carpenter*, Tech Berlan."

"Major Wright here. Temporary assignment for transport."

"Lock's waiting, Major. The Captain should be back in a few minutes with the clearance."

Jimjoy pursed his lips, then frowned again. Clearances were not picked up, but routed through the station comm system. Shaking his head, he studied the ship's lock as he stepped through the station portal and into the *Carpenter*.

Would what he was looking for be that obvious? He doubted it, but the clues were there.

"Cluttered" was the best word for the ship's lock. Although all the gear was secured, much of the additional equipment was stowed in place with brackets added without much regard for the ship's original design, leaving only enough comfortable space for a single suited individual to walk through into the ship itself.

Jimjoy studied the lock, but all the equipment appeared standard, and the lock control panel, though battered, showed no signs of recent tampering.

The man who had identified himself as Berlan waited inside the courier.

"Major Wright?"

"The same." Jimjoy fumbled with his flat dispatch case, carried in addition to his kit and his flight equipment. The flight equipment bag also included several smaller packages with rather more specialized equipment. Commander Hersnik would not have been pleased with the contents, but then again, Commander Hersnik would not be carrying out the mission. The need to bring equipment meant that he was carrying more gear than usual, and the lack of personal mobility bothered him.

At last he managed to fumble out his I.D. and orders for the technician.

Berlan was red-haired, rail-thin, and stood perhaps five centimeters taller than Jimjoy. His short-cropped hair was shot with silver, and a thin white scar ran from the right corner of his mouth to his earlobe.

"Yes, sir. Senior Lieutenant Ramsour should be back shortly. You get the top bunk in the forward space—that's the spot of honor, since you're ranking on board.

"Hope you don't mind acting as the backup, but otherwise we don't go."

"No problem, chief. Let me stow my gear. Then I'd appreciate it if you'd show me around."

Berlan looked as though he might frown, but he did not. His lips pursed. Then he nodded. "Yes, sir."

Jimjoy eyed the clean but battered control area as he passed the open portal. In the Captain's cabin, scarcely more than a long closet, he found a single large and empty locker and placed his bags and case inside.

Berlan stood waiting.

"Drives?" Jimjoy asked as he knelt by the flush hatch that should lead to the space below that contained the grav-field polarizer, the screen generators, and the discontinuity generator, not that anyone ever called it other than the jumpbox.

"Standard. Beta class." Berlan made no movement to unseal the hatch.

Jimjoy touched the access plates, waiting for the iris plates to open fully. Then he touched the locks to ensure the hatch didn't reseal on him. He still wore his shipsuit, including the hood, with only the face membrane not in place. Drive spaces had been known to lose pressure during inspections, especially when the inspector was not popular.

"Coming, Berlan?"

"If you want, sir."

"Wouldn't hurt, especially since your equipment may have been modified since installation. Ships this old tend to have some unique modifications."

As he slid into the maintenance area, two meters square, from which in-passage repairs were theoretically possible, the Major took a deep breath.

Ozone, as expected. A hint of old oil, also expected, and a rubbery sort of smell, the kind that always showed up after new or rebuilt equipment had been installed.

He waited until the tech's feet touched the plastplates, looking at the area to his right. The polarizer was untouched, clean, but with a fine misting above the exposed plastics and metal. The mist seemed to hover several centimeters above the polarizer.

"Not much to see, sir."

"Enough, Berlan. Enough."

Jimjoy looked straight at the jumpbox. The involuted blackness of the discontinuity generator twisted at his eyes, but he attempted to look around it, and at the thin power lines that ran to it. Superconductors were fine, but even a small gash could pose enough problems to turn the scout into disassociated subatomic forces. The silver finish on the lines he could see was unmarred. Besides, there were no recent marks around the field boundaries on the plastplates of the deck.

That left the screens.

"Had some screen problems last time out?"

"Why . . . ah . . . yes, sir. Nothing major, Major. But we kept going into the orange with debris."

Jimjoy forced himself to nod, as if he really didn't understand. "They fix it, or just replace part of the generators?"

"There. Pulled out the power links, replaced them."

Jimjoy followed the tech's gesture, noted the obviously newer, or at least less battered, section. He also noted, but did not call attention to the dullness of the thin power line running to the rear section of the screen generators.

"If that's all, sir . . . ?"

"That's all, Berlan."

Clink.

"Flame . . ." muttered the Major as a stylus spilled from his belt pouch onto the deck and skittered to the base of the unpowered screen generator. "Lucky it went that way."

Berlan swallowed. "Need some help, sir?"

"No. Get it myself."

"I'll give you room, sir."

Jimjoy knelt and crawled under the apron of the generator, reaching for the stylus and checking the power connections. He did not nod as he saw what he expected, but, instead, reached for the stylus and eased it away from the equipment. His hand flicked a switch into an alternate position, a switch he doubted most of the crew knew even existed.

Then he eased himself backward and stood, carefully tucking the stylus back into his belt pouch.

"Everything all right, sir?" Berlan peered down from the hatch.

"Fine. Coming right up."

Jimjoy climbed the ladder slowly, though he would have needed only two or three of the inset rungs to lever himself back into the scout's main corridor.

There were two possibilities, and he didn't like either. Lieutenant Ramsour's presence might tell him which was correct.

"The other tech?" he asked as he resealed the hatch.

"That's R'Naio. Should be back with the Captain. Wanted some real comestibles, not just synthetics."

Jimjoy grinned. "Can certainly understand that." He edged toward the control section. "Wouldn't hurt to check out the board, especially if I'm backup."

"Yes, sir. But the Captain's quite good."

"Understand, but sometimes the best can't do everything."

"Suppose that's true, sir, but it will be a short trip."

Jimjoy smiled and edged around the technician into the copilot's couch.

The control section smelled . . . used . . . and the section of the controls before the Special Operative was slightly dusty. He held back a sigh as he ran his fingers across the board, trying to refresh his skills, noting the slight differences in control positions and calibrations. The screen configuration was standard, with the power disconnects apparently operational solely between screens and drives.

The rationale was simple enough. Scouts by necessity often operated at high gee loads. Scout pilots were often inexperienced. The default system configurations allowed power diversion between screens and drives, but not between the grav-field generator and either drives or screens.

Jimjoy would have bet on two other factors, one being that the *Carpenter* ran hot. All scouts did.

With a wry grin, he eased himself out of the copilot's shell.

"You must be Major Wright," a new voice remarked.

The speaker was thin, dark-haired, hard-voiced, and female.

Jimjoy nearly nodded, instead answered. "The same. You're Captain Ramsour?"

"A very junior senior Lieutenant Ramsour, Major. And also rather new to the *Carpenter*."

"First command?"

"Second. Had the courier *Tsetung* for a bit over a standard year. Rotated into the *Carpenter* when her skipper made Major and was selected for staff college."

Jimjoy merely nodded politely.

"Major?"

"Yes?"

"What the flame did you do?"

"Enough that New Kansaw is the best assignment I'll ever get again."

Lieutenant Ramsour shook her head. "You know the board?"

"Yes. Not as current as you."

"Happy to have you here." Ramsour scarcely sounded happy, but more like resigned to an unpleasant duty. "Your gear strapped in?"

"In the empty locker. Sufficient?"

"What it's for. We're waiting for a R'Naio and a few local comestibles, since none of us care much for synthetics."

"Outbound from New Kansaw?"

"After we pick up Lieutenant L'tellen . . . fresh from post-Academy training."

Jimjoy frowned.

"Her father's deputy base Commander there."

"Wondered about that." Jimjoy looked toward the board.

The pilot followed his glance. "R'Naio should be here momentarily. She had an electrocart at the lock. You can start pre-break checks, if you want. I'd like a last look below."

"Go ahead. I'll wait. A few minutes won't matter that much." He wanted to watch her inspection of the drives.

The Lieutenant did not acknowledge his statement, but was already kneeling to reopen the hatch.

Berlan stood on the other side of the hatch, ostensibly checking the bulkhead panel containing the lock circuits and controls. As the Lieutenant dropped through the full iris of the hatch, he looked up to meet the Major's eyes, then looked away.

"Berlan!"

"Yes, Captain?"

"Did you run a full-surge through the screens?"

"No, Captain. Can't until we're clear of the station. We're at a standard lock port, not at a Service lock."

"Sorry . . . forgot about that."

Jimjoy nodded imperceptibly. She asked the right questions, although he wondered why the *Carpenter* had not been able to get a full-Service lock.

He caught Berlan's eye. "No facilities for couriers?"

"Not for a Ramsour, Major."

Jimjoy nearly choked, turned the feeling into a cough. "The Commander Ramsour? Her father?"

"Uncle." The tech's voice lowered. "She won the Armitage . . . understand they couldn't deny her pilot training . . . finished in top ten percent . . . with everyone out to bust her."

"Berlan . . . are you spreading gossip again?"

The Lieutenant looked up at the two men before flipping herself up and into the passage with a single fluid movement that Jimjoy envied.

Berlan flushed.

"Don't listen to him, Major. He thinks the whole universe is out to get me because Steven Ramsour was my uncle. But his paranoia counters my unfounded optimism." She resealed the hatch and straightened, brushing back short black hair with her left hand. The hair was too short to need brushing, but even that nervous gesture was graceful.

Jimjoy glanced at the standard embossed wings and name on her gray shipsuit—LT RAE RAMSOUR, ISC.

"Yes . . . the name is Ramsour. That's me."

Jimjoy merely nodded. The more he heard, the less he liked it.

"Have you ever heard of a Commander by the name of Hersnik, Lieutenant?"

"Hersnik? I don't believe so."

Jimjoy was convinced she had recognized the name, especially when she did not ask for his reasons for asking the question.

"*Carpenter*? Berlan, release the double-damned lock and give me a hand with your flaming fresh food." The gravelly voice issuing from the lock control panel could only be that of the missing R'Naio.

Berlan reached for the control.

The Lieutenant nodded sharply toward the control board. "Let's get you on your way, Major."

Jimjoy turned, took a step, and dropped back into the copilot's shell, this time cinching the straps in place.

"Skitter pilot, too?"

"Sometimes." He realized that the Lieutenant, while not experienced, was sharp. Too bad that she was being allowed to climb too fast, although that was also predictable. Intelligence, arrogance, grace, looks, and disguised femininity . . . and a case to prove for the entire Service—Hersnik had a lot to work with, and Jimjoy had probably handed him the solution to two problems on a platter.

He thumbed the checklist prompt.

"Power one . . ."

". . . standby," she answered.

"Power two . . ."

The checklist was quick enough, and the *Carpenter* showed in the green.

"Alphane beta, this is Desperado. Standing by for pushaway. Orbit break, corridor three. Clearance delta."

"Desperado, beta. Cleared for break. Estimate pushaway in three stans. Clearance is green. Report when clear of station."

"Beta, Desperado. Stet. Will report when clear."

"Lock links are clear, Captain." Berlan's voice was raspy through the board speakers.

Sssssssss.

Only a faint scraping sound marked the separation of ship and station.

"Don't," cautioned Jimjoy as the Lieutenant looked from the DMI to the course line display.

"Don't what, Major?" Her voice was low, sharp.

"Don't report clearance until we're actually powered."

"Sloppy procedure."

"Survival procedure."

"Care to explain, *Major*?" Rae Ramsour's face stiffened.

"No. You can trust me or not. Couldn't explain, but don't survive as Special Operative without trusting your instincts. Hersnik is out to get you and me. I set you up. Not intentionally, but I owe you. Now . . . trust me or not. Up to you."

Her mouth had dropped slightly, but only slightly, at his mention of being a Special Operative.

"Special Operative?"

"Why else would I be going to New Kansaw on a courier?"

She shook her head. "You handle the comm, then. Since you seem to think it will make a difference."

"Might not. Can't hurt, though."

Jimjoy could feel Berlan looking toward them, but the technician said nothing. Neither did R'Naio, wherever she was.

He waited as Ramsour's long fingers played across the board, watching as the DMI showed greater and greater separation from beta orbit control, waiting as the ship's acceleration built.

"Alphane beta, this is Desperado. Reporting orbit break this time. Outbound corridor three. Estimated time to jump point four plus five."

"Desperado, beta control. Understand four plus five to jump. Interrogative delay."

Jimjoy could tell that Ramsour wanted to ask the same question, but had not.

"Beta, Desperado. Require additional en route testing of equipment.

Power shunts were not available Alphane station. Proceeding as cleared this time."

"Stet, Desperado. Your clearance is green."

Jimjoy continued to watch the panel, particularly the energy tracks on the EDI, to see if beta control would launch a message torp. But the EDI showed only the station and a single incoming ship, cruiser-sized, on corridor two.

"Paranoid as Berlan, aren't you?"

"More, probably," answered Jimjoy. "Would you mind another paranoid suggestion?"

"Suggestion? Or a strong recommendation?" Her voice bore a tinge of exasperation.

"Whatever you want to call it."

"I'm waiting, Major."

"Boost your angle . . . enough that we'll end up at about plus two by jump point . . ."

"Be happy to, but won't that actually delay our jump time, not to mention the distortion?"

"It would . . . if we wait until projected jump time."

Ramsour half turned toward the Special Operative. "Major, I do not appreciate half-explained, 'I know best,' patronizing schemes. While I appreciate fully your interest in maintaining both our hides, I personally operate a great deal more effectively when I fully understand what is intended. And I might actually be able to help."

Jimjoy repressed a smile.

"All right. First, what's the normal-matter-density distribution pattern relative to a system's ecliptic? Second, what's the purpose of a jump corridor? Third, why do the normal power cross-channels not allow diversion from the polarizer?"

"So we don't get turned into particles of various sizes?"

"Try again, and would you mind boosting our angle, say—"

"Since I don't yet understand your machinations, Major, please feel free to make the correction you would find appropriate."

Jimjoy could see the woman set her jaw. She also had the legendary Ramsour impatience, it appeared.

"If you wouldn't mind." He turned his attention to the board, blotting out her coolness, and began making the adjustments.

He could still feel her eyes on him, and on the board, as her fingers jabbed at her own calculations.

"Rather a subtle course pattern, Major."

"No sense in making it obvious. It should look like carelessness, at least for a while."

"All right, Major Wright. I'll go back to basics. First, matter density *normally* decreases with the distance from the mean plane to the ecliptic. A defined jump corridor is merely a path of lower matter density leading to one of the closer points outside a system where the matter density is low enough to permit a safe jump. Third, the grav polarizer is not cross-connected to the power shunts because a courier has an acceleration capability sufficient to damage an unfielded ship and its crew."

Jimjoy nodded. "Why do we have to stay in the ecliptic?"

"Because . . . oh . . . it's basically the lowest-power, least-error approach. But how much time will you gain? And how far into the reserves . . . ?"

"Not at all." Jimjoy grinned. "I took the liberty of restoring full cross-connections to the *Carpenter*. Figure we'll be clear enough to jump in about another one point five to two standard hours. In another ten, fifteen stans, start boosting accel. Drop to zero just before jump, and shift field and drives to screens."

"Are you planning the same sort of reentry?"

"Why not? If you screw up a jump and end up too far above the jump corridor, what else can you do?"

The Captain of the *Carpenter* shook her head slowly. "Should work." She paused. "But why don't more people figure it out?"

"It's in the more obscure tactics books, but what's the most expensive part of operating a ship?"

"Energy costs." She paused, then asked, "But how does that square?"

"It doesn't." He couldn't help grinning further. "Question isn't just energy. Matter of accuracy. Too far above the ecliptic, and the standard jump calculations don't work. They include a constant for matter density. The level of variation increases exponentially with distance from the mean galactic plane . . ."

"That's a fiction."

"Mean galactic plane . . . you're right again, but it's useful in approximations of this sort." Jimjoy paused to modify his early changes to the ship's vertical course angle. "Some of the commercial freighters use the tactic all the time, especially on runs where they know the density variations. They change over time, unlike the corridors, which exist because of internal system dynamics. But the changes are slow. Problem is that military ships go everywhere, and besides, we're not at war. So why complicate the business of navigation, not to mention boosting energy costs?"

This time Rae Ramsour was the one to nod. "And every hot pilot would be trying to cut time, and flame the energy costs."

"You've got it. Also, the debris level is uneven, and over time that can play hades with screens."

"So for economic and maintenance reasons . . ."

"And to simplify procedures for young pilots, not to mention increasing the defense capability of Imperial systems."

"How? What's to prevent attackers from copying your tactics?"

"Habit . . . and lack of information."

She laughed, brittlely. "It takes energy to determine local matter variations, and since no one but the Empire has the energy . . . but what about the Fuards, or the Halstanis, or the Arm traders?"

"If they have, they aren't telling, and neither would I."

Jimjoy continued to watch the board indicators as he talked, in particular those showing the cruiser inbound to Alphane on corridor two. But the cruiser bored in toward the Imperial planet and its orbit control stations on a steady course and angle.

"Major, you are dangerous. No wonder they want you off Alphane."

"So are you, Lieutenant. And consorting with me won't help." He tried to keep his tone light, even as he tapped an inquiry into the board.

"Desperado, Alphane beta. Interrogative time to jump. Interrogative time to jump."

"Rather interested, aren't they?" noted Jimjoy.

"Beta control, Desperado. Estimate three plus to jump. Three plus to jump."

"You lie effectively, Major."

"Just doing my best to preserve the Empire's assets."

Rae Ramsour shook her head again.

Jimjoy took a look at the spacial density readout and smiled wryly. If the thinning continued at the current level, jump was less than a standard hour away.

XXXVIII

"LESS THAN TEN stans to jump."

"I have this feeling," murmured the Captain of the *Carpenter*.

Jimjoy looked at the senior Lieutenant. "Recommend sealed shipsuits for jump, Captain."

Ramsour frowned. "What else haven't you told me?"

"Call it mere instinct. But if our shields have a flaw, the loving Emperor forbid, we won't be in any position to—"

"—make repairs. Or react." The courier's Captain straightened. "Berlan, R'Naio. Seal shipsuits for jump."

"Sealing suits, Captain."

Jimjoy sealed his own suit with the plastic shield, triggering the internal comm system. "Comm test."

"Clear, Major. Berlan?"

"Hear you both, Captain."

"R'Naio?"

"Clear enough."

"Would you like to set the jump, Major?"

"If you don't mind, Captain."

"Be my guest."

"All hands, strap in for maneuvers."

"Strapping in."

"Strapping in."

Jimjoy touched the controls, shifting power from the grav polarizer to the drives. A momentary lightness was replaced by the acceleration of the stepped-up drives.

"Major . . ."

"We'll be fine." Jimjoy's voice was calm, but crisp, as he concentrated on positioning the ship for the jump. He doubted that anyone would be waiting at the fringes of the New Kansaw system, but if they were, they would scarcely be prepared for the jump-exit velocity he had in mind.

"And I thought the Captain was a hadeshead . . ." The gravelly mutter was not meant to be heard, but the internal shipsuit pickups were voice-actuated and sensitive.

Jimjoy grinned. He might yet improve Rae Ramsour's situation, if only by comparison. Even if his presence as a noticeably senior officer had put her in an impossible position.

"Two stans until jump." Jimjoy could see the Lieutenant trying not to squirm in her shell.

With less than thirty seconds before jump Jimjoy diverted all power from the drives to the ship's screens, then watched the screen indicators, bleeding some of the power back to the jump generator.

"Ten, nine, eight, seven, six . . ."

At the word "six," Jimjoy dropped all power into standby, letting the ship's cutouts take over. Weightlessness brought his stomach into his throat. As he swallowed it back into place, the wave of blackness that defined a jump flashed over him.

The blackness subsided, though the weightlessness did not, as the *Carpenter* popped back into normspace.

As he studied the controls, Jimjoy was scarcely surprised. Internal pressure was dropping to zero, and the shields were inoperative.

"Remain suited. Internal pressure loss." He began to unstrap. "Captain, appreciate it if you left power *off* both drives and screens until I see if I can locate the cause of the problem."

"You don't seem surprised, Major."

"Would have been surprised if there hadn't been a problem."

Jimjoy unstrapped and made his way to the access hatch, where Berlan had already begun to open the iris. The tech said nothing as the Special Operative slipped down into the space below.

As Jimjoy suspected, one of the superconductor lines was black. That was the easy problem.

Berlan watched as Jimjoy eased the spent line from first one socket, then the other. Installing one of the spares was done almost as quickly.

"Captain, power up on the screens."

"Powering up."

The line shimmered dusty silver.

"Screens are in the green, Major."

"Course line?"

"Estimate two plus to New Kansaw orbit control. We're at about one and a half plus on the high side."

"What's the reserve on oxygen?"

"Two full pressurizations."

The Special Operative removed the temperature probe from the equipment locker and began to sweep the lower deck, concentrating on the inside hull plates.

One of the plates behind the screen generator was noticeably colder.

"Dropping the screen generator off-line, Captain."

"Can you make it quick, Major?"

"Debris?"

"Not for another fifteen stans at our inbound."

"Stet."

Jimjoy used the manual shunt to drop the generator offline. Then he squeezed around the bulk of the generator. A neat hole had been drilled, probably with a laser cutter, at an angle to the plate, virtually invisible unless looked for. The secondary ship's screens probably had held a plug in place on the other side. When the screens failed, the internal pressure had knocked the plug out and depressurized the ship.

The sealant tube in the small equipment locker did the work.

Jimjoy repowered the screens.

"Ready to repressurize, Captain."

"Repressurizing, Major."

"Stand by for atmospheric tests, Berlan."

"Internal monitoring ready, Major."

Jimjoy climbed out from the lower deck hatch, leaving the iris open. Then he strapped back into the copilot's seat.

"Wonder you Special Operatives can even function, you're so paranoid," noted the Lieutenant. Her voice was dry.

"Some days we have trouble."

"Internal atmosphere tests normal, Captain. But it's still cold. Suggest you wait another five stans before you unseal."

"Thanks, Berlan."

Jimjoy studied the control board, looking for a discrepancy, any discrepancy. Surprisingly, he found none, and that bothered him.

"What next, Major?"

"We dock at New Kansaw orbit control, and you wait for Lieutenant L'tellen. I report planetside, and Berlan checks out all the hull plates and runs current tests on all the superconductor lines. You become more paranoid, and R'Naio poisons everyone with fresh food, assuming that any of those comestibles survived the instant vacuum packing they received."

"No more fresh food," muttered the other tech.

"I take it that we don't report inbound until we have to."

"Why give more notice than we have to?"

Lieutenant Ramsour shook her head. She said nothing, but readjusted the grav polarizer.

Jimjoy checked the screen indicators. All read in the green.

"If they're watching the system EDI, we should have an inquiry reaching us in about one standard hour."

"That the comm break point?"

"Roughly."

"Wonderful."

Jimjoy shrugged and leaned back in the shell. He eased open his face shield, closed his eyes, and let himself drift into sleep.

The comm inquiry woke him.

". . . Interrogative inbound. Interrogative inbound. This is New Kansaw control. Please be advised that this is a quarantined system. This is a quarantined system . . ."

"Now they tell us."

Jimjoy struggled erect, squinted, and checked the time. He had slept for nearly one and a half hours. More tired than he had realized.

"You awake, Major?"

"Mostly."

"You heard the message?"

"The part about the quarantine? Yes. Was there more?"

"Asked for I.D. on pain of death, destruction, and dismemberment, or the equivalent."

"Mind if I reply?"

"Not at all. You have a certain way with words."

Jimjoy coughed, tried to clear his throat.

"New Kansaw control. New Kansaw control. This is Desperado one. Desperado one, clearance delta. Departed Alphane for crew change New Kansaw. Authorization follows. Authorization follows."

Jimjoy called up the authorization codes from the navbank, then continued.

"New Kansaw control, Desperado one, authorization follows. Delta slash one five omega slash six three delta. I say again. Delta five omega slash six three delta."

He touched the screen controls, toggled the Imperial I.D flash. While such flashes could be duplicated, any sector Commander who fired on a ship that had flashed such an I.D. would have a hard time explaining it away. Still . . .

"You have a torp on board?"

"Two, Major," answered Berlan.

"Program it with the information that New Kansaw control has declared a system quarantine, and that we have informed New Kansaw control of our mission and are proceeding in-system."

"What good will that do?" asked the *Carpenter's* Captain.

"By itself, not a great deal. But after we've informed New Kansaw of our helpfulness in spreading the word . . ."

"Devious . . ." muttered Berlan.

"Why are you so determined to get to New Kansaw?" asked the Lieutenant.

"That's where I'm ordered, Captain. Failure to obey orders is a cardinal failure for a Special Operative."

Jimjoy cleared his throat again, then triggered the comm system.

"New Kansaw control, this is Desperado one. We are relaying your quarantine message to Alphane control via torp. Relaying your quarantine via torp. Proceeding inbound to assist in quarantine. Proceeding inbound to assist in quarantine."

He paused, then asked, "That torp about ready?"

"Input complete, Major. Permission to launch, Captain?"

"Launch when ready," replied the Lieutenant.

"Launching torp for Alphane."

Jimjoy tracked the thin trace of the small high-speed torp until it jumped from EDI display. He suspected that New Kansaw control also tracked the torp.

Then he forced himself to lean back in the shell, and wait. And wait.

The hiss of the old air circulation system and a faint whine from the open comm net were the loudest sounds in the courier.

"Desperado one, this is New Kansaw control. Desperado one, this is New Kansaw control. You are cleared inbound to alpha control. Cleared inbound to alpha control. Do not deviate from course line. Do not deviate from course line. We estimate your arrival in point seven five standard hours. Please confirm."

"Slight improvement, Major."

"New Kansaw control," answered the Special Operative, "this is Desperado one. Will maintain direct course line to alpha control. Will maintain direct course line to alpha control. Estimate arrival in approximately point nine standard hours. Point nine standard hours."

"Still trying to give yourself a margin, Major?"

"Not much. They never consider standoff time, and I really don't want to give anyone an excuse. For either one of us, Lieutenant Ramsour."

"Thank you for reminding me, Major Wright." The woman's tone was cooler than frozen ice.

Jimjoy suppressed a frown. He obviously hadn't thought that one through, but what could he say now?

"Sorry," he whispered, hoping the techs would not pick up on the apology.

"Quite all right, Major. Quite within the rights of a Special Operative."

He did not shrug, but felt like it. Some days, even when he won, it felt like losing.

XXXIX

JIMJOY HEFTED THE two ship bags and slipped the dispatch case under his arm. Once again he felt awkward with the amount of equipment he was carrying, but after the trip on the *Carpenter*, he couldn't exactly say he regretted it.

He looked up.

Berlan was standing by the cabin archway. The *Carpenter* only had curtains, not doors or portals as on larger ships.

"Major . . . ?"

"Yes, Berlan?"

"We appreciate it." The tech's voice was pitched uncharacteristically low. "You have to understand . . ."

"Think I do, Berlan. Think I do."

He understood, all right, but wasn't sure what to do. Rae Ramsour was a person, not a mission.

"She'll understand in time."

Jimjoy nodded, took a deep breath, and made his way forward.

Lieutenant Ramsour was perched sideways on the edge of the control couch, looking neither at the controls nor at the Major, who stood there.

"Leaving, Major?" She did not look up.

"Not quite yet."

"Thought you'd burn your way through Hades to get to your mission."

"Only because I don't have the choices you do, Lieutenant."

She finally looked up. "What choices?"

He set down the bags and eased himself onto the edge of the copilot's shell.

"Running out of time, Lieutenant. Learned a lot as a Special Op.

Learned enough to know that, one way or another, this is probably my last mission. If I can pull it off," he lied, "it's off to a desk. If I don't," he continued truthfully, "don't have to worry about desks, or choices.

"I know a lot about destruction and how to avoid it. But I made a lot of mistakes about people. Fact is . . . still making them. People matter." He laughed harshly. "Right? Special Op killer telling you that people matter? Sentimental killer and all that flame?" He shrugged. "Not much else to say. Sorry I was hard on you. Hope I helped."

Slowly, he stood, picking up the bags.

"Anyway . . . good luck to you, Captain. And to your crew." He straightened. "Permission to leave the ship, Captain?"

"Permission granted, Major." There were dark circles under her eyes. "And thank you . . . I think."

Though she did not smile, there was no bitterness in her tone, Jimjoy reflected, and that would have to be enough.

For some reason, he wondered, as he turned to activate the lock, if Thelina would have approved of his attempt to clear the air.

"Good luck, Major." Berlan, the first on the *Carpenter* to see him aboard, was also the last to see him off.

"Same to you, Berlan. You've got a good Captain."

He did not listen for any response, but stepped through the lock to New Kansaw orbit control and the pair of armed technicians who waited to escort him planetside.

XL

"THE MAIN RESISTANCE headquarters has to lie in the Missou. Hills." The Commander jabbed a pointer, awkwardly, at the wall projection. "We've cleared out all the other possibilities here on the central plains. The reeducation teams are having some success, and they would certainly have more . . ."

"If the rebels weren't so successful?" Jimjoy stood at attention, a rather relaxed attention that verged on insolence as the Operations officer summarized what he knew about the rebel positions. "How much does their success depend on your inability to find their base of operations? Do we even know if they require a fixed base?"

"Look, Major, this isn't a typical guerrilla action. We aren't talking small farmers up in arms about the Imperial onslaught. Most of the planet was held by large landowners. What we have here is a bunch of professional rebels, the same group the landowners were fighting to begin with."

Jimjoy tried not to betray the sinking feeling in his guts. "They didn't like the ecological transformations, I take it."

"Obviously. Why else would they sabotage the landowners? Remember, the Council asked for Imperial assistance when they failed to meet their repayment schedule for the planetary engineering. We didn't get called in until the minority landholders withheld their taxes and declared the High Plains independent."

Jimjoy wanted to shake his head, but did not. Instead he asked another question. "So the majority landholders claimed that the rebels and the minority landholders were somehow destroying the crops?"

"Worse than that. They were targeting the planetary diversion projects and the holdings of the landholders who supported them . . . anyone who supported the Empire."

"I see."

"That's why they have to have a fixed base. Because their operations aren't antipersonnel."

Jimjoy knew better than to dispute the Commander's facts or logic, neither of which was totally accurate. "What about a quarantine?"

"That's what we've been trying for the last three standard months," said the officer in crimson and red, "but they don't have any conventional ties or transportation, at least nothing that we can track, even by satellite sensors. They aren't a large group, never mount more than a limited number of operations, but they have cost us more than fifty million creds' worth of equipment and three squads. We've lost one Commando team and one Special Operative. They were the only ones who inflicted more damage than they received."

"Terrain too rough for conventional support?"

" 'Rough' isn't the word for it. All you can do is land on the objective and hope the ground doesn't collapse under you. Take the badlands of Noram, add the winds of Coltara, the aridity of Sahara, and the ashes of Persephone, and you have some idea of the terrain."

"Why so much difference between the hills and the High Plains?"

"The Plains sit practically on the bedrock. The hills were upthrusts where the aquifers broke out. Mess of fractured rock, silt. That's why they're collapsing now. No water supporting them."

Jimjoy again refrained from comment on the Commander's inadequate grasp of geology. "That why the area was never terraformed?"

"That and the fact that the alkalinity was phenomenal. It was too high to bother with, and too unstable. The Engineers just diverted the subsurface water tables and let it go."

"So there was a lot of vegetation there?"

"That's what they say. Supposedly, it climbed all over the cliffs, even down into the ravines. It's almost all dust and ashes now." The Commander cleared his throat and set the pointer down on the dull gray finish of the projector's console. He glanced over Jimjoy's shoulder toward the portal.

Since Jimjoy had not heard the telltale whisper of a portal opening, he knew that the other officer was hoping someone else would come in. He repressed a grin. The Operations theorists were never happy when they had to brief a Special Operative directly. It put them too close to the cold-blooded side of the mayhem. They all preferred to think of combat as either an art or unavoidable.

"I take it you want them neutralized?"

"Ummm . . . of course. Wasn't that why you were sent?"

"Yes. I was dispatched to find the quickest and most effective solution to your problem—regardless of the cost to the rebels or to the ego of Imperial forces. But no one would have dared to state that openly." Jimjoy paused before twisting the knife further. "They prefer not to ask too many questions about my solutions."

The Commander looked down at the drab and gray plastone floor, then back over Jimjoy's shoulder at the portal, and finally at the Major in his tan singlesuit without emblems or trappings—only the crossed bars of his rank on his collars.

The singlesuit was immaculate, as was Jimjoy. But neither looked traditionally military, since Jimjoy did not affect instantaneous obedience, and the singlesuit possessed no knife-sharp creases, braid, or rows of decorations.

Jimjoy knew the only military aspects of his person were his eyes. Even Admirals had wavered before them. Not that he was anything other than superbly conditioned and trained. He just wasn't military at heart, and probably shouldn't have been in the Service at all.

But he had survived for more than a decade in a field where the casualties ran eighty percent in every four-year tour.

He waited, his silence exerting a pressure on the Commander to speak.

"How long will it take?"

"Depends on what I have to do. One way or another, be finished in three months. Might be three weeks."

"Three months?"

The Major sighed. "You want a miracle. I'm here to do it. The difficult we do on schedule. The impossible takes longer. This is impossible. You can't take anything mechanized into the terrain except flitters. You don't know who the enemy is or where they are. You haven't been able to solve the problem in six months with five thousand Imperial Marines. You've lost Commandos and Special Operatives, and you want me to fix it overnight?"

He threw a skeptical glance at the Commander, who responded by stiffening and squaring his shoulders.

"Spare me a lecture about how each day costs money and troops," the Special Operative continued, his words stopping the protest from the senior officer. "Understand that. But you'll have even more delays and costs if I go off half blasted and get zapped. Now, if you'll excuse me . . . Is the rest of the material in the console?"

The Commander nodded, his face tight.

"Fine. After that I'll probably be wandering around to get a feel for the situation. Then I'll let you know what I'll need."

"What you will need?"

"Don't carry supplies with me, Commander," commented the operative as he drew the stool up to the console.

The Commander stood there, staring blankly at the Major's back, until he realized that he had effectively been dismissed by a junior officer. Finally, he turned and walked woodenly from the room.

As the portal whispered shut, Jimjoy glanced backward. "All alike. If it's not laid out in their order files, it doesn't exist. If it wasn't taught at the Academy or spelled out in Service policy, it's not possible."

He continued his scan of the background material, strictly a factual description of New Kansaw and the grain belt plains.

New Kansaw—T-type planet, variation less than point zero five from norm. Atmospheric oxygen content sixteen point five percent, and gravity point nine three of T-norm. Mean surface temperature within acceptable parameters . . . He skimmed through the facts.

The odds were that the statistics would tell him less than nothing, another fact that the Operations types never quite understood. He shook his head as he concentrated on the more detailed information about the higher plains where the Empire had expected the colonists to concentrate on grains and synde bean production.

The one number that might have some significance, he reflected, was the number of cloudy summer days. Why he could not recall, but somewhere, sometime, he had read about the need for an inordinate amount of unobstructed sunlight for successful synde bean cultivation.

Clouds usually meant rain, and rain meant moisture. Some grains did not do well later in their growing seasons with too much precipitation.

He keyed in the inquiry, more to see if the unit were connected to a full-research data bank.

Beep.

"Subject inquiry requires 'Red Delta Clearance.' "

The Special Operative gave the screen a wry grin and closed down the console. Stretching as he stood, he stepped away from the console and began to pace around the bare-walled conference room, his feet hitting on the gray plastone tiles with a flat sound.

He found it hard to give his full attention to New Kansaw. The Accord situation, especially the friendly detachment of the Ecolitans, still bothered him. Even Thelina had been professional. Only Temmilan had shown any interest, and that had been for the express purpose of compromising him.

He had made his report, hadn't even been asked any follow-up questions, which would not have been precluded by his hurry-up departure. Hersnik just wanted him dead, one way or another, without any blame on Hersnik or the Service itself.

On the one hand, the Service was concerned about Accord. On the other, the Admiralty really didn't want any new information or insights, just an excuse to act against the planet.

Running a stubby-fingered hand through his short black hair, Jimjoy pursed his lips. He could worry about Accord, about Thelina, *after* he had muddled through the New Kansaw mess. *If* he muddled through.

He grinned—what else could he do?—and headed for the portal.

As he stepped out into the humming of the main corridor, he could not avoid the senior technician, fully armed, who came up to him.

"Major Wright? Technical Specialist Herrol, sir. At your service, sir."

Jimjoy said nothing, let his eyes survey the lean-looking, dark-haired young man with the flat brown eyes. He did not nod, but it was obvious that Technical Specialist Herrol would be both bodyguard and expediter, if not assassin, at the appropriate time, should one Major Wright show any lack of suicidal enthusiasm in pursuing his assignment.

"You know where I'm quartered, Herrol?"

"No, sir."

"Neither do I. Let's find out. Where do I start?"

"You might try Admin, sir."

"Be happy to. Where is it?"

"Through tunnel three blue, sir."

Jimjoy gestured. "Lead the way."

Herrol's face was expressionless as he turned. "This way, sir."

Jimjoy followed. Herrol's mission was more than obvious. What was not obvious was how Herrol had been assigned that mission so quickly, and why. Herrol would be difficult to deal with, particularly if he knew nothing except his duty.

Jimjoy shook his head as he stretched his stride to keep pace with the technical specialist.

XLI

"SPECIAL OPERATIVE WRIGHT," announced the black-haired man as he leaned over the console. "You have a bird for me."

"Wright?" asked the technician.

"That's right," responded Jimjoy evenly. "For a recon run at 1400. Code delta three."

"Oh . . . Major Wright. Yes, sir. That will be Gauntlet one, on the beta line. Sign-off and tech clearance are at the line console central." The woman looked away, as if she had completed an unpleasant task.

"Beta line?" asked the Major. "Could you point the way?"

"Sir. Take the corridor outside until it branches. Take the left fork. That serves the beta flitter line. The maintenance section is the second or third portal on the right after the fork, depending on whether you count the emergency exit as a portal."

The words rattled from her mouth with the ease and lack of enthusiasm created by frequent repetition.

"Thank you, technician." He turned and headed for the portal through which he had just entered, but not without glancing back to catch the fingers flicking over the console before her, as if to send a message.

He looked back again, just before the portal closed, but the technician had not looked up from her console.

Once through the portal, he surveyed the corridor, empty except for two technicians wheeling an equipment cart toward one of the flight lines and a junior pilot who trudged unseeing toward Jimjoy, the vacant look of too many hours at the controls overshadowing any other expression on the young woman's face.

"Afternoon, Major," the Lieutenant said mechanically, as she drew abreast of him.

"Afternoon, Lieutenant," the Special Operative replied politely as he turned toward the flight lines, swinging the small pack in his left hand.

Jimjoy had no illusions about eluding the persistent Technical Specialist Herrol, who would doubtless appear within moments, if he were not already waiting at the flitter. Jimjoy had not told him about the flight, but Herrol would know, and would be waiting or on his way.

At the proper fork in the corridor the Major in the camouflage flight suit stopped, as if to ponder which direction to take. He wondered what would happen if he wandered down the alpha line side.

Nothing—except he would eventually be directed back to the specified flitter on the beta line, a flitter doubtless snooped and/or gimmicked to the hilt.

Shrugging, he resumed his progress down the three-meter-wide corridor of quickspray plastic and unshielded glow tubes. At the third portal he stopped, then stepped through the opening and into the maintenance line area.

"Major Wright," he announced. "Gauntlet one ready for me?"

The technician beside the console jumped, but the black woman at the board merely looked up slowly.

"Yes, sir," replied the seated tech. She gestured toward the empty seat in front of a second console. "Plug in your particulars, and she's yours. Second one back once you're on the line."

Jimjoy wondered about the guilty-looking jump by the thin technician, but said nothing as he studied the small squarish room. Three consoles, two vacant, filled the center of the space. The walls to his left and right were nothing more than arrayed equipment lockers, but whether there were plastform partitions behind the lockers he could not see. Directly behind the consoles was another portal, presumably leading outside to the line where the base flitters squatted between missions.

The Special Operative glanced back to the chief technician, who had leaned forward in her swivel, but otherwise made no move to stand up. The other technician, who still wore a faintly guilty look, at least to

Jimjoy's relatively experienced eye, had backed away, as if waiting for the Major to take a seat before bolting the maintenance line area.

"Appreciate your consideration, technician." He spaced the words evenly, fixing the chief technician with a steady glance that was not quite an order.

"Not at all, sir." But she stood up as he continued to study her, and her brown eyes finally flickered and dropped toward the plastone flooring.

"I do appreciate your working this flight in," he said more softly as he slid into the armless swivel in front of the console and began to enter his own identification, the mission code, the expected times of departure and return.

The screen cleared and brought up the maintenance records for his inspection. Jimjoy frowned as he studied them. Given the time since the flitter's last overhaul, there should have been more equipment failures, a longer history of technical and mechanical problems, and more comments by pilots.

The lack of documentation meant either lax maintenance, a light flying schedule, or something prearranged about the flitter.

As the thin technician finally made her hasty exit, Jimjoy caught the relieved look on her face as she edged out through the portal.

The chief technician had not reseated herself, but slowly paced around the area as Jimjoy studied the records.

Finally he stood. "Authenticated." He looked toward the remaining tech. "Second one back?" He picked up the small pack again.

"That's right, Major."

"Thank you." He nodded and stepped through the portal.

Outside, although the high clouds blocked any direct sunlight, the humid air seeped through his flight suit like heavy steam. Heat radiated upward from the plastarmac, and the olive-drab flitter squatted like an oversized insect waiting for its prey.

Jimjoy concentrated on the flitter as he approached, noting with amusement the carefully polished fuselage. The only way to conceal work on a flitter was to clean it thoroughly, which, he reflected with a twist to his lips, revealed that some work had been done.

The best way to conceal alterations would have been to assign him a bird straight out of the maintenance cycle, but that hadn't been done. No maintenance officer or senior tech would have allowed it. Which left an even more ominous implication.

He climbed up the handholds and triggered the pilot's side-door release. The puff of air that swept past him was warmer than the steamy atmosphere on the flitter line, but not much. After setting his equipment bag and all it contained on the seat, he descended to begin the preflight, wondering how long it would be before the ubiquitous Herrol arrived on the scene.

Rather than begin in the approved order, Jimjoy started by checking the turbines. Though the intakes showed signs of heavy abrasion, the turbine blades and casings were clean and spotless. Jimjoy filed the information for future reference as he continued his checks.

Nothing ostensible showed in the power system, but in several instances sections seemed far cleaner than normal or necessary. As he checked the connections on the tail thruster/stabilizer, he heard the hissing of the portal from the maintenance line. Jimjoy continued his preflight.

"Afternoon, Major," offered Herrol.

"Afternoon, Herrol. Ready for a recon run along the hills?"

"Been ready for a while, sir."

"Put your gear in the bird. Almost done with the preflight."

"Mind if I watch?"

"Suit yourself. Not very exciting."

Jimjoy continued the methodical checking, nodding occasionally as he went.

The skid linchpins were new. The cargo bay doors both worked, and showed signs of having recently been repaired.

At that, the Major did shake his head. He couldn't remember the last time he'd flown a beta-class flitter with fully operable crew doors. Most of the pilots ignored the door status, although a pilot could theoretically refuse to fly if the doors weren't fully operational. The only time anyone had bothered about that technicality was when the mission was a medevac or transporting brass or high-ranking civilian Impies.

"Everything looks good, Herrol. Let's strap in."

"You're done?"

"Finished a lot before you got here."

"Yes, sir." Herrol's flat voice was the single indication of possible displeasure with Jimjoy's failure to inform him about the flight.

Jimjoy ignored the tone. He had deliberately provided Herrol with no notice. The lack of advance information had slowed his assigned shadow only briefly, as had been the case all along. Jimjoy had ignored the "technical specialist" as much as possible, but invariably Herrol popped up, always unfailingly polite, usually apologizing for his tardiness, but never overtly alluding to Jimjoy's attempts to keep him scrambling.

Before Jimjoy slid into the pilot's seat and snapped the safety harness in place, he tucked the equipment bag and its contents into the minilocker under his seat.

Herrol's eyes darted to the bag quizzically, but he said nothing, and Jimjoy volunteered no explanation. The Major hoped he would not need the contents, but suspected that he would later, if not immediately.

The Special Operative began running through the checklist, answering himself as he did.

"Harnesses . . . cinched . . .

"Aux power . . . connected . . .

"Generator shunts . . . in place . . ."

Herrol watched intently but continued to maintain his silence as Jimjoy readied the flitter for light-off and flight.

"Starboard turbine . . . ignition . . .

"Port turbine . . . ignition . . .

"EGTs . . . in the green and steady . . ."

His fingers flicked across the board with the precision that had come from long practice. After clearing his throat, he keyed the transmitter.

"PriOps, this is Gauntlet one. Ready for lift and departure."

"Gauntlet one. Understand ready for lift-off."

"Affirmative. Recon plan filed. Estimate duration one plus five."

"Stet, one. Cleared to strip yellow. Cleared to strip yellow."

"Gauntlet one lifting for strip yellow."

Thwop . . . thwop, thwop, thwop . . .

The regular beat of the rotors increased as Jimjoy added power, and the flitter lifted from the plastarmac and began to air-taxi westward toward the designated takeoff strip. The one farthest from the main flight-line structures, Jimjoy noted humorlessly.

"PriOps, Gauntlet one. On station, strip yellow. Ready for lift-off and departure."

"Gauntlet one, cleared for lift-off. Interrogative status."

"PriOps, this is Gauntlet one. Lifting this time. Status is green. Fuel five plus. Departing red west."

"Cleared for departure red west."

Thwop, thwop, thwop . . . thwop, thwop, thwop . . .

The flitter shivered as the beat of the rotors stepped up, and as Jimjoy lowered the nose fractionally. As the aircraft gained speed, he eased the nose back and established a steady rate of climb.

From the corner of his eye, Jimjoy noted how Herrol's right hand stayed close to the emergency capsule ejection lever.

All the power indicators and engine readouts remained in the green.

"PriOps, this is Gauntlet one. Level at five hundred, course two nine zero."

"Stet, one. Understand level at five hundred, course two nine zero."

"That's affirmative. Out."

Beneath, the even green of the synde bean fields stretched for kays in every direction visible for the canopy. Had he looked back, Jimjoy would have seen the Impie base as an island of grayed plastic amid the seemingly endless fields.

New Missou itself was a good hundred kays south of the base, and its low structures were invisible at an altitude of less than around three thousand meters.

What else besides agricultural vistas could you expect on an agricultural planet modified to supply the Imperial fleet?

Scarcely the place for a Special Operative, but here he was, with his deadly shadow seated beside him.

The EGT flickered as Jimjoy eased the nose back momentarily to begin the rotor retraction sequence. As soon as the blades were folded back, he dropped the nose again and began to twist on additional power with both port and starboard thrusters, letting the airspeed build, rather than stopping at a normal cruise.

He was gambling that whatever surprises had been planned for him were based on timing, not on fuel consumption or speed, and he needed to be as close to the badlands as possible as soon as possible.

"Really burning up to get there, aren't you, Major?"

"The sooner the better," replied Jimjoy, half surprised at Herrol's observation. "Plenty of fuel. No reason not to use it."

"You're the pilot. Let me know if you want me to point out any of the key landmarks."

"Stet," replied Jimjoy evenly.

The EGTs remained steady, as did the fuel flows and the airspeed.

"Gauntlet one, this is PriOps. Plot indicates position ahead of flight plan. Interrogative position. Interrogative position."

The pilot smiled tightly. Didn't anyone realize they were tipping their hand? Or did it mean they didn't care?

He scanned the navigation readouts, compared them with the visual representation screen and the view outside.

"PriOps, this is Gauntlet one. Position is delta one five at omega three. Delta one five at omega three."

"One, PriOps. Understand position is delta one five at omega three."

"That is affirmative."

Not exactly, thought Jimjoy to himself. He had reported a position slightly behind the flitter's current position. He would have liked to fudge more, but Herrol's presence in the cockpit made any wild mis-statement of location out of the question, at least until Herrol's position became clearer.

"Gauntlet one, say again position. Say again position."

"Stet, PriOps. Current position is delta one seven at omega four. Delta one seven at omega four."

Herrol was leaning forward, as if to take a greater interest in the series of transmissions. The technical specialist's eyes ranged over the position plots, as if to compare what he had heard with the flitter's position on the small screen.

"PriOps, this is Gauntlet one. Interrogative difficulty with base track?"

"One, that's negative. Negative this time."

The pilot refrained from smiling. One small momentary victory for the underdog, and one which might give him a little edge.

He inched up the power again, easing the nose down a shade. Ahead, he could see the hazy lines that marked the edge of the badlands area, assuming the charts were correct. He edged the flitter more toward the starboard, estimating the most nearly direct course toward the ruined lands.

Herrol did not seem to notice the marginal change, but his apparent lack of understanding meant nothing. In Herrol's position, Jimjoy would have betrayed nothing.

The EGTs flickered, and Jimjoy held himself from reacting, mentally calculating the distance remaining between the flitter and the badlands. If he could maintain speed and altitude just a bit longer . . .

He could feel the sweat beading up under his helmet, the dampness oozing out of his pores. Always, for him, the waiting was the most difficult.

His eyes flicked across the board, across the range of readouts, but the EGTs were steady, as were the fuel flows. He tightened his lips as he saw the fuel flow needles flicker in turn.

"Gauntlet one, this is PriOps. Interrogative status."

"PriOps, one here. Status green."

"Understand green. Interrogative position."

"That is affirmative," answered Jimjoy, ignoring the second question. From the left-hand seat of the flitter, Jimjoy frowned as his eyes shifted sideways for a quick glimpse at Technical Specialist Herrol's profile.

Herrol looked tense behind the casual pose.

Jimjoy kept himself from nodding. Before long, he would have to act.

"That the badlands perimeter up there?"

"That's it, all right," answered the man in the copilot's seat. "Have anything in mind?"

"Nothing special. Not yet. Wanted to get a good picture before I make a final decision." The pilot studied the board. All indicators were normal, even the EGTs and the thruster power levels.

Herrol fidgeted in the copilot's seat, shifting his weight, his left hand straying toward the capsule ejection handle.

"Gauntlet one, PriOps. Interrogative present course. Interrogative position."

"PriOps, present course three four eight. Three four eight. Status is green. Status is green."

"One, understand course is three four eight, status green. Interrogative position."

"That is affirmative. Affirmative."

Herrol's right hand hovered near the now unsealed thigh pocket of his flight suit.

Jimjoy took a deep and slow breath before snapping full power off both the port and the starboard thrusters and pitching the flitter's nose forward.

As Herrol's right hand lurched from his thigh pocket, the edge of Jimjoy's right hand snapped across Herrol's wrist.

Crack!

The small stunner struck the canopy.

Crunnnch.

The second backhand blow crushed the specialist's throat.

Wheeeeeeeeeee . . .

"Emergency! Emergency! Ground impact in thirty seconds! Ground impact in thirty seconds!" blared out the flitter's emergency warning system.

Methodically continuing the emergency deployment of the flitter's rotor system, Jimjoy brought the nose back up to bleed off airspeed and reduce the rate of descent.

"Mayday! Mayday! This is Gauntlet one. Position is—" The pilot deliberately cut off his transmitter. He did not look at the dead man held in the copilot's seat by the emergency harness as he concentrated on his emergency descent.

The flitter was nearly over the transition area between the badlands and the cultivated High Plains as Jimjoy completed the turn to bring the flitter's nose into the wind. To his right he caught a glimpse of gray dust and cratered hills, a few marked with sticklike silver trunks of trees seasons, if not decades, dead.

He let the nose rise into a flare, then brought in full pitch on the blades as the flitter mushed into the golden and waist-high grasses that bordered the synde bean fields.

Shuddering as the blades slowed, the flitter sank into the soft ground. *Uuunnnnnnnnnn . . .*

The blades ground nearly to a stop as Jimjoy applied the rotor brake. *Thunk.*

The final stop was more abrupt than any flight instructor would have approved, and the flitter shivered one last time.

As he unstrapped, his eyes scanned the control indicators a final time, checking the EGT and thruster temperatures, both of which were still well into the red. His fingers flicked across three switches in rapid succession, ensuring that the fuel transfer to the stub tanks would continue so long as there were power reserves remaining.

Flinging the harness from him and wriggling out of his seat, he unfastened the harness that held Herrol's body in place. Then he wrenched the dead technical specialist from the copilot's seat and levered him into the pilot's seat, strapping the body into place.

That misdirection completed, he manually opened the copilot's door and scrambled out, carrying his equipment bag with him.

He half tumbled, half jumped into the grass below. *Squishh.*

His boots sank nearly ankle-deep into the damp mud from which the grass grew. He shook his head as he pulled his feet from the mud. Swamp grass between the cultivated fields and the badlands—that he had not exactly expected.

He flipped the pack into place as he moved toward the starboard stub fuel tank and began to loosen the filler neck.

Whheeeeee . . .

The sound was faint, distant, but increasing. Another flitter was heading toward the one Jimjoy had grounded.

"Don't leave much to chance, do they?" muttered the Special Operative as he wrenched off the tank's filler neck cap. Next he molded the adhesive around the small flare, and wedged both into the neck, giving the dial a twitch counter-clockwise.

Without looking backward, he began to lope northward through the grass, ignoring the squelching sounds and the tugging of the mud at his boots.

Whhheeeeeeee!

After covering the first fifty meters, he glanced back over his shoulder at the downed flitter, and beyond it at the black dot in the southern sky. He had another two or three minutes before the flare went, and perhaps five minutes before the pursuing flitter came close enough to see him.

By now he was within ten meters of the sterile ground that marked the edge of the rising and desolate slopes that lifted into the badlands. Changing his course to parallel the boundary, he kept up the long and even strides now more northwest and north.

Crummmp!

He dove headfirst into the still-damp ground. The grass, thigh-high, was deep enough to cover him, especially since he was more than half a kay from the fiercely burning wreck that had been a combat flitter.

WWHHHEEEeeeeeee . . . whup . . . whup . . . whup, whup, whup . . .

From the sound alone he could tell that the pursuing Service flitter had deployed rotors and was hovering near the burning wreck.

Scuttling along with his back below the tops of the grasses, he continued his progress away from the wreck and the hovering flitter.

WHHUMMPP!

The shock wave drove him to his hands and knees, and he lowered himself all the way to the ground.

Whheeeeee . . . whup, whup . . . eeeeee . . . WHHHUMMP!

Jimjoy eased himself around and darted another look backward.

In a perverse sense, he was gratified to have his suspicions confirmed. The first explosion had been the metallic explosives he felt someone had planted on the flitter, although he had not been able to confirm that during his preflight.

He brushed the mud and grass off his uniform as well as he could and took a moment longer to study the devastation behind him. Where his flitter had been was nothing but dispersing smoke and a flattened expanse of grass and shredded synde bean plants. What remained of the chase flitter was a burning pyre, surrounded by smoldering plant life.

Someone hadn't known much about metallic explosives. Either that or they hadn't wanted to take any chances. A good fifty kilos of metalex had blown when the heat from the fire had reached the critical point.

The ensuing explosion had turned his flitter into a mass of shrapnel, which, in turn, had claimed the pursuing bird.

Jimjoy surveyed the scene, and seeing no immediate signs of life, reshouldered the small pack and began trudging along the edge of the field, ready to turn toward the highlands when the terrain offered some cover. He tried not to shiver as he stepped up his pace almost into a trot. No surprise that someone had wanted him dead. The surprise was how many. Herrol, with his background, had to have known the uses of metalex and would never have climbed into a flitter sabotaged with fifty kilos of it. Herrol had been watching the engine instruments.

So Herrol had either gimmicked the thrusters or had been told they were faulty. The technician had been duped as well. Which meant he would have died in any case.

But Jimjoy had killed a man who essentially had done nothing except make him nervous—that and pull a stunner in the cockpit.

The Imperial Operative kept walking, listening for the sound of another flitter, keeping close to the grass and hoping that he didn't have to worry about a satellite track. He felt cold, despite the heat and humidity.

More than one person had orders to eliminate him, that was certain. And without much regard for bystanders, innocent or otherwise.

As he reached the top of a low rise, he glanced back again. More than two kays separated him from the destruction he had left behind.

He started down the other side, studying the terrain ahead. From his earlier analysis, he estimated his jumping-off point was still another three kays ahead. He lengthened his stride, trying to ignore the tightness in his gut, his ears alert for the sound of the next wave of flitters that would be coming.

XLII

As Jimjoy studied the rugged and chopped hills from his hiding place near the ridge line, he thought.

Had his analyses been correct?

He shrugged.

The rebellion on New Kansaw had been in the making for years, mainly the work of a small group of idealists—zealots, most probably. The scattered nature of the resistance, despite the overall population's sullenness, clearly pointed toward a single small group with well-prepared and preplanned bases.

His eyes drifted over the empty riverbed at the bottom of the rock-jumbled valley. Roughly one hundred kays to the east was the diversion dam which had siphoned all the water from the Republic River into the eastern side of the Missou Plains, turning what had been arid steppes into irrigated synde bean fields.

The western half of the Plains, beyond the point where he had crashed the flitter, was served by a similar dam across the old watercourse of the Democrat River. Like a wedge, the badlands separated the northern parts of the Plains.

While the diversions had changed the dry but fertile soils of the steppes into lush fields, the mere surface water rearrangements had not caused the powder-dry dust and spiked silver tree stumps of the badlands—all that remained of the junglelike growth shown on the early holos.

The Imperial Engineers had gone beyond mere dams. After charting the flows of the major aquifers, they had used their lasers and impermeable plastics to build underground dams far more extensive and critical than the two massive surface diversion projects.

The former highland jungle, according to background reports, had consumed nearly fifty percent of the area's available water. Since the steppe soils would not sustain the silverthorns and the rampart bushes, the jungle mainstays, once the surface and subsurface waters had been diverted, the silverthorns began to die out immediately.

The highlands had been the remnant of a more extensive upland forest network which had already been drying out as New Kansaw's climate edged toward another ice age.

The Imperial Engineers had not waited for the ice age. Defoliants and laser-induced fires had followed the diversion projects. Now all that remained were thorn thickets, spiked silver trunks, and hectare after hectare of drifting silver ash and dust.

In a few spots, the original dark blue dust thorns of the steppes were sprouting from beneath the silver devastation, seeking a new home away from the too damp synde bean fields.

Jimjoy shook his head again.

He couldn't say he disputed the rebels, but the whole situation was bizarre. The original colonists had opposed the water reengineering, but only because they had claimed it would not work. The Engineers had obviously made it work, and the synde bean plantations were producing protein and oil for the Imperial fleets—though certainly not in the quantities once projected by the Imperial Engineers.

The violence of the rebellion had caught New Augusta totally off guard, although the few captured rebels had claimed that the increase in the Imperial production tax from forty percent to sixty percent had ignited the unrest.

A puff of dust caught the Special Operative's eye as he continued to scan the dry riverbed and the overlooking ledges. He relaxed as he watched the small four-legged creature scuttle from dry rock to dry rock.

While he did not expect anyone or anything to appear in the open, for him to move until nightfall would be dangerous. Evening would be best. Later at night was almost as dangerous as full daylight, but not quite, since positive identification would be difficult for a satellite sensor.

His strategy had been based on two simple assumptions—water and location. He could only hope he had been right. In the meantime, he retreated back into the sheltered and overhung semi-cave and curled into a less dusty corner, stifling a sneeze.

A short nap would help, if he could sleep.

Either the heat or the silence woke him, and he rolled into a ready position, the stunner appearing in his hand even before he was fully aware he was reacting.

Both the heat, rolling in shimmering waves down the valley, and the silence were oppressive. He tried to swallow, but it took several attempts before his parched throat worked properly. He edged forward into the observation position, watching, listening. The silence was near absolute, with only the barest hint of a rustle of ashes.

Finally convinced that no one was nearby, he slipped back under the overhanging rock and retrieved his water bottle, taking a healthy but not excessive swallow. Capping it carefully, he replaced it on his equipment belt.

Then he pulled out the old-fashioned magnetic compass, useless for directions now but sufficient for his purposes, and studied the needle. Though the thin sliver of metal fluctuated, the range remained within the same bounds, reflecting the underlying low-grade iron ore. The heat buildups and the iron concentrations would provide the rebels with a near ideal barrier to any deep satellite scans. In that respect, Jimjoy wondered why no one in the Imperial services had not reached the same conclusion.

Or had they?

He listened for the distant whine of turbines, but all he could hear in the heat of the late afternoon was the soft sound of the wind beginning to sift silver-and-gray ashes from one pile to another, breaking the oppressive silence ever so slightly.

He surveyed the dry riverbed, particularly to his left, where it wound in a northwesterly fashion back toward the Imperial-controlled synde bean fields.

He shrugged and shouldered the small pack.

Not much sense in waiting, not when there was nothing he could do where he was except lead the Impies to the rebels, and that would be deadly for everyone, mostly for one Jimjoy Wright.

He did not sigh, but took a deep breath and began to move eastward toward the presumed rebel base, trying to parallel the now empty underground aqueduct that had predated the last massive restructurings of the Imperial Engineers.

With each step, the feathery cinders and dust rose around his boots. Some fragments flew higher, worming their way into every opening in his flight suit and boots. Ahead lay more ashes and cinders, more dead silverthorns jutting out like sticks—just like the ashes and desolation behind. The sunlight itself seemed weighted with ashes and death.

In the dryness, the ashes rose and fell, rose and fell, as if searching for moisture. Jimjoy's neck itched, as did his forehead, his back, and everywhere there was the slightest bit of perspiration. Ignoring all but the worst of the itches, he forced one foot in front of the other.

After a time, he stopped, easing himself down under another dust-covered rock outcropping in an attempt to reduce the chances of any satellite detection that might reach through the overhead clouds, the clouds from which no rain ever fell on the badlands.

Jimjoy shook his head, wondering if he would ever understand the intricacies of ecology, if Ecolitan Andruz would have been able to explain why it was so dead and dry where he sat and so wet it was nearly swamp ten kays westward—when the opposite had been true just a few years earlier.

With a half groan, he pulled the pack into place and resumed his hike through the ashes. Common sense indicated he should hike at night when it was cooler. Common sense was partly wrong.

Hiking late at night would have been a dead giveaway to a satellite infraheat scan, even through the clouds. Jimjoy needed to be undercover before the temperature dropped too much. At the same time, he needed to get into the rebel base, assuming it did exist where he thought it might, before the Impies were convinced he was still alive.

He put one foot back in front of the other, letting the ashes rise and fall, rise and fall.

When he stopped again, the light was dim, a dusk that was not quite true twilight. He itched all over, and the contents of his canteen were limited.

Keeping behind a still-hot boulder, he pulled out the combination nightscope and binoculars, carefully unfolding the gossamer plastic to check what appeared to be an unnatural rock overhang across the dry riverbed.

One look was enough, and he slid further behind the boulder and began to study the area section by section. The geology was less than natural, although from overhead, or from any distance, nothing would have shown, not even the concealed portal big enough to accommodate a small ACV. The lines of the portal showed that it was built for casehardened endurasteel, nothing that a full battle laser or a set of metalex charges couldn't have sliced through in a matter of minutes.

While Jimjoy had the minutes, he lacked the charges or the laser.

The rebels could only be using passive snoops to monitor the area outside the entrance, since their base had not been discovered, and since Imperial technology would have tracked down any stray radiation. Especially in such an isolated and theoretically unpopulated area.

He eased the scope back into its small case, carefully folding the light plastic. Then he sat down behind the boulder out of sight of either a satellite heat trace or a direct optical scan from the rebel base, and opened a sustain ration.

The ration tasted like rust. Although Imperial technology had the ability to produce tasty field rations, the Service did not supply them. Not since a long-dead Inspector General had noted that the good-tasting rations were subject to a nearly eighty percent pilferage rate.

Jimjoy did not bother cursing the long-dead Inspector General, but choked down the rest of the sustain, forcing himself to chew in turn the even less tasteful but still nutritious outer wrapper as a last measure. A slow series of sips from the canteen completed his repast.

After checking his pack and the small stock of supplies and equipment, he stood and began to move eastward again. He was not looking forward to the next phase of the mission. But he needed to go underground, literally, before his former compatriots arrived in force, which they would.

The Special Operative sighed silently and continued his progress along the edge of the dust-and-ash-filled watercourse. The gloom deepened into dark, and the heat began to die as a breeze picked up. The silence remained near absolute, still enough for Jimjoy to hear his own breath rasping in the evening air. Overhead clouds blocked the light from either the nebula or Pecos, the single small moon.

He had covered almost a full kay before he reached what he was seeking. What had been an access tunnel for the early settlers had been reduced to a roofless ruin partly filled with a pile of rough-cut blocks.

Still cautious, Jimjoy approached the hillside ruin slowly, staying as far from the open dust and ashes as he dared, keeping on harder rock where possible and using the available boulders and dead thickets as cover. The loose ashes inside his camouflage suit seemed to be everywhere, and he itched continually.

Less than ten meters from the ruin, he halted behind the last small heap of rock and slowly retrieved the starscope from his pack.

He studied the old maintenance building, originally ten meters square, but could see no sign of the onetime trail that must have wound through the jungle growth that had preceded the ubiquitous ashes.

He swallowed, trying to moisten his throat, and to ignore the bitter taste of ashes.

The warm night air, the taste of ash and dust, the lack of any living scents, the drifting heaps of ashes, and the gray light, gray stone, and sticklike trunks of the silverthorns all resembled a vision of Hades.

Jimjoy returned the refolded starscope to his pack, then took another sip from his nearly empty water bottle, still listening for either rebels or Imperial pursuit. Hearing neither, he shouldered his pack and stepped toward the maintenance ruin.

The doorway was vacant, without even a trace of the original door. The roofing material had been consumed by the old firestorm or removed at some earlier point. The back wall, where a large pile of stones had apparently fallen down, showed the greatest destruction.

The Special Operative glanced from one wall to the next. Only the stones from the back wall, the wall on the side of the building partly sunk into the hillside, had fallen. The other walls, except near the roofline, were intact.

Fallen stones? He grinned.

Next he studied the jumbled stones, looking for the telltale signs of traps, but could detect nothing. He sighed, and began the tedious job of removing the pile, stone by stone.

Although it had been a long day, he forced himself not to hurry, to move each stone, each bit of rubble, carefully, and to study the remaining pile before proceeding.

After he had removed the top layer, he could see the frame around the access hatch. Jimjoy nodded as he continued the methodical removal of stones blocking the hatchway.

As he stripped away the last of the old building stones, he wiped his forehead. Despite the drier evening air, he was sweating from the effort, breathing more heavily than he would have liked, and plastered with fine ashes around his neck and forehead.

The hatch cover, or doorway, was of a dark and heavy wood that, despite its plastic covering, had turned black from the heat of the jungle fires. The plastic had run and bubbled in places. Jimjoy first tapped the wood, then pushed against the blackest section. The hatchway held firm.

He ignored the nagging thought that he was not as young or as well conditioned as he once had been, and turned to the small tool kit in his pack.

Taking one deep breath, then another, he sat down and tried to relax. A few minutes more now wouldn't matter, and once he had opened the hatchway, he well might need every bit of energy.

The hatch itself was held by a simple lock and two heavy industrial hinges. With a deep breath, Jimjoy stood up and removed the short pointed rod with the shining tip from the tool kit. He began to look for a rock of appropriate size.

Thud. Thud . . . thud . . .
Clunk. Clunk.
Whhssttt!

After removing the shattered lock, he sprayed the hinges and waited. While thumps and scattered impact noises always occurred in underground retreats, squeaking hinges meant something else entirely to anyone who might be listening.

He forced himself to wait longer than he wanted, though he worried about the growing possibility of satellite detection. In the meantime, he replaced all the tools in his pack, except the stunner, which he slipped into the left thigh pocket of his flight suit, the flash, which he held, and a small coil of cord, stronger than most ropes, which he put in his right thigh pocket. Then he reshouldered the pack.

At last he eased open the hatchway, looking to see whether there were pickups attached to the hinges or the doorframe. There were none, only a rough circular tunnel which ended in less than two meters. At the end of the tunnel was a shaft. Both tunnel and shaft were unlighted.

Stepping inside, Jimjoy eased the heavy wooden hatch door shut behind him but did not switch on the flash, instead listening for the sound of steps, breathing, reactions, or anything that might indicate his presence had been noted.

Nothing.

After a time that seemed much longer than it could have been, he flicked on the light and edged forward to the rim of the shaft. The light caught a shimmer of metal and glass as he studied the shaft area. He turned the beam on it. A lamp, bulb still intact, rested in a simple bracket, with a thin cable leading from it downward into the darkness.

A series of looped metal ladder rungs, each step set directly in the laser-melted shaft wall, led downward into the blackness beyond the reach of the flash.

Jimjoy studied the rungs, putting weight on the topmost with his boots. There was no give at all. He tried the set beneath. Also no give.

Clipping the flash to his belt, he switched it off and began the descent, testing each rung.

A dozen steps down, after anchoring himself with boots and one arm, he switched on the flash and studied the rungs beneath him. No break in the ladder and no sign of the bottom.

He continued his careful and nearly silent descent, testing each rung and periodically using the flash. After half a dozen uses of the light, his arms were stiffening.

Masking a sigh, he used the belt clip to anchor himself to a rung and let his arms dangle, shrugging his shoulders and trying to relax tired and tight muscles. By all rights, he should have been sleeping.

Each movement echoed slightly, but the sound died quickly. Again he resumed the downward progress.

Later, after another half-dozen more checks with the flash, his probing leg found nothing.

Another check with the light, and he discovered a near circular opening in the shaft wall. The next ladder rung had been offset to his right. With a deep breath, Jimjoy eased himself down and into the cross tunnel, where he listened, sniffing the air as well.

The atmosphere was dry, with a faint odor. His nose itched. At that, his back reasserted the need to be scratched.

The Special Operative began scratching, as well as rubbing his nose. The ashes and cinders from the badlands had dispersed to the least accessible portions of his flight suit and anatomy.

Even as he scratched, he continued to listen. The surface underfoot was flat, not curved as would be the case with a water tunnel. The tunnel had been built for maintenance or access purposes, presumably to the deep shaft which in turn accessed the old aqueduct beneath.

The maintenance tunnel where he stood, assuming that the ladder had not gradually twisted ninety degrees, headed west, back toward the location of the original maintenance station, the one that the rebels used.

Jimjoy sat down and pulled off his boots. He was tired, and in no shape to take on anyone. No one had used the tunnel recently, and he needed some rest before he tackled the three-kay walk back.

Asleep almost as soon as he had pulled the pack under his head, he dismissed the thought that he might be reacting to an oxygen deficit.

Waking with a start, he grabbed for the flash.

He did not switch it on, listening instead for whatever had awakened him, looking for the faintest glimmer of light. But the tunnel before him and the shaft behind him both remained silent. He could feel the slightest of breezes, flowing down from the shaft and into the tunnel toward the maintenance station.

As he sat up slowly in the darkness, he realized that he had a few bodily needs.

After convincing himself that there was no one nearby, he switched on the flash. The walls of the maintenance tunnel formed a half circle. The top of the arc stood about three meters from the floor. The widest section of the tunnel was about a meter above the floor, roughly four meters wide. The floor was melted rock, as if the Engineers had laser-drilled a circular tunnel, but let some of the molten material fill up the bottom to form a roadway for personnel and equipment.

Jimjoy pulled on his boots, then used the deep shaft to relieve himself. He doubted that there would be anyone below to object. Next he finished the very last of the water, scarcely more than a few drops, and checked the time. Four standard hours was all he had slept.

As he ran his fingers over his chin and felt the stubble, he grinned, imagining the sight he must present. He shrugged and set out, keeping the flash beam low.

Like the access shaft, the maintenance tunnel was lifeless. No insects skittered through it. There were no dragons in the dark. It smelled of long-departed moisture and ashes.

Like death, reflected Jimjoy.

Close to an hour later, he became aware of a faint glow ahead. Switching off the flash totally, he lightened his steps and continued forward, straining his ears.

The tunnel ended abruptly, blocked by a rough plastic partition. The glow was caused by the light which seeped around the edges.

Easing up to the partition, Jimjoy listened.

Outside of the faint hum from what might be a ventilation system, and an even higher-pitched and fainter sound that came from either old-fashioned lighting or electronics, he could hear nothing.

He used the flash to study the partition wall. With only minimal bracing and a thin layer of plastic overcoat, the partition had been constructed as a heat-and-light barrier, rather than as anything else.

With the knife from his belt pouch, Jimjoy carved out a small triangular niche in the wall, about half a meter off the floor, to scan the area on the other side.

His caution was wasted, since the space beyond the partition was nothing more than a storeroom, generally empty, with a scattering of opened and unopened cartons. Another wall, far more solid-looking, with a metal hatch, marked the end of the tunnel ten meters farther eastward.

Jimjoy used the knife to extend his viewing niche into three sides of a rectangle, creating a small "doorway" into the storeroom. After squeezing inside, he folded the thin plastic back into position, pressing the edges together. The cuts would not be that apparent to a casual observer.

Glancing at the hatchway to the main section of the station, he checked the contents of the boxes, discovering several sets of unused Imperial field uniforms, two cases of combat sustain rations, camouflage netting, and two unopened boxes of office supplies.

He shrugged. Everything so far had been merely preliminary. Now he had to tackle the main rebel base, preferably without too much chaos, in order to obtain his own passport off New Kansaw.

XLIII

JIMJOY TOOK ANOTHER look around the makeshift storeroom before approaching the hatch. Rather than a circular hatchway, the opening in the wall was more like an old-fashioned endurasteel pressure door set on massive hinges. The wall in which it was set was solid stone, fused to a smooth finish with no indication of joinings or mortar.

Keeping close to the wall, Jimjoy eased toward the steel door, repressing a smile as he neared it and saw the sliver of light cast on the floor.

Not terribly security-conscious, the rebels, he observed. Still, he stopped to listen again, right at the doorway, not that he learned anything from the silence on the other side. The air remained dry and musty, reminding him that both his nose and his back itched. He rubbed his nose and ignored his back.

Then he slipped the stunner from his thigh pocket and gently edged the door a few millimeters. No reaction. He peered through into what seemed to be an air lock of sorts. Shaking his head, he stepped into the small room. Of course, the original Imperial Engineers would have provided both protection and access if the aqueduct had ever backed up. The storeroom had been added later.

The next door was a bona fide watertight hatch with a wheel to open it, closed, with no indication of what lay on the other side.

Jimjoy didn't bother to shrug. Holding the stunner in one hand, he spun the wheel until the dogs were released. Then he cracked the door and listened once more. The heavy metal would shield him from anything likely to be inside the station.

Other than a hum of lighting and a hiss from the ventilation system, the Special Operative heard nothing. This time he waited even longer. The rebels were probably not professionals, not at the waiting game.

At last he swung the hatch wider, peered around the bottom edge of the door, and saw an overturned table, a reddish smear across it. The sour smell of death oozed toward him.

The corners of his mouth turned down, and he bolted through the hatchway and across the room. The unitized and portable computer system with the map display still flashing indicated that the space had served as some sort of strategy or planning center.

He avoided the pool of blood and the single dead man who wore a faded purple uniform and stopped by the half-open doorway, ears cocked for any possible sounds.

This time he heard voices—male and female.

Before he could make out more than a sense of strain in the one woman's voice, the sound of closer footsteps echoed toward him. All he could do was stay close behind the doorway and wait, stunner ready.

"Pick up the most incriminating stuff, Dieler."

"What?"

"You know—maps with Imperial positions, anything with body counts, slots with data, anything to make Commander Moran happy. Nothing with blood on it."

Jimjoy smiled mirthlessly. Moran wanted bloodless extermination, like all Imperial tacticians. Like all too many modern tacticians, he thought.

"Right."

Two men stepped inside the rebel strategy center, not even looking backward.

Jimjoy let the first man pass and broke the neck of the second before the tech knew what hit him.

"Uhnnn—"

"Tech—"

Thrummmm!

Hoping that the high-pitched hum of the stunner had been less obvious than a shout would have been, Jimjoy listened intently as he dragged the figures, one dead, the other unconscious, behind the overturned table. He debated switching into one of the Marine's uniforms, but decided he didn't have the time before someone else showed up.

Moran had been smarter, much smarter, than Jimjoy had given him credit for. Jimjoy also wondered how Moran had kept track of him, what Herrol had planted on him. They had lost track of him once he had gone underground, but following his trail had clearly been enough.

More than enough to lead them to the rebels and to assault the base.

He edged the door farther open, but could hear only the voices coming from the hallway to the right.

Slipping out into the corridor, he darted toward the sounds. The first ancient doorway on the left was hanging on one hinge, and two bodies were sprawled inside, one sliced nearly in half.

Jimjoy swallowed hard and kept moving. Why the use of such fatal weapons? In close quarters, stunners were more effective, and less likely to destroy your own troops in the event of a mistake. Not to mention more humane.

Human soldiers, of course, always condemned inhumane weapons—except when necessary, which was usually.

Jimjoy slowed as he neared the almost closed door from where the voices came. He tried to listen for steps behind him or nearby as well.

"How many?" The tone was persistent, but assured.

Smack!

"How many were here?"

Smack!

Jimjoy stepped through the door, took in the two Marines and their Captain.

Thrum! Thrum! Thrum!

Only the Captain had had the time to look surprised.

The room was filled with the stink of sweat and fear, and Jimjoy wrinkled his nose in distaste. He closed the door behind him, quietly.

The woman tied to the chair did look surprised, her eyes widening as she took in the Imperial-issue flight suit . . . and the unsavory character wearing it. The other conscious figure was a man, gagged and bound to the other chair.

Jimjoy pulled the knife from his belt and stooped—once, twice, three times. When he straightened the third time, the woman's face was even whiter.

"Sorry . . . what they did was totally unnecessary. Appreciate it if you didn't scream. I intend to cut you loose."

She said nothing, but did not stop shivering. Her curly, shoulder-length brown hair rippled with the shivers.

He kept the knife low, away from her body, as he sliced the cords from her hands and feet. Then he did the same for the man, glancing back toward the door as he did so, listening for further sounds.

"How many are there? Impies, I mean." His voice was low.

"I . . . don't know," answered the woman. The man was still struggling with his gag. "We saw a lot, more than twenty, I guess, when they stormed through the portal."

"All wearing uniforms like these?" He gestured at the dead Marines as he moved back toward the heavy door, which he eased open a few centimeters.

"I think so." She rubbed her wrists to regain some circulation.

The man still had not spoken, although he had finally removed the gag.

Jimjoy nodded and smiled.

The woman shivered, and the man paled.

"Sorry. Have a few loose ends to tie up." He eased the door closed and walked back to the three bodies. He reached down and removed two stunners from the Marine corpses, checking the settings. Lethal.

He reset the stunners to the widest beam focus and to a heavy stun pattern—enough to drop the strongest Marine cold—and handed one to the woman and the other to the man. The man handed the stunner back.

"It's only on stun," noted Jimjoy.

"Kordel does not use weapons."

He realized that she had a strange pronunciation pattern when she spoke, almost a cross between Old Anglish and Panglais. "Then you use them both if anyone looks in."

"Looks in?"

"If you see a face that isn't mine, shoot. The next crew that shows up will probably kill on sight. Or you'll wish they had."

"Like you?"

Jimjoy ignored the edge in the woman's voice.

"They've already tried to kill me about four times."

"And that justifies murder on your part?" Kordel's voice was soft, although the man looked trim and physically fit.

"No time for philosophy, Kordel. Could debate ends and means forever. Violence did save your lives, at least temporarily. And, excuse me . . . I'm going to attempt to ensure that our salvation is more permanent."

He edged out the door and worked his way farther along the corridor toward the two doors ahead. He chose the one which was ajar.

There were two Marines inside—one woman, one man. The woman Marine had a knife in her hand, wiping the blood off on the torn tunic of the dead woman on the cot.

The male Marine was pulling his trousers back on.

Jimjoy eased the stunner power level up to lethal.

Thrum! Thrum!

Even before the bodies dropped, he was inside the door, moving toward the dead Marines, forcing his stomach to stay calm, trying to keep his eyes away from the body on the cot, trying to ignore the retching feeling in his guts.

"You've killed before, Wright," he whispered as he checked the male Marine's stunner. "You've killed thousands."

But it hadn't been personal, and he hadn't gloried in it. He hadn't, had he? Pushing the questions away and leaving his nearly exhausted stunner, he took the stunners from both Marines, ignoring the laser rifle against the wall. He looked to see if both stunners were set on lethal. They were.

Listening for a moment at the door, he heard steps.

"Silzir, get on with it. They've had their fun. Make a last sweep and collect whatever we've got. Lieutenant wants the place cleared."

Jimjoy stepped behind the door and waited.

Thrum! Thrum!

The senior Marine tech died before he saw Jimjoy. The other's mouth opened.

Thrum!

The Special Operative laid the two technicians beside the other bodies. Four Impies and one female rebel. Back at the doorway, he could hear no other sounds close by. The former pumping control station sounded as it must have once before, with only the sounds of ventilation and lighting, scattered voices muffled by partitions and closed doors. The air seemed to thicken around him, and he put his head down and took a deep breath.

At his end of the corridor, the only room he had not checked was the one behind the closed door directly across from him. With a quick study of the still-empty corridor and a shrug, he slipped across the few meters between the doors, pausing outside the closed room.

He could hear two voices, both low-pitched, punctuated with silence.

He eased the door opened, saw two sets of eyes widen at his strangeness.

Wwwhhhsttt!

Thrum! Thrum!

Whhsstt!

Jimjoy was already diving away from the path of the laser cutter that left a clean slice diagonally across the door—a door left quickly behind him as he dove sideways.

Thrum!

Abruptly, the room was silent except for Jimjoy's heavy breathing, the only breathing in the room.

The Special Operative's eyes flashed across the gouged plastone flooring that bore the imprints of long-removed equipment. The laser rifle lay an arm's length from the man who had trained it on him—belatedly.

Jimjoy would have shaken his head, but he was still breathing too heavily as he moved back toward the slashed doorway, wondering how he had ever managed to avoid the laser, especially since he had *heard* the lethal weapon before he had fired, even before he had started to dive out of the way.

His eyes lifted to the silent figure in the straight-backed chair.

This time, he could not keep the contents of his stomach in place, could not avoid seeing in full the use to which the laser had been put by the dead Marine, before depositing the remnants of his last sustain bar on the gouged and already brownish tiles.

The last blast from the laser, the one that had cut the white-haired rebel in two, had not been sufficient to destroy the evidence of selective dismemberment. What had saved Jimjoy had been the Marine's need to refocus the laser. Even so, the dead Imperial Marine information specialist had nearly been quick enough to get Jimjoy.

Information specialist—his stomach turned again. While he had recognized the obscure rating patch, he had not realized that the duties were quite so hands-on brutal. His missions had been clean by comparison.

Jimjoy slumped back against the wall, forcing himself to take a series of measured breaths along with a short set of muscular readiness/relaxation exercises to put himself back together. His already dubious beliefs and his stomach were taking some severe punishment, and he hoped that he had a few moments before any more Marines showed up.

After wiping his dripping forehead with his arm, smelling his own stink—part animal, part filth, and part fear—he tried to center his attention on the next job at hand, which had to be getting out in one piece with the two remaining rebels.

"Hope—" He cut off the mumbled words. He had no time left for soliloquies, maybe not even for action.

With a last deep breath, he edged up to the scored and sliced doorway. The footsteps he heard were getting fainter, as if a two-man patrol were heading to the end of the other corridor at right angles to where he stood. He went through the doorway as quickly as he could and down the corridor, trying to maintain the high-speed glide step that was supposed to be virtually silent. He could hear his own steps as a faint scuffle.

Passing the room where he had left the woman and Kordel without a pause or checking at the closed door, he stopped short of the cross corridor and listened again.

"... check ... Silzir ... ready to toss ..."

He nodded as he could hear the pair headed back his way. Dropping low, he hugged the edge of the wall just behind the counter and kept listening.

"... Commander ... pull out ... bring ... out ..."

"... casualties heavier ..."

"Not bad, not for just three squads and the battle cutter ..."

"Lucky, if you ask me."

"No luck. We get wiped, and the Commander rams a tachead in. So sorry."

While the conversation was getting more and more interesting, Jimjoy was running out of time. He dropped around the corner and fired.

Thrum! Thrum!

This time he dragged both bodies with him back to the closed door, which he opened from the side. He waited for the rebels to see the bodies.

"That you?"

"Dumb question," he muttered, ducking and peering around the door at knee height. "All right, put down the stunners and drag these two in."

"Why?"

"Do it."

Whether reacting to the sensibility in his voice or to the cold matter-of-factness, each rebel dragged a body inside. Jimjoy eased the door shut and began stripping off his bedraggled flight suit. He glanced over at the woman, whose eyes widened and who looked at the stunner she had laid down.

"Forget it. If you want to get out of here, you'd better follow my example and find a uniform that halfway fits."

His eyes held hers for an instant, and he could see her face pale momentarily.

"Yes. It's that bad. Now move."

"And how bad is that, whatever your name is?" asked the man named Kordel.

"Bad as you wish to believe, maybe worse. Three to five minutes, the remaining Marines will discover the trail of bodies. Quick HE charges, maybe a tachead, to take care of everything, including any of their own left behind. No more pump station, no more us."

"There is a way out . . ."

"No. Came in that way. Couldn't get far enough. Compression wave." Jimjoy found that his conversation suffered while trying to keep his voice low and changing into the Marine uniform simultaneously. He had chosen a senior tech's uniform, leaving the dead Captain untouched. Too many would know the Captain.

"Who are you?" the woman asked as she pulled the Marine trousers over her legs.

Jimjoy had not seen her shed her own trousers, but then his concentration had been on the closed door and his own problems in changing.

"A former Imperial on the run. Did what worked. Not exactly what they wanted."

"So honorable yet." Kordel's voice was flat. He had begun to button the tunic, looser on him than Jimjoy would have liked, but they were running out of both time and luck.

"Hardly. Didn't happen to like unnecessary killing or killings for no real purpose. That and a few other things."

"You're about halfway honest, then." The brown-haired woman had a refreshing voice, and Jimjoy wished he could have spent more time listening. He folded back the Marine blouse in a standard tuck and reclaimed the beret.

The woman shivered as she saw him in the uniform.

"You look like you belong in it."

"I did . . . once. Ready?"

"For what?"

"To walk out to the outboard cargo flitter—the last one on the right-hand side. Keep the stunners holstered. If I yell 'Run,' follow me. Otherwise we march." He shrugged. "No great battle plan, but it's our only choice."

"At least we'll be shot on our feet."

Jimjoy thought of the woman in the next room and the tortured and dead rebel leader across the corridor and nodded slowly.

"The others?"

"What's your name?" Jimjoy asked as he put his hand on the door lever, ignoring her question.

"Luren. And yours?"

"Wright. Jimjoy. Major. Ex. Special Operative."

He thought he could feel the chill settle behind him, but he touched the lever and eased the door open, stepping into the still-empty corridor.

"March," he said quietly. "Try to stay halfway in step with me, not like a parade, but as if your steps mean business."

He could hear another set of steps when they neared the corner of the corridor. He gauged the sounds, his hand withdrawing the latest stunner he had appropriated. One set of footsteps.

"Tech—"

Thrum!

Almost without breaking stride, Jimjoy scooped up the falling figure and slid him around the corner and out of sight.

The main portal lay straight ahead, with no sentries in sight on the inside. Those controlling the portal would be outside, weapons trained on the portal.

With no one in sight, Jimjoy kept his steps quick and crisp, letting the old drill patterns take over while he sorted over the alternatives. He could tell from the orders he had overheard and from the desultory mop-up efforts, combined with the tail-end brutality, that the last step would be the total destruction of the former aqueduct control center, along with total destruction of its contents.

No doubt Moran would claim the rebels had left a self-destruct system.

The missing insignia on several Marine uniforms also told another story—one confirmed by the Marines' action after taking the rebel base. One way or another, Moran had raided the disciplinary battalion for his strike force.

Jimjoy straightened as he stepped toward the open inner portal.

"Keep it moving!" he snapped. "Captain wants us out." Kordel stumbled.

"Gorski! Pick up your feet!" Jimjoy had noted the name on the uniform earlier.

Luren looked more military than Kordel did as the two marched out through the outer portal, each side of which stood jammed three-quarters open. The air reeked of ashes and blistered metal.

A single sentry stood ten meters away, laser rifle dangling negligently.

"How many more?"

"Captain's finishing up with the woman."

"How's he finishing up?"

"Told us to leave. Kept Dieler there." Jimjoy shrugged, keeping moving toward the troop carrier on the right. "Move it!" Jimjoy snapped again as he turned away and gestured toward the two rebels wearing the Imperial uniforms. "You might give some of them another call. Don't know how long the Commander's going to wait."

"He'll wait . . ." But the sentry looked back toward the portal.

All four troop carriers had the loading ramps down. None had guards outside, for which Jimjoy was glad. But then, the rebel base had supposedly been mopped up hours earlier.

His boots touched the bottom of the ramp, and he turned back toward the pair behind him, as much to shield his face from the copilot as to check on Luren and Kordel.

With a jerk, he turned back and covered the ramp in three quick strides.

Ummh.

The cargo-master fell to the stiffened hand without understanding what had hit him.

Thrum! Thrum! Thrum!

Ugh.

Thud.

Jimjoy shook himself, half coughing at the ozone from the stunner. Five more bodies sprawled around, from the pilot and copilot dangling in their harness to the single crew chief and the two Marines. More carnage, but he still hadn't seen any alternative. He had to keep moving faster than the reactions of the Impies.

"Get in here!"

Luren's face turned even paler as she surveyed the mess. Kordel turned greenish and swallowed—once, twice.

"Isn't there any other way?" asked the woman as she stood inside the cargo space, one hand on the back of a troop seat.

"Not if you want to live. And I won't even guarantee that yet."

Jimjoy began stripping the pilot from his harness.

"Anyone else shows up . . . let them inside and stun them."

"Inside?"

"Inside. Don't need bodies falling out. Besides, we've got enough lift here." Jimjoy eased the dead pilot from his seat and into the cargo space. He unlatched the copilot's harness and repeated the process. Then he turned to the pair of rebels. "Strap in."

"Why?" Again it was Luren, her brown eyes hard upon him.

Kordel stood waiting, still swallowing to control his stomach, his face alternating between unthinking blankness and thinking nausea.

"Because we're getting out of here."

"Where?"

"Accord." Jimjoy sighed. Luren wasn't going anywhere unless he explained. He had no time to act, let alone explain, and he was having to do both. "Look. Unless all three of us get off New Kansaw, we're dead. The only place to get off-planet is at the Imperial Base. So I intend to borrow a shuttle and lift for orbit station."

Luren shook her head. "That's insane!"

"Right," agreed Jimjoy. "Absolutely. Do you want to cooperate? Or do you want to get out, get tortured, raped, or worse? Like the ones I was too late to save. Do what I say or get the hades out. Your choice."

Kordel shuddered, but said nothing.

Luren locked eyes with Jimjoy, then dropped her gaze and reached for the crew-seat straps.

"No. Up here. Take the helmet, and don't touch anything." He pointed to the copilot's seat.

The Special Operative checked the ramp mechanism to ensure that all the safeties were unlocked, then donned the pilot's helmet and seated himself at the controls.

". . . three . . . do you read . . . do you read?"

"Cutlass two, can you see three?"

"That's a negative . . . you want me to send someone over?"

Jimjoy sighed. He had no idea what the pilot of Cutlass three had sounded like. But he needed to say something. He mumbled instead.

"Three here . . . here . . . breaker problem . . . up in four . . ."

"Gilberto . . . you always—"

"Clear it, two. Interrogative up time, three. Interrogative up time."

"Stet. Up in four. Up in four."

Jimjoy rushed through the first part of the checklist, gesturing at Luren to complete strapping in, hoping that Kordel could at least get himself strapped down. He used the unapproved checklist used by Special Operatives to get a bird airborne in minimum time. With the carrier ready for instant light-off, he unplugged the helmet jacks and slipped from the pilot's seat, heading toward the back of the combat carrier, looking for the emergency flare kit.

There was no flare kit, but there was a squarish case.

After twisting the seals off, he set to work, making the changes in one of the grenades, and clipping a small device to the side of the top one, and setting a timer loosely on top.

As he carried the heavy case back through the cargo space, he glanced first at Kordel, then at Luren. She was looking back at the man, who stared blankly at the open ramp.

Jimjoy set the case on the thruster console, then slipped back into the pilot's seat, plugged in the helmet jacks, and let his fingers dance across the board, listening to the audio. He levered the case onto his lap, checking to ensure that there was room for him to use the stick.

"Two. Gilberto back yet?"

"He's strapping in now, I think."

Jimjoy finished his preparations, sighed, and touched the studs.

"Three up. Commencing power up. Commencing power up."

"Negative on power up, three. That is negative."

" 'Request power up. Losing aux system. Losing aux system." Jimjoy intended to power up in any case, but talking about it might get him permission and would gain time.

"That's negative until strike team is fully returned. Negative this time."

Jimjoy brought the thrusters on line at eighty percent and started the ramp retraction sequence, not that anyone but the sentry could see the action. That had been one reason for choosing the outboard cargo flitter.

"Gilberto! Shut down, or Nedos will have your hide."

"Stet. Will be shutting down. Need to break a shunt here." Jimjoy brought all systems on line and released the rotor brakes.

Thwop . . . thwop . . . thwop, thwop, thwop . . .

"Gilberto, shut down! Merro, get your gunner trained on three."

Jimjoy poured turns to the rotors and began to lift, spraying ashes and dust over the three remaining carriers as the flitter rose into the late morning. The whine and roar through the open cockpit hatch window was almost deafening as he began to edge the flitter up and over toward Cutlass one, the command carrier.

From the corner of his eye he could see a handful of figures streaming out from the shattered lock of the rebel base, but he ignored them as he locked the thruster lever in place with his knee and one-handedly levered the heavy grenade case toward the window, sucking in his stomach and barely keeping the carrier from pitching straight down into his target.

The grenades were meant to be launched from a laser rifle with an adapter, but the fused timer should create about the same result. He hoped.

"Merro. Once three clears, gun the flamer down. Must be Ferrill. Can't be Gilberto."

"Ready to commence firing."

"Negative! Negative! He'll drop on us."

Yanking the tab on the small detonator, he plastered it on the top grenade and levered the container out. Once both hands were free, he dropped the nose, fed full power into the thrusters and rotors, and began a sprint from the area.

"Fire, Merro. Fire!"

Crump! Crump!

WHHUMMP!

The troop carrier bucked twice with the shock wave, then settled down. Jimjoy did not look back at the greasy smoke that poured upward from the chaos behind him. He also ignored the smaller explosions that occurred when the fuel supplies of the three grounded flitters ignited.

Now all he had to do was get landing clearance and steal a shuttle.

Since the base always had a standby shuttle, finding the shuttle wouldn't be the problem. Stealing it well might be. But then, what was another impossible problem?

He glanced sideways at Luren, who refused to look at him, although she periodically glanced back at Kordel, who refused to look at either one of them.

Jimjoy didn't blame either one. Their chances were terrible and getting worse. But, as he had told her, there were no longer any alternatives. None. Moran would gladly destroy half the planet to get either Jimjoy or remaining rebels, and Hersnik would be cheering him on.

"Now, Wright," he muttered under his breath, "isn't that taking too much credit?"

He did not answer his own question. Instead, he checked the readouts—less than sixty kays left before he reached the clearance call-in point. Less than sixty kays before the next confrontation. He shrugged his shoulders and tried to relax the tension.

He continued to scan the controls until he was certain that the carrier was functioning as designed. Then he set the autopilot, hoping that the cargo bird wouldn't fly into the ground. He watched the radalt for another few minutes before he eased from behind the controls and stepped into the troop space and began the distasteful job of stripping the copilot's flight suit. The pilot was too small, and since both uniforms were standard flight suits, no one would notice. But everyone would question it if a senior Marine tech landed the bird.

Kordel continued to stare straight down, with an occasional glance at the bulkhead before him, as if the rebel were still trying to gather himself together, or to escape from the nightmare in which he found himself.

Luren turned to watch, noting that Jimjoy did not change boots, and that his own matched both the pilot's and the copilot's.

"Yes, I'm a pilot, among other things."

He doubted she heard his words, although she shook her head sadly, the helmet bobbing as she did, the curly hair floating out from underneath momentarily.

Once he was wearing the flight suit, he used his own I.D. patch, the one thing he had kept besides his knife through three uniform changes. He doubted that the entire New Kansaw Base had been told that one Major Wright was persona non grata. Besides, Majors were scrutinized less intently than Captains and Lieutenants.

He scrambled back into the cockpit, noting that the flitter was less than two hundred meters above the plain. He made the corrections even before strapping back into place.

Then he shrugged his shoulders, trying to release the tension.

XLIV

JIMJOY SHIFTED THE frequency from tactical control to field, listening for traffic at the Imperial Base before announcing his presence.

". . . PriOps, Gauntlet four. Departing alpha seven. Fuel status is three plus. Time of return one plus five."

"Four, cleared for departure."

Listening, he waited, then keyed his own transmitter with the ease of habit.

"PriOps, this is Cutlass three. Cutlass three, returning TacOp. Request delta three."

"Delta three clear. Interrogative threshold. Interrogative threshold."

"Estimate threshold in one zero standard. One zero."

"Cleared for delta three in one zero. Interrogative hunting status. Interrogative hunting status."

"Status is mixed green."

"Mixed green? What . . . ? Three, please clarify. Please clarify."

"Objective accomplished. Objective accomplished. Cultass one, two, and four are strikes."

Jimjoy continued to scan the controls, mentally planning his approach to the Imperial Base and the shuttle it held. With a deep breath, he glanced sideways, then backward, to take in his two passengers—the one glancing speculatively at him, the other looking blankly at the gray metal decking.

"Interrogative assistance this time, three."

"Strike force will require outlift. Will require outlift."

"Interrogative intentions, three. Interrogative passengers."

"Negative on passengers, PriOps. Negative on passengers. Inbound for commlink. Then will resupply and join outlift."

"Understand resupply."

"After commlink, PriOps."

"Stet, three. Do you wish transfer to beta line after delta three?"

"That is affirmative."

He wiped his forehead with the back of his sleeve before shaking down the deeply tinted visor that disguised the three-day growth of dark beard.

He had thought about asking if a shuttle were scheduled for departure, but deferred. He needed the standby shuttle—after taking a few steps.

A tap on his shoulder, just as he began to line up for his final approach, brought him back to his immediate problems.

"What do you want us to do?" asked Luren.

"Drag all the bodies out of sight."

"Drag the bodies out of sight? Just like that?"

"Just like that." Jimjoy paused, then added, "When we land, just follow me and keep quiet. We'll all be heading for the main commcenter."

"Just like that?" repeated Luren.

"That's—"

"Cutlass three, interrogative time to threshold."

Jimjoy checked the EDR, then answered. "PriOps, this is three. Estimate threshold in four standard. Four standard."

"Three, please acknowledge Imperial I.D. I say again. Acknowledge Imperial I.D."

The suspicious Imperial mind, reflected Jimjoy. Only one of four flitters returns, and they want some reassurance that it's still theirs.

"Stet. Acknowledging."

He reached under the control board and triggered the cargo flitter's hidden transponder switch. The switch was in the first place he looked, although he knew all four potential locations.

"Stet, three. Signal green. Cleared to delta three."

"Understand cleared to delta three. Will report threshold."

"Stet, three."

Jimjoy's eyes flicked beyond the expanse of synde bean fields immediately before him and noted the gray of the Imperial Base structures and landing strips, and the black field tower. The fusion power plant was well beneath the base of the tower—standard Imperial design, and within a few meters of the standby shuttle, which was exactly where it should be.

"Why the commcenter?" asked Luren again, catching his attention by touching his shoulder.

"To get close enough to the standby shuttle. If you want to help, round up three or four stunners with full charges. Let me have two and keep two . . . and see if you can find an official holster for one of them."

She wrinkled her nose in reaction to either the proximity to the unwashed Special Operative or his latest request. "Can't you find a *peaceful* way to solve anything?"

"Wasn't trained that way. Besides, you rebels weren't exactly peaceful, either."

"Not after—"

"Excuse me." Jimjoy returned full attention to the controls. "PriOps. Cutlass three at threshold, descending to two five zero."

"Three, cleared to two five zero. Do you have visual on flitter at your two thirty?"

Jimjoy looked. The flitter was on a low-level departure.

"Stet. Have visual. Low level." The pilot added power as he completed the rotor deployment.

"PriOps, three descending to one zero zero. On final approach."

"Three, you're cleared to delta three. Interrogative crew service."

"That's negative until transfer to beta line. Request beta seven."

"Negative on beta seven. Beta four, five, and eight are open."

"Request beta eight."

"Holding beta eight for you, Cutlass three. Interrogative time on ground before transfer."

"Estimate one five standard."

Easing the nose upward, Jimjoy began dropping airspeed and adding power, gauging his descent to come to a full stop well clear of the tower, planning a sedate air taxi into the commslot.

The EGT on the right-hand thruster edged into the amber as he added power to bring the heavy craft into a hover. Cross-bleeding power left both thrusters in the green, but barely, as he edged the flitter toward the touchdown spot.

"PriOps, three on the deck. Shutting down."

"Stet, three."

Completing the shutdown seemed to take forever, but the clock only showed three minutes by the time Jimjoy was unstrapping.

"Have those stunners? And a holster?"

Luren pressed both into his hands, a sad look in her brown eyes. "I'm sorry I said anything. Thank you for trying."

"Don't thank me until I get you out of here safe. Let's go. You're witnesses to the nuclear arms the rebels had stored in their base.

"But—"

"I know. I know. But that's one of the few things that will get me where I need to be if anyone raises the wrong questions. And there's little enough left for anyone to dispute it by comm now." He set the stunners on the flat section of the controls, unstrapped, and attached the holster to his equipment belt.

Luren shook her head again.

Each time she seemed ready to accept him, he said or did something that set the woman off again.

For what seemed the hundredth time over the last few hours, he wondered why he was dragging the two along. Did he need some salve for his conscience? Or was he subconsciously thinking of a bargaining tool with Accord? He brushed the thoughts aside as he holstered one stunner and concealed the other, slightly smaller one in a thigh pocket.

He wished he had some of his own gear left. He'd had little enough by the time he'd left Accord, and bit by bit the rest had been used up. But all he needed was speed, force, and the luck of hades.

"Come on." He had triggered the ramp letdown already, and waited for the extension to stop.

"What do you—"

"Just follow me and look grim. Shouldn't be that hard for you."

He stepped down the ramp in smart steps, with a touch of haste, as if he were in a hurry but trying not to be too obvious about it.

"Major . . ."

The man who met him directly inside the portal to the flight tower was a tall Captain, taller than Jimjoy by half a head. The Marine Captain wore badges for combat proficiency and field command, and he was scrutinizing Jimjoy as if he had crawled from the nearest sewer.

Jimjoy did not shake his head. The Captain would be the next casualty.

"Captain. Urgent message uplink from Major Nedos."

"I'll be happy to take care of the details, Major. Since you are doubtless needed back in the . . . field." His voice conveyed a touch of disdain as he continued to survey the three scroungy-looking figures from the security of his height and impeccably creased uniform.

"I think not, Captain. But I would appreciate it if you would lead the way and verify both entry and transmission."

Their eyes met again, but the Captain, even from his superior height, looked away.

"This way."

Jimjoy knew the way, but saw no need for an uproar yet. He followed the Marine, letting Luren and Kordel trail him. The three received curious glances but no challenges as they took the old-fashioned stairs up two levels toward the commcenter.

The inner workings of the center were closed to all except restricted personnel, but several rooms with transmission consoles, directly outside the center and separated from the operations area, were available. They were seldom used, since station personnel could use their own consoles for the same purposes.

As the Marine gestured through the open portal, Jimjoy hesitated, stepping aside to let Luren and Kordel pass him.

"Go ahead, Captain. I'll need you as well." As the Captain reluctantly entered the small room, scarcely larger than a clerical cubicle, Jimjoy's hands brushed the portal controls. He turned.

Thrumm!

The Captain's face did not even register surprise. Jimjoy dragged his figure out of view behind the console.

"Not again!"

"Quiet."

Jimjoy pointed to the single console in the small room.

"Luren, sit here. Type out anything your heart desires on the screen. But type, and don't touch any of these three studs. Stand next to her, Kordel, as if you're reviewing it."

"Why?" asked Luren.

"For the benefit of anyone who may use the scanner. I'll be back in a few minutes. Just stay put. Use the stunner on anyone besides me who comes through the portal."

"Trust you?"

"Why not? Got anyone better?"

Jimjoy reversed himself and stepped back out into the corridor that led to the main commcenter. A young technician manned the access desk before the main portals.

"Major . . . were you looking for someone?"

"I was supposed to meet a Captain Tiarry here. Have you seen him?"

The technician glanced at her screen.

Thrum!

As he dragged the body out of sight, Jimjoy wished he had reset the stunner. He scanned the control board and shook his head. Totally tied with an interlocked security code. Any attempt to meddle would probably alert the entire base.

He turned his attention to the portal itself. It seemed relatively standard, despite the heavy casements.

He checked the stunner, refocused the weapon to the narrowest and most intense setting. Then he retrieved the second stunner from his thigh pouch. He stepped up to the portal, calculating the circuit placements.

Thrum!

Nothing happened. He moved the weapon slightly.

Thrumm!

The portal edges quivered.

Thrumm!

The doors spasmed, opening perhaps a quarter of the way before starting to close again.

Rippppyyyttt.

The Special Operative almost didn't clear the portal edges as he slipped into the commcenter, dropping the used and fused stunner and switching the replacement into his left hand.

Three people, the duty officer and two technicians, looked up with mild surprise.

"So sorry . . ."

Thrumm! Thrum! Thrum!

He grabbed the duty officer's stunner and jammed it into his holster, replacing the other weapon in his thigh pouch as he stepped up to the master console.

He entered the series of codes and instructions he was not supposed to know, the ones left over from the time of the Directorate, the ones used to ensure that no one captured an Imperial Base—and survived.

"Masada one, on line," scripted the console.

"Romans at the walls," he tapped in return.

"Time until sunrise?" inquired the ancient safeguard.

"Thirty-five standard minutes." Jimjoy hoped the time was sufficient, but if they didn't make it within the time limit, they wouldn't make it at all. Not after his trail of carnage.

"After sunrise?" the console asked in the uncharacteristic antique script.

"Neither legions nor the chosen people."

The console blanked, returning to its standard format. According to the program design, not even shutting the power off would stop the next steps. Only disabling the fusion power generator buried below the tower could do that.

The internal pressure on Jimjoy reminded him of another pressing need. He glanced around, trying to reorient himself to the more mundane necessities of life.

Trying to lift a shuttle on a high gee curve with a full bladder was likely to be uncomfortable, if not fatal. He sighed as he located the fresher and sprinted for it, shaking his head.

To be slowed by the merely physiological. He hoped that the minute or so spent relieving himself would not prove critical. His failure to account for nature would have amused Thelina and the Ecolitans, he suspected.

The fresher was plain, empty, and welcome. He also took several deep gulps of water from the tap, not caring if he dripped on the borrowed flight suit. Not that he would have cared even if it had been his.

Feeling less physically pressured, he left the fresher and moved back through the commcenter, with thirty-two minutes still remaining before the Masada trap triggered. Exiting through the portal was far easier, although he was ready to use the stunner, if necessary.

It was not. No one had discovered the missing tech, and he walked back to the transmission room where he had left Luren and Kordel.

"Finished? Good. Let's go."

"What have you been doing?"

". . . why . . ."

"Let's go," he repeated, setting the portal controls to lock behind them.

They were down the first flight of steps, fifteen meters from the access door Jimjoy wanted, when another officer confronted them, stunner in hand.

"You—where's Captain Tiarry?"

"Captain who?" asked Jimjoy.

"You know who."

"Tall Marine Captain who went with us to the commcenter? He's still there. Very upset."

"Now . . ."

"You would be, too, if you'd just found out that the rebels had wiped out most of Commander Moran's strike force and had managed to come up with half a dozen tacheads before he closed down their base."

"Tacheads?"

"Just class three," amended Jimjoy, edging closer while turning toward Luren. "You have that shot there?"

As he turned back toward the Lieutenant, something white in his hand, both hands flashed.

Ugghhh.

Clank. The unused stunner clattered on the landing, a crack across the muzzle tube.

Jimjoy dragged yet another body out of the way through the portal leading to the access tube to the standby shuttle.

"Someone should have caught us by now."

"They have, several times . . . but no one really believes they'll be attacked in their own base."

He locked the portal, hoping that any searchers wouldn't think about two strange Marines and a pilot in conjunction with the emergency shuttle, at least for a few minutes.

And he needed those minutes, he realized as he reached the lock portal separating them from the shuttle. With a sigh, he pulled out the sole remnant of his equipment, the small tool kit.

"No more explosives?" asked Luren softly. "No more stunning miracles? No more defenseless individuals murdered?"

"Kindly—shut—up," he mumbled, relieved that the panel controls and associated lock circuits were relatively straightforward.

Still, the perspiration was streaming down his forehead before the five minutes it took him to persuade the locked panel to open had passed.

Clank. His fingers were shaking so much from the strain that he dropped the probe as he tried to retract it. Jimjoy shrugged, eased himself off sore knees, and picked up the instrument.

"Now what? Do we go back gently, killer, and plead for mercy?"

"Oh . . . that." Jimjoy smiled and touched the access plate. This time it lighted, and the portal opened. "No, you strap in. You get the co-pilot's seat. And, Kordel, you strap in where you can. We're running out of time. So you're on your own. Try to do it right."

Once they stood in the shuttle lock, Jimjoy dogged the manual seals into place. They might get blasted, but not assaulted by a following force.

"Onward."

Neither Kordel nor Luren said a word, but followed him along the narrow passage to the control cabin.

"Kordel . . . strap in there . . . you, Luren . . . there."

Jimjoy seated himself and strapped in, studying the controls, looking at the blank panel before him that would display an instant view from the scanners once he powered up the shuttle.

First came the pre-power checklist.

"Converters . . . shields . . . shunts . . ."

Next came the power.

The blank panel filled with a panorama of the New Kansaw Base, with the flat stretch of plastarmac lined up right before the shuttle all set for an emergency lift-off.

He tapped the primary comm circuits.

"PriOps, Gauntlet one, approaching TacOps. Approaching TacOps. Will report ASAP . . ."

"Scampig Papa, at threshold . . ."

"Cleared to beta four, Papa."

Jimjoy bit at his lower lip. Gauntlet one would be reporting on the chaos he had left before much longer. He forced himself to remain methodical in attacking the remainder of the checklist, but he didn't resist a sigh when the board was fully green.

The right thruster began to scream. Then the left.

"Charon two, interrogative your intentions. Interrogative intentions."

Jimjoy was surprised PriOps would even ask.

"Missou PriOps, Charon two. Lifting for orbit control. Code Argent Black. Code Argent Black."

He brought both thrusters on line and tapped the panel stud to initiate retraction of the umbilical corridor to the tower, waiting for the light to signify a complete break.

"Charon two. Interrogative Argent Black."

Jimjoy added power to the thrusters, and the heavy shuttle began the roll out along the emergency strip.

"PriOps, Charon two. Clearance is beta theta seven. Logged with Missou commcenter."

"PriOps, this is TacControl. Request authentication from Charon two."

Jimjoy twisted the thrusters to full power.

"Charon two, this is PriOps. Interrogative authentication. Interrogative authentication."

The control readouts showed the thruster strain, but the thrusters remained on the border between green and amber as the ground speed built. The end of the emergency strip was appearing closer and closer.

"Charon two. Interrogative authentication . . . return to base."

"Missou PriOps, this is Charon two. Authentication logged in commcenter. Authentication logged in commcenter. Authentication follows. Jupiter slash five omega slash beta delta three four. I say again. Jupiter slash five omega slash beta delta three four. Lifting this time."

"What are you doing?" demanded Luren in a stage whisper from the copilot's couch.

Jimjoy ignored her as he eased the still-wallowing shuttle into the air, straight and level until he had enough speed to begin the turn necessary for orbit control positioning.

"Stalling . . . don't shoot while they're talking . . ."

"That gives you an advantage. You do."

Jimjoy dismissed the bitterness, watching with relief as the barely airborne shuttle cleared the base perimeter fencing, and as the airspeed finally began to climb when he retracted the wheels.

"Charon two. Say again destination and mission. Say again destination and mission."

"Missou PriOps, this is Charon two. Lifting this time for New Kansaw orbit control. Mission codes filed commcenter, as per ImpReg five four two."

Not that there was an Imperial Regulation 542, but that would confuse the issue for a moment or three.

Finally, the shuttle reached ramspeed, without a Marine combat flitter nearby yet. Jimjoy torched both rams, watching the airspeed build as the high-speed engines took over from the thrusters. Then he began to work with the course corrector, trying to merge his trajectory with the orbit control approach lane, easing the shuttle back toward the standard departure profile.

In another few moments, nothing from the base would be able to reach them. Then he could begin to worry about orbit control.

He darted a glance over his shoulder at the still-slack-faced Kordel, impassive as ever, and at the brown-haired woman, who continued to shake her head sadly.

"Have you thought about what you have done?"

"No. No time to think. Be dead by now."

Actually, he did think, but not about morality, which was what she had in mind.

"Charon two. Return base OpImmed. OpImmed."

"Missou PriOps, that is negative. Negative this time. Entering boost phase. Unable to comply."

Let them stew over that. The base had no long-range lasers, and no combat flitters close enough to reach them, even with tactical missiles. With the shuttle in boost, nothing on the planetary surface could reach them.

Another minor problem solved, with a mere dozen or so remaining before they could reach Accord. If they could reach Accord.

He shrugged and adjusted the steering rams. One step at a time.

XLV

HISTORY HAS SHOWN that there are two kinds of warfare practiced. The first is the use of military forces and tactics to obtain territory, power, or position. The principal assumption underlying such 'power-seeking' warfare is that the participants will refrain from actions threatening their survival.

The second, and rarer, general classification is that of total warfare, where the goal is the total extermination of at least one of the partici-

pants. At times, total warfare may be limited to the destruction of a
form of government of one participant or to the total destruction of a
specific culture or racial type, but the goal is still the total destruction
of *something*.

Governments and generals who fail to understand what kind of war
they are pursuing (or opposing) seldom choose the proper strategies or
tactics.

> *Patterns of Politics*
> Exton Land
> Halston, 3123 N.E.

XLVI

JIMJOY DIDN'T PARTICULARLY care for what was about to happen to
the Impie Base he had left behind and below the shuttle. But there
hadn't been any real alternative. What it amounted to was that he
valued his own continued existence over that of several thousand other
individuals, many of whom were totally innocent.

"Charon two, this is Missou PriOps. Interrogative passenger status.
Interrogative passenger status."

"Missou PriOps," returned Jimjoy, simultaneously adding boost,
"status is green. Status is green. Entering lift phase two."

Why was the base still operational? Before long, if it hadn't already,
the base security force was bound to discover the trail of bodies.

To his right, in the copilot's position, Luren sat quietly, but her eyes
continued to check the screens and the controls, as if she had some idea
what the readouts showed. Behind her, in the comm seat, was Kordel,
his narrow face expressionless as ever.

He only wished that either one could help in operating the shuttle.
He was tired, and it had been years since he had spent more than a few
hours with a shuttle.

"Charon two, this is Missou PriOps. Authentication invalid. I say
again. Authentication negative. Return to base."

"Missou PriOps, two here. Please say again your last. Say again your
last." Jimjoy continued the stall.

SSSSSSSSSSSSSSSSSSSSSSSSSSSssssssssssssss . . .

The scream of white noise across the audio was accompanied by a white flare that momentarily blanked the visual screen for the instant before the compensators reacted.

"What was that?"

"The end of Missou Base," answered Jimjoy evenly.

"The what?" asked Luren.

"End of Missou Base. Finis. Gone."

"You—you—you—?" finally stuttered Luren.

"How else could I keep them from alerting shuttle control? You think that Commander Moran and the Admiral would just let us fly off into the sun? After they'd sent five operatives after me? After your resistance cost them more than three hundred troops?"

"My god! Now what will they do?"

"What else can they do? They've already murdered every rebel they know about. Besides, that explosion won't have the resistance's name on it. It probably has my signature all over it."

"Are you sure? Wouldn't it be easier to blame the resistance?"

Jimjoy shrugged uneasily. "Could be . . . but they'd do that anyway if that's what they wanted."

"*What* are you?"

"Wish I knew . . . wish I knew . . . once I was a Special Operative . . ."

He kept scanning the controls, noting that the screen had dropped the glare filters.

"Where can we possibly go now, Mr. Planet-killer?"

"To Accord. Where else?"

"Accord?"

"Tell you later." Jimjoy began to make a series of minor power corrections. As he finished, with a sigh, he switched frequencies and keyed the transmitter. "Beta shuttle control, this is Charon two, beginning final boost. Beginning final boost. Interrogative status Missou PriOps. Interrogative status Missou PriOps."

"Two, shuttle control. Understand commencing boost. Say again your last. Say again your last."

"Beta, two here. Last transmission from PriOps garbled. Sensors indicate anomaly vicinity Missou Base. Missou PriOps does not respond."

"Two. Understand Missou PriOps does not respond."

"That is affirmative. No response Missou Base. No response on any frequency. Full boost this time." He shut down the struggling rams and touched the booster controls.

The surge of acceleration shoved Jimjoy back into the pilot's seat. Luren's breath whuffed from her. Kordel grunted.

"No response—two, can you return Missou Base?"

"That is negative. Beyond envelope this time."

"Stet. Interrogative your assessment of Missou Base."

"Comm status of Missou Base is omega. Comm status omega. Unable to determine other functions."

"Stet, two. Shuttle control unable to raise Missou Base. Report outer approach. Report outer approach."

"Stet, shuttle control. Will report outer approach." Jimjoy had to grunt out the transmission under the two-gee pressure.

"Why . . . are . . . you . . . telling . . . them?" gasped Luren.

"Why not? Want them to think we're on perfect orbit as long as possible. Less suspicion this way."

"Less suspicion?" Luren's laugh came out as a cough.

Jimjoy ignored her skepticism as he corrected the boost arc course, then ended up having to readjust what turned out to have been an overcorrection. The arc indicator lights finally all lined up green on the board, but the Special Operative repressed what might have been a sigh of relief as he caught sight of the projected closure rate.

Remembering his training, he did not shake his head but began cutting the boost rate, rather than having to pile on high decel later.

"What . . . next . . . ?"

The pilot ignored the mumbled comment from Luren as he continued to make the necessary course and power adjustments. He wished he could have trusted the automatic computer controls, but once he allowed the linkage with shuttle control, he lost all control of the shuttle. Plus, the automatics were rough, and no shuttle pilot ever used them except in emergencies.

To add to that, he wasn't exactly planning a normal rendezvous.

Abruptly, he cut the boost to minimum gee and began reversing the shuttle's position.

"What are you doing now?" demanded Luren.

"Whatever's necessary." Next he began feeding in the parameters for the deceleration curve. Another few minutes would have to pass before he had to begin that operation. While he waited, he studied the control readouts. Finally, he called up the farscreens, trying to see if the shuttle were close enough to scan the orbit complex.

"Insufficient data," the screen announced.

"Oh, hades," he muttered. "Not again." He checked the times, then unstrapped and headed for the suit locker.

"Now what?"

"Time to get suited up. You won't have a chance later."

"Why do we need suits? Aren't we just going to lock in?"

"Not unless you want to be sent back planetside. So if you don't want to breathe vacuum, it would be most helpful if you got into one of these."

"Would you mind explaining?"

"Simple. We won't last more than a minute if we walk through a lock. We can't exactly lock in and ask them to give us a ship, if you please, to let us get away from them for Accord."

"I knew it. More violence . . . more bodies."

"You should have thought about that a long time ago—when you got involved with the rebels." Jimjoy stopped talking as he finished struggling into the suit and began checking the connections and seals. He glared at Kordel, who cowered in the comm seat. When he turned to Luren, she was unstrapped and twisting her long brown hair into a knot at the back of her neck.

Kordel might prove useful on Accord, but for what Jimjoy had no idea. Jimjoy jabbed at the racks. "Here are the suits. Get into one now. You've got about two to three minutes."

"Do you want us to put on the helmets now?" asked Luren. She stepped toward the locker and caromed toward the overhead in the low gravity.

"No." Jimjoy caught her by the knee to slow her inadvertent flight. "Try one, and make sure you can get into it. But leave it on the rack. *Securely*. Don't need them bouncing around when we brake."

Kordel finally unstrapped himself and began to fumble with a suit.

Jimjoy finished his checkout of the single command suit and turned to see who needed assistance. Luren seemed to have mastered the process and stood quietly easing into the equipment, checking the connections as she did. She did not protest when Jimjoy adjusted several fasteners.

He turned his attention to Kordel, who held two identical suit sections and had a bewildered look on his face. Jimjoy sighed, took one section from Kordel's hand, and began to methodically stuff the man into the suit.

Cling!

"Hades!" he muttered as he let go of Kordel's shoulder clip so quickly that the other swayed toward the bulkhead in the low gee restraint.

Jimjoy swooped back before the controls and delayed the decel for another minute. Pursing his lips at the thought of having to recompute all the inputs, he bounded back to Kordel and resumed completing the simple suit-up that the resistance man seemed to find insurmountable. Then he turned to Luren and ran over her suit.

"You're fine. Strap in. You, too, Kordel." Kordel did not move. "Now." He picked up Kordel, who opened his mouth in protest, and jammed him into the comm seat, slamming the harnesses in place around the seeming incompetent.

Once back before the board, he began to recompute the decel vectors, realizing that he had gotten upset for almost no reason. He had never intended to bring the shuttle to an absolute stop in any case. Approximations would be sufficient . . . so long as the shuttle's relative velocity was relatively low when they exited.

He made the changes, rough as they were, and shifted his attention to the farscreens.

"Shuttle control, Charon two. Commencing back-brake. Commencing back-brake."

"Two, control. Interrogative status. Interrogative status."

"Shuttle control. This is two. Returning on manual pilot. Returning on manual pilot. Closure control delta. Closure control delta."

"Understand closure control delta. Do not attempt to lock. Do not attempt to lock."

"Stet. Will stand off. Standing off within scooter hop."

"Stet, two. Scooters standing by."

"Back-brake this time."

Jimjoy touched the fingertip controls as the gee force surged to four plus gees, then subsided to a constant three gees.

"Shuttle control. Two here. Interrogative courier for urgent pouch dispatch. Interrogative courier."

"Two. You're lucky about something. Both *Pike* and *Darmetier* on station."

"Stet."

Jimjoy knew there had to be some ships on station, but a courier would be best, with a small crew, high speed, and low profile. Armaments would be worse than useless. A scout would have been his next choice.

By now the farscreens were showing the general outlines of the shuttle control complex. He could make out several outlying ships, including one that bore the signature of a full battle cruiser. He did not shake his head, not under three gees. A full battle cruiser he did not need.

"Two, this is shuttle control. Suggest you increase delta vee. Closure rate above approach line. Suggest you increase delta vee."

"Stet. Increasing delta vee."

Jimjoy boosted the decel to four gees, this time waiting for shuttle control to acknowledge his actions.

"Two. You're under the curve."

"Stet. Monitoring this time."

He began backing down the deceleration according to his calculations, until the gee force was only slightly greater than one gee. He continued calculating the course line, trying to reset the decel schedule in a way that would not break the curve until the last minute, one that would not alert an already suspicious orbit controller.

Finally he found the combination he needed and entered it into the system. Fuel-wasteful, but the shuttle wouldn't be needing that fuel after he was finished with it in any case.

He concentrated on the farscreens. Both couriers' images were there, fuzzy compared with the solidity of the cruiser. The couriers were roughly equidistant from the shuttle's projected course line. He called up the EDI. One courier was distinctly colder than the other. That was his target.

Again his fingers returned to the maneuvering plot. He tapped in another small correction. The shuttle shivered as the attitude thrusters applied the necessary force.

Jimjoy keyed the transmitter.

"Shuttle . . . here . . . sssttt . . . on   path . . . again . . . borthrop . . . again . . ." The skipped words should have given the impression of a malfunctioning transmitter.

"Two, this is shuttle control. Say again your latest. Say again your latest."

". . . control . . . on top . . . maneuver . . . sstteent . . . path . . . again . . . again . . ." Jimjoy repeated his stuttered effort.

"Two, shuttle control. Your transmitter is omega. Interrogative status. Interrogative status."

Dumb question. How could he answer if his transmitter were omega?

In his efforts to set up the approach, he had forgotten to check on the two passengers/resistance refugees. He glanced sideways at Luren, whom he found looking back at him. A quick look over his shoulder caught Kordel shivering and seeing nothing.

"Two, this is shuttle control. Can you read me? Can you read me?"

". . . trol . . . trans . . . broke . . . again . . . pact . . . brothrop . . . con . . ."

Jimjoy could tell from the corner of his eye that Luren was trying to figure out why he was using a pseudo broken-transmitter routine.

The readouts showed that the beta shuttle complex was less than twenty kays away as the shuttle hurled toward its final rendezvous. The pilot/Special Operative rechecked the calculations.

"Charon two, this is shuttle control. If you read me, key your transmitter. If you read me, key your transmitter."

Jimjoy nodded. Someone was getting smart.

". . . control . . . broke . . . gain . . . say . . . roga . . . en . . ." he replied as he watched the orbit control complex grow in the screens. Less than ten kays, and the shuttle was still under the approach max lines. But not for long.

He unstrapped and flung himself from the controls.

"Helmets on. Now."

He didn't even stop to let Kordel try, lifting the man from the couch and twisting the helmet on for him. Luren had hers on fast enough for him to check the seals by the time he had finished with Kordel. His own followed.

In less than two minutes the steering thrusters would ignite, adding some velocity to the shuttle, and the single message torp would also fire, both directly toward the orbit station. The shuttle would be piling toward the cargo holding section of the orbit control, the widest section of the station and the best target.

Palming the inner lock controls, he gnawed at his lower lip as he waited for the lock to iris open. Luren needed but a nudge before he shoved Kordel in after her and jammed himself in after them both.

While waiting for the inner lock to close and for the evacuation to begin, Jimjoy linked the safety lines around the other two. Then he checked his belt harness to ensure that both needler and stunner were firmly secured, and that the emergency tool kit was also in place.

When the outer door opened, he pushed the other two clear to give himself enough room to extract the broomstick—what passed as an emergency scooter on most Imperial shuttles. Nothing more than a metal tube with limited solid fuel jets and with a padded shock damper on the front.

The shuttle began to reaccelerate fractionally within seconds of his clearing the lock, even before he managed to draw Kordel and Luren to him. Both were gesturing wildly, obviously concerned that they could not talk to him.

He frowned within his helmet as he remembered that he had not told them that their suit communicators were inoperable. He'd taken care of that earlier, since he had not wanted the Impie comm techs to pick up any stray radiation or other indication of their presence.

Jimjoy checked the drift toward the nearest dark silvery hull. It would take most of the stick's power just to kill their relative velocity, assuming he could make contact.

By now the message torp should have fired. It packed more than enough power to dent the station, assuming that all screens were not at full power.

The dark hull of the courier loomed to the right. Jimjoy touched the broomstick controls, hoping his last-minute directional shift wouldn't break the safety line.

Thud.

The dull sound vibrated, rather than rang, through his suit as the damper end of the broomstick impacted the courier hull. The thin and fragile-seeming tube bent, but the damper grips held. Forcing himself to move methodically, hand over hand, down the tube from the spidery seat, the Special Operative at last reached the hull. He began to look for the bonding pattern that would identify a recessed loop link. After what seemed nearly a standard hour, and probably took but instants, he found the first loop.

To that he attached the two safety leads that led to Luren and Kordel. To the second, located even more quickly, he attached his own line.

As he moved toward the emergency entrance that all couriers had, leaving the two hanging behind him on their lines, he hoped that neither one would panic. But they couldn't move rapidly enough for the next phase of the operation.

The courier might have all four crew members on board, or none, or some number in between. The lack of radiation he had noted earlier argued for less than a full crew.

The simplest way to take the ship would be to force both inner and outer locks and require the crew to breath vacuum. That solution might create more problems than it solved, since there was no guarantee that the courier would have adequate reserves to reatmosphere itself, or that he could guarantee that the ship would remain airtight. In addition, he did not know whether the ship was undergoing maintenance, with the more sophisticated electronics exposed.

He sighed. Nothing to do but bluff it out, if necessary.

He reached the emergency entrance, not much more than a tube big enough to accommodate one suited spacer, and used the command suit's keylock to open the exterior door. Folding himself inside, he closed the outer lock and waited for the atmospheric pressure to build. Within seconds, the light blinked amber, then green, and he touched the lever.

The inner door squealed as it opened, loud enough to alert anyone, awake or asleep, within the small ship and a sure sign that the courier's crew was lax in its inspections. The scout was under minimum gee field, indicating someone was aboard.

He was clear of the hatch and had closed it behind him, quickly making sure that the seals were in place, before he heard the woman's voice.

"Turn around . . . slowly . . ."

He did, unfastening the helmet clasps but leaving the helmet in place, just cracking the faceplate.

She wore uniform gray shorts and tunic, both obviously thrown on in haste. Still, she had reached the lock before he had cleared it, which meant that she had reacted to the broomstick's impact on the hull. She held a needler firmly aimed at his midsection.

"Care to explain, stranger?"

"Wright. Major Jimjoy Wright." He inclined his head. "My shuttle malfunctioned. Have two passengers in emergency suits tethered outside. Didn't want to explain in advance."

"We'll see. Walk straight ahead, and don't make any sudden moves. Or I'll use the needler."

"Wouldn't dream of it. But can we hurry. One was hysterical even before I put him in the suit."

"Him?"

"It happens." He turned and took a step forward, as she had indicated.

From behind him, she laughed. "One point in your favor. No man would invent a hysterical male."

Jimjoy listened. There were no other sounds. Since the woman wanted him to move forward toward the controls, it meant no one else was aboard. He could feel his own stunner at his belt, but did not look down as he carefully stepped along the short passage, ensuring that he did not encourage the other officer to pot him on the spot.

After he entered the control area, he stopped.

"If you are who you say you are, you should understand the board. Call your control point and report you and your passengers are safe."

"Fine. Where are we safe?"

"This is Dauntless two."

She wasn't even giving him the courier's name, but he leaned forward slowly, his hand brushing the equipment belt and taking the stunner with it.

"Clumsy in gauntlets," he observed conversationally, letting his armored fingers click on the flat board's surface. He touched the activation stud before she could accuse him of stalling and waited until the automatic check sequence completed itself.

". . . shuttle malfunction has impacted gamma three. Beta complex in full-suit isolation. No casualties except for possible victims on shuttle."

"Two for you," observed the woman. "Maybe one minus for drek piloting. Go ahead. Report."

His timing would have to be perfect. He touched the activation stud long enough for the tone to sound, but did not actually key it.

Cling.

"Shuttle control, this is Charon two—"

Thrum!

Clang!

He had dropped, twisted, and triggered the stunner in a single fluid motion.

She had fired the needler, but not quickly enough, and the needle had ricocheted off the overhead. The needler bounced from her suddenly limp hand as she folded into a heap, mouth open in surprise. She was still breathing.

Jimjoy did not remember resetting the stunner, but he was just as glad the shot had not been fatal. He slipped the needler up and put it in his belt where he had kept the stunner. He held the stunner ready as he swept by the unconscious officer, checking each of the closet-sized cabins and the single small room that served as recreation, mess, and meeting room all in one.

His initial assumption had been correct. No one else was on board.

He refastened his helmet as he headed for the main lock, hoping the rest of the courier's crew was not returning. Unless they were already en route, he doubted that they would be heading out until the mess in orbit control was straightened out.

With the main lock empty, he stepped inside, closed the inner door, and jabbed the bleed valve to vent the atmosphere. The outer door irised at his touch, and he scrambled out, scanning the emptiness around the courier. Nothing.

Kordel and Luren were still linked to the courier, but Luren had reeled herself into the hull and had begun to draw Kordel to her. She turned her head, alerted by the glint of his armor. Then she pointed to the still figure at the end of the safety line, and shook her head vigorously and negatively.

Jimjoy nodded in return to signify his understanding. Kordel was probably suffering from shock, space fugue, or who knew what. But it couldn't be helped. Not now.

He took over the job of reeling in the inert figure, slowly, until the man floated near his shoulder. Then he unclipped both rebels' lines from the ship and linked them to his belt. His own was attached to the courier's lock.

He could sense Luren's impatience with his slow and methodical progress—both in reeling in Kordel and in making his way back to the lock. But since weightlessness scarcely equated to masslessness, he did not speed up his efforts.

Once he had shepherded them both inside the lock, he almost breathed a sigh of relief. Instead, he used the manual lock seals to ensure that no one else would be able to surprise him.

Kordel sagged into a heap in the light grav of the courier. Aside from quickly removing the man's helmet, Jimjoy made no other effort to help him. As Luren removed her helmet, he snapped, "Crew quarters to the left. Get Kordel strapped into one of the lower bunks. Then come up here." He pointed. "Control room. Understand?"

"Yes, great and wondrous protector. I do understand."

"Wha—" Then he grinned. "You win that one."

"Everything's to be won . . ." She did not look at him as she began to struggle out of her suit.

He turned and made for the controls. He hadn't needed to hurry. The Imperial officer was still unconscious. Her short red hair framed her face like a halo. He checked her pulse. Regular and strong, and her breathing indicated she would be out for some time.

He unfastened the heavy gauntlets and clipped them to his belt, then extracted two equipment loops from the armor's regular supply pouch. The loops bound the woman's hands and feet tightly. For the moment, he left her laid out in the passage.

Luren had removed her own suit and knelt only a few meters away, easing the limp Kordel out of his suit. Jimjoy stepped around them both as he walked back to the emergency lock, where he checked the manual seals to ensure no unnoticed visitors would repeat his own entry.

Since the manual seals prevent easy exit, as well as easy entry, their use in space was generally forbidden by Imperial regulations.

Jimjoy rubbed his neck, then began to strip off his own armor, racking each piece into one of the recessed lockers by the main ship lock after he removed it.

He looked at Luren, who was still preoccupied with Kordel.

"Once you have him safely strapped in, would you please stow your suits into one of the empty lockers?"

She nodded, but did not look up.

Jimjoy again stepped around and over the pair, awkwardly, as he headed toward the control room. Before entering, he scooped up the slender officer and strapped her unstirring form onto the narrow couch behind the copilot's station. He thought about a blindfold, but decided it was irrelevant. She had seen his face, and besides, stealing a courier without murdering someone else was the least of his sins to date.

As he straightened, he watched Luren stuff an all-purpose space suit into the locker, close the cover, and sigh. She took another deep breath and headed toward him, looking over at the strapped-down woman.

"Now what?"

"She's only unconscious."

"Now you're just collecting them?"

"Got any better ideas?"

She shook her head tiredly, standing there as if waiting for him to move. He did, slipping into the pilot's couch. He scanned the board, then began to touch the controls necessary to bring the courier out of stand-down into full operational status.

He touched the audio, realized he was holding his breath as he did so. He forced himself to exhale, and to take a deep breath.

"Red four, beta secondary. Negative on transshipment this time. Negative on fatalities."

"Beta secondary, this is Medallion Strike. Interrogative instructions this time . . ."

Jimjoy listened even as his fingers began to key the courier for orbit break, hoping that the telltale emissions from the courier's systems would be overlooked as merely an emergency precaution.

He glanced up at Luren, who had been watching him from the archway between the passageway and the control section. "Strap in."

She started forward.

"Is Kordel strapped in? Look like he'll be all right?"

"Do you care, really?"

He ignored the bitterness. "Care as much as I can afford to. Any more, and I wouldn't be around to do any caring. Might give some thought to that."

"He's asleep. Whether he'll be all right or stay in that trance state, I couldn't tell you."

"Your straps secure?" he questioned, as the last of the pre-break telltales flashed green.

"Just about."

He nodded and touched the screen controls.

"Power . . . green . . .

". . . locks . . . secure . . ."

Forcing himself to remain deliberate, he went through the entire checklist, until the console screen blinked and scripted the go-ahead.

"Ship is ready for break. Insert course cube."

Jimjoy did not have a course tape for Accord, nor would he have used one had he owned it. Instead he tapped in the instructions.

"Negative cube. Unprogrammed destination."

"Insert course and acceleration requirements."

He nodded at Luren. "You ready?"

She nodded.

Jimjoy tapped in the course line—a straight shot to the nearest point in the system that would allow a jump. At maximum acceleration. As he touched the last digit and keyed the override, he automatically straightened in the acceleration couch.

The nearly instant pressure gradually pushed him back into the cushions that felt less and less yielding.

"Hades . . ." The remainder of Luren's exclamation was lost as she worked just to breathe.

"Beta control . . . beta secondary . . . this is Medallion Strike. Interrogative on outbounds. Interrogative on departures."

Jimjoy cursed silently. Medallion Strike had to be the battle cruiser, and whoever the watch officer was, he was sharper than Jimjoy would have preferred.

"Beta control." Jimjoy forced the words out distinctly, in an effort to confuse the issue. "Dauntless two, departing as precleared. Mission omega orange four. Mission omega orange four. Sector radian blue. Sector radian blue."

"Dauntless two, this is Medallion Strike. Interrogative omega authorization. Interrogative omega authorization."

The Special Operative would have awarded the watch officer a medal, had he been on the other side. With all the dullards in the Impie fleet, he had to have blasted past one of the few bright stars.

"Medallion Strike, two here. Authorization filed with beta control. Authorization filed with beta control."

Jimjoy checked the acceleration and the separation from the cruiser. He needed more time. The courier, despite its headlong acceleration and increasing velocity, was still well within range of the cruiser's long-range torps.

"Dauntless two, this is Medallion Strike. Interrogative omega authorization. Interrogative authorization. Medallion Strike stands Radian Crown. I say again Radian Crown."

Worse luck. Not only was the cruiser alert, but the ship was carrying the Imperial sector command.

"Medallion Strike, Dauntless two. Request authorization for interrogatory. Omega mission tee plus cleared."

Jimjoy grinned as he keyed off the transmission.

Even with instantaneous recall, it would take a few instants more for them to react to his perfectly legitimate, if foolhardy, inquiry. Had he been captaining an actual omega rush mission, he would have been well within his rights to ask for disclosure authorization. The sector Commander might have seen that he never again saw an assignment closer to Terra than the Far Rim, but he could have requested it.

Jimjoy rechecked the separation. Then he began rekeying the jump parameters. Next he checked the perceived special density, on the off chance that the courier might be able to try an early jump.

The density was higher than average for his solar separation. Within the confines of the acceleration shell, he frowned, waiting for the authorization he knew the cruiser would have back at him.

"Dauntless two. Medallion Strike vice Radian Crown. Authorization follows. Authorization follows. Delta victor slash five four theta. Delta victor slash five four theta. Request immediate your omega authorization. Immediate your omega authorization."

The Special Operative slowly sucked in air, thinking as he did. Finally he keyed the transmitter.

"Medallion Strike vice Radian Crown, this is Dauntless two. Omega authorization filed with beta control. Filed beta control. Omega authorization as filed follows." Jimjoy swallowed as he began to repeat the code, based on what he remembered from a far earlier authorization and updated from his more recent experiences.

"Gamma slash seven four slash four seven omega theta. I say again. Gamma slash seven four slash four seven omega theta."

Inputting the authentications would take only seconds, but it might take up to several minutes before the recheck was complete. Jimjoy hoped so, yet there was little he could do but coax the maximum sustained speed from the courier's drive and hope that the bogus authentication he had given had retained some semblance of accuracy.

He scanned the board before him, ignoring the anxious woman pressed into the copilot's shell. From his own instruments, Jimjoy could see that the cruiser had still not broken orbit. Nor were there any EDI traces for any of the smaller ships near the orbit control station. But the audio was suspiciously quiet.

With a second thought, he boosted the gain on the rear detectors, risking a burnout in seeking such sensitivity.

"Hades!"

He transferred all power from habitability and services into the drive, struggling to maintain consciousness against the immediate eight-plus gees that pressed him deeper into the couch, so deep that he thought he could feel every wrinkle in the couch liner scoring him like a knife.

HHHHSTTTTT!!!

The board went blank with the overload, but the immense pressure across his chest reassuringly continued.

Hssssssttt!

Jimjoy could only see the narrowest section of the board before him and barely feel the fingertip controls. But he waited until the blackness threatened to engulf him before he disengaged the bypass.

"Uhhhhhh . . ."

He realized that the groaning sound belonged to him and closed his mouth.

The screens swam back into sight from the swirling blackness, and he wondered why it was so difficult to move.

"Hades . . ." He fumbled for the fingertip controls, realizing that the

bypass disengagement had only returned the acceleration to the preprogrammed three-gee level. The gravity dropped to a fractional gee
level. He hoped enough power remained for jump and reentry.

He swallowed, that simple act made more difficult by the dryness
of his throat and the soreness of his entire body. The bruises he would
have . . .

1734. He had been out for only a few minutes. His fingers slowly
began to check the ship's systems and reserves. Power was down to less
than forty percent—adequate if he didn't have to evade anyone on the
other end. None of the rear screens functioned, but the system checkouts
indicated that the problem was in the sensors and receptors. He nodded
minimally, remembering that he had never lowered the gain.

Moving his head slowly to the side, he looked at the still-limp figure
in the copilot's shell.

Luren was breathing.

He strained to look behind him, but he could not see without unstrapping. He hoped the courier pilot was doing as well as Luren.

After completing the damage control scan, he waited for the results
to script out.

Jimjoy saw the figures and permitted himself the luxury of a tight
smile.

Dauntless two, *His Imperial Majesty's Ship Darmetier*, was functional,
if overstressed, and on course to the nearest jump point in the New
Kansaw system.

He checked the EDI readouts, since the rear screens were inoperative,
and nodded at the EDI traces. Rather than send the battle cruiser after
the torps, the Commander, or the bright watch officer, had dispatched
the other courier, either to attempt to track or, more likely, to report
the piracy of the *Darmetier* to Headquarters.

Definitely no turning back, reflected Jimjoy. The remaining question
was whether he could persuade Accord, or the Institute, not to turn
him over to the Empire.

The stakes were getting high enough that the Empire just might
offer enough for one renegade to make it worthwhile for even the most
discontented colonial government.

On the other hand, while the Impies might suspect the catastrophes
had been caused by one Jimjoy Wright, there was little hard proof,
especially since New Kansaw Base no longer existed—no fingerprints,
no records.

Jimjoy pushed away those thoughts and returned his attention to the controls. One thing at a time.

Jump was approaching, and with the power drains he had placed on the courier, he needed a good jump. A very good jump.

Luren groaned, but Jimjoy did not look over at her. In less than fifteen standard minutes, he would have plenty of time, since jumps were not traceable, except with far more sophisticated equipment than possessed by the distant *Pike*.

He sighed and began to make the necessary entries and calculations.

XLVII

CLING . . . CLING . . . CLING.

At the first chime of the red-framed screen at the corner of the heavy wooden desk, the Admiral did not even look away from his own work on the main screen. With the second, he frowned. With the third, he put his own calculations on hold and reached for the emergency screen.

"Admiral, sir," stammered the Headquarters commlink watch officer. "Sorry to bother you, but Radian Crown has reported a major uprising on New Kansaw . . ."

The Admiral pursed his lips but said nothing, nodding his head for the woman to continue.

"Do you want the detailed status report or the executive summary, sir?"

"Both," replied the senior officer. "Both, if you will. Feed them right through."

"Yes, Admiral. Immediately, sir."

"That will be all, Captain Harfoos."

"Yes, sir."

The red-framed screen blanked momentarily, then displayed a title— *Executive Summary—New Kansaw Anomaly.*

Cling.

The Admiral tapped the controls on his own screen, shunting his work into storage and calling up the reports from the emergency communications system. The *Executive Summary* appeared on the screen before him, and the smaller emergency screen again blanked, and stayed blank.

The Admiral began to read, unconsciously rubbing his forehead as he finished the first page of the summary.

New Kansaw—either the rebels had proved too difficult for the talents of that Major Wright . . . or, even worse, he and Commander Hersnik had vastly underestimated Wright, and Wright had thrown in with the rebels.

The Admiral frowned as he began the second page of the summary. At the end of the three pages, he called up the body of the report.

By the time he had finished the complete report, he had the beginnings of a headache. He immediately routed a copy of the summary to Hersnik, mostly to give the Commander enough information to make the Admiral's next step a bit easier.

Rubbing his forehead again, he tilted his head sideways, then accessed the report again, searching for one section.

He nodded thoughtfully as he reread the part about the destruction of New Kansaw Main Base. That fit, and it had to be Wright, although he doubted that the Service would ever be able to prove the man had actually invoked the Masada safeguards. Because the issue was clearly under seal, he would not have to go public. But action was necessary, beyond a doubt.

How Wright had discovered the Masada safeguards was another question that would also never be known.

The Admiral sighed as he checked another section for the second time, then reread the conclusion, which lingered on the screen a moment before the Admiral relinquished it to permanent storage.

He shook his head slowly at the language.

"With the limited energy reserves on the *Darmetier* and the lack of atmospheric landing capabilities, the Service anticipates recovery of the vessel in the near future."

XLVIII

JIMJOY'S FOREHEAD WAS still damp from the fresher, as was his hair. But at least he was clean, and shaved, for the first time in days.

The flight suit he wore had belonged to one of the crew members who had presumably been in New Kansaw orbit control at the time Jimjoy had appropriated the *Darmetier*. The suit's original owner was slightly shorter than Jimjoy, but a shade bulkier, and the difference in fit was not noticeable except that the flight suit's legs only reached down past the tops of his boots.

He glanced over at the control board, then at the woman in the copilot's seat, whose curly brown hair was already dry. Jimjoy had suggested that she use the facilities first once they had emerged from the jump, during the time when he was setting up the inbound course.

"You actually look presentable, Major."

"Jimjoy. Service wouldn't have me back except for an execution."

"Don't you deserve it?"

"Hades . . . but . . . probably so, at least technically."

"Technically? How about ethically?"

Jimjoy eased himself back into the control couch. "Ethically? Not sure about that." He did not say more, but the question sounded more like something a certain Ecolitan Andruz might have asked. Still might ask, if he ever got back to Accord. And he really didn't have an answer that would satisfy Luren or Thelina. Especially Thelina.

He sighed, and checked the board. He still had to get back to Accord. The brief recharge from the cleanliness and warmth imparted by the fresher was already beginning to fade, and he could feel the weight of the days of fatigue building behind his personal controls.

For another few hours, perhaps, he would be able to override it. Postpone payment for a time, but only for a time. His eyes were bloodshot and felt like they had been sand-blasted. His legs felt like he wore twenty-kilo boots.

Still, once he got to Accord and locked in—

He frowned, wanting to pound his forehead.

"Hades!" He'd forgotten the simplest thing, the last hurdle. And the most troublesome.

"Now what—?" asked the rebel in the copilot's seat tiredly. "Another battle? Another set of impartial killings?"

Jimjoy ignored her. His problem was simple. Simple and impossible. So simple he had totally ignored the obvious.

His fingers touched the controls, and he studied the display screen before him. Just under three standard hours until he was within the defense perimeter of Accord. Just under four hours of power left in the *Darmetier*.

The problem was that Accord orbit control was Imperial territory.

Stupid of him . . . subconsciously believing that once he got to Accord his problems would be over. And the *Darmetier* was a spacecraft only, with no atmospheric capability.

He sighed.

"What's the problem?" Luren asked tiredly.

"How to get through Accord orbit control. It's an Imperial station."

"Walk through. No one could have traveled any faster than we have. How would they know?"

"Not exactly the problem. This is an Imperial ship. I have no Imperial I.D. except my own, and that isn't usable. You and Kordel have none. Even if we could fake our way through and onto a down shuttle, it wouldn't take much to trace our steps. Then the Accord locals would have to return us."

"I wish you'd thought of this earlier, Mr. Kill-them-all-and-think-later. Is there any place else we can go?"

"With four hours of power left?"

Still, Jimjoy called up the navigational display and studied the representation of the system.

Suddenly he grinned. Maybe . . . just maybe . . . he could work it out.

"What's so funny?" snapped Luren. Her red-rimmed eyes peered out from the dark circles in her face.

"Nothing."

"Nothing! You don't tell us anything. You have a drugged Imperial Lieutenant tied up, and Kordel's virtually catatonic, and you're laughing."

"You're also alive," snapped the pilot.

Luren sighed and closed her mouth.

Jimjoy thought of another possible problem with his tentative solution, and his hands and fingers moved more quickly. He would have to plot a nearly powerless approach to avoid a telltale EDI track. Finally he had the figures on the screen.

"Strap in."

"Again?"

"Just for a minute or two. We're headed somewhere safer," he said, not adding the words, "I hope."

As the acceleration pressed him into the shell, he continued to watch as the course change took effect. Then he cut the power down to the absolute minimum for habitability. Any Imperial detectors might have detected the burst of energy, but not the directional change toward the fourth planet's second moon, the one with the Ecolitan research station.

The next problem would be deceleration behind the planet to mask the radiation from the Accord orbit control detectors. And that would make the approach tricky, as well as hard on both of them, since he could not afford to make gradual changes. A gradual powered approach would hand the Impies a road map.

His initial power surges could have been a ship outjumping or merely passing through, unlikely as it might seem . . . but only so long as there were no energy tracks traced in-system.

He leaned back in the couch and watched the screens.

"Now what?"

"We wait."

"Until when?"

"Until we get there . . ."

Luren gave him a disgusted look. "Do you mind if I check Kordel?"

"Not at all. At least an hour before anything else happens."

As Luren fumbled with the straps, he wondered how he would explain it all to the Ecolitans, or to Thelina, assuming he ever managed to see her again. He was assuming there were no Imperial ships in the vicinity of Permana, the fourth planet. If there were, they were all dead. He shrugged and leaned back in the couch.

". . . I said, he's fine . . ."

". . . un . . . what?" Jimjoy jerked himself awake, realizing he had not remembered dozing off. He lurched to check the time—less than an hour had passed.

"Are you all right?"

"Fine," he mumbled. "Under the circumstances." He rubbed his neck to ease the stiffness and to lessen the pounding in his temples.

Then his hands reached for the navigational display controls. He began to replot the *Darmetier*'s position. Surprisingly, the courier was within the envelope he had earlier plotted.

The next step was to program the ship's tight-beam burst sender. With the correct focus and reduced power, he should be able to contact the Ecolitan Base without alerting anyone else.

He checked the ship's position again. Still too early for comm contact.

"Would you stop tapping your fingers, Major?"

"Not Major, just Jimjoy."

"Fine, Mr. Just-Jimjoy. Would you stop tapping your fingers? It's bad enough sitting here watching you fidget, without listening as well."

"Sorry."

"No, you're not, but thanks, anyway."

Jimjoy studied the nav screen again.

"You're tapping your fingers again . . ."

He sighed.

"What are you waiting for?"

"For us to get close enough to get rescued."

"Rescued? I thought we had plenty of power."

"Not that much, not now. And we need to be rescued in order to escape the Impies."

Luren looked away. Jimjoy did not volunteer more, instead checked both the screens and his calculations again.

The broadband audio frequencies remained in a hissing near silence.

Finally, Jimjoy cleared his throat, checked the power outputs, and triggered the tight-beam sender. "Nader Base, Nader Base . . . blue Mayday . . . blue . . . Sendak . . . failure . . . estimate . . . arrival . . . estimate . . ."

"Mayday? Is it that serious?"

"Only if we don't get rescued."

"Aren't you ever truthful?"

"I am this time. We need to be rescued."

Luren shook her head again, refusing to meet his eyes.

Jimjoy watched as her eyes rested on the display screens, watched as she tried to make sense of the information remaining on the screen.

"Unidentified ship, unidentified ship, this is Nader Base, Nader Base. Request your status and estimated arrival. Request your status and estimated arrival." The woman's voice was no-nonsense, but the phrasing was decidedly non-Imperial.

Jimjoy ignored the transmission. Instead, he continued to monitor the courier's instruments, particularly the EDI.

"Why aren't you answering?"

"Because they expect me to. Because any Impie on a fishing expedition would respond immediately, and because any ship with the power level I just used wouldn't be able to hear the Nader transmission."

Jimjoy checked the closure rate and the angle between Permana and Accord. He had another five minutes before he could pour on the remaining power to kill their inbound vector.

"Unidentified ship, this is Nader Base. Request your status and estimated arrival time. Status and estimated arrival time."

Again Jimjoy ignored the transmission, continuing to monitor the *Darmetier*'s screens and to watch Luren squirm uneasily in the copilot's seat.

After a time, he touched the comm controls.

"Nader Base . . . blue . . . blue Mayday . . . arm . . . Sendak . . . arrival in one . . . say again . . . one . . ."

"You don't let anyone know the whole truth, do you?"

Jimjoy looked over at the young woman, about to answer. Then he closed his mouth.

"You don't lie, either, exactly. You never let anyone know everything if you can help it."

"You may be right." He did not look at her, but at the navigational plot, which showed the *Darmetier* had finally coasted in behind the bulk of Permana. "Strap in again."

Luren said nothing, but he could hear the rustle of the harness and the shifting of weight.

"You ready?"

"I'm fine, Major."

Jimjoy did not argue about the title, but touched the stud to start the preprogrammed decel. The pressure pushed him into his seat, and the blackness narrowed his vision to a tunnel that kept trying to close in on him. He fought it until the pressure eased.

Cling.

He shook his head to concentrate, and was rewarded with an increasing throbbing in his temples as he studied the board, noting the post-jump entrance of another ship in the Accord system. He began to calculate its inbound path against the standard parameters.

The throbbing eased fractionally as he realized the inbound ship was Accordan and on course for Accord proper.

"Unidentified ship. Unidentified ship. This is Nader Base. This is Nader Base. Standing by for your arrival. Do you need medical assistance? Do you need medical assistance?"

Jimjoy nodded in response to the inquiry, but made no move to respond.

He continued to check the plot screen, trying to calculate whether he needed to step up the decel before the ship cleared the section of transit blocking a direct screen from Accord. Finally he stabbed the override and was jolted back farther into the shell.

". . . uuufffff . . ." Luren protested.

He eased up on the extra decel and checked the parameters for near orbit around the moon. Given the six-hundred-kay diameter of Thalos, the orbit would have to be close indeed.

As he touched the controls again, the *Darmetier* shivered, once . . . twice . . .

"Unidentified ship, unidentified ship—"

"Nader Base, Nader . . . tier . . . medical . . . say again . . . med . . . stance . . . arrival ten . . ."

"This is Nader Base. Nader Base. Say again. Say again."

Jimjoy ignored the request. The base had already picked up the burst of power from the *Darmetier*, which would pinpoint the ship's location.

He was gambling that the Ecolitans would notify the Institute by their own courier, but not the Imperial orbit control station off Accord. From what he had seen on his guided tours of Accord, the Ecolitans, even plain local citizens, tried to avoid letting the Empire know anything.

With a mirthless smile, he monitored the last stages of his near powerless approach to the airless moon that orbited Permana, the fourth planet of the Accord system, and home to an Ecolitan mining-and-research operation.

"Ohhhh . . ." The gasp came from Luren as he called up the front visual. Thalos filled nearly a quarter of the main screen.

As she took in the view, Jimjoy scanned the board. The courier's EDI detection system was picking up energy sources—both in space and on the satellite itself. Those from the satellite were barely detectable, something he might have expected, given the Ecolitans' consciousness of energy usage.

He frowned as he studied the two point sources in space, in orbit around Thalos, each roughly one-third of an orbit from the other, indicating the possibility of a third identical source.

Needleboats! With their only use that of space-to-space combat, the majority of Imperial needleboats were in storage. Those on his screens appeared marginally different. Why would the Accordans be using needleboats? And where had they obtained them?

Pushing those questions away, he focused on the delicate last stages of his manual approach, trying to use the last of his power to establish a generally stable orbit and hoping that the Ecolitans would ask questions first.

The sweat beaded up on his forehead. He wiped it clean with his forearm, not taking his eyes off the screens and the readouts before him.

"Gentle . . . now . . . power . . ." The words slipped from his lips as he tried to fuse with the board, fingers adjusting, correcting, using the minimal power available, as if each erg were the last the courier possessed. He had already dropped all the screens and cut off the internal grav field.

"There!" He sat back, bouncing in his straps in the null gee, then wiped his forehead and leaned forward to reestablish a minimal gee in the courier for as long as the energy lasted. He took a deep breath and relaxed. But only for an instant.

"All right. Let's suit up."

"Suit up?"

"Right. We'll put Kordel and the Lieutenant into the bubble sled." He looked at her. "Before very long, someone will be here, and we'll need to be ready. They certainly aren't about to let an Imperial ship close to their base, even if the *Darmetier* were able to land."

"*Darmetier?*"

"Name of the courier." He was in his suit, except for the helmet, before she was halfway suited. While she finished, he located the bubble sled in one of the lockers next to the lock.

Then he checked Kordel. The man lay on the bunk, still staring blankly at the overhead, still wearing the harness straps. From there Jimjoy went back to the control area, where the Imperial Lieutenant was beginning to toss, as if the stun charges were wearing off. The last thing the woman's nervous system needed was another stun or drugs. He sighed and tied a makeshift blindfold over her face. Her hands and feet were still bound.

She might be rather uncomfortable, but for some perverse reason, he didn't want to hurt anyone he didn't have to, no matter what Luren and Thelina thought. Besides, the woman hadn't done anything wrong, except be in the wrong place at the wrong time.

Turning back to the main corridor, he found Luren suited, except for her helmet. "Turn around."

As she did, he checked over the suit connections, and found everything in place.

Clang.

"Our rescuers have arrived."

"Are they our rescuers?"

"Hope so."

He moved to the lock controls, and touched the stud to open the outer door. Through the narrow vision port he watched as two green-suited figures edged in. Both wore holstered hand weapons of an unfamiliar design.

He closed the outer lock and waited for the pressure to equalize, then cracked the inner door.

Despite the protection of her suit, Luren shivered as the cold air poured into the corridor.

Jimjoy said nothing, waiting with his empty hands in full view of the Ecolitans as the pair stepped inside the courier.

The taller one opened his faceplate. "You don't look that disabled."

"Not in the conventional sense," answered Jimjoy. "But I can assure you that both you and I would suffer a great deal if we had been forced to make Accord orbit control."

At the word "suffer," the first Ecolitan shifted weight and put a suit gauntlet on the butt of the holstered hand weapon.

"Refugees, then? You know we'll have to turn you back to the Empire, particularly if you mutinied and took the courier."

"We didn't exactly mutiny, since we weren't the crew. And I think you'll be in deep trouble if you act without contacting the Institute. You might check with an Ecolitan I once knew there. Andruz . . . Thelina Andruz."

"Who are you?"

Jimjoy grinned raggedly, belatedly recalling that he had told the man in the green suit nothing. "Sorry about that. Been a long time without much rest. My name is Wright. Jimjoy Wright. Guess you'd have to call me either a defector or a traitor, depending on your viewpoint."

He gestured toward Luren. "Can't the inquisition wait? Her . . . husband is lashed in the crewroom with deep-space shock trauma, and there's a rather angry Imperial Lieutenant trussed up and about ready to wake up in the control area. Luren here hasn't had much more than a few hours' sleep in the past four days."

"You still haven't explained why we shouldn't summon the Imperial Service." The Ecolitan's voice was cold and tired.

His silent companion had said nothing.

"Oh, that . . . it's really rather simple. You could execute me yourself—"

"No . . ." The involuntary cry came from Luren, who immediately closed her mouth.

"—but you might have a rather difficult time explaining why an Imperial courier with a defecting Major from the Special Operative section of Imperial Intelligence showed up near Accord with a commandeered courier. Even if you turn all three of us over. And you might have an even harder time with the Institute if you got rid of me without at least consulting with them. And last, if you insist on getting rid of us, how are you any better than the Impies?"

Jimjoy shrugged, then added, "And by the way, Luren and Kordel are the last survivors of the Imperial massacre on New Kansaw. You might find what they have to say about Imperial tactics and kindliness interesting."

Cling.

Jimjoy recognized the sound.

"Hold on. The grav's going, and we'll be down to emergency lights and no ventilation."

"Going?" asked the Ecolitan.

"We didn't exactly have a lot of power to play with, friend. Less than I thought . . ."

As the courier lapsed into weightlessness, the onetime Imperial Intelligence officer squinted, tried to hold back the blackness as the corridor swirled around him. Tried to hold on, to argue for Luren and Kordel, for himself, and for Accord. And failed.

The blackness of deep space swallowed his awareness.

XLIX

"SIT DOWN, COMMANDER." The Intelligence Service Commander looked at the Admiral. A hint of a faint and sad smile flickered around the corner of his lips. He inclined his head, as if to ask where.

"Over there," added the Admiral, jabbing a long finger at the single straight-backed chair.

The Commander sat, gingerly, as if the chair represented a trap into which he was being forced to place himself.

"Commander Allard V. Hersnik, under the regulations of the Service, I regretfully must inform you that this gathering represents the initial Board of Inquiry to investigate your handling and conduct of the events leading to the destruction of the Service Base at New Kansaw, with the loss of life of more than twelve thousand souls. Indirectly, your actions may have contributed to the extensive damage suffered by the New Kansaw orbit control facility, and to the loss of *His Imperial Majesty's Ship Darmetier.*

"All proceedings here will be recorded on tamperproof vitraspool, but will remain under seal, due to the extremely sensitive nature of the material to be discussed. The findings of this Board will constitute a recommendation to the Admiral of the Fleets for disposition of the case.

"Anything you say will be retained for review by the Admiral. Likewise, while in any future review proceeding, should there be one, you may elaborate upon any testimony you provide today, you may not introduce new evidence unless you can prove it was not known to you today."

The Admiral paused before continuing. "Are these conditions understood?"

The Commander in the straight-backed chair swallowed. "Yes, Admiral. Perfectly clear."

"Then let us begin." The Admiral nodded at the Legal Services Commander to his left. "Commander Legirot will serve as your counsel as well as satisfy the requirement that at least one member of the proceedings be of equivalent rank to the Service member under inquiry."

The Vice Admiral to the Admiral's right straightened in his seat.

"Vice Admiral M'tabuwe will serve as the Presiding Officer, and I will act as Inquestor."

Commander Hersnik's eyes ran from the dark-skinned Vice Admiral, clearly just promoted and quite junior to the Inquestor, to the Legal Services Commander and back to the silver-blond Admiral with the light and penetrating voice.

"May we hear the nature of the charges?" asked Commander Legirot, his deep bass voice drawing out each word.

"The charges are as follows:

"First, failing to recognize and report unauthorized actions in a subordinate officer under the inquiree's command—a violation of Code Section 4004(b).

"Second, by not reporting such actions, becoming an accessory after the fact in a criminal action, that action being the murder of a Service officer in the performance of his duty—a violation of Code Section 5020(a).

"Third, by returning said subordinate officer to a field assignment without proper debriefings, medical examinations, and loyalty evaluations, allowing an Imperial command to be hazarded and lost—a violation of Code Section 6001.

"Fourth, ordering the elimination of an Imperial officer under emergency provisions of the Anti-Espionage Act without receiving clearance from a Board of Inquiry or an appropriate Flag grade officer—a violation of Code Section 6003 and Code Section 2012(c).

"Fifth, failure to report gross violations of security at an Alpha class installation, amounting to dereliction of duty—a violation of Code Section 3007.

"And sixth, falsification of official records—a violation of Code Sections 6006(b) and 6006(c)."

The Commander in the uncomfortable chair smiled bleakly, looking at his counsel, who did not return the smile.

The Admiral turned to the Vice Admiral. "With your permission, Mr. Presiding Officer, the Inquestor would request leave to present the facts at hand."

"You may begin, Mr. Inquestor."

Commander Hersnik slowly began to envy those who had been at the New Kansaw Base. Most hadn't known what had happened to them.

L

JIMJOY STRETCHED OUT on the narrow bunk, glancing at the locked door, not bothering to stand. The door had been locked when he had awakened two days earlier, after his collapse in the courier.

At regular intervals a tray of food was slipped inside. Irregularly, the trays were removed.

The former Special Operative smiled, almost a real smile, as he waited. While he could not be certain, he doubted that the Ecolitans would turn him over to the Imperial Intelligence Service. Not after two days. They might dispose of him themselves. That was not out of the question. But if that had been their intention, they could have done so without letting him regain consciousness . . . unless they wanted to debrief him. That certainly would have been the Imperial way.

His eyes roved over the room. Standard asteroid station quarters, except for the small adjoining room with the fresher and toilet facilities. The hard rock walls and the minute fluctuations in gravity told him he was still on Thalos, awaiting who knew what.

He stretched again. This time he swung off the narrow bunk and stood, debating whether to run through his exercises again, doing his best to stay in shape for whatever might come.

With a flicker, his eyes ran toward the locked door and back to the foot of the bunk. Had he been so determined, he could have left the makeshift cell at almost any time, but he still would have been on Thalos. On Thalos with some rather worried and scared Ecolitans, and no one was more aware than Jimjoy that he now needed all the support, or lack of opposition, possible.

Someone was at the other side of the door, but he waited, forcing himself not even to look in that direction, not until there was a noise from the old-fashioned door itself.

Click.

Turning, he watched as the door opened and a silver-haired woman stepped inside. He suppressed the smile he felt. "Good day, Ecolitan Andruz."

"Good day, Major. I see you're still presenting problems." Thelina's voice carried a mixture of resignation and amusement.

"Forget the 'Major.' "

"I take it you are not interested in remaining on active Imperial service." Her voice was still dry.

He looked at her, wondering how he ever could have thought the woman impersonal, not with the piercing green eyes and expressive voice. "I have no doubt that the Empire would be most anxious that I do so. Not exactly eager to pay that price."

"I can guess why."

Before she could continue, he interrupted. "Been patient and waited, but isn't there somewhere else we could talk?"

"You're still the restless type." She paused. "You act as if it were your choice to stay here."

"Some ways it was. Not much doubt that I could have gotten out of here without any trouble at all—or not much. Probably could have taken over a good section of the base." He shrugged. "But that would have gotten everyone upset and given the local commander the perfect excuse to dispose of me. They weren't exactly thrilled with my arrival anyway."

A short laugh, half chuckled, came from Thelina. "You think you know us that well?"

"Don't know you at all. Know something about people." He smiled slowly. "Now . . . about talking somewhere else?"

"I don't see why not. Besides, I'm not about to stand and talk while you sit."

Jimjoy refrained from noting that the narrow bed was still wide enough for two.

She turned and walked back through the door she had never closed, speaking to someone outside. "Major Wright and I will be going to the small conference room."

Jimjoy moved through the doorway cautiously, nodding quietly to the pair of impromptu guards standing with the strange hand weapons. Both young, the man and woman inspected him closely, as he did them.

Although they had the look of solid training, the edge of experience was missing.

Thelina watched the proceedings, then gestured. "Follow me."

Once they were a good twenty meters down the wide corridor that had been drilled from the solid rock, she asked quietly, "And do you still believe you could have escaped?"

Jimjoy nodded. "But I'm glad I didn't try."

"So am I."

Another few meters and they stepped into a small circular room with a stone table sculpted out of the original rock. Around the circular and polished surface of dark gray were six functional wooden chairs, hand-carved, with the type of design that Jimjoy had come to regard as Ecolitan.

"Take any one you please."

Jimjoy plopped into a chair on the far side, from where he could watch both Thelina and the doorway. She made no move to close the door.

He grinned as she sat down to the side, taking a chair from where at least her peripheral vision could take in the corridor while she retained some distance from him. She pulled a small tablet from her belt, edged in dark green, as well as a stylus.

"Official record?"

"As official as we need."

"That bad?" His voice was even.

"Depends on what you mean. You left us with a bit of a problem. Two refugees and an Imperial Lieutenant ready to kill, given half a chance. Then you pass out." She shook her head.

He started to retort, then held his tongue and asked another question. "Can you help Kordel? Is Luren all right?"

"That's an interesting order of questions, Major. Especially given your background." Thelina shifted her weight in the chair, jotted something on the pad, and then pushed a strand of silver hair back over her right ear. "Space trauma can be cured. It will take time, but the Institute doesn't see any real problem there.

"The woman still doesn't know what to make of you. She insists that you ran the courier at multiple gees manually and that you didn't sleep for nearly one hundred hours."

"I had a few catnaps."

"For a hundred hours?"

"Closer to eighty."

"But you ran that courier single-handedly and manually under three-to-five gee loads?"

"Not exactly. First, there was the cargo flitter, and that was atmospheric. Then there was the shuttle, and that was a standard manual emergency lift. And then there was the courier. The courier was about three-quarters of the time involved."

"I see. But you did them all manually, and finished up in high gee with the courier?"

Jimjoy nodded.

Thelina made more notes. "Why?"

"To escape." He was afraid she didn't understand, that she thought he'd done it all because he was paranoid or macho-psycho, or both. "Look. Imperial ships are idiot-proof. Can't drop the shields and screens except on manual control. Without diverting power from screens and shields, you can't build in enough acceleration and variation from predicted course patterns to escape torps and other couriers or scouts."

Thelina continued to shake her head. "So you ran on manual for what . . . sixty hours?"

"No. Hardly. I told you. First I had to get from the rebel base to the Imperial Base. Then I had to divert their shuttle. Boosted nearly through the center of orbit control while we used suits to take the shuttle. Had to drag Kordel through open space without brace or brief. That's where he went catatonic."

Jimjoy took a breath before continuing. "After that I used a few techniques I know to get into the *Darmetier* through the emergency lock. From there it was maybe ten hours through the jumps till breakout. After we started in-system here I took a few catnaps. I did a minimum-power approach until I was shielded from Accord orbit control, then did a real abrupt decel. EDI probably registered, and might have caused them to ask a question or two, but I doubt it would have been a traceable course line."

"So she was right . . ." mused Thelina.

"Who? What? Was it traceable?"

"No, you were right. The Impies screamed about our covert activities, but didn't connect you to that EDI blast." Thelina looked into the distance that was not there in the small conference room.

"Who was right?"

"Oh, that woman. Luren. I've already talked to her. She's afraid of you and probably worships the ground she insists your feet never touch."

"For what?" Jimjoy shifted his weight. For some reason, the chair wasn't totally comfortable. "Just did what had to be done."

"I know. I know. That's why you're a problem." The Ecolitan looked at Jimjoy, and her voice was even as she asked, "Is there anything else we should know?"

"Probably a lot. Don't know what you know. Someone never wanted me to leave New Kansaw. Empire is scared to death of Accord. Couldn't prove it, but it's there. Guess is that they can't understand you. As for me . . ." Jimjoy shrugged.

"What is that supposed to mean? That we ought to take you in, like every other lost ecological nut or misfit?"

Jimjoy flushed slowly, but said nothing as he considered what the silver-haired Ecolitan had said.

After a few moments, he commented slowly. "So you're judge and jury, all rolled into one."

"For all practical purposes . . . yes."

Jimjoy continued to think, struggling to put into words what he had felt all along.

Thelina looked at the gray stone wall over his left shoulder.

The pair of de facto guards edged closer and stationed themselves within easy range of the conference table. A single female Ecolitan strode past, apparently oblivious to the drama taking place.

"You know," said Jimjoy, "from your point of view, it really might be best to dispose of me. Especially if you intend to knuckle under to the Empire. You could plant me back in the courier, drive it right into Thalos, and report the tragedy to the Empire. They wouldn't believe it, of course. But they'd accept it, and they'd believe that you were at least as cold-blooded as they were, and they'd wonder what you'd gotten from me before disposing of me.

"And you could take Kordel and Luren. Intelligence would figure they were deep plants they couldn't identify. But the Imperial Lieutenant would have to go down in flames with me."

"Do you think we could do that?"

"You're all quite capable of that. You, especially." Jimjoy shrugged again. "Besides, there's not that much I can do for you. I could destroy the Empire's control over Accord, I think, but it wouldn't be pretty, and the price would be higher than a lot of your idealists would be willing to pay. Loads of innocent people would die, just about everywhere."

He did not look at Thelina, much as he wanted to, but continued to talk to the gray stone walls. "Not much good at talking, but there's a solution to almost any problem. Most technically good solutions never get adopted because of political problems. But everyone calls the objections 'practical.' "

"Political problems?" asked Thelina, as if the question had been dragged from her.

"People refuse to set their priorities. If liberty is the most important principle, then all others should be secondary. If they are not, then, whatever you say, liberty isn't the most important. The others are just as important."

Thelina's mouth dropped open. "You really believe that?"

Jimjoy shrugged his shoulders without directly looking at her. "Try to. Haven't always succeeded."

"You're . . . you're . . . mad . . ."

"Could be. Never said I wasn't. But I try not to fool myself. Like you and your guards there." He gestured toward the pair in the corridor. "Reason why I could escape is simple. If I choose to escape, that becomes the most important item. No hesitations, no worrying. I don't like killing, and I won't if I don't have to. But if it's necessary, I will. Means you don't commit to things wholeheartedly unless they mean a lot. In anything important, you have to make your decisions first. Not as you go along, but first."

"So you think that the end justifies the means? Like every dictator in history?" She pushed back her chair and stood.

"You said that. Not me." Jimjoy stood and stretched, but was careful to circle away from Thelina, staying in full view of the guards. "If you don't decide how to balance the ends and means before you start, you don't have a prayer, not in anything important. You decide your ultimate goal first. Then you adopt a strategy that goes with your principles. Then you plan tactics. If it won't work, you either abandon the goal or decide that it's more important than one of the principles getting in the way.

"In an action profession, you make the hard decisions first, if you want to stay alive. Sometimes you make mistakes, and in the end you're dead. But that's what it takes. And that's why your guards can't hold me if I choose not to be held. They may kill me, but they won't hold me."

Thelina looked down at the table.

"No wonder they want you so badly . . ."

"Have they actually said so?"

"This morning's message-torp runs contained an All Points Bulletin. It had a holo and your description, and said you were the most dangerous fugitive ever."

"I doubt that. They just don't like the idea I might escape their tender mercies. Hurt their egos."

"Major . . . let's cut the rhetoric and self-deprecation. You are a borderline sociopath with more blood on your hands than men and women who still live in infamy. You are damned close to the ultimate weapon. I have to recommend whether we pick up or destroy that weapon. You might represent survival or total destruction of everything we hold dear. And my problem is that I'm not sure whether your survival guarantees our survival or our destruction."

"Both, probably. Any decision you make will probably turn Accord upside down." He tried to keep his voice even, but could not keep the bitterness from it as he continued. "So what's the verdict, judge? String me along until I'm not looking, or use me until the cost gets too high, and then zap me? Or trade me in for credit to buy time?"

"Why did you come to us?" Her voice was flat.

"Not sure. Suppose it was because the Empire is dead. The future's here, so far as I can see. Here, or with Halston or the Fuards. I'm not much for single-sex politics or for tinhorn dictators. That left you." And you, he almost added, but choked back the words.

"For that slender a . . . hope . . . you left that trail of destruction?"

"Hope is all you ever have, Thelina." He turned toward the wall. If they wanted to shoot, they might as well have the opportunity.

The silence drew out as he tried to pick out the veins in the barely smooth rock wall.

"Major . . ."

He turned slowly. "Jimjoy . . . if you please. Never was a very good Major."

Thelina pulled out the chair and eased into it. Her hands were on the table.

"Sit down . . . please."

He sat, quietly, but remained on the edge of the blond wood chair, his forearms resting lightly on the table.

"I am not the final arbiter. I make the recommendations. Usually they are taken." She wiped her forehead with a green square of cloth, which she replaced out of sight. "Let me ask you another question. What could you do for the Institute?"

"Besides the inside information on the Imperial Intelligence Service? Not anything planet-shaking. Could design and run a better training course for any agents you have. Know a bit about small spacecraft and their design and could probably help you improve couriers or scouts for your special needs.

"Don't know anything about ecology, biology, and all your specialties. Know a lot about killing and destruction, and when to use it, and when not to."

"Are you firmly wedded to your present appearance?"

Jimjoy refused to let himself hope. "Sort of like the way I look, but some changes wouldn't bother me. Prefer to keep Jimjoy as a nickname, since I'd find it hard not to answer to it."

"That *might* be possible." She added some notes to the tablet. "How would you handle your disappearance? And what would you do about the *Darmetier*?"

Jimjoy wanted to relax, but waited, still on the edge of the chair. "Wouldn't try to explain anything. I'd crash it somewhere where it would be found. I'd blank the last month or so from the Lieutenant's mind, if you can, and have her turn up in plain sight somewhere. And if I had a convenient body or three, I'd fry them in the wreck."

"Would you keep the ship if you could?"

"No."

"What if we can't, as you put it, mindblank the Lieutenant?"

"Drop her on some outback on a colony planet. That assumes that you haven't let her know where she is. By the time she gets anywhere, everything will be confused enough that it wouldn't matter."

"What about you?"

"All I have to offer is experience. You park me or eliminate me, and you lose it all."

One corner of Thelina's mouth quirked upward. "That was not what I meant. What would you do, given a free choice on Accord?"

"Not much doubt. Work for the Institute, however I could."

"What if the Institute wouldn't take you?"

"Try to find my own school to teach something. Work electronics on the side, I suppose."

Thelina stood. "That's that. You should be hearing shortly."

"Hearing what?"

"When you report to the Institute. What else could we do with you?"

Jimjoy's hands tightened around the edge of the table. He stood slowly, forcing his fingers to release their grip on the stone, transferring the anger and his grip to the back of the chair as he moved behind it.

Thelina looked at his face and took a sudden step backward.

His words came slowly. "Do you always play with people like this?"

"You were a little . . . unusual . . ."

He forced himself to relax, going through the mental patterns to loosen muscles and thoughts, taking one deep breath, then another.

"I see," he said. "I see. I think . . . could be interesting . . ."

"What? The Institute?"

"No . . . the wars . . ." He chuckled, but it was a forced chuckle, although he could feel the tension ebbing.

"What wars?"

Jimjoy took a long look at the silver-haired woman, but refrained from shaking his head. "All of them," he answered. "All of them."

THE ECOLOGIC SECESSION

To Kristen Linnea,
  for her determination,
  her love,
    and her desire to
    do life right.

■

"YOU REALLY THINK he's the answer to all our problems, don't you?" The bronzed woman with the long silver hair stared at the Prime Ecolitan. Her face and figure were youthful under the unadorned forest-green uniform. The intensity of her green eyes and the faintest tracery of fine lines edging from the corners of those eyes contradicted the impression of youth.

"No. I never said that." Sam Hall glanced from the tall woman seated across the wooden desk-table from him. "He has talents and a unique outlook that we need."

"He's a sociopathic killer with a few stray ideals, and he turned to us to save him from his former colleagues."

"Major Wright—"

"Soon to be Ecolitan Professor Whaler, I understand."

"—understands the business of survival. He also has a deeply developed sense of ethics."

"Just about personal survival." The green eyes flicked from the floor to the half-open window. "Sam, I don't understand you. You've devoted your entire life to your ideals and to building the Institute into a force for the good of ecology. We've worked hard to avoid the usual problems of Imperial colonies, to prepare the way for a peaceful transition to independent status. Now . . . along comes Major Wright, the most bloody-handed of Imperial Special Operatives, and you order us to make sure he doesn't get killed on our turf. Given Imperial politics, that's understandable. But then you ordered me to ensure he knew everything about Accord—about the Institute—when that knowledge could bring an Imperial reeducation team down on us faster than a jumpshift. Not only that, but you want him to report that information to the Intelligence Service. So . . . we work with him and get him back where he came from, again possibly revealing capabilities we've spent decades building in secret."

She brushed back a strand of the long silver hair, looking from the darkening western horizon to the Prime. "Then, when he's safely out of our jurisdiction, he destroys half a planet. With most of the human Galaxy looking for him, he comes running, and again you order me to take him in. If the man had learned *anything* from us . . . but he's the same old killer. He's close to the ultimate weapon—that much I admit.

He can probably destroy anything ever conceived of by civilization. We can't hide that kind of weapon."

Whhhsssttt . . . A gust of wind reminded both Ecolitans of the coming rain.

Sam Hall nodded, not agreeing, but acknowledging that he had heard her complaints. "Who will know he's here after he returns from Timor II? Especially after Dr. Hyrsa finishes with him?" The white-haired Prime briefly placed a square-fingered hand on the small stack of papers that threatened to lift from the polished wood.

"Sam, he's so hardheaded that even a complete cosmetic surgery won't hide him for long—not without a complete personality change. And that won't happen. Major Jimjoy Earle Wright has more blood on his hands than half the villains we scare our students with."

The Prime Ecolitan smiled softly, looking out into the late afternoon at the thunderclouds gathering over the hills to the west of the Institute. The line of gray that heralded rain appeared as though it would arrive before the twilight—but not by much. He said nothing, steepling his fingers.

"Sam, won't you at least tell me why?"

The white-haired man straightened in the all-wooden chair, letting his hands rest on the smooth natural wood of the table. "Times have changed. They always do, you know. The Empire's politicians respect only force—force they can see. Force they can measure in their own limited and conventional perceptions. Our biologics mean nothing to them. Does a salamander understand a jaymar's flight or stoop? Only the Imperial Intelligence Service understands the danger we pose, and, for political reasons, they refuse to tell either the High Command or the Senate.

"We lack anyone who can project force so effectively as can Major Wright. Yet that is precisely what we need. Once he establishes that Accord, through the Institute, possesses a credible military force—"

"We don't have any real space force, let alone a credible one," interrupted the woman. Her long bronzed fingers, with their short, square-trimmed nails, whitened as she gripped the arms of the wooden chair where she sat.

"You are forgetting Major Wright's considerable talents, Thelina."

"Talents!" The word burst from the Ecolitan's lips. "You act as though he could build and command a space force single-handedly."

Sam Hall waited, gentle smile unchanged.

"Sam, he's nothing but a hired killer. He'll never be more than that."

"Just like another hired killer would never be more than a cold-blooded Hand of the Mother . . . ?"

Thelina pursed her lips, but the Prime Ecolitan let his words trail off.

Thrummmmmm . . .

The light in the room dimmed as the thunderclouds and rain approached. A gust of wind riffled the handful of papers on the table that served as the Prime's desk. Sam stretched his left hand and gently held them down. "You have taken a rather strong dislike to the man. Do you know why?" His words were gentle, almost abstract.

Thelina shrugged. "Do you want a catalog? He acts as though nothing but death could stop him, and maybe not even that. He murdered more than fifty thousand innocents on Halston. He destroyed an entire Imperial outpost to escape—and then thought that we'd be impressed because he rescued two of the rebels the Empire was trying to kill. He still doesn't seem to understand that Accord is an Imperial colony, and that we have to watch every orbit we break. Worst of all, he takes apparent pride in being a one-man killing machine."

The Prime nodded. "Did you know that he's from White Mountain? Or that he had one of the highest recorded Service entrance-exam scores ever? Or that he's had his calligraphy exhibited? Or that he could have supported himself as a professional musician?"

Thrummmmm . . . thrummmm . . .

Thelina frowned simultaneously with the thunder. "I'm supposed to be impressed?"

Sam sighed softly. "No. I just thought you might consider that there is more to Major Wright than meets the eye."

"There may be, Sam. There may be. He certainly doesn't show it. Or any of those finer qualities. And all your persuasive words aren't likely to change my mind."

The older man laughed. "Words never do. Perhaps his actions will, once he returns."

The younger woman shook her head slowly. "After he fakes his own death to get the Empire off his trail. Will it work?"

"It should. The bodies will show a complete DNA match, and that's what the Special Operatives base death verifications on. The courier is equipped exactly as when he commandeered it. All that should prove his death."

"Until his oh-so-submissive personality reexerts itself and screams to the Galaxy that Major Wright is back in business destroying real estate and killing innocent bystanders."

"Why don't you help the Major change, then, Thelina?"

She shook her head more deliberately. "A man like that?"

"Will you give him a chance?"

"Only because you ask it. Only because of you, Sam, and what I owe you."

Thrummmmmm . . . thrummmmmm . . . whhhsssstttt . . .

The papers began to lift from the table, and Thelina swept out of the chair to close the sliding window to a crack.

For a long moment she looked out through the rain at the Institute, at the low buildings housing the laboratories, the classrooms, and the physical-training facilities. Under the low and grass-covered hills beyond the classrooms and the formal gardens were the underground hangars for the flitters—and for the other equipment the Empire did not know about, equipment no colony was allowed to have. That the Institute had developed and controlled such resources was only a legal technicality that would not have amused the Imperial Senate, much less the Imperial Intelligence Service.

The Prime Ecolitan watched her, a faint smile playing across his lips.

Thrummmmmmm . . . thrummmmmmm . . . The thunder rolled eastward from the mountains, and the rain dropped in sheets onto the thick green turf and the precise formal gardens.

In time, a tall woman walked down an empty corridor, still shaking her head, leaving the lean and tanned Prime looking into the darkness of the storm alone.

█ █

CLING.

"Time to jump. Point five. Time to jump. Point five."

The pilot, wearing unmarked greens, glanced over at the silent figure beside him. The other, a woman wearing the uniform of a lieutenant in the Imperial Space Force, remained facing the screens, saying nothing.

The control room flashed black at the instant of jump, that subjectively infinite blackness that ended so quickly it could not be measured.

Cling.

"Jump complete. Jump complete," the console speakers announced impersonally. "Insert course tape."

The pilot touched the console again. "Manual approach."

"Control returned to pilot."

The pilot began entering figures and inputs. A representational plot appeared in the lower right-hand corner of the main screen.

"Two plus to target. Not bad," the pilot noted to himself.

The figure in the copilot's couch said nothing. The representational screen showed the system entry corridor as clean—the only moving symbol the single red dot of the courier itself. The target—a mineral-poor planet too warm for comfortable human existence, though technically habitable—glimmered a dull silver-blue on the screen.

The remote observation station was the only other red on the screen, a technicality, since the station was in a stand-down condition and would remain so unless triggered by certain activities or by a distress call.

The pilot checked the controls, the readouts, and then locked the control settings. He stood up, wrinkling his nose at the faint remainder of decanting liquor, a lingering acridity mixed with sweetness.

With a brief head-shake, he glanced back at the screens, then headed down the narrow corridor to the crew quarters. He carried the pouch of tools he had retrieved from the small storage space behind the control couch.

Three meters aft of the control room bulkhead, he stopped and slid open a cover set into the side bulkhead, toggling the switch inside. A hatch set into the deck irised open.

After easing himself down the ladder in the low gee of the courier, the pilot began to work.

"Power flow meter . . . check . . .

"Compensator . . ."

Clink . . .

In time he came to a black cube, which he did not touch, but which he carefully checked, noting the model number and the other features. He nodded.

". . . hours since power-up . . ."

Then he shook his head. ". . . stupid . . ." He stood up from his kneeling position in the cramped power room and went back up the ladder to the control room.

The figure in the copilot's seat had not moved. The pilot ignored the still form as he reseated himself to manipulate the ship's data system once again.

"Time to programmed deceleration is point five," announced the console's measured voice.

The pilot looked at the representational screen, then called up the forward navigation screen. His fingers continued to skip across the keyboard. Then he tapped a last key and straightened, stretching in place and unconsciously brushing a short strand of black hair off his forehead.

He glanced at the copilot's seat and shivered, looking away in spite of himself before he stood and walked back down the narrow corridor to reenter the power room.

Once on the deck below, he made several last-minute adjustments before gathering his tools and climbing back up the ladder. Then he triggered the lock switch and resealed the hatch. His steps back to the control room were quick, his motions precise as he replaced the tools in their storage space.

"Point one until programmed deceleration."

With a sigh, he strapped himself back before the controls, not that such a low level of deceleration would affect the interior gravity of the courier. Only a slight *humm* and a barely perceptible jerk marked the beginning of the deceleration. The pilot watched until he was certain that the courier was maintaining the appropriate low-power approach to Timor II.

Then he unstrapped again. His destination was the forward crew stateroom—scarcely more than two bunks and the accompanying lockers. There a still form lay cocooned in each bunk, fully webbed in place. He repressed another shudder and closed the hatch.

Three steps away was the wardroom-common-room-galley, where he opened a package of dried rations and sipped a glass of metallic-tasting water. Methodical mouthful by methodical mouthful, he chewed the rations.

After rinsing the empty glass and replacing it in the rack, he headed forward.

Nothing had changed in the control room except the screen readouts showing the courier's progress and diminishing power reserves. The pilot sat down and waited, half alert, half resting.

"Programmed deceleration ending in point one. Programmed deceleration ending in point one."

The man stretched before calling up more detailed readouts from the courier's data banks. The readouts confirmed the accuracy of his piloting and of the data supplied by the Institute.

Cling.

"Programmed deceleration terminated. In-system closure rate is beyond normal docking parameters," the console announced mindlessly.

"Of course it is," mumbled the pilot. He pulled the estimated approach time from the system. Less than point three. "Anytime now . . . anytime now."

"This is Timor control. This is Timor control. Please declare your status. Please declare your status."

"Timor control, this is Dauntless two. Dauntless two. We have system power failure. System power failure."

"Dauntless two, declare your status. Are you disabled or operational? If possible, state your status in Imperial priority codes . . ."

The pilot waited for the computer-generated message to end.

"Timor control. Code Delta Amber slash Omega Red. Delta Amber slash Omega Red. Ship control number is IC dash one five nine. IC dash one five nine."

"Dauntless two, you are cleared to lock one. Lock one. Lock one is illuminated and marked by rad beacon."

"Stet, Timor control. Approaching lock one this time."

The pilot split the main screen, the left half for visual approach, the right upper quarter for a local representational screen, and the right lower quarter for a system-wide representational view. After that, he began to enter the manual approach profile, continuing to check the representational screens as he did so.

"Dauntless two, approach speed is above recommended closure."

"Stet. Will reduce approach speed."

"Dauntless two, approach speed is above recommended closure."

"Hades . . ." mumbled the pilot, his fingers on the controls. A flare of gold showed on the close-in representational screen as the last of usable power reserves flowed forth.

"Dauntless two, closure is acceptable. Closure is acceptable."

"Many, many thanks, you mindless machine." The pilot did not transmit his words as he continued to make what adjustments he could with the remaining power.

A single line of green flashed on the close-in screen, indicating a tiny vessel departing the station at extraordinary speed—a message torp. He noted the time absently, estimating that he had a minimum of roughly twenty standard hours to complete the conversion and disable certain station functions. Even as he mentally filed the information, his fingers initiated another minor correction.

In one moment of respite, he wiped his damp forehead with the back of his sleeve before the sweat ran into his eyes. Despite the chill of a control room where his breath nearly stood out as condensed vapor, he was hot.

Clunk . . . clung . . . cling . . .

"Locking complete," announced the courier's console. "Receiving aux power from lock."

"Dauntless two, interrogative medical assistance. Interrogative medical assistance."

"Timor control, negative. Negative."

The pilot made an inquiry through the direct data link.

The message screen responded. "Input Imperial power usage code."

The pilot frowned, then shrugged, tapping in an active code, though one which did not match the ship.

"Power transfer beginning," the screen responded.

Nodding, the pilot watched the power reserve indicator as the bar inched upward.

"Power transfer complete. Further transfer would limit station requirements."

The indicator bar rested at sixty percent, more than enough for the next phase of the mission.

The pilot stood, letting the harness retract, massaging the muscles in his temples with the fingers of his left hand, trying to relax. Finally, he retracted the control console into the standby position.

Kneading the tight muscles between his shoulders with his right hand, he walked back down the narrow corridor to the second crew compartment. There a single cocooned figure rested within the crash webbing.

The pilot surveyed the crewroom, not looking at the face of the courier's fourth still form, then bent and released the harness. He took a deep breath, then eased the figure out of the bunk and over his broad left shoulder, straightening as he did so. Wrinkling his nose at the acridness of decanting solution, he cleared his throat once, twice . . .

. . . cccaaaCHEWWW!!! . . . CHEWWWW!!!

He brushed the other bunk with his shoulder before regaining his balance and shifting his footing to free his right arm.

. . . cccaccCCHEEWW . . .

Ready as he was, the second series of sneezes did not unbalance him, but he was forced to wipe his nose on the back of his right sleeve. The soft coarseness of the open-weave green fabric relieved some of the itching.

Despite the courier's low internal gravity, he moved slowly and deliberately back to the control section.

Still avoiding looking at the face of the man who wore an Imperial flight suit and a major's insignia, the pilot strapped him into position.

As he straightened, his eyes instinctively went to the face of the silent form before the controls. The pilot in greens shuddered, in spite of himself, before retrieving his tools and heading back to the lock that would lead him into the observation station. "Jimjoy, old man, looking at your own dead face is enough to unnerve anyone."

Once in the courier's lock, he pulled on the heavy-duty vac suit that did not belong there and attached several tools to the equipment belt. The others went in the suit's thigh pouch. He had left the crew suits in their assigned lockers.

With a last check of the courier's lock, he adjusted the helmet and tapped the plate.

Hbssssttt . . .

As he had suspected, the station pressure was lower than the ship standard. Within the three steps he took into the maintenance lock, his suit was creating a trail of fog before the remaining condensate disappeared.

Two hatches marked the smooth gray metal of the far lock wall. A green light shone above the right-hand one. The left-hand hatch was dark.

He extracted a tool from the belt as he walked toward the left-hand hatch, trying to recall the details of the standard observation/rescue stations.

In less time than it had taken him to cross the maintenance lock, itself large enough to house the courier docked to it, he had manipulated the fields behind the hatch controls. The heavy door swung inward.

DANGER! INERT ATMOSPHERE. DO NOT ENTER. That was what the plaque over the inner door read.

He ignored the warning just as he had ignored the lock on the outer door. Shortly the second locked hatch yielded to his touch.

"This is a prohibited area. Unauthorized personnel are not allowed. Failure to leave the prohibited area could result in extreme danger or death. Failure to leave the prohibited area immediately could result in extreme danger or death."

The man did not acknowledge the words as he toggled the lighting controls beside the inner hatch. Less than nineteen standard hours before an Imperial response.

His steps vibrated through the heavy suit as he followed the corridor toward the station's maintenance section. In passing, he noted a section where planetary survival equipment was neatly racked. After he had made the necessary alterations to the courier, he would need to remove enough equipment for four people. Remove it and store it in the courier's small hold.

He hated to spend the time, but he would not have ignored the equipment if he intended to use it, not when he was so desperately wanted by the Imperials, not when he needed them to believe his life was at stake. With a deep breath, he continued down the corridor to his destination.

The clearly marked hatchway—"Maintenance"—was also locked, although it provided even less of a challenge than had the outside locks.

Inside, he studied the arrayed equipment, mentally organizing what he would need before beginning. After a time, he lifted a rodlike device and the accompanying power line reel and strode quickly back toward the courier. The station gravity—roughly one-third gee—was enough for him to carry the equipment comfortably.

Soon a stack of equipment stood by the unopened outer lock that would gain him access to the station's hull—and the courier's as well.

"Next . . ."

He removed two items from the pile and returned to the inner area of the station, where destruction of certain monitoring and record-keeping equipment was necessary. That destruction triggered the launch of yet another message torpedo, noted and ignored by the suited man.

On his return, he forced the lock on the survival storage area and began the first of several loads of assorted material. Unlike the maintenance equipment, the survival equipment went into the courier's hold—the forward one.

When he had stowed the last survival suit, he stopped in the courier's mess, slumping into an anchored plastic chair for another tumbler full of metallic water and another set of tasteless rations. As he swallowed the last neutral crumb, he checked the time. Sixteen hours yet.

That was followed by a partial desuiting, the use of certain sanitary facilities, and a sigh of momentary relief.

With a second sigh, not of relief, he began to resuit.

In less than a quarter of a standard hour, the man in greens and the heavy vac suit stood inside the outspace lock from the maintenance space, locking the power reel connections in place, first on the rod-shaped device, then to the special receptacle inside the open lock.

He touched the rod. The indicators on the cutting laser flared red.

The pilot tugged on the safety line again, making sure that the lock lines were secure before easing his way through the open hatch.

Supposedly, what he was about to do would work, according to the more obscure survival manuals that no one ever read, but he was not aware that it had ever been tried.

Inside the helmet, he smiled. In fact, the emergency conversion didn't have to work. He only had to do it well enough so that the majority of the courier reached planetside on Timor II.

His momentum carried him to the end of the line, where he steadied himself with a gauntleted hand. The dark bulk of the observation station shielded him from the direct light of Timor as he triggered the laser.

Fifteen hours to modify the courier, drop it planetside, make a rendezvous, and disappear. When the Empire eventually got around to investigating, the Service would find the bodies of the four people who had ravaged Missou Base and New Kansaw orbit control. Finish to one Major Jimjoy Earle Wright. Except that was just the beginning.

■ ■ ■

"TRANSMISSION FROM THE observation station off Timor II, sir."

"Timor II? And . . . ?"

"The remotes indicate that Dauntless two—that's the *D'Armetier* . . . the courier taken from New Kansaw—has locked in there."

The Admiral straightened in his chair. "How good is the data?"

"Good enough that Special Ops analysis insists it's a real courier."

Frowning, the senior officer sat back in the padded chair. "That's a class four planet, isn't it?"

"Yes, sir. Marginally habitable."

"Do Service catalogs show the station as unmanned?"

"Yes, sir. But with limited repair capability."

". . . makes sense . . . Wright could gut the station with his abilities . . . refuel and be off . . . before we get there . . ."

"Sir . . . ?"

"Send a corvette. Just one."

"Just one, sir?"

"One way or another, he'll be gone before the ship gets there, if he was even there to begin with."

"You think it's a setup?"

"Given Major Wright? I doubt it. That man works for no one but Major Wright. There's no sense in taking chances. Warn the corvette crew. It could be an ambush, probably set up inside the station. Have them take their time. I'd like to see if there's any indication whether anyone else is involved."

"You really don't think so, do you?"

"No. But he's outguessed us all so far."

"What do you really expect?"

"I don't know. The time delay bothers me. He's been somewhere, and that's the real question. I doubt we'll find out that."

"But we have to try?"

The Admiral shrugged. "Have any better ideas?"

"No, sir."

"Send the corvette."

IV

JIMJOY SHIFTED HIS weight from one side of the chair to the other. "You didn't mention psych treatments."

The silver-haired woman who stood at the other side of the small office met his eyes without challenge, but without flinching. "You didn't ask. And as I recall, you weren't exactly in a position to ask for too many conditions, Mr. tentative Professor Whaler."

He sighed. "Why? So you can ensure I don't upset the proverbial quince wagon?" His jaw hurt, and they hadn't even really started in on the real work.

"Apple cart," she corrected him, picking up a thick file from the desk beside her. She thrust the bound stack toward him. "Because you are, to put it bluntly, a borderline sociopath, with no recognizable form of unified ethics and no conscience." The Ecolitan looked at the man who sat in the hospital chair, his bandaged face so covered as to be unrecognizable.

"Strong words . . ." His headache was beginning to return.

"Do you want an accounting? A listing of the names, a categorization of the millions of liters of blood you have spilled, frozen, or cremated? It's all here, unless there's even more than the Institute could uncover."

"Ecolitan Andruz . . . I admitted I was scarcely perfect. But if you insist on turning my psyche inside out, you'll have less than nothing." He wanted to know why she was pushing the issue even before the major surgery had begun. "And why are you insisting on all this now?" A flash of pain scorched up his jawline, needling into his skull.

"You are already resisting. If you don't change psychologically, at least to some degree, the Empire will pick you up from your old profile within months. Is that what you want?"

"Do you want some lily-livered professor? With skills and no way to apply them? Is that what *you* want? No challenge to your expertise and authority? My so-called imbalance is certainly part of what I have to offer." He tried to lean back and ease the tension in his body, but the combination of the pain and the muscle relaxants made conscious control difficult—one reason that he had always avoided drugs.

"That is doubtless true, and for that you should be grateful. We still think we can improve some of your underlying attitudes without crippling your ability to act. That means knowing more about how you work. Whether you know it or not, you are paying a price for what you have done."

"So? I paid it. Not gladly, but I did." The dull pounding in his temples had become a heavy continuous hammering. He eased himself forward in the chair again, trying to concentrate on the woman.

"You really don't understand exactly how heavy a price . . ."

"You don't know everything, Ecolitan Andruz." His voice sharpened. "What do you want? True confessions of a confessed mass murderer? Tales of tragic triumphs in service of the mad Empire?"

"If you want to tell those tales . . . but frankly, I could care less. I'd rather see you stew in your own poisons." She deposited the heavy folder back on the desktop. "What you do is your choice, not mine."

"Then why . . ."

"Because the Prime Ecolitan insists you're worth saving. I agree with Sam's sentiments, but question the reality."

"Aren't *you* optimistic?" He didn't bother to disguise the sarcasm. Not only did his head ache, but he was getting dizzy.

"You wanted my thoughts. Your possibilities are only limited by the greatest pigheadedness I've ever seen."

He sighed, leaning forward and holding his head in both hands at the top of his forehead, where there were no bandages.

"Are you all right?"

"No. Does it make any difference?"

"You . . ." This time she was the one who sighed with heavy exasperation. "We'll talk about it later. I didn't mean to push."

"Don't bother."

"You're refusing?"

"No. Pigheaded, but not stupid. Accepting. I don't have to like it . . ." Lifting his head, he sighed again, softly, aware that sudden movements triggered the heavier throbbing. "When does this all start?"

"When you feel better." She touched the console, then waited. A tall and thin woman entered the room. "This is Dr. Militro. Doctor, this is . . . Professor . . . Whaler. I wanted you to meet each other now . . ."

Jimjoy stood, aware of the rubbery feeling in his legs, but determined to make the effort. "Not exactly pleased, Doctor, but . . . appreciative."

"Please sit down, Professor."

Jimjoy sank back into the chair, watching Thelina Andruz rather than the doctor.

"Professor . . . Doctor . . . I need to be going . . ." Her piercing green eyes rested first on Jimjoy, then upon the black-haired doctor.

Jimjoy only nodded.

"Thank you, Ecolitan Andruz," the doctor noted politely, turning again toward Jimjoy, but waiting until the heavy wooden door had closed. "Professor . . ."

"Call me Jimjoy."

"Very well. This is not a time for heavy analysis or deep thought. I would like an accurate summary of your background, beginning from when you can remember. You do not have to use names. We are talking patterns. First, though . . . how do you feel?"

"Honestly?"

"Honestly."

"Like hades."

"What if I meet you in your room when you feel better?"

"I'd like to start now . . . before I think too much . . ."

The doctor smiled. "Believe it or not, it won't be that bad."

"Not for me, Doctor, but for you . . . it will be hard to remain objective." Jimjoy grinned brittlely under the bandages, recalling the incidents on New Kansaw, on Halston, on *IFoundIt!*—just for starters. Maybe Thelina was right. He shrugged, then winced as the pain ran up his jawline again. "At the beginning . . . I was born on White Mountain, the Hampshire system. That's right at the edge of the habitable zone, lots of lakes, and rocks, and ice. Short summers. My mother was the Regional Administrator. Women run most things there, except for the heavy equipment and the asteroid mining . . ."

The doctor nodded without taking her eyes off him.

V

19 Novem 3645
Demetris

Dear Blaine,

You've already gotten the official report on old zipless. Evaluation was stretched to the limit to list the *Halley* as operable. Even at one hundred percent, we'd be outmatched by the Fuards. I preferred the Halstanis, thank you. But their new Matriarchy seems more economically oriented. Not the guys on Tinhorn, though. Once a Fuard, always a Fuard.

Rumor has it that the Fuards have some new wrinkles in the works. Right now it's close. Our training's better, at least. Tactics, too.

Understand the great and glorious Imperial Senate turned hands down on the Fast Corvette. Reports from the faxers here don't put it that bluntly. More like: "In view of the escalated costs associated with building the FC, the Senate rejected the Emperor's request to build two hundred FCs, and instead voted for a feasibility study."

A nerdy study! Out here on the perimeter, I need another study like I need a light sloop. Seriously, what's the scoop on getting something better than old zipless? And before my kids are in

Service? Not that the *Halley* wasn't a fine ship in her day, but her frames were plated before I was old enough to read about the Academy, much less go.

Helen and Jock send their best. Cindi's not old enough to, but she would if she could. Even out here, they're both a joy. Two probably is too many for someone who's "high-risk," as Helen puts it. With old zipless, she doesn't know how high.

Let me know.

Mort

VI

CRACK!!!

A single bolt of lightning jabbed from the towering thunderstorm that straddled the center of the lake.

WHHHHssstttttt . . . The first dark funnel dipped toward the skimmer as he guided it between the three-meter waves raised by the storm. By the time that funnel had brushed the wave crests to the west of him and folded itself back into the thunder-dark clouds, another funnel was snaking toward his skimmer, this time from the south, as the storm beat its way northeast.

Jimjoy could feel the whiteness of his knuckles on the tiller of the light lake craft, as much as he tried to relax and avoid overcontrolling.

CRRRACCKKK! Another bolt flared, even closer.

WHHHSTTTT . . .

CRACK!!

He glanced to his right, trying to catch sight of Clarissa's skimmer. Once again she had dared him, older experienced sister to younger brother, and once again he had fallen for it, going deeper into the storm pattern than was wise, just to prove he could do her one better.

HSSSSSSSTTTT . . . *CRACK! CRACK! CRACKKKK!*

The last flare of the lightning lashed less than a quarter kay from him, almost outside the main storm flow.

"NOOOO!" The hellish energy had not struck in the storm, where he tossed, fighting his way through and around waves he should have been able to avoid if he had only gauged the storm track correctly, but right through the blue skimmer that had almost dashed past the curtain winds and into Barabou Notch.

"NOOOOOO!!!" Not Clarissa. Not again.

"Noooo . . ." groaned the man in the hospital bed.

No one answered his groan, and Jimjoy slowly opened his eyes. The monitoring equipment focusing on him reported the change in his awareness.

"Hades . . . same dream . . . again . . ." He wanted to shake his head. Instead, he lay there for a time. The ceiling overhead was green, a pale green that reminded him of the way his stomach currently felt. Turning his eyes to the side without moving his head, he could see that the heavy wooden door was ajar. No one passed by outside.

Clarissa—how many years back? Hadn't he gotten over that? Lerra— not mother, don't call me mother—had never said one word about it. She had just gone and had Anita. Was Anita the Regional Administrator now? No, not yet; Anita was still too young. She couldn't have finished all the requirements. Besides, could she be Regional Administrator if Kaylin were the System Administrator? That was what Lerra had wanted.

He blinked slowly, feeling the wetness in the corners of his eyes, wishing it would go away before anyone came in. Dr. Militro would certainly be interested in the dream. He tried not to shiver, to push away the feelings he had felt on a slow skim back into Barabou Harbor all too many years earlier.

He slowly eased his head away from the direction of the door, wincing at the tingling in his scalp and the increased intensity of the headache he felt with the movement. The softness of the light outside indicated twilight at the Institute.

Funny, until he was actually in it, he had never realized that the Ecolitans had quietly maintained a complete hospital. Even in his previous months as a "guest" instructor, he had not noticed the facility. They hadn't so much hidden it as simply placed it within the central research complex.

Deciding to sit up, he slowly—very slowly—used the bed controls to ease himself more upright. Just as slowly, he reached for a tissue. He put it down, afraid that poking around the bandages might result in scars.

Then he noticed the stack of tapes and materials on the hospital's bedside stand. On top of them was an envelope.

He reached for it, ignoring the twinges in his head and the residual soreness in his shoulders and ribs.

A single note card was inside, and he slipped it out.

These are the materials I mentioned. If you want to qualify as an instructor, you will need to pass an examination, both in theory and in practice, on the ecological materials.

The Prime has waived, in light of your extensive experience, similar requirements in your specialties and granted you status in piloting, navigation, hand-to-hand combat, and military operations. You'll probably also receive status in electronics—practical and theoretical—and in contemporary political science, and perhaps one or two other areas. That will be enough to justify granting you the status of Ecolitan Professor . . . if you can master journeyman status material in the ecological disciplines.

These tapes and the introductory manual are the beginning.

The doctors tell me that the headaches will continue for several days, but represent no impairment of mental faculties and should not affect your learning, especially with your mastery of relaxation and combat meditation skills.

T. Andruz

"You're all heart, Thelina. All heart." Just like Lerra. He did not even bother to sigh as he studied the pile of material. Finally he lifted the thin manual that was supposed to provide an overview.

Click . . . tap . . . tap . . . tap . . .

He ignored the footsteps.

"Well, I see you're awake even earlier than Dr. Hyrsa had anticipated. We'll be taking off the pressure bandages on your face tomorrow, I think, and we'll all get to see what you look like, Professor Whaler."

"Not really a professor . . . uccouughh . . ." The cough was almost painful, both in his shoulders and in his face. Like the nurse, he had to wonder exactly what he would look like. While he had seen the profiles and sketches, there was a big difference between art and your own flesh.

Dr. Hyrsa had been careful to point out the limitations of what she, or any surgeon, could do, given his insistence on not having his muscular abilities and coordination impaired.

"We can alter the fingerprints, retinal prints, eye color, and facial bone structure . . . improve the chin. Fix the hitch in your shoulder. It will start giving you trouble before long anyway. We can extend your legs about five centimeters with the bone we've cloned from you, but that will mean at least three months of therapy and supervised physical redevelopment . . ."

"Isn't that a risk?" he'd asked, worried about the operation failing and losing his legs or their complete use.

"Any surgery is a risk, but the leg extension is relatively simple as these things go, and our unqualified success rate is above ninety-eight percent. Broadening your shoulders is a slightly higher risk, but there we have an incipient problem to correct anyway . . ."

The other problem had been the cosmetologist.

"Permanent color? Not sure I like that . . ."

"There is a slight risk, less than one case in one hundred thousand, according to the risk assessments, of triggering simple skin cancers— not melanoma. The identity chart matrices show that without a complexion alteration the other changes will not be sufficient . . ."

He had shrugged, wondering what he had let himself in for.

Now he knew. He ached all over. He had been in the hades-fired hospital for more than six weeks, and now he had headaches. He had never had headaches.

"They all say it's just a formality, Professor Whaler," added the nurse. She was white-haired and professionally grandmotherly. "And the way those Institute folks look up to you, I'm sure that you're just being modest.

"Now let's take a look at you . . ."

He put down the thin manual. It could wait a few minutes. But that was about all, from the amount of the materials Thelina had left.

His scalp half itched, half hurt. They'd warned him about that too. "And don't scratch!" Thelina had added. As if she had ever had to go through what he was undergoing. Fat chance.

". . . uuummmm . . ."

"That shouldn't hurt, Professor . . ."

"Doesn't . . . except when I cough . . ."

"Coughing's good for you. Just hold a pillow against your diaphragm if it's too much."

Damned if he'd use the pillow. Of course, Dr. Militro would point out that stoicism that served no purpose was mere masochism. He let his breath out gently and reached for the pillow laid next to Thelina's materials.

Outside, the twilight was sliding into dusk, the green of the upper hills he could see from the window fading into gray. The nurse switched on the room lights and twitched his covers back into place.

"Monitors show you're doing better than expected, and they had projected a quick recovery. Haven't had one this special for several years."

"Do you have many cases . . . like . . ."

"Like you, you mean? Distinguished scholars who want to start all over . . . not many. One every year or so. There was—but I really shouldn't discuss it, they say. They never tell us who you were, only who you are. That's better. Always look to the future. That's where we'll have to live.

"Is there anything else you need?"

"Something to drink?"

"You can have just a little bit of this." She went out into the corridor and returned with a paper cup. The cup was the first disposable thing he had seen at the Institute, either this time or in his earlier visit. For the hospital, it made sense.

"Now just sip this slowly. If it stays down, and it certainly should, you can have some clear liquids for dinner. You should be back on solid food by tomorrow. That's really just a precaution until Dr. Hyrsa is sure everything has stabilized."

He almost shivered. Stabilize? What was there to stabilize?

"Don't worry. If the doctors here can't do something, they don't. It's just that simple." She checked the nonintrusive monitors again. "I'll be back with some more to drink later."

He looked out at the twilight on the eastern hills, picked out a single star winking in the gray-purple sky, then tried to identify buildings from their outlines. He had been brought in quietly, through an underground tunnel that he had never suspected even existed, directly into the hospital area. He had not seen the Institute itself this time. The outlines looked as he had remembered them, although some of the trees were now bare in the local winter.

So far as he knew, only Thelina, the cosmetologist, and the doctor had actually seen his unchanged visage. None of them, himself included, had seen what he looked like now, or would look like once he healed and the various swellings and stiffnesses subsided.

But the dream . . . he had not thought about Clarissa's death since . . . since at least pilot training . . . perhaps longer. He started to shake his head and stopped in mid-shake as both scalp and headache warned him.

With a sigh, he retrieved the manual. Studying and learning were less dangerous than remembering. He'd understood that for a long time.

VII

JIMJOY SAT ON the edge of the hospital bed, letting his bare feet touch the warm tile floor. As the nurse stripped the last of the pressure bandages from his face, he tried to keep his shoulders relaxed. They began to ache every time he tensed up, and he wondered if they always would.

"Just a moment, Professor Whaler, and we'll have these off. Then you can see how you look." Her voice contained the professional brightness he had always associated with nurses. He didn't know which was worse, the false booming heartiness of the men or the blithe cheerfulness of the women.

"What I look like," corrected Jimjoy.

"Dr. Hyrsa is very good, Professor. You look fine. A few small bruises, but that's all. Those heal quickly. No more than a week or two at most."

Thud. The wadded-up bandages echoed in the container set by his feet.

"Bruises?"

"Not exactly. They look like bruises, but they're not."

Thud. More bandages clunked into the container.

How many kilos of dressings had he been wearing on his face alone? The shoulder dressings had been disposed of several days earlier.

"You hair is coming in nicely."

Scrttchhh.

"Ooooohh . . ."

"That was a little sticky, but that was the last one . . . and Dr. Hyrsa did a nice job—as usual. I'll even bet you'll be pleased with the results."

Jimjoy did not look at the proffered hand mirror, instead running his fingers across his face, tracing his cheekbones and his chin line. Under his fingertips he could feel the usual stubble of unshaven beard. He was supposed to have higher cheekbones, green eyes . . .

"Are you ready to look in the mirror, Professor?"

He sighed and took the lightweight mirror from the red-haired nurse, who held it practically in his face. He held the mirror without lifting it.

With another drawn-out breath, he brought up the mirror. The face was that of a stranger. Not even a near relative, but a total stranger.

He gripped the mirror tighter to keep his hand from trembling as he studied the reflected image. The face frowned at him. *His* face frowned at him.

His nose was sharper, finer, and more aquiline than his original nose. The cheekbones were clearly higher, and his chin was a touch more pointed, not nearly as squared off as he recalled. His eyes were a piercing green, much like he remembered Thelina's. But he had only a colorless stubble for eyebrows and eyelashes, and his scalp was a hairless bronze . . . or was it graying before his time? Bronze? His entire face was somehow bronzed.

Despite the itching of his scalp, he did not scratch it, but pressed the skin gently to try to relieve the sensation. He could feel the stubble of regrowing hair under his fingertips. Then he studied his hands before lifting his eyes to the mirror again. He was bronzed indeed, bronzed over every millimeter of his body.

"Are you all right, Professor?"

"Just thinking . . ."

He held the mirror closer to his eyebrows, angling it to catch their color.

"Silver . . ." His hair and eyebrows were going to be silver. Dr. Hyrsa had only told him that his hair would be lighter, much lighter. She had smiled when he had said he wouldn't mind being a blond, but she had not agreed with him.

"Silver . . . be an old man before my time."

"I doubt that. With all your improvements, you'll outlive us all. Besides, you were in excellent shape to begin with."

Despite her soft voice, her words and not just the professional tone in which they were delivered somehow bothered him. He ignored the red-haired nurse and turned the mirror up toward his scalp. Silver.

Hades! While he didn't look anything like he had, he'd certainly stand out in a crowd now. Taller, with bronze skin and silver hair . . . how could he ever do what he'd done before?

He put down the mirror on the rumpled sheet beside him. Thelina had silver hair, the same light bronze complexion, and could still disappear as effectively as any Special Operative.

Thelina? The pieces snapped together inside his skull. "Nurse—did you ever work with Ecolitan Andruz?"

"Professor, I couldn't rightly say which Ecolitans I've worked with."

"Andruz. Silver-haired. Bronzed, with green eyes, a sharp tongue . . ."

"Now, Professor, no woman would like to be characterized by her tongue . . ."

Jimjoy waited. "Silver hair," he finally prompted, trying to catch the nurse's eye as she bent to pick up the container holding the used bandages.

"You must think we have a fixation on silver hair. We deal with all kinds of hair color—brown, red, black, gray. Some have been women, perhaps with silver hair. I could be wrong. I don't remember names."

"Here," he said tiredly, picking the mirror up and handing it back. "You don't like how you look?"

"I guess I liked the way I used to look more than I thought."

She took the mirror. "Could I get you anything to drink?"

"No. No . . ." He looked down at the alternating ceramic triangular floor tiles of black, green, and gold. What else had the Ecolitan surgeon done? What other "improvements" had he blithely agreed to?

"*Whffffuuuugh* . . ." His sigh dragged out. Even his stomach muscles still ached. And the ache in his shoulders was threatening to return at any moment.

"You need to rest, Professor Whaler."

"All I've done is lie around."

"Just swing your feet up and think about it."

"Ooohhh . . ." The involuntary exclamation as he twisted drew a quickly suppressed grin from the nurse. Although stretching out was scarcely painless, the rest of his movements were silent.

In time, so was the hospital room, except for the sound of breathing.

VIII

JIMJOY LOOKED AROUND the hospital room. One compact kit bag containing all of his current worldly possessions rested on the single chair. No flowers, no cards to take with him. Just the good wishes of Cerrol—the white-haired nurse—Verea, and Dr. Hyrsa.

Although Jimjoy had hoped that a silver-haired Ecolitan would visit him, Thelina had not shown up after she had introduced Dr. Militro. Instead, she had sent two heavy packages of instructional materials with cryptic notes implying that he learn virtually every word and concept before he would be truly fit to be classified as an Ecolitan.

Since the Institute did not provide personal fax terminals, he had not even been able to fax her. Nor did he know how or where to send a note, assuming he had been foolish enough to write down anything.

With a sigh, he picked up the kit bag. It was light enough not to strain his rebuilt shoulders, even before the weeks of rehab scheduled for him, and the weeks of conditioning necessary after that.

The room was ready for its next patient.

"Good luck, Professor," called Verea from her console.

"Thanks, Verea."

The junior medical tech with the coppery hair waved briefly.

Jimjoy pushed open the wide wooden door and stepped out into the open staircase, avoiding the elevators—the only ones he had seen on Accord.

His steps were easy. He was in terrible shape, and it would be months before he was back in the condition necessary for the events to come. But his muscles were still there, out of condition as they were.

Stepping through the doors at the foot of the stairs, he saw two people—a young man in tans at the hospital information/admissions/ guard desk and a young woman in Ecolitan field greens by the front doorway. He had met the young woman—Mera—once before, in what he was coming to think of as his second life, his service as an Imperial Special Operative. She had been his driver.

Would she recognize him in this third life?

"Professor Whaler?" asked the black-haired woman.

"The same," acknowledged Jimjoy. "And you are?"

"Mera Lilkovie, student third class."

He inclined his head to her. "Appreciate your help, Mera."

"That's what we're here for, Professor."

He forced a laugh. "Not really. You're here to learn, not to transport partly disabled staff, but I appreciate it." While he could hear the deeper timbre of his voice, would the change in pitch, combined with the physical and cosmetic differences, be sufficient to pass her scrutiny? Then again, she had only driven him once, and that had been well over a standard year earlier.

"The car is outside. Do you have anything else?" Her eyes flickered to his short silvery hair that was well beyond a stubble, but still too short for all but the strictest military organizations.

"No."

"That makes it easy, then."

She showed no sign of recognition, unless she had been instructed not to. He doubted that. She turned and held the door.

Jimjoy stepped out into the hazy noontime sunshine, still amazed at the informality of his departure. That morning, Gavin Thorson, Sam Hall's Deputy Prime, and the Ecolitan in charge of all staffing arrangements at the Institute, had appeared in his room and announced that Jimjoy had been assigned permanent senior staff quarters—at least as permanent as any such quarters were—and that he would be discharged for background briefings and rehabilitation. A car would pick him up at 1100 hours local and take him to his quarters, where a minimum of linens and furniture had been supplied. And a full set of Institute uniforms, plus a few items of leisure clothing.

Jimjoy could either eat in any one of the Institute dining facilities or, once he familiarized himself with the Institute's supply procedures, cook his own meals.

Thorson had then handed Jimjoy his I.D., credit number, current account balance, and a folder containing his résumé, complete personal history, projected teaching load for the following quarter, his briefing schedule, and an accelerated follow-up course in ecologic and personal ethics for one James Joyson Whaler II. The material duplicated what Thelina had already provided.

James Joyson Whaler II—that was the first time he'd seen his new name in print. But why had the Institute delayed in identity conditioning?

Thorson had waited for him to absorb it. "Not that much of this should be a surprise to you, you understand, but we're asking a lot of you. Even so, the Prime and I welcome you back, Professor Whaler," Thorson had said.

"Jimjoy, please."

"Jimjoy it is."

That had been it. Now he was walking toward a groundcar to begin a new life for real—for the third time. He almost shook his head. That was another mannerism he would have to eliminate—or limit. He tried pulling at his chin. In time, perhaps he could replace the one gesture with the other.

He also had to learn his own new personal history—cold—before he really appeared in public.

"Professor, our car is the one on the right."

"Thank you." Jimjoy angled his steps toward the pale green electrocar. After opening the rear door himself, he tossed the small kit bag onto the far side of the seat and eased in. The twinge in his shoulders as he bent forward reminded him that he had been in the hospital for a reason.

Clunk. Mera shut the door behind him.

"You have not seen your quarters?"

"No, young lady, I have not. They were arranged while I was incapacitated."

"You will be pleasantly surprised." The car moved forward smoothly and turned to the right at the end of the semicircular drive. "All the new staff members are."

He looked back, noticing that the building where he had stayed bore no indication it was a hospital. It was not the same building into which he had once carried an injured student less than two years earlier. Of that he was sure.

That led to other concerns, such as exactly how many medical facilities existed on the grounds of the Institute, and how little he knew about the people to whom he had entrusted his life. Not that he had had many options.

"Exactly where are the staff quarters?" He paused, wondering how much he was supposed to know. "I've studied the maps, but . . ."

"It's not quite the same thing?"

"Right." Jimjoy nodded.

"Have you visited the Institute before, Professor?" Mera asked.

"Not in this particular life, at least." He forced a short laugh.

"You know, you must be very special. The Institute doesn't grant many full fellowships or professor's chairs."

"Especially not to former outsiders?" he asked.

"No. I think Professor Firion is one, and they said one of the senior field trainers was an outsider, but that's rumor."

"I'm probably asking a stupid question, young lady, but could you enlighten me on the differences in meaning here at the Institute between professors, fellows, and Ecolitans?"

The electrocar purred up a narrow road and by a stone wall. Jimjoy kept his face impassive, although he recognized the orchard. He had wondered where the road led, and it appeared he was about to find out.

"Well . . . anyone who has graduated from the Institute or passed the equivalency tests and been accepted by the Prime or the examining Board as proficient in all the required skills is an Ecolitan. Most Ecolitans are Institute graduates, but you don't have to be.

"Fellow actually means Senior Fellow of the Institute, and that takes longer. Professors are Senior Fellows with specific responsibilities. That's what makes you unique."

While Mera was practically begging for an explanation, Jimjoy let the not-quite-asked question pass him by. "And the quarters?" he prompted.

"Oh, just up the road here. You can actually take the footpath between the hills and along the brook and walk to the main grounds faster than going by car. That was to discourage groundcars when the last Institute plan was developed."

"And did it? Discourage the use of groundcars?" he asked with a smile.

"Not really. No one used them anyway."

The car swept between two massive pinelike trees flanking the narrow roadway, slowing to nearly a crawl as the pavement ended in a narrow stone-paved lot. The entire parking area was less than twenty meters long and not more than five meters wide. A vacant green groundcar was parked at the far end.

Terraced stone walkways paralleled the parking area and continued up the sloping terrain toward individual wooden structures set roughly ten meters apart. Each was two stories, with wide front and rear wooden decks, a sharply pitched roof, and large windows.

"You get the end unit, Professor." Mera pointed as she brought the electrocar to a purring halt beside the empty green car.

"New kid on the block?" asked Jimjoy. He looked at his quarters-to-be again. Perhaps a shade narrower than those farther uphill, but still two stories, with both decks, and the same detailed workmanship and contrasting dark and light woods—all in all, quarters probably better than those offered to all but command-class officers in the Empire. "All to myself?"

"Unless there's someone I don't know about. You certainly can invite anyone to share your hospitality." Mera turned and grinned at him. It was not quite an invitation.

"That tired of Institute quarters?" He grinned back.

"Not yet, Professor. But try in a year."

He started to shake his head, then remembered and pulled at his chin. "Remind me of that, would you?"

"I just might, Professor. I just might." She bounced from her seat.

Jimjoy moved more carefully, still not quite certain which movements triggered which pains. As he stepped out, he surveyed the area, from the neatly groomed bushes and short grass to the rows of low silver blooms growing beside the slate gray of the stone walks and steps.

Click . . . clunk . . .

"Ready?" asked the student.

"I can take that!" protested Jimjoy, realizing she had retrieved his bag.

"No problem, Professor. Suares would have my head if she learned I'd let you carry anything."

He cut his shrug short as his shoulders protested and followed her up the wooden steps. A cold breeze carried the scent of firs and the promise of rain. Overhead, the haze had thickened into light clouds. Toward the west, behind the lower clouds, lurked a darker presence.

Thrummmmmm . . . The thunder, faint as a half-played beat on a child's drum, whispered through the afternoon.

Stopping at the doorway that Mera had opened but not stepped through, Jimjoy followed her eyes. Beside the blond wooden squared arches of the front doorway was a plaque. *J. J. Whaler, S.F.I.*

"You first, Professor."

Jimjoy stepped into a small foyer, floored in narrow planks of close-grained golden wood. The walls—all the walls—were wooden. Well finished and satin-lacquered. Although the wood had been refinished for him, a few dents and rounded edges showed that there had been previous occupants.

Past the foyer, with its narrow closet for coats, cloaks, or whatever, and through another squared arch, this one without doors, Jimjoy stood in a single long room running from one side of the dwelling to the other—perhaps eight to nine meters. The center of the room was open to the beamed ceiling. The entire southwest wall was comprised of wood and glass with just enough wood to hold the glass. Each window on the upper level could swivel open, and sliding glass doors framed in wood ran in multiple tracks the width of the room.

To his right, a railed but open staircase rose to the second story, where it opened onto a loft. From what he could see, the loft joined two rooms, one at each side of the house.

He walked left, toward the open kitchen area and the dark bronze wooden table and wooden chairs—the only dark objects in the entire room. On the table was an oblong white card.

He forced himself to pick it up slowly. The message was neatly inscribed on the stiff card with a green triangle in the upper left corner: "Welcome home, Professor. Sam."

Home? That remained to be seen. White Mountain had been home once, too. And so had Alphane. Neither had been, though he had thought of each that way.

He set the card back on the table.

"Don't you want to see the rest?" Mera was smiling, bouncing slightly on the balls of her feet, still holding his single kit bag in her left hand.

Jimjoy repressed a frown. "Of course."

"Besides the deck, there's the upstairs."

Jimjoy took the staircase, his steps heavy on the carpeted runner.

"Your room is the one at the far end."

"My room?"

"The main suite?"

"Suite?"

"Well . . . maybe not a suite, but . . . you'll see."

He did. The room, with an oversized bed, a dresser, a bedside table with a lamp, and a table desk with a console and matching chair, had enough open floor space to look uncrowded. All the furniture was a light bronzed wood. The only fabrics in evidence were the forest blue of the quilt, the matching curtains on the two windows that flanked the bed, and the two throw pillows—cream—on the bed. Above the sliding glass door that opened onto the upper deck was a wood-slat shade that rolled down for darkness or privacy, or both. A spacious fresher/bathroom was visible to his left through an open archway.

His eyes strayed back to the forest-blue quilt. He swallowed. Once, twice.

"Like it?" Mera had set the kit bag next to the closet door.

"It's very . . . very coordinated."

"The Prime thought you would like the color."

"You picked out the furniture?"

"I had some help from Kirsten—she was my second-year roommate. We worked with the woodcrafters to get it right. The downstairs was left here, but the Prime thought this should be new for you."

Jimjoy did shake his head. How had Sam Hall known about the forest blue of White Mountain? A lucky guess? Not likely. The room was more to his taste than he dared to admit.

"It's . . . I like it," he finally admitted.

"Thank you. We hoped you would. Kirsten and I, I mean."

"You did a very nice job."

"I know, but it's more important that you like it. We wanted you to feel at home." She shifted her weight from one foot to the other.

"Thank you. Really don't know what else to say . . ."

"You don't have to. You're pleased . . . but I think it brings back old memories."

"It does," he admitted, "but that's not necessarily bad. I still think I'm going to like living here very much."

"We hope so."

"So do I. So do I."

"If you need anything else . . ."

"No . . . I'll be fine."

"There's a package on the counter downstairs. It has directions to everywhere and the times everything is open. Just ask anyone around."

Jimjoy followed her down the railed and open stairs, watching from the open door until the pale green of the electrocar had purred from sight.

Then he sank onto the couch, staring out at the gathering thunderclouds, listening to the winds of his own thoughts.

IX

27 Janus 3646
New Augusta

Dear Mort:

I'm sorry about my slowness in getting back to you, but for some reason, I just got your screen. Deeptrans is backed up again.

You're probably back out on-station now, but I'll torp this off anyway while I've got a moment. I managed to win an argument with Tech and pull new drives away from a station-keep in Sector Five and get them routed to you. The Rift hasn't been a problem, and nothing's happened in Five for a couple of decades, but robbing Peter to pay Paul will catch up with us all someday.

You guessed right on the study thing. When the cost of the FC came in, Senator N'Trosia blew quarks, and they weren't charmed, either. He yelled about two hundred years of peace and cooperation, and about how we had managed to keep the peace through diplomacy, and how there was no need for a Fast Corvette when the Attack Corvettes were still perfectly functional. Politics!

So we got a study. In the meantime, the Admiral—do you remember Hewitt Graylin, the guy who was a dec up on us, the one that set the flic records that are still standing? He's the new Fleet Admiral for Development, and he just briefed us on the Fuards' new destroyer. Why they call them destroyers and we call them corvettes escapes me. The mission's the same. Except they're more honest in their nomenclature, and their new ones are really something. Supposedly, they have instantaneous postjump acceleration, and the ability to rejump without repositioning, plus a few other things best not gone into here. We've discussed the possibilities, so you know what I mean.

We'll keep pitching, and you try to keep the old *Halley* together. Congratulations on the not-so-recent new arrival! Don't know how I missed her or how you managed it, but that's a touch of envy. We (I) failed the gene screen. Guess that's another price for being on Old Earth. Looks like adoption if we want another. I don't know. Sandy has to think it over.

Blaine

✗

"PROFESSOR, ACCORDING TO Kashin, *Theories of Warfare*, a government fully backed by a people with an ideology has an advantage over a pragmatic system. What you said seems to contradict that." The youngster with the barely concealed smile waited.

Jimjoy quirked his lips before replying. "Mr. Frenzill, Kashin included a number of qualifying statements. Do you, perhaps, remember them?"

"All other political conditions being equal . . . including real and not apparent resources . . ." Student third class Frenzill's smile had vanished.

Jimjoy studied the class. All twenty looked awake. Roughly one-third appeared to understand the argument.

"Before we go on, for the benefit of Ms. Vaerolt, Mr. Yusseff, and the remainder of the third row, I'd like to repeat the point to which he has taken polite exception. *Ideology does not win wars or battles.* Fanatics or even true believers have won wars, and they have lost an even greater number." Jimjoy paused. Three other heads showed mild interest, although Gero Yusseff was still asleep with his eyes open.

"Mr. Frenzill, what caused the fall of the Halstani Military detente?"

"The rise of the Matriarchy, ser."

"Wrong, Mr. Frenzill. That is a tautology, a definition, if you will. The Matriarchy, despite the Hands of the Mother and a strong ideological hold on the populace of Halston, had been unsuccessful for more than a generation in even gathering seats in the popular assembly." Jimjoy surveyed the faces.

"Ms. Jarl?"

"Wasn't the Matriarchy successful after the Bles disaster?"

"What was the Bles disaster, exactly?"

"Professor . . . everyone knows that. It was news for weeks."

"Humor me, Ms. Jarl. Tell me what it was."

The blonde squirmed slightly in her seat, licking her lips. "Well . . . the fusion power station malfunctioned . . . and most of the military command was celebrating nearby . . . so no one was left to stop the Matriarchy . . ."

"Very convenient, wasn't it." Jimjoy watched the students shifting their weight, realizing that he was leading somewhere. "Now, does anyone want to speculate on the probability of only the *second* power plant accident of this magnitude in recorded history occurring at a time when it would wipe out not only an entire planetary government but also the majority of the military High Command? Or the fact that the government which took over had been unable to do so through conventional means?"

"Are you suggesting . . . it was deliberate?"

"I'm not a great believer in coincidences. Are you? Would you stake your life on them, Ms. Jarl?"

"Professor?" asked student third class Frenzill.

"Yes, Mr. Frenzill? You were about to observe that I had said ideology did not win wars, and here is a case where the popular ideology won?"

"Yes, ser . . ."

"There is a significant difference between causality and apparent results. The cause of the Bles disaster is still unknown. What gained the Matriarchy power was not its popular ideology, but the annihilation of its opposition. To the degree ideology allows you to mobilize superior resources, tactics, or commitment, it will win battles or wars. But . . .

the distinction is important . . . *ideology does not win wars.* Any comments? Questions?"

There were still too many blank faces. He sighed. "All right. Your assignment, due five days from now, is a short essay. No more than one thousand words. Take a position. Give me a logical proof of why ideology wins wars or why it doesn't. Any essay which does not support one position or the other will be failed. Any essay which repeats my argument blindly will also be failed." Another look around the class, and he could see that at least three students glared at Frenzill.

"Is that clear?"

"Yes, Professor."

"Now . . . beyond the question of ideology is the main point of today's lesson. Mr. Yusseff? MR. YUSSEFF. Thank you." He waited momentarily for the groggy Yusseff to realize he was the focus of attention. "Mr. Yusseff, you may get the assignment from either Ms. Jarl or Mr. Frenzill later. Since we are attempting to analyze the basis of military power, my question to you is: Do you agree with Kashin's theorem of pragmatic causality? Explain why or why not."

More squirms around the classroom, Jimjoy noted. Despite the openness of the Institute, sometimes he wondered how much intellectual challenge the students actually got. Repressing a sigh, he waited. He liked the hand-to-hand better, but Sam had insisted on Jimjoy's undertaking the warfare course. Jimjoy suspected a lot of others could have taught it better, but he owed everything to Sam . . . so . . . all he could do was his best.

XI

THE NAMEPLATE READ:

> Thelina X. Andruz, S.F.I.
> Meryl G. Laubon, S.F.I.

With a shrug, he stepped up to the doorway.

Tap . . . tap . . . The knocks on the heavy and dark-stained wooden door were even, almost precise. Jimjoy shifted his weight from one foot to the other. He wished he weren't standing at the doorway, but Thelina had continued to avoid him, time after time. When she couldn't, she was so politely professional that the planetary poles were warmer than the atmosphere surrounding her.

The door opened silently. Jimjoy tried to keep his mouth shut. Thelina's silver hair was cut short, barely longer than his own, which, although he was overdue for a haircut, was scarcely more than five centimeters long. "Come on in, Professor." Thelina shrugged as she stepped back from the half-open doorway. Wearing pale green shorts and a short-sleeved blouse, she was barefoot.

"Professor?"

"I'm happier with titles right now."

Jimjoy followed her through a single long room with kitchen facilities at one end, including a glass-topped table in a dark wood frame, and a sitting area with chairs, two low tables with matching lamps, and a couch arrayed around a small stove at the other end. Open and railed stairs rose from the right side of the entry door to the second level. The far wall was comprised of two floor-to-ceiling windows and a set of French doors in between. Jimjoy followed her out to the timbered rear deck. Three wooden chairs were spaced around a heavily varnished dark oak table. A single half-full mug sat on the table, and a book—*Field Tactics*—lay closed beside it.

He glanced overhead, but, despite the mugginess and the overhanging clouds, he could see no rain to the west.

"Have a seat. Would you like some cafe?"

"No, thank you. A glass of water?" He took the chair opposite hers.

"No problem." Thelina slipped back through the louvered door.

As he waited, he surveyed the deck. The pattern seemed similar to the house he had just been assigned, but he'd never been in any of the other senior staff homes before. His quarters—or Thelina's and her colleagues' quarters—seemed incredibly spacious for fellows of the Institute. He shook his head.

"Your water, Professor." Thelina placed a heavily tinted tumbler—no ice—on the table before him. He caught a scent of something, perhaps trilia, before she efficiently sat down at the other side of the table.

"How about 'Jimjoy'?"

"It lacks distinction and the stature reflecting your deep and valuable experience, Professor Whaler."

He sighed. "What about . . . 'I'm sorry'?"

"That wouldn't be a bad start, Professor—if you really meant it."

"I might. If I could figure out what I said that was so offensive."

"After rewriting history? You really mean that, don't you?" She took a sip from the dark green mug. "You are even denser than . . . there isn't an apt comparison . . ." She kept shaking her head intermittently.

Rewriting history? Jimjoy sipped the water, trying to keep from frowning. Rewriting history . . . she couldn't mean that. Even if he had said something wrong or misleading in his warfare class, she had been cool to him before that. Cooler than the water in front of him. He took another sip.

Thelina touched the book, turned it over, but left it on the table, saying nothing, not even looking his way.

He took a third sip, concentrating on the taste of the water, a coolness he hadn't thought about in a long time. Even without ice it was cold. Cold and fresh. Like a lake called Newfound, where he had stood beneath the firs sighing in the winds and listened to the steady lap, lap of the water.

That had been a life, before . . . there, once, he had been happy. She had been as clear and beautiful and unspoiled as the lake itself. Christina—he wondered what might have been if he had accepted the life he had been born to instead of trying to escape. Yet here he was, trying for still another life . . .

"Professor?"

"Oh, sorry."

"Professor Whaler, I do believe you were kays away."

"I probably was, Ecolitan Andruz. I probably was."

"Probably?"

"All right, Senior Fellow of the Institute, Ecolitan Andruz. You are, as usual, one hundred percent correct. My thoughts were elsewhere."

This time Thelina was the one to sigh. "Just about the time you start to act human, you revert to the standard Imperial protocols."

Jimjoy caught her green eyes and stared directly at her. "We're too old for games, Thelina. And too much rides on us to have time for games."

She returned the gaze, so directly that he finally blinked. "Professor, that attitude is exactly what is wrong with the Empire and your thinking. First, we all die in the end. All we have is the trip through life. Without games, without spice, and without meaning and love along the way, life doesn't offer much. It doesn't help when you distort what really happened along the way. And second, no one is indispensable. Not me. Not you."

... thurummmm ... Jimjoy looked over his shoulder, toward the west. The darkening clouds and the mist lines below the clouds spelled an oncoming storm.

Whhhipppp ... A gust of wind, with the scent of rain, flipped open the back cover of the book Thelina had turned over.

"Do you want to wait for hard evidence, Professor Whaler, or shall we retire to the living room?'

"I bow to your superior knowledge, Ecolitan Andruz." Jimjoy picked up his tumbler and stood. "What about the chairs?"

"They'll be fine. They're oylwood." Thelina closed the book, picked it up, and reached for her now-empty mug. She did not look back.

Jimjoy closed the louvered door, nearly bumping into Thelina. "Excuse me." He stepped back quickly, pushing away the thought triggered by her standing so close. Why, he still didn't understand, not with her continual hostility.

Halting, he turned and watched the clouds darkening and tumbling upward even as the rain began to spatter on the deck outside. A single shaft of sunlight played upon a tree-covered mountainside kays westward. As Thelina ran water in the small kitchen, he watched the line of sunlight disappear.

"How about an amendment to my last statement?"

"No apologies this time?" She had replaced the mug with a tumbler of water. She set it on the table and eased into the chair, tucking one leg under her.

"Thelina, I am what I am. I probably should change some of that, but to apologize for what I am is hypocrisy." He sat down in the chair opposite hers and sipped from the glass he still carried. "You are right about life being a journey. That was what I was thinking about when I drifted off. But ..."

"Surely you aren't going to claim that you are indispensable?"

"Not indispensable ... not exactly. The universe, or most of the people in it, could care less whether you or I exist, or about what we do. The universe could also care less whether we enjoy life and the journey it represents.

"Now, I can't claim to know history the way old Sergel Firion and his staff do. But there have been times in human and alien histories when individuals have made a difference. There have been discoveries that no one else besides a single scientist has even understood for decades. There have been political actions taken, battles won, and conquests made that have changed history because of a single and unique individual." He paused and took another sip from the glass, grateful that Thelina was still at least seeming to listen.

"Likewise, some discoveries could have been made by dozens of individuals, and some battles and political actions were taken by possibly the worst of all possible candidates.

"As far as Accord is concerned, only a handful of individuals understands more than a fraction of the structural and political problems involved. You and I happen to be in that handful. Denying that is like denying"—he glanced out at the wet deck—"that it's raining outside. If we don't act, someone else will have to. Someone besides an ex-Imperial Special Operative and a former Hand of the Mothers." He grinned at her and waited.

Thelina met his grin blankly. "What else have you figured out, Professor? Besides the obvious? That just makes what you did worse."

"If you please, what did I do that was so inexcusable? And what is this rewriting of history?"

"Your whole warfare class is talking about it. How you pointed out how convenient it was for the Matriarchy—"

Jimjoy's stomach turned upside down.

Thelina stopped talking as she saw his face. "How can you be so perceptive and so dense? You didn't even realize . . ."

"No. It was used only as an example of how ideology by itself cannot gain control, of why force is required to obtain control."

Thelina looked at the woodstove in the corner.

He took a deep swallow and finished the water, looking for somewhere to put the tumbler besides on the finished wood of the table.

"You destroyed Military Central."

"You gave up."

"No price too high for you, Professor . . . no burden too great?"

"There might . . ." He looked at her face and stood up. "You're angry because what I've said threatens your tight little conception of the universe. Because I've put my neck on the line and think you might have to also, if you believe what you say you do."

"How can you even suggest that?"

"Because all you do is poke holes in what I've said and done. That's easy. Lord knows I've said and done a lot wrong. But you won't accept the fundamental truth of what I've said. You didn't like it when I told you in that cell in your mining station that first principles are first. I'll admit you're right. There is more to life than the end. But the Empire doesn't think that way, as you have so clearly pointed out. If you want to preserve the idea that the journey is more important than the destination, it means putting your sweet little ass on the line. Not once, but time after time. And I still don't like games. Games are different from love, and sunsets and sunrises." Surprisingly, he had managed to keep his voice even.

Thelina's face was still expressionless, although her eyes looked cold.

"I'll think about what you said," he finished. "Then . . . someday when you're in the mood . . . let me know."

Thelina remained immobile in the chair, and started to open her mouth.

"Don't bother with another flip or sarcastic answer. Good day, Ecolitan Andruz." Jimjoy walked straight to the front door, not looking back, and closed it quietly behind him.

As he walked down the wooden steps, he started to shake his head, then remembered and pulled at his chin instead. The dampness and splatter of the rain were welcome, despite the dull ache in his muscles from his ongoing efforts to regain his conditioning. All he'd wanted to do was apologize, to get a warm word or two, and now he'd made it ten times worse.

He began to run, heading out around the lake and hoping that his muscles would hurt even more by the time he reached home.

XII

"I'D PREFER YOUR permission," stated the tall, silver-haired man.

"You have *my* permission and support, but not the Institute's. Right now the Board wouldn't support such an action."

"Why not?"

"The Governor's on the Board."

Jimjoy pulled at his chin. Nothing was straightforward. He paced around the end of the table, then back again. "That's the choke point. With the Haversol System Control gone, it would take the better part of six months to mount an attack. So long as it stays, they can have a squadron here in days."

"They couldn't otherwise?"

"Oh, they could. But with no guarantee of power reserves . . . with no clear support trail . . . blocked by the Rift . . . there's not an admiral in the Service who would want to do that. Not with the Fuards looking for any weakness. Not with the Halstanis ready to use any Imperial military action as a lever to gain trade concessions from the other independents."

"*If* what you say is right, what would keep the Empire from immediately associating the action with us?"

"We might have the best motive, but the 'accident' would be staged not to have Accord's fingerprints. The Fuards would be as likely a set of suspects as anyone." Jimjoy licked his lips, pursed them together, then waited.

"All the way out here?" The other's voice was amused.

"Right now they're everywhere."

"That takes care of the military aspect, for a little while. But why won't they replace the station immediately?"

"Immediately means six or seven weeks—five tendays—"

"I understand both weeks and tendays."

"—at the earliest. If nothing is happening elsewhere in Sector Five, and if they have a spare fusactor. That's what they need."

"They couldn't just lift one from in-system?"

"No. Civilian systems aren't compatible without rework. It could be done, but it would probably take more time than bringing one halfway across the Empire." The former Imperial Special Operative cleared his throat. "Then, if we could take out the five system control stations inward from there . . ."

". . . you've effectively buffered us. Which is fine, except that there's limited political support."

"I've been working on that, too."

"The manifestos?"

"Some of them. Someone else seems to be publishing their own . . . and there's that new Freedom Now Party. They're so radical that mere independence seems conservative."

The other man laughed softly.

"I thought so," noted Jimjoy. "Is there anyone else?"

"No, but a number of us are using several other avenues."

"Not enough people."

"Not enough we can trust—at least until you take out orbit control. I assume that's the second step."

"I need a team for that. Destruction's easy. Capture isn't. We need orbit control. Need it to act as if it were still Imperial under our control."

"Buying time."

"Exactly."

"I can provide you with what you probably cannot obtain alone—for the first step. You may be on your own after that."

Jimjoy looked into the shadowed eyes of the older man.

"You're telling me that if I act, you become the target."

"Since you asked . . . yes."

"After all you've done, I'm supposed to go ahead?"

"Do we have any choice? Really?"

Jimjoy stopped pacing. "What about Thelina? Can't she help?"

"She won't approve anything you do. Not now. Not anything that threatens me, even if it's for the long-term good. She has the resources to block you. She would. By the time you convinced her, we'd have a reeducation team here. She hates what you stand for, and you don't have time to change that."

"I suppose not."

"Gavin will get you what you need. Don't let anyone else know. You're having additional medical treatment." His eyes twinkled.

Jimjoy nodded slowly. "Are you sure?"

"No. Are you?'

"No. I don't see any other alternative that will protect Accord."

"Neither do I. Neither do I."

XIII

"Captain Erlin Wheile, Technical Specialist," Jimjoy announced to the Imperial Marine at the military lock.

"Your orders, sir?"

Jimjoy handed over the folder to the Marine technician, along with the databloc that contained far more information than the folder. The folder was for people, the databloc for his ostensible destination's personnel control system—in more ways than officially intended.

"Have a seat over there, Captain." The Marine handed back the orders and the cube and pointed to the black plastic seats through the gate to his left.

Buzz. The gate opened to allow Jimjoy to enter.

"You're lucky," added the Marine. "The next shuttle to SysCon will be locking in less than a standard hour."

Jimjoy nodded politely. "Needed some luck after the trans-shipping . . ."

"Getting here isn't always easy."

"Not from Demetris." Once through the gate with his ship bag, Jimjoy hesitated briefly.

"You got all the luck, Captain."

"Right."

Jimjoy carried his baggage into the nearly empty waiting area. Both an older woman wearing the insignia of a medical tech and a young man in a general technician's uniform looked up. The medical tech immediately dropped her eyes from the chunky and aging junior officer to her portable console. The technician studied Jimjoy until Jimjoy caught his eyes and held them.

After a moment, the young tech looked away.

In turn, Jimjoy eased himself into one of the unyielding black plastic chairs, setting his ship bag at his feet.

The Council was going to be upset, very upset, when they discovered what he was doing, if they discovered. They hadn't seen an Imperial reeducation team. As for Thelina—he didn't want to think about that. She might not speak to him again, assuming he escaped from the mess he was about to create.

He shifted his weight on the hard seat, glancing over at the older technician, who was engaged in some activity with a pocket console—chess, redloc, or something more esoteric. She did not react to his scrutiny, but continued to touch the tiny keys with precise movements, far too quickly for chess, standard games, or data manipulation. If she were playing redloc at that speed, even against a pocket console's memory, she was good, very good.

The technician apprentice kept looking first at Jimjoy, then at the senior technician, and then down at the scuffed plastiles. His black hair barely covered his pale scalp, and the gray of his coverall, which retained its original creases, was still a distinct and recognizable color.

Jimjoy stretched and began to consider how he might have to modify his plans once on board the system control station. The theory was simple enough. The Empire would find it difficult, if not impossible, to maintain easy access to the systems leading to the Rift without at least some functioning system control stations for repowering and re-plenishment.

Since jump drives and functioning fusactors did not coexist—for more than milliseconds—system control stations became essential tools for conquest or control. They had the fusactors, the long-range lasers, and the overall fleet support ability. Removing the system control stations made invasions problematical and conquest impossibly expensive. Of course, removing an orbit control station wouldn't stop a cruiser with a sunburster or a planetbuster—just make it difficult. Besides, most of the time, destroying real estate eliminated the resources you needed to control in the first place.

He pulled at his chin, looking up as another Imperial technician, female and only a shade older than the recruit, plopped herself into one of the hard plastic seats midway between the two men.

"... friggin' screen jockey ... cruddy bitch ..."

Jimjoy took in the clear complexion and the angelic face with the less-than-heavenly language and stifled a grin, noting how the initially disgusted expression on the recruit's face was followed by a speculative look. The woman ignored both glances and bent down to yank her kit bag closer to her feet.

"SysCon shuttle now docking," announced the overhead speakers.

Only the recruit stiffened. Jimjoy and the two women knew the delay before the process was completed, especially if cargo and equipment were involved.

Clunk.

Wsssshhhhtttt. The familiar sounds of docking and off-loading continued for a time.

"... glad to see some new faces ..."

"Not like Vandagilt, you mean? ..."

"... I could have *died* when I saw her there ..."

Jimjoy smiled at the chatter of the two young Marines first off the shuttle. Behind them trooped a handful of technicians, most carrying full kits.

Cling.

"Shuttle for SysCon now ready for boarding."

Jimjoy straightened, but the young recruit was quicker, making it to the lock door even before the barrier had dropped away. The senior medical technician stowed her pocket screen and shook her head as she watched the youngster's haste. The physically attractive junior technician awkwardly hauled a bulging bag over her shoulder and followed Jimjoy.

No one else entered the shuttle.

Jimjoy looked around the windowless cabin with twenty utilitarian couches and strapped his kit into the locker under a couch.

"Prepare for departure for SysCon. Please strap in. Regulations require all passengers remain in their couches during the shuttle run. We anticipate locking at SysCon in less than two stans. Thank you."

Jimjoy strapped in, then stretched out for whatever sleep he could get. He would be getting precious little of that after he reached SysCon. His eyes closed even before the shuttle had unlocked from Haversol orbit control.

"Approaching SysCon."

He blinked, trying to reorient himself. Had he really slept almost two standard hours?

The medical technician was yawning as he looked her way. The recruit merely looked tired, and the other technician was still mumbling obscenities.

Clunk.

"Locking complete."

Jimjoy began to unstrap, thinking about his next steps.

To make an Empire work required standardization, and standardized equipment and installations led to standardized responses by standardized personnel. All of which made destruction easier. The technology, the patterns, and the weak points were always the same. Every SysCon station had the same in-depth defenses, with outlying sensors, remote lasers, and off-station patrol craft. All controls were centralized in the operations center.

Theoretically, the way to destroy a station's capability was to destroy the operations center. Unless you used planetbusters, or their equivalent, destroying the ops center meant suicide. Since he had decided against suicide on general principles, and since he had no planetbusters in his kit bag, he had developed an equivalent.

Cling.

"Personnel may use the forward lock. Please exit in single file."

Jimjoy retrieved his bag, letting the efficient-looking medical technician and the technician apprentice lead the way. The beautiful, if candid-tongued, technician rummaged through her oversized kit, looking for some last-minute item—like her orders or personnel dat_bloc.

Swssshhh. The inner lock door irised open. Over the shoulders of the recruit and the medical technician, Jimjoy could see that the station lock was already open.

"Step up, please."

Jimjoy eased forward as the medical technician dropped her kit back in front of the console and handed over her orders and databloc.

"Technician Meirosol?"

"Yes, Technician?"

"You're cleared to return to SysCon."

"Thank you."

"Next."

Jimjoy waited while the sentry processed the recruit.

"Next."

Jimjoy handed his orders and databloc to the sentry, a bored-looking woman seated behind a half-shielded console. Behind her, encased within a set of screens, sat a professionally intent Imperial Marine with a laser.

Jimjoy almost shook his head. The screens prevented use of projectile weapons, and the theory was that no one could get a laser power pack through the locks without triggering alarms. All true enough. But the kinetic velocity of an old-fashioned hand-thrown knife was below the threshold of the screens, and there was nothing to prevent an intruder from wearing ablative reflection thins under makeup to give himself the instants needed to disable both guards.

While there were plastic knives in his belt, he did not intend to use them, not unless the false nature of his orders was detected.

"Captain Wheile?"

"Yes, Technician?"

"You are cleared to Inprocessing. Have you been on Haversol SysCon before?"

"No."

"Take the corridor to the right. First hatch on the left. . . . Next."

Jimjoy picked up his orders and databloc, then his bag, and followed the directions he had been given, not that he needed them.

He took a deep breath as he started toward the designated hatch. As always, but particularly after his time outdoors at the Institute, the air smelled more mechanical and oily than ever.

Snnniffff . . . His nose was beginning to run, letting him know that it was displeased with the general atmosphere inside the system control station.

Ummmmmm . . . Clearing his throat didn't help. In any case, one way or another, he wouldn't be on board terribly long. After another deep breath, he stepped into the personnel section.

"Yes, Captain?"

The personnel technician looked vaguely interested, in a polite way, in the overweight officer.

"Wheile, Erlin, Technical Specialist, reporting as ordered." He handed her the orders and the databloc.

A puzzled look crossed her face as she looked at the orders, then back at him, then at the databloc. "Don't recall any inposting on you, Captain."

Jimjoy sighed. "I certainly didn't ask to be shuttled from Demetris."

"Demetris?"

"Yes, Demetris." Jimjoy's voice took on a slightly irritated tone. "Back-to-back tours like this, after all these years . . ."

"I understand, Captain, but . . . there's no advance on you. Let me check."

"The databloc should show my posting."

The technician looked at the heavyset officer, then at the databloc, and shrugged. "That doesn't—"

"At least check it—make sure I'm real."

The woman smiled faintly as she took the databloc and inserted it into the scanner. She waited.

Jimjoy could see the green light flick on from its reflection on her badge.

"It says you're real, Captain, but that still doesn't tell us what we're supposed to do with you."

"Wonderful. So what do I do? Get back on the shuttle? Return to Demetris and tell the Admiral it was all a mistake? Or will they say there's no place for me there, either?"

The technician looked apologetic. "These things do happen, Captain. Much as we try to avoid them, sometimes personnel on Alphane fouls up."

"So what do I do now?"

"I'll book you into the transient officers' quarters for the moment. We'll process what we can and request your inposting. Have a good meal and some sleep, and check back in tomorrow morning."

Jimjoy shrugged. "Anything else I can do?"

"Not really, Captain."

"So . . . point me in the right direction . . . would you?"

"Third level north, second spoke. We're on the mid-level, just inside the first spoke . . ."

Arcane as the directions sounded, Jimjoy understood them. He nodded.

"Here's your temporary badge, Captain. It's good for everywhere except comm and ops." The technician handed him the coded square bearing the resemblance of his present appearance. "It's coded to your stateroom . . . number three delta."

"The proverbial closet, I take it?"

"A bit larger, sir."

Jimjoy clipped the badge to his tunic, then hoisted his bag. "Thank you." He turned away, then turned back. "What time tomorrow?"

"Around 0900. There's no reason to get here earlier."

He turned back toward the hatch and started for the transient officers' quarters, trying to bring a hint of a waddle into his walk.

"Technician Smerglia . . . ?"

Since he had managed to get the databloc read by the station personnel system, he had less than two standard hours to get ready. The bag over his shoulder, he continued toward the access shaft that would lead to the north, or upper, side of the station. Even with his waddle walk, it didn't take him more than five standard minutes to arrive at his temporary quarters.

Three delta made a closet look spacious, reflected the Ecolitan. Just a bunk with a reading light, a narrow hanging closet, and a locker under the bunk. He shook his head as he slid the doorway shut behind him.

Clunk . . . He shook his head again as he edged the bag inside the sliding door it had not cleared. "Not even enough space to get the kit inside."

With a sigh louder than he felt, he slid the doorway shut and levered the bag onto the bunk, looking around the closet stateroom. Despite the standardization of the system control stations, some provided small consoles for visiting officers. He had not been provided with one, which meant a little more work in finding a vacant console where no one would complain.

In quick motions, he shoveled out the uniforms and clothing and placed them in the open locker—except for a standard shipsuit, which he draped over a hook in the narrow closet. The two belts he laid aside, as well as the toiletries kit and the spare pair of boots.

The bag empty, he flexed its fabric side, half twisting, until the seam opened. Removing the plastic stiffeners one at a time, he stacked them on the bunk. Then he repeated the process with the bottom. The stiffeners on the bottom were noticeably thicker and went into a second pile.

Off came his boots and the undress travel uniform. The uniform went into the locker, and on went the shipsuit. He placed the stiffeners in the pockets where they temporarily belonged. Next he reclaimed the small plastic-composite tools from the bootheels, before separating out a dozen centimeter-square cubes from the remainder of the heels. One he set aside. The rest and the tools went into the shipsuit's belt pouch. Finally, he put on the real boots and transferred insignia and badges from the travel uniform.

After a last look around the cubicle, he picked up the small black cube and placed it within the pile of clothes he had never worn, nor intended to. Although he could have worn them, doing so would have been mentally and physically uncomfortable, especially around stray voltages or eddy currents.

He opened the sliding door and stepped into the corridor, closing the door behind him. A junior officer had just passed, heading back toward the shafts leading up or down station.

He followed the woman, since the station library was usually somewhere off the main deck. No one gave him even a passing glance during the transit of three decks and a quarter spoke.

The library was empty, except for one duty technician.

"New here," he explained to the young technician, who looked blankly at him. "Arrived before all of the inposting materials. So . . . personnel suggested I come here and spend some time learning about the station. Is there a standard information package?"

"Sure, Captain, but you don't need to—oh—"

Jimjoy nodded. "Right. The woman I'm replacing hasn't left yet. So I'm stuck in one of the TOQ closets. No console, no access . . ."

The technician shook his head sympathetically, then ran his hand over short, stubbly red hair. "We don't have much privacy, sir. Just the three terminals there." He pointed to three utilitarian gray consoles on the wall.

"No problem. Better than my present closet." Jimjoy offered his badge.

"Don't need that, sir. Those are open access, the control is right here."

"Oh . . . fine . . ." The Ecolitan tried to sound bored. "Any special codes to call up the briefing package?"

"No, sir. We're all plain language here, not like the older stations. Just ask what you need."

"Thank you." He waddled toward the group of consoles.

"Take either of those on the left, sir. The keys stick on the right one."

"Thanks," grunted Jimjoy as he sat before the console, studying the setup and waiting for the technician to unblock access.

He almost nodded when he saw the standard databloc access port. Although it wasn't needed here, the Empire hated to make differing console models. He could have inputted his commands from memory, but that would have taken longer, and there was always the chance that he would key something wrong.

The screen swirled, and the face of a pleasant-looking woman appeared. "I'm LISA—Library Information System Applications. What would you like to know? You may use the menu or request other information directly by using the keyboard."

Jimjoy tapped the keys, adjusting the volume downward and calling up the standard systems orientation.

"This is Haversol System Control Station. Located three point eight standard A.U. from Haversol primary, it has been in operation in its present configuration for thirty-five standard years . . ."

The screen displayed a three-dimensional cutaway of the station.

As it did so, Jimjoy palmed a databloc from his thigh pouch and slipped it into the almost dusty scanner slot.

". . . powered by a fusactor class three, with class two screen capabilities . . . including a full aquatic exercise facility on the main deck . . ."

Now that the technician was back into whatever clandestine viewing he had interrupted to help Jimjoy, the Ecolitan smiled ruefully and touched the keys, calling up the second screen momentarily.

"Read data A . . . enscore . . . delay twenty sm . . . ex-score . . ."

"Accepted."

Then he flicked back to the briefing, using the time to locate and reconfirm the locations of his next targets. Whether or not he made it through, he'd left behind, where Thelina and Mardian would find it, an outline of the strategy he'd employed. He hadn't liked leaving a data trail, but he owed her that much, since he hadn't dared to brief them, and they probably wouldn't be all that happy about his "borrowing" the beefed-up needleboat.

He checked the time, then forced himself to wait through another series of briefing bits until he was certain that his departure wouldn't be viewed as too abrupt. He left the databloc in the scanner. It would take care of itself in another standard hour or so, or sooner if anyone tried to remove it.

Finally, he stood up.

"That's about all I can take for now."

"Huhh?" The technician looked up so guiltily that Jimjoy had a hard time smothering a smile.

"That's about all I can take for now," he repeated.

"Pretty boring, sir?"

"I've seen supply manuals more interesting," admitted the pseudo-supply technical specialist.

The technician nodded.

"But I'll probably be back later to see the rest."

"All right, sir."

"Thank you."

But the technician had already returned to whatever he had called up on his own screen.

Jimjoy waddled back to his closet, aware that he was right on schedule, as if he were heading back just before the first mess, when transients were expected in the wardroom. The door to his stateroom/closet opened to his badge, more easily this time.

Once inside, he stripped to the waist and pulled out the bottle of "fragrance." Off came the spare tire around the middle, which he then let resume its prearranged shape as a small datacase. The flat stiffener cards from his kit bag went into the equipment belt.

He reached over and nicked the corner of the black cube in the pile of clothes that were not clothes, and then stepped into the corridor carrying the datacase.

Three corridors, five salutes, and two changes of directions later, he placed the datacase into the proper fire control recess next to a heavily armored conduit. After checking the cubic detonator, he twisted the corner. Too bad he couldn't place the charge exactly where he wanted, but when the time came, it would create a large enough hole along one set of command/control axes to compound the confusion, not to mention the loss of atmosphere.

Jimjoy continued onward, glancing at the corridor lights—still glowing steadily. The ventilators pumped forth in their regular rhythm the same oily air that he had disliked for years, recirculating it through the kays of vents and filters and scrubbers.

With almost a sigh, he extended a card toward the air-lock access scanner.

Click . . .

The lock opened nearly in his face.

"You're not—"

Jimjoy's hands flashed, and the technician crumpled into meat and cloth. Jimjoy grabbed the dead man's badge from his tunic and, taking advantage of the opportunity presented, placed the badge into the scanner, tapping in a series of maintenance codes.

"Cleared for exterior maintenance," flashed the minute screen above the scanner.

Even as the screen finished, the Ecolitan dragged the dead figure into the lock with him. Although he might have wished for marauder-type space armor, the old general-purpose baggy would have to do. It did have the belt for his tools and the flat plastic squares. And, initially, he would be less conspicuous.

Once the helmet was in place, he slipped the first prepared card into the lock scanner. The light winked green. Jimjoy retrieved the card and tabbed the outer lock release, holding himself in place while the air puffed from the lock. Then he slapped the flat plastic against the thinner bulkhead membrane beside the hatch framing, breaking the seal on the thumb-sized detonator. He repeated the process on the outer wall. One down, and a minimum of twenty more to go.

The broomstick came out of its brackets without even a hitch. Fuel? Three-quarters—enough for the moment.

The interior lock lights, dim red for vision adjustment purposes, continued to provide steady illumination. The Ecolitan shook his head, wondering how effectively the virus would be able to infect the SysCon operations net. A gentle push-off with his booted feet carried him and the broomstick away from the station's hull, but toward the northern end. The air lock's outer door winked shut as the automatics triggered.

A silent burst from the front squirter slowed the stick to a slow walk as Jimjoy aimed himself toward the next lock and its lights.

"ExOps, this is OpCon. Interrogative maintenance from alpha center. Interrogative maintenance from alpha center."

Jimjoy winced inside the suit, taking in the approaching lock lights. They shed an unblinking light.

"OpCon, ExOps. Negative on scheduled maintenance this time. Negative on scheduled maintenance this time. Interrogative your last."

Clunk . . . The vibration as the stick grazed the station hull translated into sound inside his helmet. He triggered the lock and waited until the outer hatch irised open. Inside, he slapped another plastic square in place and triggered the detonator. After repeating the process on the outer bulkhead, he pushed off again. Two down.

"ExOps, OpCon. Lock sequencing indicates external operations ongoing this time. Interrogative source."

"OpCon, will check master log."

"Stet, ExOps."

The lock lights continued unblinking. Jimjoy passed the next lock without stopping, angling across to the second spoke. He'd hoped for a bit less time before the virus struck, and a more lethargic reaction from the station crew.

Clunk . . .

The third air lock was an emergency lock, as were most of the spoke locks, and Jimjoy had to practice contortions to place the charges. Another push-off, and he was headed back inward toward an equipment lock on the main frame between spokes two and three, northside.

"ExOps, we have a lock entry spaceside on lock epsilon three gamma."

"Stet, OpCon. We are sending a recon team."

"ExOps, transfer Sigma Charlie. Transfer Sigma Charlie." The comm frequency turned into a flat hiss.

Scrambled communications meant someone was beginning to take things seriously. Jimjoy glanced around, calculating where the recon team would appear. ExOps was southside, about spoke four. And the damned lights still burned steadily.

Clunk . . .

No one was near the big equipment lock, even after the double-sized hatch irised open. This time Jimjoy slapped three separate charges into place—on both exterior and interior bulkheads—before kicking free.

The broomstick crept around the edge of the main hull, within an arm's length of the composite plating. Now that the station was at least partly alerted, the last thing he needed was a radar or EDI reading.

A glint of light off armaglass caught his attention, up near the southern tip of the station. Jimjoy calculated, then angled his broomstick more directly southside.

Clunk . . .

The secondary supply lock was vacant—as it always was except in emergencies. The Ecolitan slapped six more charges in place—three interior and three exterior—and triggered them.

"OpCon, snowman on delta—"

Jimjoy smiled at the broken transmission as he pushed away. Someone had touched the wrong control, then caught on.

He angled past the heat transfer plates marking mid-station and onto the southern side, still less than an arm's length away from the exterior plating. Balancing on the broomstick, he retrieved another charge from the almost depleted supply in the pouch. With a quick motion, he pressed it against the station plates, then used the squirter to keep him close to the hull.

The idea had been to create enough chaos so that his entry into first the fusactor and then, if possible, the weapons storage bays in the armory would not be noticed. Once the security system was immobilized, or at least so erratic that no one in operations could believe it, and with the two dozen major leaks and half-dozen jammed air locks, the maintenance crews would have their hands full. Except that nothing had happened yet.

"Blowout! Section two delta! Blowout in two delta!"

Jimjoy eased the broomstick even closer to the hull in reaction to a pair riding their own sticks a quarter diameter away. They passed behind a stub spoke, number four, apparently without seeing him.

"Blowout! Section three. Lock jammed . . ."

The Ecolitan nodded, wishing that the main power system bugs had taken hold. He glanced over his shoulder.

"Hades . . ."

A single broomstick bore down on him from behind, less than twenty meters away. How had he missed it?

The heavy knife came out of the equipment belt, as did the small can of spray. Then he stopped the stick, flipped it, squirted once to kill his relative speed, and triggered the can.

The polymer spread into a glistening shield just as the laser triggered, and collapsed as rapidly as it had formed.

The knife left his hand, heading through the dissipating silver haze.

The broomstick rider tried to dodge the heavy razor-edged plastic weapon, but his accumulated momentum was too great, and his air spilled from a suit split from shoulder to hip.

Jimjoy swallowed hard, forcing the bile back into his throat, and nudged the squirter to avoid the still-flailing figure that cartwheeled past him.

With another swallow, he edged the broomstick toward the fat-looking nodule connected by the umbilical to the south end of the station. Another look at the scattered lights of the station. Still nothing. He was running out of time. But he couldn't even begin the next phase unless the virus had been successful in penetrating the SysCon operating codes.

Again Jimjoy studied the lights framing the nearest lock.

Was there a flicker? Definitely, a pulse to the lights. Once, twice . . .

He began to toggle through all the SysCon frequencies. The helmet receiver hummed, and he halted the cycle to listen.

". . . control . . . intermittent power . . . interrogative . . ."

"OpCon, interrogative status. Interrogative . . ."

". . . lost slush on tank one . . . lost slush . . . strains . . . three epsilon . . ."

Jimjoy smiled faintly and goosed up the broomstick another notch, heading toward the fusactor module. Now, within minutes, no one would have standard commlinks, thanks to his efforts in the library. And the maintenance crews would have their hands more than full.

". . . MAYDAY . . . DAY . . . spoke five . . ."

". . . spoke six . . . uncontrolled lock cycles . . ."

Still scooting along in the shadows within an arm span of the hull, he could see assorted vapor puffs and flashing lights. Ahead, the umbilical to the fusactor grew larger.

"Raider six, OpCon . . . omega black . . . black . . ."

Jimjoy shivered at the last broken transmission. Although the power cycles had disrupted the scramblers, the operations center had clearly decided they wanted him very dead. They didn't know who he was, or where—yet.

He glanced around again. So far, so good. In a few moments he would have to leave the shadows and cross the open gap paralleling the umbilical.

Crump . . . whhhsttt . . . The sounds of destruction filtered through the headset momentarily. He shook his head, thinking, idiotically, that he should be trying to pull at his chin.

Even in the sunlight no one pursued him, as the puffs of vapor continued to spill into the void.

Clunk . . . The impact nearly flattened him against the plates surrounding the fusactor assembly. Surprisingly, the broomstick had not bent. He checked the squirters. Less than fifty percent.

He inserted the I.D. code card into the scanner slot. For several moments, nothing happened. Then the access light winked green and the codeboard lit.

With a sigh, Jimjoy tapped out a code, altered but based on an older, valid entry code, and waited with a small probe.

The entry light flickered amber, and Jimjoy pressed the tip of the probe against the edge of the I.D. slot, triggering the modified pulse current. The light turned red, then green, and the hatch irised half open.

With the opening just wide enough for Jimjoy to scramble through, he barely got his left boot clear of the edge before the lock slid shut. The inner door was unguarded, opening at his touch as he floated in null-gee. The grav-fields had been shut down by the power fluctuations, but the power sections were engineered to work without grav-fields, since they provided the power for and had to precede the fields.

Inside, he pulled himself hand over hand around toward the section he wanted. Once there, he withdrew several tools from his pouch, taking off his gauntlets but leaving his helmet in place.

The adjustments were minor, and their immediate effect would scarcely be noticed amidst the power surges already racking the station. He hoped to be clear of the station before the final impact.

After replacing the panels he had removed for access, as well as his gauntlets, the Ecolitan pulled himself back to the lock, where he made two more adjustments, ensuring the outer lock would open once, and only once—to let him out, along with the extra broomstick he had unlatched from the lock wall.

It did, closing quickly enough that, again, he almost lost a foot.

"Charlie three, leak on delta five. Class three."

"Stet. Delta five with a four patch."

"Blowout in supply two . . ."

"Hades . . . get that sucker . . ."

Overhead, in his present orientation, the SysCon station presented an array of flashing lights, some hints of what appeared to be mist, and a handful of space-armored figures.

Jimjoy checked his orientation again, slowly swinging the first broomstick about. The second was tethered to him. Then he lined up the pocket EDI, trying not to think about the next step.

"If . . . if . . ."

He pressed the squirter control, letting the broomstick carry him out toward the station-keeping area. According to the postings, two couriers, a scout, and three corvettes stood off-station. The corvettes were useless.

The EDI needle seemed to match his vector.

He took a deep breath, then another, then held it and listened, as he chin-toggled from frequency to frequency.

". . . section four beta . . . secure . . ."

". . . blowout uncontained in supply two . . ."

". . . kill the frigger . . . whole section . . ."

". . . ExOps . . . no sign of intruder . . ."

With a last deep breath, he touched the squirter controls. The broomstick carried him into the shadows and toward the stationkeeping area, directly toward the dimmest of the EDI readings.

He forced himself to let up on the squirter. He'd need all the power he could muster at the other end, and he had more air than power.

Turning his head, he watched the SysCon slowly recede, its gray-and-silver bulk blotting out less and less of the stars, lock lights still flashing intermittently, puffs of vacated atmosphere still jerking forth.

How many had died? He tried not to think about it. Maybe Thelina was right—that he was nothing better than a coldblooded killer who justified his actions with simplistic principles. Had the young library tech deserved to die? He certainly had had nothing to do with wanting to crush Accord. Nor had the medical tech absorbed in her redloc game.

". . . slush two frozen . . . tank three . . . whole system's shot . . ."

". . . blowout . . . four epsilon . . ."

". . . power pulses from fusactor . . ."

He shivered and turned to watch the blackness before him, straining for the glint of metal or the dullness of composite plates, continuing to check the EDI for the slightest twitch. The broomstick carried him onward into the darkness, outward toward where he hoped to find escape—one way or another.

XIV

WAS THERE A glimmer ahead? Just off the left of the broomstick's heading? With all Imperial hulls designed as nonreflective, the dim sunlight from Haversol had not proved much help in locating the off-station ships.

Jimjoy checked the EDI, uncertain whether the needle leaned off-center.

Buzzzzzzz . . .

The alarm sounded, and the EDI display vanished simultaneously.

"Hades . . ." muttered Jimjoy, careful not to trigger the suit's transceiver. Without turning, he began to pull in the spare broomstick that had trailed behind him until he held the narrow frame in his hands, his knees still holding him on the exhausted composite-metal structure. As quickly as carefully possible, he positioned the unused broomstick next to the one he had ridden and eased from the one to the other. Only after he was in place did he release the tether and transfer it to the spent vehicle.

The mass of the used stick, however insignificant, might be necessary, and since it currently had the same momentum as he did, there was no point in letting it go . . . yet.

Then he touched the activator stud, watching the EDI display light up. The needle was definitely moving leftward, toward the glint he had seen, or thought he had seen.

The problem was his limited fuel. If he ended up heading toward a corvette, he was as good as dead. He needed a courier or scout, preferably a courier, and ideally one in a stand-down status.

". . . blowout patch gone . . . four delta . . ."

". . . power surges . . . continuing . . . non-SysCon origin . . ."

". . . frigging designs! Clamp . . ."

A vague outline appeared ahead to the left, visible as a dark patch against the stars. To the right was the darkness of the Rift, against which no hull shadow would be visible until he was nearly upon it.

He glanced down at the EDI as the broomstick coasted outward. The outline looked too solid for the kind of ship he needed, but if he didn't have some other hint before long . . . He shivered inside the suit, although he was not cold.

Twitch. The EDI needle shivered, but remained fixed. Jimjoy watched as the needle and the shadow edged ten degrees leftward off his heading. Then he studied the area to the right more intently as the EDI shivered again. Was that a small fuzzy black patch?

He almost shrugged as he touched the squirter controls, beginning a gentle curve away from the corvette and toward what seemed to be a smaller spacecraft.

". . . damned power surges . . . fusactor . . . interrogative . . . umbilical . . ."

". . . OpCon . . . negative . . . negative . . . work party . . . for fusactor . . ."

Jimjoy swallowed. His timing was finer that he would have liked, and he hadn't been able to modify any of the ship or station tacheads. So EMP detonations were going to be minimal.

The EDI needle suddenly flicked rightward. Jimjoy couldn't help smiling as the needle centered on the darkness ahead.

". . . OpCon . . . access blocked . . . lock inoperative . . ."

"ExOps, OpCon, imperative immediate access to fusactor . . . umbilical . . . interrogative release . . ."

". . . sabotage . . . interrogative . . . say again, ExOps . . ."

Jimjoy peered ahead at the darkness within the darkness, then triggered the squirters for a short burst. The EDI remained locked on the ship ahead, whose shadow loomed larger.

He keyed in the squirters for full forward thrust, trying to kill off his outbound momentum before he either flattened himself against the hull plates or went flying by and into an orbit which might be of interest to astronomers or future archaeologists, but would cease to be of much urgency to one Jimjoy Whaler. Even now the name sounded foreign.

". . . cutting laser . . . op immediate . . . laser . . . ExOps . . . do you read me . . ."

Jimjoy pursed his lips at the frantic sounds of the transmissions from behind him, even as he concentrated on guiding the broomstick to the courier ahead. He had too much velocity, careful as he had thought he had been, for the squirters to kill. He had to hit the courier—squarely—and hope the collapsible frame would function as designed.

". . . frig . . . regs . . . need that cutter . . . NOW!!!"

Whhhsssssstttt . . . The vibration of the final squirter thrust killing the broomstick's velocity fed back through the framework and into his suit.

Clunnnnk . . . Jimjoy winced at the sound. Anybody awake and on board the courier certainly wouldn't have missed his arrival.

As the broomstick absorbed the shock, he reached out and planted the sticky lock loop on a hull plate before any recoil could separate him. Even so, as he clicked the safety tether fast to the loop, he and the courier began to separate.

"Ummmffff. . ." The jolt of hitting the end of the safety line caused the involuntary exclamation.

After dragging himself back to the hull, hand over hand, he eased the first broomstick out of the tether loop and left it floating beside the courier hull. Then he began a careful scramble toward the main lock.

Along the way, he checked to ensure his remaining knife was still available for use. While the stunner might be more useful, it was what any crew would be concentrating upon.

Finally, he floated outside the crew lock.

"Well. . . ." With a deep breath, he touched the access stud, waiting to see if he needed to use his tools.

The red panel winked on as the outer door slid open.

Moistening his lips and swallowing, Jimjoy pulled himself inside, upright, to anticipate returning to ship gravity. His feet touched the deck, and he stepped fully inside, tapping the stud to close the lock.

"WHO . . . UNIDENTIFIED VISITOR, PLEASE IDENTIFY YOURSELF!"

Jimjoy winced at the volume of the inquiry.

"IDENTIFY YOURSELF!"

"Wheile, Erlin, Captain, I.S.S., Technical Specialist."

"Likely story . . ." The metallic sound of the suit speaker still conveyed the skepticism of whoever was inside the courier.

"May I come aboard?"

"You already are, without invitation." The speaker's tone was all too reminiscent of a passed-over courier skipper.

"May I come aboard?"

"Everything else is crazy—why not? Keep your hands in plain sight."

Jimjoy released his breath and keyed the lock controls for the inner door, waiting for the release inside. Finally the panel blinked, then turned steady green. The inner door irised open, and he stepped through.

A baggy-suited figure stood two meters from him, a laser aimed straight at his midsection. "Again, who are you? How did you get here? Why?"

"Erlin Wheile, Captain, I.S.S., Technical Specialist."

"Supposed to believe that?"

"Check with ExOps," suggested Jimjoy. "Had an intruder. Hit me with a stunner from about a meter away. Suit helped, but I was headed outbound, without enough fuel to get back. Only hope was an off-station ship. Bent the hades out of the broomstick."

"Likely story."

The lock closed behind Jimjoy.

"Fine. Check your screens. Is there anything around here? You think anyone is crazy enough to deliberately take a broomstick ride in the middle of nowhere in hopes of finding a ship?"

"Point, but not much of one." The speaker's voice was still muffled. "Take off the helmet—slowly. Keep your gauntlets on, and your hands in full view."

Jimjoy almost sighed. Clearly an officer with some understanding of suits. He carefully loosened the maintenance-type helmet, following the other officer's directions. As he cracked the seals, he could hear only the ventilators hissing. At least there was but a single crewman aboard.

He began to lift off the helmet, watching the other's gun-hand gauntlet.

"Bast—"

Clang . . . clunk . . . The helmet clanked off the Imperial's upper arm. *Whhsssttttt.*

Thud.

"Hades." Jimjoy managed to steady himself against the bulkhead, forcing himself to breathe, despite the fire in his right shoulder, as he looked at the fallen figure in the narrow passageway. The officer lay facedown, motionless. Although he could not see it, Jimjoy knew a heavy knife protruded from the chest of the woman. Sooner or later, it had to have happened.

Some gesture, some look, despite the disguise, had betrayed him. But Ladonna had always said she would recognize him anywhere. Especially after the *IFoundIt!* mission, when he had gotten Sashiel cashiered for incompetence.

Well, she had recognized him, or what he represented. It didn't matter which. And she was dead. And he wasn't in exactly wonderful condition. Despite the protection from the suit, his right arm didn't work. His nose protested the smell of burned flesh.

He took a deeper breath, ignoring the fire shooting across his chest, and concentrated on calling up the pain blocs, focusing on the bland but stale metallic odor of the recycled air. The effort it took made it clear he didn't have much time.

The controls were only five steps away. He took one step, then stopped. Another long step, and he crossed Ladonna's body. Step and rest, step and rest, step and rest. In more than the one-third gee of the ship, he would not have made it. Step and rest . . . all for a mere five meters in low grav.

". . . don't relax . . . don't relax . . ." Jimjoy did not realize he was vocalizing his thoughts until he recognized the voice as his own.

His right arm dangled, but his left swung the fingertip control

pad—normally used for high-gee, outside-the-envelope maneuvering—
into position.

Ignoring the checklist, he brought the board to life, checked the
power, and began to preprogram the outsystem course, the jump sequence, and the inboard course to Thalos. If he collapsed, the pre-
programming might get him close enough to be rescued. Otherwise,
he would modify the course as the ship neared each decision point.

"AlCom, this is Haversol SysCon. Haversol . . . all units . . . imperative . . . stand . . . SysCon . . ."

"AlCom . . . negative . . . negative . . ."

". . . Radian Throne . . . request . . . imperative . . ."

Jimjoy ignored the conflicting transmissions for SysCon evacuation
and alternatively for station-ships to stand off, slowly completing his
power-up and waiting for the board to wink green.

"Ready for departure," announced the console.

Jimjoy did not wait for the completion of the courier's announcement before stabbing the stud to trigger the drive controls.

"Speedline four, interrogative action. Interrogative action."

Jimjoy sighed. "Negative action. Negative action. Maintaining station."

"Radian Throne, this is Courage three. Interrogative status SysCon."

"Courage three, Radian Throne. Stand by. Clear this frequency.

"Speedline four, Radian Throne. Imperative you hold station this
time."

"Radian Throne, Speedline four," rasped Jimjoy. "Interrogative your
last. Interrogative your last."

"Radian Throne, Hawkstrike one, standing off this time. Standing
off this time."

"Hawkstrike one, negative. Negative standoff. Hold your station . . ."

"Frig you . . ." muttered Jimjoy almost under his breath, but deliberately keying his transmitter.

"Interrogative last transmission. Interrogative last transmission."

Jimjoy ignored the request from the station-keeping commander and
edged up his drive velocity. Even the motion in his fingers sent twinges
through his other shoulder. The laser should have cauterized the arm
enough so that the blood loss was minimal, but there was no way to
tell what internal bleeding might be occurring. He didn't want to think
about the nerve damage.

". . . standing by not advisable . . . AlCom . . . interrogative . . ."

". . . OpCon . . . power . . . surges . . ."

"Speedline four, return to station. Return to station."

"Stet. Returning to station," Jimjoy answered, knowing that the courier needed every instant of acceleration possible, since he could not personally survive a high-gee run.

"Hawkstrike four, return to station. Return to station."

"Negative, Radian Throne. That is negative this time. ImpOrd three point five beta forbids hazard of vessel in noncombat situation."

"Hawkstrike four, I say again. Return to station."

"Departing station this time."

WHHHHHHHEEEEEEEEEEEeeeeeeeeeeeeeeeeeeeeeeeeeeeeeeeeeee . . .

The scream of white noise—that and the EDI pegging off the register—told Jimjoy that Haversol SysCon was no longer a threat to Accord.

He could sense the control area turning gray around him, and wondered if he would be able to rouse himself for the jump . . . if he should try . . . but, damned if he wanted to give Thelina the satisfaction . . .

. . . *cling . . . cling . . .*

As if from a distance, he could hear the chiming, the distant sounds of the morning bells on White Mountain, rebounding over fresh white snow . . . or was it the sounds of evening bells from the meeting house on Harmony . . . ?

He pried one eye open, reached—and was rewarded with a searing line of pain down his right arm.

Haversol, Ladonna, the laser wound, and now the jump.

With an effort he used his left hand.

"Jump parameters outside acceptable envelope."

He squinted at the readout. Once, twice. On the third try, he could read the numbers. The dust density was above acceptable levels.

His left hand tapped out the query.

"Probability of successful jump is ninety-eight point five."

His fingers slashed the jump command stub, and instantaneous endless blackness flashed up around him. For that instant, the pain in his shoulder became a kind of pleasure, but only for that instant.

Back in real-space the searing continued, with each instant adding yet another needled blast.

Jimjoy took a breath and concentrated on rebuilding the pain blocs.

After a while, the searing receded, and he could see the board clearly enough to realize he needed to reconfigure the small remaining jump. He did, one finger at a time, one calculation at a time, and touched the jump button.

Again the blackness relieved the pressure of the blocked pain, but even in null-time, Jimjoy did not relax the blocs, just waited.

"Jump complete."

With another effort, he began to reprogram the entry curve to Thalos, that airless moon off Permana, the Accord system's fourth planet, trying to ensure that the final deceleration would occur with Permana's bulk between the courier and Accord orbit control.

As a last effort, he also programmed the Mayday message for transmission on the Institute's scrambled frequency—but only after deceleration halted.

His fingers touched the controls, and the ship began its inward curve, a curve that he hoped would bring him back. He'd done what he promised to Sam; and Thelina would never talk to him again. Why did he worry?

From that point, events took on a gauzy texture . . .

. . . did he actually adjust the curve to compensate for dust . . . ?

. . . or boost the decel power to cut closer to the Institute base . . . ?

. . . or tell the needleboat standing off the courier to just go ahead and wait until he was dead . . . ?

. . . or did the grayness roll in over him at the moment the courier entered the system?

XV

THE ADMIRAL TOOK a deep breath, then glanced up at the holo view portraying New Augusta from the air. His fingers drummed on the bare wood as he pursed his lips.

After a time, he looked back at the hidden screen, recessed into the wooden table and displaying its message only to someone sitting in the Admiral's chair.

"Haversol SysCon—Status Report.

"Facility: OMEGA

"Survivors: 87 known (10.1 percent of estimated POB/E)

"Ships: HMS PIKE (cc)—OMEGA

HMS DEGAULLE (lc)—OMEGA
HMS NKRUMAH (lc)—DELTA
HMS LEGROS (ft)—OMEGA . . ."

He skipped to the analysis, picking out phrases.

". . . simultaneous use of ANT (accelerated nerve toxin), fusactor bottle effect, tachead explosions, and wide-scale EMP effects point to a well-orchestrated military operation, rather than an accident or a terrorist attack . . ."

"Brilliant, just brilliant," muttered the Admiral. "Of course it was military. But whose military?"

". . . the Haversol SysCon 'incident' bears no identifiable modus operandi associated with past or present efforts of either the Halstani or the Fuard Special Operations teams . . ."

". . . knew that . . ." The Admiral rubbed his forehead and returned his study to the screen.

". . . the statistical comparator found the greatest similarity between the Haversol SysCon 'incident' and Imperial Special Operative techniques . . . correlation level of fifty percent plus . . ."

The Admiral shook his head before touching several recessed keys in quick succession. The screen displayed a second document.

"JIMJOY EARLE WRIGHT III
DECEASED . . ."

He skimmed through the file, again mentally noting key elements.

". . . use of EMP as a detonating mechanism during HUMBLEPIE (see Halston 'accident') . . ."

". . . ability to infiltrate and destroy installation warned against him was highlighted by his presumed destruction of the New Kansaw facility through the use of the Masada safeguards . . ."

". . . piracy of HMS *D'Armetier* was attributed to Major Wright, after diversion of a planetary shuttle into the New Kansaw orbit control . . ."

The Admiral frowned, again all too aware of the pounding in his temples. He jabbed at the controls.

"Profile of Major Wright (DECEASED) achieves 78.4 percent correlation with assumed and reconstructed modus operandi for destruction of Haversol SysCon."

The senior officer glanced at the holo view of the capital once more before touching the console controls and rereading the words displayed on the screen for at least the fourth time.

". . . wreckage of the HMS *D'Armetier* discovered on the surface of Timor II (see catalog Red 3-C). Remains of four bodies were on board. Two were positively identified by physical remnants, Imperial tag trace, and absolute DNA match. Two were tentatively identified as New Kansaw rebels—one male and one female.

"The two positive identifications were:

JIMJOY EARLE WRIGHT III
MAJOR, I.S.S./S.O./B-941 366
HELGRAN FORSTE MITTRE
LIEUTENANT, I.S.S./ A-371 741."

Finally, the Admiral blanked the screen.

"The only one, and he's dead." He reached for the hypnospray, hoping that this time the medicine would relieve the headache.

XVI

OVERHEAD WAS GRAY. Swirling, spinning gray. He could not move, his chest bound by an invisible band that made each breath an effort. Fire gnawed at his right shoulder, but he could see no flames, feel no heat on his face.

Closing his eyes replaced the gray with featureless black, but his eyelids wanted to remain closed.

"Acchhh . . ." His cough sounded strangled in his own ears as he forced his eyes back open.

The gray overhead was gray—solid gray rock. The fire in his shoulder ebbed, until he tried to shift his weight off his aching buttocks. Then it seared all the way down his arm and back through his chest. Down his arm?

Jimjoy wanted to shake his head, but knew he should pull at his chin. He couldn't, not with the padded cuffs around his wrists. Where was he? Not on Accord, not with the dark rock overhead. Thalos, where he had ended up after his first escape from the Empire?

". . . thought you were awake, but you really shouldn't be, Professor Whaler." The woman's voice was low but pleasant.

"Accccchhhhaaa . . ." Clearing his throat didn't make breathing any easier, but the dryness subsided. "Where . . . ?"

"Thalos," answered the green-clad woman as she adjusted something in the apparatus behind his right shoulder. The fires in his arm and shoulder eased. "You've been under for a while. That's hard on your lungs, but the first stages are critical, and any jerky motions damp retakes."

"Gibberish," he mumbled, because none of what she said made any sense.

"You really overstressed your system, but we've got it all under control. I'm going to put you back under for a little bit. We need another day to ensure everything takes, but you're doing just fine. Just fine.

"Now, try to relax. . . ."

Even as she spoke, he could feel his muscles begin to loosen.

". . . any . . . choice . . . ?"

"No, Professor, you don't. We can talk about the reasons later."

As the grayness dissolved into black, he understood she was talking to keep him calm while whatever she pumped into his system took effect.

When his eyes blinked open again, the overhead gray was clearer. The gumminess around his eyelids remained. His right shoulder and upper arm throbbed with a dull ache, and the padded cuffs were still in place around his wrists. A fractionally deeper breath indicated that the invisible band still encircled his chest.

He'd clearly been rescued, if rescue were the correct term, by the Institute. In what light his return was regarded remained another question. That all depended on Sam; on what he had been able to do. The dimness of the lights signaled local night, or the equivalent.

Shifting his weight did not bring the agony he recalled from his previous awakening, only a slight intensification of the throbbing in his arm.

"How do you feel?" asked the low-voiced woman from behind his shoulder.

"Better . . ." His throat was dry and he swallowed once, twice, in an effort to moisten it.

"I'd like you to try and rest quietly. I'm going to loosen the cuff on the left arm, but you'll still have to stay on your back. I know it's sore, but regrowth doesn't take in null-gee, and trying to handle partial field generation isn't possible within a field."

"Regrowth . . ." he croaked.

"Partial regrowth," she corrected. "The bone cells were mainly all right, but you lost all the nerves along the upper arm and most of the musculature. That's why the pain was so great, why you've been under sedation for so long. But don't worry. The arm regrowth took just fine. It's going to be painful sometimes, especially since the nerve confusion will take time to settle out.

"You've got some fluids in your lungs, but they're within limits. Tomorrow we'll move you into postural drainage for a bit, before letting you sit up."

"How . . . about . . . arm . . ."

"Your arm will be fine. You will need a great deal of therapy before it's normal again. How fast is up to you." She frowned as she bent over to loosen the cuff. "No, you can't start now. You'll need another few days in solution at least."

He managed to turn his head to see the molded tank attached to his shoulder and in which his right arm lay.

"I'll be back in a moment. You can wiggle your fingers on the good arm and move it *gently*. Don't touch anything on your right side."

"All . . . right."

He focused on the overhead. Would they take all this trouble if he were destined for disaster? He did not shake his head, although he felt like it.

Another set of footsteps echoed on the stone.

He glanced toward the doorway, taking in the blond-haired new arrival. The second woman eased over to his bed. Why was Meryl here? At least he thought it was Thelina's quarter mate.

"Are you awake?"

"Barely." He tried to force a smile.

"Thelina will be here in a few minutes. She's angry. Don't let her blame you." Meryl's lips pursed. "Just remember. She's mad. She needs someone to blame. Besides herself."

Jimjoy squinted up at her, trying to hold her fading image in view, at the words that seemed to come from so far away. "Angry . . . because . . . Haversol . . . ?" Each of his words took a separate breath against the invisible band encircling his chest.

"No. Because—My God! You don't even know. How could you? They called it an accident. It wasn't—"

"Ecolitan," intruded a second voice. "He's not to have visitors yet."

"Just a moment. He needs to know." Meryl bent closer to Jimjoy. Her face was damp, pale, and a wisp of hair brushed his cheek. "The

Empire—Special Operations—someone—murdered the Prime. Sam and Gavin Thorson. An accident, but we know better. Thelina wants to blame you. Don't let her."

Her hand squeezed the fingertips of his left hand, the one that he still seemed to have, and he blinked.

When his eyes reopened, she was gone. Another slow blink, and a woman in green was adjusting the apparatus attached to his right shoulder.

"You're doing fine, Professor. Just fine."

Another blink, and she was gone. Just the gray overhead above him. Solid gray. Solid, unlike the swirling gray of winter on White Mountain. Solid, unlike the black-and-gray bolts of the storms of Accord. Solid dull gray.

He could hear the footsteps on the polished rock floor.

Tap . . . tap . . . tap . . .

"Hello, Thelina." He managed to keep his throat from rasping.

"Hello, Professor." Her voice was low, almost ragged.

"Sorry . . . to keep meeting you like this . . ."

She edged up to the left side of the bed, looking down at him. Even in the dim light he could see her eyes were bloodshot. She looked from one end of the bed to the other, slowly shaking her head.

"That bad?"

"Always a flip comment, Professor?"

He sighed—almost. His breath caught with the pain in his chest.

"No . . . you bring out . . . the best . . . in me."

She studied him for a long time, not speaking.

He lay there, unwilling to say anything.

"Meryl was here."

"Yes."

"She told you about Sam."

"A little . . . an accident . . . not an accident . . . killed Sam and Gavin Thorson. That . . . was it. Said you were upset. Said you might blame me . . ."

"I found your package."

"And . . ."

"You're a bastard—a cold, unfeeling bastard. You're effective. Sam knew it. He knew we needed you. He knew you might be his death. He's the hero."

Jimjoy waited, watching the tears stream down her cheeks, understanding, he hoped, at least a small fraction of what she felt, knowing that the only man who had supported him and believed in him was dead.

"... know ... you even feel it ... a little ..."

Jimjoy nodded, not wanting to speak.

For a time, the room was silent, except for the background hiss of ventilators and two sets of ragged breathing.

"I need to go ..."

"I know ..."

Did her hand touch his, ever so lightly, as she stepped away? Or had he imagined it?

"Take care, Professor ..."

"You ... too ... Ecolitan Andruz ..."

His cheeks felt damp. But it had to be from his gummy eyes. It had to be.

XVII

12 Duo 3646
Lansdale Station

Dear Blaine:

Should have faxed you earlier. Hadn't realized how time has gone, but with the buildup out here, the increased tours, didn't seem to have a minute. If it's not one Fuard thing, it's another.

Torp trash says they blew out Haversol SysCon. That true? If you can't say, don't. But I couldn't figure anyone else who could.

Halley's down again. Converter fused solid after overjump. Managed to coast in-system here. Hell of a thing not even being able to lock by yourself, and halfway across the sector so I can't even see Helen, Jock, and little Cindi. She's a doll, but sometimes these days I think I scarcely know them. They don't know me either.

What's new on the FC? Rumor has it the Senate passed a resolution declaring it obsolete before it would be ready. Serious???

Had a near miss last month with one of the new Fuard destroyers. Couldn't believe it. Damned thing came out of jump going sideways. Ran circles around us.

Way it looks now, I guess I'll be out here longer. New I.S.S. personnel directive—extending command tours another two standard years, except for promotions. Won't be in the zone for another two. So it's two more years with the old *Halley*—if either of us lasts that long.

My best to you and Sandy.

Mort

XVIII

"WHEREAS IMPERIAL TECHNOLOGY, equipment, and expertise have been provided to colony planets at substantial risk to the provider and represent the contribution through sacrifice by honest citizenry interested solely in benefiting their fellow beings;

"Whereas said equipment and technology have been provided to endow colonists and their successors with the ability to survive and prosper;

"Whereas the peaceful use of knowledge and technology is the right and heritage of all thinking beings;

"Whereas the abuse of Imperial technology has led to great loss of human life, human suffering, and substantial loss of capital resources by the law-abiding citizens of law-abiding planets;

"Whereas the inability of colony planets to prevent the misuse and malappropriation of technology and the continued failure of these self-same colony planets to bring to justice those responsible for such great loss of life and irreplaceable resources have become evident;

"THEREFORE, be it resolved by the Senate, in accord with the Charter, and under the powers invested in this Body, that:

"The presence or use of offensive weapons upon any aerial or off-planet self-powered craft or fixed emplacement, other than those operated directly by duly constituted Imperial Forces, is hereby forbidden;

"An additional ad valorem tax of five per centum on the assessed value of all production or sale of raw materials, semifinished or full finished goods shall be paid to the Revenue Collection Service, excepting those goods produced within any planetary system which has accepted full voting membership in the Council of Systems;

"The revenue raised from such ad valorem tax shall be devoted in total to the maintenance and enhancement of Imperial interstellar capabilities in the areas of colonization, exploration, and colonial protection, including, but not limited to, shipbuilding, research, development, and training of personnel;

"The results of all research efforts funded directly or indirectly, or arising from an Imperial colonization effort, shall also be made available to the Consortium of Advanced Studies;

"And, finally, the enforcement of these provisions shall be the duty and obligation of His Imperial Majesty, as delegated under the Charter and set forth herein, modified as necessary with the further consent of the Senate for full implementation."

"Debate is now open on the measure," intoned the clerk in black.

By the lowered benches behind the rostrum, two individuals nodded to each other.

"So we spent all this money, and the little buggers aren't grateful. They want to do things their way? What else could you expect, Stentor?" His voice was nearly a whisper, designed not to be heard above the formal debate taking place behind them.

"Are we speaking candidly?"

"Don't we always?"

"Nothing. I expect nothing from the colonists. They are not the issue at all. The armed forces, the Service in particular, and the Fuards are . . ."

"You think a display of resolution by the great and glorious Imperial Senate will pacify the eagles and the Fuards?"

"I'm not really that ambitious. I merely wish to raise the issue early, to preempt the firestorm it will become later. To provide a focus so that something more extreme is not adopted."

"You think that this is the most moderate of approaches possible, then?"

"It may be still too moderate. Admiral KeRiker has proposed militarizing all orbital and space travel facilities serving colony planets, even those with locally elected governments and independently and locally supported off-planet facilities. As for the Fuards . . . nothing will pacify them."

"You may be too late."

"I may. But may I count on your voice?"

"My voice? By all means. But my vote is the will of the people's."

"I understand . . ."

XIX

JIMJOY FROWNED AT the console. Doing was so much easier than planning, especially when he had relied so much upon instinct, rather than trying to chart out all the possible variables.

Chrrupppp . . . Outside, another of the local birds called out a greeting.

Letting his hands rest below the keyboard, he looked out at the bare limbs of the T-type maple. Through the branches he could see the native grayoak, not properly an oak at all, which did not shed leaves seasonally but throughout the year, although the leaves looked like gray leather in the cold of winter and early spring.

On the maple's top branch roosted a purplish jaymar, one of the few Accord avians he recognized. Not that recognition was difficult. Jaymars had a call more raucous than a crow's, manners less acceptable than a pigeon's, and an appetite less discriminating than a sea gull's. Only their striking purpled-black feathers were pleasing—and, according to the ecological purists, their singular ability to remove carrion and/or wastes.

Chuuurrrrppppp . . .

With a drawn-out breath, he flexed his right hand, trying to loosen the stiffness of skin and muscles. Now the pain in his shoulder had diminished, using the console was no longer a chore. Returning to teaching *Theories of Warfare* had been almost a relief—except for Yusseff's sleeping in class.

Because Ecolitans had the odd habit of disappearing and reappearing—injured and otherwise—no one had asked him about the bulky regen dressing. But they had sighed at the return of his logical argument papers and his insistence on questioning fundamental assumptions. Several Ecolitans had covered for him, including Thelina, who had left him notes—most impersonal—on the two sessions she had taught on tactics under the military dictatorship of Halston—pre-Matriarchy.

Mardian, the other tactics professor, had handled the majority of the classes and had left a note. "Too bad you didn't opt for teaching years ago!"

Jimjoy stroked his chin at the thought. Without the mistakes he had made . . . but that wouldn't help him with the next phase. He needed an entire set of manuals for the crew he had yet to assemble.

"Datablocs," he mumbled. "Use of coding . . . access to Imperial datanets . . ." All of the loopholes and techniques he had developed needed to be reduced to simplified procedures for others without the benefit of his experience. At times, he was amazed at how much he had learned.

"Right . . . good for the ego . . ." He almost grinned.

Chrrrupppp . . . churuppppp . . . With a double raspberry, the jaymar flicked its tail and launched itself into the late fall drizzle.

A wisp of woodsmoke swirled above the bare branches, and Jimjoy sniffed for the welcome acridness. The closed door blocked any scent, and he turned back to the screen.

". . . system access codes . . . classified by type of system . . ."

He leaned back and tried to catalog mentally the types of systems, finally pulling at his chin before listing each one that came to mind, following each with a brief description and the probable types of access codes. By the time he finished his rough listings, the hardness of the wooden chair had numbed his buttocks, in spite of the pillow he had placed on the seat.

". . . someone's going to buy it . . ." He addressed the closed sliding door that would have been open to the upper deck of his bedroom on a warmer day. "How can you tell them everything . . . ?"

Even as he tried to outline what he knew in detail, he was beginning to gain a healthy admiration for Sam Hall. For some reason, that admiration did not extend to his former superiors in Special Operations.

Why? Because Imperial Special Operations only told you the minimum necessary, on a need-to-know basis. Why he had survived so long—besides being near suicidally fatalistic, or worse, according to Thelina—was because he had tried to learn more. As much as possible, whenever possible.

He touched the console and flipped back to the beginning of the latest document, adding a caveat on the fact that the information presented did not represent everything necessary, only what was available.

"Even that's cheating." He sighed again, looking out the wide sliding glass door. The wooden decking was now thoroughly wet, and the raindrops were splashing up against the glass.

Chhhurrrppppp . . . The jaymar sat on the railing, looking directly at him, as if to ask where the scraps were.

After making sure his latest changes were incorporated into the document, Jimjoy stood up from the console, stretching gingerly, but leaving the equipment running. Then he headed downstairs.

A faint odor of woodsmoke had drifted in, probably through the thin crack he had left in the kitchen window.

The main floor was gloomy, dampish, and he stopped by the cold woodstove. Finally he slipped the kindling in place and lit it, waiting to make sure that the pencil wood had caught before adding the wood he had split months earlier. Had it been last fall?

After closing the stove, he walked over and opened the pantry shelf. As he had recalled, there was indeed a box of stale crackers, from which he extracted a handful. He glanced at the woodstove, where a glow flickered through the micaglass. The shrouded flames made the long room seem warmer already.

Crackers in hand, his right hand, he walked to the sliding glass door onto the main deck. "Ummhhhh . . ." He managed to get the recalcitrant slider open enough to toss the crackers to the far side of the deck.

Chhurrrppppp . . .

Even before he had closed the glass, the jaymar was swooping down. Jimjoy smiled. Some brashness ought to be rewarded.

He retrieved a pearapple from the fruit bowl. Fruit wasn't his favorite, but eating the starch and sugars he naturally preferred would have left him with the rotund profile of the gray ceramic woodstove.

Chhhurrruuupppp . . .

"No, you don't get more . . . shouldn't have given you that."

Chhurrupppp . . . With another flick of the tail, the jaymar disappeared.

Standing by the kitchen counter—dustier than he liked, but not enough to encourage him to clean quite yet—Jimjoy took small and slow bites from the pearapple. Later in the afternoon he needed to walk to the physical-training center for another round of exercise and therapy. Exercise and therapy—he hadn't expected nearly so much of either.

Thrapp! Thrapp!

With a frown and a last bite, he straightened, tossing the fruit core into the composter slot.

"Coming!"

A blocky man with the muscles of a powerlifter stood on the front deck. Rain glistened on the dull green waterproof he wore.

"Professor . . ."

"Geoff. Come on in." He stepped back from the door.

Geoff Aspan stopped on the tiles and shut the door behind him, glancing toward the stove. "See you've got a fire going."

"No so much for the heat—just wanted to get rid of the damp. Right now I'm a little stiff . . . let me take that." Jimjoy took the jacket and hung it in the otherwise empty closet. "Can I get you anything? Have some redberry juice, a couple of bottles of Hspall . . ."

"Actually, even though I'm not begging, the Hspall sounds good. Can't stay too long. I promised Carill I'd be back before the kids came home. She's taking the late shift with the field team."

Jimjoy had not even considered whether Geoff was contracted—or had children—even though the other Ecolitan had helped him occasionally by suggesting additional exercise or therapy for particular problems after the laser damage.

Jimjoy pulled the bottle from the back shelf of the keeper. Cold—but it should have been. It had been a housewarming gift. Had it been from Mera and her friend? So it had been there for close to a year.

"It's cold." He laughed as he opened it. "Glass or bottle?"

"Bottle's fine." Geoff had turned one of the straight-backed wooden chairs around, sitting on it with one forearm resting on the low back and looking out at the rain.

Churrrpppppp . . .

"You got one of those pests."

"Made the mistake of letting him, maybe it's a her, have some scraps." He extended the bottle to Geoff.

"Sort of like them," mused the dark-haired man as he took the ale. "Thanks."

Jimjoy eased onto the other straight-backed wooden chair. "I like their brashness."

"I suspected you would . . . Major . . ."

Jimjoy nodded. He wondered how long before the handful of Ecolitans with whom he had worked would recognize him. "How many of you . . . ? Think it's going to be a problem?"

"Kerin and I figured it out right after you started exercising when you first came back. None of the students, except maybe Jerrite, would recognize you from techniques. Your posture is a bit different, you're physically bigger, your voice is lower, and your entire complexion is different."

"Techniques?"

"Right. You're too good to be anyone else. The problem is that Dorfman has been asking questions about where you came from. He's close to Harlinn, and he's under Temmilan's thumb."

"Temmilan . . . had worried about that."

"So did Sam. That's why he had her posted to Parundia. Her tour is up in about two tendays, and Harlinn's sweet on her."

"I've got trouble." Jimjoy pulled on his chin and looked out the window. "More than I already thought. What's Kerin think?"

"If you weren't hooked on Thelina, it wouldn't matter what she thought." Geoff snorted. "It doesn't matter anyway. She says body postures don't lie, and you're honest. Don't know that I believe the posture bit, but I agree with her." He shifted his own posture as he took a quick swig from the bottle.

Jimjoy wished he were holding a bottle, or something. "Sometimes—hades, lots of times—I wish I weren't." He wondered why he was telling a near stranger. "She's attracted—Thelina, I mean—but she has no intention of ever letting me know that."

"Have you told her how you feel?"

Have you told her how you feel? The question echoed in his thoughts, and he glanced outside, where the rain was pelting heavily again, puddling on the deck and splashing against the glass. Jimjoy pursed his lips, swallowed. "No. I've thought about it, but every time I get close, she picks a fight."

"Hmmm . . . makes it hard . . . glad Carill's more relaxed."

"She from Accord—originally?"

"We both are. Sometimes she works under Thelina. You know, Thelina's only been here four, five years . . . and she's almost as good as Kerin . . . better than me . . . on the hand-to-hand . . ."

Jimjoy, trying to keep from frowning, got up and pulled another stove log from the short stack by the stove. He slipped on the insulated leather glove, opened the stove, and dropped in the log. The three split pieces he had used to start the stove were mainly glowing ashes.

Clunk. The stove lid dropped back into place.

"Any suggestions, Geoff?"

"*Not* telling her hasn't worked, has it?"

"No." He didn't quite have to force the short laugh.

"So tell her." The training expert took another swallow from the half-empty Hspall bottle.

"That why you came over?"

"Partly . . . but mostly to let you know about Temmilan."

"Thanks." Jimjoy looked out the window, where the rain continued to lash the deck. "A lot to do, and not much time."

Geoff stood up. "That's the definition of life, Professor."

"Jimjoy. Please, just Jimjoy."

"Fair enough. I need to get back. Shera and Jorje will be home any instant, but I appreciate the Hspall."

Jimjoy walked to the front closet, pulling the other's jacket out. "Here you go. Still damp, I'm afraid."

"No problem. Let me know if I can help."

"I will. I will."

Jimjoy watched from the open doorway as the blocky man threaded his way off the deck and dashed uphill through the near-torrential rain. Finally he shut the door.

Have you told her how you feel? Why not?

"Because she'll cut you to ribbons . . ."

Shaking his head, he collected the empty Hspall bottle, rinsed it out, and set it with the rest of the glass remnants. Manual recycling was still not a habit.

Upstairs, the console waited for him to finish the training manuals no one but Sam Hall wanted. And Sam wasn't around to appreciate them.

He took a deep breath, dried his hands on the rough towel, and started toward the stairs.

XX

15 *Trius* 3646
New Augusta

Dear Mort:

Once again, I'll have to apologize for being late in back-faxing. What with one thing and another, somehow I put it off.

I don't know whether to envy you or worry about your being

out there where you can do something. You were right. N'trosia's the new Chairman of the Defense Committee. They changed the name, too, from Military Affairs to Defense. We don't want the Galaxy to think we're warmongers, do we? Anyway, the distinguished Senator has another study in hand to show that even if we started plating the frames today, the FC wouldn't be ready for fleet action for five years, and the full force of one hundred couldn't be deployed for ten. By that time, according to his study, the FC would be obsolete. So why bother to spend trillions of credits for a corvette that would be outdated before it spaced? So help me, not a single senator asked how outdated the ACs would be by then.

Then the Haversol thing came up, and N'trosia even twisted that. He claimed that the FC wouldn't do a thing against sabotage and that we needed more for Special Operations, not for ships that couldn't prevent such disasters. Not that the two are related, of course.

Looks like the Committee is buying N'trosia's argument, and if they do, so will the entire Senate.

I passed on your account of your encounter with the Fuard to Admiral Graylin. He's had several reports like yours. His theory is that they're testing us in every way they can. Last week we had a briefing on another new development. Pardon me if I'm sketchy, but you'll have to fill in the details, and I'm sure you understand why.

Rumor has it that the other fellows have come up with a way to use high-speed jump exits with a hull twice the size of their current destroyer hulls. Figure out what that means if they can build cruisers with the speed of corvettes, excuse me, destroyers. Enough said. Maybe too much said.

The gene thing led from one thing to another, and Sandy and I decided it wasn't going to work out. I understand she and Marie are on Haldane now.

Keep in touch. I'll try to be more regular in responding.

Blaine

XXI

SINCE, BASED ON past experience, he didn't have much time before Thelina cut him off or he stalked out unable to contain himself, he didn't bother to sit down—in either the comfortable chair or one of the hard wooden ones. How the Accordans found those wooden chairs comfortable he still didn't know.

"You're the head of Security."

"Since when?" She stood a meter away, her left hand on the handle of the sliding door. That close, he recalled how tall she was. Graceful and well proportioned, she didn't seem large except next to someone else.

Outside, the night wind whistled through the wooden railings whose outlines were concealed by the reflection of the room in the glass sheet of the door.

"Since before I first showed up, maybe since you left—"

"Leave it at that, please. We try to avoid bringing up your past. Grant me the same courtesy." Thelina gave a half shrug and turned to face him.

He nodded. "No discourtesy meant. But I have a problem."

"You do have a few." She continued to look him straight in the eye. Her direct study reminded him of Clarissa; why, he wasn't certain.

"Yes, Thelina, I do. Shall I start with the first?"

"Start wherever you like."

The faintest tinge of trilia reached him, and he wanted to step forward and to back away, both at the same time. "Fine. My first problem is that—"—he swallowed—"that I love you, and you do your—"

"You can't love me. You don't know me. Loving someone who isn't even in their real body means nothing. You're infatuated with Dr. Hyrsa's creation. I'm just a body to you."

He couldn't stop the sigh. "I know more about you than you think . . . but I don't want to fight about it. I've told you how I feel. You want to dismiss it—fine. You want to continue to pick fights—fine. Just think about it."

"I'll think about it—if you think about—about something else."

"Something else?"

"I shouldn't have put it that way." She gave an exasperated sigh. "I'll just ask directly. Why do you have to prove yourself to every woman?"

"I don't."

"You don't? What about your sister? Your mother? The Empire?"

"What about them? They're dead."

"That makes it worse. Now you can never prove to them that you, a mere male, deserved their approval."

Jimjoy looked away from her steady green eyes, over her shoulder, out into the darkness through the reflected scene in the glass, trying to determine whether the fast-moving clouds from the west had yet arrived overhead.

"You don't even want to face it, do you?" Her voice was so low he almost missed the words.

"Face what?"

She shook her head slowly.

"And where does the Empire fit in?"

"Empires are women . . ."

He didn't know whether to laugh or frown. "You can't be serious."

"I'm very serious, and you know I am. You just don't want to hear."

He took a long, deep breath. Then he took a second one. "I'm confused. I tell you I care for you." He looked down and finally met her level glance. "That I love you . . . and you tell me that, first, I can't possibly love you, and second, that I'm a slave to approval from women . . . and the Empire. I've opened myself up, and you use the opportunity to chop me up."

"Professor . . ."

"And can't you just call me Jimjoy?"

"No. That would make me a substitute for your mother, or your sister."

"A substitute?" Jimjoy blinked, feeling like a man walking the edge of an unseen cliff.

"I'm just the last in a long series."

"You think that my whole life is just trying to get approval? That nothing I have done is because it was worth doing?"

"You've tried to do the impossible. Time after time they tried to let you kill yourself. But you kept succeeding; you kept doing the impossible. They wouldn't give you that approval. That's why you left. I think that if they'd given you a great big medal with 'Galactic Hero' printed on it, you would have allowed yourself to be shot quietly. They wouldn't. They kept insisting that you didn't exist. So you're going to force them to admit you do.

"Why did you insist on keeping your nickname? You keep telling everyone to use it, almost like advertising. Are you trying to commit suicide? The psyprofile indicated we had to let you keep the name, unless we wanted to try to rebuild your whole personality. If we did that, we'd have a nice, useless, well-muscled, and well-adjusted nothing.

"You used the same mission profile on Haversol. You just kept pressing to get more approval. Each time you push for recognition, you also are saying, 'Go ahead and find me. Shoot me, if that's what it takes.' Don't you understand?"

"Understand what?" He wanted to wipe his forehead, but then, that was the way he felt with Thelina about half the time.

"Women are approval mechanisms. I'm attractive, bright, and as close to your physical-ability level as any woman is likely to be. I'm smarter than you are, and I have the ability to reward you. That's why you want me. If I love you, then I become the ultimate approval for you. And I won't do it. I won't." Her voice was ragged.

He swallowed. His mouth was dry, and the swallow did not help much. "Because I want you to approve of me, you won't . . . even . . . consider . . ."

"I didn't say that. I said I won't be your approval mechanism. You have to love me for what I am, not the image I fit in your twisted value scheme."

"But I do."

"You might . . . but you don't. You don't even try to learn who I am . . . as a person . . . what I like . . . what activities I enjoy . . ."

He stood there forever—that was how it seemed—balanced on that unseen cliff edge, teetering there between the unreal world reflected in the glass and the unreal world where he stood.

"I . . . never . . . thought of it . . . quite that way . . ."

"I know . . . that's why I told you." Her voice went from the gentle tone back to professional Ecolitan. "Your next problem . . . Professor?"

He wondered if he should have walked out then, but he was having trouble not shaking where he stood. So he put both hands behind his back, near parade-rest style, and took a slow, long breath. "Temmilan Danaan. She's an Impie plant, and Dorfman's her tool. He's just about figured out who I am. Kerin Sommerlee and Geoff already know."

"And since Harlinn's close to the Dorfman clan and thinks we can wait out the Empire—based on his theory of historical inevitability—

you think you'll be targeted once she returns?" Thelina looked over his shoulder toward the front door, then back at him.

He ignored the look, concentrating on her. He had heard nothing. "No. I *am* targeted. You know that. Except I'm dead. Temmilan will reveal I'm not, and that the Institute has more abilities than the Empire realizes. She doesn't understand that just uncovering me will get the Empire to act immediately."

"Why do you think so?"

"Simple. Once I'm found alive, Special Ops statistics will show that Accord engineered the suspected Fuard destruction of Haversol SysCon, that other agents have been gathered by Accord, and that Accord biotech is good enough to infiltrate anywhere in the Empire. That enough for starters?"

She nodded. "There's more, I presume."

"Third, I had started the manifesto operation—"

"You?"

"Yes, me. I started writing the things to stir up some popular support, but outside of a handful of people, it wasn't generating enough support. At first Sam didn't know it was me. He used the manifestos to build the Freedom Now Party. Except he's dead, and I don't know who followed up. Someone has—and I would have guessed you—except it didn't quite fit . . ."

Thelina tilted her head, then turned toward the shining black of the closed sliding glass door. The door shivered from the wind. Reflecting the lights in the room against the darkness outside, the image of the room moved once, twice, before settling, and revealing a figure by the stairs.

Jimjoy said nothing about the newcomer who waited behind him, although he could feel his shoulders wanting to tense.

"Occasionally, Professor—occasionally—you surprise me. Some of your manifestos are surprisingly well written."

Determined not to rise to her baiting, Jimjoy swallowed. "Thank you."

"Your reasoning is close. Meryl is the one who worked with Sam."

Jimjoy nodded. "So that was why she came to the hospital."

Thelina frowned; then her face cleared. "After Haversol, you mean."

"After Haversol, yes." He cleared his throat. "We need to increase the pressure."

"We? Exactly what do you mean?" asked a new voice, as cool as Thelina's.

Jimjoy turned toward Meryl. "Does the average person here really care? I doubt it. Most people just want to live their lives in peace. They fight when there's no choice, and sometimes not even then. From what you've said, people here are different, but I haven't seen that much difference. I'm not counting the Institute and the leadership here.

"Take your capital—Harmony doesn't feel that different from a dozen other semi-independent colonies or dependencies. You've been so successful in developing your way of life that most people truly don't understand how antithetical it is to the Empire. Or how much the Empire might come to fear Accord."

"What sort of pressure did you have in mind?" Meryl had walked over to one of the wooden chairs beside Thelina.

"A few follow-up stories on Imperial reeducation teams. Like the story they refused to cast or print on Luren . . ."

"Why would they print it now?"

"They won't, not for several tendays. Then the situation will have changed."

"You realize, Professor, that your confidence verges on total arrogance?" asked Thelina.

"There's my last problem," Jimjoy said.

"Well, don't spare us that one, either."

Meryl winced at the tone in which Thelina's response was delivered.

Jimjoy took another deep breath. "How and where do I train a team to take over orbit control?"

Meryl nodded. Thelina shook her head, not in negation, but not in approval. Outside, the wind whistled through the railing of the deck.

Finally Meryl looked at Thelina, then back at Jimjoy. "Carefully, and without the knowledge and approval of the Institute."

"I take it there's more than one Temmilan."

"Your brilliance continues to astound me." Thelina's tone was dry.

Meryl almost winced—again.

Jimjoy ignored both. "How do I get a group of Ecolitans together under the imprimatur of the Institute without the Institute's support?"

Meryl looked at Thelina, who looked back at Meryl.

"The same way we always do."

Jimjoy grinned wryly. "More explanation, please."

The two exchanged glances. "We ask for volunteers."

"Look, I'm talking about training a group that will eventually be the Accord variety of Special Operative."

"You can't call it that," observed Thelina mildly.

"I know. They ought to be more broadly trained." He cleared his throat.

Both women waited politely.

"How about calling it something like 'applied ecologic management'?"

"You also have a way with euphemisms."

"Any better ideas, Ecolitan Andruz? Like how we get the Institute to allow us to develop an accepted new discipline with apprentice and journeyman status?"

"That part's easy. We just make it a sub-branch of the field training. You're already listed as a qualified master in field training, and with the approval of the majority of Senior Fellows in a major discipline, any master can develop a more specialized sub-branch."

"I take it security, or whatever euphemism you use, is also a sub-branch."

Both women nodded solemnly, a solemnity that could have concealed laughter.

Jimjoy wanted to shake his head, instead remembered to pull at his chin. "And nobody says *anything*? What about budgets? Supplies?"

"If it goes beyond the department's budget, you have to get the Prime's approval, except for security, and that budget is approved as a whole a year in advance, with the ability to commit up to fifty percent more. But you have to answer for the overrun personally to the Prime."

Jimjoy took a deep breath. "When do you want the plan?"

"Tomorrow at the latest. You don't have much time."

"We don't have much time," added Meryl.

"Tomorrow," he agreed, looking out into the darkness. "Tomorrow."

XXII

24 Quintus 3646
Demetris

Dear Blaine:

Just received your latest. Arrived here at home rather than station catch. Too bad we can't receive torps, but they'd never know where to send them.

Sorry to hear about you and Sandy, but keep the stars, keep the stars. Wish I could say more, but what is there? Helen and I both care, wish you the best.

Some ways, I wish I hadn't heard the latest rumors. Now there's another one—about the courier that disappeared, a year ago, I guess. Was it the *D'Armetier*? Anyway, torp tissues said it showed up on a T-form planet where no one expected it and with a cargo of bodies—and no one can account for the missing time. That sort of thing doesn't play well with the crews. Any way I can refute it?

Then there's the continual battle against obsolescence. With old zipless cracking around the frames every other jump, the thought of being chased by something twice as big and twice as fast, with even better jump accuracy and exit speed, doesn't exactly improve my outlook. Talked about it with Helen, and she's asked me to consider putting in my papers after this tour.

Can you do anything? Sure, the FC isn't *the* answer. But *Halley*'s older than half my crew. It's still the latest we've got. Any hope of new development, like the CX concept? Understand you've put it out for costing and tech evaluation. That true?

New exec arrived. Querrat—Francie Querrat's cousin, graduated six years behind me. Seems as sharp as Francie—miss her, and that's another one I hold against Tinhorn—and he'll work out. No-nonsense, but the crew respects him from the start.

Not much else new. Cindi's growing like a sunplume, and Jock's learning differentials. Demetris is nice enough, but it's not home. Miss the winters. Once a Sierran, always a Sierran, I guess.

Mort

XXIII

THE WOMAN IN the faded blue trousers and gray sweater turned over the cream-colored oblong as she closed the door behind her.

"Thelina Andruz, S.F.I." was written in old-fashioned black ink on the envelope. The envelope itself was lightly sealed. How long the envelope had been there she did not know, although the heavy paper was still crisp, and there had been a light rain the night before. The ink was unmarred.

Her lips pursed, and in the dimmer light of the wood-paneled foyer she squinted at the precise handwriting, almost a bold and thick-lined calligraphy.

Cocking her head to the side, ignoring some blond wisps of uncombed hair that framed her face, she grinned. Then she cleared her throat softly. Finally she called upstairs. "Thelina. You have an invitation."

Silence.

"It's impeccably correct," she called again.

"I have a what?" Wearing a heavy terry-cloth robe and a towel over her hair, turban fashion, Thelina stood at the top of the stairs.

"I'd say it was an invitation of some sort . . . very formal . . . linen paper and black ink—like something that the Council—"

"Oh, Meryl, just open it."

"I couldn't do that. It's sealed and addressed to you. Personally."

"Is this a joke?"

Meryl turned the envelope over, holding it up so the calligraphy faced Thelina. "It doesn't appear to be."

"All right." With a sigh, the taller woman made her way down the stairs, quickly yet precisely.

"Here you are, honored lady." Meryl grinned.

"You know."

"I know nothing, but I'm a pretty good guesser."

"So?"

"Let's see."

Thelina shook her head, then flicked the flap of the envelope open with a short and well-trimmed thumbnail. "A second envelope . . . very formal indeed."

"How is it addressed? Just 'Thelina,' right?"

"You know." Thelina glared at her housemate. "Is this some sort of game?"

"No. But it figures."

"You aren't saying."

"I might be wrong."

"Never mind." The taller Ecolitan eased open the inner envelope, scanning the heavy linen card she held by the lower right corner. She read it once, then again.

Watching her friend, Meryl began to grin even more widely.

"This . . . he . . . this is impossible!"

'The good Professor Whaler?"

"You've seen his handwriting before?"

"No. How else could he address your charges? You claimed he knew nothing about the real you. You really asked for a formal courtship. He took you at your word."

"I never said . . ."

"Not in words."

"You're impossible . . . you're both impossible . . ."

Meryl held out her hand for the card.

Thelina handed it over brusquely. "*You* go."

"No. You go."

"I despise him." Thelina tucked the inside envelope against the outside one, then placed the card under both flaps.

Meryl arched her left eyebrow, holding Thelina's eyes.

"What should I wear?"

After grinning again, Meryl shrugged. "Something suitable and casually formal, in keeping with the tone of the invitation."

Shaking her head slowly, Thelina handed the two envelopes and the card to Meryl. "Men."

"Agreed." Meryl read the card, with the letters written so precisely that they almost appeared typeset.

The honor of your presence is requested at an outdoor luncheon for two at 1315 H.S.T. on the fourteenth of Septem at the lookout on Quayle Point. Refreshments will be provided . . . suitable attire is suggested. . . .

> James Joyson Whaler II,
> S.F.I.

The sandy-haired Ecolitan laid the card and envelopes on the small foyer table and followed her friend upstairs. Suitable attire, indeed, would be necessary. Especially if it looked like snow. But an outdoor luncheon?

XXIV

THE TALL MAN, bearded and bent and wearing a faded brown greatcoat, hobbled from the library's public section, pausing frequently on the staircase. His breath puffed around him irregularly in the chill early morning air.

As he reached the top step, resting against the railing to catch his breath again, a younger man emerged, black-haired, with the collar of an advocate's tunic peering above and out of a quilted winter jacket that was unfastened.

The advocate who was not an advocate looked up, ignoring both the old man and the middle-aged redheaded woman coming down, took the middle of the staircase, and bounded up the steps to street level two at a time. The steam of his breath was as enthusiastic as his pace. In his right hand he carried an envelope the size of a thin folder of standard paper.

The older man limped in the same general direction as the pseudo-advocate, somehow not quite losing sight of the young man as both made their way uphill, away from Government Square and toward the outworld commercial section.

By the time the white-haired man had crossed Carson Boulevard, the morning sunlight had lifted the frost from the still-green grass everywhere its rays had struck. Those few who walked in the early Tenday sunlight no longer saw their breath, and the frost only lingered in the shadows.

By the time the tall man had crossed Korasalov Road, he had unbuttoned the top button of the greatcoat and watched the younger man enter a low two-story building. His limp increased as he plodded after the other, mumbling through his beard, loudly enough for a passing runner to veer away with a look of annoyance.

In time he approached the locked door of the building, where he fumbled at the lock momentarily, staggered against the door-frame, as if for support, before stumbling, then tumbling inside as the heavy carved door swung open. A second runner, observing the scene, just shook his head and concentrated on keeping his pace.

Down the dimly lit interior hallway limped the oldster, stopping at last by the door he sought, where he listened quietly for a time.

Thump . . . thump . . .

The gaunt man rapped on the door, the sound of his knuckles muffled by the heaviness of the wood and of the metal beneath it. "Marissa! Open up! I know you're here . . ." He ignored the brass plate on the door's center panel.

CentraCast Business Publications
Harmony Information Center

. . . thump . . . thump . . . thump . . .

"Marissa . . . you let your father in." His voice cracked, not quite in hysteria. "I know you're in there."

The other doorways on the short hallway remained closed. All were news-related businesses, not surprisingly, since the two-story building was the Business and News Center. Nor was the lack of response surprising, not on Tenday, when most Accord businesses were shut down.

. . . thump . . . thump . . . thump . . .

"Marissa! Open this door!"

He paused and took a deep breath, waiting as if to regain his strength. After a time, he leaned toward the door.

Thump . . . thump . . . thump . . .

"Marissa, you listen to your father . . ."

The hallway remained silent.

Thump . . . thump . . . thump . . .

"Marissa . . . worthless girl . . . just like your mother . . . open this door . . ."

As he leaned back, the door opened full. The black-haired young man stood in the doorway, a stunner leveled at the disheveled oldster.

"You . . . you're not Marissa. What have you done with her?"

"There is no Marissa here. You're disturbing everyone. Please leave or I'll call the—"

Thrum.

The young man toppled forward, without even a surprised look on his face, only to be caught by the ancient's too-well-muscled arms.

Clunk. The stunner echoed dully on the scuffed wooden planks.

The tall man stepped inside the office, scanned the front room. Two consoles with battered but matching chairs, a short, squarish green upholstered love seat, two wooden armchairs, and a table, around which the armchairs and the love seat were clustered, constituted the furniture.

A single curtained window joined the rear wall and the right wall, providing the room's only light. In the middle of the left wall a door opened into an even dimmer room.

In the front room one console was turned on, a pale green square.

As he completed his near-instantaneous survey, the man in the greatcoat lowered the unconscious man. He recovered the stunner and closed the door.

With quick motions, he set the young man in a wooden armchair, the type favored by all Ecolitans, and balanced him in place, letting the arms dangle. The folder lay on top of an envelope on the operational console. The older man in the greatcoat noted its presence as he polished the fingerprints off the stunner with a cloth retrieved from an inside pocket of the worn coat. With the thin transparent gloves on his own hands, he had no worry about leaving his own prints. He levered the setting up to the maximum level before placing it in the limp hand of the unconscious man in the chair.

With quick steps he moved into the small equipment room that lay through the open door in the left wall. Two locked cube cases sat against the back wall, and several cases of fax equipment were stacked carelessly around. All but one were covered with dust.

A muffled *click* caught his ear, and he slipped from the equipment room back into the front room, standing behind the wooden chair facing the closed door.

After waiting about the length of time it would have taken someone to walk from the side building door to the CentraCast door, he lifted his own stunner.

Click.

Thrum.

Crummmppp.

A dark-haired woman slumped through the door and onto the unscuffed planks inside the office. A large envelope slipped from her hands and skidded across the wood until it rested against the throw rug on which the low table sat.

He dragged the woman inside. After extracting the key from the door, he closed it with a *click* and set her in the chair opposite the unconscious young man. He slipped the key, on its plain steel ring, into her right jacket pocket and struggled with the closures on the jacket, opening them all, but leaving the jacket on her.

His gloved hands deftly opened her belt pouch, subtracting one or two items and replacing them with several others. His nose wrinkled at the scent of melloran that enveloped her as he continued his search-and-replace efforts.

In time he shifted his attention to the younger man, adding several items to his person.

Then he replaced the contents of the envelope carried by the woman with another set of documents, and placed the envelope on the table in front of her. In turn, he lifted the several sheets of copied public records from the envelope by the still-humming console and replaced them with other copied public records.

Taking a deep breath, he looked around the room again. His eyes moved to the stunner lying in the lap of the unconscious man, and he bent down and checked the charge indicator. It would be sufficient.

Retrieving his own stunner, he set the charge as low as possible and aimed the weapon at the woman's head from a meter away.

Thrum . . . thrum . . . thrum . . . thrum . . .

Her body twitched after each shot, and by the last shot her face was slack, her chest barely moving.

The tall man took the slack hand of the unconscious man, the hand holding the stunner. He positioned the man so that he held the stunner against his own temple.

TTHHHHRRRUMMMM . . .

Clank. The body twitched once. The stunner struck the floor, where the tall man left it on his way out of the office.

XXV

(ANS) HARMONY [14 SEPTEM 3646] Local authorities are still investigating a mysterious suicide/attempted murder which took place in the CentraCast offices over the enddays. Local sources indicate the dead man was a junior Ecolitan attached to the Institute for Ecologic Studies, but his name has not been released. The woman, a Senior Fellow at the Institute whose name has also been withheld, suffered severe brain damage from a stunner bolt. The man apparently then turned the stunner on himself.

Items found on the two and in the office indicated that the woman had attempted to break off a love affair. Well-placed sources indicate that the two had often been seen together.

Other sources indicated that the woman had just returned from a temporary assignment on the Parundian Peninsula. Such assignments are frequently used as a disciplinary tool. Further comment could not be obtained from the Institute, since the official who assigned the wounded Ecolitan died several months ago in an equally unusual flash fire in a training vehicle.

Diagrams of the same type of training vehicle were found in a folder at the CentraCast office, but local authorities refused to speculate on any connections between the two incidents.

XXVI

JIMJOY SET THE second basket beside the table, checking again to see that the green linen cloth would remain in place against the light breeze from the east. With the chill of the wind came the scent of fallen leaves.

On the table were two large crystal goblets rimmed in thin bands of gold and green, two smaller goblets with the same pattern, two sets of gold-plated dinner utensils, two green linen napkins, two butter plates, two salad plates, and two luncheon plates. All the plates were of pale green china with a single golden rim. An armless chair sat behind each setting.

In the unopened basket were the various courses he had arranged for the luncheon, as well as the small bottle of Sparsa and the thermos of ice water.

He stood and surveyed the lookout. The stained wooden railings, smoothed to the finish of glass, still guarded the drop-off. Behind him, the saplar forest covered the crest of the hill from which Quayle Point projected.

With a wry smile, he recalled the first time he had climbed the hill, right through the forest. The sap secretions had ruined that set of greens. Then, like now, there hadn't been the small buckets attached to the trees, since the Institute tapped the sap only during the spring. Even upwind from the trees, he could occasionally smell their mint-resin odor.

He and Thelina had watched the sunrise, and she hadn't spoken to him then, either, even though they had walked back to the Institute together.

From where he had placed the table, the center of the Institute was visible, although the outlying training areas were not. Nor were the underground facilities. Even now he doubted that he knew of more than half the hidden emplacements—if that. The Institute was like an old Terran onion, pungent and with layer hidden behind layer.

The sun warmed his back, even as the wind from the east cooled his chest. He wore only a set of heavy formal greens. Still, the breeze was nothing more than a fall zephyr to a man born and raised on White Mountain, although those years had been two lifetimes ago.

A shadow made its way up from the Institute and across the forest as, overhead, a scattered handful of puffy white clouds swam toward the west, along the southern mountains to his right.

After a glance at the flat strip on his wrist, he reached down and pulled the thermos from the provisions basket. The dark organic-based plastic felt smooth against his fingers. 1314 Harmony Standard Time. Even though he pursed his lips, his hands were sure in filling the two large goblets three-quarters full with the spring water.

There was always the possibility she wouldn't come. He hadn't asked for an RSVP, probably a grievous breach of etiquette in itself. 1315 Harmony Standard Time. With a frown, he stared at the Institute, wondering . . . hoping.

Crunnchhhh . . . The footstep on the path was so faint, almost fainter than the susurrus of the wind, that he almost missed the sound.

Stepping away from the table, he waited.

Like him, Thelina wore formal greens. Her short silver hair glittered in the sunlight as she walked from the path and across the grass. Her eyes widened slightly at the formal setting of the table.

"You did mean formal, didn't you?"

He bowed at the waist, slightly. "The setting is formal, the locale informal, and the repast, alas, probably not up to either, or to the guest."

She inclined her head. "The speech is also rather formal."

"It's been suggested that one should know someone, their likes and dislikes, before attempting informality." He stepped forward and gestured, pulling out the chair for her.

"I think I'd better help with this." Thelina helped guide the chair she was taking into place. "Chairs don't slide on grass very well."

"I'll talk to the plant biology department about improving that characteristic." He reached for the basket. "Please pardon some informality. Do you like Sparsa?"

She nodded, her eyes traveling toward the lookout, and to the Institute beyond and below.

Thwupppp . . . Jimjoy uncorked the green-tinted bottle, then eased the sparkling wine into the smaller goblet before Thelina. He filled his own goblet and sat down across from her.

"If I might ask," she began, "where did you get such a coordinated setting?"

"In Harmony. Thought I might have some use for it in the future. At least I could dine in style. The setting would make up for my cooking."

"You do cook?"

"I'm from White Mountain. That's a long time back, but how could I be male and not cook? Certainly I'm not up to my father's standards, but . . ." Jimjoy shrugged, and waited for Thelina to taste the Sparsa.

She caught the flick of his eyes from her face to her goblet. Her hand reached for the goblet and lifted it, holding the crystal for a long instant before carrying it to her lips for a small sip.

Jimjoy followed her sample, although his was a short swallow, rather than just a sip.

"Grand Sparsa in crystal. Perhaps the second time in my life."

"You like it?" he asked, wishing as he did so that he hadn't.

Her lips quirked. "How could I not? What did this set you back?"

He smiled faintly. "If I told you, would you enjoy it more or less? Please enjoy it." He took a second, smaller sip, letting the taste linger.

"Are you—"

"No." He cut off her question, knowing where it might be leading. "I only asked you for luncheon, and I selected the lookout as a place to enjoy the best I could provide. That's all."

Her smile was part annoyance, part amusement. "Do you always answer questions before they're asked?"

"Usually not. I apologize. You wanted to ask . . . ?"

"I'll phrase it a bit more delicately. Aren't you concerned I might not fully appreciate what could be considered more than a little ostentatious?"

"That is a possibility. I had hoped that you would wait until after the luncheon to make a final judgment."

She took another sip of the Sparsa as the breeze fluttered her silver hair. "That's a fair request."

He eased his chair back, careful to avoid snagging the legs on the grass, stood, and bent to open the basket again. From the insulated plastic came the two rolls and the butter. From the bowl, after he unsealed it, came the salad. With the tongs, he deftly laid each piece of mixed greenery on the salad plates. From another small container came the nut garnish. Then he removed the clinging seal from a small pitcher, again of the same gold-rimmed green china, and placed the pitcher in the middle of the table.

Without another word, he replaced the basket and reseated himself, retrieving the linen napkin from the grass next to his chair, where it had been carried by a brief gust.

He nodded. Thelina nibbled at the warm roll, leaving the butter untouched. Then she set the remaining half roll back on its plate, picked up her fork, put it down, and reached for the pitcher. She raised her eyebrows.

"Oh, nothing special. Call it a house dressing. As close to my father's as I could make it."

Thelina poured a thin line of the amber, spice-tinged liquid over the greenery. She extended the pitcher to Jimjoy.

"Thank you."

"Thank you," she answered. Her tone was gentle. She waited until he had added the dressing to his salad before lifting her fork. "Very good."

He acknowledged the compliment with a nod and a soft "Thank you," and followed her lead in addressing the greenery. The first taste told him that, this time, he hadn't overdone the lemon, and the dressing had just the touch of tang he had wanted.

After another measured mouthful, he set down his fork along the edge of the salad plate, watching Thelina finish her salad, enjoying the relish with which she ate.

Another shadow from the fluffy overhead clouds crossed the table, and the wind ruffled the green linen.

"A little chilly when you lose the sun."

"It does make a difference," he agreed.

"You look . . . comfortable. Are you wearing just your greens?"

A touch of a smile crossed his face. "Just my greens. I'd hoped it would be a little warmer—the way the long-range forecast had predicted."

"You're not cold?"

"No. Are you?" His voice carried a touch of concern.

"No. But I took certain precautions, like thermals." She smiled. "Would this really be considered a warm day on White Mountain?"

"Not a summer day, but certainly a pleasant fall day. What about where you're from?"

She tilted her head. "Call it a crisp fall day or a warm winter day."

He stood and returned to the basket, pulling forth two insulated, self-heating containers. From the first he eased the contents onto Thelina's plate—thin white slices of meat, covered with a golden sauce containing dark morsels; split green beans sprinkled with a mist of nutmeats; and a circlet of black rice. He repeated the process with his own plate, replaced the empty containers in the basket, and reseated himself.

Although the cloud had passed and the fall sunlight bathed the table, thin wisps of vapor still rose from the plates.

"If I could, I would have managed hot plates, but that just wasn't practical."

Her eyebrows rose again as she picked up her dinner fork. "You actually cooked this yourself?"

He nodded.

"Every bit of it?"

He nodded, then grinned. "I'm out of practice. I tried each course twice over the past week. This was the first time they all worked out together, and I wasn't sure they would." He inclined his head. "Go ahead. It's better warm, and it won't stay that way very long."

Thelina took both knife and fork and the invitation. Jimjoy followed, although eating more slowly, tasting the sauce critically, noting that it had almost separated again, although he'd gotten the taste right.

"You really did this?"

"Yes."

"It's marvelous."

He nodded, knowing that it was good, although not as good as he had secretly hoped.

She stopped and looked at him, putting her utensils down. "It's not as good as you wanted, is it?"

He sighed. "It's good, perhaps even a bit better. I'd really hoped it would be spectacular."

"I'm flattered." She paused. "I really mean that. I am flattered. No one has ever done something like this for me. Especially not with their own hands."

Jimjoy couldn't help smiling. "I'm glad. Shouldn't say that, but I am." He took another bite, hoping Thelina would still enjoy the remainder of her meal after his confession that it had not reached his standards.

She did, finishing everything on her plate, and even using the remainder of her roll to catch the last of the sauce. She took another sip of the Sparsa, emptying her goblet.

He stood, refilled it, and removed all the plates, stacking them neatly in the basket.

"Could we just talk for a bit?"

He closed the basket and sat down, his forearms on the table, leaning slightly, but only slightly, toward her, noticing how her hair sparkled in the afternoon light, how graceful she looked sitting there.

"No matter how much you protest, you listen, don't you?"

Nodding, he waited.

"You don't like to ask questions, and you wait for people to talk. Sometimes, though, people won't talk unless they're asked."

"Sometimes," he responded, "people don't know what questions to ask, or when."

"You don't like women very much. You can love them, but you don't like them."

He pulled at his chin, conscious of the wind riffling the linen tablecloth and his hair, conscious that he was squinting to see as he faced the slowly lowering sun. "You may be right. And you? Do you feel that way about men?"

"Does it show that much?"

"I'm not sure anything shows, except I seem to bring out stronger feelings in people. Something, maybe a lot of something, hits you wrong. And I . . . anyway . . ."

She ignored his unfinished statement, looking out beyond the lookout. "I don't trust men. The men you trust are the ones who hurt you the most."

He took a deep breath, slowly. "You may be right about that, too. Except I'd say that whoever you trust can hurt you the most. It doesn't mean they will. They can, though. Could you trust your father?" Even as he asked the question, he wondered whether he should have.

"I don't know. He died when I was twelve. And he was too sick to care before that."

Jimjoy frowned, wondering how anyone on any civilized planet would be condemned to a lingering death.

"He was on the proscribed list."

Jimjoy kept his mouth in place. The proscribed list—there had been rumors of the device, how the Matriarchy had used it to punish its opponents long before the Military Directorate of Halston had fallen.

He pursed his lips, then looked at Thelina, and guessed. "Didn't they keep their word? Or was it too late?"

She met his eyes. "When he found out, he committed suicide."

"And you kept your part of the bargain?"

"Yes."

"Do you want to tell me about it?"

"No. But I will . . . if you'll tell me how you got from White Mountain to the I.S.S."

"All right." Even in the sunlight he could see the tenseness that might have been caused by the cold. "I have liftea or cafe. And dessert. Would you like either?"

"I'll wait on the dessert. The liftea would be nice."

He took almost the last items out of the basket—the china cups and saucers and another thermos, from which he poured.

"Thank you." Thelina immediately took a sip of the liftea, without the sugar Jimjoy was placing in the center of the table.

He added sugar to his, waiting for her to begin.

"We lived on an out-continent in one of the ring systems. That's where the Matriarchy has always been the strongest. They controlled the health network. My father was a magistrate, and he ordered the doctors, and they were mostly women, to abide by the Spousal Consent Laws . . ."

Jimjoy shuddered. Those few systems that had given spouses the right to insist on offspring observed the practice mainly in the breach— except for the now-deposed Militarists in the Halston systems and the Fuards.

". . . and somehow he came down with Ruthemnian Fever. No one would treat him, and none of the other magistrates or enforcers would insist. They might be next. I watched my mother begin to die in her own way. She pleaded, I think. It did no good." Thelina took another sip of the liftea.

Jimjoy's eyes flicked past Thelina to the jaymar climbing away from a ferrahawk. The nuisance bird avoided a stoop from the predator by darting into a saplar stand below the lookout. The ferrahawk recovered and began a circling climb away from the saplars and to regain altitude for future hunting with less troublesome prey.

"So I went to the Temple. I wasn't even twelve. My father's dying was killing my mother, and I loved her. What else could a girl do?

"They came the next day and took him to the hospital. Less than a tenday later, he was home, cured. The day after that he stepped off the Malyn Bridge. He left a note, but I never understood it. I still don't. My mother died the next spring, I'm told, after I entered training."

Jimjoy could feel his hands tightening against the green linen tablecloth, wanting to strike out. He forced his muscles to relax and took a sip of his rapidly cooling liftea.

His eyes caught hers for an instant, then dropped from the darkness he saw there.

"Did what the note say matter? Or that he killed your mother?"

"I remember enough . . ."

Jimjoy took another sip of his tea.

". . . the part . . . he wrote something like 'I cannot be bound to be enslaved and forever beholden.' And he said that I had made my bargains for myself, not for him."

"They wouldn't release you?"

"I didn't ask. What was left? No sisters, no cousins. My brother left before I could remember him."

Jimjoy drained his cup with a sudden swallow. "Feel . . . I don't know . . . compared to you, I had no reasons." He looked toward the west, over Thelina's shoulder, squinting slightly as the sun eased downward. "You know my mother was a regional administrator. Her mother had been the sector chief. Two older sisters to begin with. Kaylin and Clarissa. Clarissa was the golden girl. Tops in her class, beautiful. She could sing, she could sail, she could paint, and everyone loved her. So did I. I wanted to do everything she did. Better, if I could. The singing—actually put together a band. Male bands were a real novelty, and we did all right, but my mother was smart. She left me alone, just put pressure on the parents of the three others. Pretty soon I had no one to sing with. I couldn't paint that well, but I tried calligraphy, and Clarissa couldn't do that. She pushed me, but it wasn't nasty."

He looked down at the green linen.

Thelina said nothing.

"Kaylin came back from Cirque, the university. Selected as the Diplomate, and, of course, the Regional Administrator had a party, honoring the number-one graduate student in all of White Mountain. My father outdid himself with that banquet.

"I'd graduated from Selque, the local pre-university, number one, first man in a generation. Also won the open skimmer title that week—we used the week system there, just like on Old Earth. Plus a few other honors here and there. Not only didn't I get even a small dinner, I was gently reminded to make a tactful appearance at Kaylin's festivities and then disappear.

"Three weeks later Clarissa was killed on the lake, after I'd taken her dare. I beached the boat in our harbor and walked all the way to the Imperial Shuttleport, took the tests for a Reserve commission, and passed. They sent me to Malestra."

"Just passed?"

He laughed softly. "With a perfect score . . . for all the good it did me. I never got a letter, a fax, or anything."

"A perfect score. Did you tell anyone? Even where you went?"

"There was Christina . . . but her family had already shipped her off to Cirque, just like Kaylin. She never returned my faxes, but I really don't know that she ever got them. I was too independent, unpredictable, for her family. Maybe that's just my wanting to be that way. I faxed Kaylin once. She cut me off. I sent two hard-copy faxes. Both were refused."

Thelina pursed her lips. "Did you tell any of this to Dr. Militro?"

"Some. Not all. Not about Kaylin's party. Not about Anita."

"Anita?"

"After Clarissa's death, Lerra—she wouldn't let me call her mother—decided to have another child. That was Anita. What she probably had to live up to . . ."

Another set of clouds, grayer, thicker, passed over the sun, and a colder wind whipped the linens. Jimjoy stood up and reached for the basket, bringing out the last items, setting one before Thelina and one at his place. "Crème D'mont. Try it before we both freeze." He seated himself.

He wasn't freezing, but even with the thermals under her greens Thelina was drawing into herself.

She took a small bite, then another. "How many times for this?"

"Actually . . . none. I fix it for myself on and off." He took a bite twice the size of hers. "Just not too often."

"If this is any sample of how you cook, you're a far better cook than I am. Or than Meryl."

Her eyes met his, and their green, for once, seemed less piercing, not as if he were facing another challenge.

Even so, he wanted to look away. Instead, he answered. "This is about the best I've done. Too lazy most of the time."

"Too lazy?" Her voice sounded puzzled, and as if her teeth were about to chatter.

He reached for the thermos and refilled her cup. "Finish that while I pack this up. If I make you stay here any longer, you'll turn into a block of ice." He eased back his chair and began to replace the remaining utensils in the first basket. "Lazy?" he reflected as he removed his dessert plate. "By the time I'm in my quarters, fixing anything feels like a chore. Then again, some days everything feels like a chore."

"That doesn't sound like the Special Operative who ran himself almost to death on at least two occasions."

He smiled wryly, briefly, as he finished packing up everything except the cloth and her cup and saucer. "Suppose not. Would you believe that I'm also a coward at heart?"

"No. Not a coward. A man who could never afford to show fear, I think." She emptied the cup and set it down.

Jimjoy retrieved her cup and saucer and packed them, along with the green linen that flapped in the stiffening breeze. "Knew that anyone who wasn't afraid was a damned fool, but I couldn't ever believe it." He glanced up. Except for the far west, the entire sky was cloudy, hours ahead of the forecast. "I'm afraid I'll have to reveal some of my secrets, since we're going to have to cut this short. The weather didn't follow the forecast."

"It doesn't, not on Accord." She stood up. "What can I do?"

"If you wouldn't mind . . . there's a pack stashed behind that boulder—" He gestured to a point behind her left shoulder. While she hurried toward the rock, he began to break down the chairs, then the table. By the time she had returned, he was tying three bundles of wood together.

"You asked me to get that just so I wouldn't see how you took those apart." Her tone was mock accusing. She handed him the pack and watched as he fitted the two baskets and the bundles together. "Ingenious."

"It is. Not my idea, but I remembered it from New Avalon. They like elegant picnics there, I'm told. Waltar's made it for me. I guessed some on the design, but Geoff helped me out."

Thelina shook her head as he slipped the pack on. "Are you sure I couldn't carry something?"

"No. It all fits together. Bulky, but it's not even as heavy as a standard field pack, especially now. Shall we go?"

Thelina opened her mouth, then closed it for a moment, before finally nodding.

Jimjoy, conscious of her walking beside him, forced himself to concentrate on the path. The wind tugged at his tunic, and he could sense the chill in the coming storm. Snow—or freezing rain—but not for a few hours, he guessed.

"You've made things even more complicated now," she said as they passed the curve in the path below the saplar forest. Ahead lay the Institute.

"Suppose so. Nothing's ever turned out simple. But how do you mean it?" He could sense her shrug.

"You're no longer just the cold and efficient Special Operative or the brilliant Professor Whaler who leaves his students' preconceptions in tatters. You're not just a soulless killer."

"So what am I?"

The silence was punctuated only by two sets of steps, one heavy, one light, and underscored by the whistling of the wind.

"I don't know. I don't think you do, either."

He had to shrug, though the gesture was restrained by the picnic pack. "You're right. I don't. Once I thought I did." He took several more long steps, which she matched, as she had all along, before he added, "I've thought so more than once. I was always wrong."

The path branched in front of them, and they took the left-hand branch, the narrower one that led to the cluster of housing where Thelina lived.

"I almost didn't come."

"I worried whether you would."

"I know. I saw you checking the time. Twice."

Her tone said she was smiling, but he wasn't sure whether he should look. Finally, after an instant that seemed like eternity, he did. She was.

He couldn't help grinning, and she smiled even more knowingly.

"You're blushing" she observed, still smiling.

". . . know . . . can't help it . . ." He stopped at the steps up to her front deck.

Thelina turned to face him.

Jimjoy realized he hadn't said what he really wanted to say. Yet he had said all he could. Finally, after holding her eyes, as the wind whistled around them, as he could see her repress a shiver, he moistened his suddenly very dry lips. "Thank you."

"You won't—no, you're right . . ." For just an instant, she looked as bewildered as he felt. Then she was back in control. "I had a wonderful time, and I won't try to spoil it by trying to drag it out. Thank you."

"So did I."

"Next time will be my treat." She put one foot on the first wooden step, her eyes still on him.

He nodded. There would be a next time, at least. "Go get warm."

"I will. Thank you. I mean it. Freezing or not, I enjoyed every minute."

He didn't know what to say, except "So did I" again. So he just looked, waiting for her to go up the four steps to the deck.

She took the steps deliberately, then stopped and turned at the top. "Thank you."

Her voice was soft, slightly more than a whisper, but each word lingered in his ears.

He watched the door close before he turned to carry the picnic pack back. He had some cleaning up to do, and then some. Not that he minded, not at all. Not at all.

XXVII

JIMJOY STRAIGHTENED THE quilted martial arts jacket and brushed his short hair back. Why he bothered he didn't know, since the next set of exercises would only disarrange both.

". . . two, three . . . uhhh . . . two, three . . ." The improvements in his shoulders and the slight addition to his height, even with Dr. Hyrsa's work on his muscles, hadn't improved the overall muscular tightness he'd inherited, or diminished his need for stretching exercises.

He took a deep breath, ignoring the subdued scents of sweat, steam, and pine resin that seemed to characterize every exercise facility on Accord.

"Watching you makes me glad my parents were relaxed." Geoff Aspan grinned at the taller Ecolitan.

"Relaxed, hades. If they were *that* relaxed, you wouldn't be here." Jimjoy took a deep breath and went back to work.

Geoff grinned, then wiped the smile from his face.

". . . two, three . . . unhhhh . . . two, three . . ."

"We've got problems."

Jimjoy, catching the seriousness in the other's voice, stopped and looked up from his stretched-out position on the mat. "Why?"

"Here comes Kerin, and she's ready to kill."

"Your problem, Geoff. I only work here part-time." Jimjoy was grinning as he kept working on stretching out his back and leg muscles.

"This look's for both of us."

"How do you know?"

"You obviously haven't been contracted or married. All women have that look, and you'd better learn to recognize it. Worse yet, there's enough time before my next group."

"Mmm . . ." Jimjoy kept stretching. Thelina had such a look, except that she still didn't feel he was worth wasting it on.

"We've got troubles." Kerin Sommerlee's voice was low, but at the tone, Jimjoy got up, straightened his jacket. She turned and walked back toward the staff office.

Geoff looked at Jimjoy, who returned the look.

"We've got problems," repeated Geoff.

Jimjoy just nodded as the two of them followed her.

Kerin just stood inside the office, empty except for the three of them. "Two Impie agents, snoops, not Special Ops, hit orbit control on the way down. Same pair that were here and left right before Sam's murder."

"Accident, you mean?" asked Geoff.

"Murder."

"Thought so," muttered Geoff.

"How did you find out?" inquired Jimjoy. "About the Impies?"

"Thelina stopped by. Said she didn't know whether you were a charming liar, a lying charmer, guilty by association, or just guilty. She isn't holding her breath, but she does suggest you take the next shuttle to Thalos—the long way. She'll worry about the rest of the budget and the students. Oh, hades!"

Kerin turned to Geoff. "Here comes the entire second class. Can you get out there and keep them directed or misdirected?"

"Sure, but—"

"Thanks, Geoff."

As he left, Geoff gave Jimjoy a look. The look said: You're in for it.

"I don't know what you did, if you did, or why, but she's gone so far out on the proverbial limb for you she'll never get back. I hope—never mind." Kerin Sommerlee shook her head. "Just putting you two on the same planet together . . . we didn't even ask for you . . . Sam thought—"

"Out on a limb? Why? Supporting my training idea?"

Kerin turned from looking at the incoming group to Jimjoy, black eyes drilling into him. "Training idea? Do you really think she'll be able to conceal the fact that you plan to develop a team of killer commandos that will eventually match or exceed the Imperial Special Operatives? Do you think the Fuards would let you? Or the Matriarchy?"

"Who would believe it?"

"If it were *anyone* but you, no one."

Jimjoy sighed. "Kerin, they don't know it's me."

"Not yet. But how many more people will be the victims of trumped-up murder-suicides, or accidents? Why can't the Empire just leave us alone? Why can't you and Thelina leave us alone? Why can't my girls just grow up without living through this war you seem determined to start?"

Jimjoy looked back at her, sadly. "They can. You can. Just welcome the Imperial reeducation teams, the fifty percent income levies, and the security guards on every corner in Harmony for as long as it takes for you to become dutiful little Imperial citizens."

"That's fine for you. You haven't already lost your lover. You don't have two little girls you have to leave every time you go into the field. You don't have to wonder if you'll come back. Or if they'll remember you when you don't. Or who will take care of them when the cause has taken their mother and their father.

"What will you say to Carill when Geoff doesn't return? Or to Shera and Jorje? You'll return. We won't. The gods of war aren't merciful to those of us who don't glory in it."

"I didn't know . . ." Jimjoy's voice trailed off momentarily. "And I didn't ask you to go. I asked for volunteers. I didn't ask Geoff."

"No. You didn't know about us. But you didn't ask, either." Kerin looked at the polished stone floor. "Sam did, and now I can't even argue. He left hostages behind. So I want to blame someone . . . and you're that someone."

Jimjoy took a deep breath, absently noting that the pine-resin smell was stronger in the office. "Sorry. Still think it has to be done—if your daughters are to have a chance for what you want for them."

"You're an easy man to respect"—she looked back at him—"but a hard man to like. And probably harder to love. Thelina's my friend." She paused and caught his eye. "I don't like to lose friends, either. Or see them hurt."

Jimjoy looked away this time, swallowing. What he didn't know about people . . . what he hadn't wanted to know? He shook his head slowly.

Kerin shook her head even as he did.

For some reason, he wanted to hold her, to tell her things would be all right, to lie about the future. Instead, he forced himself to look back at her. She was staring at him, and there was darkness in both their eyes.

They stood there in the dimly lit office, neither speaking.

"You'd better get moving."

Jimjoy nodded, then reached out and squeezed her shoulder. "Thank you."

"For what?"

"For reminding me." As he slipped toward the back of the office, toward the door leading to the staff dressing room, he swallowed again, thinking about Kerin's two girls, wondering if they looked like their mother, and about Geoff's Shera and Jorje.

As a Special Operative, he hadn't had to worry about the incidentals—except they weren't incidentals. Not any longer. He moistened his lips as he began to strip off the jacket even before reaching his locker.

No, not incidentals. . . .

XXVIII

Jimjoy swallowed once, moistened his lips, and took the wooden stairs evenly.

Around him swirled the gray mist that was a combination of frozen rain and fog, lending an unreal atmosphere to the late afternoon.

Thelina should have been back from the field training staff meeting. But "shoulds" didn't always translate into reality. Especially where she was concerned. And her message had been clear. Get to Thalos. But he couldn't leave without saying what he had to say.

Chuurrruppp. . . .

The raucous call of a jaymar echoed from one of the bare branches hidden in the mist.

Jimjoy grinned fleetingly as he stepped up to the door, pleased at the scavenger's call of support. At least he felt it was support of some sort.

Thrapp. Thrapp.

He waited, hearing the muffled sound of feet on the wooden floor inside, wondering whether Thelina or Meryl would open the door.

A sliver of golden light, followed by a breath of warm air—trilia-

and cinnamon-scented—spilled onto the porch where he stood as the door opened.

"Oh. . . ." Other than offering momentary surprise, Thelina's face was unreadable.

"Sorry. I'd just like a moment, if I could."

"Come on in." Thelina still wore a set of field greens, muddy beneath the knees, and a set of heavy greenish socks. "I just got back—literally." Her left hand flipped toward her legs. "As you can see." A smudge of dirt or mud on her left cheek almost appeared like a bruise, and her short hair was damply plastered against her scalp. She stepped back.

Jimjoy closed the door and glanced into the main room. Even from the foyer he could feel the warmth of the fired-up wooden stove. "Too cold to get cleaned up yet?"

Thelina nodded as she gingerly eased herself into one of the straight-backed wooden armchairs closest to the stove. "I'm also too tired. Sit down. You had something in mind?"

Jimjoy took the other wooden armchair, sitting on it at an angle to face her. He looked at her face, catching the almost classical lines as she closed her eyes momentarily. The warm light of the lamps and the flicker of orange from behind the mica of the stove lent a hint of softness to the cleanness of her features, to eyes and a nose perhaps a touch too strong in full sunlight.

What had she been like before?

"You had something in mind?" she repeated.

"Sorry . . . just thinking." He straightened up in the chair. "You put yourself directly on the line for me. Why?"

"I didn't do it for you. I did it because your program is the only chance Accord or the Institute has—and because I promised Sam I would, no matter how I felt about you."

"Hades . . . Sam could have ensured a successor . . . couldn't he?"

"Yes."

Jimjoy turned in the chair, glancing through the glass of the sliding door at the mist outside. Beyond the far deck railing he could see only vague outlines cloaked in gray.

"Either he didn't want a successor, or . . ."

"Or?"

"Nothing." He understood, he thought. All of the first-class strategic brains at the Institute were women. And Accord was not the Matriarchy, but an Imperial colony.

"Nothing? You came over here in the rain to bother an exhausted woman for nothing?"

He sighed. "No. I came to thank you. I came to tell you that I still care for you, and I came to admit that you were right. I was attracted to a facade at first. I admit it. But I've seen enough to know that the facade isn't a facade, that it reflects you. And I wish Sam simply could have named you his successor."

"Me?" Thelina sat up, looking surprised for the first time he had known her.

"Seems clear to me. For the most part, once you leave Sam and Gavin Thorson out, the sharpest of the Senior Fellows are women. You, Meryl, Kerin, Analitta . . ."

"What about you?" Her voice was softly curious.

"Me?" He felt like an echo. "I'm too new, too unknown. Too much of a lone wolf. I could do something about as big as my training group." He broke off. "That was why I came—to tell you how much your support meant, especially when you don't care that much for me." He stood up and faced the window, where the twilight had begin to darken the mist and reduce the visibility further.

"Anyway . . ."

"That's not quite what I said." Her correction was also soft, though her voice did not sound tired.

Jimjoy shrugged without looking back at her. "I don't know that I'll see you again for a while." If ever, he thought, the way things are going now. "And I wanted you to know"—he swallowed—"that you were right . . . and that I still care for you. Didn't want to leave without telling you." He turned and looked at Thelina.

She had left the chair and taken a step toward the door, not exactly toward him, but not avoiding him, either. She stepped to the glass beside him.

For a time, nearly shoulder to shoulder, they watched the mist swirl around the deck and the trees beyond, slowly darkening with the twilight. As they watched, he realized again how tall she was, something hard for him to believe for all her grace. Finally, his right hand found her left, and his fingers slipped into hers.

"Why do we fight so much?" he asked softly.

"Because I don't trust men, and you don't trust women."

"Could we try?" His fingers tightened around hers, but he did not dare to look at her.

"Only one at a time . . ."

She returned the pressure, and he could feel the strength in her long fingers. As strongly as he had pressed, she had answered.

Jimjoy turned toward her, and found her turning to him, her eyes looking into his. He found his hands touching her cheeks, drawing her face toward him, even as her hands found his shoulders.

Outside, the darkness dropped through the fog like foam from the fast-breaking night.

In time their lips dropped away from each other, and they stood, wrapped in each other, unwilling to let go, holding to the moment.

"I'm still filthy . . . and tired . . ."

Her breath tickled his ear.

"Do you want a shower?"

"Not a joint shower . . . not yet. Remember, I hardly know you." But there was laughter in her voice.

"I hardly know me."

"We'll get to know you together . . . slowly . . . Jimjoy."

"That's the first time you've ever used my name."

"I don't believe in easy familiarity."

"I've noticed," he whispered dryly.

She laughed again, softly, and he marveled at the hint of bells in her voice.

"Well, it's about time you two got that over with," announced a voice from the foyer.

They turned, not quite letting go of each other.

Meryl was grinning with every tooth in her mouth showing. "Now, maybe you can concentrate on planning the revolution."

"That may be hard," noted Jimjoy to Thelina, "since you'll be here and I'll be on Thalos."

"Security has to inspect *all* installations periodically. I'm overdue for Thalos."

He wrapped both arms around her, bear-hug fashion, and she reciprocated.

"Good thing for us lesser mortals that you two confine your affections to each other. A hug like that would break anybody else's ribs," Meryl remarked from the landing as she headed up to her room.

"I have to go . . . the shuttle . . ."

"I know . . . but . . . I do inspect, Professor, and don't forget it."

"How could I? How could I?"

XXIX

JIMJOY GLANCED AROUND the rough-hewn rock room, then at the group of twenty-plus fourth-year students and apprentices packed inside it. When the asteroid base had been built, it had not been designed for large meeting rooms.

Part of their training would consist of using new equipment to enlarge the quarters and facilities on Thalos, since the Institute would need additional off-planet facilities—hopefully for a long time to come.

In the meantime, the room was already getting uncomfortably warm, increasing the odor of oil and recycled air.

"You all know why you're here, I presume . . ." His tone was not quite overtly ironic.

Mera Lilkovie, in the third row, nodded.

"So why doesn't someone tell me?"

"Because Accord is about to rebel against the Empire . . ."

". . . we want to be free . . ."

Jimjoy waited until the words had died down.

"All of what you say is true, in a way, but no one yet has wanted to tell you the rest of what's going on . . . and I don't, either. But you deserve it, and anyone who doesn't want to stay on this team *after* I explain doesn't have to. But you *will* spend six weeks on one of the asteroid stations. And you'll understand that, too, after the explanation."

A few frowns crossed faces in the back.

"It's very simple. Without a new Prime, there's no real authority at the Institute, and no one wants to take chances. If we wait until that's sorted out, Accord will be under military occupation with a military reeducation team in place. I've seen military reeducation." He paused. "How many of you have . . . seen the debriefing on what happened on New Kansaw?"

This time nearly the entire room nodded.

"New Kansaw is the third system which has been 'reeducated' in the past decade. Unless we do something, Accord will be next."

"But . . ."

"How . . ."

"... against the resources of the Empire ..."

Once more he waited until the murmurs had died down.

"You were all approached because you are troublemakers of a particular sort. You prefer action. You tend not to take anyone's word for anything. You're going to have to take mine—since we're going to succeed.

"Without a fleet, without a large standing military force, we will quietly become independent and probably free a large number of other Imperial colonies or dependencies as well." Jimjoy managed to keep a straight face.

"Wait a stan, Professor. Just how do you propose this miracle?"

"By doing the impossible. First, we will take over Accord orbit control and operate it as if it were still Imperially controlled—except for some obvious gaps in information we will not pass along. Second, we will undertake certain steps to ensure that the Empire cannot mount a full-scale military attack against Accord."

"... right ..."

"... so obvious ... and so wrong ..."

This time the muttering went on for a while.

Finally, Jimjoy stood up straight. *"TEN-HUTTTTTTTTT!!!!"*

The sound reverberated through the chamber, stilling it, though none of the students and apprentices physically responded to the ancient command.

"Thank you. The Institute does not believe in either exaggeration or hyperbole. I am here to train you to help accomplish both tasks. Successful completion of this course entails advancement to journeyman status in applied ecologic management tactics—a new field for the Institute, but the privileges and status are just as valid and real for all the newness.

"As the old saying goes, that is the good news. The bad news is that half of you will be engaged in extremely hazardous efforts and about thirty percent of you may not live to see advancements to Senior Fellow status. Of course, if enough of you don't undertake this effort with me, we'll all be dead, exiled beyond the Rift, or on the mushroom farms."

He looked over the group—quite silent as the implications of what he had said penetrated. "I realize fully that I have given you insufficient information for an informed decision. Any more information for anyone not committed to the effort will cost lives of those who are.

"I can only stress that I am personally completely committed and that I'm not associated with losing ventures." He paused and glanced across the open and young faces. "Some of you may know I almost didn't survive several of my ventures and that Accord is my home by choice, not birth. Some of you will die. I wish there were another way. Neither I nor the other Institute fellows associated with this effort can see one.

"This is not a lark, and it is just the beginning of a long struggle. Those of you who choose to join the team will go down in history— one way or the other. You have until tomorrow to make your decision."

Then he turned and walked out. His steps echoed off the stone and into the silence.

XXX

"*ROOSVELDT*, CLOSURE IS green. Delta vee on the curve. Commence backburst."

"Stet, OpCon. Commencing backburst."

Jimjoy moistened his lips, listening. He glanced over at Arnault, watching the youngster check the small tank he carried for at least the fourth time in as many minutes. Lined up behind Arnault, the rest of the squad waited, each Ecolitan carrying some apparatus vital to the operation—a tank, laser welders, or cutters. Everyone carried stunners. The only weapons intended to cause death were the knives in Jimjoy's belt.

"*Roosveldt*, delta vee excessive. Increase backburst. Increase backburst."

"OpCon, increasing backburst."

Jimjoy tapped Arnault on the shoulder. Arnault nodded and tapped the next Ecolitan apprentice.

Jimjoy wanted to shake his head. Mounting an operation mainly with apprentices was crazy, but they had to start somewhere, and the handful of Senior Fellows who would have been helpful were too valuable to risk.

"*Roosveldt*, increase backburst. INCREASE BACKBURST . . ."

WHHHHHSsssssttt . . .

The steering jets kicked in with nearly full power with less than fifty meters remaining between the Accord transport and the orbit control station.

"*Roosveldt* . . . delta vee on curve . . ."

Clung . . .

At the sound of the locks matching, the modified cargo hatch slid open a mere meter. Jimjoy was the first out, riding a beefed-up broomstick, with Arnault and Keswen right behind him.

"OpCon, *Roosveldt*. We are setting out a maintenance party. Need to check the steering jets. Too much lag between control and response."

"Stet, *Roosveldt*. Maintenance party cleared. Next time, find out before you try to lock . . . if you wouldn't mind."

"Sorry about that, OpCon. We poor colonials have to make do."

"Don't take it out on us hapless Imperial functionaries."

Jimjoy aimed the broomstick toward the fusactor umbilical, touching the squirter controls, first to steady his heading and then to ease the speed up.

Glancing back, he could see that the last two Ecolitans, the two behind Arnault, were straying too far from the station hull. He motioned once. Nothing. "Hades." Touching the squirter, he slowed just enough to let Arnault ease up beside him.

Tap.

Arnault looked over. Jimjoy motioned again, gesturing for the two broomstick riders behind Arnault to move closer to the hull plates. This time Arnault nodded and dropped back to pass the word. The two offenders closed with the station, and all four broomsticks glided along in the shadows.

"OpCon, interrogative time between call for backburst and response."

"You don't know?"

"Come off it, Hensley. I know what our instruments show. When I called increased backburst, that's what the tape shows . . ."

"Hades . . . wait—we'll see if there's a visual . . ."

The *Roosveldt* was locked in on delta three, the closest main lock to the southern tip of orbit control. Five needleboats lay dead, shrouded, in a hundred-kay semicircle around the control station. The only ships locked in at the station belonged to Accord.

So far, so good. Jimjoy gave a hand signal and flared the squirters to slow the broomstick.

The umbilical to the fusactor was less than fifty meters away.

After another set of hand signals, Jimjoy brought the broomstick to a halt, suspended at a wide black band that separated the station junction plug from the silvery gray of the umbilical.

As Jimjoy took the tools and began to remove the collar, Arnault eased the tank into position while Keswen set up the laser. Marcer took control of the broomsticks and watched the nearby locks.

"*Roosveldt*—"

EEEEeeeeeiiiii . . .

The commscrambler crew had managed to get their equipment installed and operating, which meant that the station crew had no internal/external transmission capability—except for torps.

Now, if the ventilation crew had managed as well . . .

Jimjoy grinned and chin-toggled down the helmet's receiver volume as he pulled the collar away from the plug, carefully tethering it. He would need it later, once the station was theirs.

He put the thought aside as Keswen moved the laser into position.

Four quick slices and the heavy bolts were severed. The laser was also out of power.

Jimjoy eased himself up to the connecting points and began the business of manually separating the connectors, making sure that he touched nothing except each connector.

Eeeeeee . . . The scrambled sound of the jammer died away as the station lost all power except for the reserves. He would have liked to maintain scrambling longer, but his team needed communications, and the mass of a self-powered jammer would have been difficult to handle for his crash-trained crew.

Jimjoy toggled up the comm volume. "Interrogative status project green." Back on the broomstick, he guided himself toward the Accordan ship.

"Project green is go. Project green is go."

Jimjoy nodded at the sound of Paralt's voice.

"*Roosveldt*, are you crazy? This is an Imperial station."

The ship did not answer.

"*Roosveldt*, answer me!"

"OpCon, this is Commander Black. The *Roosveldt* is not responsible for this effort. We are."

"Who the hades are you?"

Jimjoy did not answer, instead checking behind him and motioning Arnault and Keswen closer to the station hull plates. Hensley, assuming he was the senior officer in OpCon, still had two operating lasers, two torp ports, and twenty-four hours of emergency power.

"Commander Black, energy concentration in beta three. Energy concentration in beta three."

Jimjoy sighed and pulled the red bloc from his equipment belt, thumbing the release.

One hundred keys out, five needleboats powered up, screens searching for the commtorp the station was about to launch.

"You friggin' Fuards . . ."

"We're—"

"SILENCE!" boomed Jimjoy, cutting off the incautious rebuttal of some outraged Ecolitan. Right now they were better off if the station thought that it was the victim of a Fuard sabotage effort.

"Captain Green," continued Jimjoy, back to a normal voice, "status of nutcracker." His feet touched the personnel lock still beside the ship lock. One Ecolitan looked him over, stunner lowering in recognition of his identity.

Jimjoy thumbed the entry stud, and the light began to blink.

"Commander Black, nutcracker is beta green."

"Stet."

Inside the lock another apprentice, too close, looked him over. Jimjoy made a mental note. Too many people where they couldn't do any good. Then he entered the station, heading toward the armored and self-contained operations center.

So far as he could see, only green-suited Ecolitans were moving. In the main corridor he stepped over two unconscious figures—one male, one female.

"Commander Black, green team, station is secure except delta five, and OpCon."

"Status delta five?" Jimjoy concentrated. Delta five? Electronics shop? Of course, the clean rooms probably had self-contained atmospheres.

"Delta five blocked, with power cut. Two holdouts, without suits."

"Drill it. Use the cutter from red team with a power adaptor, and punch a half-dozen holes in the side bulkheads."

"Stet, Commander Black."

Jimjoy stopped at the heavy metal emergency doors to the Operations Center. Four young green-team members turned as one to look at him.

"Slate?"

Even as Paralt handed him the square of plastic and the stylus, Jimjoy was jotting a question he didn't want OpCon hearing, since he was certain that the OIC had already put the automatic frequency band monitors into full operation.

"Welds on torp ports three/five?"

Paralt shrugged, then took the slate back. "Blue team. Reported start."

"Blue team, Commander Black. Interrogative status. AFFIRMATIVE OR NEGATIVE ONLY."

"Prime affirmative. Secondary negative this time."

EEEEEEEEEEEEEEEEEEEEEEEEEEEEEEEEEEEEEEEEEeeeeeeeee . . .

Jimjoy winced as the white noise jolted through his helmet receiver. Some had realized that the communications benefited the invaders more than the invaded.

After chin-toggling down the helmet communicator volume, he wrote on the slate: "Send messenger. Report when all torp ports sealed."

Paralt read it and nodded, handing the slate to the Ecolitan next to him. With a start, as her helmet turned toward him, Jimjoy realized the messenger was Mera.

He took the slate back. "Casualties?" he wrote.

"One—Nerat. Sliced own suit. Blew," was the reply.

Jimjoy shook his head. Carelessness was the greatest enemy. Wiping the slate, he jotted out the next steps for Paralt:

"Swivel joint—plan 1. Force gas through line one. Min. 140."

Paralt shrugged as though questioning.

Jimjoy scrawled below his command: "OpCon hold out forever. Bring up main cutters after torp ports. Have to cut through. Reconnect direct supercon line from fusactor to laser. Ten hours!!!"

Taking a station was so damned much harder than destroying it. He hoped they had ten hours without an Imperial ship arriving unannounced, although he had planned on that possibility. Even a courier would require three-plus hours to make it from system jump entry to Accord orbit control.

He gestured to the young Ecolitan, signifying he was leaving. Next he had to gather the red team back and install a direct power line from the fusactor to the laser cutters needed to open the Operations Center. All that getting the gas into Operations Control would do would be to reduce the possibility that someone else got killed.

In the meantime, he needed to ensure that the blue team was securing the station and removing all the Imperial personnel.

With another sigh, he stepped up the pace toward the lock, chin-toggling down yet another notch the noise generated by the OpCon signal converter.

So . . . no one took an Imperial station?

He grinned as he walked on. The grin faded as he thought about the next steps—including how to handle the first Imperial ship that docked and knew the station crew, or wanted to wander around.

Taking the station wasn't the biggest problem—keeping it might be.

XXXI

"Of those who claim the Empire is necessary for survival, ask for whose survival—ours or the Empire's.

"Of those who assert that Imperial unity is necessary to prevent rebellions and wars, ask why the number of wars and rebellions remains constant century after century—even as the Empire has grown mightier and mightier.

"Of those who declare that the Empire is necessary for the wise allocation of resources, ask how allocation is possible when the cost of transport between systems makes it infeasible for all but the most precious of goods.

"Of those who fear aliens hidden in the stars, ask why the Empire has enslaved those few found with less effort than ruling us.

"Of those claiming peace as the reason for Empire, ask why the Empire maintains the mightiest fleets and forces of all time.

"Of those who claim the Empire promotes free movement of peoples, ask why the Empire conquers and enslaves those who would leave peacefully."

> *Query I*
> Manifesto series
> Circa 3640 O.E.E.

XXXII

He glanced toward the small room's privacy lock, a small brass device on the narrow and golden plastic door. The Ecolitans hated plastic, but carrying wood to an off-planet station just wasn't practical—not to Thalos, and especially not to one of the smaller outspace research stations.

"What are you thinking about?" She lay next to him on the narrow bunk, her left hand massaging his too-tight shoulders, her strong fingers working across his bare skin.

"You." He wanted to stretch. At the same time, he did not want to move away from the silkiness of her skin against his. With her beside him, the gray moon-rock walls seemed immaterial. They could have been back on Accord.

"Besides that . . ."

"You . . . yesterday . . . when you got here . . . and my heart . . . and I couldn't say anything." He edged closer to her, drawing in the scent of trilia.

"You've come a long way. But besides me . . . what are you thinking? There's a corner of your mind somewhere else." Her hand stopped, then traced a line from his shoulder to the back of his neck.

Jimjoy shivered, not saying anything, not really wanting to speak.

Thelina's hand rested lightly on his right shoulder.

Finally he stretched, shrugging his shoulders but letting himself drop back against her, hoping she would nibble his ear, or something equally pleasant. "What else is there as important as you?"

"You *are* planning a revolution . . . when you're not thinking licentious thoughts." The warmth of her words tingled his neck.

He took a breath. "Try not to think about it sometimes. We're asking a lot . . . maybe far too much . . . trying to outtrain the Impies without enough time."

Her hands kneaded the muscles at the base of his neck. "They did well with orbit control."

"Not bad. But that was close to home. We had all the advantages, and we knew everyone's habits and schedules. We still lost one person and had three other casualties. That's a lot . . . under the circumstances." He leaned back against her, savoring the feel of her skin, her uncovered breasts against his back.

"You're too tight. Roll over." She pushed him away as he started to pull toward her, to move between her long legs. "The other way—onto your stomach."

He sighed, louder than necessary, then took another breath, trying to relax with her warm legs straddling his, trying to enjoy her fingers probing and releasing the tightness in his lower back.

"You worry . . . about the SysCon expeditions?"

"Be a damned fool not to. Somewhere . . . someone . . . taken precautions . . . don't know what they are . . . pickups . . . problem . . ."

"What about the more experienced ones?"

"Geoff? Analitta? Kerin?" He grunted and stopped talking as her hands dropped to the backs of his legs.

"If you don't keep talking, I won't keep massaging."

"And then . . . ?" He made the question as suggestive as possible.

"I'll leave and inspect something else. This was *supposed* to be an inspection tour . . . Professor." She leaned down and kissed his neck.

He shivered as her breasts brushed his bare back.

"The experienced ones . . ." she prompted.

"The way you do that . . . experience . . ." he gasped.

"That's not what we were talking about." Her laugh was gentle. "What happened?"

". . . made them . . . draw straws . . . couldn't risk them all . . . tried to persuade Kerin and Geoff not to go . . . small children . . . turned me down . . ."

"You're going to let them?"

He sighed again, withdrawing from the pleasure of her hands at her question. "Couldn't stop them. They made a scene. I rigged it the best I could, but they insisted—Geoff and Kerin did. Yelled about how I couldn't do everything dangerous. Palmed Kerin's straw—don't tell her! Geoff grabbed before I could do anything. Insisted I needed some experience on the Fonderal mission, since it was the last one."

"Too many observers?" She leaned away from him, her back erect, moving beside his thighs, balancing on the narrow space between his legs and the edge of the bunk.

Jimjoy nodded, half turning toward her, feeling his eyes widen as he saw her body. "Too much observation for me . . ." His hands were greedy as he reached for her.

Thelina only put out her hands to his shoulders to break her fall toward him, and only for an instant before she drew his face and lips to hers.

XXXIII

TO THE RIGHT—that was what the map in his head said. But a map wasn't like *knowing* it. The broad-shouldered man in the counterfeit uniform needed to place the next charge by the connector lines servicing the recycling system.

The corridor was dim, especially for someone accustomed to field work planetside, and no short-term intensive training would change that. Gray steel and plastics of all shades, the corridor smelled of oil, sweat, and ozone.

His boots clicked faintly on the hard plastic underfoot, plastic that had lost its resilience years earlier. Only the minute fluctuations of his weight told him that his time was getting short.

How had anyone done it? Especially single-handedly.

He picked up the pace, then slowed as an officer emerged from the corridor junction in front of him.

"You! Technician! Your badge isn't current."

"Sir?"

"You don't belong on this level." The officer had a stunner in his hands, aimed squarely at him. "Move, *Technician*."

The blocky man shrugged. "What can I say, sir? These new rigs . . . this new badge, that new badge . . . what difference does it make?"

"Your section chief will think it does. So will you after a week in confinement." The officer gestured with the hand not holding the stunner, which remained trained squarely on the technician. "Past me and up the lift."

"There's no lift that way, sir." He knew that from the drills, as well as from the hidden challenge tests. "Do you want me to take the right branch or go back?" He kept moving slowly ahead, but as though he were still trying to follow the impossible instructions and avoid the stunner.

How much time? The Imperials were getting edgy, too security-conscious.

"That's right." The officer gestured again. "Who's your section chief?"

Thud

Thrummm.

The stocky man blocked a scream—his own—at the line of pain searing the edge of his shoulder. The Imperial officer lay in the intersection of the two lower-level corridors, his neck at a disjointed angle.

He scooped up the stunner from the gray plastic floor tiles with his good right hand, trying to flex the fingers of his left as he did so.

Time! So little left. He forced himself into the junction, checking both directions. Momentarily clear. Only the next charge was critical before he could break off and meet the rest of the team. He began to trot, fast enough to cover the remaining few hundred meters quickly, slowly enough that he might not seem too out of place. Total secrecy was out anyway. And the badge business had to be a reaction to Haversol.

Whhhp . . . thewwwp . . . whhhp . . .

At the next junction he slowed, bringing the stunner up.

Thrum.

Another officer toppled. The blocky man jumped the body, landing awkwardly and off-balance, mainly on his right foot.

One more turn, and the proper piping/angle configuration appeared. A quick glance over his shoulder told him that the corridor remained clear—for the moment. He laid down the stunner. One, two, three flat cards went into place. He pressed a small cube on the outermost and nicked the corner off, taking longer than he should because of the shaking in the fingers of his left hand.

After retrieving the stunner, he turned and scanned the main corridor. Still clear. He could make the fingers on his left hand work, but their control wasn't going to be very good for fine work for a while. He picked up his steps until he reached the next junction, where he slowed, easing the stunner up at the sound of boots, and holding back from the intersection.

A technician eased into the intersection, holding a stunner, but checking the far side first.

Thrummm.

Thud.

The real technician dropped into a heap without another sound, except for the muffled *clunk* of his weapon hitting the tiles.

Beyond the junction, to the right, lay the maintenance lock that was his immediate goal. He slapped the glowing green stud, which blinked amber as the inner door opened.

Three suits. He checked the air supplies and took the center one, belatedly remembering to touch the panel to close the lock behind him, violating two safety precautions simultaneously. After setting aside his equipment pouch and tool belt and extracting the remaining explosive cards, he fumbled forth the all-plastic arrow gun and set it aside also. With the quick motions he had practiced so often on Thalos, he donned the suit, double-checking each connection. Finally he secured the suit and adjusted the equipment belt and retrieved the cards and tool pouch. Two of the cards he placed against the thinnest plating on the inner wall of the station, nicking the detonator cube.

Both broomsticks came out of their bulkhead brackets. He touched the red stud, which flashed. An alarm began to howl, although the hissing and sound loss told him that the lock pressure was dropping. As the outer-door iris widened, he slipped two more cards and a detonator into the plate interstices.

The suddenness of stepping from the low grav of the lock into null-grav off the hull plates brought his stomach up into his throat. He swallowed, wondering how much time remained. Again he remembered the procedures and chin-toggled the helmet communicator.

He tethered one broomstick to his belt and brought the other broomstick to him and himself to it, awkwardly settling into the seat. Then he touched the squirters.

"OpCon—emergency! Intruder, level three delta. Casualties."

Time? How much longer? Three delta? Who had that been? He corrected his drift to remain within elbow length of the station hull plates. Who?

You, he answered.

"ExOps, interrogative exterior maintenance this time."

"OpCon, that's a negative."

"Open lock, four delta."

"That's our bandit. Squad beta on target."

He glanced over his shoulder, seeing nothing but the regular exterior station lights and continuing to guide the broomstick toward the fusactor tether. He touched the arrow gun at his belt.

". . . friggin' Fuards . . . their asses . . ."

"Silence on the net. Silence on the net."

"OpCon . . . power . . . inter . . . say . . . surges . . . interrogative . . ."

A faint smile crossed the suited man's lips as he curved around the remaining quarter of the station's southern end—only to catch sight of two figures in marauder suits broomsticking toward the fusactor.

Marauder suits meant trouble. While he edged his own stick deeper into the hull shadows, he followed the Marines toward his and their destination. His left hand still trembling within the suit gauntlet, he left the arrow gun hooked to his belt. Against armor, he had to be closer, much closer.

"OpCon on emergency power. All hands! All hands! SysCon red omega. Red omega!"

Hades. This would be the last SysCon taken from within. *If* they could take it. Time? How much? He gave another touch to the squirters, closing more quickly on the Marines before him.

"Bandits on the southland! Bandits on the southland, OpCon."

"Stet. Omega measures. Omega measures."

The blocky man in the maintenance suit fumbled with the arrow pistol. Before him, one of the marauder suits balanced a laser rifle. Unless he stopped the pair, they would stop Niklos and Keswen, and none of them would make it to the pickup. Unless they took out the station, the modified needleboat wouldn't be able to make the pickup.

Another squirt, and he could see the distance narrow. Almost close enough. He raised the pistol, squeezed the wide trigger.

The first shot missed. At least nothing happened, and the plastic missile continued unseen into the darkness. He steadied himself and squeezed again.

"Frig—"

"Beta under fire."

One marauder broomstick veered. Stick and figure split and bounced separately and slowly against the station hull. The laser and power pack proceeded on a gradually diverging course, tumbling end over end toward the SysCon fusactor.

The other broomstick and its rider turned.

"Idiot," murmured the man with the arrow pistol as he squeezed the trigger again.

No sound—but the second Marine jerked as the plastic explosive blew open the front of his suit.

Tasting sudden bile in his throat, the survivor guided himself past the faint mist and tumbling body and toward the fusactor tether, where he could make out two figures.

He retrieved the green light/reflector square from the tool pouch, attached it to his shoulder, adjusted the position, and touched the stud to illuminate the light badge. He didn't need his own team turning an arrow gun on him. The two others triggered their badges, the green lights winking from their shoulders as they continued to work on the base of the fusactor tether.

That they were targeting separation meant real problems.

"ExOps, OpCon. Interrogative status squad beta."

"Negative status. Negative status. Have dispatched follow-up squads."

He touched the controls for the broomstick's forward squirters, coming to a near dead stop by the others. He gestured, not wanting to use the helmet comm.

Keswen gave him a quick series of motions, indicating a lock problem and the need to cut off power to the station.

The solo Ecolitan nodded and gestured toward the lock.

Keswen shrugged and returned to working on the connectors.

The single man touched the controls on the squirter, easing himself toward the bulbous end of the fusactor module, where he found that the standard entrance control plates had been replaced with an armored key and combination plate.

For a long moment he studied the arrangement, reflecting that the changes did not extend from the plate area itself, which indicated the possibility that the underlying circuitry had not been replaced. With a half shrug, he went to the carryall pocket in the maintenance suit.

Two squares, one cube, to begin with. He placed all three, nicked the cube, and climbed far enough around the bulb not to get punctured by the shrapnel from the explosion. The plates seemed to twist ever so slightly just before he put his feet down.

He waited until he felt the slightest shudder in the plates under his boots.

"Bandits! Detached the southland. Detached the southland."

"Friggers! Blast . . ."

At least twenty broomsticks aimed toward the bottom end of the fusactor tether as he scrambled for the lock.

Forcing himself not to hurry, and ignoring the dampness on his forehead, he carefully picked away the remaining shards of plastic and plate to uncover the exposed circuit lines. There were three, each of which he pulled from a shattered circuit bloc. He trimmed the ends to expose bare metal.

He touched the black and red together. Nothing. The red and green. Nothing. Finally, the black and the green. The outer fusactor lock irised, jerkily. He staggered inside, dropping to one knee on his return to artificial gravity. On his feet, he slapped the interior controls to close the outer lock behind him. The inner lock door had no security combination, just a standard plate, which he pressed.

He wasn't supposed to be the one working the fusactor. That was Keswen, but Keswen was at the tether, and if—but Keswen wasn't going to make it in time. He glanced over the standard control board arrangement, trying to recall the backup briefings at the Institute and, later, on Thalos.

The bottle controls were in the third panel . . . was it from the right?

They roughly matched the control layout. So he should count from the left. He stepped around the locked control board. Among the tools in his pouch was a long-bladed screwdriver. Two quick twists and the panel dropped off, bouncing off his suit boot.

His forehead was sweaty and clammy all at once, and he wanted to wipe it, but the only option he had wearing a suit was to press his forehead against the helmet pad.

"Ha—" He hadn't even considered that the fusactor was pressurized, but it had to be. Off came the helmet and the gloves. After wiping his forehead and taking several deep breaths of the stale power-section air, he began methodically to check the connections. A series of increasing magnetic bottle constrictions—that was the goal—each one building up the residual force within the bottle.

Three-quarters of the blocs uncovered were useless, clearly serving other functions. Attaching the program probe to one bloc, he pulsed it, leaning back to watch the power boards. There was a flicker on the output monitor. He pulsed it again. A larger flicker, a brief output drop before the return to normal. But the field size remained constant.

"Hades . . . never said it would be this hard or take so long . . ." Outside, he knew, the Marines were wearing down Keswen and Niklos. Against twenty what could they do?

He tried another bloc. Nothing. And another. Still no reaction. A fourth. The field strength monitor edged down.

He took a deep breath before looking around the control room. Fine—except he hadn't the faintest idea of how to program the parameters.

His stomach felt like lead.

"Carill . . . don't want to do this . . ."

Clank.

He hadn't locked the outer lock door.

Clung.

After scrambling over and around the control board, he threw himself into the lock and began to twist the manual locks into place.

Clang . . . hummmm . . . buzzz . . .

"Hades . . ."

The Marines were outside. He was inside, and unless . . . His heart was as cold as his guts as he walked back to the panel and the power probe.

Don't think about it. Don't think about Carill. Don't think about Shera . . . Jorje . . .

Pulse bloc two. Adjust.
Pulse bloc four. Constrict the field.
Pulse . . .
Constrict . . .
Pulse . . .
Constrict . . .

XXXIV

23 Decem 3646
New Augusta

Dear Mort:

I'll have to be quicker than I planned. First comes the good news. I was selected below zone for Admiral, and that means a boost to the Planning Staff. I'm looking forward to it, or think I am. With the situation out in your sector, I may not be as enthusiastic once I've moved and been briefed, although it's likely to be another month or so at the earliest.

There's more of the bad news. The FC has definitely been scrubbed. We did put the CX out for review, costing, and tech evaluation. We didn't lose totally, because a lot of the better features of the FC are incorporated in the CX, plus we've got the high-speed jump entry-exit thing licked—at least in theory. That ought to help a lot, *if* the Senate will approve it. The problem is we'd still be six, seven years away from deployment. What are we—you especially—supposed to do in the meantime?

With all the Fuard efforts, some of the "colonies" that really aren't colonies are trying to get actual independent-member status. Because of the higher imposts for colonies, the Senate hasn't wanted to grant them actual independent status. The honorable Senators finally did act, though. They passed a law making it so punitive for any colony that they have to rebel.

So a bunch have already started making noises—or worse. Worst is Accord—you know the place—combination free enterprise/ecological nut system out on the Parthanian Rift. The idiots took over their own orbit control station. No problem—except that there have been a few more Haversol-type "incidents" out there, and there's no convenient repowering for a full battle group. The Fuards have been really rattling their sabers. Anyway, you can figure out the logistics of that one! None of the politicos understand why you can't just dispatch a battle cruiser with a planetbuster. They also haven't figured out how you get that far without SysCons to repower—or, if we actually succeeded, how you collect revenues from assorted dust and debris.

The Social Dems, N'Trosia's boys and girls, are screaming about our procurement budget again. They want to put the credits into programs "socially" more valuable. They claim all our spending hasn't stopped the colony unrest or the Fuards. Forget about the difficulty of handling either one with inadequate and obsolete equipment. The worst part is that all of the rhetoric's bound to have an impact. How can it not when he's the Chairman of the Defense Committee?

I've got to get back to the work screens, trying to get caught up before I go over to Planning. Sorry about the bitching to you, but you always were a good listener. I'll try to keep you posted. My best to all four of you.

Blaine

XXXV

THE THIN MAN in the pale green laboratory coat looked up at the two visitors. His mouth twitched as he glanced from one to the other, from the man—two meters tall, silver-haired, bronze-skinned, and with green eyes that seemed to cut like a scalpel—to the woman, perhaps one hundred and eighty-five centimeters, just as silver-haired and bronze-skinned, with eyes as cold as the snows of Southbreak.

"Professor Stilsen, Ecolitans Whaler and Andruz. From the Institute. Ecolitan Andruz heads field training, and Ecolitan Whaler is in charge of applied ecologic management tactics." The young man in field greens inclined his head, then stepped back and closed the door.

"Field training and tactics . . . seem a far field from micro-genetic management," offered Stilsen, looking at the hard copy beside his console.

"Not so far as you might imagine, Doctor," offered Jimjoy. He gestured at the console and the hard copy. "Even though I understand a little about your work, I still found it hard not to expect a traditional laboratory setting."

"I'm sure you have a great deal to do, Ecolitan."

"And you'd like to know why we're here." Jimjoy laughed not caring if the laugh was false. "Fair enough." He glanced toward the small table and four chairs in the corner. Papers dribbled from an untidy stack in the center of the table. "Do you mind if we have a seat? While it won't take too long, we can't be quite that brief."

Thelina smiled, and her eyes warmed momentarily.

"I understand. I apologize for the disarray. My colleagues kindly refer to it as creative chaos. Would you like anything to drink?"

"No, thank you," answered Thelina in a low voice.

"No, thank you," added Jimjoy. He pulled out a chair for Thelina.

She raised her eyebrows, and her eyes raked over him.

"Simple courtesy," he said softly.

Stilsen swept the papers which threatened to drift from the stack and onto the brown-and-orange braided rug into a separate pile. Then he pulled out a chair for himself, the one closest to his console. He glanced at the image on his console screen, almost regretfully, and sighed. "How may I help you?"

Thelina glanced at Jimjoy.

He pulled his chin. "According to your last quarterly report, you have demonstrated some considerable success in bacterial 'parasitism' . . . and I'd be interested in learning how applicable that technology is."

"Applicable? Rather an odd choice of words, Ecolitan Whaler."

Jimjoy looked at Stilsen, levelly, directly.

The Professor looked away almost immediately. Then he coughed and cleared his throat. "I have to assume you are referring to my success in slowing down bacterial reproduction patterns by decreasing the internal tolerance to self-generated toxins and waste products."

"I did read about that . . . but I was more interested in the other ones. About replication of parasitic borer characteristics in a wide range of pests . . . and I was also interested in your references to spread vector distribution."

"I was afraid of that."

A faint smile crossed Thelina's lips at the scientist's response.

"Ethical concerns, doctor?"

"Partly, and partly . . ." Stilsen shrugged.

Jimjoy swallowed. "What do you know about Accord's current situation vis-à-vis the Empire?"

Stilsen smiled almost apologetically. "More than I would like, Ecolitan. Even with the careful management of news on both sides, it is clear that some sort of hostilities are imminent."

"Hostilities have already broken out, Doctor. We have been forced to take over Accord orbit control and quarantine all Imperial Forces in the system. The Empire is gathering a task group and a reeducation team to deploy here."

"I don't see how I can help . . . not in that time frame."

"I think we can buy some more time." Jimjoy shrugged. "But we need to deliver a message to the Empire that we can destroy the ecology on any planet we choose."

"We're not in that class, Ecolitan." Stilsen's voice was cold.

"If we're not, Doctor, or if we can't get there hades-fired quick, then you and I and most of Accord will be dead before the end of next year."

The scientist glanced down at a brownish-black spot on the orange section of the braided rug. "Are you the new centurions, then?"

Thelina looked baffled.

Jimjoy shook his head slowly. "No. We cannot compel anything. Came to request your help. But to keep the Empire from totally annihilating us, we need to demonstrate that we can destroy a planetary ecology. We could build a planetbuster. That won't work. Everyone *knows* that poor little Accord couldn't build the fleets to deliver enough of them to matter.

"Ecological war is another thing. People believe that a handful of little bugs can multiply and divide and destroy an entire food chain, whether it's true or not. They will believe that Accord can do that—whether we can or not."

Stilsen shook his head. "I don't think you understand. There are at least four of us who can do what you want. I'd rather do it willingly."

"Why?" asked Thelina.

"Because there are good ways and bad ways to get there. Some ways would leave a planet destroyed forever. Others will have just as devastating short-term impacts, but relatively insignificant long-term environmental effects—besides mass starvation." His last words dropped like acid rain.

"Do you have an alternative?" asked Jimjoy quietly.

"Do you?"

"I'd try to build that planetbuster and destroy Alphane."

"You mean it." Stilsen's voice was matter-of-fact, unquestioning. He turned to Thelina. "Could he do it? Personally?"

"Yes. He's already done worse—at least in some ways."

Stilsen's pale complexion grew paler as he glanced from one Ecolitan to the other. "And if I go to the Prime?"

"You know as well as I do, Doctor. Harlinn will dither, call three committee meetings, and put it out for study. The study completion date will be considerably after our demise under the Fourth Battle Group—or whatever they call the Fleet reeducation team. There is absolutely no pressure I can bring upon you to help us out. At any time, you can call a halt to this . . . starting right now." Jimjoy stood up. "I appreciate your patience. After you have a chance to think it over, one of us will be in touch with you."

Thelina rose. "Thank you, Doctor. This puts you in an impossible position, I realize. Too many evils in history have been justified in the name of survival. Perhaps this would be one of them."

Jimjoy added, "You don't know whether we are trying to preserve something unique against an implacable opponent or whether we are trying to bring down a great civilization for personal gain or vengeance."

Stilsen stood up. "I don't know whether any end justifies such means."

Jimjoy handed him a folder. "Before you decide, you might read through these. Then check with some sources you trust to see how true the stories are. We'll be in touch."

"I'm sure you will be. I'm sure you will be." Stilsen inclined his head. "And now . . ."

"Good day, Professor."

"Good day."

The door closed with a firm click.

The two Ecolitans walked unmolested down the corridor and out through the research station doors. The station rested in a meadow. The meadow, clearly artificial with its green T-type grasses and flower beds beside the building, was surrounded by the darker native conifers, with a scattering of corran trees.

The Institute flitter waited on a section of the narrow stone-paved road that arrowed for a break in the trees.

Jimjoy pre-flighted the flitter, more to ensure lack of tampering than for concern that the aircraft had become less airworthy in the short time they had spent with the research station staff.

"What do you think?" asked Thelina as she watched him strap in.

"What do I think? Why ask me? You understand people far better than I do." He clicked the straps in place and began the checklist. "What do you think?"

"He wants to help, but he won't, not unless the Institute encourages him."

Jimjoy nodded as he continued the checklist. "We've avoided Harlinn as long as possible. Probably can't be avoided any longer. Won't be pretty."

"Ha!" Thelina's laugh was short and sarcastic. "When you say that . . ."

"Hold on." The whine of the turbines through the open side windows cut off the rest of her comments. "Close the side ports. We'll need to plan strategy."

Though she frowned as she strained to hear his words, Thelina nodded.

XXXVI

"YOU ASKED FOR the meeting, Ecolitan Whaler," said Harlinn, acting as Prime.

Jimjoy reflected. Trying to express what he had in mind would be hard. "I did." He looked around the office. Thelina would listen. So would Kerin Sommerlee. The history philosophy types were out, as were the pure scientists. He wished he knew Althelm better—the economist could be the key. "It's time to put all the cubes on the screen. All of you know some of the pieces. First, most of you should know that the tactics group has taken over the control and actual operations of Accord orbit control. Some may have wondered why an Imperial Battle Group hasn't tried to take it back.

"Unless we act together they will. Right now they can't. The tactics group has managed to destroy two more Imperial SysCons—"

"SysCons?" asked someone from the corner.

"Imperial System Control Stations—fleet repowering and restaging bases, usually placed in a stable orbit around an outer planet gas giant."

Jimjoy cleared his throat and continued. "Anyway, we've destroyed the two along the Arm. After the accident at Haversol, that means the Impies can't attack us with a full fleet unless they replace the SysCons. Right now they can't commit the resources, not so long as their problems with the Fuards continue. But they can gradually replace those stations, or slowly shift resources toward us. And that they will do, until they've built a fleet out here." He looked around the Prime's office—he still thought of it as Sam's.

"Are you telling us that you've single-handedly declared war on the Empire on behalf of Accord—whether we and the Institute like it or not?" Harlinn's face had become paler with each moment.

"I could say I've just speeded the process. After all, the Empire already has doubled the imposts and declared that it will control every bit of research the Institute will ever do. That's just for starters." Jimjoy held up his hand to still the mumbling. "But I won't insult your intelligence.

"Yes. For all practical purposes, I declared war on the Empire. No mealymouthed apology will stop the Imperial Forces. Only good strategy and applied force. You can help me, or you can wait for the citybusters and the reeducation teams. Those are your options." Jimjoy waited for the outburst.

"What!"

"Madman . . ."

"Sam was a fool . . ."

"Wait . . ."

". . . historical inevitability . . ."

". . . give him a dose of his own medicine . . ."

". . . hire mercenaries, and this is the result . . ."

"WAIT A MOMENT!" Kerin Sommerlee's voice cut through the incipient arguments, and the grumbles died down as faces turned toward her. "Arguing over the past won't solve anything. Even executing Ecolitan Whaler wouldn't solve anything, and personally, I'd have to ask who would bell the cat. So we might as well hear what else he has to say. Then we can decide." She turned to Jimjoy. "Before we hear anything else, what were the results of your attacks? No one here seems to know. You indicated success. How much success?" Her face was pale also, and once again Jimjoy wanted to hold her and tell her that everything would be all right. But he couldn't lie.

"You should know that the destruction of the Haversol SysCon was total, along with three or four ships. Accord suffered one slight casualty, but the Ecolitan involved recovered and is back on duty. The Cubera mission involved a three-person team, two of whom were wounded. One will require complete visual reconstruction from laser burns. The Cubera station was totaled. Five Imperial ships were also destroyed." Jimjoy paused, hoping Kerin would not push.

"You mentioned another mission?" Finally, Althelm asked a question.

One look from Kerin to Althelm indicated that both wanted it on the table. Jimjoy had not told anyone but Thelina of the morning's report from the *Jaybank*.

He took a deep breath, conscious that Kerin was intent upon him. "The recovery needleboat for the Fonderal mission reported back just before this meeting. I do not have all the details of exactly what happened. The mission was successful in destroying the Fonderal SysCon."

"What about the team?" Kerin's words were evenly spaced.

"I'm sorry. The team did not make its rendezvous. The station fusactor approximated a very small nova. Six Imperial ships were destroyed. The *Jaybank* lost all screens and barely made it back. That was one reason for the delay."

Jimjoy met Kerin's gaze, watching for the tears he knew she was holding.

"Thank you, Professor Whaler. Is it fair to say that your missions have, with four Accord deaths and three other casualties, cost the Empire close to twenty ships, military control in three systems, four if you count Accord, and killed close to two thousand I.S.S. personnel?"

"That's a fair approximation."

The silence was absolute. The group in the Prime's office looked from face to face, anywhere but at the tall bronze man with the silver hair.

Jimjoy cleared his throat. "It's like this. If you want freedom, then you want it more than anything else. That cuts two ways. You all understand that you can't destroy freedom on Accord to fight the Empire. That way, you lose before you begin. That's why I didn't try to coopt the decision-making process or position the Institute for a coup. I just gathered enough people and resources to force the issue while there was still time.

"Second part is harder. If freedom is important, then anything else is secondary. *Anything*—that means your life, your family, your children, politeness, decency, and restraint. The question the Institute faces is simple. How much are you willing to give up for freedom?"

He held up a hand, as if to forestall a second set of objections, although no one seemed ready to raise any—yet. They were still in shock. "I'm not saying freedom at all costs. Some costs are too high. But we need to pare away the unnecessary restraints on our actions. We're in a war, whether you want to call it that or not. Can we afford to say, as the philosophy types have been insisting, that we must restrict our attacks to purely military targets?

"We'll all be dead, and Accord will be a large pile of dust orbiting a G2 sun, if we follow that course. If we kill off the population of Imperial planets, the same thing will happen."

"So you're saying we can't win?"

"I never said anything of the sort. In war, all targets are potentially military targets. What stops the other side from exterminating your civilians and innocents is the fear that you might do the same. You don't have to strike at noncombatants, but it helps to have the capability."

"We don't have enough weapons to hit military targets . . ."

"What's a weapon?" asked Jimjoy.

"Needleboats, tacheads, lasers—you know better than I do."

Jimjoy nodded. "You're right. I do. What about fusion power plants, hands and feet, rivers, meteors, rocks, sand, and forest fires?" He could see Thelina purse her lips. "What about disease, plague, and pestilence? Crop failures? Drought? Aren't all these potential weapons?"

Harlinn waved away the words. "Against the Empire?"

Jimjoy stood, trying to bite back the words. "A weapon is something you use to damage your enemy. I'll take an effective nuclear 'accident' any day over an outmanned needleboat. A series of crop failures over outnumbered recruits. The collapse of economically viable markets and the reduction in imposts at a time when the Empire is facing challenges from both the Fuards and the Matriarchy."

"I take it you are also willing to consider purely economic means?" asked Althelm.

"No. Pure economic means never work in this sort of situation by themselves. They can give greater weight to military and biological weapons."

Althem merely nodded.

"I've given you the current situation. Do you think the Empire will accept any surrender offer without prostrating us? Without wiping out Harmony and the Institute to the last man, woman, and child—unless we give them no choice?"

"You haven't given *us* much choice."

"You never had much choice," countered Jimjoy. "If you thought you did, you were living in a dream world. To face the Fuards, the Empire has to change its entire internal political and social structure— *or* find other sources of knowledge, technology, and cannon fodder. Unless Accord and the brighter outsystems fight, the Empire will find increased exploitation far, far easier."

"So you made the choice for us." Harlinn's color had gone from white to red. "You single-handedly decided we would face down the Empire."

"No." The iron in Jimjoy's voice stilled the room. "The idea was Sam Hall's. That's why the Empire murdered him. And Gavin Thorson. That's why you were proposed as acting Prime . . . you couldn't decide to cross the room without a committee. I'm not a politician. I've talked to most of you personally, and nothing happened.

"The Planetary Council has met and dithered, and dithered and met. In the past three years, six outsystems have been brutalized by Imperial reeducation teams. At least three members of the Institute have been targeted by Imperial agents, and two Imperial Special Operative teams have been assigned to report on and/or disrupt Institute operations. One former fellow was an Imperial agent reporting directly to the I.S.S. Special Operative section."

Jimjoy gave a theatrical shrug. "What do you want? Individually engraved invitations to a reeducation camp?" He made his way toward the door as the figures in green stepped aside from him. "It's your decision. If you decide the Institute will support the independence effort, then I suggest you select someone to act as coordinator. In the meantime, I'm going after some volunteers who understand their lives and future are at stake."

The silence lasted well after he was outside the Administration building.

XXXVII

THE ADMIRAL PURSED his lips as he reread the screen for the second time, although his memory was good enough that he could remember the salient points without any reinforcement.

After taking a sip of water, he replaced the glass on the replica wooden desk with which all admirals were furnished. He stood. His long steps carried him into the open space between the desk, with its concealed console, and the empty briefing table.

First, the loss of Haversol SysCon. The loss of Cubera SysCon. The loss of Fonderal SysCon. Haversol *could* have been an accident, or more probably the work of a terrorist or small group. Three in a row meant organization, like something the Fuards would cook up. Then, of all things, across in Sector Four, the destruction of Sligo SysCon with an asteroid barrage.

Now, a report from his last agent on Accord that the first three SysCon destructions had been engineered by some unknown professor, with an equally unknown background, and a small "tactics" team.

The Admiral rubbed his forehead. Either the agent was lying . . . how could one small group from an obscure if brilliant ecological college possibly have the materials and expertise to destroy three stations, capture an orbit control installation without a warning going out, and annihilate fifteen-odd ships, including two cruisers? Especially without the knowledge or support of the college head or the Planetary Council?

His steps carried him back in front of the desk. He stopped and took another sip from the glass. His headache was definitely returning.

The comparator didn't help either, insisting that the closest match to the methodology was that of Imperial Special Operatives. Great help there—the death of every single operative over the past decade had resulted in a body and a complete DNA match. The Service was very thorough in ensuring its dead operatives were indeed dead.

He glanced at the holo of the Academy at Alphane. The view that overlooked his desk was the view of the Spire, its facets glittering in the gold-white light of noon.

Some days he just wanted to go back there and teach, make it all sound so simple, instead of trying to figure out what information meant what and why.

He took another sip from the glass.

How could anybody be building another team of Special Operatives? Especially in a nutty place like Accord? A system supposedly in revolt, and yet the Planetary Council had yet to decide what to do. He shook his head again, wincing at the stab of pain across his forehead.

XXXVIII

JIMJOY TOOK ANOTHER deep breath, looking up at the five steps to the front deck. The unseasonable warmth of the day, combined with the moist odor of decaying needles and leaves, made him think of the spring that was not yet due, not until the suffering of a winter not begun had been endured. Weak but warm sunlight beat through the patchy clouds. Part of his walk had been chilled by their shadows.

On each side of the stairs, at the top, was a carved bird—a ferrahawk on the right and a jaymar on the left. Geoff's handiwork. The jaymar was golden, with black feathers of a different wood. The ferrahawk was clearly black oak, almost glittering in the midmorning light.

He swallowed, trying to force down the lump in his throat. Hades, why hadn't he taken the Fonderal mission himself? Or the negotiations off Tinhorn? Or let someone else come here? But after the meeting with Harlinn, he had practically run here. He couldn't let anyone else bring the news.

Finally, he started up the stairs.

Peering at him through the window on the stair landing was a small dark head. Shera and Jorje, wasn't it? The boy had to be the younger, then, the one with the serious expression watching the stranger climb the steps to the front deck. A stranger who should not have been a stranger, and who regretted again never having taken Geoff's invitations to stop by.

He paused by the wooden jaymar, taken by the delicate sturdiness of the carving. On some planets, the single bird would have been worth a month's earnings of an advocate or a systems engineer. Here—it was there because a man had loved to create beauty.

Jimjoy swallowed again and stepped up to the door. On the wooden plate was a hand-carved scroll: *Geoffrey & Carill Aspan.*

He hadn't known they had shared names in a time when that was the exception, not the rule. But he kept finding out there was a lot he didn't know. He raised his hand to the knocker beneath the carving.

Thrappp . . . thrappp . . .

The door opened. A dark-haired girl, broad-shouldered, with blue eyes, whose head reached perhaps the middle of his chest, held the door.

"Good morning, Professor Whaler."

"Good morning, Shera."

A tentative smile played around her mouth. "How did you know my name?"

"Your father told me." Before she could ask, he added, "Is your mother in? I'd like to talk with her."

"Who is it, dear?" a woman's husky voice called from the landing.

Jimjoy could see that the house's internal arrangement was similar to his, except that it seemed to have a larger upstairs—probably three bedrooms.

"It's Professor Whaler, mother!"

"I'll be right down. Show him in, and then come up here. I have an errand for you and Jorje."

"Mother!"

Jimjoy almost smiled.

"Please, Shera. I need your help."

The girl turned back to Jimjoy. "Would you come in, Professor?"

"Thank you, Shera. How old are you?"

"Ten standard." She held the door more widely and stepped back.

Jimjoy nodded, visually measuring the girl. She would be a tall girl, and she was already striking. Geoff was proud of them—had been proud of them. He moistened his lips and swallowed.

He stepped inside. A mirror with a hand-carved light oak frame hung over a small table. His face, somber and cold, stared back at him from the center of the oval glass.

"Professor?" Carill Aspan had black hair past her shoulders, loosely bound with a red band at the base of her neck, skin darker than Jimjoy's bronzed complexion, and brown eyes. A hint of tears hovered in her eyes. Almost as tall as Thelina, she wore a faded green tunic and trousers. Her feet were bare.

"Jimjoy Whaler . . ." he didn't know what to call her. "Carill" sounded too informal.

"Carill Aspan."

For a moment, neither moved.

"Did you have an errand you were going to send Shera and Jorje on?"

"Oh . . . I forgot." Her eyes said she had forgotten nothing. "Shera? Jorje?" As she spoke, she walked into the living area and pulled a slip of paper from the simple secretary that stood against the wall. Writing quickly, she jotted down several sentences and folded the paper over.

"Yes, mother? Jorje's still on the landing."

"I need both of you to take this to Cerla. Jorje!"

"Coming . . ."

Jimjoy and Carill stood in the space between the foyer and the living room, waiting as Jorje took one slow step after another down the wooden stairs.

Shera glared up at her brother even as she struggled with a light jacket. "Come on."

"Rather not."

"Jorje . . . please?"

"I'm coming." His last step took him to the main floor, where his mother extended a dark blue jacket. He did not protest as she eased him into it. Neither did he help, with arms as limp as overcooked pasta.

"Would you both take this to Cerla? If she's not home, ask Treil or Gera if they know when she will be back." Carill glanced from Jorje, who remained under her arm, to Shera. "Do you understand?"

"Yes, mother. We take the letter to Cerla. If she's not there, we check with the neighbors to see when she will be back. Then we come tell you. What if Cerla's home?"

"Then you come back with her. All right?" Carill had her hands clasped tightly together.

"All right. We won't be long." Shera extended her hand to Jorje. "Come on, slowpoke."

Jorje looked back at his mother, dark eyes almost liquid, before his sister opened the door and tugged his arm.

Carill looked at her son. "Go on, Jorje. I'll be here when you get back."

The boy slowly transferred his eyes from his mother to the floor.

"Come on."

Jimjoy kept his face relaxed, wanting somehow to hold both children, feeling like his silence lied to them both, as he and Carill watched them march down the steps.

Jorje glanced back once, twice, three times, until the walk took them out of the open door's direct line of sight.

Click. Carill shut the door. "Shall we go into the main room?"

Jimjoy nodded.

"Would you like any liftea? Geoff said . . ."

"No thank you. Not right now."

She stood, then waved vaguely. "Sit anywhere you like."

He waited for her to take a chair. Not surprisingly, she sat in one of the wooden armchairs, perched on the edge. Jimjoy took the one across from her.

"It's about . . . Geoff . . ."

"Yes. The recovery boat arrived this morning—"

"No . . ."

"Geoff did what he had to . . . but they didn't make it back." The words felt like lead in his mouth. "I'd asked him not to volunteer . . ."

"He told me." The tears seeped from her eyes. "He was afraid he wouldn't come back. He left a letter . . . told me not to blame you . . . if it happened."

Jimjoy felt his own eyes sting. Geoff had never mentioned it, not that he would have. "He didn't tell me. He wouldn't have."

"No . . . he wouldn't."

"I'm sorry. It's not enough . . . nothing is . . ."

"If it weren't for Geoff, I could hate you, Professor."

"If it's easier that way," he offered.

"We talked about it." She sniffed, pulling a faded handkerchief from somewhere, blotting her cheeks. "You talk, but you never think . . . it's always someone else . . ."

He nodded, hoping she would keep talking, wishing he had brought someone else, someone whose warmth would have eased the pain. His eyes burned.

". . . Geoff . . . he didn't want to go . . . he said he had to . . . that too many people would die if the missions failed . . . was he right . . . did it make any difference? Don't lie to me."

Jimjoy swallowed. "He was right. His mission succeeded. He brought us the time to hold off the Empire." He hated the pompous sound of his last words. "He gave up everything just to give us hope . . . just hope." He swallowed again, his mouth dry.

"You liked Geoff."

Jimjoy nodded, not having the words.

"He liked you, respected you . . . one reason why he went . . ."

Her words were like knives, even though she meant them as a kindness to him. A kindness to him? His eyes focused on the floor, picking out the lines of the planks.

"Professor . . . ?"

He looked up at Carill's tear-streaked face, knowing his own looked as streaked.

"Thank you."

"For what?" He wanted to bite out the words. For what? For killing your lover, your husband, and the father of your children? For destroying the one man who might have been my friend? For leaving Shera and Jorje fatherless? Instead, he repeated the words more gently. "For what?"

"For caring. For being the one to tell me . . . and for hurting."

Jimjoy shook his head. "I didn't want to come."

She wiped her eyes again. "But you did. Geoff said . . . if anything happened . . . you would . . . saw you on the steps . . . I knew . . ." She put her face in her hands.

Jimjoy stood up and walked the three steps toward Carill. Each step felt like he was moving in high gravity through syrup. Finally, he stood behind the chair and put both hands on her shoulders.

Neither said anything as a shadow from the overhead clouds darkened the deck behind Jimjoy, cutting the light that had poured into the room. Nor did either say a word as the small cloud released the sun and the light resumed.

Thrap!

"Mom! We're back. Cerla was home."

"Carill?" asked a woman's voice.

Jimjoy straightened and walked toward the doorway, toward the red-haired and petite woman in a blue blouse and old-fashioned skirt, toward Shera and, hiding behind his sister, Jorje.

Swallowing, Jimjoy stopped short of Cerla. Carill was almost step for step with him, although he had not heard her leave the chair.

"This is Professor Whaler . . . Geoff's friend. Cerla McWinter . . . she's an old friend of mine."

Cerla's blue eyes raked over Jimjoy, took in his face, and looked to Carill. "I told Brice I'd be staying here tonight."

"Thank you."

Jimjoy felt out of place, invisible in a private communion occurring around him. He glanced at Jorje, saw the coldness, the stony expression.

"Jorje . . . ?"

The boy looked at the floor.

Jimjoy knelt until his eyes were level with the dark brown ones. Shera stepped aside. "Your father asked if I would be your friend."

"Daddy's not ever coming back."

"No, he's not. But before he left, he asked—"

Without a word, Jorje turned and began to run—out through the front door, down the steps.

"Jorje!"

Jimjoy stood, then sprinted after the child, just trying to keep him in sight. As he ran he felt like pounding his own head. Why couldn't he have said something softer? More appropriate?

By the time he took the stairs two at a time and vaulted the corner flower box, he had caught up enough to see Jorje take the path toward the gardens.

Jimjoy slowed his steps, attempting to keep them light.

The sky darkened again, and a gust of wind ruffled his hair. Ahead, the path narrowed and twisted through a saplar grove, where the tangled and leafless branches twisted back on one another.

Sciff . . . sciff . . . sciff, sciff, sciff . . . Only the sound of the boy's shoes and Jimjoy's boots on the gravel path filled the grove.

Sciff . . . sciff . . . sciff . . .

Jorje ignored the polished oylwood jungle gym and plodded past the bedded-down flower gardens toward the soccer field.

Sciff . . . sciff . . .

Jorje circled the south end of the field and took the path that led upward into the preserve. Underfoot the gravel became clay and wood chips, and both sets of steps, cushioned by the dampness, subsided into near silence.

Halfway to the gazebo that overlooked the south end of the Institute, Jimjoy slowed his steps to match the boy's tiredness.

Jorje continued to plod upward, one step at a time.

Jimjoy followed, also one step at a time, trying to give the boy as much space as possible, but not wanting to lose sight of him.

At the top, Jorje slumped to the ground, not at the gazebo, but leaning against a railing post at the overlook. He did not look back, but down at the Institute.

Jimjoy waited at the edge of the clearing, at the top of the path.

The clouds began to thicken, and the wind to rise.

Jorje did not move, slumped, watching sightlessly.

Jimjoy shifted position but stayed, letting the boy keep his space, checking the weather, wondering about the coming chill that would signify the end of the brief spring interlude in winter, hoping the entire Institute wasn't out looking for the two of them.

As the wind began to whine, Jorje straightened up, but did not leave his post.

Jimjoy waited.

As the sky turned darker gray, Jorje stood and turned. He walked straight for the path where Jimjoy stood.

The boy's steps took him to the tall Ecolitan. He looked up at Jimjoy and then down the path.

The two of them walked back down toward the Institute, not hand in hand, but side by side.

XXXIX

JORJE WATCHED SILENTLY from the landing as the tall Ecolitan walked down the steps and into the afternoon mist that heralded the reappearance of winter.

Jimjoy had not looked back.

Overhead, the clouds from the southwest continued to thicken. A touch of frosty rain brushed his face, and his breath steamed in the quick-chilling air.

His steps lengthened as he headed toward Thelina's quarters. After the less-than-satisfactory meeting with Harlinn, and his effort to break the news of Geoff's death to Carill, he needed . . . something.

Thelina was not likely to be too sympathetic, nor was Meryl.

A figure appeared from the mist, ghostlike, heading toward him.

"Professor Whaler," called Althelm. Bundled in a heavy green parka and a green stocking cap, with only his unbearded face uncovered, he stopped.

"Yes," answered Jimjoy neutrally.

"You were rather convincing, if a trifle brutal." A trace of Althelm's thin white hair protruded from beneath the cap.

"Wasn't trying to be brutal, just to lay out the facts. I've—" He caught himself and stopped, trying to rephrase the words that would have indicated too much about his past. "I've seen enough of Imperial responses to know that the Empire isn't interested in sweet reason or freedom—only in tax levies and self-preservation."

Althelm shrugged, a gesture that incorporated a shiver. "You are doubtless correct, but that can be a hard truth to face. I would like to continue, but unless you are from Sierra or White Mountain, you should already be a block of ice, and my entrophy is carrying me too quickly in that direction—bad physics, I know, but pardon my excesses. We economists are known for our inaccuracies with hard numbers. In any case, my best wishes, Professor." He inclined his head, stepped around Jimjoy, and disappeared into the mist.

Jimjoy shook his head, realizing that even he felt a bit of chill, wearing only a set of medium-weight greens. He debated heading home first, but decided against the detour, since Thelina's and Meryl's was on his way in any case.

The steps to Thelina's front deck looked even more forbidding than those to Geoff's home had.

After a deep breath, he took the stairs two steps at a time, then paused. His hand reached to knock on the door.

"It's about time." Thelina's eyes took in the greens, the lack of a jacket, the dusting of ice on his hair and shoulders. "Where have you been?" she asked quietly. Like him, she had on the greens she had worn at the meeting.

"Telling Carill about Geoff."

"You look like it." She stepped back and held the door open. "Would you like something warm?"

He nodded. "Liftea?"

"The kettle was just on. It shouldn't take long. Something to eat?"

"Anything light—I can get it," he protested.

"Just sit down, and take the couch. You hate the armchairs."

Jimjoy eased onto the couch, taking a quick look through the closed sliding glass door at the light snow beginning to fall across the deck.

"Here's the liftea. I hoped that would be where you were. How did it go?" She perched on the edge of one of the chairs.

Jimjoy did not answer, instead taking a sip from the dark, heavy mug, then looking again at the light snow outside.

Thelina waited, not quite tapping her toes in impatience.

Finally he shrugged, took another sip of the tea. "Didn't want to walk up those steps. Didn't want to tell her that I'd killed Geoff."

"Is that the way you really feel?"

"Not that I killed him, but that he'd be alive if he hadn't been my friend. Wasn't a friend to him. He was to me." Jimjoy took another sip of the liftea, welcoming the scalding taste. "One afternoon, almost a year ago, he came over, told me he recognized me. Just wanted me to know. We talked. Or he talked. And he asked me why I hadn't told you how I felt about you. If he hadn't asked, I never would have told you. So, in a way, I owe loving you to Geoff, too."

The snow outside began to swirl, although Jimjoy could only see the flakes closest to the window as the twilight dropped into darkness.

"Let me get you something to eat. You're as pale as that snow outside." Thelina hopped to her feet and headed for the small kitchen.

Jimjoy sipped from the mug and looked at the snow, not seeing it.

"Here you are." Thelina resumed her perch on the chair. "It's simple, and not up to your standards, but . . ."

"Thank you."

On a small tray were a stack of crackers, two types of sliced cheese, a sliced pearapple, and three thick slices of meat. He nibbled at a pearapple.

"How is Carill?"

"She's all right. A friend, somebody named Cerla, is staying with her."

"How are you?"

Jimjoy wanted to talk about Jorje, about the boy's reaction, his running away. But he couldn't. He took a cracker instead, put a cheese slice on it, and ate both in a single bite. Then he ate another.

"Guess I'm all right. Easier when I didn't have to worry about people." He folded one of the beefalo slices and began to chew, gesturing at the plate for Thelina to help herself.

"No, thank you. We ate earlier." In response to his unspoken question, she added, "Meryl went over to the Tielers for the evening."

Another period of silence followed, and Jimjoy took the second slice of beefalo, chewing it methodically. He followed with cheese, then finished off the pearapple.

"I worry about Shera and Jorje."

"You were there a long time."

"Jorje ran away, all the way to the top of the nature lookout. I followed . . . tried to give him space. Just waited for him. Took a while."

Thelina shook her head slowly but said nothing, balancing a mug of something on her knee.

"He didn't say anything . . . just ran out the door and kept running."

"You followed him?"

"Enough to make sure he was all right, that somebody cared." He looked at the snow, already beginning to taper off, before taking the last sip of tea.

"You knew. . . . Do you wish someone had followed you?"

He shrugged. "Little late for that now."

For a time they sat there, not speaking. The snowfall had stopped by the time Jimjoy shifted his weight, swallowed, and looked up.

"Just the beginning," he mused. "Hardly taken any real casualties . . . and they're all scared."

"Aren't you?"

Jimjoy smiled wryly and briefly. "I know what's coming. Just don't know what to do. Except I need to get to Thalos and start building up what space capability we can. Get me out of sight and get that job started. You and Meryl can do whatever has to be done here. Far better than I could right now."

Thelina set her mug on the table beside the half-eaten plate of food she had prepared. Then she moved to the couch, settling herself on Jimjoy's left, not quite touching him.

"You don't have to go tonight, do you?" Her tone was lighter.

"No." His hand found hers, but he only squeezed it, and let his shoulder rest against hers, trying to draw in her warmth, wondering if she could lift the chill inside.

XL

"FINE. WE'VE GOT hulls for another fifteen needleboats. We've got drives and basic screen units. And no controls and no jump units." Jimjoy looked at Mera, then at the console blinking back at him.

The small office, with two consoles side by side and its single ventilator and rough-melted gray mineral walls, smelled of ozone, oil, and stale Ecolitans.

The apprentice who had just recently been a fourth-year student looked back at the Ecolitan professor. "Not bad, considering how little time we've had."

"Right," he snorted. "Except that without the micros for the screens and the grav-field controls, all we have is well-designed junk. There's still no response from the Institute. If we had just two lousy chip bloc machines . . ."

Jimjoy stood up and glared at the console, as if it were the nonresponsive Institute. He shrugged. "Going over to the magic shop."

"When will you be back?"

"Whenever . . . whenever."

"Don't forget that fax cube."

"Oh—thanks." Jimjoy picked up the cube he had made for Jorje. For the past day it had rested on the console because he had kept forgetting to send it.

"Do you think Jason can do it?"

"I can hope." He shrugged again, then lowered his head to clear the hatch, easing it shut behind him.

His boots echoed in the empty corridor, the sound bouncing from the melted rock beneath to the melted borehole walls and back again. This latest addition to Thalos station had not been developed with long-term comfort in mind, but with cobbled-together equipment as a manufacturing/staging/facility.

While some of the Impies had probably learned the Institute had hidden facilities off Accord, trying to locate and neutralize them without an in-system base would require more resources than they could afford, not to mention better intelligence. Not even Harlinn knew exactly where the new facility was located.

Jimjoy looked back over his shoulder. Mera had not left his/their office.

At irregular intervals, hatchlocks punctuated the corridor. Jimjoy entered the third hatch on the right, south of his office. Inside, before a small console from which ran a handful of silvery cables, sat a youngster with short, nearly stubbly black hair. He did not look up from the console, which displayed a three-dimensional circuit bloc design.

Jimjoy watched as the bloc was rotated on the screen, broken apart, and reconfigured. Finally, he coughed.

"Oh—Professor!"

"Jason." Jimjoy inclined his head. "Any luck?"

"Yes and no. I think I can adapt standard fax transceivers and an obscure design probe, plus other assorted junk, into a screen controller . . . or a reasonable facsimile thereof."

"But we only have enough of that stuff for one or two boats?"

"Maybe three—if the shop doesn't make any fabrication errors."

"Forget that."

Jason nodded slowly.

"What about grav-field and jump units?"

"Do we need grav-fields on all the boats?"

Jimjoy pursed his lips. "Probably not. But that means heavier hulls and more reliance on the screens."

"We can design around that."

"The jump units?"

"That's the hardest. I can build one from the subcomponents, but I don't know enough and we don't have the documentation to redesign from other stuff."

"I was afraid of that. Who makes them?"

"Veletar, Osmux . . ."

"That's Imperial?"

"Yeah."

"Where do Halston and the Fuards get theirs?"

Jason shrugged.

"*If* I can ever get the grounders to answer, I'll see what we can find out. Can you rebuild faulty units?"

"If the two central blocs are intact. Those you don't play with."

"Maybe we can find a good scrap merchant . . ." Jimjoy took a deep breath, let it out slowly. "Thanks, Jason. Go ahead and cannibalize anything extra to get two of the new boats semioperational."

"What about Ecolitan Imri?"

"I'll talk to Imri." Jimjoy repressed another sigh. The mining/research station commander was not going to be too happy. Then again, she'd be less than happy if an Imperial fleet were to plow through the system.

He shrugged as he bent over again and left Jason in front of his screen, designing another way to accomplish the impossible.

XLI

THE TALL MAN eased the laser into position, readjusting the settings.

Hssstttt . . .

Nodding, he eased the laser into the next position, resetting the equipment, wishing he could shake his head, but not daring to. The basic equipment was good, but precision microcontrollers would have made the job easier—much easier. The Institute had never considered Thalos as a mainline production facility, only as a source of those few raw materials not easily available on Accord—and mainly for orbital or outsystem use.

All the controls and microblocs had been produced planetside or imported. Now the imports weren't possible, and microengineering equipment was scarce, even for the few independents that dared circumvent the Imperial embargo.

Hssssttt . . .

He continued the laborious process until the two sections were welded together. After carrying the assembly to the storage area, he began the equally laborious process of storing and racking the laser and the welding heads. The morning shift would be arriving shortly and one more unit would help—some, at least.

With a last look at the equipment, he slipped on the more formal green tunic he would need for the rest of the morning.

He shrugged as he eased out through the crude lock into the main section of Thalos Base.

"Good morning, Professor."

He looked up sheepishly at Mera. "Good morning, Mera."

"A little midnight welding? Along with the twilight electronics? Or the lunchtime power systems?"

"Not midnight, just early morning. They needed a little help."

She shook her head, then turned and left him standing there. Mera did not argue, but left her position clear, quite clear, without ever raising her voice.

He took a deep breath and let his feet carry him toward the mess. His stomach growled, reminding him that he had not eaten since . . . had it been the afternoon before?

If they only had micros, or chipbuilders, or— But why not ask for an entire fleet? The needleboats would be fine for delivering biologicals, if they got the biologicals, if they could build the boats. If . . . if . . . if . . . He shook his head angrily.

He'd sent two messengers to Thelina, and still no answer. No answer at all, but he couldn't leave yet, not until the standard defenses were functioning and the station had managed to damp all EDI detectable radiation.

He slowed as he approached the mess, his steps dropping to a mere quickstep. His stomach added another sound effect to the echo of his boots.

"Morning, Professor," called a voice. Gilman, about to become an apprentice and another member of the needleboat framing crew, waved as he headed back in the direction from which Jimjoy had come.

"Good morning, Gilman."

This time he pulled at his chin, then ducked to step into the mess-room. Most tables were empty this early.

On the heat counter were various hydroponics. No synthetics. The

Institute did not supply synthetics. You ate real food of some sort. Better real dried kelp than tasty synthetic beef.

Jimjoy chose real and dry muffins with a large dollop of pear-apple preserves, a slice of cheese that seemed more holes than cheese, and an empty mug. Carrying the mug to the beverage table, he filled it with old-fashioned tea, a variety even more bitter than liftea, and scooped in enough sugar to rouse departed dieticians from graves parsecs away.

He sat at the end of an unoccupied table.

"Good morning, Professor."

His mouth full, Jimjoy only nodded to the stocky man who eased himself into a chair to Jimjoy's right.

"How is your needleboat project coming?"

Jimjoy took a sip of the tea, so bitter that even a mug saturated with sugar could not remove the edge. "Well as expected."

"Do you really think needleboats can defend us against a fleet?"

"We can build needleboats. Can't build cruisers. No one's selling any these days, not that I know of." The muffin crunched as he bit into it and sprayed crumbs over the green cloth covering the table.

"Do you think the Impies will attack Thalos or Accord first?"

Jimjoy shrugged as he devoured the second dry muffin.

"They say you were once an Impie. Is that true?"

Jimjoy stuffed the hole-filled cheese into his mouth, wishing Thelina would send the equipment he wanted, and wishing Imri's deputy would stop making a practice of quizzing him at meals. "Yes. I've also been a Fuard, a Halstani, a true-believer, and a Swartician."

"A Swartician? Where . . ."

"On Swartis, of course." Jimjoy almost smiled. As far as he knew, there was no Swartis system. He stood. "Have a good day, Ecolitan Ferbel."

Now all he had to do was figure out how to get hold of three dozen jump units. Too bad you couldn't fit people in torps . . .

He dashed toward Jason and the magic shop. The micros had to be the same, and that was what they needed, not all the power and hardware connections. At least that was what he hoped, but Jason would know, and three dozen torps, or even ten dozen, shouldn't be impossible to find. Obsolete ones might do as well, might even allow them to develop new torps.

XLII

"GO AHEAD, ECOLITAN." The shuttle copilot, doubling as disembarking officer, nodded.

Raw damp air gusted into the shuttle, and the copilot edged toward the protection of the corridor to the control area as she continued to watch the handful of passengers—virtually all Ecolitans—line up to file out. The single exception was a woman nearly two meters tall, wearing the beige and blue of the Halstani diplomatic corps. She stood halfway into the control area, talking to the shuttle pilot.

Jimjoy stepped onto the landing stage. He had carefully avoided the Halstani diplomat, and his tactics team had not volunteered his role, other than as an Institute instructor. Jimjoy's hands were empty as he glanced across the white ferrocrete—almost grayish in the winter light—before heading down the half a dozen wide steps from the shuttle.

Thelina—why hadn't he heard from her? Before he had left for Thalos, she said she would let him know when he should return planetside. That had been nearly three tendays earlier, and he'd heard nothing. He pulled at his chin, continuing to study the port area as he reached the bottom of the shuttle steps.

Roughly thirty meters in front of the port terminal, a single figure paced slowly back and forth on the pavement. Beyond the terminal waited several groundcars painted green, and a sole commercial taxi.

Two flitters with Institute insignia rested on the ferrocrete. One was for Jimjoy, but he did not head directly toward either, but toward the terminal and the Ecolitan in greens. Even with the Empire's blockade on Imperially based traffic, there should have been more activity.

The man in greens turned toward Jimjoy.

Jimjoy took in the deliberately slow steps, caught sight of the face, took a step left, then dived into a roll right, pulling the knife from his belt.

. . . hsssstttt . . .

Thrummm . . . thrummm . . .

Whunnk . . . thud . . .

EEEEEEEEEEEeeeeeeeeeeeeeeeeeeeeee . . . The shuttle's siren began to scream.

Jimjoy covered the remaining open space between him and the nearest flitter in a zigzagging and irregular sprint, ignoring the woman in greens with the knife in her chest and the stunner by her outstretched hand. A woman dressed deliberately like a man.

The flitter pilot already had the turbines turning by the time Jimjoy threw himself through the crew hatch.

"Lift it!" Jimjoy cranked the crew door shut from a prone position. Had someone already gotten to Thelina?

"Yes, ser. Lifting!"

Jimjoy finished cranking the crew door as the rotors began their regular *thwop, thwop*. Then he eased up into the space between the pilot and copilot.

The pilot, a chunky black woman with "Iananillis" stenciled on her flight suit, lifted the flitter, asking without looking at him, "What next?"

Jimjoy glanced at the copilot, a thin, sallow-faced younger man with limp black hair. His name patch was blank, but Jimjoy noted the partly unsealed flap of the right thigh pocket.

"Field unit three?" he asked Iananillis, suspecting the worst.

"Yes, ser. Do you have a destination?"

"The Institute will be fine . . . for now." He looked at the copilot. "Jimjoy Whaler, Tactics." He had raised his voice almost to a shout to override the sound of the turbines and to penetrate their flight helmets.

Both a knife and a stunner were in his hands, so quickly that neither pilot had seen them appear.

"Set it down! There!"

Iananillis looked at Jimjoy, then at the other pilot, her hand tightening around the throttles.

Crack!

Her face paled as she looked at her suddenly limp hand, wrist fractured from the unbladed edge of the knife.

"Don't try it." He doubted that either heard his words, but both respected the weapons. Either that or the look on his face. His head nodded toward the pad at the end of the shuttleport. "There! Now!"

Iananillis glanced at her copilot, who gingerly took the controls and began a slow flare into the pad.

Jimjoy grinned. In the other's place, he would have done exactly the same.

Thwop . . . thwop, thwop, thwop . . .

As the flitter settled onto its gear, Jimjoy's hands touched the harness locks. "Out . . . leave the helmets . . ."

The unnamed copilot left holding his ear. Jimjoy had been rougher than necessary in insisting that his helmet remain with the flitter.

Before the two had cleared the rotor path, Jimjoy had the pilot's helmet in place, although it was tighter than he would have liked, even with two of the shim pads quickly sliced out. Harness in place, he torqued up the turbines.

"Greenpax one, terminus. What is your destination?"

"Terminus, one here. Lifting for Diaplann."

"Understand Diaplann."

"Stet."

Jimjoy kept the flitter low, below two hundred meters, and well clear of the shuttleport, noting as he circled south that both the former pilots of his flitter were running toward the terminal and waving at the second flitter.

Diaplann was southwest of Harmony. Although Jimjoy did not intend to go there, he eased the flitter into a southwesterly course and began a transition into full thrust and rotor retraction.

As the turbine whine increased and the forest-green flitter screamed over the southwest highway, he began to cross-check the course line for the Institute against the rising hills beneath him. Harmony sat farther north of the mountains than did the Institute, even though they were at roughly the same latitude, because the range curved gently south about fifty kays east of the Institute.

Once he got beyond the first hills, his course line would change.

He shook his head, automatically increasing altitude to maintain his ground clearance. Seeing Sabatini in greens at the shuttleport, dressed as a journeyman and carrying a stunner, was a good indication that Harlinn had made a decision, a very unofficial decision. The flitter pilots had just confirmed that. Earlier in the year, Thelina, Meryl, and Geoff— he winced at recalling Geoff—had begun to shift personnel in the field training divisions, partly on skills and partly on loyalties.

None of them would have sent a pilot from field unit three. Unfortunately, that and Sabatini's presence meant Harlinn had his own organization.

Jimjoy smiled faintly. Nothing like a civil war within a revolution. He wondered if all revolutions were this messy.

"Greenpax one, Greenpax one, this is Harmony control, Harmony control. Request your course line and elevation."

"Hades!" He dropped the flitter's nose and inched up the throttles, leveling out less than fifty meters above the conifers on the rugged hillsides below. Still another ten kays before the first plateau lines.

"Greenpax one, this is Harmony control. Request your location. Request your location."

He eased the flitter even lower, not that Harmony control had ground-to-air missiles. He'd checked that out earlier. But he didn't know who controlled Harmony control at the moment.

In fact, stupid as it sounded upon reflection, he didn't know who controlled what. Accord was so libertarian—so disorganized—that once you got beyond basic principles of liberty, it was difficult to get more than a small group to agree on any specifics. Any good revolutionary was going to have to sell his or her wares under basic principles and avoid discussing specifics, or be discussing specifics still when the first Imperial fleet arrived.

Underneath the flitter flashed a narrow road. The conifers began to thin, showing reddish sandstone as the hills steepened. Beyond the tabletop mesa covered with native gold grass and scattered ferril thorns, conifers, and bare red sand, the ground dipped into the transverse interrange valley. The valley stretched northwest, eventually paralleling the Grand Highway, to a point twenty kays short of the Institute. Without detailed satellite coverage, which Accord didn't possess, he would be virtually invisible to Harmony control for that part of the trip. They might guess, but they wouldn't *know*.

"Harmony control, terminus. Do you have a location on Greenpax one?"

"That is a negative, terminus. Negative."

"Thank you, Harmony control."

Jimjoy smiled behind the dark plastic face shield of the too-tight helmet. That seemed to answer one question. The controller at the shuttleport was on his side, getting Harmony control to indicate they had no idea where he was headed. Either that . . . He shook his head. The possible mind games weren't worth the effort. He'd know when he got to the Institute.

In the meantime, he continued to scan instruments, airspace, and the ground beneath, looking for any sign of unfriendliness. At his speed and altitude, his greatest danger was impaling himself and the flitter on some terrain feature—like a rock spire—that he didn't see.

The high clouds would have helped against satellite detection, but without a concentrated down-array, that wasn't a problem either. That left other aircraft and pilot error as his two biggest threats. In his state of mind, pilot error was the biggest threat.

Already he could see the end of the valley ahead. The first time he had made the trip to the Institute, it had been by groundcar. Now he was traveling as fast as he could push the flitter, and the distance seemed minimal.

His fingers toggled the receiver through the major frequencies.

Nothing but static, and he left the frequency selector on control as he raised the nose and began the climb back over the front-range hills.

". . . control . . . location . . . one . . ."

". . . negative . . ."

He frowned. Someone was still looking for him.

Ahead, he could make out the hills behind the Institute, but not the buildings. He crossed the Grand Highway and dropped the nose. For a number of reasons, a high-speed approach was advisable.

The flitter screamed in over the south side of the Institute at less than two hundred meters. Abreast of the lake, Jimjoy flipped it ninety degrees to the ground, dropped full spoilers, cut the turbines, and brought the stick nearly into his lap, watching the airspeed bleed off.

As it dropped below two hundred kays, he punched the rotor deployment and eased the flitter upright, nose high, to bleed off more speed.

Thwop . . . thwop, thwop, thwop . . .

With the aircraft under full rotor control, he brought the flitter back around into the wind, scanning the space before the Administration building. At least a squad in field greens was deployed around the building. Two figures stood at the end of the walk to the circle drive. One, the shorter, waved a projectile rifle, indicating he should land.

The other, light-haired—was it silver-haired?—raised a hand. Jimjoy took a deeper breath and began his flare, easing the flitter into the open grass in the middle of the circle. At least Thelina was there, even if she didn't seem wildly enthusiastic about his arrival.

Even as the skids eased onto the grass, his fingers began the steps to shut down the flitter. Then he noticed that one of the Ecolitans—the one who had waved him in for a landing—had her weapon trained on him.

He raised both hands for a moment, then continued his shutdown.

Thelina stood outside the rotor wash, shaking her head sadly. Two Ecolitans, wearing field two patches and carrying the projectile rifles they were not supposed to have, were behind her. Neither was watching

Thelina. One left her rifle loosely trained on the flitter. The other scanned the area around the Administration building.

As he shut down the turbines and continued through the checklist, bringing the rotors to a full stop, he noted the other Ecolitans in field greens scanning the area. He took off the helmet slowly, feeling his ears tingle. As he set it on the console, he rubbed his temples briefly with his right hand, then opened the cockpit.

The Ecolitan who had focused her rifle on him had now lowered it slightly.

Thelina waited for him to walk to her, not even lifting a hand, although he thought he saw a brief smile.

He wanted to put his arms around her, but she was waiting for him to get close enough to hear, and her body posture was formal—almost stiff.

"Congratulations, hotshot." While her words were sarcastic, her tone was soft, almost sad. "You precipitated another crisis, just by refusing to take the right precautions and then waiting too long."

"Waiting too long?" Jimjoy was puzzled.

"I sent you a message . . ."

Jimjoy was shaking his head.

"You didn't get it?"

"No. That's why I took the first shuttle I could. I expected something; you told me you'd be in touch. I didn't tell anyone . . . that's why, when that flitter team zeroed in on me and was from field three . . . and Sabatini was the clincher."

"Field three? Sabatini? What happened at the port? What did you really do? Harlinn tried to lock us up. Didn't use enough force—"

Her posture wasn't stiff, he realized. "How badly are you hurt?"

"I'll be all right."

"Let's see Hyrsa. You can tell me on the way."

The dark-haired woman who had watched him nodded at his remark. "I'll get a groundcar, Professor."

"I'll be fine," protested Thelina.

"Are things under control?" he asked.

"Yes. Kerin's squad took over comm, and that boy Elias—Elias Elting, the one you carried to the infirmary that night—he literally pulled Harlinn from his flitter, along with some very interesting files.

"His partner, Mariabeth, made copies and circulated them to everyone, immediately. That quieted the few who were actively resisting."

A groundcar purred up, stopping well clear of the grounded flitter.

"Is there anyone here who can get that flitter to maintenance?" asked Jimjoy loudly.

"Yes, ser. I can." The voice came from the other Ecolitan who had been guarding Thelina. "Ytrell Maynard, journeyman forest spotter."

"You have it, Ytrell. And thanks." Jimjoy nodded toward the groundcar, offering his arm to Thelina.

"Thank you, but no. It doesn't hurt as much if I walk alone . . . carefully. Probably just a cracked rib. I remember the last set, and this isn't that bad."

"Who?" asked Jimjoy. "Harlinn doesn't have it in him."

"Talbot, loyal to the Prime to the end." She started to shake her head, then pressed her lips together and stopped.

Jimjoy glanced at the other Ecolitan, who had continued to scan the area as the three had walked to the groundcar, finally catching her eye. "She took Harlinn's staff alone?"

"Yes, Professor. We were spread thin."

Jimjoy looked over at the groundcar driver. "You know the driver?"

"Yes—Altehy. She's fine. Helped Kerin with comm."

Jimjoy held open the groundcar door, again extended an arm for Thelina.

"Thanks . . ."

He hurried around the forest-green car and entered from the other side. "Medical one—do we know who's on duty?"

"Most of the senior staff," answered Thelina. "This wasn't without some casualties, unlike some operations."

Altehy eased the groundcar back and turned it to avoid the flitter, where the journeyman spotter was pre-flighting the turbine inlets.

"All right," began Jimjoy.

"You first."

He shrugged. "When I didn't hear from you, I set up Mera and Jerrite with instructions—"

"Jerrite?"

"We're also a little thin. You have Kerin, and . . . Geoff . . . Anyway, I set them up with a series of contingencies, including some pretty detailed plans. That was one thing that delayed me. Then I took a needleboat to orbit control, and I spent some time with them—with some more operating plans and procedures for handling various types of incoming traffic and ship classes. Like no direct locks for anything big enough to carry a squad of storm troops."

"You *have* been busy."

"Details, details. Much easier to *do* something than organize it."

"You've learned that?" Her tone was dry, although her posture was stiff.

Again he wanted to hold her, to tell her he would protect her, even as he realized that he was having trouble protecting himself. "Thelina . . ." His voice was low.

"Yes?"

"Please take care of yourself. Please."

Surprisingly, she just turned her head toward him.

He bent over and brushed her lips with his. "You mean too much to me." For a moment his vision blurred. He shook his head and swallowed, then took her hand, which was reaching for his, and held it, gingerly, afraid that the slightest pressure would cause her to tense the muscles over her injured ribs.

"Thank you for saying it," she whispered back.

"I care."

"I know." After a pause, her voice went from a whisper to a normal tone. "About the rest of your trip?"

Jimjoy did not release Thelina's hand, but cleared his throat. "Took the first shuttle possible down after I briefed Derrin. Did you know there was a Halstani diplomat coming in from orbit control? Trans-shipped on one of the independent traders."

"You get her name?"

"Something like Mariel. Didn't get too close. A little nervous about Halston," he reminded her.

"They wouldn't recognize you now."

He shrugged. "Anyway, I didn't get too close. Stepped out of the shuttle. Two flitters waiting, and then Sabatini, disguised as a man, just waiting."

"And? You commandeered the wrong flitter?"

"Sabatini tried to take me, and then I commandeered the wrong flitter."

"Dead or unconscious?"

"Probably dead. Had to use a throwing knife."

"Professor, Leader Andruz . . . Medical one," interrupted Altehy.

Jimjoy bolted from the groundcar, scanning the area around medical one, but, again, seeing only a light guard force from a field team, field team one this time.

He held the door and offered an arm. Thelina used both arm and doorframe to ease herself into a standing position.

Two Ecolitans with rifles stood by the entrance.

"Professor, Team Leader . . ."

"The Team Leader has some ribs that need looking at," volunteered Jimjoy.

Thelina grimaced at the explanation, but said nothing as they entered.

Jimjoy punched the button for the lift. Climbing stairs was hades on sore ribs.

"So . . . after you chose the wrong flitter? Did you impose murder and mayhem again?" Thelina glanced from the student Ecolitan at the information desk to Jimjoy and back to the lift door, which was opening.

"No. Broke one wrist, ordered them out. Iananillis, I think, and someone I didn't know. Then I told Harmony control I was heading for Diaplann. I did until I crossed the range, then took the valley parallel to the Highway."

They stepped into the empty lift, and Jimjoy punched the square panel for the second floor.

"Now, quickly, what happened here?"

"There's not much to tell. Harlinn started trying to isolate us. He must have had a few we didn't know about to have gotten my message to you. I thought Daniella was a safe bet."

"She might have been. Has anyone seen her?"

"Oh—I thought she was with you."

"Could be another casualty of Harlinn's. You and Meryl started organizing, and Harlinn sent some troops from field three to round you up?"

"Sort of."

The lift door had already opened, and Jimjoy, out of habit, scanned the area. Dr. Hyrsa was talking to one of the medical technicians.

"Thelina! Are you all right?"

"No. She's not," answered Jimjoy.

"Let's get a look at you." The doctor's voice was no-nonsense.

Jimjoy followed as the physician led Thelina down the right-hand corridor.

"Professor? I'm not sure . . ."

"For the moment, I'm staying."

The doctor looked at Thelina, who smiled faintly.

"I wouldn't try to make him leave . . . yet."

"Oh, I wouldn't have guessed it from the way you two abused each other."

"Times change," said Jimjoy.

"So do people," added Thelina.

He could only shrug, as the doctor pressed a stud beside a closed door. Jimjoy stepped around the two and looked inside from a crouch. The examining room was empty.

"We are secure here, Professor," commented Dr. Hyrsa.

"I worry."

Both women exchanged glances.

Jimjoy smiled sheepishly. "All right. I'll wait outside."

Thelina looked at him. "I'll be fine. I'm not made of glass."

"I know." He stepped outside, again checking the corridor.

He ought to be checking in with Meryl, who was probably in Harlinn's office by now, running the entire Institute. But Thelina and Meryl and Kerin had done well without him. Better than he could have done. He shrugged again and leaned against the wall, waiting to hear from the doctor and hoping that Thelina's ribs were only bruised and not worse.

"Professor?"

He looked up, recognizing the copper-headed nurse. "Verea. How are you?"

"Are you all right? You looked worried."

"Oh . . . I'm fine. Nervous, but fine. Thel—Ecolitan Andruz is being checked over by Dr. Hyrsa. Bruised ribs, I hope." Seeing the look on the nurse's face, he continued. "Instead of cracked or broken ribs, I meant."

"Andruz? Oh, she's the one!"

"What was she doing? Being a hero?"

Verea ignored his soft sarcasm. "They say she personally disabled Harlinn's entire personal guard, including Talbot."

Jimjoy raised his eyebrows. Talbot was bigger than he was, and in good shape. While Jimjoy *thought* he could have taken Talbot, Thelina was giving away at least ten centimeters and thirty kilos. "She's good," he admitted, "but I hope the price wasn't too high."

"So do we, Professor. So do we." She started to leave, then paused. "But it's nice to see you have a soft spot somewhere."

Jimjoy frowned. What had he done to Verea?

Click.

He turned toward the sound, so quickly that he found Dr. Hyrsa taking a step backward. "How is she?"

"Better than she has any right to be. Mostly bruises. She has a partial hairline fracture on one rib. How she got that . . ." The doctor shook her head. "She will be *very* sore for a while."

"Will she be staying here?"

"Not as long as she is careful. Right now we're a little overbooked, thanks to your revolution, Professor."

Jimjoy pulled at his chin, which felt stubbly. Why was it his revolution? "All right if I wait?"

"It's likely to be a while. We're fitting her with an inflatable support splint. Also getting some painkillers and supportive regenerative capsules. You could wait downstairs . . ."

Since the doctor's suggestion wasn't totally suggestive, Jimjoy nodded. "Thank you. Will you tell her?"

"I'll make sure she knows." Dr. Hyrsa turned back toward another room, presumably toward another injured Ecolitan.

Jimjoy started for the stairs, wondering just how many people had been hurt in the takeover of the Institute. As he opened the doorway to the upper landing, his mouth opened.

Stacked on the landing was a suspense cart, with three coff-wombs, the portable equipment humming. The chill from the coffinlike enclosures radiated from the cart.

"Excuse me, ser, but please keep away from the equipment." An orderly, or the equivalent, straightened up from adjusting something. She wore a stunner. "Pardon me, Professor. I didn't recognize you. What are you doing here?"

"Checking on the casualties," Jimjoy responded, hating himself for the partial lie, but not retracting it.

The woman nodded. "We did all right, considering that bastard Harlinn had a hidden armory. These are ours. Dr. Hyrsa thinks they'll make it, if they can hang on until there's a free operating room."

"All of you did the impossible," Jimjoy temporized.

"Just following your example, Professor. Take care." She returned to monitoring the equipment and the vital signs of the coffwombs' occupants.

Jimjoy started down the stairs, again wondering what in hades Thelina had been doing, and feeling guilty that he had been so concerned about her relatively minor injuries, and, as he thought about it, even more guilty that he had been exposed to so little of the danger. Clearly, a lot of young Ecolitans had suffered much worse.

He stepped through the doors on the main floor.

"Professor Whaler! Professor Whaler!" The speaker was a youngster in greens, so fresh-faced he had to have been a first-year student.

"Here!" Jimjoy called unnecessarily, since the young man was already making a beeline for him, thrusting an envelope forward.

The impromptu waiting area was not filled, but several younger Ecolitans, wearing splints, bandages, or vacant looks, turned to view Jimjoy. The faces of at least half carried a degree of respect that verged on awe.

Jimjoy took refuge in the envelope, which had written upon it "Professor James Joyson Whaler II."

Inside was a single sheet of paper.

Please come to the Prime's office as soon as possible (after you've reassured yourself about Thelina). Remember, you are this revolution's hero. So don't disclaim it.

Meryl Laubon

Jimjoy swallowed and refolded the paper into the envelope, then turned to the youngster. "Do you have a groundcar?"

"Yes, Professor."

"Good. I need to head back to the Admin building. Can you take me, and then return to pick up Leader Andruz and bring her after the doctors are finished with her." At the alarm in the youth's eyes, he added, "She's fine." Or mostly fine, he thought.

Act like a hero . . . remember? He stopped at the door and turned to the faces that had followed his progress. "Today represents a giant step toward freedom and self-determination. All of you have proved what can be done." He paused, then added in a lower tone, "But remember, this is only the first step on our way back to the stars—our stars."

Since he couldn't think of anything else to say, he didn't, but let his eyes cover the dozen or so wounded before he turned.

He had to remember not to walk through the student Ecolitan in his preoccupation to reach the groundcar and Meryl.

XLIII

20 Trius 3647
Lansdale Station

Dear Blaine:

Why me? Last thing I need is an incident with a brand-spanking-new Fuardian S.D. Mucker was out to crumple *Halley*'s fields, no question about it. Flaunted his superiority. Just wanted us to know how good he was.

Two to one I get an inquiry or a reprimand. N'Trosia and his let's-not-make-trouble attitude. If I'd even had an "obsolete" FC under me, the outcome would have been different. But you do what you can.

Speaking of that—what's the status of the CX? We really could use something like that out here, as if I hadn't already made that clear enough. Poor old *Halley* isn't up to the rough stuff. We lost most of the converter, strained the whole front-frame structure.

More rumors again. I know you can't comment, but thought you might like to know what's circulating. My techs say a six-month extension is planned for duty in Sectors Five and Nine. One for the crews on the Rift and one for us. Speaking of the Rift, I haven't heard anything new, and that's always a bad sign. Between the ecologs and the Fuards and the damned and honorable Senate, I.S.S. is hurting.

I'll have my time in by the end of this tour, even if I'm not extended. Helen wants me to put in my papers, and I'm going to have to think about it. There's no reason to stay in if OpSec flashes a black one on the dossier for this.

Sorry for the complaints, but I have the feeling you're the only one back there listening. Jock still talks about going to the Academy, and I'm not really sure how I feel about that. Helen sends her love.

Mort

XLIV

MERYL WASN'T IN the Prime's office, but in the one next to it, the one that Gavin Thorson had occupied. The sliding window was ajar, with a definite chill from the outside filling the office. She was juggling her attention between two screens and a stack of notes. Her hair was mussed and oily, and a smudge of grease across her left cheek resembled a bruise. Her eyes took in Jimjoy.

"She's fine—relatively. One slightly cracked rib, being splinted," Jimjoy responded to Meryl's raised eyebrows.

"That's what she thought. That wasn't what I was about to ask."

Jimjoy shrugged. "Sorry. I got your message. Don't think I've fouled up too much, except for the incident at Harmony, but that was unavoidable."

"It probably was," responded Meryl. Her tone failed to agree with her words.

"Look," said Jimjoy, trying to keep his words even, "your messenger didn't reach me. I'm trying to develop space-based system defenses with no input from planetside. None. I sent two of my own messages—"

"Who?"

"Kermin Alitro and Jose Delgado."

"We got them, and that's why Daniella was sent back."

"I told Thelina. She never got there. Either to orbit control or to Thalos." He looked around the room, taking in the two standard all-wooden armchairs, the cluttered console top, and the two mugs half filled with cafe. Then he looked down at the blond woman.

Meryl looked up from the consoles at Jimjoy. "You men aren't worth a damn at patience, or at balancing personal concerns. You came down here either because you didn't have any confidence in us or because you hadn't heard from Thelina."

Jimjoy flushed, knowing exactly what she was talking about and not wanting to admit it. "You didn't even have a revolution before I got here."

"We didn't need one until you got here."

A gust of wind from the sightly ajar window threatened some of the papers. Meryl leaned forward and slapped them back into place.

Jimjoy glared at her. "You don't really believe that. You'd already be dead or in a reeducation camp. And you know it. If you want me to admit I was worried about Thelina . . . I admit it. But I kept asking for expertise and key supplies. I got no expertise and no supplies, and not one explanation.

"I needed micros for the ships we're building. I needed to know whether we had any progress on the biologicals. You can't design and build delivery systems without knowing the biological parameters.

"I needed more pilot trainees. I got neither trainees nor reasons." His voice was rising in intensity and volume, despite his resolve to keep it quiet. "Patience is *not* a virtue when there's no time."

"So you got your revolution, Professor, and there are at least one hundred unnecessary casualties. If we'd had two more tendays, we'd have had none." Meryl looked right through him.

Jimjoy ignored the steps behind him.

"Do we control Accord?"

"No," answered another tired voice. Thelina stepped around him. "We control the Institute, plus all the planetside field stations, plus the shuttleport. You control—I presume—all the off-planet facilities."

Jimjoy shrugged. "Then we need to take Harmony."

Meryl looked at Thelina. Thelina looked at Meryl. Both looked at Jimjoy, waiting.

A faint odor of hospital or disinfectant or both wafted from Thelina.

Jimjoy wrinkled his nose, trying to repress a sneeze, before going on. "You don't take cities. You put a supervisor in the police office and a coordinator in every media outlet. You suggest certain news stories, and you make sure the police continue to enforce civil laws. You disband the Planetary Council and call for new elections immediately—with the stipulation that since the Empire has repudiated and embargoed us, the Council will function as the civil authority. The Planetary Governor gets shipped back to the Empire."

"What if someone revolts?"

"Not many will. Liquidate their property and use the proceeds to pay for damages and their transportation to an Imperial system. Let them keep the balance. Anyone who wants to can leave—provided they can find transportation. If the word gets out, and it will, half the high-priced independents will show up looking for passengers."

"It might work," admitted Thelina.

"I doubt it," argued Meryl.

"Give it a try," suggested Jimjoy.

"Fine," snapped Meryl, "but who signs the documents? Who acts for the Institute with Harlinn a hopeless vegetable?"

"You," suggested Jimjoy.

"Not even Accord is ready for a female Prime."

"Then call yourself something like the acting Deputy Prime, pending formal selections. That will get them used to the idea. If they don't buy it, it gives us time to come up with someone else."

Thelina edged over to one of the wooden chairs, wincing as she lowered herself into a sitting position. Jimjoy stepped toward her, but she gave the slightest of head-shakes to wave him off.

Jimjoy and Meryl waited for her to sit down.

"And you? What do we do with you?" demanded Meryl.

"Me?" Jimjoy paused and took the other chair, the one closest to Meryl and her console. "You answer my questions, send me what supplies and the experts you can, and the bodies to crew what I'm building."

"What exactly are you building?"

"Mostly beefed-up needleboats. You had the hidden production facility on Thalos. We've about tripled its capacity. We're trying to design for the biologicals' delivery. And we're working on smart rocks, even big dumb rocks—anything that can disrupt an Imperial squadron."

Meryl rolled her eyes. Thelina grinned momentarily as she watched her friend.

"How soon can we persuade you to get back to smart rocks?" asked Meryl.

He looked toward Thelina. "As soon as—"

"You can't wait that long. No pressure on the ribs for at least a couple of tendays."

"—we can make some plans and I've had a chance to fully discuss a few things," he amended, wanting to throw up his hands. "We still have to take over Harmony and put together at least a shell of an official government. That way, it will give the Halstanis and the Fuards the ability to communicate openly, at least on the pretext of investigating to see if we are a truly independent system. And it will make it that much harder on the Empire to keep calling it a rebellion or a civil war. That won't change the I.S.S. plan now, but the longer we can exist as an independent force, the sooner it might cross their minds that they'll have to deal with us."

"You talk about taking over government as if it were easy."

Jimjoy sighed, then leaned forward to pat down a stack of papers that threatened to lift off the flat surface with another gust of wind. He glanced over at Thelina. She shivered slightly, wincing as she did.

Jimjoy stood and walked around the console and past Thelina.

Clunk. Jimjoy winced at the sound, realizing he had used far more force than necessary. He turned and headed back to the uncomfortable and uncushioned wooden chair.

"The room smelled of Thorson's mints," observed Meryl.

"We'll survive." Jimjoy looked from her to Thelina, who mouthed, "Thank you."

"Besides," he added, "this way you won't have to chase hard copy all over the room."

"Always pragmatic."

"Harmony," insisted Jimjoy.

Meryl shrugged. "All right. How would you implement your ideas?"

Jimjoy pulled the chair closer and restacked the papers on the edge of the desk to get a clear spot.

Thelina sighed, very softly. Her eyes went from her friend to her lover and back again.

Meryl cleared one console screen, coughed softly, and met Jimjoy's eyes unblinkingly.

Jimjoy smiled wryly. It would be a long afternoon.

XLV

JIMJOY GLANCED OVER his shoulder, through the clear glass of the window to the pair of flitters waiting on the grass in Government Square. A squad of Ecolitans in full field gear, including projectile rifles, cordoned off the flitters, technically a poor defense position. But the squad's mission was not to defend, but to state the Institute's power. The second squad, the unseen one, was there to protect the men and women in plain sight.

Then there was the third squad, the grim-faced men and women who controlled the corners of the theaterlike Council room.

Jimjoy took a last look at the scene outside before heading down the steps from the landing to the heavy wooden double doors into the Council chamber.

One of the heavyset planetary guards glared as Jimjoy approached.

The guard glanced at the tall Ecolitan, then at the armed Ecolitans, before letting his eyes drop toward his now-empty holster.

Taking over the chamber had been simple. Jimjoy and his three squads had arrived well before dawn, opened the building, and quietly disarmed everyone who arrived for the meeting. Then the flitters had been landed in the square.

Jerold caught sight of Jimjoy, stopped riffling through his notes, and waited for the Ecolitan to reach the smaller podium serving the elected delegates when they wished to bring an issue before the Council.

A series of murmurs swept over the nearly full gallery as the two hundred or so spectators caught sight of Jimjoy. Of the other eight members of the Council, five were present—four men and a woman. The woman, Charlotta deHihns, also watched from her carved dark wooden Council chair as Jimjoy approached. Only one of the men did, the white-haired Sylva Redark. The other three refused to look up as Jerold stepped to his podium.

Tap . . . tap, tap, tap . . .

"The Planetary Council will come to order. The purpose of the meeting is to discuss possible Council action in response to the Imperial embargo of the entire Accord system." Jerold paused, moistened his lips, coughed gently, and finally cleared his throat. "The Institute of Ecological Studies, less formally known as the Ecolitan Institute, has petitioned the Council for action. Therefore, the first speaker will be the representative of the Institute, Senior Fellow and full Professor of Applied Ecologic Management, James Joyson Whaler the Second. You have the floor, Professor Whaler."

Jimjoy stepped up to the podium, looked at the Council members in their chairs on the dais slightly above him, and swallowed. With his back to the gallery, he hoped his Ecolitans had been effective in removing weapons from the spectators and the few media in the gallery above. "Members of the Council, citizens of Accord. Today we face a decision. Should those of us who live in colony systems, those of us who have left the ecological disasters of overpopulation, overindustrialization, and mindless mechanization—should we continue to pay for the sins of an Empire that has repudiated us? Should we surrender our freedom of thought to the Imperial reeducation teams? Should we surrender our schools, our customs, and our personal freedom in the hope that, by some miracle, those few who do survive the Empire's tender mercies *may* see their grandchildren gain a fraction of the freedom and prosperity we now possess?

"The Institute cannot guarantee victory—only a chance at freedom and self-determination. The Institute cannot guarantee comfort or prosperity—only the chance to make our own future. The Institute cannot promise that any success will come easily—only a fighting chance for that success.

"The first step in that effort is to declare that we are free of the Empire's heavy hand. For this Council to freely step down, to declare that it will hold free and open public elections for delegates, and that those delegates will select the next Council. In the interim, the Council will express to the Empire our determination to remain free and will continue to minister to the needs of Accord.

"The Institute proposes no major changes in our way of life—except that the Institute will undertake with all of its resources the defense of the system. In return for that defense, the Council will provide reimbursement for those expenses it and the newly elected delegates deem reasonable.

"The Institute will accept and train volunteers, but not anyone coerced into volunteering. The Institute will work to guarantee the physical safety of any individual who wishes to leave Accord permanently until that individual is embarked upon a neutral vessel.

"Our recommendation is spelled out in detail in the document presented to the Council and released to the people and the news media." Jimjoy paused. "I respectfully request that the Council unanimously adopt the proposal."

Jerold stepped to the Council podium. "As acting Chairman, I bring the proposition to the Council and recommend its adoption. Is there a request for debate?"

The five remaining Council members exchanged glances. Charlotta deHihns, with a faintly amused smile, gave a minuscule and negative shake of her head.

Jimjoy waited. According to the script, nothing should happen, but scripts were no guarantee, even with three squads of armed Ecolitans to view the play.

"The Council will consider the proposal. All in favor, signify by voting in the affirmative. All opposed, in the negative."

Six green lights flashed on the voting board.

"The ayes have it. The proposal is adopted as presented."

"Mr. Chairman!" added Jimjoy. "I request that the Council set the date for elections as 20 Quintus."

"The proposal on behalf of the delegates is that elections be set for

20 Quintus. Is there any debate?" Jerold's forehead was damp and shiny.

Again, according to the script, there was no request for debate.

"There is no request for debate. The question is on the proposal to set elections for delegates on 20 Quintus. All in favor, signify by voting in the affirmative. All opposed, in the negative."

Six green lights flashed.

"Mr. Chairman, on behalf of the delegates and the free people of Accord, the Institute thanks you."

As Jimjoy spoke, Jerold produced a white handkerchief and wiped his forehead, then shook it as if to fold it. "There being no other business—"

At the flash of white, Jimjoy dropped from the podium.

Crack!

Thrum! Thrum!

As a single Ecolitan lifted a limp figure from the center of the media gallery, three others watched the crowd, weapons leveled. Two others pointedly turned their weapons on the Council.

"Traitor . . ." hissed one voice.

"Impie swine . . ."

"Served them right . . ."

Jimjoy stepped up to the delegates' podium again before the audience could fully recover. "Mr. Chairman, now that the Council has accepted the proposal and recessed, and you have declared your intention to leave Accord, I strongly suggest you accompany us to the Institute. Under no other circumstances will we be able to guarantee your safety.

"On behalf of the delegates, I declare the Council in recess until its replacements can be elected by the new delegates." He turned and walked out, not looking back, praying that his troops could keep him from being gunned down.

Once through the double doors, he turned right and sprinted down three steps and through a single door to the de facto command post.

There, Elias half stood as he burst in. "Professor! You all right?"

"Fine. This time they missed. Amateurs. Hades, a white flag yet. Can you alert the relocation team to get ready immediately? We'll see some Impie symps at the Institute within hours. Use the old transient quarters." Jimjoy took a deep breath. "Have you heard anything from the Halstani independents?"

"The latest word is that the *Blass* is en route. Ready to take up to three hundred. Nothing else. Meryl says that the planetary police will cooperate. They don't like us much, but they like the thought of either Impie reeducation teams or chaos even worse."

"That figures." Jimjoy pulled at his chin, aware that the gesture still wasn't perfectly natural.

XLVI

"WE JUST CAN'T do that kind of pilot project here, Professor," Stilsen added slowly. "We just can't. The risks are too high." He took a sip from the steaming mug of cafe.

Jimjoy tried not to wrinkle his nose at the odor. Unlike most I.S.S. officers, or former officers, he disliked cafe. "I thought you did most of the design work on the computer."

"We do. That takes most of the time, and, these days, we can predict with better than ninety percent accuracy that we'll get what we designed." Stilsen set the mug back on the edge of the table.

"But?" Although Jimjoy didn't see exactly where the genetic engineer was going, he had a good idea.

"You want biohazards. I understand the need. But what good does it do you if it escapes here? The idea, as I understand it," continued the scientist in a drier tone, "is to inflict damage on the Empire, not on Accord."

Jimjoy laughed softly. "Point well taken, Doctor."

"That means some other place."

Jimjoy pulled at his chin. "What sort of environment do you need?"

Stilsen looked from the blank console to the orange-and-brown rug, then at the wall. "Really . . . nowhere is suitable. . . ."

Jimjoy understood. Stilsen was agoraphobic, spacephobic, or both. "I'm not sure we're talking about the same need. A production or test facility doesn't need someone of your caliber. Besides, we can't have you isolated—"

"Isolated?" Stilsen's thin face expressed puzzlement.

Jimjoy shrugged. "Sorry. Thought it was obvious. We need to build several isolated, full-grav, asteroid-type outposts—only two- and three-person stations where you do the testing and production. If something goes, you lose one station and three people, not a town or a continent."

Stilsen looked down again. "I can't ask anyone to do what I wouldn't do."

Jimjoy took a deep breath, almost sighing. "I don't think you understand, Doctor. The odds for survival are probably better on one of those stations than here on Accord, particularly if the Empire ever figures out what you're doing." His eyes caught those of the genetic engineer. "If your design and preliminary work are as good as you think, the people on those stations will be fine. Besides, you're going to pay your own price, and we both know it."

Stilsen's smile was brief. "Odd you should say that. I was thinking that about you."

"Me?" protested Jimjoy. "I'm just doing what has to be done."

"Sometimes . . . sometimes that's the hardest thing of all."

Jimjoy pulled at his chin, then glanced at the closed door. "The Institute can probably supply some of the production station personnel."

"Anyone but Kordel Pesano."

Jimjoy frowned. The name was vaguely familiar, but he couldn't place it. "Why? Who is she?"

"He. He's a refugee from some Imperial colony, just recently, the past year or two. He is a first-class plant geneticist and molecular level engineer. I would recommend that he become my backup, assuming he is willing. Since he is at the Institute, would that really be a problem? Also, I was told he suffered space trauma, and going back into space so soon might not be wise."

Kordel . . . space trauma? That Kordel?

"I see the name is familiar."

"Sorry. At first it just didn't register." Jimjoy tried to keep his face moderately concerned. He'd been the one to rescue Kordel from the fall of New Kansaw, and the one who had given Kordel space trauma. Luren—the other refugee—was in field training, insisting she would be a needleboat pilot. With her determination, she might, even though she was a shade old for it.

Jimjoy almost laughed as the irony touched him. Late? Here he was, probably a decade older than Luren, starting a third career.

"You find something amusing?" Stilsen's voice was suddenly chilly.

"Only my own limitations, Doctor. Only my own failings."

"Professor Whaler, you are a strange man. I saw your address to the delegates. You manipulate people, and yet you act as if you do not want to. You are a leader who has appeared from nowhere, with rumors of a bloody past, yet you have obvious concern and compassion." Stilsen shrugged and picked up his mug. "At a time when we need a leader, you arrive. Very strange."

Jimjoy cleared his throat. "I can have the first stations within the next three tendays. Can you have the personnel ready? If you can get me the specs and the type of equipment you need, I'll also get to work on that."

Stilsen laughed softly. "You can't work miracles that easily, Professor. All this is custom-designed." His arm swept around the office, gesturing more to the entire research station beyond the office walls.

"Tell me what raw materials and components you need to duplicate it, and we'll start there."

"You'll have a first list tomorrow."

Jimjoy stood up. "Thank you, Doctor."

"I won't thank you, since there really isn't much choice, is there?"

Jimjoy met the genetic engineer's gray eyes. "No. There isn't."

XLVII

A WHITENED "L" from the air, the marine research station overlooked a near-circular bay carved from the solid cliff line that divided sea and land.

Thwop . . . thwop, thwop, thwop . . . thwop, thwop . . . The sound of the rotors echoed through the half-open flitter window.

Even with the side windows open and the airflow from the flitter's descent, the heat and humidity had glued Jimjoy to the seat cushions. Below, the sea was nearly glassy in the midday sun. Jimjoy flipped up the helmet's dark lens, squinting against the flood of light just long enough to wipe his steaming forehead with the back of his flight suit's sleeve. Then the lens came down.

"Equat Control, this is Greenpax four, commencing approach at marine two." He lifted the nose to flare off more airspeed.

"Stet, Greenpax four. Please advise on departure."

"Control, will do."

He lined up the flitter for touchdown on the pad farthest from the cliff edge. With the high-density altitude at the equatorial latitude, he at least wanted some ground cushion for lift-off. Half aware of the empty seat next to him, he wondered what Thelina was up to. Then he frowned. With Meryl and Thelina effectively running the Institute, anything was possible.

He brought his attention back to the flitter, noting that the turbine EGTs were almost into the amber. After lowering the nose fractionally and easing back on the throttles, he let the airspeed rise another ten kays. The area around the bleached concrete pad was vacant. Even the tattered, fluorescent green wind sock hung limply in the glaring midday heat.

As the flitter dropped toward touchdown, Jimjoy flared sharply, kicked in the turbines, and lowered the flitter onto its skids—all in a near-continuous maneuver to avoid any air-taxiing in the high-density altitude. The wind sock bounced in the rotor wash, shaking the thin wooden pole on which it was mounted.

Jimjoy cut the turbines and began the shutdown checklist.

Thwop . . . thwop . . . thwop . . .

As the rotors slowed, a head peered from the nearest building—the first one Jimjoy had seen on Accord that was climate-controlled. Waves of heat reflected off the bleached white concrete—no plastarmac at remote outposts.

After securing the rotors and the turbines, Jimjoy removed his helmet and unstrapped, stretching and peeling his damp flight suit from the pilot's seat cushions. His back was soaked from the humidity, and his forehead was dripping again. As he stepped out onto the concrete, he felt the heat roll up from the hard whiteness underfoot.

"Professor Whaler?" called a young man standing on the golden grass next to the landing pad.

Jimjoy nodded and turned toward him.

"Alvy Norton. I'm the junior marine biologist here, so I get sent out in the midday sun." He wore sandals and shorts and a short-sleeved tunic, both items of clothing of an open-weave green fabric bleached to an off-white.

"I see why you recommended an *early* morning arrival."

"It gets warm," answered the marine biologist. "Unless you've been here, it's hard to understand just how warm. Let's get you inside. You're not dressed for this."

"No," agreed Jimjoy. White Mountain—even at the equator on the hottest of summer days—got nowhere near as warm. In recent years, only New Kansaw, with its dusty plains and ash wastelands, came close. "I've seen worse, but not on friendly terms. This is friendly territory, isn't it?"

"Usually. Unless you're here to cut Dr. Narlian's budget." The marine biologist grinned briefly, then turned toward the door from which he had earlier watched Jimjoy land.

"That wasn't exactly what I had in mind. I wanted to ask about some potential applications of the station's research." By the time the two men had covered the fifteen meters or so separating them from the doorway, Jimjoy felt drenched, and the sweat was beginning to pour down his face. "Whew!"

"It is a little more comfortable inside, but not exactly temperate either," warned Norton as he eased open the door.

Jimjoy stepped inside the station, aware of two things. First, the station temperature was a good ten degrees cooler. And second, the corridor in which he drooped was still as hot as a warm summer day on White Mountain. Initially, the interior seemed dimly lit, but after a moment of adjustment he realized the wide polarized glass windows on the right let in a surprising amount of light.

"You see what I meant."

"I do," agreed Jimjoy, looking around as he followed the biologist along the corridor, which stretched the entire length of the structure. He wiped his forehead with his sleeve again, more to keep the sweat out of his eyes than in any real hope of stemming the flow.

The corridor walls were of local stone plastered over with a light green cement or stucco, the floor of polished gray stone. As they turned a corner at the end of the building, Jimjoy paused to look out at the glassy sea. A narrow ramp, not visible from the air, cut down through the rock and presumably toward the beach below, although Jimjoy could not see the end of the ramp.

"Dr. Narlian's office is this way."

"Oh . . . yes. I was just admiring the view."

"You really can't see all that much from here. If you have time later, and if you are interested, I could show you the cliff observation stations." Alvy Norton looked from Jimjoy toward the open doorway at the end of the corridor five meters ahead, then back at the senior Ecolitan. "Professor . . ."

Jimjoy pulled himself away from his study of the ramp wall cuts. "Sorry." He followed the sandy-haired junior biologist into the office ahead.

Norton cleared his throat, looked respectfully at the petite woman seated between a pair of console screens, and announced, "Dr. Narlian, this is Professor Whaler. From the Institute."

The office contained the two consoles, a conference table with two chairs on one side and a single chair on the other, a pair of old-fashioned filing cabinets, and what appeared to be a drafting board. A worn dark green rug covered most of the floor, with perhaps ten centimeters of stone exposed between the rug and the green stuccoed walls.

When Arlyn Narlian stood up, Jimjoy realized exactly how petite she was, since she barely would have reached the middle of his chest. Her face was elfin in shape, with olive-shaded and unlined skin. Her short hair was as much silver as black. The black eyes were sharper than the narrow and aquiline nose.

"Greetings, Professor. Have a seat." She nodded toward the pair of wooden armchairs—which looked even more uncomfortable than the ones Jimjoy had experienced at the Institute. "Thank you, Alvy." The doctor's voice was controlled, yet almost musical.

The junior biologist closed the door on his departure.

Jimjoy moved next to one of the chairs but did not sit down, waiting for the doctor to reseat herself or move.

Arlyn Narlian did neither, instead surveyed the taller Ecolitan. Finally, she spoke again. "What weapon do you want from me?"

Jimjoy smiled. "You've obviously thought it out. What makes sense?"

"Good." She smiled in return. "At least you're more than a mere figurehead for that pair at the Institute. Your address to the Council actually said something, besides giving people someone to rally behind." She pulled out the single chair on her side of the table. "Sit down."

Jimjoy followed her example, and the two ended up facing each other.

"You upset Stilsen. He still shakes when he thinks about it."

Arlyn's hands rested on the table, which, Jimjoy realized, was wider and lower than normal, clearly modified for the doctor's needs. His legs did not quite feel cramped, but they would if he remained for any length of time.

Jimjoy shrugged. "I couldn't expect any less."

"Why did you start with him?"

"As opposed to you?" Jimjoy met the hard dark eyes. "Most Imperial planets get their food supplies from land-based cultivation. Wanted a temporary impact, not total ecological destruction."

She nodded. "What about New Providence?"

"Good example, but there's only one."

"So why are you here?"

"I could be wrong. And you might have a better idea."

"I like you, Whaler. You don't play games. You know what you want, and you'll admit you aren't infallible. And you're actually pretty good-looking."

Jimjoy managed to avoid swallowing at the last remark.

"I'm direct in *everything*, Whaler."

"I see." He managed a laugh.

"Are you committed?"

"Yes. It's hard enough to be honest in just one relationship."

"Fair enough." She looked like she actually might sigh before the near-wistful expression vanished. "I have a list of potential ideas which might help on a range of planets within the Empire. Basically, they're fresh water breaks in the food chain. You're right about the ocean link."

The doctor leaned back and retrieved three pages of hard copy, which she then slid across the polished surface of the wide gray-oak table.

Jimjoy scanned the list, which categorized each biohazard by target planet, the probable degree of success, the timetable, and any restrictions on delivery/application. "Most of these look good. A couple we can't deliver under the parameters you've listed." He inclined his head. "I'm impressed. Very impressed, especially considering I did not explicitly state my reasons or ask for assistance in advance."

He considered asking her what she wanted, then deferred. He knew what she wanted—the remarks about Stilsen had told him. "I can't promise immediate control of the research programs, but I can obtain immediate independence from current research department budget constraints. Obviously, if our efforts are successful, the Institute will have to be completely reorganized."

"Can you promise that?"

Jimjoy laughed. "In writing? No. But if you can produce what you have listed here, and especially if you can get Stilsen to act . . . Do you want to take a real chance?"

"Try me." Even though her hands remained on the table, her voice still musical, a touch of intensity edged her words.

"How about running the outspace research production facilities?"

"Fine. Send me the details, and I'll be there."

"They're not complete yet, but be at the Institute a tenday from now." He pushed back the chair. "Thank you."

"My pleasure, Whaler. My pleasure." Arlyn Narlian stood as he did. "I'm sure Alvy would be more than pleased to show you around."

"I'd be pleased to see it as long as I don't spend too much time outside."

"That shouldn't be a problem. And now . . ."

"I understand. You'll be receiving a package shortly."

Tap.

"Come on in." The doctor addressed the door.

The nervous smile of Alvy Norton filled the space between door and frame. "Yes, Doctor?"

"Professor Whaler would like a *short* and cool tour . . ."

"No problem, Doctor. It would be my pleasure."

Jimjoy inclined his head to her. "Thank you again."

"Thank *you*, Professor. I look forward to working with you."

Jimjoy turned and followed the junior marine biologist.

XLVIII

"CHECKLIST COMPLETE," JIMJOY muttered. Although the cockpit was empty, he tried not to cut corners. Sloppy pilots ended up dead pilots. Slowly, he released the harnesses and pulled off the helmet, still damp from the bath he had taken in the equatorial humidity of Dr. Narlian's marine research station.

As he cracked the cockpit door, sliding it open, a gust of wind fluttered the sleeves of his flight suit. For an instant, The chill was welcome. Then, as his breath turned white in the late afternoon air, he reached for the leather flight jacket, carrying it out of the flitter. He stood on the grass next to the aircraft, shrugging the jacket on over the thin flight suit.

"Professor?"

Two Ecolitans were headed toward him—Fervan, head of flitter maintenance, and Eddings Davis, who had inherited Gavin Thorson's duties.

"Professor?" said Davis again.

Jimjoy turned and nodded. He didn't feel like talking.

"We have a problem with the sym—the refugees . . ."

"Can't say I'm surprised. Excuse me for a moment." He turned to Fervan.

"How was she?" asked the stocky white-haired man.

"Smooth most of the way. Turbines tended to overheat more than the specs on approach, but they admitted at Equat that it was as hot as it ever is—more than ninety-five percent relative humidity. No wind. Might have been the conditions. DRI worked fine on Harmony. Couldn't pick up the Equat beacon until the last one hundred kays. Might be beacon placement." He paused, coughed. "Then again, maybe the crystals for some of the freq subs are off."

"We'll look at them both. Any problem with rotor vibration?"

"No. Smooth there. Blade path seemed sharp, none of that flutter like on the last flight."

"Thanks, Professor. Appreciate your taking this one."

"No problem."

Fervan waved to a woman in a green parka who was steering an electotrac toward the flitter.

In turn, Jimjoy touched Eddings' arm, nodding toward the path that led to the transients' quarters and away from the maintenance line and its ramp into the underhill hangar.

"What's the trouble?"

"Some of the refugees have been here nearly three tendays—"

Jimjoy raised his eyebrows. "That's a problem? They're warm, fed, safe, and there's medical care."

"Professor, do you know who most of them are?"

Jimjoy could guess, unfortunately, after Jerold's assassination attempt. "Probably rich Imperials, second children's children . . . scared that they won't make it on their own, with enough money to live anywhere."

"Right."

Jimjoy sighed. "The poor can't and won't leave. They figure it will be worse anywhere else, and they're probably right." He shrugged as he continued toward the old transient quarters, waiting for the rotund Eddings to explain. The wind whined softly, tugging at his uncovered head.

Eddings hunched further into his jacket.

"I still don't know the problem."

Eddings did not answer.

At the top of the low hill separating the disguised flight line from the rest of the Institute, Jimjoy stopped, glancing back to the west, where the white-gold sun hung suspended in the winter haze just above the mountains. For several moments he just looked.

"All right, what is it?"

"Credits," blurted Eddings. "They're scared. They can't get to orbit control. They're afraid the Empire will blot out the whole planet any day. Not enough independent transports are ignoring the Imperial boycott . . . bribes . . ."

Jimjoy pulled at his chin. "Are our people taking bribes?"

"Mostly . . . no. Thelina gathered them all together a couple days ago, right after you left. She said that anyone who took a bribe would go with the refugees and their money."

Jimjoy frowned, then nodded. "Now they're getting nasty? Have they tried the hostage routine?"

"Not yet, but some of them are thinking about it."

"So . . . who's stirring this up? Jerold?"

"No. He's gone. Remember, Meryl Laubon threw the real troublemakers on that Halstani transport. That's another problem. The ones left feel slighted."

"Hades!" Jimjoy wrinkled his nose as they approached the end of the transients' quarters. A pair of third-year students, armed with stunners—permanently locked on nonlethal, Jimjoy knew—and wrapped in winter parkas, stood by the low brick gateway.

"Professor."

"Any problems?" He addressed the woman who had addressed him. Her companion, a young man half a head shorter, watched the double doors at the end of the two-story timbered building.

"No, ser."

Jimjoy wrinkled his nose again. "What in hades is that smell?'

Eddings looked at the ground, then at the waist-high brick wall. The woman student guard looked at Eddings, then at Jimjoy. The man kept watching the double doors.

Finally Eddings spoke. "It's the building . . . ser . . ."

"Don't tell me they can't be bothered to clean up!"

"Not exactly. It's neat, but there are a lot of people . . ."

"Damnation!" Jimjoy straightened up. "You!" He pointed to the woman, who was at least as tall as Thelina. "Come with me. Eddings, get a load of mops, sponges, clean-up supplies, and stack them right outside those doors there. In the next twenty minutes. Understand?"

"But . . . they won't . . . already suggested . . ."

"I'm not suggesting this time." Jimjoy turned to the student. "Let's go." Ignoring the young man, who had shaken his head, he marched straight to the double doors, ripped the right one open, and stepped through.

Even through the first door, the smell was sour. Inside the second door, the odor was rank, not of unwashed bodies, but of mildew, urine, and sewage. The hallway was dusty, but nowhere wet, and along the thirty meters before the doors and stairs at the middle of the building were gathered small handfuls of well-dressed, if wrinkled-looking, individuals, some in the latest Imperial styles.

He stopped by the first group, three men close to his own age, all slender, tanned, and hollow-eyed.

"If you're here to fix the plumbing, it's the first door to the right," offered a blond man.

Rpppppppp . . .

Without thought Jimjoy lifted the smaller man straight off the floor by his imported silk tunic, bringing him right up to eye level. "*You* are the one who will clean the sanitary and shower facilities. Every one of you. When this place is clean again—*then* I'll see about sending in a plumber."

He dropped the stunned man in a heap, turning to the second man, dark-haired and olive-skinned.

"Don't touch me, peon."

Snap!

Thunk . . .

The olive-skinned man looked stupidly at his broken wrist, then at the pieces of the plastic knife on the stone floor.

The student guard glanced around, bringing her stunner to the ready, as the others in the hallway turned toward the four men.

"You are here because the Institute offered to protect your miserable lives. The Institute is providing food, shelter, and medical care. Every student or staff member here cleans up after himself or herself. You're no different from us. Cleaning supplies are being delivered to that door." Jimjoy pointed to the double doors through which he had come. "If you don't want to end up back on the streets of Harmony—or worse—I suggest you get to work."

Jimjoy looked at the third man, nearly as tall as he was.

The redhead looked back. "Who are you? What right—"

"Whaler, James Joyson. I represent the Institute—"

Thud.

Clunk.

Jimjoy shook his head, looking down at the unconscious man and the miniature stunner. The three should have tried to jump him at once. He glanced around, reached down, and scooped up the weapon, slipping it into his flight-suit pocket. "Come on." He headed toward the next group, an older man and three women.

"Whaler, your name is. When do we get off this planet?" demanded the man with the thinning brown hair and double chin.

"When a ship comes that will take you. After you clean up this mess."

"We didn't make that mess," protested one of the women.

Jimjoy glanced at her, reevaluated his judgment of her age, and replied to the teenager. "It doesn't matter who did. I just want it cleaned up. Period. Do you understand?" His eyes raked the group.

No one would look back at him.

The next group was more submissive. "Yes . . . so sorry . . . we'll talk to the others about . . . form a committee . . ."

"Just get it cleaned up. How you do it is your responsibility."

Jimjoy kept moving, putting out the word, more curtly with each group, aware of the fatigue of three long days piling up. He still hadn't had a chance to talk to Thelina. He shook his head as he neared the building's center doors.

A little girl peered at him from an open door, as if she wanted to say something. For some reason, she reminded him of Jorje, despite the long braided hair and the green velvet jacket and matching trousers.

He stopped and knelt down.

"Yes, young lady?" He tried to keep his voice low.

She said nothing, glancing back into the room. A woman stood behind her, and the girl's hand twined into her mother's trousers—also green velvet.

Jimjoy waited, ignoring the student guard's impatience and continuing glances up and down the corridor at the muttering groups of refugees.

The girl looked down.

"Go ahead, honey," prompted a low, almost sultry voice.

Jimjoy's eyes flickered toward the mother, who looked only at the top of her daughter's head.

"Mr. Ecolitan, why do we have to go? Rustee couldn't come. I love Rustee. Mommy said you wouldn't let him come. Is that true? You made me leave Rustee?" Tears seeped from the dark-haired girl's eyes.

Jimjoy glanced from the girl to the slim woman whose trousers the girl clutched with her left hand, a woman whose features matched the girl's.

"Rustee is her pet gerosel."

Gerosel? Offhand, Jimjoy wasn't aware of the species, but there wasn't room for pets. That he knew. Not when so few ships ignored the embargo.

"Can I take Rustee?"

"No . . . I'm sorry . . . you can't take Rustee."

"I hate you! Go away!" She burst into another round of sobs.

Jimjoy straightened, trying not to swallow, catching the same dark look from the mother as from the daughter. He nodded to the mother curtly and turned. "Let's go."

A couple looked up from an embrace under the stairwell as Jimjoy burst through the first doors. They seemed to shrink away from him, but he ignored both and pushed open the doors to the fresh air.

"Hades . . . not made for this . . . drek."

"Ser?"

"Sorry you had to go through that. Should have let them stew in their own messes." He glanced around, then turned his steps toward the end of the building through which he had entered, studying each window as he passed. Some were ajar, but they all seemed in working order.

The single male guard took a deep breath as Jimjoy and the woman returned.

"Professor, Ecolitan Davis told me that the cleaning supplies would be here as soon as he could round them up."

"Fine." Jimjoy pulled at his chin. What else did the refugees need?

He pursed his lips. All the little girl knew was that she had to leave her pet behind because one Jimjoy Whaler said no. The adults—they got better than they deserved. But the children? And these were probably the luckiest ones.

"Can you two handle it?" he asked.

"Yes, ser," the pair chorused.

"Good." His voice softened. "Take care."

As he walked away, he could hear the woman begin to tell about the trip through the refugee quarters. He closed the top seam on the flight jacket.

The sun poised itself on the edge of the western mountains, and Jimjoy listened to the rising wail of the wind as he headed toward Thelina's office.

XLIX

JIMJOY POKED HIS head into the small office to the left of the now-empty Prime's office. Unlike Meryl's office, Thelina's did not connect directly to the Prime's. From the right-hand office, Meryl acted as Deputy Prime. Even though the Institute never had such a function, no one questioned either the title or Meryl. Not since Jimjoy's actions with the Council.

Jimjoy's incipient smile faded. Thelina was out.

Instead, Kerin Sommerlee was sitting there, the faint late-late afternoon winter sunlight pooling on her and the left side of the desk/console. Like Thelina, she had cut her blond hair short. She was using the console, her fingers awkwardly tapping at the keyboard studs.

"Oh . . ."

She looked up. "Professor . . ."

"Jimjoy."

She shook her head. "I don't know as any of us—Thelina excepted—will ever think of you that way."

"Guess I'll never be accepted—"

"I didn't say that, Professor." Her tone was tart, as was her expression.

"I know. No time for self-pity. Where is she? Thelina, I mean."

"She didn't tell you?"

Jimjoy swallowed. The look on Kerin's face told him that Thelina was up to something less than perfectly safe. And after the mess with the refugees . . . "Where . . . is . . . she?"

"She said you'd know, that you'd agreed on certain duties . . ." Kerin moistened her lips.

"And she asked you to stand in for her?"

"I agreed to. It had to be someone that field three and Harmony civic would listen to."

Jimjoy nodded. "Did she say where she was headed?"

Kerin grinned ruefully. "She said to tell anyone who asked to check with you or Meryl."

"When did she leave?"

"Yesterday morning."

Jimjoy nodded again. Her reluctance to come with him to deal with the scientists made a lot more sense. She still didn't fully trust him. He sighed. "Anything else I ought to know?"

"Not really. There are a lot of details . . . police units all over the planet are faxing in reports about possible Impie agents. Althelm has taken over trying to locate that micromanufacturing equipment you need . . . has a lead from an independent out of Gersil. It's likely to cost the equivalent of—I don't know what . . . the number is enormous."

"*If* it meets Jason's specs, and *if* they can deliver within two tendays, pay whatever it takes."

"It's that important?"

"It's that important. You might check with Meryl on how to negotiate on it. She's far better than I'd be."

Kerin shrugged. "We have a few merchant types around here."

"I understand. You handle it."

She almost grinned.

"I'm going over to see Meryl."

Kerin nodded, took a deep breath, and looked back at the console, avoiding his eyes.

He pulled at his chin, wondering exactly what sort of danger Thelina had taken on. Then he shrugged and turned, slipping out into the corridor and walking the ten or so meters toward Meryl's office. Currently, with Harlinn's permanent indisposition, the Prime's office served as a conference room and a neutral meeting ground.

Meryl's door was closed.

Thrap!

"Yes?"

"Jimjoy . . . mind if I come in?"

"You will anyway."

He opened the door and eased inside. Meryl glanced up from a stack of hard copy and a screen surrounded with amber flashing studs. Her window was firmly closed, and she wore a dark green pullover sweater.

"Where is she?"

Meryl provided him with a nervous smile, which vanished almost simultaneously with the sunlight. Symbolic or not, the sun had finally dropped behind the mountains. Now the trees on the hillside had turned even grayer.

"I understand you've been busy laying down the law for our poor, depressed Imperial refugees."

Jimjoy sighed. "If getting them to understand that the Institute doesn't provide maid and valet service and that they'd hades-fired well better act like responsible adults—yes—but some people, like the Empire, don't understand anything but force."

"That you can deliver."

He took another deep breath. "When necessary . . . I suppose . . . The children bothered me. They don't understand. Guess I didn't, either." He straightened. "Where's Thelina?"

"She didn't tell you?"

Jimjoy sighed. "She's up to something dangerous, and she's not about to tell me."

"You think she should?" Meryl seemed to be wrestling with her hands.

"Yes."

"Why? You didn't tell her about your suicide attack on the Haversol station. She found out about that from Dr. Hyrsa, when no one was sure whether you'd even live."

"But . . ." Jimjoy could almost feel the woman's words physically piercing him. He glanced over his shoulder, as if hoping Thelina might appear. Then he looked back at Meryl, who sat in the straight-backed chair, the hard copy piled across most of the flat spaces around the console.

Had Thelina really taken it that way? "Wait—she wasn't even talking to me at that point!"

"That doesn't mean she didn't care, or wouldn't have liked a little notice. You effectively declared war on the Empire. As you have told more than a few people with pride."

Jimjoy winced at the coolness of her last words.

"You have trouble treating her as an equal," continued Meryl. "Yet she's saved your life at least twice. All the professed love in the world won't be enough unless you really change."

"Change?" Jimjoy looked at Meryl. "I wanted to know where she was, and you talk about my needing to change. Change more?"

The slender blond woman stacked the small pile of paper on the console and stood up. "Would you like some tea? If I have to explain this, I need something warm. My throat's sore. There's a kettle set up in Sam's office." She shrugged. "Sorry. I still think of it as his."

"Suppose I do, too." Jimjoy also shrugged. Meryl was going to take her time, for whatever reason. Was she stalling to keep him from stopping Thelina?

"No, I'm not stalling. She's well off Accord. So relax, if you can."

Women! Besides reading minds, they were always suggesting that he consider something else. That was why he had left White Mountain. Or was it? "Liftea would be fine, if you have it."

"Either old-fashioned tea or liftea. Sam didn't like cafe."

"Liftea." He followed her toward the Prime's office and watched as she turned on the gas on the single burner.

Outside, the light dimmed further, leaving the Institute in darkness, with scattered lights appearing in the twilight. Meryl touched a plate and the soft ceiling lights came on in the almost stark office, empty now of most of the books and all the memorabilia. The table that had served Sam as a desk was bare except for a crystal paperweight with the green Imperial seal caught within it and an empty wooden tray that had contained papers.

Clink. Meryl took two cups from the shelf and set them beside the burner. "Did you expect to find Thelina dutifully waiting for you?"

Jimjoy swallowed, looking away from Meryl's directness to the dark outline of the upper hills. "Not dutifully. Surprised that she hadn't even told me."

"I asked you before, but you didn't answer. Did you tell her about your Haversol operation?"

"No. She would have stopped me."

Meryl snorted. "How? How could anyone really have stopped you? You had Sam's backing. You could have told her as you were leaving. Why didn't you?"

Jimjoy frowned. Unfortunately, Meryl's question made sense. Why hadn't he wanted to tell Thelina? He did not meet Meryl's eyes, instead focused on the crystal paperweight with the symbol of the Institute within it.

"When you put it that way . . . I'm not certain." He looked at the blond woman. "What do you think?"

"Do you really want to know?"

"No." He forced a short laugh. "But I'd better."

Meryl favored him with the faintest of smiles, then glanced at the wisp of steam beginning to escape the kettle. "It's only what I think—"

"Which is usually pretty close to target," interrupted Jimjoy.

"—but you try to avoid any advance approval, particularly from women. Sam's death really hurt that way. He wasn't a threat to you. You know Thelina, Kerin, and I have to run the Institute right now, and subconsciously you're back working for women—for your mother or your sisters. You chose it this time. It wasn't an accident of birth. And it's tearing you up—"

"Wait a minute. I went to Haversol *before* Sam's death."

"You still didn't want to get female approval." Meryl sighed, then turned off the burner and poured the boiling water into the green porcelain teapot. "It should steep for a bit," she added in almost an aside. "Why do you think we've tried not even to suggest your role, except when you ask?"

"Trying to tiptoe around the frail masculine ego?"

"You said that," noted Meryl tartly. "You have no reason for a frail ego. You've accomplished miracles—even if some have been miracles of destruction and escape. The problem is that you don't like yourself, deep inside."

"So what does that have to do with my not telling Thelina and her not telling me?"

"She doesn't trust men, and you don't trust women. If you don't trust her enough to tell her, how can she trust you?"

Jimjoy pulled at his chin once more. "You're saying that I have to trust her before she'll trust me?"

Meryl said nothing, instead poured the tea into the two cups. "Would you like sugar?"

"Did she tell you not to tell me?"

"Would you like sugar?"

Jimjoy sighed. "Yes, please. Two, please." He felt like tapping his fingers on Sam's desk, cursing feminine logic, and walking out. Instead, he looked at one of the hard wooden chairs, then took the heavy cup from Meryl and walked toward the middle chair. Despite the darkness outside, the flight jacket felt warm, too warm for his being inside.

Meryl stood beside the empty Prime's desk-table, cradling her cream-and-green cup in both hands, letting the steam drift into her face, as if warming herself, despite the heavy sweater she wore.

"Why don't you sit down?" he suggested. "At least for a moment."

Meryl nodded before easing herself into the chair nearest the desk.

Jimjoy sipped the liftea, too hot for more than sips. "What about trust?"

"What about it?"

"You said—"

"What I said was perfectly clear. You have to trust Thelina."

"She doesn't have to trust me?"

Meryl looked up from the cup she still held in both hands. "She has. She recommended the Institute accept you. She offered her whole career as hostage to developing your Special Operatives. She risked her life against Harlinn's bodyguards. She gave herself to you—even with her background. What else do you want? Don't you see? She had to do something without telling you, if only to deliver a message."

Again Jimjoy was forced to look from the intensity in the woman's eyes. What else did he want? What did he want? His eyes flicked from the floor to the window and the growing blackness of the western horizon, then back to Meryl. "Trust is a shared orbit?"

"I could almost hate your mother—and your father." Meryl took a deep sip from the cup, then brushed a wisp of blond hair back with her left hand.

Jimjoy didn't ask why. He knew. "Where is she? I know, based on the way I handled Haversol, you have every right to make me wait until she returns." If she returns, he thought to himself. "But I would like to know."

"She's in the New Avalon system, trying to negotiate an arrangement with Tinhorn."

Jimjoy winced. "An arrangement?"

"She thought she could use some former chips as a lever to suggest it was in the Fuards' best interests to let Accord salvage some old destroyers—minus weaponry, of course."

"Do they know who she is?"

"No. She has the history as an Institute operative to operate on her own."

"But the former chips?"

"She got someone to call them in for her. And that's all she told me."

Jimjoy pulled at his chin, then took a long swallow of tea, almost welcoming the burning it etched down the back of his throat. "So we wait?"

"No. You keep doing what needs to be done. Just like she did, just like I'm doing."

His eyes refocused on Meryl, her words recalling that she had been Thelina's friend and confidant far longer than Jimjoy had known Thelina. He swallowed. "Sorry . . . hadn't thought about it. Stupid, but I hadn't. Is there anything I can do?"

Meryl finished her cup of tea, then stood. "No. But understanding late is better than not understanding at all, Professor."

"I wonder." He stood. "The cups? Anywhere to wash them?"

"Thanks for the offer, but I can handle one extra cup. I would have had the tea anyway. Just leave it here for now."

"You sure?"

"Yes." She poured a second cupful from the teapot. "This goes back to the office." Then she set her own cup down and reached for his.

Jimjoy handed it to her. "Thank you."

She nodded as she set his cup beside the kettle. "What's next for you? More persuasion on the research establishment?"

"Dr. Narlian may do that for me."

"She could . . . but be careful."

"I see you've met the doctor."

"It only takes once." Meryl shook her head slowly. "What else?"

"Work with Analitta and Gersin to see if we can complete the off-planet research production post-designs."

"You aren't actually doing design work?"

Jimjoy smiled briefly. "They're better at that than I am. A whole lot better. Just give them the power and size parameters and the requirements. Plus pep talks. Then I'll try to find some more leads on bioweapons. And hope a lot . . . and try to trust."

"Thelina should be fine." Meryl lifted the teacup and started back toward the doorway to her office.

Jimjoy followed, not necessarily agreeing. The Fuards weren't trustworthy, but right now there was nothing at all he could do. Except trust—and he didn't like the feeling. "Let me know."

"You may see her first." Meryl's look seemed momentarily wistful as she set her cup next to her screen, where several more lights were now flashing, two of them changing from amber to red.

"Then we'll let you know."

Meryl took a deep breath and settled herself behind the console, looking back up at Jimjoy as he stood there. "Please do."

He nodded, not knowing what else he could trust himself to say, repressing a sudden shiver inside the heavy jacket that suddenly failed to warm him.

L

8 Quat 3647
New Augusta

Dear Mort:

Urgency does happen—sometimes. I took your faxes and record to Graylin (Fleet Development), and he agreed to fight if
N'Trosia pushed for a black flash on your dossier, but it won't
come to that. N'Trosia doesn't want the incident to be brought
to light, other than as an unfortunate and unavoidable accident
for which no one was to blame, not with his talk about the Fuards
being reasonable people and with the Declaration of Secession
from Accord hitting the tunnels. So it looks like you're clear.

The manpower and operations costs for Sector Five (Accord)
hit the Defense Committee, and they nearly hemorrhaged.
N'Trosia was screaming, right in the hearing room, about the
mismanagement of diplomacy by the I.S.S. He demanded to know
how we thought we could conduct diplomacy with warships and
no compassion. Then he told Fleet Admiral Helising that the
Accord Secession was the direct result of the I.S.S.'s preoccupation
with weapons of death and destruction.

Anyway, the long and short of it was that they scrapped the
CX, at least for now, and compromised on more spare parts and
limited retrofits for the Attack Corvettes. From what you said and
from what I'd gathered, I wanted my new boss, the head of Plans
and Programming, Admiral Edwin Yersin, to point out the problems. He declined, not because he didn't agree, but because
N'Trosia had the votes. So it goes.

I wish I could offer more hope from the capital, but now it
comes out that we've already lost a bunch of ships to the eco-
freaks. They call themselves the Coordinate of Accord, and they're
dignifying their little rebellion with the catchy title of the Ecologic Secession. Between N'Trosia's compassion, limited budgets,
and a few missing SysCons, any application of massive force—
trust you know what I mean—is currently out of the question.

Then, the asteroid miners out of Sligo are trying the same thing. There our supply lines are clearer, and something might happen. But who really knows these days?

The Fuards are complaining about the three-system bulge again, you know, out your way, and where that will lead is anybody's guess.

I heard from Sandy again, last month. She left a delay cube for me, said she was on her way to Accord. Latest trend, of course, is to be fashionably ecological, but she, once more, will take it to extremes.

I shouldn't ramble on, but sometimes you just wonder . . . *Enough is enough. Give my love to Helen and the kids.*

Blaine

LI

THE BOULEVARD WAS almost deserted in the midafternoon freezing drizzle, a few hardy individuals in waterproof parkas sloshing through the few centimeters of puddled slush that covered the precisely cut gray stone sidewalks.

An occasional groundcar whined to or from Government Square, hissing across and through the combination of ice and rain that covered the roadway.

Jimjoy, his parka collar turned up, paused to look at the display in Waltar's, then smiled.

"Think Spring!" proclaimed the graceful script in the window. There, for all Accord to see, underneath an open umbrella, was a copy of the formal picnic set he and Jurdin Waltar had designed. As he studied it, he realized that Jurdin had simplified the set and improved the design in several minor ways, allowing the final backpack design to be even more compact.

On a whim, he pushed open the door.

Cling. A gentle bell rang as he stepped inside.

"May I help you, ser?" asked a young man, a youngster still of school age, with slicked-back black hair and a fresh-scrubbed and clean-shaven face.

"Is Jurdin in?"

"No, ser. He's out at the workshop. He said he wouldn't be back until late. Is there anything I can help you with? Or Dorthea? She's in back."

Jimjoy shook his head. "No, thank you. I just wanted to compliment him on the picnic set in the window. You could tell him I stopped by, if you would."

"Ser? You are . . . ?"

"Oh, sorry. Just tell him Jimjoy Whaler, and the picnic set."

"Whaler . . . yes, ser! I didn't recognize you. That was some talk you gave, ser. Are you going to run for Council? My whole family thinks you should."

"Run for Council? No, that should be somebody like Jurdin. I wouldn't make a good Council member."

"You aren't going to run?" The boy's tone was almost hurt.

Jimjoy smiled gently. "Young man, politicians have to make people happy. Spent my life doing things that made people unhappy, telling them things they didn't want to hear. Somebody has to but people would be unhappy hearing from me all the time. Better I stay with the Institute."

"You could still be an Ecolitan, Professor."

"No, I don't think so. Ecolitans should stay out of politics. All we did was make sure that the people get to choose their own politicians. We're idealists, most of us, and idealists make poor politicians." He shrugged. "I appreciate your support. Just make sure you choose an honest Council."

"Are you sure you won't run?"

"I'm sure. I may not even be planetside for the election. How could I be a Council member when I'm not here?"

Cling. The bell signaled the arrival of a figure in a hooded coat.

"Do you have any snigglers?"

Jimjoy nodded at the youngster. "Just tell Jurdin I was here."

"Yes, ser." All seriousness, the boy turned to the woman who had arrived. "Yes, sher. We have two, four, and eight meters. They're racked in the third aisle at the end . . ."

Jimjoy stepped out into the rain, heading uphill to Daniella's. With the intricate silvered spiral over the door, the stop stood out from the others.

Whssssttttt . . . splattt . . .

Slush from a passing groundcar sprayed on the stone centimeters from Jimjoy's boots as he pulled open the heavy wooden door. Inside stood a single, heavy display case, unattended, as it had been the last time he had come.

Jimjoy swallowed, then stepped up to the case. No one was at the jeweler's bench, but he could see Daniella's broad back through the open door to the supply room.

"Daniella?"

"Be there in just a moment." Her head, covered with a thatch of thick and short gray-streaked brown hair, did not move.

Jimjoy waited.

"All right—oh, Professor! I think you'll be pleased." The near-elfin voice failed to match the solid and muscular body to which it was attached.

Jimjoy smiled back at the jeweler. "You're the one who looks pleased."

"I am. You will be, too." She went to the heavy metal case, more like an antique safe, and, after easing out a metal shelf, extracted a small box. "Here you are." Daniella laid out a soft black cloth, then, after opening the box, laid the ring on the cloth.

Jimjoy nodded, trying to keep the grin from his face. Thelina would have thought he was totally insane.

The ring was simple—two green diamonds, large enough to be noticed, not large enough to be called rocks, set in a platinum silvered to the shade Jimjoy had specified. The two stones flowed into each other, yet remained separate.

"I had to modify that design, Professor, just a touch. Here . . ." She pointed. "And there. Otherwise, a hard knock at the wrong angle and you could lose the stone."

"That's fine. Looks better that way, anyway."

"Thought so myself."

"You're the expert."

"Mind if I use the idea again?"

"Could you wait a while?"

Daniella grinned, wide white teeth sparkling. "You want her to know how special it is?"

Jimjoy nodded. "Spacer . . ."

Daniella shook her head. "Got to watch those women spacers, Professor."

"That's what she'd say about me." Jimjoy handed over a stack of notes, the total nearly depleting the funds remaining from his few Imperial assets.

"Thank you." Daniella carefully replaced the ring in the hand-carved black wooden box and handed it to him.

"Thank *you*." He nodded and slipped the box into an inside pocket of the parka, making sure it was securely sealed before stepping back into the wind and freezing rain outside the jeweler's.

His steps were quick and light as he made his way toward the port to catch the afternoon shuttle back to orbit control.

LII

JIMJOY SCANNED THE controls, checking the EDIs and the far-screens yet another time. Theoretically, they were not in Imperial space, but the last thing they needed was for an Impie ship to see the distinct energy signatures of the *Roosveldt* and the *Causto* three sectors away from the Rift.

He looked at the representative screen again, wishing Broward would hurry in closing with the *Causto*. He hated to ask, even with tight beam laser comm. His fingers drummed on the edge of the finger control panel.

Mera Lilkovie grimaced as she looked pointedly at his left hand.

"All right. All right. Just wish Broward would move that tub."

She shrugged, as if to ask whether impatience would speed the transport.

Jimjoy watched the *Roosveldt*'s image cross the dashed green of the congruency perimeter on the representational screen.

Cling. His eyes flashed to the farscreen, noting the EDI entry. The system was supposedly uninhabited, like the one for which they were heading, and the presence of another ship was a definite warning—either military or an independent.

His fingers scripted the inquiry, even as he watched the *Roosveldt* close up to his ship.

"Incoming ship is Imperial scout. Probability ninety-five percent," the screen answered.

Jimjoy touched the laser comm stud. "Bellwar one, interrogative jump to salvage one. Interrogative jump."

From the copilot's couch, Mera Lilkovie again glanced at him and his finger tapping.

He kept his eyes on the screens. He also ignored Athos and Swersa

n their crew seats. The incoming scout was too far away to track the
wo Accord ships, and near positive identification limits—possibly just
)n a border recon run. But the coincidence bothered him.

"Black control, one ready."

"Jump at my mark." He paused. "Now . . . MARK!" As soon as he
aw the shimmer on the screen, he pressed the jump control, hoping
le had not waited too long.

The blackness of the jump was as instantaneously endless as ever
)efore the *Causto* dropped out at the edge of the target system—con-
aining only three gas giants and two undeveloped rock balls.

Cling.

Jimjoy pointed the *Roosveldt*, well behind the beefed-up needleboat,
hen scanned the entire system.

One brightly pulsing blue dot and four fainter dots appeared at the
)rbit line of the fifth planet, right where they were supposed to be.

2214 Universal—leaving nearly two standard hours until the ren-
lezvous target time. That the Fuards were already there indicated how
uccessful Thelina had been, or how badly they wanted the Empire
)verextended on the Rift.

"Bellwar one, interrogative estimated closure."

As he waited for Broward's response, Jimjoy tried to keep a frown
rom his face. Having allies, hidden or otherwise, like the Fuards was
lot his preference. Bad as the Empire was, the Fuards were worse. But
,vithout the Fuards, the Empire would already be down on Accord. He
)ursed his lips and took another deep breath.

He hadn't liked the Fuards. He hadn't liked Thelina's negotiating
he "salvage" arrangement with them, and he still didn't. They were
)erfectly capable of potting both the *Roosveldt* and the *Causto*—and not
,ven worrying about it. But they wouldn't have offered four obsolescent
;hips as bait. For the fledgling Coordinate of Accord, one or two mil-
;ary ships would have provided plenty of bait.

"Black control, estimate closure in point two five stans." Broward's
oice was as gravelly as usual.

Jimjoy had offered to let the senior civilian captain take the lead in
he operation, but Broward had declined, politely, insisting that mili-
ary operations be run by military types.

Jimjoy had not pressed, and neither had mentioned the exchange
;ain.

"Stet. Changing course to destination line. Maintaining current in-
,ound vee until closure."

"Understand current vee, new course direct to destination."

"Affirmative."

"Stet, black control. Estimate closure in point two stans."

Jimjoy nodded and continued to scan the screens, hoping they would remain empty. If anyone else showed, the Fuards were capable of anything. While they clearly wanted to provide the ships, the transfer location and method were designed to keep the ships' origin as quiet as possible for as long as possible.

"System clear, except for target," announced Athos from the small console tucked into the space behind Mera. Swersa, behind Jimjoy, coughed but said nothing. She was there to bring back the oversized needleboat.

"Let's hope it stays that way," muttered Jimjoy.

"It's Fuardian territory, Professor," offered Mera.

"Nominally, but you'll note it sits on a big area of uninhabitable systems with Halstani and Imperial systems nearby. They want us out of here in one jump. Even want to be able to claim we strayed here."

Cling.

Jimjoy checked the screens. A faint line of dashed blue ran from the bright blue dot—an outgoing message torp, probably reporting to Fuard HQ the arrival of the great Coordinate armada, reflected Jimjoy. He shrugged his shoulders, trying to release the tension.

"Black control, estimate closure in point one."

"Stet."

Still no traces of Impies or Halstanis, but Jimjoy kept scanning the screens, watching, and hoping they stayed clear. And, for Mera's sake, trying not to tap his fingers too much.

Finally, the Accord transport crossed the dashed green line on the representational screen.

"Bellwar one reporting closure."

"Stet, accelerating at point five this time."

"Accelerating at point five."

Swersa coughed softly behind Jimjoy. Mera glanced from the pilot to the *Roosveldt's* second pilot. Athos said nothing.

Not quite three-quarters of a standard hour later, screens still clear, except for the two Accord ships and the five blips that represented the Fuard contingent, Jimjoy began deceleration.

"Commencing decel at point five five this time."

"Understand commencing decel at point five five."

"That's affirmative," responded Jimjoy.

"Killing inbound jump carryover?" asked Mera.

Jimjoy nodded. His eyes burned slightly, probably from too much concentration on the screens. But neither the *Causto* nor the *Roosveldt* carried any offensive weapons, and flight would be their only defense should an unfriendly armed vessel appear.

He sighed and began another wait, watching as he waited, again hoping that the system would stay clear. He could see Athos stretching out, but Mera continued to track the screens as the two Accord ships crept toward their rendezvous off the fifth planet.

After yet another interval, the screens indicated lock-on of the Fuard cruiser's EDI trace.

"Confirmation matches Fuard light cruiser parameters with a probability of ninety-five percent," the console scripted.

"Bellwar one, decel at point two."

"Black control, decel at point two this time." Broward's voice seemed even more filled with gravel than usual.

"Stet." Jimjoy fingered the comm controls, setting standard Fuard frequencies. Then he tapped in the message—all burst-sent copy.

"Green are the orchards of Jericho, and yet the walls have tumbled."

The receiving screen lit almost immediately.

"Loud are the trumpets in the name of righteousness and the host of the mighty."

Jimjoy nodded and tapped in the plain-language message. "Standing by for salvage operations."

This time, there was no immediate answer.

Mera looked at Jimjoy, who concentrated on the screens.

He sighed. All four faint dots vanished from the representational screen, leaving only a blue dotted ghost for each. "Screens down on the salvage ships. Probably disembarking crew."

As if to confirm his observation, a small blue dot separated from the bright dot that was a cruiser and merged with the first ghost dot on the representational screen.

"Bellwar one, close to standoff point."

"Following your lead, black control."

"Stet."

All three Ecolitans and Swersa watched as the shuttle moved from host dot to ghost dot and finally back to the cruiser.

The comm screen flashed again. "Hulks cleared for salvage. Past owner disavows any responsibility."

Jimjoy added his own follow-up. "Approaching this time for salvage."

"Cleared to approach."

Jimjoy coughed softly, then triggered auditory communications with the *Roosveldt*. "Bellwar one, cleared for approach to salvage operations this time."

"Black control, following your lead."

"Stet."

The Fuard cruiser remained stationary, hanging off the four destroyer hulls, its heavy screens pulsing at full power, as the *Causto* and the *Roosveldt* eased to within broomstick distance of the "salvage."

Jimjoy's fingers darted across the board, checking and cross-checking to ensure that the *Causto* was stationary with respect to the four hulls, particularly the nearest hull.

"Bellwar one. Commencing salvage."

"Stet, control. Let me know when you're ready for support crews."

"Will do."

Jimjoy unstrapped. "Swersa. She's yours."

"Thanks, Professor." The muscular second pilot of the *Roosveldt* had unstrapped and was stretching in place. "You do nice jumps. Better than Broward."

Jimjoy laughed softly. "His are safer."

"Could be. Could be."

The Ecolitan professor glanced at the other two Ecolitans. "Ready? Let's suit up and get moving. Sooner we clear those hulls and get out of here, the happier we'll all be." He led the way to the needleboat's lock.

After a time, three broomsticks glided up to the nearest of the four obsolescent destroyers hanging in the darkness off the fifth planet of a gas giant system that had only a catalog number. Unlike the light-absorbing composite plates of Imperial ships, the destroyer's hull was a softer, almost silvery dark gray. From a distance the color was as invisible as the darker plates of Imperial ships, but closer, it made broomstick navigation easier.

Behind the trio of broomsticks rested two ships—the bulbous Accord transport and the needleboat from which the broomsticks had come. Beyond the "salvage" loomed a dark, sleeker shape with the silvery hull and faint crimson screen shimmer of a Fuardian cruiser nearly three times the size of the Accord transport.

Jimjoy wanted to pull at his chin or shake his head. He still wished he had been able to see Thelina and to discover how she had engineered the ship transfer. But all he had received was a brief message outlining the details of the pickup and the cryptic notation that she was working on "Phase II." Whatever Phase II was, even Meryl didn't know.

Clung . . .

The lead broomstick touched the plates, and Jimjoy flicked the squirters to kill any recoil.

"How do we get inside?" asked Athos.

"Manually." As Jimjoy suspected, the electronics to the main lock had been stripped away. After tethering his broomstick to a recessed ring, he slid back a cover plate covering a small wheel and began to crank. The crank turned easily, indicating that it had been used frequently.

The slab air-lock door eased open, revealing a lock wide enough to take all three figures. Even though the ship was in stand-down condition, without grav-fields, the three Ecolitans entered the lock oriented feet-to-deck.

All the equipment brackets on the lock walls were empty. Mera opened the emergency locker—to find it empty as well.

Once inside, Jimjoy twisted the inside crank to reverse the process. Although the interior wheel also turned easily, by the time he had finished, his forehead was damp and his arm muscles were tight. "Whew . . . little unplanned exercise . . ."

"No electronics?" asked Athos.

Mera had asked nothing so far, instead concentrating on the engineering details of the unfamiliar structure.

"Probably as little as possible. We'll have to do manual course and accel/decel calculations and inputs." He turned toward the inner lock, thumbing a heavy button to flood the lock with ship's air.

. . . *hhhhssssssss* . . .

A faint buildup of frost covered all three suits.

"Damn . . ."

"No dehumidifiers," stated Mera flatly.

"Probably inoperative. Have to fix that." Jimjoy checked the gauge he'd brought along with his tool pouch. "Pressure's a touch low, but steady." The inner lock controls—a heavy switch—were in place. He toggled the switch and waited as the inner door opened. The corridor was empty, as empty as the lock had been. Any movable equipment not essential to ship operations had been removed.

As the three floated in the corridor, Jimjoy toggled the inside lock controls, then, after the lock had resealed, began to crack his helmet seal. "Stale, but all right." He took off the helmet, but did not rack it or set it aside, instead fastening it to his shoulder strap. Not that he expected the ship's hull to fail, but without the added protection of screens, he preferred to have the helmet close.

The two others followed his example.

Hand over hand, Jimjoy edged himself toward the control section without looking to see whether Mera or Athos followed.

With the screens off, the control room was a steel-walled box, irregular gaps showing in the control board itself and in the equipment bulkhead behind the second row of consoles. Two control couches—pilot and copilot—faced the board. Behind the control couches were three smaller consoles, each with a couch.

"How big a crew?" asked Athos.

"Eight or nine, depending on the mission." He leaned over the board and tapped two studs in sequence. "Thirty percent. Not too bad, if the others are like that. Might not even use all the surplus from the *Roosveldt*." Pulling himself into the rough approximation of a sitting position—as well as possible in null-gee without actually strapping in—he began to run through the analysis programs, nodding or shaking his head as the outputs appeared on the small screen on the board itself.

He ignored the look that passed between Mera and Athos as they noted his familiarity with the controls. The older Fuard systems clearly didn't allow the flexibility of detailed split screens, instead tracking outputs to predetermined screens. "Rigid and idiot-proof . . ." he mumbled.

Mera and Athos exchanged looks a second time before Mera began to try to puzzle out the board in front of the copilot's couch.

Abruptly, Jimjoy tapped several controls and sat up. "It works. For now, at least. Let's see what it looks like below." He eased around Mera and pulled himself back into the central fore-aft corridor.

Floating just off the plastic-coated metal desk in the destroyer's stale air to inspect the hatch to the lower deck, Jimjoy used the suit's belt light to supplement the dim emergency lights. Around the squarish hatch were heavy scratch marks in the dark purple plastic finish. The hatch itself was a single piece of metal which slid into a recess under the deck, unlike the irised double hatches of Imperial ships.

He nodded. The Fuards used steel, probably asteroid-smelted, and far less composite and plastic than Imperial ships.

"What do you think?" asked Mera and Athos nearly simultaneously.

"Don't know. Let's see." He used the manual control wheel to crank open the hatch on a solid steel ladder leading to the deck below, and the drives, and screen, grav-field, and jump generators. Then he pulled himself into the narrow space at the foot of the ladder among the equipment.

Every single unit was at least a third again as big as the comparable Imperial equipment.

He shook his head ruefully, but he couldn't keep a smile from his lips. With all that power . . . But that led to the next question. He disconnected the light from the equipment belt and focused it on the thin line of silver that ran from the converter to the jump generator. He repeated the tracing process with the screen generator and the grav-field equipment.

"No cross-connects," he murmured. Not that he had expected anything else. The Fuards were known for their straightforward, brute-force, energy-intensive approach.

"Cross-connects?" asked Mera.

"Not the time for an explanation, but I needed to see these to make sure. Power flows run straight from the converter to each separate system. Probably has a tiered logic in the converter distributor . . . drives, jump accumulator, screens, and grav-fields. Logic system is based on normal loads. Ship is overpowered, but the logic fields act as a governor. No reason we couldn't cross-connect and shunt power from screens or grav-fields to drives."

Athos, floating down the ladder, shook his head. "You've lost me, ser."

Jimjoy finished his inspection and clipped the light to his belt. "Just a matter of expectations. Change the performance envelope of the ship . . . probably have to make it automatic . . . most of our pilots couldn't handle it without more training time than we have, but it would throw off the Impies."

Mera nodded. "What's the standard deviation on a fire control system?"

"Depends on distance. Call it an average of less than five percent max on a deep-space solution."

"So a variation in acceleration/deceleration . . ."

"Right."

"You two," muttered Athos. "It's like an abbreviated code." He moved himself back to the main deck of the former Fuard destroyer.

"How long will it take?" asked Mera.

Jimjoy shrugged and turned back toward the ladder, waiting for Mera to head up. "First we've got to get these home—looks like they'll make the jumps. But we'll do it in full suits. Screens are generally first to go. Once we're at Orbit Dark, we'll need to check out all the equipment, see what needs to be replaced. Then, if we have time, you can start on the modifications."

"Hold it. Can't we fix some things here?"

Jimjoy snorted. "Terms of transfer were *immediate* removal. The Fuards don't want anyone to prove that they're supporting a revolution that just *happens* to keep Imperial Forces tied up half a quadrant away from the Empire/Fuard border systems."

Mera sighed. "Nothing—"

"I know. Nothing we get into is simple. We did get four ships, and they're better than I'd really hoped for. Even if it will take some work."

"How much work?"

"Depends. First on the checkout of the existing gear. After that, mostly on how much supercon line we need and whether you can round up enough and if we have someone who can change the converter logic without blowing the entire system."

"Me? You keep saying 'me,'" observed Mera, her voice rising slightly. "I'm not even officially even a graduate."

"You will be. Who else? Thelina says I can't do everything. I'll give you a written set of performance requirements, and you'll have to figure out how all four ships can meet them. In the meantime, you're going to learn how to pilot this on the way back. Now . . . up you go."

Mera gave herself a gentle shove with her suit boot and drifted up along the ladder and through the hatch.

Jimjoy followed, slowing at the opening between the decks, then pulling himself to a stop in order to crank the hatch closed.

"Three more to go. Then we'll have to crank out the course lines, jump points, and get the hades out of here." He headed for the main lock, not mentioning once again that he would feel happier, much happier, outside of Fuard-controlled space.

LIII

THE THIN BLOND-and-silver-haired Admiral looked at his younger counterpart. "Hewitt, are you telling me that we can't win against those eco-freaks no matter how much money you get?"

"No." The dark-haired Admiral smiled easily. "I'm saying N'Trosia can't afford to give me the funding, or the time, it will take."

"And you think Intelligence can persuade him otherwise?"

"Not necessarily. I just thought you ought to have a full understanding of the situation. I came across an interesting report, two or three years old, from one of your Special Operatives . . ."

"Yes?"

". . . on Accord. I thought you might have a continuing interest in
he situation." The younger Admiral smiled again, sitting comfortably
a the leather-padded armchair.

"I can't say that I recall that report."

"You probably have so many it's hard to keep track. This one was
y a Major Wright. I tried to track him down, but your office indicated
e was a casualty of his last assignment."

"Major Wright? Can't say the name rings a bell."

"That's odd. He was the one who handled the Halston HUMBLEPIE
peration. I would have thought—"

"Hewitt, what do you want, really?" The older Admiral counterfeited
sigh and leaned forward in his swivel.

"Me? There's nothing I could possibly ask for. No amount of re-
urces will really undo the damage in Sector Five. Most of that seems
) have been caused by some group at least as effective as your Special
peratives, I might note. I can't plan actions in areas that have no
apport or operating SysCons. Hades, I can't even recommend them as
good return.

"If the first report by Major Wright—I did mention that there were
vo that showed up in my files, didn't I?—if that first report is correct,
ose eco-nuts could create a great deal of ecological damage on Imperial
lanets."

The older Admiral nodded, still smiling. "I don't recall another re-
ort by a Major Wright, but supposing there were such a report, I'd
e interested in what it had to do with Fleet Development."

The younger Admiral shrugged. "As I was saying, the Senate can't
ommit adequate resources for Sector Five, no matter what. Sector Nine
another question—a purely military one, which is appropriate for
ilitary solutions."

"You don't think that the Accord example won't cause problems
aroughout the Empire? What about the Sligo revolt?"

"Sligo is in Sector Four. Those hard-rock types have always been
alcontents. If you want to make an example, do it there."

"You would support such an example?"

"Me? I'm just a very junior member of the staff command. I was
aly making an observation."

"And do you have any other observations, Hewitt?"

"I'd be very surprised if the late and unremembered Major Wright
as deceased as the files say."

"That's an odd observation."

"Perhaps. Leslie was the Comm Officer at Missou Base on New Kansaw. Call it slightly personal."

"I see. You'd question a complete dead body with a total DNA match?"

"Only where Accord is concerned, but there's really nothing that can be done there. Might as well leave the Rift alone. That might not have happened if the Service had better equipment, if we hadn't been forced to rely too much on Intelligence operations, if we could have built the FC or the CX—but I ramble too much. . . . It is too bad that the Honorable Chairman of the Galaxy's most prestigious Committee continues to try to run all aspects of military policy. One of these days, who knows, he might even start in on Intelligence operations, revealing another set of sordid details." The younger Admiral laughed. "It's so enjoyable testifying before him and that know-everything young staff of his. Just hope you never get that pleasure."

"You do have some interesting ideas, Hewitt. Have you thought about retiring and writing them down? It might be a fascinating exercise in fiction."

"Hardly. I have shared them with a few highly placed friends, but . . . what can I say? Our best bet would be if the Senator took up some hazardous sport like skim-gliding on Sierra, but he's far too devoted to his job. The only thing that would stop him would be a sudden stroke or an accident. Hardly likely these days, though it does happen."

The older Admiral nodded. "Interesting speculation, but you still haven't told me the reason for your visit."

"No real reason. I was over here and thought I'd stop in. Wondered if you had any thoughts on how we could concentrate on Sector Nine and our friends the Fuards. That's what we ought to be doing. Then they'd have to come to economic terms with the Matriarchy. If we'd done that to begin with, Accord wouldn't have dared . . . but I'm rambling again. What's done is done." He stood up slowly, as if requesting permission to depart.

"Well, Hewitt, you do have some intriguing thoughts, and someday you might think about writing them down."

"There's too much to do, right now . . ."

"That's true." The older Admiral stood. "I appreciate your stopping by. Give my best to the Chairman the next time you see him."

"Oh, I'll leave that to you. Our hearings are over, for a while anyway." He turned to go, then paused as if to add something, then stopped. He looked back. "Have a good evening."

"You, too."

LIV

JIMJOY TIGHTENED THE straps holding him into the control couch in the weightlessness of the Ecolitan-designed and Thalos-built needle-boat. He mentally reviewed the checklist, cataloging the items, occasionally stumbling at the not-quite-familiar order.

"You can start the checklist, Luren." He glanced over at his temporary copilot.

While the needleboat's overall design was an improvement, for the Institute's needs, on standard I.S.S. configurations, the new checklist took a little extra time for someone trained on the older design.

Luren did not have that problem, since she had been trained on the new Institute design.

Jimjoy watched as she began.

Her once-long curling brown hair had been trimmed nearly as short as Thelina's, and, according to Kerin Sommerlee, she had a near-natural aptitude for the martial arts and hand-to-hand. Her piloting skills were adequate, but not nearly so natural. Her determination was the compensating factor. Jimjoy had watched her spend her limited free time helping build the new boats with Jason and his team, as if by knowing every structural and engineering detail she could increase her skills.

Jimjoy pulled at his chin, glancing from the boards to the representational screens, still wishing he were doing the piloting.

"Converter . . . stand by . . ."

"Screens . . . up . . ."

Her motions were deliberate and practiced, not yet automatic.

Jimjoy's eyes surveyed the cabin, where no essential item was beyond the pilot's reach. The forward display screen showed mostly the black of space, sprinkled with the white scattered stars of the Arm, contrasting with the formless dark of the Rift. In the right-hand corner of the screen lurked an indistinct gray object, PAA #32, the asteroid his team had just finished converting into a two-person biohazard research/production station.

"Checklist complete, ser." Luren did not look at him, but continued to scan the controls and screens.

Jimjoy's fingers touched the small square of controls beneath his left hand. "VerComm, Jaymar two, departing Bold Harbor three this time."

With the time lag, he didn't expect an answer, but VerComm needed to know he was en route to the last station setup. Mera and Jason had already left with the big transport, the lasers, and the remaining fusactor.

Behind him would come the *Roosveldt*, trundling in the supplies and the equipment required by Drs. Stilsen and Narlian.

Jimjoy smiled as he recalled the meeting between the two.

"Stilsen, we don't need all that junk. This isn't research; it's war. We *know* what to produce. After we win, then you put in for all the goodies, when everyone's grateful—or, in our case, scared stiff." That was how Arlyn Narlian had attacked the cautious Dr. Stilsen.

He looked over at his copilot, still wondering if he should have switched the rotation. "It's all yours, Luren. Get us over to Bold Harbor four."

"Yes, ser."

He watched as her fingers flicked easily across the simplified board.

Waiting until the faint pressure pushed them back into the couches—this particular boat had yet to be fitted with grav-fields—he scanned the readouts on the board.

Then he triggered three studs. "Simulated emergency. Simulated emergency. Your decel is scheduled in three minutes."

Jimjoy had blocked the transfer of power from the converter to the drives.

Luren froze the board, then began to unstrap.

Jimjoy smiled. "What do you plan to do?"

"Unless an instructor freezes power, the only thing that will produce that blockage is either a converter malfunction or a short supercon line. There's no way to tell the difference without looking."

"Strap back in. How would you tell the difference?" Jimjoy unfroze the board. His actions had really been a trick to see if she would have tried to do *something*. Sometimes the best course was to do nothing, at least until you knew what to do. Luren had been right. Under the circumstances, she could have done nothing from the controls.

"I'd check the supercon line first, ser. Then the plug end from the converter . . ."

Jimjoy nodded. He still had another five requirements on which to test Luren.

"The board's open. Without any net increase in total power output or time of arrival, change our approach vector by at least ninety degrees. Don't hurry it. You have plenty of time." He kept his voice even, wishing in some ways he didn't have to double as check pilot, but he needed to know the new pilots' capabilities, and the Institute was short on top-flight pilots, even after co-opting off-duty time from the Accord line people, like Swersa and even Broward.

He leaned back, pretending to relax, wondering if he looked as much at ease as he tried to project, watching and hoping Luren would be able to figure it out. Then he could drop the next one on her.

He almost pulled at his chin. Instead he cleared his throat and glanced at the representational screen, glad that the only EDI traces on the system board belonged to Accord. How long that would last was another question.

LV

THE ADMIRAL FROWNED as he read through the report, still wondering how Graylin had come up with Major Wright. His head was beginning to throb again, and he reached for the glass of water, sliding out the small console drawer containing the capsules.

Water and capsules ingested, he turned back to the screen, again skimming through the information.

"Whaler, James Joyson, II . . . no known record outside of limited data bases prior to 3645 E.A. . . . Professor at Ecolitan Institute . . . applied ecologic management tactics . . . expert in field tactics . . . reported as besting system champion in hand-to-hand (open) . . . unexplained absences . . . reported as 'brilliant' instructor . . . inspires great loyalty . . ."

The Admiral rubbed his temples, then tried to massage out the tightness between his shoulders with his right hand before jumping to the last lines of the report.

". . . comparison between Wright, Jimjoy Earle, Major (Deceased) and Whaler, James Joyson, II . . . inconclusive. Physical parameters at limits of surgical alteration possibilities, even given assumptions of Accord biosurgery . . . psyprofile comparison indicates seventy-five percent congruency . . . equivalent to clone or identical twin raised in differing environment . . ."

He shook his head. What good would it do him, assuming he could spare the operatives, if Accord could clone the man again? Especially if he weren't even Wright? What if they had debriefed Wright, taken tissue samples, and cloned him—then murdered him on Timor II? With their technology . . .

He rubbed his temples again, hoping the capsules would take effect, waiting for the news bulletins.

LVI

JIMJOY WATCHED AS the suited junior Ecolitan realigned the drilling laser to follow the fracture line on the screen. Then Jimjoy shifted his study overhead, trying to pick out one of the needleboats orbiting the asteroid.

He'd gotten the idea from the reports on the way the Sligo miners had taken out Sligo SysCon. The concept was relatively simple, although the mathematics and the hardware for the remotes had proved beyond his pilot-oriented abilities. He would have turned to Jason again, but Jason was working too many hours trying to refurbish the destroyers and complete and upgrade the needleboats.

After several complaints, Meryl had finally drafted Orin Nussbaum, one of the senior specialists in mathematical constructs and analytics. Orin wouldn't dirty his hands with assemblies or with the tedious programming. So he instructed the brighter students, some of whom looked like they might learn enough for Orin to return to Harmony.

That would be fine with Jimjoy. Not a day passed when he was on Thalos that Orin didn't corner him. The food was boring. The maintenance staff preempted his latest modeling run with a power failure. The student Ecolitans were too interested in big yields instead of proper dispersion.

Even thinking about it, though Nussbaum was eighteen million kays away, started a faint throbbing in Jimjoy's temples. With Thelina somewhere unknown, he had enough to worry about. The thought of her still tackling another unnamed mission she hadn't even shared with Meryl twisted his guts whenever he let himself think about it. Damned near four tendays since he and the *Roosveldt* had "salvaged" the Fuard destroyers, and no one had heard from Thelina.

He moistened his lips, conscious of the sour smell of the suit, a smell that he was enduring more and more these days. The work grew faster than the trained hands. He took a deep breath.

"Professor, team one has the drive borehole complete. They want clearance to bring in the installation group."

"Stet. I'm on my way." He began to pick-bounce his way across the mostly nickel-iron asteroid—a little more than a kay in diameter, but located—for the next three standard years at least—along entry corridor two toward Accord.

"Jeryl, careful with the laser."

"Yes, Professor."

A greenish light blinked overhead, a periodic signal that the space tug was still standing by, waiting to bring in the simplified fusactor and drive unit.

"Professor, team two has an anomaly."

"Hold on the boring until after I check team one. Until I get there, split the remotes and take team one's over to their staging area."

"Stet."

In the center of a laser-melted circular space twenty meters across stood a laser boring rig and two suited figures, looking toward him.

"Meets all the specs, Professor. Five nines."

Jimjoy repressed a sigh and studied the readouts on the borer and on the tripod. The anchor holes for the drive unit met the five nines required, and the nickel iron underfoot was vapor-melted more than level enough for installation.

He nodded, then realized the motion was inconclusive within the suit. "Site one is ready for installation." He switched frequencies.

"Perch two, site one is ready for hardware. Triggering beacon this time."

"Perch two here. Understand site one is ready for hardware." Analitta's voice was crisp, cool.

"That's affirmative. Haylin standing by with anchors."

"Coming in this time."

"Stet."

Jimjoy turned toward the man in the yellowish suit, toggled back to the working frequency. "Haylin, you've got the anchors."

"Yes, ser."

"Just follow Ecolitan Derski's directions. And answer her questions, if she has any."

"Yes, ser. You're going to team two?"

Jimjoy bobbed his head. "Some problem there. You can still call me if you need me."

"Yes, ser."

Jimjoy turned back toward the other borehole, where he had left Jeryl. "Team three, interrogative status of borehole."

"Depth at point two five. Hardness within point zero zero five."

"Stet. En route team two this time. Report when you bottom out."

"Will do."

Jimjoy picked his way out of the depression where Haylin had pre-pared the site for drive installation and toward the other borehold, and where Mariabeth had reported an anomaly. Ahead, he could see the thin pole with a green pinlight, presumably still attached to the drilling laser.

"Team three?"

"Holding as requested."

Mariabeth, in another dirty yellow suit, was standing by the flat plastic screen connected to the laser unit.

"What's the problem?"

"Looks like some sort of drastic density change, ser. Drops off from the standard nickel-iron density . . ."

Jimjoy frowned. If the damned planetoid had an unbalanced core, the whole project was shot. The fragmentation had to follow a pro-grammable dispersion. Otherwise . . . He shook his head.

"Have you been able to determine how far that extends?"

"It's not too bad horizontally—not much more than five meters." She touched the display controls. "See . . . it's like a soft rock tube at an angle."

Jimjoy frowned again. It didn't look too bad, but . . . He glanced around and toggled the frequency shift. "Perch two, interrogative link with VerComm."

"That's affirmative."

"Tell Nussie that we're sending him a geology mass problem. Need a placement recalculation based on real-life geology. Somebody missed an interior spike. Should have a complete data profile within point five. And, Analitta, tell him this takes top priority of *his* time. No students. Him."

"Yes, ser."

Jimjoy switched back to common. "Mariabeth, you heard that?"

"Yes, ser."

He smiled. He thought she had switched frequencies with him. "You understand the data needs?"

"Yes, ser."

He touched her suit's shoulder. "Take care of it. Bring me a cube as soon as you can. I'll be on Perch two, trying to calculate what borehole latitude we have in terms of the physical limits and geology."

He took another deep breath and began to pick his way back to where the tug was approaching to off-load the fusactor and drives. Trying to develop smart and destructive rocks could be frustrating as hades, between Orin Nussbaum and unscanned geology.

LVII

THE SUITED FIGURE rechecked the laser rig, the anchors, and the readouts on the condensers. Purity still well above ninety percent.

EEEEEEEEEEEEEEEEEEEeeeeeeeeeeeeeeeeeeeeeeeee . . .

The scream of white noise from the helmet receivers stunned her, and she had to jerk her chin twice to toggle the volume off. Her hand grasped one of the anchor struts as she stood on the asteroid surface, wobbling and shivering from the intensity of the sound.

Finally, she shook her head, and with careful quick steps headed back toward the tug, scanning the star-studded sky. Overhead, she could see Ballarney, the gas giant, like a dull red ball the apparent size of her gloved fist.

Nothing in the Belt skies seemed different. She shook her head again, then concentrated on reaching her tug.

Once inside the *Jeralee*, the thin miner only cracked her helmet before moving forward and slumping into the tug's control couch. She flicked the board activation stud and watched as the three functioning screens lit up.

Her left hand, the one that would have showed a map of scars and welts had it not remained gloved, clenched and unclenched as she waited for the old equipment to come on-line.

Clung.

Her gloved fingertips carefully punched out a query.

Hmmmmmmmmmmmm.

Again she waited.

Her eyes widened as she took in the EDI indications on the representational screen, mouthing the numbers. ". . . thirteen, fourteen, fifteen, sixteen of the mothers . . ."

As she watched, the old system laboriously scripted the parameters.

"EDI traces match Imperial warship configurations. Three cruisers, twelve corvettes, three scouts. EDI shifts indicate course for Sligo."

"Hades!" She pursed her lips.

Finally, she tapped the comm stud.

"All Belters! All Belters! Impie fleet en route Sligo. Impie fleet en route Sligo. Pass the word."

She slapped off the comm stud, not really wanting to be the target of an Impie homing torp, shaking her head again.

Then she sighed and closed the helmet, preparing to head back out to shut down the equipment. Sligo wouldn't be needing the metal, and she would need every erg of power she had. It would have to last for a long time. A very long time.

LVIII

JIMJOY REACHED FOR the door to the closet that served as his stateroom/sleep quarters when he was on Thalos. The gray plastic door set in gray rock, opening from a gray rock tunnel, depressed him. At least it did at those times when he wasn't too exhausted to care.

The corridor was empty, not surprising in midmorning, but the asteroid reconfiguration work didn't exactly require rigid adherence to a planetside schedule.

He opened the door slowly and stepped through, loosening the helmet from the shoulder straps as he did so and setting it on the shelf, also carved from the rock. Then came the suit gauntlets. Finally, he began to strip off the armored maintenance suit, all too aware of how rank he smelled, even to himself.

Only the faint hiss of the station ventilators and the muted clicking of the suit connectors broke the silence.

Glancing over at the narrow bunk, Jimjoy noticed a white oblong on the green blanket. His eyes widened and his hands dropped from the suit connectors. In two quick steps he had the envelope in hand.

"James Joyson Whaler II," read the scripted black ink.

A sigh of relief escaped him. He'd tried to avoid thinking about where she had been and what she had been doing. He shook his head and pushed the thoughts away, concentrating instead on the envelope.

Jimjoy smiled wryly, knowing the handwriting had to be Thelina's, although he had only seen the crisp note she had left him in the hospital—the one suggesting he had better hades-fired become a decent ecologic scholar if he intended to join the Institute. His fingers seemed to fumble over themselves as he eased open the lightly sealed flap of the faintly greenish linen envelope.

A second envelope rested inside the first with the single name "Jimjoy" written upon it. From the unsealed inside envelope he eased out the formal card.

The honor of your presence is requested at an indoor luncheon for two at 1315 H.S.T. on the fourteenth of Sixtus at the look-in on Thalos Station (Alpha Three-D). Refreshments will be provided. Suitable attire is suggested.

Thelina Xtara Andruz
S.F.I.

As he read the card, then reread it, his smile grew broader.

After a moment he frowned, letting his hand with the card drop. Why now? The time to have replied to his formal luncheon invitation would have been months earlier, before they had become so intimate. Was she trying to tell him something?

He pursed his lips, then lifted the card again, rereading each word, finding nothing beyond the words themselves.

Finally he set it on the shelf, propped up by both envelopes, and continued to unsuit. He glanced at his wrist. Only 1043 H.S.T. That gave him time to get ready and still dash off the fax message for Jorje that he had promised himself he would send.

As for Thelina . . . he was glad he had taken care of a few advance preparations of his own.

Still . . . He pulled at his chin momentarily before racking the heavy suit on the wall brackets.

LIX

ALPHA THREE DELTA, on the station's top level, was the end of the Ecolitan station farthest from the tactics/manufacturing section added by Jimjoy's team.

Jimjoy checked the time. 1313 H.S.T. Thelina had not kept him waiting, but had arrived on the minute, and he intended to return the favor. In his pocket rested the package he had brought from Harmony for her.

As he turned into the number-three corridor, he passed through a simulated wooden archway. His eyebrows lifted. Underfoot, the laser-melted stone was covered with green carpet. Thin synthetic carpet, but carpet nonetheless.

The doorway to three delta was not the standard old-fashioned doorway, but a modern, heavy portal. Jimjoy frowned as he touched the entry stud.

Cling. The soft chime rang in the empty corridor.

Jimjoy glanced around, but the corridor remained empty. After the portal irised open, he stepped through into a small wood-paneled foyer. On the right was a small wooden table, on which rested a simple green porcelain dish. Above the table was a half-meter-square wall-hung mirror framed in dark wood. Directly before him was a solid wood doorway—closed.

He fingered the small black wooden box in his belt pouch again, then stepped up to the doorway. He turned the solid bronze lever and pushed. The door opened silently. As he stepped onto the heavy dark green and plush carpet, Jimjoy swallowed.

Overhead, through a clear crystal dome covering the entire ceiling, swam the dayside of Permana. Above the planet sparked the lights of two thousand Arm stars. The combined luminescence filled the room with a summer-evening twilight. Below the planet simmered the darkness of the Rift.

By the single table in the center of the room stood Thelina, wearing a single-piece dark green silken jumpsuit with a V neck. A silver chain glinted on the bronzed skin below her neck. She had let her hair grow, long enough to be swept back with combs that matched the dress and to impart a softly regal appearance to her face.

A single white candle burned in the center of the table, which was covered with pale linen and set with silver, crystal, and china.

In his clean working greens, the most formal clothing he had on station, Jimjoy felt pedestrian—extraordinarily pedestrian.

After easing the door closed behind him, he inclined his head to Thelina. "You look . . ." He shook his head. "It's . . . hades, I missed you . . ." The words seemed to catch in his throat. He wanted to hold her tight, to crush her against him—to shake her for going off where she might have gotten killed without saying a word. Instead, he just stood there, looking at her in the starlight under the crystal dome, watching the woman who looked like an ancient goddess of the night.

"I'm glad you could make it, Professor." Her voice was light, not sarcastic but not romantic, either.

He swallowed, glad he wasn't close enough for her to see how hard it was for him, and nodded again. His eyes burned momentarily. It was as if she wanted to go back to when he had started courting her. Didn't she know how much he cared? Or did she care? He swallowed again. "The timing . . . was a bit close, and I am afraid . . . I did not have the most appropriate attire. This . . ." He gestured down at his working greens. ". . . was the best available."

"I had wanted to respond to your luncheon invitation in kind, but we never seemed to have the time on Accord. I'm sorry you had so little notice, but I wanted to surprise you."

He took another slow and deep breath before stepping toward her and the candlelit table. "You certainly did. No idea you were here . . . or that this . . . was here." Up close, she looked even more stunning, despite the darkness under her eyes.

"Would you like a seat, Professor?"

Jimjoy sighed softly. "Thank you." He took the seat and watched as Thelina slipped into the chair across from him.

"I'm not about to try to match your abilities with cuisine. Instead, I sought a little help. I hope you don't mind."

"No. Though you overestimate my abilities." He glanced around the space, easily the size of a conference room.

"Yes. It's normally a conference room for the station commander, but Imri let me borrow it."

With the starlight and the candle, Jimjoy found it hard to remember that it was midday, not evening. "Hard to remember that it's lunch." He glanced up at the silvery bulk of Permana.

"It could be evening, if you wish."

He finally was able to smile. "Suppose I do."

"Would you like some Hspall? Or something else?"

"Hspall is a little strong. I've been mostly awake for the past day and a half. Water until I have something to eat. What about you?"

"Two of us, then." Her hand reached for the crystal.

He lifted his glass to hers. "To your return, lady."

"To your efforts, Professor."

Clink. As they sipped, Jimjoy watched Thelina's face, noting for the first time the exhaustion in her eyes, the tension still in her body posture, as if she were for some reason on guard against him.

A doorway to Jimjoy's left opened, and a woman entered, carrying two plates.

"Salad," observed Thelina.

"Salud, perhaps?"

Thelina frowned.

"Sorry. Ancient pun, meaning greetings, health, something like that." He paused. "When did you get back?"

"Ten stans ago. With the *Vruss*—Halstani independent. I used your shuttle service from orbit control." She put down the glass, let both hands rest in her lap.

"Do they know who you are? Or were? The Halstanis?"

"They know who I am. I doubt they know who I was. That person is officially dead, like a certain Imperial Major. But you never know."

"Must have been quite a strain on you."

"How are the destroyers?"

"From what we can see, two of them can be beefed up almost to light cruisers. Jason thinks the Fuards don't really understand ship interconnectivity. The ships could make the difference."

"Will anything? Honestly?" Her voice was flat.

Jimjoy shrugged. "Thought this was supposed to be a relaxing time."

"Sorry. I'll try."

"Thelina . . . you don't have to force anything, or try anything . . ."

A faint smile crossed her lips. "Remind me of that in—say—five years."

Not catching the implications he knew were there, Jimjoy smiled in return, faintly. "We've diverted most of the needleboat crews to get all four back in shape. How did you manage it?"

"Negotiating was the easy part." Thelina took a bite of the salad. "Setting up the negotiations wasn't."

Jimjoy lifted his fork and speared a section of the crisp, almost purplish greenery.

Crunnchhh . . .

"It's priolet, very crunchy," noted Thelina with a smile. "It's also tart, but that should make it more appealing to you."

Ignoring the innuendo, he managed to swallow the first chunk of tangy greenery without further sounds like a rock-crusher, but used his knife to cut the remaining salad into smaller bits, following Thelina's example.

"How do you like it?"

"Taste is good, but it makes me feel like mining machinery. Who eats this? Hard-rock miners?"

"No. It's a delicacy in Parundia. Originally came from Cansab. No miner could possibly afford it."

Jimjoy pulled at his chin, then took another bite. The second tasted better than the first. "It does grow on you," he admitted.

"That's appropriate." For the first time, her voice held a touch of music.

He smiled, sneaking another glance at her as he finished off the salad, and realizing exactly how hungry he had been.

Thelina set her fork aside without quite finishing the salad, tilting her head to the side almost quizzically. She said nothing.

For a time neither did Jimjoy; he studied her face and tried not to look below the necklace that glittered on her skin. Something about the lunch . . . he couldn't quite finger it. He took a sip from the goblet instead, noting absently the seal of the Institute etched into the crystal. "Are you all right?"

Thelina shrugged. "It's always a strain, and I worry about what I'm going back to."

"Meryl and Kerin seem to have things pretty well in hand."

"I talked to Meryl on the tight-beam a while ago." She smiled again. "She said the same thing about you."

Jimjoy pulled at his chin, then sipped from the goblet. "I've managed, with a lot of help."

"Meryl said you were working on something new—called sharp stones?"

Jimjoy laughed. "Another pun. I got the idea from reading the Sligo reports."

Thelina shook her head. "Poor people. I suppose that is our fault."

"They've been looking for a reason to hit the Empire for years. They finally did, and that gave the Impies an easy way out." He took another sip from the glass. "In another four or five days we have to meet on that at the Institute, Meryl says. Figure out how to brief all the new delegates and Council members."

"Has the Empire made any demands?"

Jimjoy shook his head. "Just a general announcement regretting the necessity, but reminding all the colonies that the great and mighty Empire does indeed collect its debts—one way or another. Not phrased that bluntly."

"Of course. Let's talk about something else."

"All right. The view is lovely, and the stars are spectacular, though not as spectacular as you."

"That sounds a bit too practiced . . ."

"You've caught me out again, dear lady." He gave an exaggerated shrug. "What can I say?"

The woman who acted as the waitress appeared and removed the salad plates, returning immediately with two dinner plates.

Jimjoy did not recognize the entrée, except that it appeared to be some sort of fish, garnished with fruit. He glanced at Thelina.

"Go ahead." She laughed. "With your connoisseur's palate, you should like it."

"I might," he acknowledged, taking a small morsel of the fish that appeared almond-colored in the light from the stars and the solitary candle.

Thelina followed his example.

The taste was a lemon-electric shock, tempered with plum fire.

"Ansellin . . ." he murmured after savoring that single morsel. He looked at Thelina. "How . . ." The two fish on the table represented as much credit as . . .

"Don't worry. They were a gift from the past."

Jimjoy wondered who would make that kind of gift, either so casually or from such deep feeling. He put down his fork, his stomach suddenly churning, the corners of his eyes threatening to burn again.

Rather than look at Thelina, he studied the ansellin in the dim light, noting the uniform texture, the even color. In time he took another sip of water from the nearly empty goblet.

"Your family was from Anarra?"

Thelina nodded.

Jimjoy shivered. Anarra—most fanatical of the stronghold planets of the Matriarchy. Anarra—whose Eastern Sea was the sole provider of ansellin. Anarra—founding chapter of the Hands of the Mother. He shivered again.

"Don't you like it?"

Jimjoy wanted to let go of the tears he held in. Instead, he raised

his eyes to the shadowed face across the table from him. "It's . . . Thelina, there aren't any words . . . never taste anything like it again."

"I doubt either one of us will."

Silently, Jimjoy took another morsel, trying to savor the lemon-
electric tingle basted with plum fire, wondering again at the prices she
had paid, wondering how he could ever have thought he had suffered.

Wordlessly, he put down the fork.

"You don't like it?"

He said nothing, afraid his voice would break, his fingers twisting
around the bottom of the crystal goblet as he swallowed nothing, and
swallowed again.

"The price . . . perhaps too high . . . too rich . . ."

Thelina's lips pursed, tightly. "It wasn't that kind of gift, Professor."

"I knew that, Thelina. That just made the price a whole lot higher."

Her lips relaxed, but her eyes never left his. "How would you know?"

He swallowed, concentrating on the technical reasons. "Spent some time
in the Institute archives. Trying to find out more about the culture and
background of a lady. In addition to everything else, ran across something
called *The Anarra Complex*. Very detailed . . ." He took a deep breath.

This time, Thelina's eyes rested on her plate.

Jimjoy used the silence to regain his composure, trying not to think
beyond the moment.

"Do you think it's accurate?"

"The tone was so understated, so clinical, so dispassionate. Yes, I'd
say it was probably a living hades for anyone with sensitivity and intelligence." Like you, he wanted to add.

"You can't love someone because you pity them."

"Someone told me I had to get to know them, and that I couldn't
possibly love without knowing them. I've tried, even when you haven't
been around."

"You've shown more overt emotions, compassion, sympathy, understanding, even tears, in the last stan than the universe has seen for you
in thirty-odd years. I do love you, in spite of myself, but please pardon
me if I'm just a little skeptical of this gush of emotionalism."

Jimjoy shrugged. "Can't say I blame you. Can't even say I understand
it myself." He used the linen napkin to blot his forehead, catching the
remnants of his own tears under that cover. "All I know is that you've
turned everything upside down. Until I saw you tonight—this afternoon, I mean—I didn't even realize it. Not fully," he amended, thinking of the black wooden box.

Thelina arched her eyebrows. "Do you want to explain?"

"No. I can't explain. In between each project, on each solo flight, before I collapse every night, I've been going over what's happened . . . I've wanted you, for you, not for Dr. Hyrsa's artistry, since the first time we talked in the formal garden more than two years ago. Yes, I know. You were only doing your duty. But I think I've just about reordered a section of the Galaxy because of you. Hades, neither Helen nor Jaqlin nor Terrisa had anything on you . . ."

"For me . . . you committed mass murders, insurrection, and plot genocide and rebellion? What an incredibly touching thought."

He shook his head, aware his thinking was muddy and his common sense nonexistent. "That's not what I meant. You know that." He finally eased out the black wooden box and slid it across the table. "Lost the words. Maybe this will say it better."

She looked at the box, then at him. "You should take it back. I'm not what you think."

"Neither am I. But it's yours. It couldn't be anyone else's." He lowered his ragged voice. "Go ahead. Open it."

She fumbled with the catch, then eased open the carved cover, looking with frozen eyes at the twin green diamonds of the ring.

Jimjoy waited.

"Do you expect me to fall into your arms in abject gratitude, longing for you after days of deprivation from your masculine charms?"

Jimjoy sighed, not looking away from her. "No. I expect that you will take your physically, spiritually, and intellectually exhausted body and mind and collapse somewhere and get some well-deserved rest. I intend to do the same. Then, say in about twenty-four stans from now, I hope you'll think about what I said, and why I gave you the ring." He looked across at the open box still sitting before Thelina. "Not an hour goes by that I don't think about you. Does that mean I love you? That I'll always love you?" He shrugged. "I don't know. I think I know. But you could be right. Perhaps all I want is your body, and the rest doesn't count. I don't think so."

He met her eyes, ignoring the tears seeping from his own. "Until tonight—this afternoon, whatever it is—I didn't understand. Maybe I still don't. Now . . . I know, I think. Call the ring a courtship ring, an engagement ring, a promise that I'll do my best never to stop courting you. How can I say I may have lost you by loving you too hard too soon . . ." He shook his head, finally standing up, ignoring the light-headedness that threatened his balance.

"You need me to love you without always physically wanting you. Until I saw you tonight—now, this afternoon, I mean—I didn't understand. For me, the two have always gone hand in hand. Right now they can't, not if I want a future with you. It's hard . . . hades-fired hard."

He reached down and across, squeezing her hand, then releasing it. "Thank you . . . for sharing, for telling me before it was too late . . . and for giving me another chance to love you." Jimjoy straightened up. "Will I see you tomorrow? Or do you have to leave immediately?"

"Tomorrow." Her voice was a whisper.

He did not look back, but concentrated on putting one foot in front of the other as he made his way off Alpha three delta and back toward the much ruder, unfinished rock walls of the tactics section of Thalos Station.

LX

NEW AUGUSTA [14 SIXTUS 3647] Seven black atmospheric fighters thundered over the Capitol. An honor guard of the Imperial Space Force stood watch as a black casket passed into the shuttle.

The shuttle lifted on the first stage of its mission to consign Emile Enrico N'Trosia to the flames of Sol, to the heart of the Empire he served, first as an Imperial officer, then as a Senator, and finally as Chairman of the Senate Defense Committee.

N'Trosia, always a partisan of an efficient military, was combative to the end, fighting off the effects of multiple brain aneurysms for weeks.

The Emperor proclaimed a day of official mourning. . . .

—*FaxStellar News*

LXI

THRAP! THRAP!

Jimjoy rolled over, then automatically found himself on his feet. He stared from a half crouch at the back of the gray plastic door, shaking his head mainly to clear the remnants of an unpleasant dream sequence in which Thelina rode a blue skimmer toward a thunderspout . . .

"Yes . . ." he croaked.

"May I come in?" asked Thelina from outside.

"Hold on." He grabbed for a thin robe he had never worn. Together with the shorts he slept in, the robe could help him pretend to be decent.

Despite his plea, the door opened about the moment he had stuffed his arms into the robe's sleeves.

Thelina, wearing a green shipsuit and carrying a small kit bag, eased the door shut and set down the bag. "Sleeping late, I see."

He rubbed his eyes. "Didn't get to sleep very early, or for very long. How about you?"

She rubbed her arm. "Imri didn't give me much choice. She said one of us two idiots needed the rest."

Jimjoy looked at her, not really knowing what to say, feeling grimy and disoriented.

She edged closer. "I'm sorry."

"For what? You were right. You've always been right."

"Not always. Not last night—or yesterday afternoon."

He wanted to hold her, but stood there, waiting, afraid to reach for her.

"I have to go, but . . . not like yesterday." She looked down. Finally, her green eyes met his. "Would you hold me? Just hold me?"

He nodded, his arms going around her as she stepped into them.

As he held her, she began to cry, softly, as if she refused to acknowledge it. His arms tightened around her, just a touch. At the same time, his composure dissolved with hers, though he did not shudder, but let his tears flow, knowing, this time at least, they were shared.

In time she cleared her throat. "I have to catch the shuttle."

"I know." He let go, let her step back.

"Jimjoy . . . it's hard for me, too . . . but don't stop . . ."

"Don't think I could." He swallowed.

She looked deliberately down at her left hand.

His eyes followed hers.

"It's beautiful. You designed it?"

He nodded.

Her hands brushed his cheeks before their lips touched.

"I do have to go."

"I know."

"I'm still scared . . . and it's not fair . . . but I am. I can't help it. Please keep understanding."

Jimjoy swallowed and drew her to him, trying to hold her tightly enough to reassure her, not tightly enough for their closeness to lead beyond reassurance, yet being all too aware of how little clothing lay between them.

"You have to go . . ." His voice was husky.

"Yes . . . oh, I really do . . ."

He shook his head as she grabbed for the kit bag, then almost smiled as she bestowed a quick kiss on him and opened the door. "Let me know when . . ."

"Next tenday . . . the delegates . . ."

He watched, a bemused look on his face, from halfway out his door as Thelina ran down the corridor toward a shuttle that would certainly have waited for her.

LXII

20 Sept 3647
Somewhere

Dear Blaine:

You were right about the impact on us. As you can see, I'm not at Lansdale, and who knows when I'll see Helen or the kids next. We're on what amounts to a permanent rotation, trying to guess about Tinhorn's next probe.

Will it do any good? Beats me. I'm just a skipper trying to keep the plates together. The Sligo mission froze a lot of my crew. Lucky I didn't have anyone with family there. Suppose it was necessary. After all, whoever it was did destroy a SysCon and a good thousand innocent individuals. Whether busting Sligo and the three million people on it will deter a system like Accord is another question. Those eco-freaks are nuts. You even said so.

Rumor mill—once again, the rumors are in advance of the official notifications—says that Accord has racked up more than twenty I.S.S. ships to date, not to mention three SysCons. No wonder we're stretched thin out here. There's another rumor that—somehow—the ecotypes managed to "salvage" a bunch of "obsolete" Fuard destroyers.

Hades! Bet those obsolete S.D.s pack twice the power of the *Halley*. And if Accord's as inventive as the rumors say, that spells big trouble in Sector Five. Not sure I wouldn't rather be facing the Fuards. At least, it's only rat and dragon, not declared war. So far.

Helen and the kids went to Sierra—officially home leave. But I feel better about that, especially after . . . anyway . . . See what you can do to get us *something*.

Mort

LXIII

JIMJOY LOOKED AT the flat card, reading again what he had written.

> You have brought me light
> so bright that the sun dims,
> so true that the shadows of my past
> vanish into forgotten nightmares.
>
> You have brought me love,
> a flame so hot that suns retreat
> from its intensity,
> and so dangerous that death
> will not limit you.
>
> Most of all, you have given me
> back to myself, and I would do
> the same for you,
> in loving you.

The calligraphy was good, but he wished the words were better. The three words which summed up his feelings had been so overused for so long they would have been meaningless. He pulled at his chin and slipped the card into the envelope bearing her name.

He was due at the meeting to discuss what the Institute should say to the recently elected delegates and Council members. His recommendation was likely to be too blunt to be accepted. Shrugging, he pocketed the envelope and stepped out the doorway into the early winter drizzle.

Glancing uphill and to the left, toward the other complex where Thelina and Meryl lived, he descended from the front deck slowly, deliberately. No one else moved in the morning chill. After clicking up the collar of his foul-weather jacket, he turned his steps toward the Administration building.

What else could he say to Thelina? What else could he do? A romantic he was not, nor was he someone who gloried in the company of people. He moistened his lips and took a deep breath, smiling faintly at the cloud of steam he exhaled.

As he reached the crest of the path, the one spot from where he could see both his quarters and the main Institute complex, he looked back again through the shifting drizzle. No one was out around the quarters complex.

Ahead, a scattering of student Ecolitans, all in forest-green foul-weather jackets, followed the walkways between the buildings. For all the crises, the normal life of the Institute continued for most.

"Good morning, Professor."

"Good morning," he responded to the youngster who dashed past him toward the teaching labs.

His steps carried him past the history/philosophy/tactics classrooms.

"Professor Whaler?"

He stopped, not recognizing the student, dark-haired, thin, male. "Yes." His voice was casual.

"Ser. . . . is there any possibility you will be teaching the theories course next term?"

Jimjoy shrugged. "I don't know. I probably won't teach that course until next fall, but that's . . . still up in the air."

"Oh. Really wanted to take it . . ."

"Professor Mardian is quite good, and he'll be handling it if I don't."

"He is good, but I've already had him for the basics course . . ."

Jimjoy smiled at the student. "I'd like to, but there are a few other . . . commitments."

"Were you really an Imperial agent, ser?"

Jimjoy forced a laugh. "Don't believe everything you hear."

The student looked away, almost as if embarrassed.

"Son, let's put it another way. If I had once been an Imperial agent, I'd probably be embarrassed about it and wouldn't want to talk about it. If I hadn't been one, I'd also have to deny it. And if I had been an agent for another government, I certainly wouldn't volunteer that. More important, what's past is past. You can't deny what you are or what you've done, but you don't have to be bound by it, either. What I do now is what's important."

"You believe that." It was a flat statement, almost unbelieving.

Jimjoy laughed softly. "Most of the time, at least."

"Thanks, Professor."

Jimjoy wiped the drizzle off his forehead and away from his eyes as he watched the youngster dash off. He nodded absently to several more students as he made his way to the Administration building.

Once inside the main doors, he shook his coat and tried to get most of the moisture out of his hair. He took the inside working stairs to the second floor, which allowed him to reach Thelina's office without passing by the main conference room across from the Prime's office.

Thelina's door was ajar. He stopped, listened. Silence.

He stepped up to the door, rapped softly, and slipped inside. As he had thought, the office was empty. In a quick motion, he took out the envelope and placed it on her chair. As he straightened up, a brownish-tinged and ragged-edged paper half under another sheet caught his eye. The paper shade screamed of out system origin.

The covering sheet was a brief notice of schedule changes, signed by Meryl. Scrawled across the upper left-hand corner were the words. "Thel—see any problem here? M."

Jimjoy glanced back at the door, feeling guilty, and eased the second sheet out from underneath. His eyes flicked through the fax copy, picking out the key phrases quickly.

"[Anarra, 20 Julia 3647] . . . untimely death of Matriarch K'trina Veluz . . . poisoned ansellin . . . traditional Bremudoes method of assassination . . . likely to shift foreign policy . . . successor in State Counselate . . . K'rin Forsos . . . considered a pragmatist . . ."

He slipped the copy back in place, replacing the covering sheet. No wonder orchestrating the diplomatic relations with Halston had been a strain on Thelina. He wondered what other extremes had been required.

Poisoned ansellin. He couldn't repress a shudder, thinking about their starlit luncheon/dinner.

Clunk. Through the half-open doorway he heard the conference room door close.

He eased out from behind the desk and from Thelina's office. The corridor was vacant, except for a figure walking along at the far end of the building. Jimjoy replaced the door in the ajar position in which he had found it, then turned and headed down the hall.

He could hear voices, some of them already heated, from ten meters away through the closed doors.

LXIV

"IT'S THE BEGINNING of the end," said Sergel Firion sadly.

"Now that they've decided to break up planets, why even bother with this nonsense of telling our brand-new politicians that everything will be fine?"

Jimjoy frowned, pulling at his chin. After nearly a standard hour, no one had come up with an outline of the stand to take in briefing the new members of the reconstituted System Council, which replaced the old Planetary Council. Now Sergel was preaching doom and gloom. Jimjoy wondered if the entire leadership of the philosophy department had been owned by the I.S.S.

Meryl shifted her gaze from the head of the philosophy department to the former Special Operative. Thelina looked at Meryl, then back to Jimjoy.

The silence in the Prime's office dragged out.

Jimjoy glanced through the open door at the recently completed portrait of old Sam Hall, then back at Sergel. "No," he finally said slowly. "I'd say that we've won. Believing we've lost is exactly what the Empire hopes."

Sergel caught the eyes of Marlen Smyther, serving as his personal advisor.

Marlen straightened and cleared her throat before she began to speak. "This former . . . military officer . . . he claims that the loss of our strongest ally . . . the destruction of the entire planet of Sligo . . . constitutes a victory. Would you care to define a loss, ser?"

Sergel nodded.

Jimjoy looked from the almost smiling Marlen to the pensive Sergel. "A loss, sher," replied Jimjoy, refusing to give either Ecolitan any title, "would be surrendering when victory is possible."

Even Meryl looked puzzled. "Would you explain that in more detail?" Her tone was neutral.

Jimjoy shrugged. "Seems simple enough. They couldn't persuade Sligo to stay within the Empire. They didn't have the ability or the resources to attempt a conquest. So they had to destroy it. The Empire hopes that we'll give up, because they can't rule us. All they can do is destroy."

He looked around the room. What was so painfully obvious to him was clearly not obvious to anyone else—except Thelina, on whose face discomfort warred with amusement. "Let me try again. The Empire needs control. It needs the resources of other planets. The ecology of Old Earth has never fully recovered from the ecollapse, and Alphane cannot shoulder that burden alone, particularly with the population growth that it is experiencing now. Any prolonged conquest effort requires *more* resources, not less. The Empire doesn't have those resources, not to deal with more than a handful of planets. Someone in the High Command has obviously realized that and wants to send a message before anyone else realizes the Empire's vulnerabilities."

"You can't be serious . . ."

"Truly insane, Whaler . . . truly insane . . ."

The voices were low enough not to be easily identifiable, but Jimjoy marked the insanity comment as coming from Sergel. He shrugged again and stood, looking from one face to another.

"You asked for my opinion. It's just that—an opinion. However, I'm not the one who destroyed an entire planet. No one does that lightly. So why did the Empire do that, with all their fleets and Imperial Marines? It has to be an admission of weakness. They just told the Galaxy that there was no way they could reclaim Sligo and its resources.

"Either that, or the Empire is so rich and so powerful that an entire planet full of human life means nothing. Take your pick. The result's the same."

"I think I see what you mean." The speaker was Kerin Sommerlee. "Either we can win, or we can't live under that kind of Empire."

"Isn't that a rather presumptive conclusion?" Sergel's voice was pensive.

Jimjoy decided to ignore him, head of the philosophy department or not. At times like this, he wished the Institute would get its act together and agree on a permanent replacement for Sam Hall. So far everyone just seemed happy to accept the compromise he had suggested, with Meryl in effect running the Institute's day-to-day operations. "Either way, we have to fight, and we can. We can show that the Empire is both callous and weak and that we know it. Second, we can point out the obvious to the Halstanis and the Fuards—and then show we have the ability to destroy the ecology of both Old Earth and Alphane. If the Empire can't support its core population and can't conquer anyone else . . ."

"Absolutely insane . . . absolutely . . ."

"We're not savages . . ."

"They'd just destroy Accord . . . and then where would we be?"

Jimjoy waited for the exclamations to die down.

Then he sighed once. Loudly.

"Let's get this straight. First, you don't have any choice. Because we've already been identified as stirring up this secession movement, everyone in this room is dead if we don't win. So is most of Accord. We attack, or we die. That's your choice. Second, if you think things will get easier for those you leave behind if you do choose surrender . . . forget it. The Empire won't take assurances, but blood. Does anyone remember what happened on New Kansaw?"

He scanned the room. Thelina had shaken her head minutely at the New Kansaw reference. Most of the others were looking at the floor.

"So far, by destroying the key system control stations, by planting ideas and rumors, by indirect action, we've managed to avoid an obvious and direct response from the Empire. By obtaining diplomatic recognition, we've managed to retain some trade and obtain critical technology. Sligo was not known for subtlety, and they took a confrontational stance before they were ready to back it. They were also practically next door to the Fleet headquarters.

"That made it easy for the Service to send a message without over-extending itself. Accord would be different, and don't think the Empire doesn't know it. What they're trying to do is to isolate us through force and fear, and if we play dead and let everyone else do it, we *are* dead."

"That's fine in theory, Mr. Ecolitan Whaler," noted Marlen, "but we don't exactly have a fleet to put up against the Empire."

"We do have a fleet. We have the equivalent of one small fleet, or two without capital ships. That's more than most independents—not Halston, Tinhorn, New Avalon, of course. But we don't need more than one fleet. We need applied knowledge, applied psychology, and some applied mayhem and leverage. And some unique weapons. We have all that. All we need to do is apply it."

"And you think the Empire will stand aside and give us that time?"

"That's about all they'll give us. They're still hoping we'll capitulate. If they made another move right now, with both Halston and the Fuards as jumpy as they are . . . it's too great a risk, especially as far out as we are. Their fleets could be blocked near the Rift."

"So . . . they will be spending the next few tendays getting ready to move against us . . . and you're proposing we do the same?" asked Sergel.

"We don't have a choice. We have some time. They won't expect an immediate reaction to Sligo, and they'll give us time to think about it. And we should make noises about thinking about it."

"But what can we do, really do?" asked Kerin Sommerlee.

"Spread the faith . . . spread the ecological faith to new converts . . . while working like hades to stop the one fleet they might think about throwing at us."

"The one fleet?" prompted Meryl.

"No one will admit it publicly, but they can't back down without some sort of armed confrontation. Otherwise everyone will be trying to rebel. Whatever the cost, we have to destroy that one fleet totally. If we do, then the Fuards will try to gobble up something like the three-system bulge, and the Halstanis will pressure the independents into changing their high-tech and info trade patterns." Jimjoy shrugged. "At that point, as far out on the Arm as we are, Accord suddenly becomes either ignored or a potential ally."

"Ally? You've got to be crazy."

"I said potential. We still have more in common with the Empire than the Fuards do, and the Empire needs a peaceful border with us to address them."

Thelina nodded with a faint smile.

Tap, tap . . .

Meryl applied a wooden gavel, bringing the mutters around the room to low whispers or outright silence. "We still need to agree on exactly what to tell the new delegates and Council members."

Thelina stood up. "If Professor Whaler is correct, and so far at least his analyses have been more accurate than those of, say, the philosophy department, then we have very little to say. We provide them with the outline just employed by Professor Whaler. If we can beat back the Empire, we gain great credit. If we don't, no one will be alive to care about it."

The silence became absolute.

"Any questions?" asked Meryl softly. "Then the suggestion as proposed is adopted as Institute policy, and the meeting is closed."

Jimjoy almost smiled as he caught the brief eye exchange between Thelina and Meryl, but he kept his face impassive.

". . . can't believe it . . ." muttered Marlen as she and Sergel left.

". . . impressive . . ." murmured another voice Jimjoy could not identify.

Meryl motioned to Jimjoy.

He made his way slowly to where she stood by the Prime's desk. "Yes?"

"You're clearly elected to brief them. I've already scheduled it for tomorrow morning. Do you have any problem with that?"

"Same place as before?"

"Yes. The main Council chamber."

He shrugged. "Why me?"

"Who else will they believe? You told them there would be free elections, and there were. You can tell them about sweat, toil, and tears—or whatever you chose to call the coming disaster . . ."

"Tomorrow's fine. Then I'll have to get back to Thalos, unfortunately."

"Why so soon?" Meryl looked at Thelina, who had turned from a brief discussion with Althelm and was headed toward them.

"Because we need to stage a preemptive strike within the next two tendays. That's as soon as Arlyn will have the first load ready."

Meryl frowned. "Isn't that pushing it?"

"We have to strike and announce it first. Preferably to the whole Galaxy. Has to be done before they launch a fleet. Then, when we destroy their retaliatory strike, we're even. Otherwise they have to retaliate again."

Meryl and Thelina both nodded. Then Thelina frowned.

"We'll discuss this later," Jimjoy added hastily. There was no way he wanted to discuss who was going to pilot the missions to either Alphane or Old Earth. Besides, he wanted Thelina to read the card he had left her, and to talk to her personally.

Thelina and Meryl both raised their eyebrows as they looked at him.

He shrugged. "After I deal with the Council."

"We will discuss it," said Thelina softly, but her voice was firm.

"I know. I know."

LXV

JIMJOY ADDED TWO split logs to the fire, noting that his supply of split wood was getting down to near zero.

"What happens when you're never here . . ."

Outside, the freezing drizzle of the morning and afternoon had changed into a freezing mist that drifted down in the twilight almost like snow, swirled occasionally by the gusty winds out of the north.

Should he have been more direct? Asked Thelina to have dinner directly?

He glanced at the kitchen. If he had to eat alone, it would be rich and fattening. His eyes went to his wrist. 1643. Still early, especially if she had work to do after the interruptions that were bound to have followed the noontime meeting that had led to his assignment to brief the Council.

He pulled at his chin. How unlike the Empire. A briefing would have required a staff and days of preparation. Instead, here he was, one former agent, part-time professor, and full-time troublemaker, off to tell the unpleasant truth.

The Imperial conditioning persisted. Upstairs was the third draft of his remarks, briefing, whatever it would be. A good chunk of the afternoon had been devoted to that—except for the time at the commissary to pick up the ingredients for dinner.

1645. Still no Thelina.

"Do you just expect her to read your card and show up? You're nuts, Whaler," he told himself as he closed the woodstove.

WWWWhhhhhhhuuuuuuuu . . . The wind outside picked up, threshing the icy crystals on the deck.

Moistening his lips, he walked back to the kitchen and checked the ingredients—standard chicken, lightlons, the herb pack. In the cold box were the chilled and lightly brandied fruits. The skillet was laid out.

"And so is your common sense. . . ."

1648. He glanced out the small garden window, then walked to the narrow slit window by the front door, peering through the glass into the darkening ice crystals and snow swirls.

Nothing. Not a soul outside.

With a sigh, he walked to the closet and pulled out his parka. He had hoped . . . but if the mountain refused to budge, he wasn't going to stand on pride.

He eased into the heavy coat, yanked on a pair of thin black gloves, and checked the time again. 1650. No Thelina.

According to her schedule, her last meeting had been at 1500. He rubbed his forehead and stepped to the door, easing it open.

A gust of wind nearly tore it from his fingers, and he clutched it, using his other hand to grab the lever and close it behind him.

Thud.

He started down the steps. Should he try the office—or home?

As he reached the bottom step, he glanced in the direction of the main Institute complex. No one in that direction. Then he looked toward the other quarters complex and began walking. Even if Thelina intended to see him, the odds were that she would go home and talk it over with Meryl, unless she were really angry. In that case— He winced and kept walking.

Although the temperature was not much below freezing, the wind and the dampness of the tiny crystals and flakes chilled as they whipped by his uncovered ear.

Jimjoy followed the path around the corner and stopped. Ahead was a woman headed his way. Then he resumed walking. Who ever she was, she was too small for Thelina, or even Meryl.

"Chilly afternoon, Professor, isn't it?"

"Oh . . . yes. In more ways than one, Cerla." He managed to remember the woman's name, the one who had helped Carill. "Take care."

"You, too."

Was he crazy to think anything could change?

Thud. A muffled door slam echoed down the hillside as he turned his steps up the rough stone path toward Thelina's.

He loved her, and he thought she loved him. But was love enough? Or was there too much in his past for her to accept? He took another deep breath, blowing steam into the darkness. Another figure appeared on the path leading toward him.

A glint of silver . . . he found his steps quickening . . . then he was running, and damning himself for caring with every step.

For a long moment, he could see her standing there . . . stock-still.

His footsteps faltered . . . and he slowed.

Then, suddenly, she began to hurry toward him.

"Oooooofffff . . ."

She almost rebounded as his arms encircled her, and his left foot started to slide on the instantly treacherous grass beside the path.

Stumbling, he managed to plant both feet, holding on to Thelina as if he never wanted to let go.

". . . do want to keep my ribs . . ." she mumbled into his coat.

Jimjoy slowly eased his hold.

"Came to find you . . . worried . . ." His words were uneven, hesitant.

She drew back slightly, studying his face. "Why?"

He forced a grin. "Ask you to dinner."

"Serious?" She smiled briefly. "After the way I pushed you off?"

"Deserved it, especially after thinking about it. Why I . . ." He paused. Had she even gotten his note? "Did you ever get back to your office?"

"My office?"

Was she hiding a smile?

He nodded slowly. Had she read it? Was it too sentimental? Unrealistic? His stomach turned to ice, colder than the snow falling around them.

"I read your poem . . ."

"Not poetry," he protested. "Just how I feel . . ."

"Jimjoy . . . writing that took more courage than storming Haversol."

"It was hard."

"But you did it." Her gloved hand touched his cheek. "Did you mean it about dinner?"

He swallowed and nodded.

"Good. We need to talk—about us, not revolutions and institutes—and I could use a good meal." She eased out of his hug, somehow keeping his right hand in hers as they walked back toward his quarters.

The snow had shifted into a heavier fall. The footsteps he had left in the dusting that had already fallen were covered now.

"Any fallout from the meeting?" he asked, not wanting to deal with anything heavier yet.

"No. Everyone's relieved that you'll be the one facing the Council."

He squeezed her hand. She returned the pressure.

"Sort of unreal, like a white fantasy," he offered as they reached the steps to his front deck.

"If I weren't so cold, I'd stay out here and watch it with you."

Jimjoy took the hint and started up the stairs. "There is a fire going."

"Good."

The warmth billowed out the door as he opened it.

"You weren't exaggerating."

He closed the door, made sure the latch caught, and turned to help her out of her parka—except she had it off and was hanging it up.

"Sorry—just habit."

He shook his head. No matter what, Thelina would be independent.

"What were you thinking?"

"That I'm still not used to you being extraordinarily able, independent, and feminine."

She smoothed her hair unconsciously and stepped toward the stove. "Feels good."

"Would you like liftea, cafe?"

"Liftea, please."

He put on the kettle, wondering whether she would follow him or sit before the stove to get warm.

She stood at the end of the kitchen island, her back to the woodstove. "Why did you write me?"

"Because I love you. Because saying that isn't enough. Because . . . words don't come easily."

"You spoke well today. You were outstanding when you dissolved the old Council."

He set out the teapot and two large cups. "That's different. You know it's different. No sugar, right?"

"No sugar." Thelina flexed her shoulders.

He waited for the kettle to boil, not clear what else he could say.

"Did you mean what you wrote?"

He nodded, then answered, "Yes. Hard to write it down."

"Because you don't trust women?"

"Partly. Partly because I don't trust me."

"You don't want to love me?"

"Sometimes I think about that. Then I think about how empty everything seems. Sometimes I feel like I'm just going through the motions. You . . . you always seem so alive."

The kettle began to bubble. He lifted it and poured the boiling water into the teapot. Then he replaced the kettle and turned off the burner.

Clink. The heavy earthenware lid clattered as he placed it on the teapot.

"Jimjoy?"

He looked up from the cups and the teapot.

"Do we have to circle around everything?"

He looked back at the teapot.

"Do we?"

He took a deep breath. "When you want to talk about things, I always feel like you're ready to cut me down. Like there's something else I didn't understand, or something else I did wrong." He swallowed. "When we make love, I know you care, and I know you aren't ready to cut me apart."

He looked down at the counter, then lifted the teapot and began to pour into first one cup, then the other.

"Don't you see?" Thelina stepped around the island and stood almost behind him. "I need to talk to you. I need you to be able to hear my complaints, my fears, to make me feel special. When you want to love me without that, I feel used. I know that's not what you mean . . . now. But that's what it could become."

Jimjoy turned to face her, one cup in hand. He wanted to hold her, but that wasn't what she had in mind. "Let's sit down where you can get warm."

She took the cup, and he reached for his, following her to the other end of the room. He took one end of the couch, which, although upholstered, was neither soft nor cushiony. Nothing created by Accordans was soft or cushiony.

Thelina sat at the other end, leaving half a meter between them.

He shifted his weight, holding the cup in his left hand, to face her. She looked toward him, but crossed her left leg over her right, her body facing the stove. "You feel . . . used?" he asked.

"Not always. Sometimes I feel like all you want is a body. I feel what I want and feel doesn't count, and that everything will be all right so long as we make love. And it won't be."

Jimjoy swallowed. "That's not . . . Maybe in a way, though, it is how I feel . . . because words—women's words—have hurt so much."

She transferred the teacup from her left hand to her right. The fingers of her left hand squeezed his free hand gently, warmly, but only momentarily. "We can work this out."

"How?" He sipped from the cup, not looking at her. "If every time I want you without hours of conversation you feel used . . . ?"

"It's not every time. It's the pattern." She uncrossed her legs and set the cup on the low table. "That's why your note was so important. For you especially. Why your coming to find me was important. I knew you wanted me to come to you. I just couldn't."

"*Uncouugh . . .*" Jimjoy almost choked on the tea. "*Uuuchhhhuffff . . .*" He cleared his throat before setting his own cup down and turning to face her. "Wait a moment. I heard your door open and saw you coming toward me."

Thelina smiled, almost sadly. "I couldn't wait any longer. Wrong or not, I was going to come to you."

He wanted to reach for her. Instead, he said, "I thought you should come, but I couldn't wait either. I kept looking at the time, and looking outside, and looking at the time."

"Jimjoy . . . ?"

"Dinner can wait."

This time he did move toward her. She met him, her hands reaching for him, her lips wordless, but warm.

Outside, the snow continued to fall.

LXVI

JIMJOY LOOKED AROUND the small, squarish room, which he had stopped to see again. Why, he couldn't say. The last time he had been here was after he had told the previous Council to resign. The stone walls of what had once been a lower-level storeroom were damp, exuding a chill. Almost expecting Elias to be manning the command post that had long since been removed, he glanced down at the briefing papers, then folded them in half.

He couldn't read from a prepared text. He just hoped what he had planned would come out right.

With a shrug, he opened the door, carrying the folded papers in his right hand, and stepped out onto the staircase that led upward toward the speakers' foyer outside the main Council chamber. The public foyer was on the other side of the building.

At the top of the stairs waited two guards, dressed in the maroon of the planetary police. The foyer, a good ten meters deep and fifteen wide, was empty except for the three of them.

"Professor Whaler?" asked the taller police officer, a woman.

Jimjoy nodded.

"If you would care to wait—either here or . . ."

"Here is fine." Jimjoy sat down in one of the dark-wood armless chairs standing by the closed double doors to the Council chamber. He didn't really know what to do with the briefing papers, so he finally folded them in half again and tucked them into an inside tunic pocket.

"It may be a few minutes."

He nodded. All deliberative governmental bodies ran late, and even Accord's fledgling Council had apparently succumbed to the virus of rhetorical delay within the first tendays of its founding. He hoped he could keep his own efforts brief.

Both guards kept glancing at him, but whenever he looked in their direction, they were studiously surveying some other part of the speakers' foyer.

After a time, he stood up again and walked over to the largest portrait on the wall, roughly life-sized and full-length, framed in gilded wood and covered with lightly tinted permaglass.

"Ross Beigner deHihns, Chairman of the First Planetary Council of Accord, 3421–3438."

With the perfect blond hair, blue eyes, straight nose, firm lips, lightly tanned skin, the first Planetary Council Chairman looked just like the young man whose family had purchased a planet on which he could test his ecological ideas. Jimjoy smiled. If his readings between the lines of the histories were correct, that was what had happened. Next to the first Chairman's portrait was the portrait of the third Chairman, an even tighter-lipped and white-haired Ross Beigner deHihns III, 3454–3456.

There was no portrait of the second Chairman. Jimjoy frowned, trying to remember.

Click.

"Professor Whaler?"

He looked up to see one of the double doors open. Another police guard held the door. "The Council would appreciate having your briefing, ser."

Jimjoy nodded, stood, and walked through the door—and almost halted.

The spectator gallery was overflowing, as was the media section. The section reserved for delegates had more bodies than there could have been delegates elected in the past two elections.

Jimjoy moistened his lips and forced himself to continue an even pace to the speakers' podium. As he stepped up to the podium itself, he noted that the entire row of pinlights was lit and bright green. He swallowed. Every media outlet possible was here to record what he said, including the Fuard and Halstani outlets.

Instead of shaking his head, he cleared his throat softly and swallowed, then surveyed the galleries, the delegates, and finally the Council.

"Council members, delegates, and honored guests . . . you have asked the Ecolitan Institute of Accord for a public briefing on the status of the Institute's efforts in supporting and enhancing the efforts of the Council in obtaining true independence from the United Confederation of Independent Worlds." He paused. "Still . . . an Empire by any other name is still an Empire."

A light murmur of amusement rippled from the spectator gallery.

"Our current situation is critical. That is no surprise to any of you. Working together, we have made great steps toward standing alone. The Coordinate of Accord has obtained diplomatic recognition from the Matriarchy of Halston, the Fuardian Conglomerate, and the Independent Principalities of New Avalon. We have signed trade agreements with Halston, and with several of the non-Imperial independent systems.

"In this effort, the Institute has been able to assemble, through salvage, purchase, and construction, a space force equivalent to two Imperial fleets without the largest capital ships. . . .

"To date, Accord forces under the direction of the Institute have taken control of all space and off-planet facilities within the Accord system. . . . We have also neutralized the Imperial system control stations—military staging points—in all three Arm systems with direct jump access to Accord. . . .

"Our research efforts into biological processes have indicated the possibility that certain biologicals can be used, if necessary, as weapons. While the Institute regrets the necessity, we are prepared to use such weapons to guarantee our survival. We admit that the threat or the limited use of such weapons is blackmail. But the Empire's decision to destroy the entire planet of Sligo was an attempt to blackmail all colony planets into remaining hostages for Imperial plunder. . . ."

Jimjoy tried not to hurry, but still to cover clearly the points he felt needed to be made.

"There is no possibility that the Empire will surrender Accord without at least one attempt to destroy Accord itself. There is no possibility of surrender, unless all leadership and independence are forfeited for the next several generations. . . ."

Even without looking, Jimjoy could sense the stiffening when he declared "no possibility of surrender." Even the more independent Accord politicians were still politicians, looking for the possibility of compromise.

"In short, ladies and gentlemen, we cannot compromise; we cannot surrender. The Institute believes we can win a military victory sufficient to earn peace, but we cannot buy the peace, nor can we negotiate except through victory. We must earn victory, and no victory can be earned except through blood. Some children will be left without mothers or fathers. Some parents will be left without children.

"The alternative is a reeducation team, slavery for all Accord, and children without futures, without parents, and without hope.

"Regardless of the Council's decision, the Institute will oppose the Empire, holding to the ideals for which it was founded and by which it lives."

Jimjoy nodded to the Council, knowing his presentation had been too brief, probably too emotional, and not exactly what anyone had wanted to hear. "Thank you, members of the Council, ladies and gentlemen. If you have any questions, I will be happy to answer them to the best of my ability."

For a long moment there was silence throughout the chamber. Then the murmurs began, first as whispers, then as normal conversation.

Jimjoy stood at the podium, ignoring the Council and trying to gauge the reaction of the spectators and the delegates.

"Professor Whaler," began Clarenz Hedricht, the newly elected Chairman, "one aspect of your closing remarks troubled me greatly. You said, if I recall correctly, that the Institute will continue to oppose the Empire, regardless of what the Council decided. What if the council decides that the only hope of survival is an agreement of some sort with the United Confederation of Independent Worlds? Would the Institute make that agreement meaningless by continuing to fight?"

Jimjoy caught the nods from some of the new Council members, most of whom he did not know.

"Mr. Chairman, I appreciate your concern that the Institute not undermine the elected role of the Council. First and foremost, however, the Institute believes in freedom and self-determination. Therefore, I can assure you that the Institute will stand behind any Council decision which leads to that freedom for all people in the Coordinate." Jimjoy wanted to wipe his forehead. Instead, he waited for the follow-up he knew would come.

"Professor, you seem to be indicating that the Council is free to exercise its will only so long as it does not consider what the Institute views as surrender. That may be fine for those of you without families or ties to lands forged through centuries, but such fanaticism may be too high a price for those of us less . . . idealistic."

Jimjoy nodded at Hedricht. "The Institute is not composed of soldiers, nor of cast-steel fanatics. Most of the Senior Fellows have families and children. Most have come from generations of Accordans. Some of them have already died in this struggle and left children. Others know they will die. No one wants to wake up in the morning thinking it could happen to them." He paused, moistened his lips, then continued. "But the Empire—and it is an Empire—will not accept a settlement other than total capitulation. Not unless it is forced to. The Institute must force the Empire to settle on our terms. Nothing else will ensure your survival."

"Are you saying the Institute will fight, even if we order you not to?"

"Mr. Chairman, the Institute made possible the first totally free elections ever held in this system. Since I am not the Prime Ecolitan, I cannot definitively declare that the Institute would ignore such an unwise request." He looked squarely at the Chairman. "But from what I know, I think it is fair to say that the vast majority of Ecolitans would reject such a request. And so would most thinking Accordans—"

"Professor!"

Jimjoy ignored the Chairman. "You have asked me the same question three times, and each time you have asked it, it becomes clearer that your interest is not the freedom of those who elected you, but the power of the Council. The Institute is based on ideals, and stands apart from politics. As idealists, we will do what must be done. So long as I stand, no Ecolitan will enter politics. So long as I stand, power will serve principles, rather than principles serving power." He paused again, then looked at the Chairman and asked in a lower voice, "Are there any questions of *fact*?"

"Professor?" The speaker was a heavyset man at the far right end of the Council table. "Meyter Nagurso, Parundia sector. Can you provide any support for your contention that the Institute can in fact force the Empire to terms?"

"We have so far been able to nullify the Empire's ability to project a fleet into our system. We have regained sufficient trade to offset the Imperial embargo's effect on high-tech micros, and we have developed the fourth largest space force in the area surrounding the Empire. We are currently developing additional weapons and are completing an in-

depth system defense network. Nothing is certain. But if we can with-
stand a first Imperial attack, further pressures by other united systems
along the Imperial borders are likely to provide a considerable incentive
for the Empire to grant us independence without further hostilities.
We may be required to demonstrate our ability to carry war to the
Empire, and the Institute has developed such a capacity. I will not
expand upon that at this time."

"Thank you."

"Professor, how long before you expect an armed response by . . ."

"Ecolitan Whaler, is it true you have built a large fleet of obsolete
needleboats . . ."

Jimjoy answered the remaining questions one by one, providing detail where he wished and avoiding it where possible.

Tap, tap, TAP.

Finally, Clarenz Hedricht stood at the Council table. "Professor
Whaler has been most patient, most unusually candid. The Council
appreciates your willingness to brief us, Professor. Thank you."

"Thank you, Mr. Chairman." Jimjoy stepped down from the podium
and walked down the aisle in near silence, wondering as he did so how
much damage he had created. He kept his head high, even as he asked
himself what else he could have done.

Once outside the chamber, he did not wait for the murmurs or the
private condemnations that might occur. Instead, he nodded at the two
police officers, and with a polite "Thank you," left through the lower-
level door, heading for the flitter waiting for him on the green.

Jimjoy gave the pilot, Huft Kursman, the signal to light-off the
flitter as soon as he crossed the first stone walkway. Kursman responded
with a thumbs-up and the whine of the starter.

Jimjoy stretched his steps, but did not run. As he climbed into the
copilot's seat, he looked at Kursman. "Lift off as soon as she's ready."

"Stet, Professor. A little too much truth for them, ser?"

Jimjoy shrugged as he pulled on the helmet. "Didn't stay to find
out."

Thwop . . . thwop, thwop . . . thwop, thwop, thwop . . .

As the rotors came up to speed, several media types, fax rigs slung
over shoulders, hurried around the corner of the stone structure.

With a wry smile hidden behind the dark visor of the helmet, Jimjoy
waved to the lenses as the flitter lifted.

LXVII

"DID YOU HAVE to be quite that blunt?" Meryl's normally composed face was slightly flushed. Whether the additional color came from the viral infection she was fighting off or from anger was another question.

Jimjoy sat down in the chair, taken aback at the intensity of the first words she had addressed to him as he walked into her office. He thought about answering, then shrugged. "What would you have had me say? That a negotiated settlement was possible? That we all will live happily ever after without any sweat, toil, or tears? That every one of us has laid his or her life on the line so that another generation of irresponsible politicians can bargain away the gains bought by those lives?"

He shook his head, then fixed her with his eyes. "I meant what I said. No Ecolitan is going to mess with politics, except over my dead body. The Institute will never bow to the politicians. We made them to serve the people, and they damned well are going to serve the people. Not the other way around."

This time Meryl sat back. "You feel rather strongly." Her raspy voice was barely above a whisper.

"I do. I'm not a figurehead. I never will be." He looked out the window into the high and hazy winter clouds.

"So what do I do when half of those politicians are calling for your head?"

Jimjoy grinned. "Tell them the same thing, except with the finesse that you have. Tell them that the Institute stands for freedom first and foremost, and above partisan politics. We intend to remain that way, thank you. Do you want us to remove our protection of all your children and advise the Empire that Accord no longer has an armed forces?"

Meryl smiled crookedly, then blew her nose. "What if they agree?"

"They won't. They're not stupid. They just want to control the power behind the power. And we can't let them—ever."

"I wish I had your confidence."

"Meryl, I don't know how to manipulate people. This morning showed that I don't. But I know power and structures. Trust me on this one."

She took a sip of water, then whispered back, "Do we have any choice?"

"Not really."

"I didn't think so. Neither did Thel." Another sip of water followed.

"Where is she?"

"You're changing the subject. You always do when subjects get unpleasant."

Jimjoy laughed ruefully. "You're right. But where is she?"

"Visiting Dr. Hyrsa."

Jimjoy's stomach turned. "Now what?"

"Not for herself. Your comments about deaths and casualties got us thinking. We really need to build up a more dispersed emergency health care system. What happens if the battle of Accord vaporizes the Institute? She went to talk to Erica about that."

Jimjoy pulled at his chin. Still so many details unresolved, unplanned for, and less and less time remaining.

"You look worried."

He nodded slowly.

"Well, don't tell anyone. If nothing else, your confidence has been beamed all over the planet. After that performance, the Empire will probably want your head—again." The acting Deputy Prime Ecolitan coughed twice, then took out another tissue.

"What else is new?"

"They'll take a planet to get it this time."

Jimjoy's stomach twisted slightly, even though he nodded again. "We'll have to see that they don't get it." He stood up. "See you later."

Meryl only nodded in return, transferring her attention back to the screen and its priority lights, still clutching yet another tissue in her left hand.

LXVIII

2 Oct 3647
New Augusta

Dear Mort:

Wish I had been more timely in responding, but, as you know, all hades has broken loose. First, N'Trosia died of those aneurysms, and the media had a field day speculating about the probability of natural occurrences. Then the Halstanis recognized the Coordinate of Accord, and the Fuards did the same.

For whatever reason, the Fuards have notified us that they have junked the Treaty of New Bristol—officially this time—and are required to develop adequate self-defense capabilities, independent of the Empire. So Hemmelman, N'Trosia's successor, has "requested" the Planning Staff to brief the Committee in depth on the implications for the I.S.S. and has asked Intelligence to provide an assessment of probable Fuard actions.

Hemmelman seems more open to fleet modernization and agreed to our request to reopen the CX question—next year. What we'll do in the meantime, I don't know. It's no secret that we'll be hard pressed if anything else comes up, particularly if it's a goodly distance from Sector Five.

Scary thing about Accord is that their war leader, or whatever he's called, has thought rings around the tactics staff, even Intelligence. Showed up from nowhere. Did they just make him with their biotech? Who knows? Wish we had some like that. Then we might never have gotten into this mess.

Glad to hear that Helen and the kids had a chance to take home leave and trust they will be able to enjoy it for a while . . . a good, long while.

If anything definite occurs, I'll let you know. Hang in there.

Blaine

LXIX

"THERE'S ANOTHER REASON why you can't afford to be a hero." Thelina looked pale under her bronzed complexion.

"I'm not trying to be a hero."

"You're not? Then why did you try and hide this mission? Like the one that took out the Haversol System Control? Why have you put off discussing it for the past tenday?" She glanced across the deck into the late fall afternoon.

Jimjoy followed her glance, wondering where the year had gone. The sky was a crisp blue, cloudless, and the sun hung over the western mountains. With all the time he had spent on Thalos, it seemed as though he had been in some sort of suspended animation so far as the seasons at the Institute went.

He sighed softly. "I didn't want you to worry."

"Going off in the middle of the afternoon to get yourself killed isn't going to make me worry?" She twisted in the hard chair.

"Let's stop arguing." He straightened. "You said you had a reason. Not an emotional reaction, but a reason." He paused. "And why haven't you come to see me? It's no harder for you to get to Thalos than for me to get here."

Her green eyes met his green eyes. "Sometimes, even though you try so hard . . . sometimes . . ."

He sighed again. "Sometimes—sometimes what?"

"Sometimes you are so predictably male and dense."

His guts twisted, like they had at the formal under-the-stars luncheon, and he found himself moistening his lips, squeezing them together, then moistening them again. He swallowed. "That bad?"

"You can't help it, not yet. Not when you see the truth and don't want to face it." Thelina turned even paler. "Excuse me . . . just a—"

She was gone toward the facilities.

Jimjoy looked after her then out through the open slider, swallowing as the breeze ruffled his hair. Despite the unseasonable warmth, the air held a hint of chill. His stomach churned, though not nearly so badly as he imagined Thelina's was doing.

He understood now, but was it better to be understanding or dense?

Most times he would have said understanding, but he still had to go. What was worse was that he might have to do it again, when the Empire returned the favor.

Standing up from the uncomfortable chair, he paced over toward the deck, half listening for Thelina's return.

With the slightest of whispers of boot leather on polished wood, he turned and hurried toward her. Taking her hands before she could draw them from him, he met her eyes.

"Do you want to tell me? Or me to tell you?"

She looked down.

"You . . . we're going to have a child. Is that so bad?"

Thelina's eyes charged his. "You said 'we.' Will it be 'we' if I'm left like Carill, like Kerin? How many times can you go out there and come back?"

"Who else is there? It won't work if we can't deliver it to Earth itself. And let them know we can."

There was a long silence.

"Why didn't you train anyone else?"

"I've been training all year. So has Analitta. So has Imri. So has Broward."

Her hands squeezed his. "Don't you understand? I refuse to be a single parent so that you can be a hero."

He sighed. "Don't *you* understand? I don't want to be a hero. But I have to act like one. That's my only chance of getting back." He remembered what Kerin had said to him nearly a year earlier, about his having no hostages to fate. No hostages to fate?

"I did want to ask one question," he added, knowing he was changing the subject, and knowing he was being extraordinarily unwise. "How . . . ?"

"I lied. Just like you did. For a good reason."

"A good reason?" He bit off the retort he almost made.

"Would you listen?" Her voice was as gentle as he had ever heard it.

He shrugged. "I have been listening. I've been listening to you for two years. You're usually right." Except about military tactics, he thought.

"I love you. I love you, not the hero image that isn't you. I want you to want to come back."

He looked down. There it was . . . what he'd been looking for through three lifetimes, what he had refused to admit he wanted. And he'd set it up so that he had to risk losing it, because everything rested on his being able to deliver one ship full of the deadliest biohazards ever developed to the most heavily guarded planet in the human Galaxy.

"I . . . want . . . you. Have to . . . come . . . back . . ." He shook his head.

This time, Thelina, pale and trembling, drew him to her.

LXX

"WHY YOU?" SHE had asked.

Who else had there been? A year of training wasn't enough. His own ten-plus years might not be enough.

She had sighed and turned and looked out into the woods behind the deck.

Now he was in the best of the Accord couriers, a ship stripped of everything but minimal screens, overgeneratored, overpowered, and underprotected. A ship carrying two hundred minitorps filled with the nastiest of self-reproducing biohazards possible, and two thousand shells filled with the hardiest versions of the nasties. All because . . . because . . . why? Because he had to strike the heart of the Empire before the Empire struck Accord? That was what he had told the Council, and Meryl, and Thelina. Now he wasn't exactly sure of that any longer. Or was that because he really didn't want to be in the courier, screaming down from above the ecliptic on Old Earth?

He forced himself to concentrate on the audio channel, flicking from one frequency to another.

"Satcom five . . . EDI register Hammerlock one . . ."

"Belter three . . . ETA is five plus . . . five plus . . ."

With a frown, he keyed in the Imperial tactical frequencies, hoping that the comm guard this close to Old Earth was more lax than in the Arm and toward the Rift.

He could smell his own sweat. That and an odor of fear. His fear.

"Artac . . . monitor three, inbound . . . sitmo . . ."

"Clearance amber three . . ."

"Stet . . . monitor three . . ."

In some ways, coming to understand Thelina, and himself, had just made things worse. He was thinking about the future, and thinking about the future could be fatal when he needed to concentrate on the present. He wiped his forehead and tried another band.

. . . sccertitiss . . .

With a tight grin, he touched the on-board scrambler and entered a code-breaking program.

... *sccctrtttscchhh* ...

He tried a second. And a third.

... *tresascrrtttsss* ...

It took another thirty minutes and most of the descrambler program before he got something intelligible.

"Ellie five taccon, Turtle three. EDI scans normal. Continuing this time."

"Stet, Turtle three."

"Turtle four, this is taccon. Interrogative scans. Interrogative scans."

"Ellie five, Turtle four. Scans negative."

The Impies could have used tight-beam lasers, but lasers were limited by speed-of-light considerations, unlike standing jump wave. The compromise was usually scrambled standing wave.

Jimjoy listened as he wiped his forehead and studied the readouts on the board in front of him. The *Greenpeace* was damped tight, coasting at an angle to the system plane, like an anomalous piece of cosmic junk, emitting no radiation except a minimal amount of heat.

His chances—not exactly good—depended on the accuracy of his initial course plot and on his ability to use the earth's atmospheric shield. The reentry course had been designed to let the ship coast at high speed until it intersected the normal out-system shipping points serving the L-5 nexus. But no courier carried equipment sophisticated to plot and set that precise a course from a third of a system away with only one of two bursts of energy. The idea was that he would be able to make an adjustment or two near the shipping levels without creating immediate attention.

He could have done the job by setting a real cometary orbit and letting the ship drift into position. The problem with that was he would have died of old age before the courier reached Old Earth, and Accord would have long since lost.

The compromise was a ship with no radiation leaks, no outside energy expenditures, sprayed with nonreflective and energy-absorbing coatings, but traveling at high speed. All he had to do was make one or two course changes, swing around Old Earth, and launch a mere two hundred minitorps, followed by two thousand shells which would light up every satellite detection system possessed by New Augusta.

Of course, there was the small problem of getting the ship back above the ecliptic before the Imperial Forces could react.

He checked the readouts again, then the screens. Old Earth was showing a disk, as was the moon. So far, so good.

Strange, to look at them from above. The techs had initially protested his determination to rely on sampler densities and an average of pre-calculated values to determine jump and entry points as far in-system as possible.

Thelina had worried right along with them. "What if you're wrong?"

"A little bit won't matter. A lot and I'm dead. Nothing else will work."

"Will this?"

He had shrugged. There hadn't been much choice, not after the stinks he'd made. Besides, of all the Ecolitans, only Broward and Analitta had experience equivalent to his. And Broward wasn't at ease in small ships.

There was a risk in everything. He had awakened with cold sweats, thinking that Thelina had fallen back into the Hands of the Mother on her Halston mission. Now, with the diplomatic recognition from Halston, followed by Tinhorn, Accord was receiving more independent shipping, and access to the high-tech designs and critical microblocs necessary to complete outfitting the needleboats. Thelina had made it all possible, but he still had nightmares.

Wiping his forehead again, he waited, listening.

The courier's velocity was too high to be natural, even for the oddest cometary, but before he was detected, he hoped to make the last course change to set his final-approach angle.

"Ellie five, Turtle two. Negative on scans."

The courier pilot checked his own passive EDI readouts. The spread of the outer orbital picket was wide enough. Not a real detection line at all—but a mere precaution. The real detection arrays, the ships he had bypassed by his angular approach, were farther outsystem and concentrated on the possible standard approach corridors. An above-ecliptic approach like Jimjoy's was neither practical nor advisable in most circumstances. Since the calculation of jump points was problematical at best, nonstandard approaches would, over time, destroy a lot of ships.

Jimjoy wiped his forehead again to keep the sweat from his eyes. The control area temperature was normal, about fifteen degrees centigrade, but it seemed hotter, and the moisture endless.

He laughed, abruptly, and unstrapped, heading for the small fresher unit. Last chance he might have to relieve himself before he discovered whether he was a lucky fool or a dead idiot. As he left the controls, he twisted the audio up to full volume, then half pulled, half floated toward the fresher. The grav-field generators had been pulled to allow for beefing up the drives and more converter power.

"Turtle three, Ellie taccon. Interrogative screens."

"Ellie five . . . negative this time."

"Turtle three, we have enhanced negative optical at plus five. Coordinates follow. Plus five point four three. Sector red. One eight three relative. Direct feed to your taccomp."

"Stet, Ellie. Receiving feed. No EDI from sector red. Plus ten to negative ten. Interrogative negative optical."

"Negative optical—no radiation, no emissions. Detected from crossing other optical sources."

"Stet, Ellie."

"Turtle three. Understand no EDI."

"That's affirmative. Negative on EDI this time."

Jimjoy took a deep swallow of metallic-tasting water before heading back to the controls. His mouth was dry even after he drank. He listened while he strapped back in and readjusted the audio. They had him. But did they know it?

He wiped his forehead again, glanced at the elapsed time clock, and took a deep breath. The next few hours would be long.

With a sigh, he began recalculating his options. If . . . if the Impies decided he was the space junk he looked like, in another hour he might be able to pull off a quick burst to adjust course.

"Ellie taccon, three here. Negative on EDI. Negative on RAD. Negative on enhanced optic."

"Stet. Request you continue monitoring area. Probably essjay."

"Stet. Will continue periodic sweeps."

Jimjoy let out his breath, wiped his forehead. He was temporarily safe, until he had to make a course correction. He began to plot out the alternatives available for the spacing and timing of the second correction, displaying them on the navigation plot. He shook his head as he studied the courses.

No matter which one he took, the gee forces required would be close to his tolerances . . . and the ship's.

"Turtle four, Ellie taccon. Request sweep in sector green, two seven three relative, negative point three."

"Stet, Ellie five. Sweeping this time. Initial negative on EDI or enhanced optical."

Jimjoy wiped his forehead with the back of his nearly soaked sleeve, studying the course options again.

"Turtle three, Ellie taccon, interrogative status of essjay."

"Three here. Status is constant. No EDI, no optical on heat, conforms to hard cometary profile."

"Ellie taccon, Turtle four. Have reading at two six nine relative, sector green, coordinates to your taccomp."

"Stet, four. Stand by."

"Standing by."

Jimjoy moistened his lips. The Impies were jumpy. Too jumpy. He looked at the options, selecting one, the one holding off the course change until the last possible moment. Then he ran the inquiry through the plot computer.

"Probability of success exceeds point nine eight."

He winced. Someday, those two-percent chances would turn on him. Still, the representation screen showed him "above" and fractionally inside the orbit line of the Imperial ship that seemed to be Turtle three. Every minute counted now, because a torp would be on a stern chase, rather than a closing vector.

"Turtle three, this is Ellie taccon. Interrogative peacekeeper status."

Jimjoy's stomach twisted. His fingers reached for the controls, plugging in the contingency course he had hoped not to use.

"Ellie five, three here. Status is green at point eight. Interrogative status check."

"Stand by, three."

Jimjoy watched as his own screen sketched out the near-suicide course line. The basic idea was simple enough—full power straight at Earth. Full decel just before hitting the edge of the extended radiation belts, and then using the planet to sling the *Greenpeace* at right angles to the ecliptic, distorting the magfields and hopefully messing up communications and detection long enough for Jimjoy to reach low-density space and jump.

"Turtle four, Ellie taccon. Interrogative peacekeeper status."

"Ellie five, status is green at point nine."

"Turtle three and Turtle four, stand by for peacekeeper release."

Jimjoy squinted, touched the control to bring the variable stepped acceleration program up from standby. Finger poised, he watched the representation screen. He had needed another twenty standard minutes, and he wasn't going to get them.

"... *sssssss* ..."

Jabbing the acceleration controls, he keyed in the variability. The abrupt frequency shift told him enough.

"*. . . oooofffff . . .*" The sudden power surge drove him back into his couch.

On the screen three blue dashed lines flicked from the picket ship closest to him toward his position.

Jimjoy blanked the screen receptors, moistening his lips. For a moment he hung weightless as the courier dropped its acceleration to zero and changed course line. Then he was jammed back into the couch even more forcefully. Each course led to Earth, not always directly, with ever-increasing speed.

His fingers called up the scrambler program and the frequency hunter. He might as well try to find out what they were up to as the courier scrambled sideways at an acceleration well outside the standard Imperial profile.

"*. . . sccctttcchhhh . . .*"

Using the fingertip controls, he tried one of the earlier programs.

"*. . . sctttccchhh . . .*"

And another.

"*. . . sctttchhhh . . .*"

Then he punched out the analysis. He had to squint against the acceleration to try to read the figures. The pattern seemed logical, and he tried another combination. Just then, the acceleration stopped. His stomach lurched upward in the weightlessness.

EEEEEEEEEEEEEEEEEEEeeeeeeeeeeeee . . .

He felt that the courier ought to be shaking, even as he knew tac-heads in space didn't create atmospheric effects.

EEEEEEEEEEEEEEEEEEEEEeeeeeeeeee . . .

The courier was programmed to halt all acceleration at tachead detonation, as if to indicate to the Impies their efforts had been successful.

EEEEEEEEEEEEEEeeeeeeeeeeeee . . .

One glance at the representational screen told him that either Turtle three had incredibly poor tracking or the courier had been extraordinarily effective in evading the three-torp spread. His fingers dropped the evasion system into standby and called up a course line recalculation.

He pulled at his chin as he noted the courier course and speed. Course was fine—directly at the northern hemisphere of Old Earth. Speed was well above the minimum necessary to turn both Jimjoy and the *Green-peace* into the finest of interstellar dust.

He noted the resumption of audio lock as he began to refigure power outputs, trying to determine the range of escape options.

". . . status . . ."

"Ellie five, EDI traces lost at time of detonation. Scans reveal no EDI, no optical, and no enhanced heat."

"Stet, three. Continuing cross-optical scans in sector orange this time. Interrogative remaining peacekeeper status."

"Status is green, at point five."

". . . mothers . . ." mumbled Jimjoy, his mouth dry again. L-5 control would come up with another enhanced optical scan in roughly five standard minutes, cross-check it within another five, and have another spread blown out, probably with all five remaining tacheads.

He called up the course line projections, marking his own position in ten minutes, and asked the plot computer to provide options for evasion, still toward Old Earth.

"Turtle four, interrogative status of essjay target."

"Ellie five, four here. Negative on EDI at any point. Dust dispersion indicates standard comet profile."

"Stet, four. Continue scanning this time.

"Turtle three, interrogative sector orange."

"Negative on EDI or optical."

"Stand by for peacekeeper release. EDI traces prior to detonation indicate Charlie Alpha courier."

Jimjoy wiped his forehead, wishing the duty officer on the L-5 control station were not quite so persistent, and checked the course line and the preprogrammed evasion pattern—with a healthy decel built in after the initial turn.

Approximately two minutes before detection. He swallowed, letting his fingers reach for the evasion kick-in.

Knowing he was probably too early, he jabbed the stud.

"Three. Coordinates . . . release. MARK!!!"

Jimjoy released his breath just as it was knocked out of him by the courier's quick acceleration.

Before he had recovered he was thrown against the straps by an even more brutal decel kick.

EEEEEEEEEEEEeeeeeeeeeee . . .

EEEEEEEEEeeeeee . . .

EEEEEEEEEE . . .

The screams of the three tacheads battered his ears, while another attack of weightlessness assaulted his guts.

Blinking, he scanned the screen, noting that the corvette's torps had been almost as wide of the mark as on the first salvo.

"Turtle three, interrogative status. Interrogative status."

"Negative EDI. Negative optical."

"Interrogative peacekeeper status."

"Status is green at point two."

"Stet. Standby.

"Turtle four, interrogative time to omega three."

"Ellie five, four here. Estimate point two five to omega three. Point two five."

"Four, stand by."

After scanning his own screen, Jimjoy could see the L-5 operations coordinator's problem. Turtle three was nearly out of torp range, and would have to leave station to chase a small courier-sized ship that could be a decoy. Turtle four could cover, but only by leaving an even larger uncovered area, and it would be another ten minutes before the enhanced optics would sort out to discover whether the target still existed.

Jimjoy smiled. One set of problems passed. The smile faded as he contemplated the courier's power levels—less than seventy percent, with the bulk of the power requirements yet to come.

He shook his head before he began fiddling with the comm freq hunter. L-5 was surely trying to talk to either Lunar Control or inner orbit control.

"... *sccctttcchhhh* ..."

After a time, he managed to lock in with the correct scrambler keys, the ones Accord was not supposed to have, courtesy of the *D'Armetier*.

"... recommended patrollers along upper green, inbound two eight zero, dispersion ..."

"... this is absolute interdict. Say again, absolute interdict ..."

Not that the decision to vaporize him was any surprise. He had one surprise of his own left—his decel pattern. Or lack of pattern.

He took a swallow of warm water from the squeeze bottle and replaced it in the holder, watching the time run down and the distance decrease.

"Hawkstrike one, Lunie Prime, Charlie inbound on roger three. Roger three."

"Understand roger three. Negative EDI, negative optical, negative lock. Negative on laser focus."

"Stet, one. Coordinate feed follows."

Jimjoy watched the screen and listened, knowing he could do nothing else, suspecting they wanted him to move, to provide a burst of energy for them to lock in on.

Not yet.

"Prime, one here. Coordinates accepted. Negative on EDI lock. Negative optical."

Jimjoy could hope. The *Greenpeace* was aimed nearly straight at the patroller. With no radiation and no optical parallax . . .

He wiped his forehead. Just another minute or two and the *Greenpeace* would be silently whipping by the patroller, perhaps as close as thirty kays, and as effectively as distant as half a system away.

". . . bastard's here somewhere . . ."

"Silence on the net."

Jimjoy almost grinned. Too close in without energy sources for locks, and they were blind . . . and once he hit Earth's magfield . . . if he hit it.

"Hawkstrike one, charlie should be three zero zero, immediate local. Immediate local."

"Prime. One here. Negative on indicators."

Jimjoy waited, fingers ready to trigger the final inbound evasion.

"Prime, Hawkstrike three. Parallax indicates charlie is absolute orange, coordinates follow."

"All units fire on mark . . ."

Jimjoy slapped the control activation, watched his vision tunnel into darkness with the sudden acceleration, then expand, then drop away again.

". . . MARK!!!!"

EEEEEEEEEEeeeeeeeeeeeeeeee . . .

Clunk.

Jimjoy didn't like the last sound, but the board indicators showed nothing as the *Greenpeace* plunged toward Old Earth's upper atmosphere.

". . . absolute orange at two five . . ."

". . . beams on Charlie . . ."

Three lights flashed red as the lasers of the nearest patroller locked on the courier.

Jimjoy flicked up the screens to avoid being fried.

"EDI on two five."

"What in hades is it?"

". . . almost in the mag-field. Interrogative laser punch."

"Trying lock-on . . ."

Jimjoy flicked another evasion macro.

". . . lost . . . lock-on . . . reacquiring this time . . ."

His neck ached. His stomach muscles were knotted; his forehead was clammy; his mouth was dry.

Another check of the decel parameters. He kicked in another acceleration jolt, then cut the power. . . . waiting.

Amber on the nose. . . . amber on the lower hull . . . amber on leading edges . . .

"Charlie's inside the mag-field, touching oscar . . ."

The stress lines climbed.

He jammed the drives to full decel, letting the courier drop further toward lower orbit, out of the patrollers' reaches, assuming the atmosphere didn't ablate what was left of the hull.

Jimjoy could feel the heat leaching through the hull, could feel the strain placed on the supercon lines, on each and every system, without checking the rows of red-and-amber status lights flashing on across the board.

His fingers flicked three studs.

". . . torp sequence one . . . complete . . ."

He forced himself to wait, mentally counting for a minimal separation, before triggering the second sequence.

. . . *eeeeee* . . . *eeeeeee* . . . *eeeeeee* . . .

The wave receivers were deaf and blind once the courier was so far within a planetary mag-field. Jimjoy grinned grimly. The Impies certainly couldn't shoot now, not when the traces of the upper atmosphere and the mag-field made torps impossible. He was too high for missiles, and particle beams weren't allowed inside lunar orbit.

So all he had to do was survive the drop orbit and pick an exit course—blind where the Impies weren't lined up to pot him.

The course was set. No real choice there.

He triggered the second torp drop, then added the first hazard shell drop.

". . . torp sequence two . . . complete . . ."

Most of the warning lights had dropped off the red and into the amber—except for the hull thickness/integrity warning. Would he have a hull left?

He noted the deviation from the lead to the exit course and attempted an adjustment. The courier slewed, then straightened.

". . . torp sequence three . . . complete . . ."

The next round of hazard shells followed.

By now, as close to the upper atmosphere as the courier was, the only workable instruments were the laser plotter and the internal systems.

"... torp sequence four ... complete ..."

He checked the energy reserves. What reserves? If his exit course weren't perfect ... He pushed away the thought and concentrated on the next drop.

"... torp sequence five ..."

The process seemed to telescope. Scan, calculate, release torps, release shells. Scan, calculate, release torps, release shells ... and start all over again.

"... torp sequence ten ... complete ... hazard shell drop away ..."

He shook his head, aware that he and his shipsuit were dripping and that every metal surface was pouring heat at him. Another head-shake and he called up the exit profile, then punched the red stud.

... eeeeeeEEEEEEEeeeeeeeee ...

The interference began to drop almost immediately as the courier plunged skyward through the magnetic south pole.

Twenty percent, nineteen percent, eighteen percent—Jimjoy cut the acceleration, feeling his exhausted stomach flip-flop again.

"... interrogative ... intercept ..."

"Ellie five, Hawkstrike two, that is negative. Bogey's outbound beyond Hawkstrike return envelope."

Jimjoy glanced at the representational screen, watching his own track sprinting away from Old Earth at nearly a right angle to the ecliptic.

Next time, next time, the Impies would be ready for the above/below the ecliptic approach. Which was fine with Jimjoy, because there wouldn't be a next time.

If either Narlian or Stilsen were correct, Old Earth was going to be far too busy trying to survive to worry about Accord. Still, he continued to watch the screen, wondering if any heroes were going to chase him into the uncertain dust densities below the ecliptic.

"Ellie five, Hawkstrike three, releasing this time."

Jimjoy held his breath as the nearest I.S.S. corvette released a full spread of tachead torps, watching as the blue dashed lines appeared nearer and nearer on the representational screen.

EEEEEEEEEEEEEeeeeeeeee ...
EEEEEEEEEeeeeeeeeeeee ...
EEEEEEEEEeeeeeeeeee ...
EEEEEEEEEeeeee ...

EEEEEEeeee . . .

When the earsplitting comm interference ceased, Jimjoy was still squinting. Then he laughed.

The disruptions from the tacheads had destroyed his residual EDI track, and the *Greenpeace* was outbound, shuttered and without EDI emission. By the time L-5 control could get clear enhanced opticals, he would have jumped.

No matter that he'd probably require either a tow or a power transfer before getting far in-system at Accord. That he could handle.

He began setting up the jump coordinates. His mouth was still dry, and he reeked of sweat and fear. But he could set a homeward jump.

LXXI

"COMMANDER BLACK, PERCH two. We have lock-on. Estimate rendezvous in point two."

"Stet, two. Glad to see you." Jimjoy eased back in the cushions of the control couch, waiting for the space tug. He had his all-too-clammy vac suit on, except for the helmet, which he had on his shoulder straps.

"Not so glad as we are to see you. Someone promised to make life very hard on us all if . . ." Analitta didn't finish her sentence.

"I understand."

"By the way, interrogative success probability."

"Packages were all delivered. How the garden grows depends on the package designers." Jimjoy's voice was ragged, he realized. "Their scarecrows were a bit shocked at the delivery service. More later."

He checked the representational screen again, confirming the closure of Analitta's tug, then switched to visual. He could see only a dull silvery blot representing the *Percheron*.

Cling. The alarm signaled the end of the power reserves. With the reserves went the screens—and the air pressure. He pulled on his helmet and plugged in the belt jack to the ship's comm system.

"Holy drek. . . . Commander . . . any atmosphere there at all? Hull looks like a cheese grater. I've seen Swiss cheese with fewer holes."

"I'm suited."

". . . least he can't breathe vacuum. . . ." Jimjoy smiled at the voice from the *Percheron*.

"Don't be too sure," commented Analitta to the unknown speaker.

"Hold tight, Commander. Commencing lock-on this time."

"Understand lock-on. Be careful of my cheese grater."

"Stet."

The *Greenpeace* shuddered as the magnetic locks brought the ships together.

"Perch one, leave your crew aboard."

"Interrogative your last, Commander."

"I'm slow, Perch one. We don't have a confirmation that some of my packages aren't still hanging tight. I'm walking across. Have a decontamination crew for my suit. Same for me. Send an inquiry to Narlian requesting advice."

"Oh . . ."

"Yeah . . ."

Jimjoy shook his head as he eased himself from the lock. While it wasn't likely that *anything* could have survived his departure from Old Earth, Narlian and Stilsen had engineered their cargo to take extremes of temperature and pressure, or lack thereof. And the *Greenpeace* might be better off in a terminal solar orbit, with a sure sterilization.

His feet touched the tug's hull, and he took step after careful step toward the main lock.

"Commander . . . Professor . . . ?"

"The same."

"Just step into the little lock. We'll flood it with a decon gas. Once the lock's clear, leave the suit and your clothes there. Dr. Narlian says there's nothing that you personally could carry."

"Narlian . . . she was waiting?"

"Waiting? She's been pacing around Thalos Station for the last twelve hours, biting off any head that came in range."

Jimjoy closed the lock, wondering how soon he could see Thelina, glad at least that this time he was a live coward, a sneak poisoner, a thief, what have you, rather than a hero.

He didn't look, smell, or feel like a hero, not surrounded with purplish decon gas in the lock of an ungainly space tug after abandoning a courier he'd turned into shredded metal.

He waited for the lock to clear, to begin the trip back to Thalos Station and, more important, back to Accord.

LXXII

12 *Novem* 3647
On-station

Dear Blaine:

Now it's my turn to be late in responding, but, as you noted in your last, all hades has broken loose.

Right after we got the media reports on the attack or whatever it was on Old Earth, activities here went crazy. Is it true that *something* got loose inside the L-5 picket line, pulled a double orbit, and made a right-angle ecliptic exit off the south pole? But no one is saying what happened . . . if anything.

The attack has been all over the media, but not the results. We've seen more close calls in the last week than in the previous year. They seem to be probing everywhere.

We've had two converter replacements since my last. Neither the ship nor I nor the crew is up to this for much longer, but all rotations have stopped, and we've even had some transfers. The squadron lost two ships for "redeployment." They won't say where, but everyone knows.

The problem is we're going to pay for it, now and not next year or the year after.

Haven't heard from Helen, but that's not surprising, since not even much official stuff is reaching us right now.

Have to close if I want to get this off, but see if you can do anything—I'll even take old needleboats!

Mort

LXXIII

THE ADMIRAL WITH the silvered-gold hair swallowed the two capsules and rubbed his temples.

"You're taking them too often," he reminded himself in a low voice.

His fingers reached for the screen controls, then paused. After a moment, he shook his head and called back the draft report, searching for the section that had troubled him, flicking down the lines.

". . . as demonstrated by the rapid success of the mutated core borers, the anchovy virus, the high-speed wheat rust . . . Ecolitan Institute has established capability to disrupt if not destroy . . . food chains . . . on any Imperial planet . . .

". . . independent confirmation by . . . Herbridge University Biotech Center . . . indicates genetic engineering capability to wage antipersonnel campaign . . . Directorate's excesses would be mild by comparison . . .

". . . Intelligence unable to pinpoint Ecolitan production facilities . . ."

The Admiral winced and rubbed his temples again before continuing. The words before him were almost a jumble, though he knew them nearly by heart.

". . . Fuards massing in Sector Nine. . . . stepped up production of new S.D. class vessels . . . restriction in public travel in the area of the three-system bulge . . .

". . . Halstani announcement of closing the University of Teresa's High Science Center to Imperial scientists . . ."

He focused in on the key paragraphs.

"Based on these factors, the Intelligence Service concurs with the recommendations of the Planning Staff and Fleet Development Branch. Military action against Accord—even if successful—will result in even greater casualties to Imperial Forces, staging bases, and personnel. More important, given the rapid mobilization of Accord and the desperation of its leaders, no military action against Accord is likely to prove successful without at least a three-fleet action.

"In addition, the single large fleet-action limitation established by the Defense Committee makes it extraordinarily difficult to guarantee success and could further weaken Imperial Forces. Finally, to date, the

Accord Coordinate has used only a single ship to deliver biological weapons targeted against food chains. In any prolonged conflict, this restraint would not be continued.

"Under such conditions, the Fuardian Conglomerate could consider acquiring disputed boundary territories of greater value, both economically and strategically, than the Accord system.

"Therefore, the Intelligence Service strongly recommends against overt military action against Accord."

The Admiral rubbed his forehead and looked over his final recommendation again. "Damn you, Hewitt . . ."

With a sigh, he tapped the stud releasing his hold on the recommendation, then touched the comm settings. "Darkman . . . put our recommendations in final . . . send a copy to Planning . . . and leak it to the usual sources."

"Yes, Admiral."

The Admiral did not respond. His temples were throbbing, and it would be another four hours before he could take any more of the green capsules.

"Damn you, Hewitt . . ."

LXXIV

OUTSIDE, ON THE bedroom deck, a light covering of snow swirled in the gray morning. The sliding door rattled in its frame.

Jimjoy sat on the edge of the bed, formal greens on, kit bag by the door.

"I know. You have to go." Thelina sat beside him, silver hair tousled, wearing a faded green sweatsuit.

Jimjoy looked down. "I shouldn't have come at all, but . . ." His hand gripped hers too tightly.

"You were here only one day."

He grinned. "It was a good day."

She punched his arm. "You're impossible."

"I know. Takes that to stand up to you."

"You're really impossible."

Shaking his head, he stood up, not letting go of her hand and lifting her to her feet as well, drawing her to him, bringing her lips to his.

"Mmm . . ."

Finally he let her speak, not that she was struggling that hard.

"Jimjoy . . ."

He waited, her head on his shoulder, his eyes fixed on the shifting clouds, not wanting to let go of her.

"Don't be a hero . . . we need you."

"Try not to do anything stupid," he whispered.

She stepped back, forcing his arms from her, and met his eyes. "Listen to me, will you? We need you. Not just me. Not just our child. All of us need you. The only reason I have to let you go is that your little fleet needs you to protect us. But every one of them would lay down their lives for you. If it comes to that, let them!"

"But—"

"Listen to me, you big dumb hero!" Tears began to form at the corners of her eyes. "You're what holds it all together. You *have* to come back. Don't forget it."

For a time that seemed forever and all too short, the two of them clung to each other.

"You'd better go . . . or I won't let you."

"Suppose so." He ignored the burning in his eyes, touched her lips with his a last time, and stepped back. Then he picked up the kit bag.

They went down the stairs side by side.

LXXV

"BREAK OUT IN corridor two," announced the pilot, her low voice crisp.

"Stet." Jimjoy wished he, and not Analitta, were at the controls of the *Adams* instead of overseeing the operation. But he was the closest thing the Coordinate had to an admiral, and the last thing he needed was to worry about the details. That alone was enough to make him shiver.

"EDI registers multiple breakouts," continued Analitta.

Jimjoy's combat screen confirmed her announcement. Three reddish lights pulsed, followed by a second set of even more intense lights. He recognized the formation. "Green forces, plan Beta blue. Plan Beta blue."

"Interrogative timing, Commander."

"Move it. Now!"

As the faint whine of the overhauled drivers began to build, the reengineered and renamed *Adams* swept toward the preselected position behind Donagir, the largest satellite of the system's sixth planet. Jimjoy began keying instructions for the five torps waiting in the ex-Fuardian destroyer's message tubes.

"Gilman?" Jimjoy's voice did not rise. His fingers completed the instructions and sent them to the five torps. He swallowed as he continued to track the EDI traces on the screen.

"Yes, ser." The apprentice's voice wavered.

The representational screen showed the five green sparks streaking from the *Adams* toward five separate points surrounding corridor two.

"Send a message torp—regular torp—to Thalos control. Tell Imri the Impies have sent a full-fleet battle group. Down corridor two." He rechecked the screen. Eighteen red dots paraded down entry corridor two in a general V shape, aimed straight at Accord. Three were scouts, from the EDI profiles, followed by twelve corvettes and three battle cruisers.

Destroying the three capital ships was imperative. If necessary, Accord could survive anything the corvettes could throw. They weren't big enough to carry planet-busters. "Tell her to use evacuation plan two. Evacuation plan two."

"Yes, ser. Evacuation plan two for Thalos Station."

Jimjoy concentrated on the screen, wishing he were closer, without the data lag, but knowing that the four destroyers had to be saved for a better shot at the cruisers. He wiped his forehead with the back of his hand, waiting.

"On course to control point beta, Commander."

"Stet."

The first two green blips dropped from in-system jumps nearly on top of the lead scout. A third blip did not appear.

Jimjoy pulled at his chin. One needleboat down to the dust buildup—despite jumping in from above the ecliptic. The two green dots, half the size and intensity of the scout, closed on the Imperial ship. Abruptly, one green dot flared and vanished. The remaining needleboat continued to close.

This time the red dot flared and disappeared. The needleboat jumped off the screen.

Three more green dots appeared abreast of the corvette at the tip of the right wing of the Imperial formation, one appearing almost on the Imperial ship.

Jimjoy nodded, wondering how really close the needleboat had been.

"Time to station twelve plus."

"Thanks, Analitta."

All three of the green dots on the screen flared, as did the corvette they had bracketed.

"Hades . . ." Jimjoy wiped his forehead.

Beside him, Gilman took a noisy and deep breath as he calculated vectors and closures.

"Enemy continues to accelerate, Commander," the apprentice said.

Jimjoy smiled. If the Imperial commander continued that tactic . . . He pulled at his chin. Nothing was certain.

The Imperial battle group edged inside the dotted blue arc on the screen that signified the orbit of Rachelcars—planet eight.

Three more needleboats flicked out of the ecliptic at another corvette on the Imperial formation's left wing. A second corvette seemed to crawl toward the ship under attack to bolster the defense.

One needleboat disappeared—without the flare of destruction. Then a corvette toward the middle of the Imperial formation flared and vanished. At the same time both remaining needleboats flared and disintegrated under the fire of the two wing corvettes.

"What happened?" asked Gilman.

"Our boy jumped into the formation. Blind suicide shot. Took a corvette."

The seven pilots and their needleboats, and their hard-won electronics, from the Accord forces had cost the Imperials two corvettes and a scout.

At that rate, calculated Jimjoy, use of all sixty-one needleboats would still leave the three battle cruisers and three or four corvettes—more than enough to deliver the planetbusters carried by the cruisers.

"Gilman, forget the vectors. Get on the scramblers and see if you can find out their tactical wave freqs. They may not be using them yet. I'd be using tight-beam lasers."

"On the scramblers, ser."

"Thanks."

Jimjoy wished he could do it himself, but trying to anticipate what the Imperial fleet did next was more important. The relatively tight formation indicated their knowledge that Accord had no capital ships to speak of.

On the screen another pair of green dots materialized, back on the right flank of the Imperial fleet, this time each releasing a pair of torps, torps which flashed heavy dotted lines on the screen toward the rearguard corvette.

Jimjoy held his breath. Each of the special torps carried double tac-heads and a few associated leftovers from obsolete technology—a mod-ification of the old X-ray laser. Jason had thought it might work once or twice—at least until the corvettes overlapped screens.

The blue dotted lines converged on the corvette.

The Imperial ship did not so much flash as fade off the screen.

Jimjoy exhaled.

A single needleboat appeared above the Imperial right wing, the bluish tint on the screen indicating relative elevation, only long enough to launch another pair of torps before jumping.

"Negative on standing wave frequencies, ser."

"Keep at it, Gilman. Try and find a carrier near the orange."

"Yes, ser."

Jimjoy's eyes watched the special torps, realizing that the needleboat pilot had launched one toward the lead battle cruiser, on an angle between the guard corvettes. He shook his head. The cruiser's screens should be able to take that punishment.

The first torp flashed into another corvette, which glimmered, flashed on and off, then faded from the screen.

"Estimate three plus to station, Commander."

"Stet." Jimjoy watched as the second torp flashed against the lead cruiser's screens. The cruiser remained on the screen, but the dot image shifted from red to amber.

"Hades!" Jimjoy's hands flicked across the message torp controls, then to the command control. "Greenpax blue, target bulldog lead. Wedge one. Wedge one. Mark! Target bulldog lead. Immediate target. Immediate target."

"Targeting bulldog lead this time. Targeting lead."

Jimjoy's fingers clenched, then tapped the edge of the tactical screen as he watched the Imperial cruiser's image flicker from red to amber and back, clearly struggling to maintain screen integrity. Two Imperial corvettes began to move forward from the area of the trailing battle cruiser, as if to ward off further attacks.

Six green dots appeared in a wedge above the uppermost corvette on the leading right edge. The green wedge angled toward the struggling cruiser.

"On station, ser."

"Stet."

The lead needleboat launched two standard torps toward the single corvette between the wedge and the cruiser, then flared into oblivion.

The two needleboats now in the lead launched torps—standard torps—toward the corvette, whose screens flicked red-amber but held.

The leftward needleboat disintegrated under the return torps from the corvette, while a trailing needleboat launched a single special torp toward the corvette.

Jimjoy watched, his fingers tight around the edge of the screen controls, as the pair of Imperial corvettes continued to move forward to intercept the Accord wedge.

Abruptly, the single corvette between the wedge and the ailing cruiser faded from the screen under the impact of the special torp, but not before knocking out the needleboat which had launched it.

The four remaining needleboats in the wedge kept accelerating toward the battle cruiser, whose screens continued to flicker.

"Locked on carrier wave, ser. No transmissions."

"Put it on audio, Gilman." Jimjoy's eyes were locked on the screen as he began to calculate. Assuming the Imperial fleet commander realized Accord's apparent desperation and the Impies' limitations shortly . . . The figures appeared on the second screen.

He stopped for a moment to watch as two more needleboats vanished under the concentrated forces from the cruiser and one of the approaching corvettes. Then the two trailing needleboats launched four special torps—all at the cruiser—and jumped.

Jimjoy hoped they made it out as he watched the torps converge on the cruiser. He pulled at his chin momentarily. So far, Accord had lost at least twelve needleboats, possibly three more to dust/jump destruction. If he had counted correctly, only a handful of the beefed-up special torps remained.

"*Ssssssssssss . . .*" The low hum of the Imperial standing wave frequency punctuated the sudden silence as Jimjoy and his crew watched the Imperial battle cruiser flare into sudden oblivion.

"Greenpax blue, stand by for red charlie. Stand by for red charlie." Jimjoy was calling off the pick-off attempts, knowing the Imperial commander had realized he could not afford the losses of a standard approach.

"Hammerstrike, Hammerstrike, this is Radian Mace. Commence Omega Delta. Commence Omega Delta."

Jimjoy nodded, watching as the Imperial Forces drew closer together and began to accelerate, shifting slightly toward Accord itself, crossing the faint dotted line on the screen that represented the orbit of Eyres, the gas giant seventh planet. Eyres itself was on the other side of the sun.

The close-in screen showed the battle group around him—three other destroyers and ten needleboats.

Shortly, it would be their turn.

"Commander, status check. Thirty-four needleboats operational, four destroyers."

Jimjoy winced. The dust had done more damage than the Impies. But the needleboats couldn't stand and fight. That left in-system jumps.

He checked the screens. "Commence red charlie. Commence red charlie."

The Coordinate squadron slipped from behind Donagir and into an intercept course with the Imperial fleet.

Jimjoy continued to calculate, measuring the vectors and comparing the possible errors.

Then he began to reset the last set of sharp-stone drive control programs.

"Commander, Accord forces, this is Radian Mace. This is Radian Mace. Request your surrender to lawful Imperial authority. Request your surrender to lawful Imperial authority."

Jimjoy sighed.

"Saying anything, Commander?" asked Analitta conversationally.

"Should I?"

"Tell them to do the anatomically impossible."

Jimjoy grinned. Only Analitta would paraphrase swearing and still have it sound worse than the vulgar original.

"Radian Mace, this is Greenpax black. Request your departure from Coordinate space. Request your immediate departure from Coordinate space."

"Greenpax, this is Radian Mac. Without immediate and unconditional surrender, no terms are possible. I say again. Without immediate and unconditional surrender, no terms are possible."

"Radian Mace, Greenpax black. Concur. Without *your* immediate and unconditional surrender, no terms are possible."

For several long minutes, the Imperial frequency remained silent.

"Did you mean that, Commander?" Gilman finally whispered.

Jimjoy continued to watch and listen. He had more than meant it. Unless Accord could totally annihilate the Imperial Forces, their victory would not be convincing enough to persuade the Fuards of the Empire's weakness and to allow the I.S.S. to recommend granting Accord's independence.

"Greenpax, this is Radian Mace. Your position is unacceptable. Accord remains an Imperial colony. Request your immediate and unconditional surrender."

"Radian Mace. We regret your last. So will you." Jimjoy regretted the flipness of his last transmission even as he spoke it. He took a deep breath and triggered the drive control commands for the sharp stones, wondering what the Imperials would think when three EDI traces appeared, indicating ships larger than the largest Imperial battle cruisers.

The screens indicated less than five minutes before his small fleet reached torp range to strike at the main body of the Impie fleet.

Three needleboats bracketed the lead Impie scout. A coruscation of torps, screens, and energy concentrations flicked back and forth. The scout and two needleboats disappeared.

Two more needleboats engaged the remaining scout. One needleboat and the scout vanished.

"Red charlie one. Red charlie one."

Three of the remaining needleboats and two destroyers—the *Dinvair* and the *Wett*—created a wedge aimed at the rightmost of the battle cruisers.

Between the small Accord formation and the battle cruiser were four corvettes. One of the corvettes launched a series of torps. The *Dinvair* flicked its screens outward momentarily to deflect three of the torps. A single needleboat, unable to shake the remaining torp, jumped.

Jimjoy shook his head. Too high a dust density.

The *Wett* countered with two special torps. Both bypassed the corvettes, but dissolved against the battle cruiser's pulsed screens.

Jimjoy eyed the representational screen. The three large EDI tracks continued to close.

The Imperial Forces edged closer, bringing together the interlocking screens necessary to resist the X-ray laser torps and to keep the needleboat jump tactics from picking off another corvette.

"Target purple. Target purple."

One corvette lagged in joining the Imperial formation, and the Accord wedge curved away from the main body and toward the corvette.

A hail of torps, several short-range laser pulses, and the isolated corvette's screens failed. Then the corvette disintegrated.

So did one more needleboat.

"Green frank. Green frank," ordered Jimjoy.

The Accord forces eased into an in-system course—a rough wedge formation on each side and ahead of the advancing Imperials, whose force concentration made the needleboats almost useless.

Only the two battle cruisers and six corvettes remained, but so long as they remained in the tight-globed formation, nothing short of suicide jumps from the destroyers was likely to penetrate the interlocked screens.

Nothing conventional, corrected Jimjoy. He checked the massive EDI traces.

"Twelve standard minutes until avalanche one," he announced to his own crew, not daring to broadcast the timing to the Imperials.

One of the wing corvettes showed some acceleration away from the center.

"Greenpax blue, target straggler. Target straggler."

One of the needleboats darted closer and released a single torp. The corvette's screens took care of the weapon, but the Imperial ship eased back into the interlocking screen protection.

The Imperial formation eased across the imaginary orbit line of Ree-lee—planet six. Two EDI-seeking torps peeled away from the battle cruiser and toward Donagir, the moon behind which Jimjoy had staged the Accord forces. Jimjoy hoped the research personnel had evacuated the station proper.

"Commander, the Impies are accelerating."

"Stet. Understand acceleration." He rechecked the calculations.

He couldn't understand why the Impies remained in formation, not with what appeared to be three giant battle vessels sweeping in toward them.

"Maybe they don't believe their screens," he muttered.

"They think we're bluffing?" asked Analitta.

"Less than three minutes. Then it won't make any difference."

He triggered the command circuit. "Green Charlie. Green Charlie. EXECUTE GREEN CHARLIE."

All the Accord ships split away from the Imperial fleet at flank acceleration.

On the representational screen, for a full minute the Imperial fleet continued down entry corridor two unopposed.

Coming outbound on the entry corridor were three massive green EDI tracks, each track an iron-nickel asteroid propelled by a fusactor-powered drive system.

Slowly, the Imperial ships started to spread away from the battle cruisers.

Jimjoy wanted to scream at the Impie officers, to tell them to forget order, forget discipline, to get the hades away from the oncoming asteroids.

The Imperials still seemed to regard the asteroids as a mere obstacle, as three corvettes and one cruiser edged leftward and the other corvettes and cruiser edged rightward—just as if the asteroids were nothing besides heavy and unwieldy lumps of metal.

Jimjoy continued to calculate, his finger on the override.

The figures matched—one minute and thirty standard seconds before the automatic triggers.

Jimjoy jammed the override. "Full shutters! Full shutters!"

Just before the shutters activated, Jimjoy could see a handful of dashed torp lines leaving one of the Imperial battle cruisers—not toward the Accord forces, but in-system.

"Hades . . ." He wished he knew their targets, not that it mattered now. From the distance they had been launched, the torps couldn't affect an atmosphered planet. Thalos Station, and the outspace research facilities, were another matter. He doubted the Impies had data on any locations except Thalos. He wiped his forehead, hoping Imri had completed evacuations of the vulnerable sections of the station.

Inside the *Adams*, all the displays showing exterior inputs went blank.

The Commander of the forces of the Coordinate of Accord wiped his forehead.

Gilman looked over at Jimjoy, then looked away.

"Permission to unshutter, Commander."

"Wait one, Captain."

"Standing by."

Jimjoy refigured the energy paths. "Clear to unshutter, Captain."

"Shutters down."

The representational screen displayed hundreds of objects where the Imperial fleet had been. All but two were clearly fragments of the three asteroids that had carried citybusters in their centers.

The two remaining Imperial ships were both corvettes, both apparently shielded by the bulk of one of the battle cruisers. The screens of one were in the amber. The other looked untouched on the screen.

"Imperial ships, this is Greenpax control. Request your immediate surrender. Request your immediate surrender."

Jimjoy noted that the *Fitzreld*'s screens were also amber, another casualty, and two more needleboats were missing.

If they could get the two corvettes, that would be some help in rebuilding. He triggered the transmission on the Imperial frequency again. "Imperial ships, this is Greenpax control. Request your immediate surrender."

"Greenpax control, this is *Suleden*. Dropping screens this time. Dropping screens this time. Would appreciate medical assistance."

Jimjoy noted the corvette with the ailing screens had dropped them into standby.

"Stet, *Suleden*. Please stand by."

The second corvette, which had still not responded, began to step up acceleration toward Accord. In the confusion following the asteroid bombardment the corvette had continued to track in-system of the Accord forces.

"Hades!"

He touched the command circuit. "Greenpax blue, you have local control. Accommodate *Suleden*. Swersa, join up to Greenpax control. Greenpax needles"—he looked at the remaining clear needleboat numbers—"two seven, two nine, and four four, join to Greenpax control."

Swersa, Broward's former copilot, had command of the *Wett*.

"Captain, let's see if we can catch that bastard." Jimjoy again wished he were at the controls. Instead, he concentrated on the screen. The corvette couldn't destroy Accord, but even corvette tacheads could do a great deal of damage to places like Thalos and Harmony.

"Stet, Commander." Analitta already had the *Adams* in pursuit of the unnamed Impie corvette.

"*Suleden*, medical assistance arriving via needleboat."

Jimjoy nodded. Broward, coerced away from the *Roosveldt*, had the mop-up in hand.

The corvette had dropped screens to half power—just enough to hold off a single needleboat—and channeled screen power into drive energy, almost reaching needleboat speed in a mad dash toward Accord.

"Commander, request permission to cross-connect."

"Granted, Captain."

The *Adams* did not immediately gain on the corvette, but the gap began to narrow fractionally.

Jimjoy began running vectors and speed options through the taccomp.

"Needle two seven, interrogative torp status."

"Status green at point five."

"Two nine, interrogative torp status."

"Status green at point seven."

"Four four, interrogative status."

"Status green at point two."

The last pilot's voice rang familiarly. Luren. Somehow, he was glad she didn't have the most torps left.

"Two nine, request intercept on charlie target. Coordinates follow." He touched the laser tight-beam control, letting the taccomp send the data package.

"Greenpax control, coordinates received. Proceeding."

"Why, Commander?" asked Gilman.

Jimjoy took a deep breath, not moving his eyes from the screen as the needleboat began to race away from the *Adams*. "Because we need to slow him down before he can drop a half-dozen tacheads all over Accord." He wiped his forehead again.

On the screen the needleboat edged slightly off a straight stern chase and continued accelerating. Jimjoy nodded. It would take most of the needle's power to complete the maneuver, but even an unsuccessful attack should delay the corvette.

"Accord orbit control, this is Greenpax control. Single bandit charlie inbound this time."

Orbit control had three needleboats for a last-ditch defense, but Jimjoy doubted they would be necessary. The corvette seemed intent on reaching Accord itself, not orbit control.

The representational screen showed orbit control's full screens flicking into place. What it did not show was any EDI traces on Thalos. Again Jimjoy hoped that Imri had completed evacuations to the outlying stations. While the screens would prevent actual physical penetration, they would not prevent damage from second shocks and ground movement.

"Greenpax control, understand single charlie inbound this time."

"That's affirmative. Coordinates two seventy relative, orange, plus point zero two."

"We have charlie on screen. Good luck, control."

Jimjoy and Analitta watched the screens. Behind them, Broward took over the *Suleden* and continued to gather the scattered Accord forces. Before them, Accord grew in the screens.

Needleboat two nine, after pulling abreast of, then in front of, the corvette, continued to move in-system, almost to within multiple planetary diameters of Accord, before beginning a tight turn.

The Imperial corvette edged away from the needleboat, as if for an angled pass.

Jimjoy swallowed hard, visualizing the corvette's strategy, and hit the command circuits.

"Orbit control. Launch needles on north hemi swing to intercept torps. Coordinates and intercept parameters follow." His fingers managed to catch up with his words, and the taccomp burned a string of figures.

As he spoke, five torps flashed from the still-turning corvette toward Accord.

"Greenpax control, orbit control. Launching this time. Coordinates received. Intercept probability point five to point seven."

"Understand point five. Do what you can." Jimjoy shifted to the outfront needle. "Two nine, shift target to torps."

"Already shifting."

While he spoke, two torps flickered from the needleboat toward the corvette's citybusters, followed by a third torp, and a fourth.

One needle torp intersected one of the Imperial torps. A quick flash appeared on the screen.

"Commander . . ."

Jimjoy, catching the tone in Analitta's voice, refocused on the corvette, which had continued to turn back toward the *Adams*.

". . . he's head to head . . ."

"Hades." Jimjoy's forehead felt suddenly damp. Whoever turned first was most vulnerable to torps. Too late a turn and a laser punch was certain. But the Imperial pilot wasn't about to turn.

"Two until impact."

A green dot accelerated from beside the *Adams*, burning toward the corvette.

"Keep the faith, Commander." Luren's voice.

Jimjoy stared momentarily, protesting that the needleboat would break on the corvette's screens.

"Oh . . ."

All the screens went black.

Jimjoy looked down at the blank plot board, fighting back the tears no one would understand, swallowing before looking up, quickly wiping his forehead and cheeks with his sleeve as if to wipe the sweat alone off his face.

"What—" Gilman broke off as he looked at Jimjoy.

"She . . . jump-shifted . . ." mumbled Analitta.

"Right through his screens," finished Jimjoy. "Yeah . . . all that kinetic energy . . ."

"Brave frigging lady."

Jimjoy nodded, swallowed, and stared at the blank screens.

As the screens returned to normal, Jimjoy noted that Luren had been accurate. Very accurate. Not even a single fragment remained of either ship.

"Where to, Commander?" Analitta had left the *Adams* heading toward orbit control.

"Thalos Station. We need to put her back together. See what help we can provide. Build more needleboats—just in case." He looked into the depths of the representational screen. "Just in case."

"Greenpax control, this is orbit control. Looks like we only got one of the four that got here."

Jimjoy didn't like the sound of the ops officer's voice.

"Interrogative targets."

"Precise coordinates unavailable. Impacts projected at Harmony, plus or minus five kays, unknown point on the equator, and Parundia City, plus or minus ten kays."

"Interrogative impact force." Jimjoy's voice was tired. It could have been worse, but Harmony . . .

"Impact in Harmony area, estimate forty kaytee. No estimates for other targets."

"Stet. Greenpax control proceeding Thalos Station. Return needles to Accord control."

"Understand needles to remain Accord orbit control."

"That's affirmative this time. Have them restock and stand down."

"Stet, Greenpax control. Congratulations, Commander."

"Don't . . ." Jimjoy caught his tongue. "Orbit control?"

"Interrogative, Greenpax control."

"Just . . . keep the faith . . . keep the faith . . ."

LXXVI

THE SMOKE LINGERED over the area ahead, bitter, oily, with a char to it even weeks after the firestorm. The tall man, wearing only his undress greens despite the chill of the short winter days, walked toward the security perimeter.

"Ser, you can't go there—ser! HALT!" The sentry, scarcely old enough to have finished secondary school, lifted the stunner rifle.

The silver-haired man stopped and turned, fixing his green eyes on the young civil guard. "I beg your pardon?"

"Ser—that is—" stammered the girl.

"I know. I know," answered the Ecolitan as he stepped closer. "I've been away." In a lower tone, he added, "For too long."

She stepped closer, close enough that for an instant the plumes of white they exhaled in the cold air touched.

The worn greens caught the sentry's eyes, as did the single gold-and-green triangle on the man's collar.

"Ser . . . I'm sorry." Her eyes flicked just away from meeting his, as if she were inspecting his shoulder. "I didn't recognize you."

"That's more than all right. I won't cross the perimeter. I'd just like a last look." He paused. "Why don't you come with me?"

She looked around, as if to see whether anyone were watching.

"I doubt if it matters now, young lady. The biologic teams start in first thing in the morning."

Jimjoy began to walk toward the iridescent red plastic strip—held waist-high by a line of wooden stakes—that encircled the stricken area.

"Yes, ser." But she still looked back over her shoulder as she followed him. Behind them, uphill, was the abandoned Regency hotel. With a good section of central Harmony, it would be coming down in the days ahead.

The stone-paved street continued—rubble-strewn—beyond the thin warning line, marking the residual radiation barrier, down toward the dark, water-filled, unnatural lake that still steamed. Beyond the barrier, little was recognizable.

There had been mastercraft shops—places like Waltar's, where Jurdin had set out the picnic set developed from the one he had made for Jimjoy, or Daniella's, or Christina's, the little bakery he had always enjoyed. Now there was charred wood, if that, seared stone, and lingering radiation.

Farther down, at the blast center, where the old Government Square had been, was the unnatural lake whose murky waters steamed in the winter air.

Dr. Narlian declared she could decontaminate the whole place, and she probably would, Jimjoy reflected.

Beside him, the young sentry said nothing, looking nervously at the

destruction, then behind them, then at the tall, silver-haired man with
the green eyes that seemed black.

Jimjoy took a deep breath, still looking downhill at the ruins. Had
he delayed on Thalos just on the excuse of rebuilding the Accord forces?

"Ser?"

"Yes, young lady?"

"Pardon me. . . . Are you . . . ?"

"For better or worse, Jimjoy Whaler—sometime Professor at the
Institute—onetime Defense Commander of the Coordinate." He did
not wait to see the possible distaste in her eyes and turned his glance
back to the destruction he had failed to prevent. He should have developed an evacuation plan for Harmony. But he hadn't. He had only
thought in terms of preventing the planet's destruction.

The odds said he had done well. Odds weren't towns. Odds weren't
people. People like Jurdin Waltar, like Daniella, or Geoff Aspan, or
Luren. Luren, whom he had saved once only to sacrifice again.

"Ser?"

He repressed a sigh, waiting for the inevitable question. "Yes?"

"Thank you."

"For what?" He kept his voice soft. For what, young lady? For losing
over forty needleboats and their pilots? For provoking a war that could
have lasted forever and destroyed the most promising culture produced yet?

"Just . . . for being there. For doing what had to be done."

Jimjoy turned to the youngster. "Aren't those just words?"

"No, ser. I heard you talk to the Council. I heard them talk for hours
afterward. They were afraid to say anything. They were afraid to act.
Sometimes, somebody has to act. . . . Sorry, ser. I didn't mean . . ."

Jimjoy touched her shoulder gently. "You're right, and you're wrong.
Have to act, but it always costs more." He gestured downhill. "They
don't care, not when they're dead."

"Will you do it again—if the Empire comes?"

Jimjoy shrugged. "I could lie. I won't. I'll do it again, only so no
one else has to." Then he laughed. "Sounds so frigging noble. I'm not."

He turned and walked back uphill.

"Ser?"

"I'm on duty. Good-bye."

"Good-bye . . . and thank you. . . . Again."

"For?"

"Like you said . . . for being here."

He began to walk toward the groundcar that would take him to the
shuttleport and to the flitter to the Institute.

LXXVII

28 Novem 3647
New Augusta

Dear Helen:

I wish I could be with you and the children now, or that I could have been the one to break the news. I've put this off longer than I should have, and I know that a medal—even the highest honor bestowed—is cold consolation for a man like Mort.

Mort was right, and he fought for what was right. He fought knowing he didn't have the best ship and knowing that he'd been betrayed in a lot of ways by the government he supported. Because he gave everything and more, I've done something that maybe you wouldn't like, and maybe you would. I don't know, but I couldn't take the thought that Mort faced down a pair of brand-new Fuardian cruisers for nothing.

You may have seen it already, but right after the report came in, I gathered up all the faxcubes Mort had sent me, and every-thing else I could lay my hands on, and with a little help I whee-dled an appointment with the Privy Council. I laid everything out—Mort's tapes, the maintenance failures, Graylin's resignation (he resigned because they refused to listen on either the Accord fiasco or the failure to build adequate ships to deal with the Fuards), and some other matters. I told them what Mort's death meant. The Council took it to the Emperor. That was what led to his speech to the people. Even if he didn't get Mort's name right, it was important that Mort got the credit.

Some people are claiming I did it to get Graylin's job. I won't turn it down if it's offered. I don't think Mort would have wanted me to refuse. I didn't do it to get Mort a medal, and I didn't do it to get me a job. I did it because the problems won't go away by ignoring them. I did it because men and women like Mort need better ships.

We're going to get the CX. It's too late for these fights. The Fuards have the three-system bulge, and we'll have to accept some sort of terms from Accord. We don't have the ships or the technology. But we can when Jock or Cindi enters the Academy—if they choose to. That's up to them, but because they're children of a man who won the Emperor's Cross, their admission is automatic. Perhaps they'll reject the Service. I hope not, because we need them.

I wish I could offer more comfort, more warmth. You and Mort had so much, and I always looked at you two in awe. I've tried to do what I can, to give some meaning to what Mort had to do, and I hope you understand.

Blaine

LXXVIII

FROM THE COPILOT'S seat, Jimjoy took a deep breath, exhaling, trying to get the stench of burned wood, charred flesh, and death from his nostrils. He hated to think of the immediate aftermath of the attack. The situation on Thalos had been bad enough—with just secondary damage.

On Accord itself, the casualties had been the western half of Harmony, the equatorial marine research station, for whatever reason, and Parundia Town proper. The Institute had been spared.

Just from one corvette with a few remaining tacheads. He shuddered, thinking how little would have been left had battle cruisers gotten through.

A flash of light seared across the western horizon, visible even in the bright winter sun.

"Know what that was, Professor?" asked Kursman.

"Oh, that? Suspect it was either a large chunk of former spacecraft or a sharp-stone remnant."

"Sharp stone?" questioned the pilot.

Belatedly realizing he had never briefed the planetside Ecolitans on the details of the space defenses, Jimjoy shook his head slowly, then pulled at his chin. "A chunk of one of the asteroids we threw at the Imperial fleet."

"Oh . . ."

Still smelling death in his nostrils, despite the airflow through the cockpit, Jimjoy let the subject drop.

As the Institute appeared in the flitter's front windscreen, Kursman eased the nose back, bleeding off airspeed, and began rotor deployment.

Thwop . . . thwop, thwop . . .

"Greenpax ops, Prime one, on final descent this time."

Jimjoy glanced at the final lineup, noting that Kursman was not lined up for the flitter area, but for the open grass opposite the main Administration building.

More unusual was the small crowd of Ecolitans gathered here.

He looked again, realizing that the crowd was not nearly so small, perhaps several hundred people—all in green.

He looked over at Kursman, but the pilot appeared intent on making the landing, and with the westward approach and the sun cascading across the dark helmet visor, Jimjoy could only make out a determined set to the young pilot's jaw.

Jimjoy shifted his glance to the instruments, relieved that Kursman was on target for a letter-perfect approach.

The last thing he wanted was a welcoming committee, especially after the carnage in Harmony and the destruction of Thalos topside. At least he'd had enough sense to order the evacuation to the outlying Thalos facilities. That had held down the casualties there. You couldn't evacuate an entire planet, but he should have thought of Harmony. He should have. It was the only real target on all Accord—except for the Institute.

Thwop, thwop, thwop. . . . The increasing volume of the rotors brought his attention back to the flitter and the waiting crowd. He had sent a message to Thelina, not to the entire Institute, hoping to see her first, to explain.

He pulled at his chin and straightened in the copilot's seat as Kursman executed a perfect flair and touchdown in the center of the grass patch before the Administration building.

"We're here, ser," Kursman turned to Jimjoy, a wide grin on his face, even before starting the shutdown checklist. "I'll get us shut down as quickly as possible."

Jimjoy nodded and looked beyond the rotor blade path at the crowd. He thought he saw Thelina, tall, silver hair swirled by the rotor wash, in the small subgroup closest to the flitter. He slowly pulled off his helmet.

Thwop, thwop . . . thwop . . . thwop . . . The rotors came to a halt.

"Shutdown complete, ser."

Jimjoy slid open his door and stepped out into the silence, glancing from one side of the crowd to the other, catching one set of eyes, then another. All of them were waiting. He almost shrugged, instead raised his hand in greeting, knowing there was nothing he could say. Nothing at all.

The silence persisted, except for a few whispers, as he started toward

Thelina. With her were Meryl, Elias, Dr. Narlian, and a man he did not recognize at first. He thought, then remembered. Clarenz Hedricht, the Council Chairman. Obviously, he hadn't been in Harmony when the tachead hit.

The group stepped forward toward him.

Jimjoy focused on Thelina, whose face remained almost impassive, and whose tunic seemed too tight in front. She carried a small carved box.

Regardless of the crowd that began to curl around to see what was happening, Jimjoy wanted to run to her, to hold her.

Her eyes reached him, and she mouthed, "No. Not now."

The group of four stopped. Since it was clearly expected of him, he stopped, too. They couldn't be doing this, he thought. Not now.

"James Joyson Whaler." Meryl's voice was pitched to carry to the entire group. "You have put action above ceremony. Results above position. You have never spared yourself in following your principles. You have set an example for all future Ecolitans.

"Today, following that example of avoiding ceremony, of doing what should be done, we are gathered together. We declare that for your example, for providing leadership when all Accord needed leadership, for inspiring and motivating all people, and for bringing freedom to the entire Coordinate, the Institute's electors, the Ecolitans of Accord, officially recognize what has long been unofficially known.

"Welcome home, Prime Ecolitan Whaler."

Jimjoy did the only thing he could. He bowed his head momentarily to accept the tribute, then raised his face to Thelina and the crowd, letting the tears fall where they would as Thelina stepped forward and placed the single gold pin on his chest, a golden triangle within a green circle.

"Sam's?" he whispered.

She nodded.

His hands held her elbow to keep her from stepping back. "I'm no hero, and I came back, and I love you."

He could see the tears in her eyes, and instead of releasing Thelina, he pulled her to him, gently, not wanting to let go, feeling every curve of her against him, including the new one, the one that would be named Geoff or Luren.

A sigh seemed to come from the crowd.

"All right," whispered Meryl. "A little is understandable, but . . ."

Jimjoy tightened his grip on Thelina, then let go, linking her arm in his and turning to face the Ecolitans, his chosen people.

He raised his arm again and smiled, and began to walk with Thelina toward the future.

EPILOGUE

"SUMMARY:

"Detailed psyprofile comparison between Wright, Jimjoy Earle, III, and Whaler, James Joyson, II:

"Initial physical parameter comparisons, based on updated analysis of Ecolitan Institute capabilities [see H-G, sec. 32], indicate a physiological congruency range of 73%−94%.

"Psychological analyses, including statistical correlation of surface carriage indices, Mahaal-Pregud overlays, and Aaylward Socionormic Scores, indicate a congruency range below 45%, equivalent to environmental/genetic similarities or cultural congruency of point five on the Frin Scale.

"In numerous recorded observations, Whaler's actions—accepting the sacrifice of two other needleboats, entering a permanent marital contract, and displaying visible emotion—signifying a significantly less sociopathic and a more emotional personality than that of Major Wright . . .

"Conclusion:

"Despite conflicting evidence {see Appendices I-IV}, direct and indirect psychological evidence, DNA-matched physical remains, and an absolute match of implanted Imperial identification tags confirm the death of the following Imperial officer:

> "Jimjoy Earle Wright III
> Major, I.S.S./S.O./B-941 366."

> —*Termination Records*
> Vol. XL (3646–3648 I.E.)

CPSIA information can be obtained at www.ICGtesting.com
Printed in the USA
LVOW102306231211

260981LV00001B/33/P